Earth's Custodians

PAUL CUDE

GRAB A FREE 'WHITE DRAGON SAGA' STORY

FREE STORY: As new friends face ruthless enemies that have designs on not only their bodies, but their minds as well, will an ancient mantra come to their rescue? Treachery, intrigue and a bare faced lie lead to gruesome negotiations. Will a cold hearted, duplicitous, double-crossing dragon fire the opening salvo in a wicked and unwarranted war, or can virtue and the moral high ground turn things around at the very last moment?

A Selfless Sacrifice is available for free when you join Paul Cude's newsletter at www.paulcude.com.

CONTENTS

Prologue   1

1   Snowbody Does It Better   8

2   A King And A Prayer   14

3   Splitter!   17

4   Ambush Amateurs   21

5   Not A Snowball's Chance In Hell   27

6   A Surprising Blow   34

7   The Strongest Of Bonds   48

8   Fan Of Steel   53

9   Shattered Illusions   62

10   Shadow Hunter   72

11   Circumvent, Circumvent, Circumvent   78

12   A Grim Truth   81

13   A Handy Surprise   88

14   Silent Running (Well, A Fast Walk)   90

15   Stampede   93

16   Cold As Steel   107

17   Biting Back   122

18	Flash In The Pan	133
19	Malevolent Majestic Maniac	149
20	Strawberry Blonde... Really?	153
21	Deep ****	160
22	What Would Admiral Ackbar Say?	166
23	Sub-Zero Success	176
24	Steel Yourself	182
25	Confrontation Bound	192
26	Staring Into The Abyss	194
27	Holey Moley	202
28	Pipe Dream	207
29	A Bridge Too Far	212
30	Shafted	221
31	Hoodwinked	233
32	A Room With A View	242
33	Snow Point Hanging Around	249
34	Sucker Punch	252
35	A Surprise Return	266
36	Tooled Up	268
37	Bluffing, Huffing and Puffing	270

38 Gatecrashers   280

39 Deese Guys And Their Disguise   287

40 You Can Choose Your Friends But Not Your Family   291

41 Steeling Fleet Street Back From The Enemy   343

42 All Creatures Great And Small   351

43 I Love You! I Know!   405

44 Pain Relinquishing The Chain   412

45 Definitely Not Winging It   446

46 Macabre Magical Madness   455

47 Into The Hornets' Nest   505

48 Swamped   508

49 Committed To The End   526

50 Racist   532

51 Captain Courageous   570

52 An Abrupt End   574

PROLOGUE

Overcome by exhaustion, unconsciousness had finally got her man, or in this case... DRAGON! Not so much asleep, as just not awake, the naive young hockey player trapped in his human persona, grunted, grumbled and struggled against the bonds that held his torso in an uncomfortable, upright position as events that had led up to this particular low point in his life played out deep within his mind.

A guilt-ridden sigh slipped through his cracked lips as he involuntarily shook his head. Memories of all the subterfuge raced rampantly through his subconscious as wave after wave of regret washed over him. If only he'd seen through all the tricks and lies. With all the opportunities he'd had, he, Peter Bentwhistle, could have stopped everything. Even right at the very end, he'd still had a chance, on that cold, frosty November evening on the Astroturf in Salisbridge, the one place on the planet he truly thought of as his home. Against all odds he'd battled the monster all on his own, stopped him from stealing the laminium deposits, and avoided death, albeit only just. But despite his best efforts, the evil dragon known as Manson had somehow escaped justice, something that had cost the planet and its denizens dearly. If he'd only been braver, stronger, smarter... then the scheming psychopath of a dragon could be in custody now and hundreds of thousands of lives might well have been spared. Deep down it tore him apart to know that he'd been so close, and yet so far.

Skipping ahead now in something of a blur, images of his friends Tank, Richie, Gee Tee, the king and of course FLASH, skittered through his mind.

That fateful day with the king was supposed to have been about him, but it seemed like a lifetime ago that anything within his sphere of influence had turned out okay. That day certainly hadn't. Being presented to Flash, the ex-Crimson Guard, who at the time was knocking hard on death's door, had also introduced the three friends to a world of danger and malevolence that would have seemed like fantasy to them before. But it had been done, and thankfully Flash had been saved, albeit at a cost. Sorrow, regret and a deep sense of loss welled up inside him as he thought about the price his friend had paid. To be stuck in a false human shape permanently, losing the ability to return to one's natural dragon form seemed like a punishment only the gods could dish out, if indeed they even existed. But that's what had happened, and at least outwardly, his pal had moved on.

Thoughts focused on Flash's predicament, his mind turned to events on that fateful Saturday... the one where he'd lost two of the things he loved the most. Adrift in the depths of his unconsciousness, it didn't stop the tears from dribbling down the cheeks of his bruised and battered body as he recollected with crystal clarity what had happened, the heartbreak from that day still tearing him up inside.

A terrific game of hockey followed by all the usual banter and shenanigans at the sports club with his teammates was how it had started. Not only that, but the love of his life, the petite blonde bar worker with whom he'd only recently engaged in a forbidden romance, had flirted with him throughout the afternoon, causing his heart to beat faster, filling him with a sense of contentment that he'd never ever felt before. Of course it didn't last. In fact, things went to hell faster than a dragon hurrying to the toilet.

Upon finding a bomb in their beloved clubhouse, one of many planted across the planet, sheer luck combined with Tank's outstanding magical knowledge had allowed them to save the residents of Salisbridge at the cost of the obliterated building. But that wasn't all. As events played out, he'd had to not exactly lie, but not exactly tell the truth. And this had come back to bite him badly a little later on, with his beloved Janice dumping him like a barrel of toxic waste. The world wasn't nearly so lucky, suffering one of the most outrageous attacks it had ever seen, with the death toll for both dragons below ground, and humans on the surface, in the hundreds of thousands. On top of all of that, he thought he'd lost one of his two best friends, Richie, in the Salisbridge blast. In fact, she'd survived, but only just, and at great personal cost. Through a combination of magic, she'd been transformed into a human. Because of this, the dragon Council wiped her memories, forcing her to remain on the surface for the rest of her life. In conjunction with his friend Gee Tee the master mantra maker, he'd come up with a plan to save her, but he had no idea if it had worked. All he knew was that she was somewhere on the earth's surface, and just like the rest of the human population, was oblivious to everything that had gone on and the threat that events here in the dragon domain currently presented to the planet.

Imperceptibly, the pictures he had of Richie in his head wriggled and writhed, before once again forming a face, one that he knew only too well. So well in fact, that his body was currently chained back to back with the owner... Tim! Caught up in the explosion at the clubhouse with Richie, magical residues had caused Tim, a very normal and completely unexceptional human, to turn into a...

DRAGON! Taking a little time to manifest itself, at first the medics treating his injuries hadn't realised quite what had happened. Soon enough though, they found out. And it wasn't just any dragon he'd transformed into. It was a totally white dragon, a complete anomaly, and something foretold in a prophecy thousands of years old. What were the chances? But here he was, out of his depth, with no knowledge of where or what he was, let alone what he was supposed to do to fulfil the ancient foretelling. Worse still was to come. Along with Peter, they'd both been captured by Manson and his forces, and brought here, to the council building, as the effort to capture the current monarch of the domain continued in earnest. All in all, quite the predicament the two of them found themselves in. Right at this very moment, unconsciousness favoured reality for the pair of them.

Not a million miles away, other beings slept a slightly more peaceful slumber, but only through sheer exhaustion. Sitting upright against a rocky wall in an unfamiliar nursery ring, Tank, the third member of the dragon friendship trio forged in Purbeck Peninsula during their youth, snored slightly in his false human form, his huge tightly shaven head lolling to one side, his mind tortured by events of the last couple of days. Evading death by a hair's breadth thanks to Flash at the monorail station in Salisbridge, along with all the other passengers there, it was only when he'd awoken that he realised the true horror of the situation he and his friend found themselves in. Dangling precariously from a hastily fashioned gallows in the middle of the Salisbridge market place, surrounded by burning pyres piled high with the rotting corpses of dead and dismembered dragons, it was all he could do to swallow down the sick that kept racing up from his stomach. So realistic was the memory, the sense of smell from his time there made him involuntarily gag, despite the fact that he remained in the land of nod. Brutally tortured alongside Flash, with most of the skin flayed from his body, it was only the timely arrival of his boss, Gee Tee, the famed mantra maker, his best friend Richie, with her dragon memories intact, and unbelievably, a ragtag bunch of humans from the sports club above where he plied his rugby craft, that had saved him. After a chaotic battle, some ancient magic from the recesses of Flash's mind and a considerable amount of healing from some of the locals, he'd recovered enough to join what little resistance they could mount. But on finding out the true scale of the evil being perpetrated across not only the dragon domain, but the earth itself, things looked more than a little bleak. A surprise to be sure then that one of his two best friends, Richie, was tasked with leading the force that remained, despite being stuck in human form.

Cutting through any hint of bureaucracy, Richie instantly dispatched Flash to Antarctica, in the hope that he could rescue the naga king from his forced imprisonment, thereby nullifying Manson's blackmailing of the naga race. The hope was that the ex-Crimson Guard would find willing reinforcements on the way. In the meantime, they'd followed their de facto leader to the capital and found temporary sanctuary here, at the Hampton Court nursery ring. Fed and watered, the dragon force combined with a few human oddities slept, in an effort to regain their strength and stamina for what was to come.

Lost and alone, despite the fact that her pale, freckled face nestled snugly against Tank's finely honed chest, it felt as though her memories had been scattered throughout time. In one instant all she could remember was playing in the charity lacrosse match, celebrating afterwards, and then ending up at the Indian restaurant with her friends in town that night. From then onwards, after she'd slipped the exquisite ring she was supposed to keep safe for Peter, onto her finger, her world had descended into turmoil. Visions of vast underground cities populated by impossible prehistoric beasts flooded her very being. Flying, breathing fire and gobbling down gigantic sticks of charcoal swam throughout her consciousness. But it wasn't a dream, or anything like it. These memories belonged to her. It took some time for it to sink in. She herself, just like her friends Peter and Tank, were dragons, residing for the most part in the dragon domain, deep beneath the planet, their overriding goal to guide and protect humanity wherever possible, driven by an ancient prophecy divined far in the past by a conglomerate of races. Acceptance wasn't easy at first, but once the memories started they didn't seem to want to stop. After that it was easy... well, almost. Resentment bubbled up beneath the surface of her very being. The dragon Council had taken away everything from her. She didn't like that. Suspecting that something diabolical was going on deep beneath the surface of the planet, she'd been tempted to leave her dragon kin to whatever mess they'd gotten themselves into... but only briefly. It wasn't in her nature to back down or shy away from conflict. So the decision was made in all but an instant. What she hadn't counted on was the stubbornness of her human friends. In the end she'd had no choice. They'd had to accompany her down the rabbit hole.

What a trip that had been, first hooking up with the master mantra maker... Gee Tee! The look on her friends' faces had been a treat, and almost worthy of placing their lives in danger. Almost! Surprise and awe hadn't lasted long, and with the help of the dragon shopkeeper's ample supply of weapons and well of exotic magic, they'd overcome a force four times their size and had saved both Tank and Flash from a rather painful death.

As she tried to piece together the images of what had happened, nagging doubts surfaced briefly. There and then, and against all odds, she'd been chosen to lead. Once it was clear it was no joke and there was no turning back, that cold, calculating part of her took over. An inkling of regret deep within spat in her direction, in nothing more than a futile gesture over the torture she'd committed to gain the information that she'd needed. It had been necessary, that much she knew. After that, things became stunningly clear. She'd sent Flash to Antarctica, the one place on the planet he feared to go. That... she felt regret about, but once again knew that she had no choice. The threat to the nagas Manson controlled had to be neutralised. There was no other way.

And so they'd headed here, on their way to rescue their king. Only there was more to it than that. There always was. Briefly she wondered if they'd forgive her for what she was about to do. She hoped they would, but could completely understand it if they couldn't. It was Tank, the gentle giant whose form she currently slept across, his massive arm wrapped around her, a huge comfort, who she worried about most. He wouldn't like it, not at all. In essence he didn't have to. All he had to do was go along with it, something she hoped he'd do without much fuss. In only a few short hours, she'd find out.

A darkness the like of which the world had never known was spreading across the planet, a pervasive cancer infiltrating every nook and cranny. It wasn't obvious, quite the opposite in fact, by design. But it was there, and it was mounting one final push. Nagas and dark dragons disguised as humans had long since slipped into the surface populace, ready to act, ready to rain down terror and destruction. Whilst in the depths of the secret dragon domain, the purveyors of evil, the wicked minds behind all the dastardly deeds, rallied their troops, ready and able to take the keys to the planet's stronghold, knowing that everything the earth had to offer was nearly theirs. It was only a matter of hours away now...

1 SNOWBODY DOES IT BETTER

It was freezing. The scroll that Yoyo had unfurled was now solid, the letters barely visible. But it didn't matter. They had nearly reached their destination. Things had progressed well over the last hour or so, if not as fast as he'd hoped for. They'd had to move from their previously sheltered position, to one much more exposed, in order to line up the hole they were drilling, with the area beneath the ice where they hoped the captives would be. By the young dragons' calculation, they should come out within thirty or so metres of the largest heat signature down there. That hopefully, would be either Fredric, Peter's grandfather and founder of the Crimson Guards, or the naga king, or maybe both.

A shimmering ripple in the snow next to him caused Flash to turn. One of Yoyo's band of young dragons had appeared beside him. Despite his supposedly eidetic memory, he couldn't remember her name. It didn't matter.

"Two more minutes and we should be there," she shouted over the howling gale that assaulted their small team, the superbly developed camouflage suits taking the full force of the extreme weather in this, the harshest environment on the planet.

He nodded his understanding back to her.

"I don't want to hang around. As soon as we're through, I'm going in. I'll scout ahead as we agreed. If it's safe for you to come down, and you're needed, I'll let you know."

She acknowledged with a nod of her head, before disappearing completely in front of him, due mostly to the suit, with the relentless snowfall playing some small part.

Abruptly another sizeable shape materialised on the other side of him this time. He could tell it was Yoyo, because he was holding the frozen scroll in one of his camouflaged hands.

"Are you sure you want to do it this way?" he leaned in and shouted, his voice barely perceptible in the horrendous weather.

"It's best for all concerned," replied Flash, mentally readying himself for what was to come. "In essence, I should encounter little in the way of resistance. With all of you standing by up here, ready to get us out, hopefully we'll be gone before anyone even notices."

Yoyo nodded, despite the worried expression that sat across his hidden face. This, as far as he was concerned, was the most risky part of the mission. It was unpredictable. Who knew what actually lay down there? Of course it should be the prisoners that Flash had seen when he'd been captured and escorted there. But there was no knowing for sure. Not until he got down there anyway. He didn't like it, but knew better than to try and change his young friend's mind at this late stage. All they could do was remain vigilant, ready to act, and hope things went to plan.

The dizzying red light from the cutting beam of the mantra they'd been using winked out, leaving them all shrouded in darkness. Flash knew it was up to him now. Trudging through the snow, over to the lip of the precarious looking hole just about wide enough for him to fit through, he whipped off one glove, gave a quick thumbs up before instantly slipping it back on again, and with the mantra ready in his mind, leapt into the darkness.

The sensation of air zipping past him saddened him, because it reminded him of flying, something given his bodily circumstances he was never likely to do ever again. A sharp piece of ice, jutting out from the hole's edge caught him on one arm, startling him back to reality. Mentally chastising himself for getting distracted, he reminded himself to complete the mission. It was an important one, probably the most significant of his life. Given everything that was happening on the other side of the world, this could quite literally mean saving the planet as he knew it. Focused, he called forth the mantra, the words of which were already poised in his head.

Yoyo, with Flash's permission, had connected a mental tether to his friend, just before he'd plunged into the darkness. It should in theory allow the two of them to communicate, even with the former Crimson Guard over a kilometre deep beneath the very ice and rock they stood on. If he encountered any difficulties, at least he would be able to warn them.

It wasn't fancy, it wasn't... FLASH! That made him laugh. So many puns. It was very simple and elegant... just the right mantra, at just the right time. All it actually did was make the air thicker, which in turn cushioned his descent, allowing him to control the speed with which he dropped through the hole. The one down side was that the mantra couldn't thicken the air enough for him to just stop or even hover. There was no way to halt his motion and all the energy related to it. Sooner or later, he was going to have to hit something, to grind to a halt. Although a concern, it was something he'd deal with when the situation arose. For now, he maintained his focus, kept an eye on the walls surrounding him and the drop below for any sign of light or anything unusual, ready to fight at a moment's notice. He hoped he wouldn't have to, but he knew it was a distinct possibility. Any way you looked at it, he had to get the naga king out of there alive, and back to where he could do some good, not just for his friends' sake, but for the whole planet.

Surrounding the hole, they all waited fearfully. Some knelt, others just stood and craned their necks, what for, who knew? They certainly weren't going to see anything, not at that distance, even with their amazing dragon senses. A tinge of fear ran through Yoyo as he looked around him. The wonderfully designed suits the others wore flickered occasionally as the snow bounced off them. He wondered what he'd got them all into, and if indeed he really should have in the first place. It was too late now, but that didn't stop him regretting it. Would they all make it back? Would the mission succeed? Just two of many questions at the forefront of his mind, right at this very moment. Very soon, he would have his answers.

Earth's surface. London, England.
Dressed in TFL overalls and high visibility jackets, the two beings skulking in and around the dark tunnels adjacent to the underground tracks between Waterloo and Bank stations on the Waterloo and City line, deep beneath the capital, looked to be going about their business with their normal dedicated professionalism. If not for the two bodies each had killed with a single gunshot to the head, locked away in a tiny little store room, tucked some way back from the track then it might have just been workers going about their daily business... but not so. Mischief was up to no good, and had designs on creating as much chaos as was... not quite humanly... possible.

Orders had come down from on high, well at least through their group leader. They were part of a cell of eight, and knew only the other seven beings. Apart from that, they'd had no contact with the outside world. Their instructions had been clear: create as much confusion, disruption and devastation as possible, keep the authorities busy and off guard, almost mirroring what had gone on deep beneath them some time earlier.

Caution and subterfuge had been thrown to the wind, speed now the name of the game. So the two moved quickly, their destination burned deep within their memories, thoughts occasionally turning to what the rest of the cell were up to... no doubt somewhere else in the capital about to unleash a very different form of pandemonium. Ducking back into a dark recess as a tube train came rumbling along the track directly in front of them, their superhuman powers allowed them to see directly into the carriage and focus solely on the subjects there going about their daily lives, despite the speed with which the train travelled. One of them, the subordinate of the two, wondered for a split second about the humans that he'd just witnessed. Were they happy? Did they have families? Friends? What were their goals in life? Had they achieved them? If they hadn't, he knew it was unlikely now that they ever would. Soon the world would darken... forever. And everything they knew would be but a distant memory.

'Enough of that though,' he thought... 'back to the task at hand.'

As the fading light of the tube train became but a distant speck, and the rattle of carriages echoed off down the blackened tunnel, the two of them rushed out onto the tracks, mindful of the ever present threat of electrocution, knowing that even their magical abilities would not protect them from that. Sprinting now, the two travelled about half a kilometre in the same direction as the train that had just passed them. This was almost the furthest point between the two stations, and the most difficult part of the track for the emergency services to access, thus compounding the turmoil once it all happened.

With no time to lose, both of them stood opposite each other, grabbed the rail nearest them, and began to feed their murky magic into their hands. Streaks of brilliant purple and wicked dark green energy bled into the thick metal they were holding on to, sparking and arcing similar to that of a welder's torch. Mere moments later the rails started to melt and run like the wax of a candle. The two continued their mischief up the track for some five or so metres before deciding their work was complete. Taking a moment to admire the now nonexistent rails, only the flattened waxwork outline visible in the limited light, both beings sprinted off in the direction of the nearest exit to the surface which was about a thousand metres away. Spotting the concealed side tunnel with their magically enhanced vision, both ducked into it, followed its twisting path until they reached the narrow flight of stairs, which they duly climbed, all the time discarding the high visibility jackets and the stolen overalls. Reaching out with their minds, checking for anything unusual beyond the door that they stood behind in total pitch black, they both came up blank. Their path to freedom seemed perfectly okay. Taking deep breaths, they opened the door, slipping through in but a split second, joining the throng of unsuspecting passengers heading away from the station. Dressed in smart suit and tie ensembles, they blended in seamlessly with their surroundings. Three minutes later they found themselves in a black cab nearly two kilometres away, imagining the upcoming carnage the impending tube train was about to face.

2 A KING AND A PRAYER

For all he was worth, he'd hoped it would take them longer, much, much longer. But it hadn't. They'd arrived at the council building side of the bridge about an hour ago. A magical battle of epic proportions had been waged for over forty minutes. Nagas, as that's what he assumed they were, combined with some very unusual looking dragons, the like of which he'd never seen before, had surged across the chasm between the two buildings, in wave after wave of full on assaults. It was reckless, careless, a casual waste of life. For that very reason he detested it. In the end, the compact dragon force, trapped in the king's private residence, had little choice but to do the one thing they'd hoped not to. They'd blown the bridge to smithereens. Well, I say blown, they did in fact ignite the mantra that had been cast over it when they'd first retreated back over it. By their count, over a hundred nagas had tumbled to their doom, plummeting clumsily into the relentless depths. After that, it had all gone quiet... even the aerial attacks from the strange looking dragons had abated. Nothing could be seen on the other side. No doubt the enemy had regrouped out of sight, knowing that their prey was well and truly TRAPPED!

"The shield's holding fine si... George," whispered Amelia Battlehard in his ear, having just checked the integrity of the crackling blue hemisphere of light that boxed them all in.

"So it should," he replied, much more gruffly than he'd meant to. "It is, after all, powered by this." Holding up his hand, he showed off the awe inspiring magical ring that adorned it.

"Sorry," she mumbled. "It's just that I feel at such a loss for what else to do."

Opening his eyes, for they'd been closed throughout

the exchange, he exhaled and forced the tiniest of smiles onto his weary, weathered face.

"You've done all you can and more Captain. Your professionalism and dedication are a credit to your training. There's no one else I would wish to have at my side, right at this very moment."

A bubble of pride burst within her, spreading quickly to include all her appendages, especially her tail. The king always knew the right thing to say. That's probably why he was king.

"This, stupid as it seems, is one of the hardest parts of a battle... the waiting. Inevitably in my experience, there always is some. It saps the concentration, dulls the brain, and lulls everybody into a false sense of security. Over time, I've learnt to sharpen my wits, imagine every possible scenario, every weakness, every strength... all of the possible combinations, every facet of every assault. I play them out in my mind, developing defensive and offensive strategies along the way. You'd be surprised at what you can learn, the holes that you can find, in any and every attack, and just how important that information might yet be."

"Don't you find it distracts you from what is about to come?" asked the young captain, wide-eyed.

"Not at all," he shrugged. "Most of my consciousness is still here, in the present, alert and ready to act. It does stop me getting bored and complacent though, and I would have to say that I owe my life to such an exercise, at least twice."

"Thank you for sharing with me George. I'll be sure to give it a go. I'm not quite certain how well it will serve me in the future though."

The king almost let out a chuckle at that. Turning to face the young guard, and with the biggest smile he could muster on his face, he raised his voice so that all around him could hear.

"Things are desperate, there's no point in pretending

otherwise. Have I been in a situation quite as bleak as this before? Probably not! But I have been in circumstances where I thought I would die, where I had no right to survive. Fate, however, always had other ideas. All these states of affairs had one thing in common. I never gave up... not once. No one here should either give up hope, or stop believing we will get out of here in one piece. While I grant you a rescue of any sort is unlikely, it is not entirely impossible. So as your king, I order you all to BELIEVE, and to fight for the life that each and every one of you deserve, the life that these beings are trying to deprive you of."

They all heard, and despite how dire things seemed, the words did buoy them just a little.

3 SPLITTER!

So in synch with the world above, the planet wide mantra that turned the fierce orange glow of the surrounding lava into a dawn-like spectacle, crept across the underground domain of the dragons, throughout the United Kingdom. In and around the capital, the fresh morning blush revealed the previous day's death and destruction. Fires raged, thick cloying smoke circled high above, searching out the few direct routes to the surface. Murder and decay wafted on what little breeze there appeared to be.

Awoken after barely an hour, she slipped out from his warm embrace, but not before negotiating one of his giant arms, that was not far off the size of her waist, before stalking off into the shadows. Quietly, so as not to disturb the rest of the makeshift camp, as that was now what the circular courtyard of the nursery ring had become, she turned the handle on the towering stone fountain, that the young dragons based here normally drank from. A high pressure jet of water flew up from its base, splashing not only her face, but the rest of her front as well. Shaking the water from her hair, and ringing out her top at the same time, she didn't know whether to laugh or cry. Glad of the drink, she was comforted by the fact that no one had seen what had happened. Spying her target in the distance, curled up not far from the dazzling looking purple, blue and scarlet looking female dragon that had suggested using the tunnels, whose name she'd subsequently learnt was Sunset Streak, she set off around the outside of the courtyard, hugging the darkness. It wasn't long before she approached his ancient scaly face, having been determined not to sneak up on him, for fear of how he might react. She needed to speak to him as a matter of urgency, but wasn't sure how, or even if she should, wake him up. 'Carefully,' she thought on the how. Whilst still thinking, one heavy looking eyelid rolled back in front of her, revealing a giant eyeball, bigger than a football, focused solely on her.

"Good morning child," purred Gee Tee, quietly.

Instinctively she took a step back.

"Morning," she managed to squeak.

Rolling his head, first from side to side, and then back to front, the old dragon gave a huge yawn, before settling his attention back down on his visitor.

"To what do I owe this very welcome visit... child?"

It had all seemed so easy while she'd been thinking about it. But now that she had to voice some small part of it to another being, her idea, no, plan, seemed all the more crazy. It had plagued what little sleep she'd had, which she'd taken as a sign that it was the right thing to do and that she should press ahead with it. So she did.

"Your... glimpse into the future. I need to ask you about it."

This got the old dragon's attention, causing him to adjust his posture ever so slightly.

"Go ahead child. What is it you need to know?"

"I was wondering if you witnessed me in any of your visions?"

'Every being on the planet always wants to know about themselves. I thought this one might be different,' he mused, opening his mouth, about to speak.

"Is that all?" he growled, much more harshly than he'd intended, disappointed by the actual question itself.

"And any of the other humans, or Tank."

With a barely discernible nod of his head, the master mantra maker silently admonished himself for jumping to the very wrong conclusion about the young dragon leader.

"It was all very vague little one, but I'll try and recall what I can."

At this, she smiled.

"I did, as you're well aware, see Tank, swinging from that hastily erected gallows, as well as you and your band of intrepid humans. Of course, all of that has now come to pass."

Purposefully staying silent, so as not to disturb his train of thought, she wasn't sure what she hoped he would say.

"There were structures, here underground, one of which I'm pretty sure was the council building. After that, it's all a bit jumbled I'm afraid. I saw Tank in chains being led away, and what might have been the big one... you know, the one I gave the backpack to..."

"Ahhh... Hook, you mean."

"Yes, that's it... Hook," added the old shopkeeper. "It did look like him, shrouded in the shadows; that said, I suppose it just might have been Flash. Sorry I can't be any more help."

"You're sure you didn't see either Janice or myself?"

"Positive," replied Gee Tee. "That's not to say you weren't there though. There were lots of other beings being led off into the darkness, any of which could have been the two of you."

Richie rubbed the tiredness from her eyes, contemplating what the old dragon had said.

"Can I ask why it's so important, little one?" remarked Gee Tee, asking the one question Richie truly dreaded.

A very long and uncomfortable pause punctured the air between the two of them. She didn't want to say anything, but she knew she owed him more than that. In the end, she narrowed it right down to its most basic form.

"It all boils down to a decision, and almost certainly an unpopular one at that. Everything, however I look at it, seems to depend on that one choice. Almost as if the fate of all we do rests on that. I don't know what to do. It makes no sense. In fact, it seems utterly crazy. But I can't get it out of my mind. It won't leave me alone."

Blinking furiously a few times, before leaning his head to one side, the old shopkeeper gave what he'd heard careful consideration.

"Dragons in their entirety have long since lost touch

with their feelings. And I'm not talking about love, hate, sadness and joy, if that's what you think. Long ago, each and every dragon learned to trust their feelings, their gut instinct. Over the centuries, that intuition has been lost, waylaid, much to the detriment of our race. If I have one piece of advice for your quandary, it would be to go with what you feel is right. I bet your hunches nearly always pay off... am I correct?"

She nodded a reply.

"Then if I were you, I would follow them. Whatever you have to do, know that you'll be supported by everyone else. It might seem at times like you're alone, but in reality that's very much not the case. We all love you, support you, respect and admire you. When the time comes, we'll all be there to back you up. That you can count on."

"Thanks... you've been a great help," she just about got out without shedding a few tears, wondering where on earth all that had come from.

Abruptly the old dragon let out a huge, rapturous chortle, startling at least half a dozen other dragons in close proximity from their slumber. That made Richie smile... one that might be her last for a very long time.

4 AMBUSH AMATEURS

"Impregnable! Impregnable! I'll give you impregnable!" screamed the raging Manson, smashing his ornate walking stick into the human shaped naga's stomach, causing him to double over in agony. Now on the floor, the slithering reptile tried desperately to get some words out, but he'd been winded badly, and could achieve nothing comprehensible. He figured he'd have time, time to get up, time to explain, time to fight again. His understanding of the being he'd been reporting to was incomplete to say the least, something he realised a little too late, just, in fact, as the deadly barbed blade that had appeared from nowhere at the bottom of the walking stick, sliced into his chest, and was then dragged down towards his pelvis. The beast's last expression was one of complete shock and horror. Manson turned and walked away, but not before kicking the bloodied corpse in the back for good measure. All the beings gathered knew to stay quiet. All feared his temper, even his very subdued and quiet father, standing off to one side on one of the lower levels of the council building, adjacent to the exit that led to the courtyard and the recently demolished bridge that would have taken them across to the king's private residence.

"Why, oh why, does it have to be so difficult?" muttered Manson, to no one in particular, all the time pacing back and forth. The others, heads bowed, were all too scared to meet his gaze... all but one that is.

"I seem to be continually surrounded by imbeciles," he spluttered, looking for someone else to help express his anger.

"These things happen, my love," whispered Earth, soothingly.

Turning to face her, he mentally ordering the blade at the bottom of his walking stick, to retract... with the tiniest of clicks, it did just that.

"I just want it over, that's all," he uttered, all traces of anger gone from his voice.

"I know," she replied softly. "It will be, and soon. We just need to be patient for a little while longer. We have them right where we want them. They have nowhere to go, and not nearly enough supplies to hold out for any real length of time. We can afford to wait them out if necessary."

Manson glanced over his shoulder in his father's direction. Barely contained fury swirled across the old dragon's face, causing a deep down fear to come bubbling up inside him. His dad had always been able to do that to him, for as long as he could remember. In some ways, he was pinning his hopes on his father getting rid of all of his anger, resentment, frustration and despair on the current king of the dragon domain, the knight that so long ago had thwarted his treacherous plans. He hoped that after Troydenn had punished, tortured and ultimately killed the dragon king, it would relieve the burden he was carrying, and would enable him to become much more rounded and less likely to take things out on him. That was his wish anyway.

Turning back to face his soon to be queen, he ran the back of his hand across her purple lined cheek, marvelling at the smooth texture of her skin. Her gaze felt like the warm sun beating down on him. Everything was right in the world when she was with him. They'd been separated for too long. From now on, they'd be together, until the end of time.

Pulling himself away from the almost hypnotic stare of his heart's desire, he barked at the lieutenants of his army that remained.

"Pummel their defences from a distance. I want flying sorties throughout the day and night, at random, unexpected times. Try every form of magic you can think of. Keep them busy, on their toes, on edge, all of the time.

I want no let up. But I want our losses kept to a minimum. No huge forces, no all out attacks. Not yet anyway. We'll grind them down, wear them out. Lack of sleep, the constant threat of attack and not knowing what will happen next, will test their loyalty to the dragon they've sworn allegiance to. Make it so!"

The beings, some dragon, one or two naga, zipped off in the direction of the troops under their command, all eager to be away from under the twisted gaze of their soon to be king, some troubled at the thought of failing, given exactly what they'd just seen.

Earth's surface. New Delhi, India.
Day had just turned to dusk, although the stifling heat remained as she wove her way deeper into the throng of people, all out to spot a bargain. Meena Bazaar in the Old Delhi district was one of the busiest in all India, and at this time of day was almost guaranteed to be jam-packed full of people. Unsurprisingly, it was making her journey all the more difficult. The noise didn't help. Customers haggling, merchandise being dragged along the ground, and the squawking, barking and howling of all sorts of exotic animals made it hard for her to focus as a headache like an exploding volcano threatened to burst through her skull. Zigzagging briskly through the swarm of shoppers against the backdrop of vendors selling anything from paintings to all types of clothing, a vast array of bags to every colour of fabric imaginable, she continued to hold the scarf across her face, both to conceal her identity and protect her from the choking smog that had once again enveloped the city and its denizens. Ten days ago this had started, and there seemed little likelihood of it abating any time soon. What harmed the city and its residents had presented her and her kind with an opportunity, one she was eager to capitalise on. Right now, secreted in two small vials, protected by sturdy metallic pockets at the front of her belt, concealed

beneath a swathe of clothing, sat a poison so powerful and indiscriminate that it had the potential to bring countries to their knees. She didn't need to do that, or indeed kill the millions that the toxin could do quite easily. Instead she needed to overwhelm. Engulf the population, the emergency services, create a situation that the city would struggle to contain, and so in turn spread fear and panic across the rest of the country. That would be enough to leave her deeply satisfied.

Meandering through the crowd like water through a flood plain, in the distance she spotted her exit from the market, a route even more densely packed with people than those she'd already traversed. Of course it would be busy, given that it was the most direct route to the Jama Masjid, India's largest mosque, able to seat almost twenty-five thousand people.

'A staggering achievement really,' she thought to herself. 'These humans, when they put their minds to it, can achieve almost anything. It's a shame it has to come to such a crushing end for them. Anyhow, that's not really any of my business. All I want is for the king to be free, and for our race to be back in the chilly waters we've been used to for all these years. The fate of these bipeds is not my concern,' she continued to tell herself. 'We resided on this planet long before them, and will still be here long after they cease to exist, something that may well be coming much sooner than they think.'

Packed in tight like a tin of sardines, she shuffled forward whenever the crowd would allow it, coarse grains of dark yellow sand brushing in and out of her toes as she did so. Between the shoulders of two men dressed in dark brown clothing, she just caught a glimpse of one of the Jama Masjid's two fifteen metre high minarets dominating the skyline directly in front of her, and although her near perfect memory recalled exactly where she was heading, seeing the ancient mosque offered up a small crumb of comfort, knowing that she was on the right track.

It took her ten more minutes to reach her goal, which was crazy given that it was just two hundred metres away, but the crowds really were that bad. With most of the people continuing on to the famed mosque, she slipped off left down a narrow thoroughfare, seeking out the darkness and plentiful shadows it provided. Physically concealed, she let her mind wander out in front of her, checking for anything unusual, or anyone that had no real reason to be there. It was clear, for now at least. Following the twisted path, after a few moments she reached a deserted little courtyard at the end of a cobbled road. Parked in front of her was an old dark red Citroen estate, just as she'd been assured it would be. With no time to lose, she raced around to the right rear of the car, and felt about on top of the tyre. Sure enough, her slim, pale hand found just what she was looking for... two sets of keys. Grabbing them tightly, she stood up and quickly unlocked the car. Sliding behind the wheel, she stuck one of the keys in the ignition. Fearful of something going wrong, she turned the key and, to her mild surprise, the old vehicle chugged into life first time. Relieved, she wasted no time. Jumping out, she locked the driver's door before checking the rest of the car was secure. Hastily making her way to the back of the vehicle where its exhaust was spewing out toxic clouds of diesel fumes, with one hand firmly holding her scarf in place over her face, she withdrew one of the vials from her belt with the other. Loosening the rubber stopper of the vial, she leant down and shoved the poison as far as she dared up the vehicle's exhaust pipe, knowing that its volatile mixture would ever so slowly leak out and combine with the diesel emissions from the car. Pollutants from the burning of fuels reacting with the sunlight's heat and fine particles in the atmosphere had many days ago formed the cloud of smog that hung over the city like dry ice at a disco. Unsustainable levels of traffic, high temperatures, sunshine and calm winds had led to increasing pollution levels nearer the ground, closer to where people were respiring. The population were already suffering from eye irritation, inflammation of the lungs, chest pains and most commonly, asthma attacks. Her little addition to the car's output wouldn't kill, at least not a fit and healthy human being. But it would exacerbate the side effects of the smog that were already there, making them much, much worse, creating havoc from normality, overloading the city's already overworked infrastructure.

Creeping back into the shadows, the low roar of the car fading into the distance behind her, she started to head in a south westerly direction, towards the suburbs of New Delhi, past the airport, heading for another battered old vehicle, where she would once again repeat the process with the other vial tucked safely in her belt.

5 NOT A SNOWBALL'S CHANCE IN HELL

Exiting the mantra-made shaft at speed, tucked tightly into a ball, he extended his senses all around him. The pinprick of light he'd seen had so quickly materialised into a dimly lit frozen cavern. Having looked, taken it all in and decided on a course of action in but a split second, he exerted all his will, ordering the mantra to move him as far right as it could, all the time spinning, his head tucked tightly between his knees, anticipating the looming impact that he knew, at the very least, would hurt like hell. He just had to get this right. His life, and many others, depended on it.

The camouflaged ball of fast moving energy that he was, bumped the side of one of the cavern's frosty walls, burning a hole in the specially designed suit, while at the same time scraping the skin from part of his left arm. Ignoring the brutal onslaught of fierce pain, he rushed towards the curved base of the icy floor, mentally wished himself luck, closed his eyes, erected the strongest shield he could, and waited.

The vast cavern, in which an unexplained hole had appeared not minutes before, abruptly shook violently. Jutting icicles and boulders tumbled from its ceiling, smashing inadvertently across the shiny, slick floor. A cascading echo the likes of which the cavern had never seen, ricocheted throughout, its harsh, rough notes seemingly trapped forever more.

Flash hit the curved base of the wall like a rocket. Still tucked in a ball, he shot across the slippery surface, eventually smashing into a collection of stalagmites tucked away in one darkened corner, finally coming to rest. Dizzily, he got to his feet, desperate to get his bearings, knowing time was of the essence.

Leaning over the shaft, waiting for any type of signal at all from his friend, he could sense the nervousness of the young dragons around him. It was only to be expected he supposed, given that they were here, in the harshest environment the planet had to offer, the only thing currently keeping them alive, the protective suits, the result of the youngsters' ingenuity, cunning and never ending imagination. Whether the suits would hold was pretty near the top of his worry list at the moment, not currently wishing to voice any concerns as to how long they were designed to last in these surroundings. Furthermore, he just wanted to get the naga king, and get out. This place gave him the creeps, and not just because of the cold. There was something else, something dark, mysterious and dangerous... something to be afraid of. His thoughts turned briefly to his wife, Rose, wishing dearly to see her again. But something deep inside told him he wouldn't, that he'd got himself in far too deep this time. So deep in fact, that he'd never return to the domain, and the dragon he so loved. Leaning over a little more, silently he willed his friend on, as the snowflakes battered his shrouded body.

On getting to his feet, he'd slid back into the wall, behind the remnants of the stalagmites that he'd just wiped out, unable to resist checking out his arm, the pain was so bad. A huge chunk had been taken out of the suit, exposing his elbow, or rather a significant bit of it that had the skin missing, bone and blood both showing. Swallowing back the bile that threatened to rise in his throat, he dipped into his well of magic and poured it out into his arm, relieved to feel the familiar healing tingle of it washing over his damaged limb.

Cautiously, he peered out from his hidey hole. From where he was, there was nothing to see but a chilly white landscape. Knowing that the hole in his suit compromised his ability to blend in seamlessly, and with a nagging sense of urgency tugging away at him, carefully he trotted off, all the time hugging the icy wall of the cavern, in the hope that he would be at least partially concealed.

Out of nowhere, the mantra had gone off, waking him from the only kind of slumber available in a place like this, interrupted and infrequent. Just like 'he who must be obeyed' had said it would go off. Everything was set. Everything was ready. THEY were in for a big surprise.

From the corner of one eye, Yoyo could just see two of the camouflaged figures conversing with one another. It was hard to make them out, but if he watched the snow very carefully, he could just spot their outlines by the way the flakes, some nearly the size of tennis balls, impacted on their suits. From his reckoning, it looked as though Tina and Hillier were the two chatting, but both had now stopped, and were on their way over to him.

Taking a step back from the massive borehole in front of him, Yoyo made space for two of the most inventive young dragons of the lot, as they fought against the wind to reach him. Opening the mask of his suit just a little, he shouted as loud as he could to be heard against the roaring force of the snow storm.

"What's going on?" he enquired.

Tina pulled back her mask ever so slightly.

"I think we have a problem," she stated, with the kind of urgency Yoyo had never seen in her.

"What is it?" asked their mentor and friend, concerned.

Hillier reluctantly pulled back his mask.

"A few minutes ago, the heat tracing mantra detected something down there. It wasn't much, and it didn't last long, but there was certainly something there."

"Thoughts?" asked Yoyo.

"Best guess," added Tina, "is that of a mantra being set off. It's a pretty good bet whoever's down there, knows that we're here."

'Damn!' screamed Yoyo inside his own head. 'What the hell are we going to do now?'

Before he had a chance to even ask the two youngsters, Hillier piped up.

"If this is as important as you've led us to believe, I really think we have to get down there, and fast," he yelled over the shrieking wind.

'It has to be something else... doesn't it?' Yoyo told himself. But even inside his head it sounded lame. Whoever or whatever was down there had been expecting visitors. That changed everything. They had, for better or worse, to go and join Flash, and hope that they were still in time. Yoyo could never remember being this afraid.

Back pressed flat against the chilling wall, Flash peeked through a small gap in the ice, to see what lay around the next corner. The sight that greeted him turned his stomach. Stretched out on the cold ice, a ragged, flimsy looking dragon body in its natural form lay for all to see, the extent of the injuries inflicted on it all too evident. Both wing membranes were gone, scales were missing, bones jutted out at impossible angles and sickly, thick patches of green blood littered its legs, arms and back. This, Flash knew, was a dragon that had been tortured in the most unimaginable way possible. Even a dragon's worst nightmare wouldn't have got close to what had gone on here. A cold rage boiled up inside him at the thought of what the now deceased dragon had gone through. Anger pumped through his veins, ran through his blood, seeped into every living part of him. Beings would pay for this. Maybe not now, but he vowed there and then to hunt down whoever had done this and play a major part in their own nightmares. Just as he was about to move on, satisfied that nothing untoward awaited him around the corner, he caught sight of the chains binding the dragon to the icy wall in the background. Tank's whispered message came back to him, there and then. He thought about trying out the mantra on the chains in front of him, but had no idea just how draining it would be. If it took too much out of him, he might not be able to free the naga king, and of course Fredric, Peter's grandfather; he hadn't forgotten about him. But to have some laminium with him to boost his powers, was indeed a temptation. In the end, he decided against it, knowing that he would have chains from either of the prisoners he'd come to liberate.

Skulking around the corner, he could just make out the faint buzz of the flickering light, interspersed with the sound of gurgling water.

'Oh my God,' he thought. 'I'm here, I'm actually here.'

Using the giant dragon's corpse for cover, he scrabbled along the ice to its tail, where he stopped, all the time making sure to keep his damaged, exposed arm flush against it. Popping his head up briefly, he took in the scene before him. There, right in front of him, stood both the naga king and Fredric, Peter's grandfather and creator of the 'Crimson Guards'. He felt almost giddy with excitement knowing that in only a few moments' time, they would all leave this place forever. With pride swelling in his chest at what he'd accomplished, he stood and boldly started to walk towards the two prisoners.

He'd told them they were under no obligation to do this. Just as he'd thought, they weren't having any of his warnings. As they'd all said, they wouldn't have come this far if they hadn't meant to follow it through. He'd tried to explain just what they might be facing, and exactly how dangerous that might be. But typically, they didn't seem to care. He didn't know what more he could do. He didn't want to send them in after Flash; he cared for them a great deal. The sensible part of him knew though, that they might be the difference between winning and losing, here today. And that in turn might have consequences of epic proportions. So without further ado, Yoyo explained exactly what they were going to do once they reached the bottom of the icy shaft.

A few steps in, he suddenly wondered how he should reveal himself. He'd thought only moments ago that he should just stroll up to the naga king, remove his mask and introduce himself. Now, that seemed a very risky thing to do, given that he had no idea just how the naga monarch would react. So he'd changed things on the hoof, deciding to reveal himself to Fredric first, with a view to speeding up their escape and making things run a bit smoother. Padding along the ice as quietly as he could, he made his way over to the old dragon, who was currently doing one handed push ups on the icy cold cavern floor.

Abruptly Fredric stopped, the bulging, taut muscles in his right arm easily supporting his weight, as he looked over his shoulder for something he knew to be there, but could not actually see. Flash was amazed. He could have sworn he hadn't made any noise at all, even though it was clear that Fredric knew he was here. Without further delay, he brought up his arm, and peeled off his mask. The look on Fredric's face was an absolute picture.

"Hi," was all Flash could think to say. Looking back, that was probably the lamest introduction in the history of introductions.

Fredric jumped to his feet. His bonds rattled as he did so.

"Hi yourself," he said, smiling. "You're the youngster we had the pleasure of meeting, albeit rather briefly, if I'm not mistaken?"

"I am," replied Flash.

By now, the normally docile looking naga king had taken a keen interest in what was going on, and had slithered as close as his chains would allow.

"I've come to free you," said Flash. "There's little time to lose. The dragon kingdom and the world above it are in dire need of you both."

"I hope you have a way to release us from these chains," uttered Fredric, a sense of hope etched across his face.

Flash was just about to tell him about Tank's mantra, when he caught the tiniest movement in his peripheral vision. Clearly Fredric had too. They both turned, to find the evil, villainous looking jailer, seemingly having appeared from nowhere, standing not twenty metres away. Flash turned, already in fighting stance, waiting to destroy anything standing in his way. And this one being didn't look nearly tough enough to give him any trouble. Just as he thought this, dark shapes from almost every corner of the cavern slithered into view, some sliding out from beneath the ice, others dropping down from the ceiling, half a dozen or so slipping around the rock face Flash had previously navigated, looking like Olympic speed skaters, so fast was their cornering.

As the evil jailer cackled with delight, Flash turned his head to look at Fredric. The hope that had been carved into his face moments ago had disappeared. There must have been thirty or so nagas surrounding them in the cavern. Flash hadn't been prepared for all of this. Half a dozen or so he could take, but not this. Never this!

6 A SURPRISING BLOW

They'd all been watered (in Richie's case, quite literally) and fed. Dragons encircling the humans roared with laughter at the dumbstruck looks their charges gave the cooking equipment... a faint glimmer of amusement on a very dark day. For their part, the humans were fascinated by the sheer size of the pots, pans and utensils. Hook was keen to find out what a dragon portion of breakfast looked like, and was desperate to try one. In the end he had to settle for a helping of beans, bacon and dragon toast (toasted with the flame from a dragon's mouth) three times the size of a normal human amount. Everything was cooked to perfection.

Sitting in and around the still slightly stunned humans, dragons wolfed down industrial amounts of bacon and beans, the occasional crunch of dark charcoal being gobbled up interrupting the whispered conversations. Having taken his seat with the others, Gee Tee mused about just how good the breakfast was, something he continually reminded Tank about, much to the rugby player's annoyance.

Almost as soon as it had started, it was done, and the motley group of dragons and humans were ready to move out. All but one of the *tors* had decided to stay at the nursery ring, much to Richie's disappointment. They had, however, gained nine of the older students, with the much younger ones having been forbidden to join by the *tors* with them, considering the doomed quest nothing short of suicidal.

A standing semicircle of dragons and humans surrounded Richie, the raggedy bunch waiting for their instructions, humans at the front, dragons behind, apart from the old shopkeeper who sat slumped on the world's biggest cushion, off to one side.

It was time!

"You've chosen me to lead you," Richie announced to the gathered crowd. "In doing so, you've sworn your undying loyalty to free our king and take back the kingdom that is rightfully ours. Now is not the time to falter. We all need to be strong, brave, courageous and fearless. Everything, the fate of the underground domain that we love so much, the future of the planet even, depends on us and our actions today. It won't be pretty, it won't be nice. All of us will have to do things we won't want to," she said, knowing that hers was only moments away. "Some of us won't be coming back."

Richie paused, letting a long silence encompass the courtyard. She wanted them to think about what was to come, how dire things were... the severity of what they were about to embark upon. The stoic look on all their faces told her they were doing just that. After what she judged long enough, she resumed.

"Here and now, we're going to split into two forces. One to take back Fleet Street, hopefully allowing us to get communications with the rest of the world back online, with the other heading to the council building, its primary mission to rescue the king. That comes before anything else. Secondary to rescuing the monarch is defeating Manson's army, no mean feat given how badly outnumbered we are. Everyone here is to use whatever means possible to accomplish those tasks. Today, everything will be forgiven and forgotten, on that you have my word. I take full responsibility for every single act that occurs today. You will all have to be ruthless, efficient, brave and bold. You'll need to seize opportunities when they arise, using all your training and knowledge. If we're to succeed, you'll have to think outside the box, use your imagination to create magic, mayhem and misery. Use your anger. Unleash those primal instincts that you all keep bottled up. Today is not a day for regrets. One day. One chance. One outcome!"

Again, another pause, this time for effect, letting her words sink in, inspire.

"So now to the teams! I don't want any questions, arguments or suggestions. My mind is made up. In an ideal situation we'd have hundreds, if not thousands of dragons to take on Manson's army. We don't. So we just have to live with it, and do the best we can. Gee Tee, master mantra maker and the wisest dragon I know, will lead the group to retake Fleet Street. You need to follow his instructions without question, no matter how bizarre they may seem. He, and he alone, is the reason we are currently in any state to fight. Most of you would already be captured or dead if not for him. Remember that! Sam, Taibul, Emma and Angela, having worked so well together back in Salisbridge, you will be the human contingent. I'd like you," she said, pointing to one of the dragon healers who had helped heal Flash when he was saving Tank from his injuries during the previous battle, "to go. Along with all of you," she ordered, splitting off half a dozen of the Salisbridge dragons from the main group with a wave of her hand. Gee Tee smiled inanely at seeing the beautiful female dragon he'd only just got acquainted with, head his way. Richie went on to assign five of the nursery ring students, as well as the only *tor* to volunteer, to Gee Tee's group.

"I know as fighting forces go, this is incredibly small, but there really is no other choice. You may find you'll be able to pick up other dragons along the way. Hopefully what you'll be up against will be minimal. The rest of you will be going to the council building." What she'd missed out from that was the 'with me'. "There are two things I haven't mentioned so far, so listen up. Your strengths lie in your togetherness. Work in sync, fight and stay strong for one another. Watch each other's backs. You are stronger as a team. That I truly believe and could very well make the difference today."

Richie swallowed, dreading what she had to do next, as

those gathered around her looked on.

"For those of you not going to Fleet Street, a more dangerous mission I cannot imagine. But it has to be done, and done today. What you'll face at the council building, we really don't know. But you can assume you'll be dealing with beings who have no compunction about using deadly force. Torture and murder will be top of their agenda if they capture you. Remember that. Fight for your lives, for the lives of others, those around you, those that have already been killed by these twisted monsters. Fight with everything you have, right up until your very last breath, should it come to that."

Richie ran her hand through her curly brown locks, noting how matted and tangled they were. So far she'd shied away from it, but she knew if she didn't blurt it out now then she just wouldn't, and everything would be lost. So that's exactly what she did. She blurted it out.

"Tank will be leading this group," she stated, pointing directly towards her friend.

Eyes bulged, jaws dropped, looks of confusion spread across all of those gathered, not least Tank, who had absolutely no idea what was going on. Closing her eyes for a split second, she tried to compose her thoughts and filter out the turmoil of everything inside her mind. To an extent, she succeeded. By now though, whispered grumbles had started to spread across the crowd. Knowing that her leadership was hanging by a thread, she fought to find the right words.

"Most of you are rightly confused about what I've just said. While I'm not sure I can explain to your satisfaction, I will endeavour to do my best."

Gee Tee looked on, from his laid back position on the gigantic cushion.

'This,' he thought, 'was what she was talking about earlier. Oh my, what exactly have I done?'

"There's something I have to do. It could change everything that happens today. I don't want to do it. I don't want to be alone. But it has to be like this. I'd much rather be alongside all of you, going to the council building. If I'm saying I'd rather be fighting Manson's army than attempt the task I've set myself, perhaps that gives you some idea of what I will face. And no, I'm really sorry, I can't tell you what it is. But know this. I'm not running away. This is important. I will be there for the fight. I might be a little late, but rest assured... I will be there."

The restlessness faded. She'd regained their trust... well, almost.

"There's nothing much else to say that hasn't already been said. Follow those in charge. Give your all, for dragons across the world, and our beloved monarch. WE WILL PREVAIL!"

"WE WILL PREVAIL!" the crowd shouted in return.

"Sort out your things. Both teams will move out in five minutes."

The beings dispersed, some checking their equipment, others adding some last minute essentials or saying goodbye to friends on a different team. All were doing something, all except Tank and the master mantra maker. A knot in her stomach, she walked over to them both.

"What the hell?!" exclaimed Tank, before either of the other two could say a word.

"I'm sorry," Richie mumbled.

"SORRY!" Tank yelled. "What good is that? Tell me, how on earth am I supposed to lead this lot?" he motioned to everyone else who'd been in the crowd.

Richie started to flush crimson. She'd never seen her friend so upset. All the neat planning she'd done in her head was coming unravelled. She was sure she'd got it spot on, but that was clearly not so.

"Tank," whispered a soothing, soft voice. "Calm down. There really is no need for all this," managed the old shopkeeper.

Tank turned to face his employer, his mentor, his

friend. Anger and confusion melted away as he did so. He found it hard to be upset around the old dragon these days.

"I don't think your friend here would have put you in charge if she didn't have total and utter faith in your abilities," continued the old dragon. "You ask how you're going to lead this peculiar mix of humans and dragons. Undoubtedly... with ease. You have a better grasp of the world around you than almost any other dragon I've met. You're logical, and yet have the most fantastic imagination. For you to lead these beings into battle will not require any qualities you don't already possess. Of course you lack the stomach for the really dirty deeds that may be necessary today, but you have others around you that will almost certainly make up for that. In short... you'll make a fabulous leader. Just believe in yourself."

Tank was completely taken aback. He'd never heard the master mantra maker talk like that.

By now the humans, Janice, Hook, Sam, Taibul, Emma and Angela, had surrounded all three of them and were listening intently to the conversation. The wise old shopkeeper hadn't finished though.

"Perhaps instead of losing your temper with your friend, you might want to consider exactly what she will face on whatever singular quest she's set herself."

This time it was Tank's cheeks that were flushing. He chided himself for not knowing better.

"It's me that should be apologising, Rich," he opined. "Of course I'll do what you ask. It was just a surprise, that's all."

Richie smiled meekly at her strapping great friend, a massive weight taken off her mind. It was then that she noticed the others, the humans that had accompanied her on this crazy, roller coaster ride of a journey. She urged them to come in. They did so.

"Listen," she said. "I'm truly grateful for your company and efforts today. But now, I'm so sorry to have gotten you all involved. If anything should happen to any one of you, I'll be absolutely crushed."

They all looked on, not knowing what to say. That is, until the wisest of them spoke up again.

"It'll be alright. Let's not forget that despite what you think, we're not alone in all this. Young Flash is undoubtedly even now freeing the prisoners in the Antarctic, while working out how to get back here fast enough to be of some good. As for the king, well, let's just say he and I go way back. Most might see him nowadays as frail, past his best and weak. Let me assure you that is not the case. We've had our differences of course, but I'll tell you now, there are few warriors as mighty as he still is. Under that charming and caring demeanour, beats the heart of a fierce and cunning warrior. If that army of Manson's is trying to take the sovereign and the seat of power, he's in for the surprise of his life. George will unleash hell on his sorry little arse."

Despite the seriousness of the situation, Janice, Emma and Angela all giggled at that last comment.

"Pay heed to what I say little ones... it can still go our way," continued the master mantra maker. "We will all need a little luck, all the courage we possess, and for others to do their part. But I truly believe we can prevail."

They all reflected on that, for a moment at least.

"And now I think it is time to take my leave, and my team," whispered the old dragon. "Say your goodbyes little ones. You have one minute." With that, the old shopkeeper leant down and embraced Richie for all she was worth. It was a touching gesture and one the young lacrosse player really appreciated.

"Good luck," he whispered in her ear.

"You too," she replied, kissing him on the cheek, forcing a smile onto her face, before moving into the huddle of humans.

Tank had made his way over to his former boss, and now associate, with both silently looking into each other's eyes, neither giving anything away.

"It will be alright youngster."

"I know," replied Tank, lying.

Both had so much to say, both struggled to get the words out. In the end, Tank threw himself at Gee Tee, wrapping his human arms as far around the old shopkeeper's stomach as they would go.

"I'm sorry to have dragged you into all this," babbled the young rugby playing dragon.

Gee Tee chuckled.

"I think it's me who should be sorry. Sorry for what you went through back in Salisbridge, sorry that I've not expressed my appreciation more often for all your efforts over the years. You do know how much I care about you, don't you?" queried the old dragon.

Tank just nodded. That was all he could do with tears streaming down his cheeks. He loved the old dragon like a father. It was only now that he was willing to admit that to himself. He never wanted to let him go. But let him go he did. Before they parted though, the old shopkeeper had a little something for the dragon he loved like a son. Reaching into the seemingly bottomless pouches surrounding his stomach, he pulled out the replica of the king's ring that they'd both spent so much time working on.

"Why on earth did you bring that?" asked Tank.

"I'm not entirely sure. I thought at some point one of us would get as far as the ruler and who knows, perhaps it will come in handy. Looks like it's not going to be me, so perhaps you should take it," said Gee Tee, offering out the eye-catching replica.

Tank let the old dragon drop the spectacular ring into the palm of his hand, not taking his eyes off the striking piece of jewellery for one second. Now that he thought about it, he supposed it could be of some use. With that in mind, he tucked it away in a tiny little pocket on the side of one of the walking boots that he'd managed to procure.

He knew it would be quite safe, and no one would even think to look there. With nothing more for it, the two nodded to each other and went their separate ways.

Meanwhile, Richie and all the other humans were saying their farewells. Hook and Janice both shook Sam and Taibul's hands, before embracing Emma and Angela, whispering words of encouragement and luck. After that, it was Richie's turn. She wished them all the best, hugging each one tightly, fearing it might be for the very last time, until it was Janice's turn. Both women stood facing each other awkwardly. There was plenty of friction between the two of them, there nearly always had been. It was unnecessary. They both loved Peter, one as a best friend, the other as a lover and a confidant. Neither had really seen this. Neither had budged an inch. But here they were, after everything they'd been through over the last day, violence, desperation and that love for the hockey playing dragon thrusting them together, an invisible bond linking them in their desire and determination to get him back at any cost.

"Are you going to be okay?" asked the diminutive bar worker.

A beaming smile broke out across Richie's face.

"It's nice that you're worried for me. I'd be far more concerned about where you're going if I were you."

"Oh I am. But I need to see him. Need to have him back. You see I love him with all my heart. It's as simple as that."

"I know," whispered Richie, stepping forward to hug her friend. "I love him too. Don't worry, we'll get him back. I have something to do, but I'll be there... I promise!"

Looking deep into Richie's eyes, Janice could see that she meant every word she said. Giving the lacrosse player a nod, she stepped back to join the others.

Richie strolled up to Hook, marvelling at how well he was coping with the giant, heavy water pack attached to his back.

"You're stronger than you look," she said, smiling.

"So are you. But now we know why... pesky dragon! I always knew there was something special about you... wouldn't have guessed in a million years that it would have been this though. Who would have thought it, eh?"

They both burst into laughter. When the moment was over, Richie's face took on a serious edge.

"Look after them," she uttered. "Never give up hope, no matter how desperate things appear."

Hook embraced her uncomfortably, given the huge weight on his back, and replied,

"I will, I promise."

With that, the humans turned and headed off to their respective groups, who by now had all gathered to leave. Richie turned to see Tank waiting off to one side and strolled purposefully over to him.

"So this is it then," he announced.

"I guess it is," she replied.

"What the hell are we doing Rich?" he asked, shaking his head. "The whole world's gone to hell, relying on us to save it."

"Yeah," she said, smiling. "Who'd have thought it?"

Tank stepped forward and wrapped his tree trunk arms around her. She embraced him back, for all she was worth.

"We'll get both Peter and Tim back," he whispered.

She nodded, her head rubbing up and down on his well defined chest. Pulling back a little, she gazed up into his face, lost in so many thoughts.

"I'm so scared, Tank," she finally admitted.

"I know. We all are. But what can you do but listen to your own advice. For as long as we've known each other, you've always been the strong one, both fearless and imaginative. Use each and every one of those well honed qualities today, and we'll get through this, meeting up again on the other side. A dragon couldn't wish for a better friend," he said, once again holding her tight.

She started to cry. All the time, both groups looked on, not knowing what to make of things.

Thirty seconds later, it was over. They parted, knowing looks in their eyes, Richie adjusting Aviva's laminium dagger that was secured in the makeshift holster in the small of her back. Tank marched over to his group. All together, each and every one of those departing quietly exited the nursery ring, past the *tors* guarding the only available way out. Once outside in the darkened streets and alleys, they split up into two discernible groups. As this happened, Richie bounded off down the main thoroughfare, slipping into the shadows, like a hand into a glove, a foot into a shoe. In the blink of an eye, she was gone. Once the two parties had split, they crept off in different directions, none of the individuals looking back at the others, thoughts firmly focused on the mission at hand, and travelling unnoticed through the eerie streets of war torn suburban London.

Earth's surface. Salisbridge, England.
Arriving home from work a little later than normal, he turned his key in the lock, strolled inside and laid his briefcase on the kitchen table. Glancing around the place, he found it more than a little odd that things remained totally unchanged from when he'd left the house much earlier on in the day. Not usually one to pry, curiosity tinged with worry made him go and knock on his roommate's bedroom door. After banging quite hard three times in a row and calling out his name, the normally reserved insurance worker named Gavin did something so unthinkable, it sent a shiver down his spine and made his head swim. Turning the handle, he opened the door and poked his head inside. In the midst of a tidy bedroom with everything 'just so,' rugby memorabilia adorned almost every free space. Magazines sat on the bedside table, photographs sat piled on the window sill, shining awards

adorned the dark brown wooden shelves. Gavin had seen the inside of Hook's room before and so none of it came as a surprise. What was odd though, was that there was no rugby kit either dirty or clean, lying about, that and the fact all of the rugby player's work suits were still hanging up untouched and the bed clearly hadn't been slept in. Something seemed totally and utterly wrong. Vowing to give his friend until the morning to turn up before he thought about a further course of action, the insurance worker strolled back into the kitchen, his thoughts having turned to what he'd be having for dinner.

Ten kilometres away, another bewildered being knocked frantically on a front door, puzzled at the lack of a car outside.

'Normally he'd be long back from work,' she thought. Drawing her phone once again out of her handbag, she hit send on the number she selected. In big bold letters the name SAM appeared at the top of the screen. Listening intently, she waited patiently, hoping to hear his voice. It wasn't to be. Just like the other dozen or so times she'd tried in the last twenty-four hours, the phone went straight to voicemail. Ignoring the chance to leave yet another message, she hit the cancel button and headed back across the road towards her car. Worried that something untoward had happened to her boyfriend, Susan climbed into the driver's side and thought about contacting the police. After a moment or two of thought on the matter, she decided against that course of action. It wouldn't be totally unusual for him to be caught up at work would it? And what would the authorities do? Very little probably, since as far as she could tell, he hadn't been missing long, if he was even missing at all. And so still more than a little concerned, she punched the button to start the engine, slipped it in gear, and sped off up the road towards her house, thoughts firmly focused on what to do next.

With the evening shift over half an hour in, the restaurant only had a couple of diners in it, both of whom were just tucking into a stack of poppadoms and the side dishes that accompanied them. One of the waiters behind the bar finished writing down a takeaway order. No sooner had he put the phone down, than it rang again. Picking it back up as he passed the previous order off to one of his colleagues, he politely asked how he could help, before grabbing his pad and a pen. Off to one side, just out of sight of the diners, hidden away in front of the door to the kitchen, two waiters, one much older than the other started to chat.

"What do you think has happened to him?"

"I don't know. All I do know, is that his father is extremely worried."

"That's understandable."

"It is. But it might be us that pays the price."

"Why?"

"Because nobody stopped him from taking the knives, or going off with that gang from the sports club."

"Taibul's a strong willed boy. None of us could have stopped him."

"I know that, and so do you. But I very much doubt his father sees it that way. And since he owns this place and pays our wages, we'd all better be on our best behaviour and watch out. I for one can't afford to lose this job."

Nodding, his co-worker agreed, before flitting off into the kitchen to see if the couple's next course was ready.

Sitting perched on the flowery white sofa, they listened carefully once again, hoping that this time their beloved daughter would finally pick up on her end. As her husband held out his mobile in front of them, a slight crackle coming over the speaker echoed around the immaculate front room, Emma's mother wiped away yet another set of tears with a folded white tissue, unusually not bothered about smearing her makeup. Unsurprisingly the phone, just as in the previous attempts, did not connect. It filled them both with more dread and fear than they cared to admit... even to each other. Finally, not only did he dare think it, but he said it out loud.

"I think it's finally time we called the police."

Sniffing profusely, the tears having started to gush once more, his wife nodded her agreement. Their daughter hadn't come home on Saturday night, something on its own that was cause for concern. But it was now Monday and there'd been no sign of her and she'd skipped work. Having phoned all her friends, as well as her employer, they were now reaching their wits' end. And while neither wanted to admit the seriousness of the situation, having the police involved very nearly confirmed their worst fears.

In Angela's case, it was very different. She worked from home as a graphic design artist, and her friends were the lacrosse players she trained with midweek and played with at the weekend. It was unlikely that anyone would miss her for at least a few days yet. And by then, things would probably be all over one way or another.

7 THE STRONGEST OF BONDS

Sitting shackled, back to back on the shiny, polished floor of the council building, Peter and Tim's hands were bound by the strength sapping chains behind them. They'd been thrown there a few hours earlier and had been left mostly undisturbed.

Although he didn't know exactly which floor of the giant monolith they were on, Peter did at least have a rough idea. How? Because if he leant forward as far as he could, pulling Tim's currently unconscious body with him a little, he could just manage to peek round the corner in front of him, which afforded a view out of one of the panoramic, wraparound windows. That scene hadn't changed since they'd been here. Off in the distance some way, and about a hundred metres above them, a striking hemisphere of blue energy crackled and rippled, shielding a huge part of the now exposed cliff that made up the side of the king's private residence. If he looked really carefully, he could just make out a much darker colour beyond the, for now, impenetrable barrier. He knew it marked the entrance to the private residence, somewhere that held fond memories for him, a location once accessed by the magnificent marvel of engineering of a bridge that had earlier in the day been obliterated. Briefly he wondered who was responsible for the wanton destruction. It didn't make much sense, to him anyway, for Manson to have demolished the bridge, especially with so many nagas on his attacking force. As far as he knew they couldn't fly, but given everything that had occurred over the last couple of days, he wouldn't have been at all surprised to learn they could. That only left the king's force.

'Things,' he thought, 'must be really desperate if they've destroyed their only way out.'

Coughing and spluttering from behind startled him

back to the present. Gingerly, Tim came round.

"How are you feeling?" whispered Peter.

"Rotten," rasped Tim. "Where are we?"

"The council building in London," replied Peter, having completely forgotten that Tim would have no idea about dragon cultural landmarks.

"Anything happen while I was out?"

"Not really. They've checked on us a couple of times, but nothing other than that." Peter continued to tell Tim about the view of the sporadic attacks on the king's defences. Tim was aghast to learn that they'd cut off their only route to safety.

"What do you see happening now?" asked the newly formed dragon, after a moment of quiet contemplation.

Peter wriggled around, trying to get a bit more comfortable and stop the burning pain in his shoulders and biceps. He didn't succeed.

"Nothing I've seen bodes well for any of us," he blurted, almost before thinking. "The king's force is well and truly trapped, and I can't begin to think where any help would possibly come from. I'm sure there must be dragons somewhere fighting to get here and protect the monarch, but I don't doubt for one minute that Manson would have had some contingency for all that."

"And us?" Tim asked, thinking that he was addressing the elephant in the room.

'Two dragons and an elephant, that's funny,' he thought, letting out a brief chortle.

"Something funny?" enquired Peter.

"The whole thing I suppose," muttered Tim, downcast. "Dragons, a battle for the planet, I'm the new Messiah or whatever it is I'm supposed to be, and us... about to die. You've got to laugh."

Peter thought about it for a moment, and then started to chuckle uncontrollably. Tim joined in. All sense of time became lost as the two of them existed in their own little bubble. Eventually the moment passed and they came crashing back to reality with a certain sense of inevitability. The giggles banished, Peter considered Tim's last question carefully.

"I can't see any way out for us. Even if we could escape from these blasted chains, we'd still have to fight our way past Manson's army, and you wouldn't get very good odds on that being successful. If I'm honest, things are as bleak as they're ever likely to get. Sorry!"

"I appreciate your candour, my friend," Tim whispered.

Peter could feel the newly crowned White Dragon, from the renowned prophecy, shake uncontrollably. He wanted to comfort him, and felt helpless beyond belief at not being able to do so.

"So there's really no hope for a rescue then?" Tim asked quizzically, a minute or so later. "You're not just saying that so I wouldn't get my hopes up?"

Peter slumped forward, as far as he could go anyway.

"I can't for the life of me see where it could possibly come from. Unless the king has something unbelievable hidden behind that shield, then the chances of us ever seeing another sunrise are remote at best."

The two friends sat in silence, contemplating the seriousness of the situation both they, and the world, found themselves in.

Earth's surface. Washington DC, United States of America.

Yawning and stretching his arms out to form the 'Y' from The Village People's famous song, he took another hit from his strong, black coffee, hoping it would add a dash of alertness to his sleepy disposition. Normally he did his best work at around one in the morning, but today he was struggling to concentrate, feeling tired and a little run down. Perhaps he was coming down with something. That would be just typical. Stuck in this unnatural form, with these oh so fussy and particular beings who were always ill, almost at the drop of a hat, it would be just his luck to pick up some germ or other that he wasn't resistant to. They'd warned him about that before he'd set out on his mission. BLAH! Sinking the rest of the cup of Java, he sat up straight, pulled his chair in as far as it would go, and, determined not to be affected by any bug, computer or otherwise, tilted the two giant LCD computer monitors to give him the ideal viewing angle for what he was working on. Feeling comfortable, and more awake than he had in some time, he glanced over to his right, out of the full frame glass window of his Georgetown condo. Despite the late hour, he could just make out boats from their lights, sailing up and down the Potomac. Momentarily he wondered what they were doing. Surely not a pleasure cruise at this time of night. Part of him wished to be on the water, or at least slightly closer than the four hundred or so metres away he now found himself. He was supposed to have been grateful, that his so-called masters had found him this condominium so close to the water's edge. But in truth, all it did was remind him of what he'd lost, and what he was fighting for. Turning back to the huge screens, after taking a giant breath, he began.

To him, despite how tired he was, and just how racked with loneliness he felt, delving deep inside a piece of software from his desktop computer felt almost instinctive. And that was, of course, why he found himself in this precarious position. His software manipulation skills had got him noticed, unfortunately, and now he was to weave his completely different magic on creating what he considered a meaningless diversion, hoping the pathetic humans would look the other way. He'd been tasked with building and then unleashing a devastating form of ransomware, a malicious type of software that blocks access to the victim's data, until they pay a fee. That was just fine with him, especially given that he'd done the exact same thing on at least three previous occasions, and made rather a lot of money from it. The issue he had with what he'd been tasked to do, was that the software would just block the victims' access, even if they tried to pay the money. There was no collecting the cash. It was simply a way of taking as many computers as possible out of action to once again cause as much chaos as possible. Bright, intelligent and articulate as he was, he figured that much the same was taking place across every part of the globe, and that it wouldn't matter to those higher up in the chain of command if he skimmed just a little off the top.

Solely focused on the task at hand now, his mind lost in the lines of code on both monitors, his body reacted almost on autopilot, his fingers but a blur on the black keyboard, the noise of the keys music to his ears. His aim was to modify the 'WannaCry' worm that spread viciously across the internet in May of 2017, unprecedented in scale, infecting more than 200,000 computers. He'd chosen this virus because unlike most ransomware attacks which are typically carried out using a 'Trojan', legitimate files designed to trick the user into downloading them, or opening them as part of an email attachment, the 'WannaCry' worm travels automatically between computers without user interaction. A tall ask even for him, he knew that if he were successful, his masters would be utterly delighted with him.

Fingers gliding over the keys long into the night like a master musician, by the time the sun bounced off the boats and reflected off the silky river surface, his toil was complete, with a working virus ready to be dispatched at the touch of a button. Now all he had to do was allow the tricky little beast to run riot across the internet. The more computers infected, the better.

8 FAN OF STEEL

Privileged couldn't begin to describe her feelings, given that she'd been chosen from hundreds and hundreds of nurses to look after him. She had, of course, been to every match, got every book, magazine and had all the other merchandise. In short, she was a true fan. Not just of the Indigo Warriors, but of laminium ball itself, and that meant that looking after HIM was nothing short of a real honour. Up until now, it had been her dream job. But about fifteen minutes ago her dream had turned into a nightmare... a nightmare in which she currently found herself hiding in a supply cupboard alongside other members of the medical team, all afraid for their lives.

Confusing didn't begin to cover it. Only as recently as a few weeks ago he was unable to speak or communicate in any way, shape or form, so severe had been his injuries. In that time, he'd come a long way. He knew it was all down to the miracle medical team that cared for him twenty-four hours a day. Not only had they done a terrific job with his body, but had also pieced back together his splintered mind. Over the last week or so, he'd finally remembered who he was and just how he came to be in such dire straits. A laminium ball player, who'd have thought. And then there was THAT bomb. Memories flooded through him, like it had only just happened, sending a shiver along his powerful, brand new tail. Gazing at his reflection in the tinted glass that separated the room he was in from the next, he marvelled at the craftsmanship of the dragons that worked here.

'The job they've done is amazing,' he thought, as he ran both hands across the shiny new scales that made up his sleek belly. It was an odd feeling, that's for sure. The scales felt smooth, flexible and wafer thin. They weren't weak he knew, but they were brand new, fully regenerated. How? He didn't know the details. But what he did know was that they hadn't hardened yet and taken on that almost impossible to penetrate trait that gives dragons everywhere great peace of mind and makes them such formidable warriors. This combined with the fact that his wings had yet to reach their desired size, and the missing fragments of his memory, had made his decision seem even more remarkable. But when things had gone to hell, only a matter of minutes ago, something deep inside him had stirred, screaming at him to fight. Given his nature, it didn't take very much for him to comply.

During his enforced stay here, he'd been cut off from everything in the dragon domain. No news, no telepathic papers... NOTHING! At the start, he hadn't missed what he hadn't known, but as his memory started to come back, he felt the need to understand what was going on in the outside world. Still they hadn't told him. It drove him crazy, like an itch he just couldn't scratch. But some time ago, he'd overheard a conversation between a few of the staff. Clearly they'd thought him asleep. Their mistake! What he'd heard had both fascinated and terrified him in equal measure. Apparently, deadly bombs had gone off across the world, unleashing devastation beyond anything ever known. Dragon and humankind targeted. It was unbelievable, almost as if made up inside one of the humans' books on the surface, something he kept hearing about, and wished at some point to see for himself. At the moment, he wondered if his current predicament was somehow linked to that cataclysmic event. He supposed it was, but he had no idea how. All that he cared about was surviving whatever was going on and getting the staff that had done so much for him, out of here alive.

Looking down at the broken body of what he assumed to be a naga (he'd seen pictures and learnt all about them, just like every other dragonling) lying there at his feet, neck snapped, appearing for the most part like a child's broken toy, so impossible was the angle of his head, he wondered how many more were scouring the building. Procuring the vicious looking sword his attacker had worn at his hip, he decided it was time to go on the offensive.

Opening the room's door just a smidgen, he checked to see if the corridor was clear. It was. Making no noise at all, he swept out and headed off towards what he assumed was the entrance to the facility, knowing full well the rest of the staff had barricaded themselves in, further back where he'd come from. Unsure of where the entrance was, he had no memory of arriving, and up until ten minutes ago he hadn't left the room they'd been treating him in. Abruptly he dived into a secluded alcove off to his right, hidden from the main corridor by a giant potted fern, which looked as though it had come straight out of the rain forest. He'd heard voices coming from somewhere in front of him, in a strange tongue he didn't understand.

'It must be the attackers,' he thought, his shining, newly grown body hidden by the thick canopy of the plant. Nerves threatened to overwhelm him, but his character crushed them instantly. That's who he was. Using all his dragon senses, while gripping the deadly looking sword tightly, he tried for all he was worth to figure out what was coming his way.

Tasked with taking the medical facility, the group of nagas were small, well organised and had split up into ones and twos on entering the building. Two comrades in the corridor that Steel found himself secreted in, had just decided to split up, given the limited resistance they faced. One delved into a walkway, off to his left, while the other continued slithering forward in the direction that Steel had just come from.

Mind feeling fuzzy, muddied and unclear, he knew that if a dragon had been approaching, he would have been able to make out the details from where he was hidden. But because he assumed it was another of those beings, the best he could do was just to know that it was heading in his direction, all the time hoping it was alone. Pretty sure it was, he couldn't be entirely certain, which bothered him a lot. Coiled up like a spring, ready to strike, he took one long deep breath. Slithering into view, it wasn't until the naga passed the huge potted plant that it realised something was wrong. By then, it was too late. Steel leapt out with all the speed and agility of the athlete that he was. Wielding the sword at waist height, he put all his power and strength into bringing it around. Instinctively the naga turned and tried to dodge out of the way, but the deadly dark blur of metal was already destined for its goal. A target well found. Cutting almost all the way through, the blade sliced into the naga's circular waist, forcing the slippery being to thump to the floor, making far too much noise for Steel's liking. With thick, clear liquid oozing from the snakelike body across the polished floor, the naga seemed intent on uttering some final words. Fearful of it being a spell of some sort, Steel brought the sword back over his head, and then in one swift blow, decapitated the helpless beast. Aghast at what he'd just done, he did his best to hold on to his stomach contents, unfortunately to no avail, with the pot plant gaining a rather new and unusual mix of feed. Aware of how much danger was still out there, he couldn't fathom whether or not to try and hide the body parts lying there in front of him. In the end, he resolved not to bother, figuring speed was now of the essence. Taking a fleeting look at the gleaming black metal of the lethal looking sword in his hand, he decided, despite never having used one before, that he was now, most certainly, an aficionado. Pushing away that thought, he took off after the other naga, the one who'd been talking to the beast he'd just killed, before slipping away down the walkway.

Barricaded in the store room at the far end of the

facility, the medical staff had cast half a dozen mantras across the entrance, assuming that would be enough to deter even the most hardened attacker. Shields of various sorts, noise reduction mantras and even a perception puller, should take their mind right off the door, if they got this far, thought their leader. But currently, those weren't the subject of conversation.

"We can't be hiding away in here. It's repulsive."

"What exactly do you suggest?"

"We should be taking the fight to them. Teaching them a lesson they won't forget."

"Did you see what they did to Arthurituris? Not only what they did, but just how easily they did it. We wouldn't stand a chance. Our best hope is to wait here until they're gone."

"You mean cower in fear like frightened animals too afraid to stick up for themselves?"

Her worry wasn't helped by the bickering doctors. She wasn't so much scared for her own life, but for that of her patient. In the end, it all got too much, forcing her to speak up, when normally she wouldn't.

"What about him?" she interrupted.

"WHAT?" replied one of the specialist medics.

"STEEL! What about Steel?"

"H...h...he...he's probably found some cubby hole or other to lay low in, doing very much the same as us."

She snorted in derision.

"What's that supposed to mean?" asked the medic, not used to a nurse questioning his judgement.

She'd had it, and decided to speak her mind.

"The greatest laminium ball player in a generation... hiding away? You must be off your head. I very much doubt there's a braver, more courageous and fearless dragon on the entire planet. And let me tell you, the very last thing he'll be doing is hiding. We need to get out there and support him. He's our responsibility. His life was placed in our hands. So this isn't quite what we bargained for. Nevertheless, we should still be doing what we signed up to do, no matter what the price."

The small room suddenly felt very claustrophobic. You could scoop up the tension with a spoon.

The acerbic doctor, whose idea it had been to hide in the store cupboard in the first place, flushed totally red... jaw, cheeks, ears, nose, the lot. Tiny little flames squirted from his nose, looking like flares launched from a boat in trouble. He couldn't remember the last time one of his decisions had been questioned. More to the point, he couldn't believe it was by a NURSE!

Padding along very quietly now, hugging one wall, gripping the sword for all he was worth, he'd sprinted after the other naga, well at first anyway. Having made his way down the corridor, only to be confronted by a huge number of rooms off to either side, not wanting to give away his position, he'd chosen to move slowly, and try to catch the beast off guard. It was only when he was half way down that he spotted it, amazed that he hadn't noticed it before. There in the middle of the walkway, was a very thin layer, almost a film really, of clear liquid. Gazing off down the corridor, he could see the film weave gently from side to side, almost showing the naga looking through the windows in the doors of each room. Most interesting though, was that the film disappeared under a door at the end of the passage, off to the right.

'This is where it has to have gone,' he thought to himself as he stalked after it, not sure whether to lie in wait outside the door or to follow it in. As it happened, the decision was taken out of his hands just as he reached the entrance. Without warning the door came crashing open, the wriggling beast smashing through, both it and Steel each as surprised as the other. With the naga starting to mutter something under its breath, Steel belatedly swung the evil looking sword around. Faster than Steel could believe, the naga slipped out of the way, sliding off to one side, and then rolling back up to its full height on the other side of the corridor. The sword clattered into the door, smashing the glass in the window as it did, scattering the tiny little fragments everywhere. As all of this happened, Steel started to feel... muzzy, as if a thick fog had washed over his brain. Worse still, his vision had gone double, and now there were two corridors, and two nagas both grinning inanely.

As a laminium ball player, chosen at a very young age to be such, he'd never had to learn a lot about offensive mantras and spells. It just wasn't taught. Only those mantras allowed in the game, and a few other simple ones, had been on the curriculum. That was the same for all the players everywhere. Their sport required them to focus on that only and give their all. And so they did. So it was that Steel now found himself in a real bind. Outmatched and outgunned, so to speak. But he was nothing if not resourceful, which was one of the reasons the fans loved him so much. And so wading through his syrupy mind, inventiveness his friend, he selected what he hoped was the right mantra, ignored his double vision and put all his hope, belief and willpower, which was more than a match for any other dragon in the kingdom, behind the magic he cast.

Grinning like a Cheshire cat, the naga was just contemplating finishing off the dumb dragon, when out of nowhere an invisible weight crushed him against the corridor wall. Forcing all the air from his lungs, the confusion spell that he'd been casting on the dragon vanished completely. Disbelief turned to fear as he searched for the words that would save him.

Steel could feel his personal shield expand all around him, crushing the naga up against the wall, squeezing the very life out of him. Pushing ever on, willing it to grow even more, become even stronger, he was pleased to see the results of his improvised attack when his vision returned to normal.

Needing air or at least one breath anyway, the invisible force was everywhere, holding him against the wall. Desperately he tried to slither out beneath whatever it was, but his way was blocked all around. With panic taking over, he lashed out, flicking his tail as far as it would go. But it wasn't far enough. As the blackness that had started around the edge of his vision encompassed it all, his own sickly gurgle was the last sound he ever heard.

Steel crumpled to the floor, back to the wall, facing his opponent. Inside he knew he had no time to waste, not if he wanted to save the staff. But he had to rest, just for a few seconds. Panting heavily, all he could think was,

'That was too close.'

Earth's surface. Salisbridge, United Kingdom.
Meanwhile, back above ground in the historical city of Salisbridge, the local police were run ragged, trying to solve the mysterious disappearance of a multitude of individuals. Over the course of twenty-four hours, officers had been dispatched to a number of properties where missing people had been reported. Collating all the evidence back at the station had done them little good, up until the point the final call came in. On attending one of the city centre's Indian restaurants, both policewomen listened intently to the owner's seemingly outrageous story about what had happened the previous Saturday night. Only when the establishment's CCTV footage was reviewed did the officers start to take things seriously... so seriously in fact, that they had to pass things up the chain of command pretty damn quick. The kicker for them had come when they'd recognised the other missing persons they'd spent the best part of a day searching for. On seeing the group arm themselves after the woman in question had suffered some sort of fit on the floor in front of all the other diners, nothing about what had happened made the slightest bit of

sense. As the owner of the restaurant continued to badger them about the whereabouts of his son, both officers couldn't help but gaze out of the huge plate glass window which afforded a fabulous view of the city centre and in particular the ancient Poultry Cross, wondering just what had happened that fateful night. So many questions presented themselves. What had been wrong with the woman writhing around on the floor? Why did the group all need to be armed? Where had they gone? How had they avoided the CCTV covering the Poultry Cross? Was all of this done on purpose and pre-planned, or was it something off the cuff? Up until the point where the woman had become unwell, everything looked as though it were a normal Saturday night out.

'If only the restaurant's surveillance had extended further than the pavement outside,' one of the officers thought to herself. According to all the staff they'd interviewed, the group of armed men and women had headed out of the restaurant, the CCTV had confirmed this to be true, and then the woman who'd had the fit had somehow, if their accounts were to be believed, shimmied up the pole on which the council run CCTV cameras were situated, and disabled the camera before shimmying back down and joining her comrades. Moments later the whole group disappeared from sight, and not a word had been heard from any of them since. It was a total and utter mystery, one the colleagues were determined to resolve.

An hour after reinforcements were called for, four detectives, one of them being Tina, the Salisbridge lacrosse player and teammate of some of the missing persons, and several support officers arrived at the scene right in the middle of the city, causing heads to turn and whispers to run rife, something that wasn't really unexpected given that it was market day and the city streets were full of people shopping and going about their business. As the new arrivals settled in, the two officers started to explain to them all what they'd just uncovered.

9 SHATTERED ILLUSIONS

The bombardment was intense. Rippling in places, the translucent magical shield looked as though it would fold in on itself, the constant noise unsettling. It made the dragon troops and the surviving councillors nervous. The king, however, seemed lost in thought, no doubt considering the beings just the other side of the bottomless chasm that separated the two forces.

Amelia Battlehard had done all that she could and now found herself looking out through the constantly changing, blue tinged, transparent shield. With little concern for her own wellbeing, she worried over the safety of her troops and more importantly... the monarch! To say things looked bleak was an understatement. Just from what little they knew, the force they were facing was monstrous in size. It didn't help that they had no way of communicating with the outside world. Whatever had been done to ensure that, it had been well planned out in advance, before being carried out to perfection. She wondered how they'd done it, and if somehow she could have stopped it. Thoughts of help turning up whistled through her mind, but for the life of her, she couldn't see where it would come from. They'd had their knees cut out from under them, flailing around, outnumbered and outgunned with nowhere even left to run. Would she run if she could? It certainly wasn't very dragon-like. But if it kept the head of state alive and allowed him to live to fight another day, then she supposed she would.

"Penny for your thoughts, Captain?" whispered the king, having sneaked up behind her.

"It's difficult to know where to start, Your... George."

The slightest smile meandered across his face at the use of his name.

"I know things look pretty hopeless now, but don't

give up hope. There's always a chance, and I don't know about you, but I believe in being ready for when that one opportunity presents itself. It will come along, of that I have little doubt, Captain. Focus your mind on that. All is not lost."

Amelia Battlehard forced a smile onto her face, acknowledging the king's words with a slight nod of her giant prehistoric head. For a few seconds they both stood and stared out at the continuous magical onslaught that was meant for them.

It was the ruler that broke the silence.

"I suppose it's time. I had hoped to avoid it if at all possible, but we are way past that now."

The captain, a quizzical look on her face, opened her mouth to speak. The king got there first.

"Releasing the magical creatures from the capture and detainment facility in the basement of the council building would seem to be a prudent precaution given our current circumstances, don't you think?"

"Aaahhh," nodded the captain, having wondered when the time would come, and just what effect releasing the beasts might have on their opposing force.

Suddenly looking more weary and tired than any had ever seen him, the sovereign slowly closed his eyes and, in his mind, reached out to the presence inside the ring on his finger. Presence was really the only way to describe what he'd come to think of as a constant companion, occasional friend, powerful ally, and irregular confounder. Bright searing blue, green and yellow lights blared inside his mind as he wriggled around uncomfortably, looking for the tiny magical power source that he knew was continually keeping all the dangerous creatures in check. Like scouring a dream, or being captivated by a long lost memory, his mind pressed on, until he eventually found what he was looking for. As he approached what appeared to be a red metal wheel, sitting above a row of green and blue lights, on an out-of-this-world console, he could hear the ring's worried whispers echoing around his mind.

"Are you sure this is the right thing to do?" it asked. "Some of those creatures are valuable in so many other ways. Their properties, knowledge and abilities make them a threat in their own right. If the enemy were to capture them, they would have access to some most unusual and powerful magic. What about the safety of the creatures themselves? Surely they don't deserve to meet their end in a fight that isn't theirs?"

These were all questions that the king had asked himself over the last few hours. It was a risk, that was for sure. However it played out in his mind though, he could see no course of action other than to release the deadly predators, and hope that they would make their way out of the building to relative safety, and that they could be rounded up and brought under control after this crisis had been averted, if indeed such a thing were even possible. On top of all of that, they just might inconvenience their enemy and provide enough of a distraction for... for what? An escape? Unlikely! For the chance of a counter attack? In that lay madness. But who knew? Perhaps fighting madness with madness was all that was left. So with the ringing thoughts echoing throughout his head, George, muscles straining, despite the fact that this was all playing out in his mind, turned the red wheel anti-clockwise until all the lights on the console turned red. It was done. Now all they had to do was wait and see if it made any difference.

Half a dozen nagas disguised as humans had been assigned by Manson to break into the basement of the council building and ascertain the situation of the beasts in the capture and detain level. He'd stressed it was an important task, leaving unsaid that he was looking for some very old and powerful magic. Nearly ten hours they'd been at it, and still they'd barely scratched the door, let alone looked like getting in. Bathed in the green light from the lamp above the entrance, it almost seemed to be mocking their efforts. Of course none wanted to report back to the psychopathic Manson that they'd failed to get in, so they continued, throwing magic, might, mana and metal at the seemingly indestructible door beneath the faintly pulsing green light.

Powered by the king's ring, the mantras used in the basement of the council building to contain the highly magical and, in general, deadly creatures that resided there, are among the most complex and powerful on the planet. Not only designed to keep said creatures separate from each other, they also replicate, down to the finest detail, the exact environment of each and every specimen in their care, as well as looking after each individual's needs on a minute by minute basis. Those beings contained want for nothing, and never go hungry, go without company or fear for their lives. This is how the dragons rationalise their incarceration of the mythical monsters. Massive amounts of power are required to maintain the mantras, with the king's ring really the only viable option as a source, given the huge consumption.

Eerie green light surrounded each huge cell, showing that the mantras were working, and that the beasts within were contained. Row upon row of pens faded off into the distance for as far as the eye could see. Also, it was cold, like the frozen aisle of a supermarket... another precaution in case the worst should ever happen, and the creatures were somehow set free. Most would be slowed by the chilliness, but not all. With no one there to see, and without a sound, the green lights of the pens suddenly switched off, throwing row after row into darkness. Brutally the silence was shattered by piercing shrieks, ungodly wails, the clattering of hooves all accompanied by the underlying sound of scuttling, hissing and buzzing. If nightmares were ever to come to life, this is how they'd do it.

Standing back from the shield, the king examined all the troops around him. Some were sharpening their talons on the side of massive chunks of rock, others exercised, while a few sat on the ground, meditating, their thoughts somewhere far, far away. He envied them. Since having witnessed TROYDENN'S image on the computer monitor, it was all that he could think about, the hell that his ex-friend had gone through, and the twisted, dark thoughts that clearly now consumed him. For him to be here now, heading the dangerous, deadly, despicable army, clearly intent on taking the planet, the suffering he would have endured must have been unimaginable. All he knew now was that whatever happened, things didn't bode well for his survival.

A tiny tickle surprised him enough to jolt him away from the morose thoughts. It was the ring, indicating that his will had been done, and all its power had been diverted away from the basement of the council building, and transferred to the shimmering blue shield he stood in front of. He was grateful for that, hoping that the extra power might buy enough time for a solution to present itself, but wondered exactly what was going on in the bottom of the adjacent building.

It started as a swarm. Nifoloa to be precise, their buzzing sounding like a million miniscule drums all beating at once. Angry drums at that. With what they'd perceived as reality abruptly torn away from them, and the outer layer of protection stripped from around their pen, with the absence of the mantra, they started in unison, all hacking away at the walls with the single sharp tooth that they each had, the one that was the size of a man's finger. In only a matter of moments, they'd shredded their way through one of the walls and were flying in and out of the passages between all the other pens, looking for a target into which to inject their deadly poison. That was just the start.

In a far off darkened corner, amongst the howls, mewling, baying and whistling, a decidedly angry pack of skrikers gnawed a small hole just above ground level, and were currently fighting each other over just who should go through first. Paws, fur and teeth flew. Savage, bloody wounds abounded. Thick dark blood pooled on the floor.

Usually more at home in a waterborne environment, dozens of camaheutos skittered along the outside walls of the pens, having already gouged out dozens of tiny little gullies beneath their prison's walls with their razor sharp clawed feet. Natives of Chile, they had no trouble in thinking of a human as prey. They might well even consider taking down a dragon, should the opportunity present itself. Confident didn't really do them justice. However, they were unaware of what other dangers lurked in the bowels of this building.

Exhausted from their efforts, the half dozen nagas that had been tasked to break into the basement all sat either on or against massive unopened crates, just opposite the unbreakable door. Their mood was dour, thoughts of retribution for their failure from the psychopath Manson ran through all their minds. Without warning, the constant green light that had been their companion and their enemy throughout their tireless efforts flickered off into nothing, accompanied by the tiniest sound of well oiled metal moving. Immediately they were all on their feet, astounded at what had just happened. Knowing looks and what passed for smiles on the false human bodies they wore were all evident as the group as one approached the seemingly unpowered door. 'Manson will be pleased,' was the gist of what was running through each of their minds. The leader, by virtue of some kind of seniority, grasped the metre long metal handle and yanked it brutally downwards, not really sure what to expect. Both magical and physical seals were broken. Fetid, damp air could be faintly heard escaping. As their leader pulled the door open, the others looked on, pleased at having completed their assigned tasks.

The wicked chill that had up until now covered the entire underground level started to dissipate. Nearly all the creatures were benefiting from this. Their metabolisms kicked into life, as did their survival instincts.

Blissfully unaware of what was going on, the nagas in their human forms headed confidently into the dark. It hadn't occurred to them that the door unlocking all by itself could be a bad thing. Why indeed would they think that the creatures inside were anything but contained? And the noises? Having never entered the council building, let alone that particular level, they all just assumed that the noises were what passed for normal here. Boy, were they in for a surprise.

In a darkened corridor, over half a kilometre away from the nagas, five camaheutos were meeting another species for the very first time, and were determined to express their dominance. Having surrounded the group of ten centimetre long serpents, both in the corridor and up on the walls, the camaheutos almost sparkled with confidence at the thought of their first real meal being only moments away, despite it being only a mere mouthful. Breaking ranks, a lightly coloured, audacious camaheuto decided not to wait for its brethren and bounded forward with intent and purpose, determined to skewer its meal with the razor sharp claws on its feet. Just as it reached striking range, two of the tiny little serpents opened their mouths in unison, and exhaled. The daring and rather reckless camaheuto was instantly frozen to the spot in mid strike, one leg raised, poised to attack, the other firmly planted on the ground. With their bulging confidence shattered, the other camaheutos gradually retreated, watching as the group of serpents slithered their way slowly up, onto their frozen friend and began to gnaw into his still very alive flesh. A species so at the top of its food chain, had never been put in its place quite like the camaheutos had today, by a tiny group of echeneis. This was only the start of the battle for supremacy.

Still blissfully unaware of the situation around them, the nagas strolled purposefully deeper and deeper into obscurity, pleased at having gained not only access to the top secret basement, but approval from the ever moody Manson. Thoughts of how happy he'd be with them when they told him about the magical marvels contained here spurred them to press further into the basement, despite what most would have described as very disturbing noises, and now smells.

The skrikers eventually escaped from their pen. Not one looked unharmed, with most missing fur, teeth, and in some cases... LIMBS! They prowled through the darkness, using their enhanced senses for all they were worth. Their world had vanished in an instant, replaced by this cold, noisy labyrinth. Despite the rivalry amongst them, they were a pack in the conventional sense, and couldn't wait to encounter whatever was out there.

In the depths of the gloom now, a skittering had the entire group turning as one. Nothing was there. But the faint noises, ones that they had all assumed were the norm in this state of the art containment facility, were now growing louder and more concerning, coming from every direction. They looked to their leader for guidance, but he had very little. One of them piped up that they should return to their natural state, something that they could all agree on straight away. A head to toe grey shimmering encompassed each member of the entire group. In less than five seconds, their bogus human shaped bodies had been replaced by their much darker natural forms. Satisfaction at having changed was greeted by a, "HISSSSSSSSSSSSS," from nearly all of them. Confident that they could neutralise any threat that presented itself, they slithered further into the basement, all of their abilities enhanced by their snakelike forms, thoughts of glory, praise and ultimately freeing their king haunting their imagination. Little did the nagas know that they had now become the hunted.

A dozen twisted corners away from the slippery nagas, a cautious group of gaki crouched nervously in the all-encompassing black. Monstrous legends from the Far East, their bodies were humanish, with bulging great bellies that constantly, much to their annoyance, rumbled and spluttered. That wasn't what made them so fierce though. Their bodies were either bright, blood red, or brilliantly neon green, showing themselves up even though there was absolutely no light to see in. As if this weren't bad enough, they each had the heads of horses or cattle. All had three eyes. Sharp talons, horns and bony protrusions littered their bodies, each on its own a deadly weapon, but together acting like a whirlwind of razor blades. Rumoured to feed off the souls of evil men and women, they were all still taken aback at the world they'd known being snatched away from them. Some were angry, others frightened, one or two intrigued. But what they all were was ready, ready for whatever came their way. Bizarre, frightening, otherworldly could all have been used to describe this tiny fighting force, amongst any number of other fighting forces, most blissfully unaware of the others. Just how much longer could that last?

As his leader glided off into the distance, one of the nagas stopped to inspect a section of wall beneath what looked like a faulty light, wrapped in caged metal. There appeared to be some kind of writing, but it was obscured by a thick layer of ice that now seemed to be melting at quite a rate. At home in the cold, the naga had no problem scraping away the frost to reveal what lay beneath. On doing so, he exhaled sharply, the peculiar sounds all around instantly becoming clearer and much more defined. Ironically he was frozen to the spot, momentarily anyway. But his instinct for survival was ingrained in his very

DNA, allowing him to fight against the fear that held him temporarily paralysed. But what to do? The others were too far away to call out to. Well, they weren't, but only if you wanted to attract the attention of everything else in here. And from what he'd just learnt, that could well be much more than they could handle. But he certainly didn't want to go any further into what he now thought of as more of a prison/zoo, particularly as it was most likely that all of the inmates were now roaming free, probably tired, scared, hungry or a combination of all three. All he was sure of was that their little group was in a whole world of trouble.

Reaching out with his mind, he tried to pierce the wall of telepathic noise that threatened to shut him out. To his amazement, he'd done it and had managed to attract the attention of their leader. Just as he was about to report what he'd found, the leader swatted his contact away, much as one would do with an annoying insect on a hot summer's day. He couldn't believe it. Trying again with no luck, the leader had totally shut himself off. That made up his mind, there and then. Nothing was worth this. He'd face that psycho, Manson, rather than everything that he knew to be in here, free and unencumbered. Glancing one last time in the direction that the rest of the small group had headed off in, he looked at the sign, shook his head in disbelief, and slinked his way as fast as he could back the way they'd come. The melting ice from the sign continued to drip onto the floor. The words could just be made out.
NO LIGHT
NO CONTAINMENT
GET OUT
RAISE THE ALARM

Perched atop a high building that had been ravaged and destroyed, only its bare rock structure left intact, Richie sat with her back against the wall, shrouded in black. Even with magically enhanced vision, it was unlikely anyone would be able to spot her, that's how well she was concealed.

So far she'd only managed to travel a few kilometres since leaving the Hampton Court nursery ring. It had been slow going, with marauding gangs of nagas seemingly everywhere. Having stuck to the shadows, biding her time, she'd become impatient and frustrated. Knowing this wouldn't serve her well, she'd decided on a different course of action, one that she hoped would get her to her destination much quicker. Leaving the ground at the first available opportunity, she'd shimmied up the first four storey building that she'd come across, well... what was left of it anyway. After that, it had been rooftops all the way... up until now. Sitting watching, hidden from all and sundry, the only thought that ran through her head currently, was,

'How odd.'

It had been going on since before she'd got to this particular rooftop. Deciding to interrupt her progress, she'd dropped down into her little hidey hole, puzzled at what was playing out at ground level, about half a kilometre away.

Surrounded by a quartet of raging fires, three nagas were tearing into the bodies of half a dozen dragons. When I say tearing into, I mean eating of course. It was disgusting, repulsive... gross! They tore and chomped, ripped and gorged, all out in the open, lit up by the fires for all to see.

The bile in her stomach bubbled, but not nearly as much as the hatred inside her. She seethed. Not only did the spectacle disgust her more than anything she'd ever seen, but it pushed her to the very edge of reason. More than anything she wanted revenge, retribution, vengeance. Stoked by the laminium in the dagger tucked behind her back, she knew that making her wishes come true was a real possibility. But the responsibility she'd been entrusted with by not only the beings that had chosen her to lead, but by Flash who'd given her the insight that led her to be here, alone and uncomfortable, crushed any thought of violence against the sick group down below. As well, there was something else... something that niggled at her. She couldn't fathom what it was, but something about the whole thing was just WRONG! Of course what they were doing was wrong, but it wasn't that... something else was going on.

As she stared silently out across the smouldering visage of a gutted and razed London, huge areas reduced to ashes, a flicker of movement in the corner of her eye captured her attention.

Two of them rose from behind a clump of houses. One was smoky blue all over, a giant of a dragon, small protrusions running the length of its back. The other was mostly brown, but with just a hint of green running along its belly, spiralling out along its tail. Not as large as his friend, the fierce look on its face more than made up for its lack of size.

Richie observed the two dragons as they headed at speed towards the filthy, vile group of nagas. Deep down inside, she wished she were with them, adrenaline pumping, ready to do the right thing and send the depraved serpents deep into the realms of hell. But as she watched, too far away to make a blind bit of difference to the outcome, alarm bells started to ring inside her head. Letting out a tiny gasp, a single teardrop trickled from her left eye, plotting a course straight down her cheek.

The two determined dragons were on a high speed course for the centre of the three nagas, who, if they'd even seen the dragons heading their way, weren't concerned at all. And by the looks of things, with good reason. Dark shapes from out of the rubble and ruined buildings, in a concentric circle, with the dragon munching nagas at the very centre, appeared as if by magic. Richie looked on as the shadowy beings weaved their hands and fingers intricately, releasing a torrent of spells in the dragons' direction. They had no chance. The smoky blue one managed to erect a half decent shield as his friend, having been hit by a streak of rippling black energy, plummeted towards the ground. 'Smoky', as Richie now thought of him, had a tough decision to make... she urged him to run, knowing full well just how outgunned he was. Maybe if he had, right at that very first instant, he might have got away, but of course he didn't. She watched as he dropped down, trying to recover his friend. By now, the dark shapes were on the move, weaving in and out of the burning wreckage and debris, homing in on their prey. Valiantly lifting his friend's shattered body above his, 'Smoky' attempted a dash for the skies. But it wasn't to be. By now the dark shapes had all materialised into nagas, and they had all but surrounded the two dragons. It had been a trap all along, designed to prey on the dragons' sense of righteousness, designed to stoke their anger and get them to attack. More tears flowed for Richie as she sat huddled in the shadows, watching her enemy tear each and every bone from both of the dragons' bodies. For her now, the simmering anger had turned to fear. What on earth had she got herself into? And how were they supposed to defeat an enemy so barbaric and brutal? These were the questions that ran around and around her head as she sat and waited for the sordid, sickening beasts to move on.

Earth's surface. Cripple Creek Reserve, Australia.
Weather conditions were absolutely perfect for what they had in mind. And so here they were on the riverbank of a

small creek, about to set free one of God's true miracles... FIRE! Lowering the tailgate on the dirty white beat up pick up that they'd bought for $500 two days earlier, both grabbed a petrol can each, before heading in opposite directions along the stream's bank. At roughly fifty metre intervals, they stopped, poured a line of fuel throughout the dry scrub and then moved on, repeating the process five times each, before returning to the truck. It wasn't subtle, clever, or technologically advanced, what they were doing. But they'd been ordered to raise hell, create havoc and have the humans running for their lives. And so this is what they'd decided on. No one would question a couple of mates heading off out into the countryside for the weekend. And who didn't carry a few spare cans of fuel around with them these days? This was of course Australia. Having double checked the weather forecast in an effort to maximise casualties and the fear factor, they'd set out into the Blue Mountains, west of Sydney, to carry out their dastardly plan. The two had been in Australia for months, blending in, carrying on in their day jobs, going about their business, meeting up in the local bar most evenings, joining in with the revelry, whilst at the same time trying to remain aloof. It worked for the most part, with the locals liking them enough to be considered regulars, but having not quizzed them about what they did, or where they came from. As far as they were concerned, anonymity was key and had been maintained as much as possible. Ian and Steve (those were the names they'd been assigned, totally at random) had gotten to like those they'd met around these parts, with neither having had a quarrel with or a bad word to say about the humans they dwelt alongside. But at the end of the day, they were totally and utterly loyal to their race, devoted to their leader, and dedicated to the idea of freeing him from evil's grip.

So when the emails arrived, no consideration was given to the humans, despite them not really wanting to hurt them. It wasn't really even a matter of choice. And so the plan had been devised, without even that much careful consideration. It was hard to see what could go wrong with something so basic. Forest fires were always breaking out on their own this time of year. They were just giving nature a little nudge in the right direction, figuring that if they started it in the right place, and with just a little luck with the weather conditions, which were supposed to be very much in their favour, then it just might be possible to initiate a blaze that engulfed the whole of the mountain range. Potentially it could spread as far along as Newcastle in the north, and as far south as Wollongong. If so, then millions of people could be affected, and that was just in Sydney and its outlying suburbs. All they had to do was hope that the wind stayed with them.

Having met up back at the pickup, Ian grabbed the last can of fuel and wandered one hundred metres over to the edge of the forest. Reaching the third tree in, he unscrewed the cap and began shaking petrol all over its massive trunk. Once he'd finished that one, he started on the next, and then the next. After five minutes, he'd drained the can and, discarding it on the floor, took out his lighter. Glancing back over his shoulder, he could just make out Steve back at the truck, ready to light one of the streams of fuel adjacent to the creek. Igniting the lighter, he squatted down and lit the base of the tree nearest to the edge of the forest. Instantly the flame took, caressing and licking the side of the huge trunk, before leaping off up into the branches, while a trail of fire shot along the parched scrub to the next tree. It was mesmerising and Ian found himself hooked on the beauty of the searing blaze. That is until a shout came from back over his shoulder. It was Steve, urging him to run, as the fuel he'd already lit had developed into what could only be described as a roaring inferno. Turning instantly, Ian sprinted back towards the creek, while Steve jumped in the pickup, started the engine and drove off back up the red dusty track they'd come down, stopping only momentarily to wait for his mate.

With a sea of yellow, orange, red and blue consuming everything in its path visible in the rear view mirror, the two of them knew better than to stick around. Flooring the gas pedal, the back wheels of the truck spun as sand flew into the air far behind them. As the tyres finally gripped the sun scorched surface, the truck took off up the track, disappearing around a sharp bend that would lead them back to the main road. By now, thick plumes of dark black smoke bellowed into the bright blue sky behind them. The wind had picked up, as was its wont, and now a howling gale threw fire not just from tree to tree, but carried it for hundreds of metres. In the friends' wildest dreams, they could never have imagined their plan starting off so well.

11 CIRCUMVENT, CIRCUMVENT, CIRCUMVENT

Doubts festered in his mind, but he did his best not to let them show, and instead focused on the words of his friends. It was hard. This was as far out of his comfort zone as he could imagine. Abruptly he stopped, as clenched fists in front of him flared into life.

'What now?' he wondered, a tiny part of him wishing he were at the tip of the spear. His conscience, at least, that's what he assumed it was, chastised him immediately. Knowing he was their leader and as such should act like one, he'd done the smart thing by putting the dragons with at least some experience in battle at the front and back of their attack force. Nineteen had seen some sort of combat action before, and despite that being some time ago, it should in theory stand the group in good stead. Crouching in the archway of a shattered and battered home, the remains of which he could see had been ransacked in what looked like the mother of all battles, his thoughts turned to the dragon, or dragons, that had lived here up until only a matter of hours ago. Had they survived? If so, where had they gone? Would they ever return? Would things ever be the same again? Lost deep in his thoughts, he couldn't help think of his friends, Richie, Gee Tee, Flash and of course Peter, whose whereabouts were currently unknown, but were assumed to be in the company of the evil dragon Manson, somewhere in the direction they were headed. A hand on his shoulder, from the dragon in front of him, startled Tank from his reverie.

"There's some kind of naga encampment up ahead. It looks quite substantial. What do you want to do?" asked the yellow and purple tinged dragon.

This wasn't their first encounter with the enemy, and he had little doubt it would be their last. So far they'd managed to circumvent any resistance they'd found. But he was well aware that on each occasion, it cost them a considerable amount of time, something they couldn't afford to lose. He sensed that some of the dragons under his command were itching for a fight, especially those that were battle hardened. Momentarily he questioned having put most of them at the front. They could of course lead them all straight into a confrontation whenever they liked. But he knew that trust was everything, and that if he, and they, didn't have that, then all was already lost. Whispering so quietly that no human would ever hear, he told the dragon in front to pass the message on that they would once again avoid confrontation, and continue to use stealth to their advantage. He watched uncertainly as his orders were passed down the line, from dragon to dragon, in front of him.

Janice knelt on the hard rock, Tank's mighty frame encompassing everything in front of her, Hook taking up position directly behind her. Although having heard not a sound, she could see that Tank had sent instructions to the head of the force. Briefly she wondered what they were, before deciding it didn't really matter. It was too late to turn back, and to be honest, the only thing that currently concerned her, was the fate of the one she loved... PETER!

Earth's surface. Salisbridge, England.
"Thanks once again for letting me know. If I find out anything, I'll be sure to pass it along," and with that he hung up the phone on his desk, used his thumb and forefinger to stroke his moustache and pondered the meaning of it all.

For the second day in a row both Peter Bentwhistle and Richie Rump had failed to turn up for work. Not unusual in itself you might think, but there'd been no communication... nothing to say that either of them were unwell, or that there'd been any kind of emergency in their lives. And Al Garrett found this all most disconcerting. Of course he'd dealt with employees just not turning up before. Some had left for other jobs, others had just drifted off into the ether, never to be heard from again. But not these two... it just wasn't their style... plus they both held considerably important posts. Peter, as head of security, was a vital part of Cropptech's protection, and knew a great deal of confidential information about its workings both at home and abroad. And although Miss Rump didn't quite have the same stature, she performed an integral role in the running of the business. It wasn't often that the company's owner was both puzzled and concerned, but here and now he was. And not just a little. Over time he'd come to trust the young man implicitly, and even now was honouring his heroics in recovering the stolen laminium some time ago by having the site of the wrecked clubhouse cleared and then rebuilt to a much higher standard than it had been before. It was no mean feat, and something that came at incredible expense. Garrett was no stranger when it came to helping the local community; he cherished and valued each and every one of his employees and their families. Sitting in his office, taking a tiny sip of his piping hot coffee, he couldn't help wonder where the two youngsters were, and whether or not they were okay. Very much wishing they were, he vowed to keep an eye on their attendance. If another day passed without them showing their faces, he'd have some of his outside contacts look into it. After all, the company was nothing without its best employees, and he regarded these two as some of the finest they had to offer.

12 A GRIM TRUTH

A fierce burning pain shattered his brief slumber. Blinking uncontrollably, he tried to turn his slump into a more upright position. A world of hurt blossomed in his back, shoulders and neck. It was all he could do not to cry out. Then it all came flooding back. Instinctively he arced his head as far back as it would go, determined to check on Tim. He was of course still there, asleep but not soundly, judging from the ragged breathing and whispered mutterings.

Sitting up as much as the bonds that held them together would allow, Peter delved inside what currently passed for his body, trying to get some idea of the damage that had been done. It really only took a matter of seconds. It didn't look good. Broken ribs, damaged vertebrae, two fractured fingers, a badly bruised kidney, and that was before he'd even got to his mashed face. A real sense of helplessness bubbled up inside him. With just the tiniest trickle of dragon magic he could revert back to full health in an instant, but that had been denied him... he assumed by the bonds that tethered him to Tim. Try as he might, he couldn't for the life of him see how things could get any better. Exactly at that point, they got worse.

The sound of multiple footsteps, and more frighteningly, the familiar tap... tap... tap... tap that accompanied them, startled Tim awake, causing Peter more pain as the supposed White Dragon fought against the shared restraints.

"Ahhhh... if it isn't the king's favourite pet, and everyone's preferred punchbag. Not pleased to see me... BENTWHISTLE!"

Manson towered over the two friends, using his walking stick for support, the biggest, smuggest grin in the world etched across his face. Just as Peter thought it couldn't get any more dangerous, Manson's queen, EARTH, the elderly looking human who was clearly some sort of dragon and ROSEBLOOM all appeared from around the corner. Peter's heart sank. This was it... the endgame. It wasn't the first time he'd thought that. Each previous time he'd been convinced that he was going to die. Here and now, he was sure somebody would. The look in Manson's eyes was even crazier than usual, if that was at all possible. This time... he was right on the money!

"I still maintain we should kill them," offered up the elderly frail dragon in human form. "What possible use could we have for these two weaklings?"

Peter hadn't taken his eyes off Manson's face. The blood lust there was plain to see. It looked as though the other dragon's words would be enough to convince him to finally do it.

"NO! They may yet have a part to play in all this," said Earth, the words rolling off her lips as smoothly as beads of water spinning off a leaf.

The old dragon screwed his face up into a snarl. Manson seemed to be considering both options.

"They deserve to die," piped up Rosebloom, hoping to sway the argument in favour of his preferred outcome.

Manson turned to face the old dragon, both sharing the same thought at exactly the same time.

Tim shook uncontrollably. Peter's anger flared for all the good it would do him.

Bowing his head, Manson took two strides towards his father. Without warning, and faster than all of the enhanced beings could see, Manson, with all the force at his disposal, brought round his walking stick, smashing it firmly into Rosebloom's stomach, dumping the dragon councillor on the floor with a ground shaking THUMP, momentarily winded.

"Is now a good time to tell him?" asked Manson.

"As good a time as any," replied the old dragon, Earth looking on.

Rosebloom rolled over, looking to get back to his feet, but thought better of it with the tip of Manson's walking stick hovering only millimetres from the end of his nose.

"What... what's going on?" stammered the dragon councillor, fearfully.

"What's going on," exclaimed Manson, "is that it's finally time you learned the truth."

"The truth? The truth about what?"

"The truth about what really happened to your father," put in the old dragon.

"I don't understand," uttered Rosebloom nervously.

"You see, things with your father didn't go down quite the way you seem to think."

"The dragon Council captured, tortured and killed him for daring to oppose them," whispered Rosebloom.

"That is what you might have been led to believe," continued Manson.

"By you," insisted Rosebloom.

"Quite," replied the old dragon.

"But," chipped in Manson, "Osvaldo became a liability with his drinking and bragging, blabbing to all and sundry about what he was involved in, and just how powerful he would become. We had little choice but to dispose of him. In fact, it's safe to say that he was never really the quality of dragon we were looking for."

Rosebloom looked up in wide-eyed astonishment. Peter and Tim didn't know what to make of what they were hearing. Where was this all going?

"You'll be interested to know that we killed him slowly, and took great pleasure in doing so. He took days to die, in the most agonising way possible."

"Why?" asked Rosebloom stunned.

"Because we could," answered Manson.

The sickening tale came as little surprise to Peter, as he had a fairly good idea of exactly what Manson was capable of. Visions of him destroying the van full of human beings on the Astroturf on that cold, winter's night came flooding back to him.

"Why tell me all the other stuff?" snuffled Rosebloom.

"Because," gloated Manson, grinning manically, "we needed your cooperation. Where else were we going to get all that juicy information from? And how else were we supposed to sabotage the council building? Without your help it would have been very difficult to implement our plan. Your assistance has been pivotal."

Up until that moment, Rosebloom had considered himself a rather clever dragon. Not only that, but superior and of better breeding than most. But all he felt now was... FOOLISH! They'd played him for all he was worth... targeted his weaknesses, preyed on his supposed superiority. For the first time in what seemed like forever, tears streamed from his eyes.

Peter almost felt sorry for the duplicitous councillor, almost... but not quite. He'd betrayed him and nearly got him killed as well as, from the sound of things, putting the king and many other dragons in severe danger. No, he didn't feel sorry for him. In fact a small part of him hoped he was about to get his comeuppance. Be careful what you wish for.

"So you see," uttered Manson, "your usefulness has run its course. What to do? What to do?"

Rosebloom, shaking violently now, his cool and cocky exterior long since shattered, opened his mouth to speak.

"I can still be of use to you," he pleaded desperately.

"I don't think so," drooled Manson. "In fact, I would go as far as to say that you're more of a liability than your father ever was... a liability that needs quieting... permanently."

It was then that he got it. This was no test, no game. They were going to kill him here and now. The foolishness he felt at being so blatantly used was instantly washed away by the rage at how he'd been duped, and how they'd killed his father, Osvaldo. Head bowed, hunched up on the floor, he hoped they thought he'd come to accept his fate.

In a way, he had. But that tiny little spark inside him that was all dragon, remote and buried from the coward that he'd become over time, had found its way to the surface, after being lost for decades. He might have no way out, but one thought spurred him on. He wasn't going alone.

'They're going to kill him,' was all that Peter could think, shaking his head at the futility of it all. Dragons were supposed to coexist peacefully with everyone and everything. How the hell had it come to this?

Tim was living in perpetual fear. Fear of dying, fear of living in this strange new world and body. Fear of the torture that he knew they would at some point inflict on him. All he wanted was to go back to being a human and forget all about this underground nightmare.

Manson took a step forward, bringing his walking stick up above his head as he did so.

A tiny voice inside Rosebloom shouted, "THIS IS IT!" With the determination and courage that had never once showed its face during the course of his long and duplicitous life, he struck like a coiled snake, unleashing every last micron of energy, power, magic and speed into his attack, eager not to die alone.

Peter watched Rosebloom turn from shivering wreck to speeding bullet in units of time that were barely measurable. Even to his enhanced senses it was still all a bit of a blur. He had no love for the councillor, but now found himself rooting for the peculiar dragon in what he hoped would be the end of Manson, and just maybe an end to the hostilities.

Like a frozen statue, Manson seemed stuck in time as Rosebloom leapt up and flew at him with everything he had. As the particles of air in the room looked on, there could only be one outcome. And from the expression on Manson's face, he knew he was in trouble.

Air boiled, thrummed and crackled, becoming thicker, so much so that you could almost cut it with a knife. Every part of Peter's skin felt prickly.

With nothing more than a flick of her fingers, Manson's queen, Earth, unleashed a torrent of deadly purple lightning at Rosebloom, catching him mid-flight and then holding him there, trapped like an animal at a zoo, helpless for all to see. The traitorous councillor writhed and wriggled, shouted and screamed for all the good it did him, his floating mass only centimetres away from its target... MANSON!

Peter gagged slightly, the overpowering smell of burnt scales and flesh almost too much for him.

Tim sat bound to Peter, goggle eyed, absolutely terrified at the events unfolding to the side of him. If the purpose of this demonstration had been to induce paralytic fear into The White Dragon, then it had succeeded beyond any doubt.

After being momentarily lost for words and surprised at the speed, viciousness and, ultimately, courage Rosebloom had shown, Manson had now recomposed himself, after of course showering his queen with his brightest smile, a small thank you for the timely and most welcome save. Fingers still shooting lethal lightning, she returned his grin with interest, all the time her hair snaking about almost of its own accord, making her look like an ancient Medusa.

Ghostly grey, pungent smoke floated up from nearly every part of Rosebloom. His screams had turned to howls as blood dripped from his body and he tried to squirm his way out of the magical trap. But it was not to be.

"It's a shame you didn't show that kind of backbone when you worked for me," snarled Manson.

Both Peter and Tim recognised that what was left of the councillor was trying to spit into Manson's face, without very much luck. Not only was the air too thick and full of sizzling lightning, but the councillor was just too dehydrated and near death. Turning his head towards his new queen, Manson uttered two words:

"FINISH IT!"

She did. The increase in power to her lightning was intense, enough to force Peter and Tim to close their eyes and look away. Over the blistering assault on Rosebloom's body, the two friends could make out Earth's squeals of pleasure. It terrified both of them to their very cores.

And then without warning it was over, the bright, violent light fading, the crackling and sizzling of the magic replaced by the sound of Earth panting like an exhausted dog. Fighting off the urge to vomit, and really not wanting to, Peter opened his eyes. His imagination had long since run away, but somehow the sight that greeted him was worse. On the floor in front of Manson, Rosebloom's charred cadaver lay smoking away, every bit of it blacker than the darkest lump of coal. Manson strolled over and embraced Earth; the elderly dragon disguised as a human, Peter noticed, looked on disapprovingly.

Bile rose in Peter's throat at the sight of them celebrating their cold and heinous act.

Manson turned and headed in the direction of the two bound friends, kicking the charred lump of flesh on his way.

"This," he pointed at the corpse with his stick, "is what awaits not only the two of you, but the rest of the weak willed dragons and each and every one of their pet humans," he spat. "Now you'll have to excuse me," he said, turning and walking back to Earth and his father, "I've got to go and make sure your friend the king isn't getting too comfortable... laters."

With that the three of them trooped off, leaving the two friends sitting in front of the scorched carcass, pondering their own fate.

13 A HANDY SURPRISE

Surrounded and outnumbered, Flash couldn't believe the situation he found himself in. Fredric, Peter's grandfather and founder of the elite Crimson Guards, shot him a look. A look that said he wanted very much to join the fight, wanted to bet his life, wanted to be free one way or the other. As the captive dragon stretched them taut, the unbreakable chains jingled briefly, just to the side of Flash.

A chuckle, half cackle, half laugh, resounded around the cavern from the foul smelling, deranged looking being that headed across the ice towards them. Fredric's face contorted with rage at seeing the jailer, all smug and full of himself. He had no doubt it would cost him a beating later, or worse. He didn't care.

"How nice of you to join us... dragon," the jailer spluttered in broken English, still considering whether or not his enemy actually belonged to that kind of race.

Swallowing nervously as the nagas closed in around him from all sides, Flash put on a brave face.

"This has to stop now!" he demanded, puffing out his chest.

Howling with laughter, the filthy jailer spat in his direction.

"What makes you think you're in any position to make demands? Look around you. This is only going to go one way. And as luck would have it, we currently have a vacancy for a new guest," he said, pointing to the crumbled corpse of Bag O' Bones off in the distance.

A sickening terror climbed up Flash's legs at the very thought of being incarcerated in this frozen hell. His stomach flipped, while his arms went weak.

'Better to die fighting than be captured and held here,' he thought to himself, setting his mind on a reckless course of action. With the nagas closing in, forming an impenetrable semi circle, Flash started picking out targets, determined to take as many as possible with him. Just as he did so, he caught sight of something ridiculous, directly behind the nagas in front of him. Wavering in mid-air, a hand, seemingly attached to nothing, palm facing him, fingers outstretched, just hovered there. At first he thought he was dreaming. Then the more rational (ha) explanation hit him, as the thumb on the hand tucked into the palm, followed quickly by the closest finger. Time slowed. Every fraction of a second became a minute to Flash. He knew what was happening. It was a countdown. Clearly Yoyo and the others were present in the cavern now... but a countdown to what? That was the question.

Another finger dropped on the hand. Flash plundered the depths of his mind for the right mantra. Hundredths of a second later, he had it ready to go.

'A concussive blast in a 180° arc, perfect,' he thought.

The second from last finger dropped.

The jailer moved in, close enough for Flash to smell his sickeningly cloying breath, a mixture of rotting fish and whale innards if he wasn't mistaken. The former Crimson Guard's stomach howled in protest.

As the last finger dropped, in his mind Flash spoke the words, putting all his belief and intent behind them. Immediately, all hell broke loose.

Unleashing the blast, Flash caught them all by surprise and took the jailer and the first row of the surrounding nagas off their feet. On top of that, colourful magic had appeared from all around, to devastating effect.

It was on. GAME TIME!

14 SILENT RUNNING (WELL, A FAST WALK)

Gathered in the ruins of a burnt out shop, the eclectic group were all on guard, even the human contingent. They'd yet to travel even two kilometres through the battered and torn fire and smoke filled landscape since leaving the Hampton Court nursery ring. All of them were stunned at the utter devastation of the attacks. Their upbeat mood had quickly changed on seeing the first dragon corpses. A couple by the look of things, taking their dragon egg to the nursery ring. Evidently no mercy was shown, no quarter given. From the position of their bodies, they'd died trying to protect their offspring, with the egg itself having been smashed to pieces. Fragments of shell lay strewn throughout the debris. If the group needed a reminder of the brutality of the events they'd found themselves tangled up in, then this had certainly done the trick. Some of the humans had been sick. At least half a dozen dragons looked pale, almost in shock. It wasn't exactly the kind of start to his leadership that he'd hoped for. So here they were, in the first real defendable position they'd come to. With all those not on lookout duty taking on water, the old shopkeeper wondered how his friends were doing on their separate missions. Silently he wished them well, wondering if he'd ever see them again. These were dangerous times; the future was hard to fathom. Falling rubble off in the distance startled him back to the present. Letting out a huge yawn, he padded over to the gathered group.

"We've stopped for two reasons. One, so that we can all take on some much needed water. And two," continued the old dragon, "so that I can apply something that might just give us an edge."

One or two of the dragon faces in his tiny audience

perked up noticeably.

"It's a little mantra that SHOULD render everyone here totally and utterly silent in everything they do, other than their speech."

He was rewarded by a collective intake of breath. The experienced warriors amongst the dragons had a very good idea of exactly what this could do for their chances. Motioning for those on lookout duty to rejoin the group, Gee Tee pushed his glasses as far up his nose as they would go, closed his eyes, relaxed his body and focused his thoughts. Eventually he found the solace he was looking for, but not before getting slightly disappointed at how much longer it now took. In his youth, he'd have been ready to go in the blink of an eye, but now just finding that state of mind was a struggle. Old age, no doubt, just like all the other things that niggled him about his body. Trouble remembering, clumsily knocking things over, deteriorating vision and feeling the need to pee almost as soon as he'd just gone... he was sure if Tank had his way he'd be wrapped up in some kind of rubber pants, sooner rather than later. Imagine that... a dragon in rubber pants. It doesn't bear thinking about, well... unless that's your thing.

Cleared of all thoughts, he let his mind call forth the words he'd last whispered in the Mantra Emporium with Tank, when Peter had wandered in right at the end. Briefly the air in and around the ruins shimmered, like glitter being sprinkled onto a picture by a small child. And then it was done. None of the group moved... at first. Then one or two of them tentatively padded across the broken rubble of the shop. Gasps of surprise abounded all round at the effectiveness of the old shopkeeper's magic.

Knowing full well that every second mattered in what they had set out to achieve, Gee Tee figured that, with their movements shrouded in silence, they could perhaps pick up the pace a little. Not running exactly, but more of a fast walk. That should at least get them back on track, and might well prevent any nasty surprises from the enemy.

"It's time to move out," he whispered, a large part of him really not wanting to. As the force picked up their belongings and arranged themselves in their previous order, with the humans in the middle, himself towards the front and one or two of the more combat experienced dragons at the front and rear, he once again thought of his friends, hoping that they were safe.

15 STAMPEDE

Irritated, that's how the leader of the small group of nagas felt. Whatever was so important, why not just say it in person, he thought. Telepathic contact was so draining and unnecessary. No doubt he'd made some terrific discovery about one of the species down here. BOO HOO! There were hundreds of different beings held captive here, and he was going to catalogue at least a dozen before it was time to go back and report to their so called leader. He knew if he didn't, things would go very badly. Although he'd not been told to do so, his imagination played out some brutal scenes, with Manson asking him time and time again as to why he hadn't used his initiative and made detailed notes. So he was damn sure that's what he was going to do, and as far as he was concerned, the more the merrier.

Back towards the entrance of the underground enclosure, the relative silence was pierced by the ripping and twisting of metal, a small hole at first, made much larger in only a short space of time. Without warning a massive claw began to peel back the alloy of what only a few moments ago was the wall of one of the cells, and then another, and then another, until the gap was large enough for the first of the creatures to clamber through. Which it did. A scorpion's body, nearly the size of a car, its venomous tail darting this way and that, clearly looking for a suitable target. Although unusual in itself, that wasn't the weirdest thing. Exactly where the head should have been, mid-way between two thick, meaty claws was instead the torso, head and arms of a human. Long, mangy, matted dark hair ran halfway down the back of the first male to make it out, anxious to see the outside of the prison he'd only just discovered had held him and his friends. It wasn't long before there were scorpion men as far as the eye could see, well if you had night vision, which indeed they all did. Their clacking pincers added to the ever building noise.

Elsewhere in the basement, creatures from only the darkest of nightmares roamed. Eagles with two heads soared above the cells, occasionally dive bombing other species. Pixiu... winged lions darted through the air, from one walkway to another. Asena... blue maned wolves, skulked in packs throughout the darkness, on the hunt, but on the hunt for what? Conaima... giant were-jaguars padded softly this way and that, most on the lookout for their next meal, the rest guarding their newly born young. The evil trumpeting and stamping of a giant elephant beast off in one corner caught the attention of more than one group of animals. All had the same reaction. Whatever that was, it was to be avoided at all costs. All of that combined with the shape-shifting venomous snakes, myrmecoleon, a sort of ant/lion hybrid, hundreds of fire breathing gnats, a group of scaled apes, all having four arms, a pack of vampiric lizards that were spitting lightning, and something called an asag, if the name on the cell was anything to go by, a giant hideous rock demon. More and more species were coming to the fore. How long would it be before they escaped the basement good and proper?

It started out of nowhere. Using one of their ancient hunting techniques, one single nifoloa had used its razor sharp tooth to secret itself beneath one of the alleyways, the rest of the swarm sitting on a wall just around the corner.

All aware that something was wrong, but not knowing exactly what, the group of nagas were more hesitant now. They slithered to a halt at a four way intersection, each facing in a different direction, all looking out for trouble.

Tapping into all his magic, he'd tried to contact his missing comrade telepathically, ironic given that he'd rejected his last attempt. But there was nothing. No connection... just a fuzzy kind of background static. He ordered the others to try, but they had no luck either. Something was wrong, and despite not having had any communication with the different species that were contained here, only moments before he'd come to the conclusion it was time to get out, even if it meant facing the wraith of Manson. His thick, forked, snake-like tongue hissed from his mouth as he opened it to tell the others of his decision. Excruciating pain blazed into existence deep within his tail, forcing him to temporarily lose his balance.

"Whoa... are you okay?" asked one of his comrades.

"I... I... I..." was all that the leader could get out.

Surrounding their stricken colleague, the others hoped to gain some insight into what had happened. But before they could, a fierce buzzing came out of nowhere, igniting their threat sense and alerting them to a much more imminent danger.

As one, the nagas slithered in closer to their wounded leader, instantly erecting magical barriers in front of themselves. Using their heightened supernatural senses, they focused in on the eerie buzzing heading their way. Similar in form to wasps, but with one long pointed tooth, seeming almost way too big for their bodies, especially in flight, the swarm circled around the trapped nagas, one of their number occasionally attacking the shield, a sharp electrical discharge and singed wings the cost of doing so.

Much closer to the entrance, the one which the group of slippery serpents had spent many hours trying to open, the separated naga slithered silently through the darkness, encouraged at the thought of being so close to getting out, determined to barricade the door from the other side once he'd done so. Poking his head around a corner, he was rewarded with the outline of the outer door to the basement in the distance, backlit from the light outside. Making a madcap dash for it, he abruptly drew up as a darkened, four legged shadow stepped into his path.

About four feet tall, and looking more than a little sorry for itself, the rays of light from beyond the door did just enough to illuminate the creature in all its splendour. Wary at first, that is until it became apparent to the naga exactly what it was, still shrouded in gloom, he was dealing with.

'A unicorn,' he thought to himself.

"Hello little fella," he whispered through the darkness, all the time snaking slowly towards its shady profile.

Stamping its feet gruffly, the foal let loose a little grunt, causing the naga to smile at the thought of having some good news for the maniac Manson. Unicorns were rare, rarer than rare. The fact that the dragons had some incarcerated down here boded well. Their magical powers were legendary, with numerous potions and possibilities available from their extracts. Sliding to a halt, the naga reached out with one hand to stroke the unicorn's mane. Nervously the creature shied away, understandably really, turning around a little to face the very pleased with himself naga. It was then that the pale beams of light, seeping through the door out of the basement revealed the real silhouette of the beast. Not one horn on top of its head, but two, something that changed the very nature of the being a hundredfold. Immediately, the slippery serpent slinked backwards, desperate to get away, but the ra-hoon, as that's what it was, was having none of it. Incisors bared, it stalked after the naga, the terrifying tapping of its hooves on the cold metal floor signalling impending doom. Petrified and desperate, the snake-like monster shimmied one way and then darted the other, hoping against hope that the beast was dumb enough to fall for a very over the top dummy, and that he could get out and close the door behind him. Not a hope. The ra-hoon whirled with the grace and speed of a stallion, clamping its fierce teeth around the naga's scaly tail, about two metres from the end.

"Aaaarrrrgggghhhhh!" screamed the naga in agony, trying to wriggle free.

With a snarl and a cunning look that gave away not only its intelligence, but something of its devilish nature, the ra-hoon crunched down, severing the naga's tail from its squirming body. Shaking the appendage free, tossing it ten metres in the air as it did so, the unicorn lookalike bore down on its prey. With no way to balance now, the naga toppled over, trying to access all its magic for what little it would be worth.

'Everyone knows that ra-hoon are immune to any kind of magic, don't they? What the hell are they doing here, in the council building?' were the last thoughts the naga ever had, before a group of much smaller ra-hoon trotted out of the shadows and began feasting for all they were worth.

Their commander strewn on the floor in the middle of them, the party of nagas were holding their own against the deadly nifoloa. The individual that had attacked their leader had been suitably blasted to smithereens by a crackling bolt of green lightning, preventing any more damage being taken from inside the magical shield that they all now shared. Currently the conscious nagas were having a telepathic discussion about just how they were going to get their principal back to the entrance. They'd pretty much just decided that they'd need to take out all the attacking nifoloa, something they thought was pretty much doable, when trouble started appearing on all sides.

The junction, or more like crossroads, that they were situated in the middle of, had just become a magnet for half a dozen species, hungry, desperate, down on their luck, and angry about having had the world they knew and loved torn away from them. Stumbling upon two enemies (the nagas looking like a prolific source of food) brawling pushed all the right buttons on their internal fight or flight decision making process. Flight was never really an option.

Half a dozen snarling wolves bounded towards the struggle, their fluffy blue manes ruffling as they took one last flying leap, the sound of their jaws snapping at the nifoloa echoing off into the darkness. Looking out from behind their magical shields, the nagas were unable to believe what they were seeing.

One of the wolves that had hung back was just about to join the rest of its pack, when four thick, meaty, brown scaled hands whipped it up off the ground, causing it to howl like a banshee briefly, before trying to strike out at its attacker with its claws and needle sharp teeth, to little or no effect. The grinning, prehistoric looking primate rolled its eyes, before snarling right into the face of the helpless beast. Its massive scaled muscles rippled as it tore each of the wolf's legs off, one by one, only to discard them and move in closer to where the real action was.

The sound from the fight was off the scale now. Buzzing, howling, snapping, clacking, the sound of breaking bones and agonising screams were like a beacon in the dark. The creatures contained here weren't timid and shy, but the worst of the worst the mythical world had to offer. That's why they were there. Most of them liked nothing more than a good fight and had no concept of losing. To them, this was why they lived. For the nagas at the centre of it all, things were just going from bad to worse, despite the fact that they were safely holed up behind their magical barriers.

As one of the wolves swallowed a nifoloa whole, and was about to look for the next one, a giant pincer ripped a swathe of its stomach open to reveal blood and internal organs. It slumped to the floor, barely able to pant, let alone call for help, as the scorpion men moved forward together, their pincers weaving in front of them, all the time nipping at the buzzing enemies in the air.

In the recesses of one of the paths, just back from the main event, the scaled apes had been set upon by the frighteningly vicious winged lions known as the pixiu. At first the apes had thought nothing of the flying monstrosities, that is until in one fell swoop, one of the beasts had torn off half an arm at the elbow, biting clean through the primate's protective scales. This had sent the group into a wild frenzy, causing them to exact revenge. One of the pixiu had been downed by two apes working together, one throwing the other high up into the air when one of the creatures had dared to try and attack again. The sheer weight of the ape had brought the creature down and, while not defenceless on the ground, far from it, there were now three primates, rolling around beating the living daylights out of it.

Amidst the chaos of battle proper, two-headed eagles joined in the fun, constantly bombing the nagas' shield as they tried to pick off a nifoloa or two. One or two had been successful, while most had just been harmlessly turned away by the magic.

Inside the barrier, things had just gotten worse, if that were possible.

"He's stopped breathing," said one, from down by their leader's side.

"I don't care about him," shouted one of the others. "You need to get back up here and help us reinforce these shields."

"Alright," he replied, giving his former comrade one last look, before joining the remainder of their force.

"What if we gradually moved off in the direction of the exit, while still maintaining the shields? The beasts seem to be content fighting each other. Plus they might consider our former comrade's body as food, creating a distraction, and buying us some valuable time to form an orderly retreat."

As a group they considered this, despite all thinking it was deeply disrespectful to the naga that had led them for a few weeks now. But nobody could come up with anything better, so they decided to go with that. A few centimetres at a time the unit, with their shields still up, steadily retreated back in the direction from which they'd arrived.

A scaled ape ran at full pelt towards his friend, well, brother actually, who held his hands out low in front of him, ready to use every ounce of strength he had to toss his sibling high in the air, ready to bring down another pixiu. So far the primates had managed to topple three of the nightmarish beasts, but at some cost. All but these two were missing arms, with one lying prone on the ground from a nasty head wound. The fast moving ape, getting his timing just right as one of the flying lions circled above, came sprinting up to his sibling, lifting his right leg up, straight into his brother's hands. With all the might he had, his sibling lobbed him high up over his head, speeding towards his target.

BOOOOMMMMM!!!

A rocky fist the size of car swung out of nowhere, punching the ape even further up into the air, accompanied by the sound of bones shattering. The primate died on impact. Its brothers and the flying pixiu scattered for all they were worth as the fist's body appeared from out of the darkness, revealing a giant, hideous rock demon. Walking like a constipated robot, each tiny step shook the walls and the floor of the basement, creatures of every kind scattering before it. Moss and lichen draped from its armpits and the top of its legs made it look like a swimmer having just exited an ocean full of seaweed. Mostly different shades of grey, occasional worn away rock revealed a subtle white undertone. Beneath its eye sockets, malevolent purple light shone out. From somewhere deep within, it roared.

Intrigued as to why the creatures were all scattering in different directions, the nagas watched in horror as the rock demon stomped ferociously out of the black, heading towards them. Panic and a sense of self preservation took over. Each slippery serpent made the same decision at almost the exact same instant. That decision went something like this: "Sod this! I'm off!" Each retracted their shields around just themselves and slithered away on any course other than the one from which the rock demon was coming, completely ignoring all the other enemies.

Amongst those still remaining where the nagas had made their stand, a strange sense of unity had arisen. Waves of creatures banded together and were hurling themselves at the nightmarish rock demon, who in turn tried desperately to either stamp on them, or crush them with his mighty fists. For the most part he was too slow, but one or two of the wolves caught glancing blows, sending them skittering back into the dark. The nifoloa had fared better, but hadn't so much as dented its thick, rock skin with their deadly teeth.

Of the nagas who'd fled, only one was managing to stay ahead of the game. Two had been taken down by the group of four armed scaled apes, although not many of their complement still had the correct number of limbs. Using all of their magic and knowhow, the nagas gave everything in the struggle against the primates. The turning point in the whole encounter was the fact that the apes' scales, much to the nagas' surprise, offered an amazing amount of resistance to their magic. Brilliant green lightning bolts fizzled and sizzled, scorched, singed and burnt, but not much else. With little in the way of offence, the only real option for the two was to turn tail and flee, which they did, only to be tripped up in the darkness by the remainder of the apes' party. After that, it was all over, as the frenzied creatures pummelled and mashed their bodies into a disgusting slush, from which they could be seen slurping many hours later.

Another had slithered for all he was worth, but had become momentarily confused on leaving the running battle with the rock demon, and instead of heading towards the exit, had in fact travelled deeper into the basement. By the time he realised his mistake, for him, unfortunately, it was way too late. Being constantly harangued by two pairs of double headed eagles, his concentration was elsewhere when it should have been on his immediate environment. He never saw the punch that pierced his protective shield, catching him side on in the middle of his head, forcing him to roll off into the shadows and come up fighting. Conjuring up a raging ball of fire that illuminated his ambusher, a battered and bruised scorpion man, missing one of his pincers, he tossed the deadly magic towards its target, trying hard to ignore the ringing in his ears. Within metres of the scorpion man, the fireball exploded, causing him to rear up in surprise, all the time crying out in agony. With his target damaged and on fire, the naga assumed he'd done enough to earn a brief respite. Not so. Flames pouring from every part of him, the scorpion man gave one defiant charge just as one of the two headed eagles swooped out of the shadows and took an almighty chunk out the naga's tail. It was the tiniest of distractions, but it was enough. In what turned out to be the throes of death, the scorpion man, with one last Herculean effort, sidled around and brought down the huge stinger on the end of his tail, burying it straight into the bemused naga's chest. Both creatures collapsed where they were, both roaring with pain, both unable to move, the poison working in mere moments on the naga, while the scorpion man took much longer to die, in more pain than any being had a right to suffer.

That just left one. And he was snaking towards the exit at quite a rate, determined to raise the alarm. That is until a gentle hissing up ahead caught his attention. Wary beyond belief, he put as much of his magic into the shield around him as he could, and slowed to a halt. Peeking out from behind one of the gloomy corners, he could just make out a tangle of snakes slithering about in the middle of the path to the exit. Panting rapidly from having pushed himself so hard, for fear of death, from behind him the sound of many creatures racing to keep up sent a wave of fear rushing through him, as he considered all the options available. He had to get past, he just had to. But what to do? A flying leap was all that came to mind. It wasn't impossible, but it would need to be in excess of four metres from the look of things. That was pushing it he knew, however, he was out of options. So without any fuss or last thoughts, he shot off round the corner, knowing that speed was the key. Slithering from side to side on the cold stone floor, the reassuring heat he could feel from the friction gave him hope. He approached as close as he dared, the snakes seemingly oblivious to his presence, and then using the muscles in his tail, kicked off, judging it to perfection, but for one thing. These weren't just any snakes. These were shape shifting snakes, and the moment he left the ground, two of their number dissolved completely, appearing a fraction of a second later as two hulking great snow beasts, eight feet tall, covered in thick, white matted fur all over and a set of teeth that would have put a great white shark to shame. Abruptly, the naga slammed into the first one's chest, bouncing off and landing smack bang in the middle of the band of reptiles. Immediately he was peppered with bites, the serpents slithering over him, fighting for position. The poison here wasn't as quick to take his life, it just paralysed him. So there he lay for over an hour as not only the snakes tore tiny fragments off him, but the other creatures he'd been battling against earlier joined the feast, while at the same time fighting off the snakes. Through a gap in the wriggling and sliding serpents that covered his head, he could just make out the exit, the one they'd spent so much time trying to break into. If only he could go back, go back and change things. As his life force ebbed away, he watched all the different creatures, tentatively at first, make their way through the door and out into the council building proper. By the time he died, it was a positive free for all stampede of exotic and magical creatures.

Earth's surface. Coari, Amazon River, Brazil.
With the sound of the thick, brown river water gurgling

and wriggling only a matter of metres away, the three men and two women slipped silently through the rickety door, closing it as tightly as possible behind them. Flicking the switch, bringing the room's solitary light bulb to life, all five of them formed a circle on the hole-ridden, partially rotted floorboards. Instinctively they joined hands, something necessary for the magic to work, at least on the level they were looking for. One of the women, dressed head to toe in green, her dark skin looking rich and magnificent against the different shades, started to chant, softly at first, rising with every second that passed. One by one each of them joined in, all in tune, sounding very much like an award winning choir by the end. As their song continued, a barely noticeable drumbeat started up on the metal roof above their heads. Lost in the words and rhythm of what they were doing, one by one the individuals opened themselves up, exposing their true selves, letting their magic and power be harnessed by the chant itself. Wisps of supernatural power in every different colour imaginable arced across the room, bouncing off walls, ricocheting off the ceiling, clashing with one another, exploding in tiny clouds of multicoloured madness. Drizzle turned to teeming rain, the thump of the drops hitting the roof sounding like a military beat, so loud now that it almost drowned out the chanting, which itself had reached fever pitch. Amongst those gathered, eyes rolled, extremities shook uncontrollably, heads flopped, madness reigned in their eyes, briefly anyway. By now the din had become almost deafening. How the surrounding townsfolk couldn't hear was yet another mystery, but magic had a way of doing its master's bidding, even on a subconscious level at times. Wisps turned to multilayered explosions, every possible combination of colours running riot inside the small shack, the roof, now being battered from the torrential downpour on the outside, and the violence of the magic on the inside, popped up and down nervously on the flimsy wooden supports that held it in place.

Hearts raced, ears burned, eyes were nearly overloaded by the sensation of bright, brilliant, bold colours. And then, almost as suddenly as it had all started... there was nothing. No noise, no colour, just the dull, white light of the bulb, casting long, thin shadows in the corners, barely showing up the treacherous holes in the floorboards. As the five of them returned to the here and now, each wiping sweat from across their faces, the woman who'd started it all spoke up.

"That should be enough to keep the rain flowing for weeks. We'd best leave this place and quickly. The Amazon is already high, and it won't take much for the flooding to start. We do not want to be anywhere near here when this gets out of hand. I suggest taking the first boat upriver out of here in the morning."

The other four all nodded in unison.

"Where do we go?" asked one of the men.

"We'll just head upriver, and away from here. Pucallpa might be our best bet, but that's at least a week away. Let's just get on the move. I'm sure any orders they have will reach us just like the last lot did."

As they boarded the well travelled boat, all of them thought back to the scruffy, dark skinned boy, wearing nothing but a tattered pair of shorts, if that's what they could be described as. Perhaps that's what they'd once been, but now looked like a gathering of holes, off on their family holidays. During one of their trips for supplies, the boy had approached them, and despite them all trying to shoo him away, he remained very persistent, claiming that they should follow him as he had something of great value for them. Sure that it was a scam, and knowing that many a foreigner was lured away to a rather untimely demise in this very manner, eventually the child did something that captured all of their attention. He uttered the word, "propositum," something they all knew to mean 'objective'. Needing no more convincing, they followed the boy to a secluded riverside about four kilometres out of town. There he recovered a hand written letter that he'd hidden beneath the roots of a huge overhanging tree. Gathered round, the group eagerly read their orders. They were to use their abilities to create as much mischief as they could up and down the waterway they were on. If lives were lost... so be it. After reading the letter, they all knew there were two immediate priorities. So one of the men retrieved his lighter from the side pocket of his dark blue backpack and immediately set fire to the paper, letting the charred remnants of it drift out over the meandering river, while the other four took care of the boy. There could be no witnesses. Now was not the time for any mistakes.

16 COLD AS STEEL

They watched, stony faced and cold hearted as one of their number was killed right before their eyes. The murder was not only unexpected, but something of a feat given the identity of his attacker, a dragon now slumped against the wall in the narrow corridor on the monitor they were watching in the control centre. He looked scrawny, weak... almost kind of new. But there was no mistaking the strength of will that he carried. Any enemy with that much endeavour and courage would be hard to take out, but take him out they would. Their instructions were to leave no being alive, and raze everything to the ground. As the shattered dragon on the screen crawled to his feet and limped back down the corridor, the two of them started to hatch their plan.

Deep within the barricaded store room, the rather awkward discussion had turned into a full on argument, the nurse with the conscience having finally had enough, telling the specialist medics, and the acerbic doctor whose idea it had been to hide away in the first place, exactly what she thought, in no uncertain terms. She figured it would cost her the job that she loved, but there were more important things at stake currently, and she knew there was a very real possibility of not making it through the next few hours alive. Most of the medics had come round to her way of thinking, wanting to go out into the facility and back up Steel in whatever way possible. It was only really the doctor in charge, a research scientist, and two of the other nurses, that were all for staying hidden.

"I really think we need to be going out and supporting our patient," pleaded one of the junior medics.

"Don't you understand?" argued one of the nurses. "It

just isn't safe. How can it possibly be with all of those beings out there? There's no easy way to say it, but our patient is almost certainly lying dead in a corridor somewhere. We need to stay here until help arrives."

"Well said," stated the doctor in charge, "it's not what any of us wanted to hear, but she is almost certainly right, I'm afraid."

It was just then that the squabbling reignited, with everyone talking over each other, shouting, shoving, with things getting more than a little heated. It made her mad. It really did. Those words... 'Lying dead in a corridor.' Not one of them knew him like she did. He was a fighter, a winner, a dragon who would never quit. And now he needed them more than ever and here they were, fighting like love struck teenagers, while all the time cowering in fear. Enough was enough. It was time to act.

He ached all over. Worse still, his head was spinning like a forgotten coin in a tumble dryer. But, picking up the lethal sword, he soldiered on, carefully, afraid but glad to be alive, ready for whatever else life would throw at him today.

It hadn't taken them long to find what they were searching for. The dragon computer systems were almost as easy to hack as the human ones that they so often had to infiltrate. There on the computer screen before them, lay a schematic of the facility and the access to the environmental controls they'd been looking for. They'd guessed right. A medical compound such as this one did indeed have the ability to rigorously change the temperature within, just in case a dangerous pathogen needed containing. Struggling to contain their laughter as they dialled the setting down to its coldest, the nagas looked forward to the short taste of winter they'd missed so much during the preceding weeks, knowing full well just what it would do to any dragons left alive inside the place.

"YOU NEED TO LET ME OUT!" she all but screamed at the doctor in charge and his cohorts, who stood between her and the exit.

"No can do, I'm afraid," he replied smugly. "I was put in charge here for a reason, nurse, and that reason is that my judgement and experience makes me the best dragon to run this facility, and look after all the dragons in it."

The last couple of words came out laboured, a cross between a pant and an asthmatic trying to catch their breath. Odd, everyone seemed to think. That is until they all started to feel it... in their chests and throats at first. An icy chill, much in the same way as drinking the coldest drink possible leaves a biting sensation when it's gone... refreshing on a hot day, not so much at any other time. One of the medics spoke up first.

"They've adjusted the temperature. What are we going to do?"

Everyone looked to the doctor for some guidance. He just stood there, clueless and gormless fighting to see which one would win.

"If we stay here, we'll all be too cold to do anything. I say we find Steel and fight."

The nurse who'd suggested he was already dead opened her mouth to speak, but 'Nurse Conscience' cut her short.

"You're right, he might already be dead. But I'll fight with my dying breath without him if I have to. Much better that way than hunched over, locked in a store cupboard, frozen to death, like the cowards they take us for. I'm done hiding from these cockwombles. I say it's time to take the battle to them."

A rousing cheer reverberated around the small room from everyone but the doctor and his followers. Reluctantly realising he had little choice, he removed the magic in the form of shields, mantras and supernatural locks from the door, and let the others slink out into the corridor. With the last one through, the four of them closed the door, once again applied the defences and wondered if they had indeed done the right thing.

It was only when he started to shiver, that he had any idea that something might be wrong. He'd felt terrible since the encounter with the naga. His head hadn't stopped spinning, and at first he'd thought that whatever was going on was a result of that. Plainly now he could see that it wasn't. The temperature was dropping fast, causing his muscles to burn, legs and arms to shake, and the mother of all headaches to form behind his face. It felt like the worst brain freeze in the world. Staggering on with much more urgency now, almost sprinting into unknown rooms, whereas only a matter of moments ago caution had been the watchword, he knew he needed to find wherever the temperature was being controlled from. And he needed to do it fast. On his way out of his room when this had all first started, he'd gotten a sense that a lot of dragons were holed up in the furthest reaches of the compound, barricaded in from what he could make out. He couldn't blame them. He was as afraid as they were. Only he was used to channelling his fear, something he'd already used to his advantage, and was doing so now to power himself on. If he didn't get that temperature back up, those dragons, the ones that had nursed him back to health, would all die in the most excruciating agony. Determined to prevent that at any cost, he raced around the next corner.

There were eight of them altogether, all being led by 'Nurse Conscience', all heading towards the control centre, where they knew the temperature was being regulated. It was a struggle. Dragons hate cold more than pretty much anything else. As well as the physical pain it causes to them, it can have some other rather disturbing effects. It stops them using their natural gases to produce a flame, or flames in some cases. While not life threatening, it does cause inflammation of the stomach lining and what can only be described as the world's worst case of indigestion, not something a dragon needs. Cold can also make a dragon far less bendable than normal. Most dragon scales when warm are supple, lithe and flexible. But once the temperature changes, they become susceptible to not only a build up of ice in the minuscule gaps between the scales, but the scales themselves can become brittle and easily broken. In the early stages this can slow a dragon down considerably, while in much colder conditions it can lead to an agonising death. A dragon's wings can also be affected by a drop in temperature. The receptors that sense air temperature and currents can become numb, making the appendages all but useless, flight impossible and cause difficulty in walking because they won't stay tucked in behind a dragon's back where they are supposed to be. The entire group of staff were all suffering from the early stages of this but, to their credit, they were all managing it really well, given just how dire things looked. Creeping towards the end of the corridor, which itself was just along from the control room, 'Nurse Conscience' carefully poked her head around the corner, before swiftly darting it back out of sight. She held up one finger to her lips for all the others to see. None of them moved a muscle. With their attuned dragon hearing, a kind of slip-sliding motion echoed from around the corner somewhere. At first it got louder, seemingly heading in their direction, before tailing off completely. Counting to thirty in her head, she turned to the others and began whispering.

"That naga came out of the control room. It looks like now's our chance. I don't know if there are any more in there. It might be empty, or there might be fifty of his friends all waiting for us. But the longer we wait, the colder we get, and the less chance we have of surviving. I say we go in, guns blazing for everything we're worth. What do you think?"

Each and every one of them nodded eagerly in response. That settled it. Magic at the ready, they moved with all the speed they could muster.

Unusually for dragons, they huddled together to keep warm. Currently though, it was doing little good. It hadn't occurred to them that the storeroom they'd hidden in was dedicated to strange medicines, and had any number of abnormal pathogens been in the building, this was one of the most likely places for them to be stored. With that in mind, the air temperature and recycling system had not one, not two, but three vents into this pokey little room, which as it stood, was one of the coldest parts of the entire building. Still though, they all refused to come out.

Catching his breath in a relatively small cubby hole beside a three metre high stack of drawers that contained all sorts of medical supplies and one off mantras, he rested the deadly, and now because of the cold, rather heavy sword against the wall. His courage had started to wane. He'd searched high and low for something that would lead him to the control room, without any luck. And without finding that, he knew there was little chance of surviving for more than a matter of minutes at most. The tiniest fraction of a fraction of a fraction within him screamed that he should find a way out, but that wasn't him. He wasn't leaving. Not without the others. If nothing else, he knew that. But things were now desperate. His head had gone from spinning to a kind of fuzzy, muzzy feeling. His limbs, wings and tail all tingled. Pins and needles if you like, with an added dash of pain. The only way he could possibly conceive of getting out of here was if the control room was right around the next corner. If it wasn't, they were pretty much all doomed.

Extending his magical senses as far as they would go, while all the time on the lookout for the one dragon that they'd seen on the security cam, he slithered down another identical corridor, taking in the bracing and refreshing chill the air had to offer. It was a faint reminder of what he thought of as home. Smiling at having won the bet to be the one out here on the hunt for the cold, weak and defenceless dragon, he knew that under different circumstances he'd have thought it unsporting. But everything they'd been doing was to get their king back. Without him they had nothing... he'd been away too long. He could almost taste his monarch's freedom, and after that... retribution.

They hit the door at speed. Two of the medics had insisted on going first, something 'Nurse Conscience' had little problem with, fully aware that there would only be a few seconds in it. She knew she'd get her chance. As the door crashed off its hinges, twisting and writhing up in the air as it did so, the singular naga, its body swaying from side to side in front of a computer console, was the picture of surprise as eight enraged dragons tore through the opening and headed straight for him. If he'd managed to erect his shield he might have had an outside chance. But he was surprised, and slow to react. In his panic, he chose the wrong option and decided to go on the offensive. Lashing out with sickly green bolts of magic, the naga gave himself over to his power, one hundred percent.

They were, of course, much slower than they should have been, the cold, even now, taking its effect. But they were dragons. Born to fight, born to win. It was ingrained in their very DNA. Odds didn't matter. Not now. Not ever. In truth, the naga never really had a chance. His poisonous bolts tore through the wings of one of the leading medics, sending him spinning off to one side, before crashing into a bank of servers. One of the nurses had a bolt pierce her thigh, causing her to slump clumsily to the floor mid run. But by now they were on him and had already showered him with a whole host of brutal dragon magic. One had used a medical mantra designed to cut through scales during dragon surgery. It superheated the air into a fine beam strong enough to penetrate almost anything, tearing through the naga's chest, clean through to the other side, hitting the far wall. The next two dragons both had the same idea, now that they lacked their flame. Part of their jobs involved cutting, sometimes organs, sometimes bone, scale, muscle or tendon. You name a body part, they've probably cut it at some point. As they'd charged in, not knowing what to expect, the thought that had come to the fore in both of them was that it was easy enough to cast if you'd had the practice (which they had). The mantra in question could produce one, two, or many more, tiny, metallic circular spinning blades, with edges so sharp you could almost slice the air itself. Presently, eight or so of these blades were flying through the air, all at different angles, all headed for the stunned looking naga. 'Nurse Conscience', fifth through the gap where the now battered and smoking door had stood, readied the power within her. She was angry about everything that had happened today, and was more than happy to help destroy the cause of things. Unfortunately for her, she never got the chance. Stunned from the hole that now traversed his torso, the naga could do nothing against the spinning blades heading his way. Instantly, they all found their mark, all piercing his slippery, grey flesh. It was over before it had started. As a group they stood still, not exactly admiring their handiwork, more... taking stock. A split second later they realised they hadn't finished. While three of them tended to the injured, the other three tossed the naga's remains into a corner, and started to check out the computer, with a view to making things much more toasty.

Nipping around the corner of an intersection, reflecting on his decision to part with the sword, on the grounds of it being far too heavy to carry in his weakened state, the distraction and the fuzziness in and around his head almost cost him his life... almost, but not quite. The naga sent to find Steel had just slithered backwards out of a room marked 'Solar Recovery', in which three giant dragon sized beds lay, atop which stretched fabulously strong solar lighting and heating, designed to revive and rejuvenate sickly dragons, particularly those that had suffered the effects of severe cold. Just getting his head around what the beds were designed to do, the naga spun round only to find Steel directly in his path. Both were equally shocked to find the other one just standing there, and both recovered their wits at exactly the same time. Spinning three hundred and sixty degrees, the naga whipped his tail around with ferocious force. Steel leapt back, but the tail managed to catch the talons on his left foot, rolling him off balance into a small table full of books, newsletters and research papers. With Steel in a crumpled heap, the naga slithered over, determined to press home his advantage. But Steel, despite every bone in his body aching from the freezing cold air, wasn't done. Rolling onto his knees, he grasped the trunk of a huge potted palm and swung for all he was worth. The pot on the end of the plant shattered against the naga's skull with a resounding thud that echoed off down the corridor. Unusually unsure of himself or what action he should take next, an unaccustomed momentary lapse gave the confused naga a chance to get back into the fight. From the look on his face, he was determined to make Steel pay for what he'd just done.

A decision had been made, albeit just a little too late. They'd all finally agreed that they should leave the store cupboard and try and either find the others, or somewhere warmer to hole up. The problem now was that it had gotten so cold, the doctor was struggling to access his magic and remove the mantras put there to stop the door from being open. And the longer he couldn't do it, the colder it got. Ironic really, given the lengths they'd gone to in an effort to prevent the door from being accessed.

"You need to reverse the effects and get the temperature up quickly," implored one of the medics treating the injured nurse in the control room.

"I'm trying, but I've been locked out of the environmental system. It's going to take me a few more minutes I'm afraid."

"I don't think he's got a few more minutes," stammered a nurse watching the bank of monitors on the other side of the room. As one, they all gathered, apart from the dragon that was trying to crack the computer. There, large as life, was Steel, being pummelled and beaten amongst the remains of a table, barely able to bring his hands up in front of himself for protection. No doubt the cold had taken its toll, more so on his newly reformed scales than it had on any of the others watching.

"He needs an injection of heat... and fast," put in the nurse that had called them over.

That was stating the obvious.

"What about the solar recovery room?" suggested 'Nurse Conscience'.

"I'm not really convinced he's got time to lie down and be recharged. I can't be sure though."

These medical staff, she thought, were unlike any she'd ever worked with. They were always so arrogant and sarcastic, more often than not missing an idea or a point entirely.

"I don't mean to go and lie down on. I mean, is it possible to overload the beds and make that entire area hot?"

"Ohhh," replied the sarcastic one, scratching his bony jaw line. "Maybe it is, maybe it is," he mumbled, wandering over to one of the other computers. "Is it just the environmental controls you've been locked out of?" he shouted over to the other dragon, working hard to get the heating up to speed.

"As far as I can tell," he replied.

With blinding speed, and no thought other than overloading the solar recovery beds, commands were punched in, sliders moved, safeguards and alarms overridden.

Feinting one way, with all the speed he could muster, Steel then rolled the other. Done a little faster, it would have fooled his naga assailant, but the cold and the beating he'd taken over the last few moments had caught up with him. A solid mass of tail whirled round, sending bits of paper fluttering into the air, before catching him a glancing blow on the top of his thigh, forcing him to cry out in agony, a new and unusual experience for him. Slithering back to the far side of the corridor, the naga now had a huge mocking smile covering his serpent-like face, as Steel, doubled over on the floor, tried desperately to pull in a decent breath, puffing and panting like an overworked husky, not needing to look up to know exactly how much trouble he was in. As he ran his fingers across his ribcage, trying to feel the damage he'd taken, his hands shook uncontrollably. If he was any judge, it was continuing to get colder, playing right into the hands of his foe.

"You certainly don't lack spirit," remarked the naga, barely a scratch on him, despite Steel's best efforts. "But I think now it might be time to concede defeat. I'll make it swift for an honourable dragon like yourself."

He supposed for some in his position, it might be tempting. But that wasn't how he rolled. If the naga couldn't see that, bigger fool him.

"Swift?" gulped Steel, now shivering all over.

"Think of it as a measure of respect, from one warrior to another."

After a momentary pause, still on his knees, Steel nodded and said,

"Do it!"

Slithering closer, Steel seemingly done, the naga gathered up the magic in his mind, ready to release it in one fell swoop. Pulling in a breath, Steel flooded every cell in his body with everything he had left, determined to go out fighting. From the very corner of his right eye, Steel could just see his opponent about to do exactly as he'd asked. Without hesitation, the laminium ball star threw everything into his shield, expanding it as far as he dared, before rolling up onto his feet and throwing himself at the naga. The slippery beast nearly choked on his magic, if that were possible. One second it was there, the next he was being knocked to the ground by an invisible force. Some of the magic released, all by itself, not finding its target, instead lighting up the walls of the corridor on both sides. Steel just let himself go. In the preceding moments, he'd told himself to do anything and everything to prevail, that the lives of those dragons who had nursed him back to health depended on it. It was all or nothing. So on hitting the naga full on, he withdrew his shield and let rip with a stunning mantra, putting all the belief and willpower he had left behind it, while at the same time punching, kicking and scratching for all he was worth. In truth, he'd gone berserk, without even knowing it. To the naga's credit, he gathered his wits about him quite quickly, but not before admonishing himself for being tricked. As he righted himself, throwing the pathetic looking dragon off in the process, he had one thought. 'NO MORE MISTER NICE GUY!'

Steel's head smashed straight through the glass separating the corridor from the solar recovery room. Half of his body had gone through the wall. Plaster dust blossomed into a small nuclear cloud. Razor-sharp shards of glass tinkled to the floor, those that weren't embedded in some way in the laminium ball player. With all the effort he could marshal, he tried to stand, well... pull himself out of the wall. Try as he might, he couldn't move. The cold very firmly had him in its grip.

Helpless to intervene, all they could do was watch the screen, apart from the two at separate computers, who were working feverishly.

"It needs to be now," begged 'Nurse Conscience'.

"Nearly there."

Never before having felt so powerless, she stared at the screen as the naga slinked back to an upright position, having tossed Steel almost through the wall like a rag doll. She willed him to get up. Get up and fight. Briefly she thought he would, but as the naga approached, full of magic, Steel's limp body hung there, half in, half out of the wall... totally static.

Wary of being fooled again, the slippery serpent, scratched, bruised and more than a little shaken from Steel's desperate attack, hung back a little, pulling in refreshing breaths of replenishing cold air. He had no more time to waste. No doubt his partner had monitored everything that had gone on and would berate him on his return, something he wasn't looking forward to. It did seem a shame to have to kill this one though. He'd fought valiantly enough. If it were down to him, he would just leave him here with his wounds. But it wasn't. And the orders had to be obeyed, that he knew. Reluctantly, he prepared himself for the grisly task.

BOOOOOOM!!!!!!!! The wall, windows, Steel, the naga and the entire corridor were suddenly engulfed in the mother of all fireballs. In the blink of an eye, the partition disintegrated, the glass melted, the naga was pelted with fiery debris and Steel... well, Steel embraced the warmth, the fire... the HEAT! It was glorious, delicious, overwhelming... almost. All he wanted to do was stand in the middle of it all and soak it up. But he was aware now that the cold had been peeled away and recognised just what the naga was about to do to him, and how much of a threat it still presented. So without hesitation, and as much for the others as for himself, he attacked with everything he knew. With the roles reversed, the naga tussled with the heat as Steel had been struggling with the cold, and after being hurled back down the corridor from the explosive force of the fireball, as well as being pelted with wreckage, the naga didn't stand a chance. Steel was on him in an moment, and almost as a mark of his respect, finished it instantaneously. With the explosive force of the fireball having passed, Steel stood in the middle of the burning wreckage, thick black smoke wafting all around him, burnt, battered, bruised and beat. Most importantly though, he was still alive. A tiny whirring further back down the corridor caught his attention. The security camera mounted on the ceiling turned in his direction. He could sense the dragon presences behind the technology.

"Thank you," he mouthed in its direction. It moved up and down in response. Plodding over to one of the only remaining pieces of wall, slowly he slid down it until his giant scaly bottom hit the floor. Slowly shutting his eyes, he savoured the heat from the blast and the fires all around him, waiting for them to come and find him.

Discovery was the watchword of the next two hours. Heroic staff in the control centre had to use all their wits to work out how to reverse the temperature change, which eventually they managed to do. As the staff arrived to find their injured patient, Steel couldn't remember ever having been so pleased to see other dragons. Heading back to the store room in the bowels of the building, the discovery there was nothing short of grim. After spending over an hour breaking in, they found that the doctor and his followers had all frozen to death. Everything was covered in a thick layer of frost, despite the temperature having been reversed. Devastated, they all realised there was no time to dwell on the tragedy. After a heated discussion it was decided, pretty much unanimously, that as a group they should leave the facility. It was just too dangerous to remain. No doubt others would come when they noticed the nagas were missing. Staying on the move appeared to be the best option.

Next came a discovery that totally rocked Steel. They'd all decided they needed a leader, one voice, if they were to go outside into the fray. It took no time at all for 'Nurse Conscience' to nominate Steel and everyone else to second him. He was about to discover if his laminium ball leadership skills translated into battle. If nothing else, things weren't going to be dull.

17 BITING BACK

Where dragon domain magic was concerned, they were the most knowledgeable in Manson's entire force. Made up of academics, priests, librarians and archaeologists, the group of eight had been almost exactly mirroring the nagas who'd spent so long trying to break into the magical creature containment area in the basement of the building, only on a different level entirely, in more ways than one. Theirs, one floor up, was a much more important assignment, in terms of both difficulty in gaining access and in what lay beyond the sealed doors. They were Manson's most trusted advisors, or so they thought. Their task? To find a way into the council chamber and purloin all of the artefacts and items in there. Ever since the first alarms had been raised in the building, complex magical shields, hexes, spells and mantras had aligned themselves in the protection of that particular room. Gaining access had been one of Manson's chief objectives on taking the building, and he was growing increasingly frustrated as each hour passed. Constant reports of their progress, or lack of it, had been relayed regularly. They didn't need to see him to get a sense of his dissatisfaction. It was plain and clear in the communications they'd received. Doubling their efforts, no stone, magical or otherwise, was left unturned.

And so it was that the archaeologist, a particularly crotchety dragon called Ned Hardtoignite, after spending over two hours with his head buried in a very dusty and withered old tome, and having disappeared off for twenty minutes or so, approached the others at the grand old doors to the impenetrable room.

"I think I may have something," he announced.

"Really?" quipped a few of them together.

"Yes really."

"Do tell."

Taking a breath, while at the same time organising all the information he'd discovered inside his head, the others looked on, waiting impatiently. He began.

"As we know, the power here is intrinsically linked to the consciousness within the king's ring... as far as we can tell, anyway. It's a good bet that the safeguards on this door are in some way connected. I think I've found a way to fool the door into thinking we have the ring."

From the looks on their faces, he knew he had their complete and undivided attention. He just hoped he was right.

"So what's the plan?" asked one of the priests inquisitively.

"Legend has it," explained Hardtoignite, "that tens of thousands of years ago, an envoy of the dragon king at the time was betrayed by the leaders of the lands he was trying to bring together. On the pretence of an alliance, the envoy, on the instructions of the king, was ordered to the land in question, that we now call Scandinavia but was then known as Ahrensburg. The leader of this cold and desolate territory was renowned for his hatred of the bipeds of his land, and for just how brutally he hunted and tortured them for sport. Not only that but the dragons he ruled lived in poverty and constant fear. It was hoped that by bringing Ahrensburg into what was rapidly becoming a growing coalition of dragon states, all under one supposed banner, that these traits, amongst other distasteful practices, could be outlawed and everyone could benefit from a much more cohesive and stable planet. It was all a ruse, however. The Ahrensburg leader had no desire to align himself with anyone, let alone dragons he considered weak and submissive. So when the envoy, a brave, battle hardened dragon called For'son Flail arrived, he was greeted in the usual way. All the diplomatic courtesies were extended, with a huge feast laid on in his honour. A fabulous time was had by all. By now you can probably guess where this is going. Each and every diplomat in the group of visiting dragons was poisoned, with For'son forced to watch as his defenceless retinue were slaughtered in front of him. Vowing retribution whilst trying every form of magic he knew, he was tortured for weeks, before eventually succumbing to the same deadly poison. This one event started a war that would last over twenty years, one of the deadliest in the planet's history. Some two decades later, what was left of For'son's body was repatriated, on the orders of the king himself."

"That's all very interesting," exclaimed one of the librarians, "but what the hell has it got to do with getting us into the council chamber?"

"Patience my friend, patience. I'm coming on to that."

"I do hope so. As someone who's spent nine decades working in a library, you can be sure I've had my fill of tall tales."

Ignoring the librarian, Hardtoignite continued.

"It turns out that the king and For'son had a much deeper relationship than anyone first knew. They had both fought alongside each other in an earlier time and had maintained that friendship throughout the ages. Distraught at the loss of his friend, it's rumoured, and it's only a rumour, that the king, in tribute to For'son, had an expensive, intricately crafted ring made to honour him."

"You're telling us the ring that the king had made is the one on the current monarch's finger."

"It would appear so."

"So exactly how on earth does that help us?"

"When the king had the ring made, he made sure the crafting dragons included some of For'son himself."

All listening intently, the rest of the group inhaled simultaneously.

"Not just any bit of For'son either. Supposedly his... heart!"

"Nooooo," the group voiced as one. "How is that even possible?"

"Whether from the poison, the torture or from For'son's own magic, the heart inside his recovered corpse had crystallised completely. On the king's instructions, the crafters took part of that, shaped it, and now it adorns the ring that sits on our current king's finger."

Total and utter silence enveloped them. It was nothing short of a revelation, if indeed it was true.

"I still don't understand how this helps us."

From behind his back, the dragon produced something covered in a white, cotton cloth, about the length of a man's arm, and proceeded to unwrap it as the rest of the group eagerly watched. Moments later, Hardtoignite revealed what was inside. It was a model of a dragon standing up, wings spread, teeth and talons bared. Incredibly intricate, the quality of the work was majestic, some of the best any of them had ever seen. But still the group were perplexed, something that showed across their faces. Before they had a chance to ask, Hardtoignite resumed.

"Crafting the king's ring took a number of dragons nearly ten months in all, working around the clock each and every day. It was a full time job, with no days off and all of them sharing the same accommodation. But they were the best of the best and exceptionally professional, so the hardship didn't bother them in the slightest. There were, however, times when it was only possible for one or two dragons to be working on the ring itself. So to keep themselves amused, distracted, relaxed, call it what you will, the dragons used their combined skills and took turns to create a model in what little spare time was available to them. A model of the dragon in question... For'son. It was, in their eyes, a tribute to a brave and daring dragon and a chance to practise and develop their skills. After the ring was created and presented to the king, much fuss was made over the crafters, and rightly so. Their work was of the highest order and their services were now hugely in demand. From what little I can make out, the model," he said lifting up the representation he held in his hands, "was discarded and forgotten. Sometime after, it was recovered, and although not really recognised for the part in history it represented, it has ever since been sitting in the relics and artefacts section of the Council's storage wing, two floors above where we are now standing."

Considering carefully what Hardtoignite had said, none of them had ever heard this story. Perhaps that was the idea.

"So just how does that model get us through the door?"

"You see the craftsdragons," explained Hardtoignite, "used the available material around them to pursue their... let's call it a hobby."

"Again, how does that help us?" enquired the librarian.

Holding the reproduction of For'son out in front of him, the archaeologist stated,

"Look at the eyes and tell me what you see."

As one, the entire group leaned in closer to get a look at the model dragon.

"Oh my God."

"No... It can't be. Can it?"

"That's unreal."

"It looks exactly the same colour. Is that even possible?"

"Indeed it is," added Hardtoignite, "difficult to believe, but ultimately it's true. I gather the pupils in the eyes of the dragon model were made out of the off cuts from the jewel which now sits in the king's ring."

"Which means," cut in one of the academics, "that it might be possible to fool the magic into thinking the king, and more importantly, his ring are trying to enter the council chamber."

"Exactly," stated the archaeologist. "Shall we?"

Approaching the large silver double doors, images of newborn dragons exploring the world for the first time, as well as some just escaping from their eggs, all being overseen by a kind looking dragon face, carved into both, were ignored by the bold interlopers on their mission of evil. Holding the model of For'son up to the centre of the huge entrance, Hardtoignite closed off his mind and focused all his thoughts in casting the mantra that he hoped would gain them access to the precious artefacts within. Fuelled by optimism and having forgotten everything around him, he filled his intellect with the same words the cooks used when they entered with the prepared food for the Council meetings. He knew he had to get it just right.

'Patefacio, patefacio, solvo vestri obfirmo quod permissum mihi obduco,' he thought, directing all his will towards the firmly closed doors. Eyes screwed shut, the tiniest hum in the world disappeared into the background and was immediately followed by an ordinary click. The heavy doors started to pull back, the sound of monstrous metal moving slowly growled back at them. Hardtoignite opened his eyes to the beaming smiles of the others. After back patting all around, the small group entered the chamber. Much to their surprise, and discomfort, it was cold, extremely cold. Long gone were the usual fires and spit roasted meats, blackened ash the only sign they had once been there. Crusty black lava spewed out across the white and gold flecked marble pillars that adorned the room. Two of the academics marvelled at the prophecy agreement depiction on the floor as they entered, but the others just walked over it, more interested in what they came for. Ignoring the grey, granite, trident shaped table as they passed it, the giant, gold coloured abacus the size of a bus sat lonely against the far wall, beneath the tapestry made of dragon scales. In their own way, the interlopers were making a small piece of history, in a room that positively reeked of it. Ignoring everything, and with the academics having caught them up, they all stopped in the furthest corner from the entrance. Dark, freezing and positively reeking of deadly magic, more so than the rest of the room, wooden bookshelves with an array of magical items were faintly illuminated by a cool, blue glow. Water dripped and splashed onto the floor from the ceiling and the shelves. Small patches of melting ice covered one or two of the items and the occasional corner of the shelves. It felt to the dragons exactly how it looked... DANGEROUS, COLD and DARK!

It was a treasure trove of rare magical items. Daggers, bows, leather armour (dragon sized), gauntlets, bracers, belts with deeply disturbing engraved buckles, a set of folded robes, a compass, pocket watches, a leather Stetson, a gnarled staff, half a dozen wands, a set of lanterns, an array of jewellery including rings, necklaces, brooches and an assortment of hat pins, as well as all alone, almost begging for some company, an *'alea'* exactly the same as the one Peter had inherited. Light of one sort or another shrouded most of the items. A thick, dull, all absorbing brightness exuded from some, whilst others radiated a dazzling, white halo in and around their majestic forms. The contrast was immense. Standing stock still for a moment, the small band looked on, utterly flabbergasted at what lay on the shelves before them.

"We should catalogue it all first," noted one of the academics.

"Agreed," piped up a librarian. "Dividing it up into light and dark to start with might help."

Each nodded their agreement.

From out of nowhere, one of the priests yelped. "Owwwww!!!!"

"You okay?"

"No," said the priest rubbing a spot on his neck vigorously. "Something bit me!"

"In here?" replied one of the others sceptically. "It's been sealed for goodness knows how long."

"I'm just telling you what happened," declared the priest. "It really hurts!"

"We really don't have time for this," insisted

Hardtoignite. "We've already taken long enough getting in as it is. I for one want to get all of this stuff catalogued and up to Manson as quickly as possible."

On that, they could all agree.

With them splitting into two groups of four, taking dark and light relics respectively, they immediately got on with their assigned tasks. One of the academics checking the light sided objects, made straight for the artefact that had first caught his attention... the *alea*. With a quick flick of his wings, he bounded straight up to the high shelf that it was on, grasped it firmly in the palm of his hand and drifted back down to the floor, his landing as light as a feather. Not bad for a being of his size. Studying the object in the palm of his hand, with thoughts about its history and magical significance running through his mind, he was startled from his reverence by a loud CRASH off to his right, as the dragon priest, the one who claimed to have been bitten, the one who had been studying a gorgeous set of light tan leather armour a little further into the corner, had abruptly collapsed on the floor. Instantly, the entire group stopped what they were doing and rushed over to him. One of the librarians knelt down towards his head while Hardtoignite listened to the unmoving dragon's chest. Others looked on in horror at what was happening.

"I can't feel a pulse," queried the one at his head.

"There's no heartbeat. Breathe damn it, breathe," fumed Hardtoignite from the stricken priest's chest, driven now to frantically beating it.

"Uhhhh... guys!"

"NOT NOW!" screamed Hardtoignite, beating the dragon's torso furiously with both of his hands.

"YOU REALLY NEED TO SEE THIS!!!"

Hardtoignite hung his head helplessly over the body of the dead dragon, anger and despair welling up deep inside him. Why was it going so wrong? Why, just for once, couldn't things go exactly as planned? And just what the hell could be more important than trying to save the life of one of their own? Standing up, he turned to face the others, who all, oddly, had their backs to him, staring back towards the entrance. With his patience about to snap, he shoved two of them aside and made his way to the front. It was only then that he saw what was so important. Only then did it dawn on him just how much trouble they were all in.

The fighting in the basement had taken its toll. Corpses of all shapes and sizes littered the walkways and corridors. Blood and other bodily fluids pooled together in rainbow like puddles. Limbs, tails, paws and heads lay precariously scattered about. It was a crime scene investigator's nightmare. But it had all stopped, well, apart from the rock demon, who was still very much on the rampage. Mainly, it was the ra-hoon's doing. After devouring the naga that had tried to escape, the thinned out herd had headed deeper into the containment facility, eventually coming face to face with the horde of different creatures all trying to destroy each other. Smart didn't really do the ra-hoon justice, because they were cunning as well. They could see things for what they really were, now that they'd escaped captivity. And so with one concerted telepathic blast, that quite literally stunned everything (with the exception of the rock demon) around them into submission, they began to outline, to all the species there, just how they should proceed, and how working together in this strange new world that they'd suddenly found themselves in, would benefit one and all. For most of them it made sense, for the rest, it was too scary a prospect to say no. So they didn't, and agreed to tag along, always on the lookout for an opportunity to gain an advantage.

Downright terrifying couldn't begin to describe it. How they'd got in without making a single sound was incredible.

But they had, and now Hardtoignite and the rest of his followers stood facing them, wondering just what to do.

Having found their way up a plush stairwell and onto the next floor after leaving the basement proper, there were few beings about, with the exception of two solitary nagas patrolling the corridors in their human forms. In all honesty, they never really stood a chance, each overwhelmed by a considerable number of different species, each dying in a totally different way, neither able to send a warning to any of their brethren. Leading the way, the ra-hoon had arrived just in time to spot the dragon group gaining access to the council chamber, and had watched for a few minutes, before being lured by the promise of supernatural power radiating from the room, enticing them ever forward. Had they wanted to ignore it, they couldn't, the pull and seduction of the magic was just too much. Having taken in the situation, the ra-hoon gave the order. They would go in as one, quietly, without the dragons knowing. Only when they were all lined up, would they be ready to fight, and reap the magical rewards that lay somewhere in that chamber. Silently they moved into position.

In all of his nearly two hundred years, he'd never seen anything like it. An array of magical creatures, some of which could only come from legend, he thought. He just had to be dreaming, that seemed the only possibility. But he wasn't. An angry snarl from the lead asena snapped him away from thoughts of legends and fame, its blue mane rippling as it did so. And then it hit him. An attack force sent by the king to take back the building. If that was the case, then it was a masterstroke, that of a genius. On some level he was correct. While the sovereign now had no control over what the magical escapees did, he was at least hopeful that their release would result in the maximum amount of chaos possible. If only he knew.

Now that the dragons knew they were there, suppressing the noise was no longer necessary. Vile looking brown lizards scuttled back and forth, their forked tongues constantly whipping in and out, accompanied by crackling green bolts of lightning that lit up the air in front of them. A squadron of dark yellow gnats weaved in and out of the hovering pixiu, spraying tiny cones of fire out in front of them, making sure to avoid injuring their flying lion allies. One of the scaled apes beat his chest, with just two arms instead of the usual four. The rest of his kind followed. As the terrifying sound thundered around the room, causing the shelves with all the magical items on to shake, nifoloa buzzed, two headed eagles squawked, snakes hissed, the scorpion men's pincers clacked together, while all the time the leaders, the ra-hoon, looked on, waiting for the dragons' next move.

Dragon pee could peel the paint off a car in but a split second. It took all of the small group's concentration not to start redecorating the council chamber. Little choice about their next move was afforded.

18 FLASH IN THE PAN

Snow and ice hung in the air, making it all but impossible to see more than a few feet in any direction as the walls of the cavern shook from the explosion that he'd unleashed only moments earlier. Head ringing, having been thrown back into a formation of stalactites, the ex-Crimson Guard knew he had to contain the fear and pain that threatened to engulf his false form of a body. Everything depended on it. And so, as he'd done many times before, he compartmentalised everything within him, tossing it all down the darkest, bottomless chasm lying deep within his mind and stoked all the rage he possessed, knowing that now was not the time to hesitate or show even the merest hint of mercy. Now was the time to do what had to be done. Not just for his survival, but for the others in this icy hellhole, and ultimately... the planet itself.

Bounding to his feet, he bumped straight into a disoriented naga trying to get its bearings. Without hesitation, he added some magic to a punch, carefully aiming at the gills on the side of the beast's head. With a sickening THWUMP, his hand pierced the glistening scales of his foe, right up to his wrist, eliciting a wet gurgle and a garbled cry for help. Knowing that he had no time to celebrate taking one of the enemy out, particularly as he'd just noticed the damage done to his supposedly camouflaged suit, he reverted back to his age old battle mantra... NO MATTER WHAT HAPPENS, KEEP ON THE MOVE AT ALL COSTS!

Throughout the cave, well... prison actually, debris settled, senses returned, anger presided. Above it all, the high pitched jingle of chains rattling bounced across the walls, as both long term detainees, Fredric and the naga king, desperately tried to enter the fray, with very little success.

Furious nagas rolled and wriggled in an effort to free themselves from the ice and snow into which they'd been tossed, needing to be upright to unleash the supernatural power at their disposal, but before some had a chance, invisible assailants rained down innovative, brilliant, bright magic, choking some, piercing others, crushing yet more unseen. It went some way to evening up the odds, but with each encounter the imaginative camouflage suits were damaged, revealing different members of the impromptu rescue effort, almost literally painting a target on each and every one of their backs.

Aware that now was not the time to hold back, Yoyo, using all the belief and willpower he possessed, launched a devastating concussive wave of energy at a pair of murderous looking nagas attempting to sneak up behind Hillier, who'd just garrotted one of their kind with pioneering new magic. Had he the time, Yoyo would have gushed with pride. However, his attention was needed elsewhere.

True to his battle beliefs, Flash hadn't stopped moving, a virtual twister, only a few parts of his body visible, slashing and kicking, punching and blocking, decimating the naga fighting force almost singlehandedly. Abruptly the blur that he was found himself caught unaware by a heavy metal chain around his legs. Momentum stifled, he crashed clumsily into one of the slithering serpent-like beasts intent on doing his friends harm. Without a thought, vicious chain lightning rocketed from his fingertips, deep into the eye sockets of his foe, instantly boiling the naga's eyeballs, effectively rendering him out of the fight. Before he had a chance to ascertain the threat that had brought him to a halt, roaring pain erupted across the base of his back, forcing him down to his knees, causing his head to spin. Grinning inanely, the jailer, Joshim, looked on, the massive barbed metal chain he'd just raked across Flash's back hanging limply by his side.

Everything, that's how much he gave. In all the decades

he'd been incarcerated, he'd never wanted to break free quite as much as he did now, wanting to join in, fight, give his life for those who had clearly come to rescue him. But it was all in vain, as the chains didn't budge, not even an inch, still disappearing off into the wall of ice that effectively rendered him useless, when his skills were much needed.

Almost alien in comparison to Fredric's mind, the naga king's thoughts were much the same as those of his caged compatriot... wanting out, wanting to join in, wanting revenge. But he too couldn't move, the taut chain restraining most of his magic, only able to look on in horror at the scene unfolding before him.

Water dripped and splashed throughout the cavern as wayward magic danced off the walls, boiling molecules, breaking rock, decimating ice, causing needle sharp stalactites to come rocketing down from their age old formations on the ceiling, spearing one or two of the murderous nagas. Yoyo and his band of fearless, inventive dragons fought valiantly against overwhelming odds, parts of their bodies visible through the simmering steam that threatened to envelop everything around them, their protective camouflage outfits torn apart amongst the chaos.

Knees almost stuck to the ice, Flash glanced up at the smug jailer, ignoring the disorder and confusion from the battle raging all around him. Deep within, he knew it was a risk to focus solely on one opponent at a time like this, but anger flooded through him at what had occurred here, and now he decided it was time to finish things once and for all. Mustering his magic instantly, a wave of superheated air shot out from his right hand, aimed directly at the wicked jailer. Enhanced with a trickle of mana, he bounded up, the material from the suit around his knees ripping, staying firmly glued to the frosty floor, as he followed his attack. Air rippled and sparked in a familiar shape... that of a giant rugby ball, encasing the psychotic jailer. Briefly, Flash thought of Tank, wondering what hell he was encountering on the other side of the planet, but only for a microsecond, if that. Launching himself at the wicked Joshim, who'd by now harmlessly deflected away his magic, which was meant as more of a distraction than anything else, Flash caught him around the midriff and wrestled him to the ground, as the glinting metal chain swung around in his direction. Letting fly a powerful uppercut to the filthy jailer's chin, Flash failed to notice as the cold metal of the chain snaked around his neck. By the time he did, it was almost too late. Rolling off to one side, both hands gripping either end of his improvised weapon, Joshim's muscles bulged as he pulled the chain taut, strangling his surprised opponent. Pain from the snow and ice burning his exposed knees prevented him from seeking the clarity that he needed, and so instead he slipped both his hands beneath the chain currently choking him, while at the same time he kicked back, giving everything he had, for all the good it did him.

Fredric's glistening muscles strained with exertion, enhanced with what little magic he had available. Still the chains wouldn't give as he looked on helplessly as the jailer, not five metres from where he stood, appeared to gain the upper hand in his battle with the dragon who'd come to free them. Desperately, he racked his brain for anything that could be of use, anything that could help that dragon. But for the life of him, nothing came to mind. If they could come just a little closer, then maybe he could help. Just one strike, that's all he wanted. That would be enough, he knew, to end the pitiful existence of that sorry jailer. Ready and waiting, he willed the beleaguered dragon into range, but by the looks of things time was about to run out.

Things had gone from bad to worse. Flash now found himself face down on the ice, choked by the chain, his hands able to do little to alleviate the pressure around his neck, the jailer's knee digging painfully into his spine.

Inside his mind, he felt as though things were nearly at an end, and wished for nothing more than to experience his true form one last time. From nowhere, that little spark of fight, the one that had saved him on so many occasions, burst into life, urging him not to give up, to scrap, to give everything he had left. So that's what he did.

With a sickening chuckle that reverberated around the cavern, amongst the still raging battle, Joshim took great delight in squeezing the life out of what appeared to be the group's leader. Rolling waves of pleasure inundated him at the thought of yet another life taken, and knowing just how pleased his master would be with his work. Mere seconds away now, he was fully aroused by his deplorable deed. Nothing sated his desire like taking a life.

Blue in the face from lack of oxygen and the cold of the ice, with just a little push deep within his mind, he let it go. Or more likely, just removed the restraints, the restraints surrounding his magic that is. Milliseconds later, it burst forth, engulfing both of them in a raging torrent of pent up energy and furious power, whisking up ice, rock and some of the other combatants in its wake.

Putting the final touch to dispatching yet another murderous naga, Yoyo turned to see Flash struggling on the floor, about as far away as it was possible to be, a ragged, emaciated being straddled over him, throttling the hell out of him. Taking a step forward, about to rush over and aid his friend, from out of nowhere a massive invisible explosion of energy tore away at everything, knocking the healer back on his ass, straight into one of the alien looking icy formations that made up some of the walls.

Clumsily, Flash landed head first on the ice, almost within reach of Fredric, starved of oxygen, totally out for the count, at least one of his legs broken. Joshim, meanwhile, had been drilled into a solid rock wall littered with glowing fungus and was just now trying to shake off what looked like a severe concussion, noting the naga corpses scattered around him that had fared far worse from the dragon leader's misdirection. Sparing a fleeting look for the metal chain, almost instantly he disregarded it, instead pulling out what looked like a needle sharp screwdriver the length of a man's arm, previously fashioned and used to torture Bag O' Bones. Ears ringing, head spinning, he staggered towards the leader's prone body, determined to end it and quell his blood lust.

For all he was worth, Fredric screamed at the top of his voice for the dragon to get up, get up and face his foe, the disorientated jailer that even now was heading his way. With no luck, he began kicking bits of ice towards the unconscious dragon's face, hoping in vain that might rouse him. But he just lay there, unable or unwilling to get up.

Incapable of making any sense of the fuzziness inside his mind, he tried desperately to remember where he was and what had happened, but it all seemed just out of reach. All he knew was that he was cold, much colder than he'd ever been in his entire life, and that his magic was gone. In a dreamy haze, he wished for the sun to beat down on his scaled wings and warm him up, as it had done many times before.

Reaching the motionless body of the attack force's leader, Joshim took great pleasure in Fredric's anger at what he was about to do. So much so that he thought a little amuse bouche was in order before he feasted on the main course. With little concern about what was going on around him, he charged at Fredric who he knew only as the dragon that would reveal nothing. Not for the first time, he found the well honed and physically imposing dragon up for the fight, but without the magic that was his birthright, he never really stood a chance. Imbued with power, the sick jailer kicked down hard, straight through his knee cap, a deafening CRUNCH his richly deserved reward. Not stopping there, he rained down a series of brutal punches into his prisoner's face, splintering his cheek and breaking his nose. About to get lost in his blood lust, it was then that he remembered the reason he'd come over here and the pain he still felt from being tossed into the cavern wall. Throwing one last punch into Fredric, he returned to his feet and picked up the menacing looking screwdriver that he'd disregarded during his charge.

Flash, meanwhile, had all but come round, albeit still mightily confused, but had one last goal in mind before he gave up for good, and could see it only a couple of metres away. So as Joshim continued his assault on Fredric, Flash pulled himself across the ice, his broken leg sending brilliant spikes of pain up his back, tears instantly freezing on his cheeks. Just as the jailer had finished his assault and had bent down to retrieve something from the ice, Flash reached his goal and with what was left of his willpower, searched his memory for the words he needed.

Back in Salisbridge, before he'd boarded his ride to the surface, before he'd put on the boots and travelled halfway across the world, his friend, Tank, had told him about the chains... what they did, not how to break them of course... they were unbreakable. Apparently though, they could be changed... changed to something that would almost certainly benefit those on his side, those fighting to be free. And so reaching out with one hand, watching as the jailer approached wielding some kind of terrifying weapon, Flash gripped Fredric's tethered chain, and with what little belief and willpower he had left, whispered the words.

Disorientated, but still in one piece, Yoyo once again prepared to enter the fray, taking a moment to decide what to do. It was then that he noticed it... the jailer advancing on Flash, waving about something sharp and deadly. Bringing forth the most powerful magic he knew, he let rip with brilliant purple shards of energy, hoping against hope to strike the jailer down, but not really believing such a thing was possible from so far away.

Amused at his opponent making a grab for one of the unbreakable chains, Joshim, in his heightened state, was almost in total frenzy now. There could be no denying him this, nothing was going to stand in his way. The life was his to take. And with no ceremony, no fuss, just a roar that was pure, unadulterated pleasure, he thrust his rust ridden, achingly sharp screwdriver straight through Flash's heart.

Tense couldn't do justice to how Hardtoignite and his comrades were feeling right at this very moment, facing off against all the creatures from the capture and containment level. Throughout the cold, dark and foreboding council chamber, crusty black lava adorning most of the marble pillars, an undercurrent of magic was almost tangible. At the back, by the door, the orchestrators, the ra-hoon, waited, letting their new subjects take the lead. Formidable as they might be, their enemy stood little real chance against the combined fighting force of the creatures here. Schemes, plans and plots whirled throughout the intelligent creatures' minds, barely able to contain their excitement about what was to begin, eager to see if their predictions would come to pass.

Although generally quite self absorbed, it hadn't taken long for Hardtoignite to realise there really was no other way out than to fight. With that in mind, he'd briefed the others telepathically on what he thought was their best chance of success. It relied wholly on surprise, with them all throwing everything they had into a major area of effect attack at exactly the same time, targeting the entire force in front of them. Inside their telepathic connections, a timer was counting down, and currently stood on seven.

Unfortunately for them, the asenas could smell the magic they'd concocted for their private chat, and took that as a sign to attack. And so they did, their brilliant blue manes waving majestically as they took off at full pelt towards Manson's caught-off-guard force of priests, academics and librarians, who were standing still, nervously waiting for the timer to reach its conclusion.

Hardtoignite reacted first, unleashing his magic on the count of four, before his comrades had even thought to act. Striking dead centre, that first devastating attack killed one or two of the impossibly rare magical creatures on impact, as well as destroying a huge chunk of the massive trident shaped table, but forced the rest to scatter randomly throughout the room, negating Hardtoignite's plan of hitting them all at once. As things went to hell, magic exploded, energy rebounded, creatures roared, cried out and went berserk, savagely assailing their opponents, killing them all in the most brutal of fashions... scaled apes feasting on intestines, pixiu scrapping over discarded limbs, wicked brown lizards lapping up bodily fluids, with the nifoloa plunging their single giant tooth into anything that remotely resembled food. All the time the ra-hoon looked on from the doorway, taking a keen interest in just how long it would take their task force to destroy these so called superior beings. Not long as it turned out. Not long at all.

In the midst of the battle deep beneath the Antarctic, pure unadulterated ecstasy rolled through every atom of his body as the menacing screwdriver slid through the leader's heart, eliciting a laugh that was so vile, so sickening, that even the devil himself would shy away from it. Given everything going on around him, it would have come as a surprise to find that the most magical thing going on right at that very moment, not just in that cavern but across the entire planet, was only an arm's length away.

He died. The jagged metal length of the screwdriver had pierced his heart. There could have been no other outcome. But fate, if that's what it was, had other ideas. Microseconds before he'd been killed, he finished mouthing the words... Tank's words, the mantra that he'd recounted, the one that would turn the unbreakable chains restraining the prisoners into laminium. Instantly the magic had taken effect, and as the weaponised screwdriver had plunged deep into Flash's false form of a body, something wholly supernatural had happened in his immediate vicinity. If time had slowed right down, it would have gone something like this.

As the tip of the screwdriver entered Flash's flesh, he finished reciting the mantra. Immediately and with little fuss or indication, the metal in the unbreakable chains that had spent decades restraining Fredric, transformed into pure laminium. In less than a heartbeat, very much like the metal, Fredric was reborn. Unimaginable, that's how it felt. Like a harsh winter's day suddenly turning into the height of summer... darkness into light... a strong spirit crushing hopelessness out of sight. In less than a hundredth of a second, Peter's grandfather totally repaired his destroyed kneecap, broken nose and splintered cheek, flooding them with just a fraction of the absurd amount of power he found himself possessed of. Flushed with magic that had been missing from his life and body for so long, his mind reached out into his surroundings, exploring, searching, looking to see how he could best be of use. In that instant, he developed a very real and personal connection with Flash, whose skin, like Fredric's, brushed firmly against the metal of the chains. There and then, they were one. Flash, Fredric, the chains... there was no telling them apart. For all intents and purposes, they were one entity. And so as the screwdriver slid deep into Flash's heart, extinguishing his long and eventful life, the part of the entity that was Fredric called on the almost limitless supply of power at his disposal and reversed what had just happened, acting much as a god would. A billionth of a second after Flash had died, the screwdriver's barbed and sharpened shaft disintegrated, leaving just the worn wooden handle in Joshim's grip. Infused with magic, the damage to Flash's heart was undone, along with the deadly wound. As the magic flowed across both beings, and the metal linking them, the ethereal power, almost of its own accord, found something else, something unusual, something incredibly wrong, all the way down at the subatomic level.

Instinctively and without any guidance from either of the beings, it righted a wrong in the blink of an eye, returning that which once was, and should always have been. Satisfied at its work, and having all but topped up both beings, the magic retreated back into the chains, stored and waiting, ready to be called upon at a moment's notice.

Dumbfounded and momentarily confused, the expression on Joshim's face was priceless, as he stood there, wondering not only where the rest of the screwdriver had gone, but how the hell the leader, strewn out in front of him, had just opened his eyes wide, a tantalising smile spread across his face.

With the chaos of the battle still raging all around them, their own private war broke out there and then, the vile little jailer roaring with fury, his temper boiling out of control. Instantly he leapt at Flash, diving full force, his chipped yellow teeth bared in a snarl, the flimsy looking rags adorning his body flailing out behind him. A new found awareness having inundated every atom of his being, Flash found himself vaguely amused by what he knew now to be a rather pitiful attempt at an assault. Ready, willing and more than a little able, he flooded himself with as much power as he dared, and readied himself to take down the depraved little beast. From out of nowhere, a high pitched whine sliced through the cold, frosty air, only centimetres above Flash's face. Common sense told the ex-Crimson Guard that he should remain flat on the ground and so he did, grateful to let the huge chunk of laminium chain bypass him. The jailer, on the other hand, was not nearly so lucky. Having ripped the chain fully from the wall of ice that had so long contained it and him, Fredric had whipped it around using all his newfound magical power, catching Joshim full in the face, mid-dive. Metal carving through bone and flesh had never felt so satisfying, as the unedifying form of the distressed jail keeper ploughed into the base of a nearby wall. Sure he could leave Fredric to the sweet revenge he knew he must have craved, Flash leapt to his feet and, powered by magic, rejoined the fight, determined to assist Yoyo's ragtag band of dragons in ridding themselves of the rest of the fighting force.

Striding barefoot across the frozen floor of the cavern, chest puffed out, magic oozing from every pore of his glistening body, Peter's grandfather approached the broken form of the most wicked being he'd ever encountered. Part of him wanted to exact revenge, make him pay for the evil deeds he'd carried out over the course of decades. It was more than part of him... most of him in fact. But that tiny part of reason which had long since been responsible for keeping him sane throughout his captivity, roared at him to get it over with, if for no other reason than to help the others and get a better understanding of the much bigger picture. And so without further ado, Fredric called forth the might of all of his supernatural power and with a fury built up over decades, unleashed a devastating magical attack that no being on the planet would have been able to defend against. Air atoms imploded, fire and electricity forked out of Fredric, crossing the gap between the two enemies in the blink of an eye, incinerating every last molecule of the depraved jailer, leaving only a steaming, charred outline scorched into the ice. Briefly soaking up the wave of satisfaction that rolled across him, it was then that his professionalism and training kicked in, and the former founder of the Crimson Guards returned, the outcome of the underground battle now totally and utterly assured.

Earth's surface. Primm, United States of America.
Having just finished brushing his teeth for what seemed like the hundredth time, he sucked in a breath mint, hoping against hope that it might just brighten up his senses and get rid of the stale, musty cigarette odour that permeated the whole of the room he'd paid handsomely

for. Buffalo Bill's hotel and Casino! Come to Primm, see the sights, stay in the lap of luxury. What a crock! Any cheap, roadside motel would have been cleaner, and CHEAPER! Still, he did at least blend in. There was a conference of some sort. He wasn't sure who was running it or what it was for, but the attendees were nearly all single businessmen. And so the hotel was full to the brim with them, ideal for him and cementing his cover almost perfectly.

Strolling out from the pathetic excuse of a bathroom, he wandered over to the window and gazed out over the rollercoaster layout that surrounded much of the car park, towards the mountains off in the distance beyond the sand drenched plains, dotted with towering electricity pylons. What a truly dreadful place this was, he thought, longing not for the icy wilderness that he thought of as home, but just a body of water, any amount of water... a creek, a lake, a reservoir... anything. Just not that godforsaken swimming pool that so many of the single businessmen had now decided to descend upon, forcing every female even thinking about a swim to scatter like bathers at the beach sighting a fin cutting through the water.

Watching tumbleweed tumble, and tiny grains of sand carried on the ever present breeze disperse in a multitude of directions, his thoughts turned to what he was here to do. He'd been tasked... no, ordered to bring Las Vegas, north of his current location, to its knees. How he went about this was left to his discretion, but that was what he'd been told. And he would carry out those orders to the letter.

Not at all like most of his race, he was an exceptional type of inventor, which was unusual in itself and caused him to be shunned by most like him, that is until they wanted something only he could achieve, he who could combine magic and technology like no one else on the planet. Nothing was beyond his means. Possibility was only held in check by how far his imagination stretched.

Quite far, as luck would have it. Turning away from the window, he strolled across the beer stained carpet, all the time ignoring the smell, to the singular table adjacent to the breakfast bar. Opening the dark duffel bag, he reached in and pulled out a shiny silver tube, about fifty centimetres long and four centimetres in diameter. Spinning it round in his hands, he admired it from every possible angle, occasionally taking pride in his false reflection in the window. It was a marvel of technology, even by his standards, and had taken him nearly six months to fully develop the idea and turn it into a functioning prototype. Well, five functioning prototypes, to be exact. Over the last week, he'd planted the other four in what he hoped were strategic points circling the city of Las Vegas.

The first he'd hidden in a tyre yard in Pahrump, off to the west. Having scouted the location during daylight hours, it had been no great shakes to break in at night and hide the seismic shocker (that was the name he'd come up with for the devices) amidst the looming tyre towers. Even if they were looking for it, nobody would have a hope in hell of finding it. He was quite proud of that.

The second had seen him slip on his hiking boots and head out onto a little used mountain trail east of St George which itself was east of Las Vegas. The walk was exhausting, but paid dividends. He'd found the perfect place to bury the next shocker. Once again pride ran through him at the thought that nobody would find where he'd put it. It was almost the perfect crime, although nothing untoward had come about so far.

Next he moved on to India Springs north of the gambling metropolis, but not before spending a day recovering from his exertions on the mountain trail, back in his hotel in St George. Sunburn had been something of a problem. Of course he could have magically adjusted his form with just a few words and removed it, but others had seen him on his return and so lying low for a day seemed the appropriate resolution. He'd gotten away with it and learned a valuable lesson for the future with that one. He'd cleverly buried the third shocker beneath a lonely Joshua tree on the outskirts of town, having taken a walk with all of his human photography kit. Nothing too unusual in that.

For the fourth shocker, he'd crept up through the mountains in the pitch black, not such a difficult task enhanced by his magical legacy. Over the course of half the night, he'd snuck into a huge solar farm south east of Vegas and, using some magnets of his own design, had attached the shocker to the back of one of the tens of thousands of solar panels at random. The odds of anyone finding it before it was used were astronomical... lottery winning odds in fact.

And so here he was in Primm, looking to locate the last of the five seismic shockers and get the hell out of dodge before setting his cunning plan in motion, via a cell phone, from a long, long way away. Having had a good look around on his way into town, he'd examined and then discarded a few locations already. There'd been a fountain directly outside one of the filling stations. It didn't look as though anyone would pay too much attention to it, but he couldn't be sure and so had opted for something else. There'd been quite a bit of vegetation surrounding most of the parking lots and malls, all of which he could have used, but still he couldn't settle. It was only when he pulled into the hotel lot and saw the rollercoaster track surrounding half the hotel, that he knew he'd found the answer. And so that's what he settled on. Under the cover of dark he'd take a walk, claiming that he needed to clear his head. And then using some of his own magnets, he'd attach the last seismic shocker to part of the roller coaster. It should blend in seamlessly with all the other metallic elements of the design. Once far enough away in a few days' time, he'd dial in using the number only he knew, setting off the magic which, when combined with the technology, would cause ground quake after ground quake, powerful enough to do some serious damage to the world's number one gambling city, spreading fear, chaos and confusion throughout. Las Vegas wouldn't know what had hit it.

19 MALEVOLENT MAJESTIC MANIAC

Slumped forward, balanced precariously on the edge of unconsciousness, the faintest of sounds, getting ever so slightly louder, made his ears prick up like prey fearful of a predator. Shaking his head, hoping to rid himself of the cloying fuzziness that seemed a constant companion since he'd been shackled, he wondered whose footsteps he could hear approaching, and if indeed his time was finally up. Sitting up as straight as he could, not knowing what to expect, shooting streaks of pain blossomed down his neck and across both his shoulders as he struggled against the weight of Tim, who, from the sound of it, was fast asleep. What he wouldn't give for that. Eyes glued to the corner from which the footfalls were fast approaching, mentally he steeled himself for what was about to come. In reality, it did little to prepare him for this. HER!

Cloaked in a shimmering, dark brown dress that sparkled like diamonds in places, he was inexplicably drawn to her overgrown fingernails and the matching polish that adorned them. Thoughts of her drawing blood across his neck outside the council building in front of the huge army flooded his consciousness. Her words startled him out of one nightmare and very much into another.

"Ahhhh... the king's little pet. Lovely!"

Behind his back, he could feel his arms start to shake, as Tim's soft snoring tickled his ears. For a split second he hoped his friend, The White Dragon, would stay asleep for as long as possible, avoiding the terror he himself was currently experiencing.

Leaning casually against the wall, delicately tracing the purple crisscrossing lines of magical madness across her face with one of her extensive fingernails, Manson's queen surveyed the two prisoners in front of her, fully aware of the effect she was having on the one that was awake.

"Substantial injuries you have there. It's a shame, really, that you can't access your magic. Just a tiny sliver is all that's needed."

Through the mist in his head and the pain from his binders, he found it hard to ignore her goading, knowing full well the extent of his injuries and just how much of a mess his face and body must be. So instead of barking out the first retort that jumped up into his head, he just looked on, wondering what the point of her visit was. Perhaps she was just bored, and her sadistic nature needed some amusement. Well he wasn't going to bite... so to speak. He would sit, watch, ignore and take it, even if it meant a beating or worse, something that seemed almost impossible given his current state. A tiny part of him thought about provoking her... stoking her rage, nudging her into a frenzy in the hope that she would get it over with quickly, rather than face the long, lingering, torturous death he was sure Manson had planned for him. But hidden away beneath all the layers of pain, hurt, frustration and self pity, there was still some fight left, bolstered by a determination to see his friends once more, no matter what the cost. And at the back of all of that, burned a light shining brightly, bottled up, kept under wraps, out of the way, for fear of it being discovered: his feelings for JANICE! He knew it was best this way. It was unlikely that they would betray him, but these beings... he had no idea of the extent of their powers. Rumours of creatures able to read thoughts, delve inside another's mind, rummage around and extract information at will, had been around since the beginning of time, but who knew the very real possibilities of this new fighting force? If there was even the remotest chance that they could do this, then he knew he had to keep the memories buried, safe... away from prying eyes, or rather, minds.

"Locking away all your secrets?" she ventured.

Swallowing nervously, he wondered exactly what he'd given away.

"You are an odd one," she announced, padding carefully forward. "I can't yet figure out what an all-powerful being like the king would want with something so weak and pitiful."

Not for the first time... he assumed this was it. In some ways it would be a relief, if it weren't for his friends. He already felt that he'd let them down... particularly Richie, who he knew was somewhere on the surface, blissfully unaware of her true identity, her true heritage, and would suffer the same fate as the rest of humanity when the time came. It broke his heart, because he wasn't able to see a way out, not even a fighting chance for the king and whoever he had alongside him. Not against these odds.

Kneeling down, the fetid aroma of her breath brushed against his face as she leaned in close and whispered,

"I don't suppose you'd like to enlighten me about your relationship with the dragon monarch?"

Tears had built up behind his eyes over the course of the last few seconds, ready to burst through the flimsy dam holding them back, at any moment. Unsure of quite why his relationship with the king was so important, he didn't really care that much. All he knew was that they wanted to know, and that in not giving in, he could fight back and show in his own private way, just how strong he really was. And so even though the tears burst through, he remained stoic, his expression not wavering, all thoughts of giving in gone, despite the fact that her face hovered less than a centimetre away from his.

As fate looked on, smirking at this particularly bizarre turn of events, even by her standards, something unexplained sat hanging over proceedings, something breathtakingly obvious but to the two of them, as both beings watched one another. Not so much tense, as an air of anticipation, if you'd asked Peter how long it had lasted... it could have been anything... days, weeks, a lifetime. It was, however, more likely a minute, no longer. Without warning, Earth got silently to her feet, filled with more questions than answers. Of course she could have extracted them from him the hard way. But something... something nagging at the back of her mind was holding her back, the same something that had drawn her here, now. Not able to recognise it for what it truly was, almost certainly clouded by the madness in her mind, she skulked back to find her love, keen on an update on exactly when the world would be theirs.

20 STRAWBERRY BLONDE... REALLY?

Slipping through the fires, sticking to the shadows, Steel and the rest of the staff from the medical centre crept ever forward through the capital, avoiding trouble wherever possible. Through shared magic, enhanced senses allowed the small band of mainly nervous dragons to skirt encounters with fearsome dark dragons and parties of raiding nagas.

Skulking around half a dozen blazing fires, longing for the warm embrace the flickering flames promised, the tight knit group, led by the fearless laminium ball player, ducked into the still smouldering wreckage of a row of shops. Abruptly Steel raised his right arm, clenched fist in the air for all to see. Each and every one of them stopped still in total silence, their magical abilities heightened, on the lookout for the slightest hint of danger. From between two huge mounds of twisted metal stepped an almighty ginger coloured dragon, dancing balls of brilliant, bright green electrical energy charging and crackling away in both of his hands, ready to be used in an instant. With words to his shield mantra at the forefront of his mind, ready to be cast into being immediately, Steel stepped forward, almost offering himself up in an effort to protect those who had chosen his leadership.

Confident that he could not only singlehandedly dispel the ginger dragon's magic, but also take him down if need be, it was then that the cool rush of air washed over him, kicking his dragon danger sense into overdrive. Landing with a muffled thump, having been skulking high up above between a pair of blackened, burning rafters, a squat, angry looking dragon, a snarl of epic proportions carved into his face, appeared off to one side, two massive balls of raging fire rotating ominously, one in each hand. Magic pumping through what felt like an almost new body, Steel considered his response in less time than one flap of a hummingbird's wings.

Over the course of the last eight hours, they'd seen what they considered the enemy on numerous occasions. Nagas similar to the ones that had invaded the medical centre seemed almost commonplace, along with unusual feeling dragons, armed with odd looking bastard swords, each one brandished with a terrifying darkened sunburst on his or her body. Both ambushers here, although clearly presenting a threat, looked nothing like the other forces they'd encountered. That in itself was enough for him to take the chance. Throwing his arms up in the air and wings open wide in a gesture of submission, he still retained those words for the shield mantra, ready to cast it in but a fraction of a moment.

"Hold fire. We're not your enemy," whispered Steel, much to the surprise of those cowering behind him.

"I very much doubt that!" growled the tetchy little dragon off to one side, the magic in his hands crackling and spitting furiously.

"Hang on a minute," declared the well built ginger dragon taking two steps forward. "I know you. You're that laminium ball player. The captain..."

"STEEL!" Steel announced, hoping to diffuse the somewhat tricky situation sooner rather than later.

"That's right," added 'Ginger'. "What in hell's name are you doing here?"

"It's a long story," replied Steel, "but the gist of it is that the medical centre we were all in was attacked by an unknown force and so after taking them down, this is where we find ourselves. Ultimately we're looking to find out exactly what's going on and see if there's anything we can do to help. You?"

'Ginger', clearly the friendlier of the two, answered for them both.

"As is not untypical for us, we'd had a hard night on the sauce and as far as we can work out, we passed out in the cellar of an abandoned shop... something that, from the look of things, probably saved our lives. On coming round, we spent days clearing collapsed rubble away from the only exit, almost succumbing to dehydration. In the nick of time we managed to get out, only to find our beloved capital city in this state. Since then we've salvaged and hidden, avoiding clusters of those terrible beings wherever possible, desperate to get out, but the entire city seems to be in lockdown. You're the first true dragons we've encountered... alive, anyway. Vicious groups of marauding dragons are everywhere, all armed with the same murderous looking weapons. At first we thought them to be the King's Guard, but that was before we witnessed them slaughter a group of defenceless female dragons. Since then, we've given them a wider berth than the slithering reptiles. And so here we are, skulking, hiding, determined not to get caught."

Gritting his teeth, forcing down a smile... he just had to ask.

"Ummmm... and the... nail polish?"

Scared out of their wits at the turn of events, and only there because of Steel, the group of staff from the medical centre all at once looked down at the ginger dragon's talons. Sure enough, bright pink and yellow paint intricately covered each and every one of 'Ginger's' razor sharp talons, making it look as though he'd had not just a day's free pass to the nail salon, but a week's.

Preparing to scrutinise 'Ginger's' response, out of the corner of his left eye Steel just caught the faintest of smirks from his pent up partner.

'This should be good, by the look of things,' he mused.

"Huhhhh," sighed 'Ginger', realising he had nowhere to go and that his partner clearly wasn't going to come to his aid.

"Well... you see, DomCon here," he said, motioning to the full-of-rage, stunted looking dragon, off to one side, "and I are members of a sandskimming club and often spend time socialising with the ladies' teams there. What I failed to mention in my previous account, and the reason that I was in such bad shape, was that very stupidly after finishing drinking with DomCon (the full-of-rage dragon) I decided to continue drinking with a small, hardcore group of females. All I can remember after that is being escorted back to the cellar by them, where DomCon had told us he would be. On eventually waking up, not only did I have the hangover to end all hangovers, but I'd been made up to the nines. We've managed to get most of it off, but despite searching high and low over the last few days, nowhere can we find any nail polish remover. It would seem, for the moment, I'm stuck with it."

"Female dragons... eh? They sound like absolute monsters."

"You don't know the half of it," uttered 'Ginger', his partner tittering in the background.

"So what's your story... short stop?" enquired Steel.

DomCon just gazed at the ground, unable to make eye contact with the confident laminium ball captain.

Sensing that things would go no further until this group learned the truth, 'Ginger' stepped in, hoping to spare his friend at least a little misery.

"Dom the Con came about because of a suspended jail sentence imposed after two King's Guards caught him at the scene of a supposed burglary. He maintains that he was only walking past the 'Pink Flamingo' bar, minding his own business at 3am in the morning when... 'SMASH!' the entire frontage, including the massive window and frame, came crashing down into the street for no apparent reason. Both King's Guards on patrol nearby arrived at the scene to find Dom here peering suspiciously inside the gaping chasm that was once a window, clutching a number of inflatable flamingos that had been used as window dressing, firmly to his chest. Once questioned, he claimed that he was just tidying them up, waiting for the authorities to arrive. Because nothing valuable was taken, his jail sentence was commuted, although still to this day he maintains that the whole thing just happened without him touching anything. So from then on, he became known as DomtheCon which soon became just DomCon."

"Smashing!" declared Steel, much to the amusement of the others in his group.

"Don't start all of that or his eyes will 'glaze' over," added 'Ginger'.

Dom, still gazing down at the ground, just shook his head.

"He must have been 'shattered' after such a long night," continued Steel.

"Quite possibly," chipped in 'Ginger' once more. "I still wonder though if he might not have been 'framed'."

They all smiled at that, even the increasingly embarrassed DomCon.

"So what now?" asked Steel, loosening his stance, but not entirely lowering his guard.

"What do you mean?"

"Well..." continued the laminium ball captain, "clearly it's a challenge staying under the radar of whatever's going on. And although not ideal, I would suggest that teaming up is the way to go. There's no doubt we'd be stronger together than on our own." Both 'Ginger' and DomCon paused for thought, taking in the offer.

"You don't mind if we have a couple of moments to talk it over, do you?" asked 'Ginger'.

"Be my guest," ventured Steel.

Both dragons, looking quite a sight, ambled over to a pile of rubble, 'Ginger', a hulking monster of a formidable opponent despite his agreeable demeanour, dwarfing his pent up partner, who resembled the typical pocket rocket, looking as though his fuse had already been lit.

Much sooner than Steel expected, the two reached an agreement and turned to face the famed laminium ball player and his entourage.

"We're in... if you'll have us. What's the plan?"

For a split second he considered not telling them, but dismissed it out of hand almost immediately. Everyone else knew... why shouldn't they?

Explaining that they had, as a group, all talked it through, deliberating long into the night, opinions had been split between heading towards Buckingham and the council building, fearing what was happening there and for the king's safety, or sneaking off to Fleet Street because if there was anyone that would know what was going on in the rest of the world they would be there, at the centre of the telepathic papers. Also, if this was purely a localised event, it might be possible to use the telepathic facilities to alert the rest of the world to what was going on and send a shout out for help. And so it had been narrowed down to those two options, with the eclectic group being pretty much split down the middle. In the end it came down to their leader... Steel! After careful consideration, he had opted for the Fleet Street option and so as quickly as possible he explained why to both of his team's new recruits.

Both nodding in agreement all the way through, 'Ginger' and DomCon certainly couldn't fault the brave laminium ball captain's logic. A rallying call to arms across the rest of the dragon domain should certainly clear the mess up quickly and efficiently, unless of course this was happening planet wide, something that was pretty much unthinkable.

With the extended group about to set off once more, 'Ginger' thought a proper introduction appropriate.

"My name's Jar Man," he stated, smiling.

"Most probably call you 'Ginger' though, don't they?" put in Steel.

"Strawberry Blonde!"

"Sorry!"

"I'm not ginger... I'm strawberry blonde."

"I heard... I'm just sorry."

"Oh... very good... not only a laminium ball superstar,

but a comedian as well."

"Just kidding... it's great to meet you Jar Man, you too DomCon. Now you're part of my team, and with that, you have big boots to fill. On the plus side, there's nothing that I wouldn't do for you. We're all in this together. Those cockwombles that have done this to our domain have no idea what they've let themselves in for. Let the games commence."

21 DEEP ****

Shrouded in oily black shadows, she weaved in and out of the industrial pipes that made up the sewage reclamation plant. Logic told her that her enemies wouldn't be anywhere near a place like this. It had no real strategic value as a target... all it did was process the industrial waste for the whole of London. But these were strange and uneasy times. She knew better than to take anything for granted. Slipping silently into a dark recess, she stopped to catch her breath, the comforting reassurance of the laminium dagger's hilt nestling against the small of her back. Of all the places in the dragon domain, it just had to be here! But Flash's instructions had been quite clear when he'd whispered them in her ear, just before taking his leave, back in Salisbridge, what seemed like a very long time ago. Running her hands through her dark, curly locks, the superstar lacrosse player wiped away the sweat from her forehead with the backs of them. It had been tough going to get this far. Marauding gangs of dragons, nagas, and a mixture of the two were everywhere. Skirting around, above and below, had cost her valuable time. But in reality she'd had little choice. Taking them on alone would have been suicidal, despite having the advantage of the all powerful dagger. So, using her magic to the best of her ability to help keep her concealed, she'd trudged on, taking her time with every footstep, quieter than a spider sprinting across a carpet. Truth be told, it had drained her as much mentally as it had physically. But now she was here... here where, she'd been led to believe, the very start of the secret entrance began. All she had to do now was find it. And of course avoid falling into the humungous silos of dragon poo that were spread out all around her.

Craning her neck as far back as it would go she instructed the magic inside her to find her night vision.

Suddenly the murky gloom she'd been looking at, high above her, jumped out, casting everything in an outstanding overall shade of blue. Jutting out from the side of a craggy rock face, a rusty looking yellow balcony, housing a myriad of conduits, ducts and pipelines, swam into view. Excitement welled up inside her on seeing the number 34 printed on the back of the control panel sitting off to one side. This was her destination. All she had to do now was get up to it. During the course of normal operations, this would not have been a problem for anyone working here. Of course, how could it have been... all they had to do was flap their wings, and... BOOM! There they were. But not so for her... not here, not now. Even if she'd been able to transmute back into her natural form, something deep inside her screamed that she shouldn't. Maybe it was a trap, perhaps the place was being watched? Who knew? All that she did know was that she had to get up there and quickly. Not to mention quietly, and unseen.

Exiting her hidey hole before crawling nearly two hundred metres on her belly across the oil splashed floor beneath a series of interconnecting pipes that fed either directly in, or directly out of the huge excrement containers, by the time she reached the starting point of her journey upwards, she was absolutely shattered, not to mention nursing rather sore knees and elbows. Without a second thought, she bounded up the first series of pipes, using the kinks and twists in the smaller ones as foot and hand holds, gaining as much as thirty metres or so in height, but then finding herself only about a quarter of the way up the ever imposing giant vat of poo off to her right.

Crouching down on top, the concealed lacrosse player tried to map out the next part of her precarious route in the dark, all the time extending out her senses as much as she dared, on the lookout for anything out of the ordinary. While at first glance it appeared that there were numerous ways to reach the balcony that was her destination using the array of pipes to climb up, by tracking each one through, her senses seemed to almost always hit a snag. After a matter of moments it became obvious to her that there was actually only one way, a route that would consist of using the only, rather fragile looking pipe that extended right out above the waste silo housing most of the dragon excrement. Perhaps it had been designed with that in mind, putting off any would be interlopers, or anyone whose curiosity had got the better of them. Anyhow, at least now, she knew what she had to do. Steeling herself, and focusing all her thoughts on getting to that tucked away little balcony, she started off, determined to carry on in much the same way as she had been for some time now: putting one foot in front of the other, taking her time, concentrating on getting it right and remaining hidden. It was more important than ever now.

A little over an hour later she found herself at eye level with her destination, some hundred or so metres from the balcony's faded yellow metal rails. One problem alone presented itself, one last obstacle to overcome: a rather flimsy looking pipe, which was rusted in places and was about the diameter of one of her delicate little feet. And of course it cut directly across the open topped silo of dragon waste, the surface of which bubbled away some thirty metres below. Part of her wanted to sprint for all she was worth, covering the distanced in but a moment or two. But now was not the time. Patience was the key, and so ignoring the eye watering fumes that almost made her gag, she started across, cloaked in darkness, one foot in front of the other, sweat caking her neck and meandering down her back. A few paces in, she knew there was now no turning back. As the hideous stench of tens of thousands of dragons wafted over her, the heat clawing at her feet and shins, carefully she placed one foot in front of the other, having long since reined in her magical abilities. This was all about her physicality, something she never had any doubts about, being the athlete that she was. And so it was that with only one minor hiccup (a very dubious piece of the pipe, almost in the middle creaking like a worn out rocking chair) she made it across to the balcony before sliding gracefully through the bars, relieved to be supported by something much more substantial. Pulling in a deep breath, she turned around, taking in her route before looking down at the drop and exactly what it would have entailed.

'I didn't think we could be in anymore poo given the current situation,' she thought, 'but I so very nearly was. When this is all over, I'm going to have the biggest and longest bath in the world.'

Mind back on the task at hand, she turned around towards the control panel and the maze of different sized pipes that ran alongside and above it. Checking each one, it took her a while and some yoga-like twisting of her body to find what she was looking for. Exactly as Flash had described, there was a gap. But it was infinitesimally small. So tiny in fact, she had a hard time believing that even her lithe little body would fit through it, let alone that of either Flash or the king. But she hadn't come all this way for nothing, and so with nightmarish thoughts of what her friends were currently going through plaguing almost every waking moment, she ducked down on her back and, head first, began pushing herself through the darkness by her toes, managing to scoot along only a metre at a time. It was painfully slow going, as well as blindingly uncomfortable. But after thirty or so metres, the claustrophobic gap opened up into more of a duct, giving her almost enough room to crawl. Stopping briefly to catch her breath, instinctively her hand brushed against the hilt of the dagger, making sure it was still there. Of course it was (she could feel the cold metal nestled against her back) but it felt reassuring just to touch it. Continuing on, the duct remained the same size, providing just enough room to crawl, but not enough to sit up or get even remotely comfortable. Rounding a sharp bend, a giant notice on her right hand side stood out. It read, "Section 312b." Odd that she hadn't seen any other notices, but she figured this one had a purpose, just as the ex-Crimson Guard had explained. Pulling herself along until she was level with the sign, rolling over, she turned to face the opposite wall... no mean feat given her confinement. Running her fingers along the smooth metal, she felt some small imperfections progressing vertically off to one side. Forcing the edge of her thumbnail into the biggest one, she gently tried to lever the metal. Surprisingly, a small panel about the size of a human hand popped off, revealing a dark recess. Reaching in, all she could feel was fabric. Whilst Flash had told her about the secret entrance and the concealed cubby hole, he hadn't disclosed what was in it, only that she might find it incredibly useful. Grabbing a handful, carefully she began pulling out what turned out to be a black as night cloak. In that instant all her hopes were dashed. She was wearing a cloak... alright, not quite as dark as the hidden one. But she'd hoped for something much more, something that would give her an edge in what was to come. To say that she was disappointed didn't really do the situation justice. Lying on her side, spreading the cloak out as much as the space would allow, she wondered why Flash had made such a fuss. It was so unlike him... at least she thought so; the gaps in her memory, whilst fading slightly, were still very much there. About to disregard the newly found garment, it was then that she felt it, or rather not. As she'd pulled the fabric across her arm, something very strange happened. A coarse, cold numbness passed through her, only it wasn't so much physical... more in her mind.

'Odd,' was all that she could think. Slipping off the dark brown cloak currently shrouding her, she clumsily managed to slip on this new black as night one. Pulling the hood up and wrapping the front right across her body, suddenly she understood exactly what it was, and just why her friend thought it so important.

'It's imbued with laminium! It can stop anyone from sensing me.' Memories from her early days in the nursery ring flooded back, particularly one class discussion which had centred on magical objects rumoured to be at large. One such rumour focused on a cloak very much like the one she'd just discovered. It was believed to have existed centuries earlier, but had been mislaid during the course of a dragon battle. If what it could do was true, and she was quite sure it was, then it might let her get unbelievably close to the action without anyone knowing she was there. Silently she thanked the ex-Crimson Guard, wishing him well in whatever endeavour he currently found himself caught up in.

22 WHAT WOULD ADMIRAL ACKBAR SAY?

Ironically, not ten kilometres away, Tank and his merry band of renegade dragons were experiencing almost exactly the same smell as the one Richie had so recently discovered, whilst trudging through a fetid river of waste deep beneath the Buckingham area of London. Janice and Hook were appalled at the almost motorway sized sewer that they found themselves on the edge of, deep beneath the underground dragon city. It was much too dangerous to do anything other than stick to the perimeter, as they'd been told the waste in the middle could be anything up to thirty metres deep. Scary enough you'd think, but the smell... oh the smell! Janice had nearly passed out on climbing down here. It was all she could do not to be sick. One of the other dragons had cast... now what was it called? Oh that's right... a mantra, on all her clothes, making them as fragrant as a fresh summer's meadow. It had helped, that's for sure. Hook though, being the tough rugby player that he was, just sucked it up (not literally) and carried on regardless, wading through God knows what (well, he knew), mind focused on his backpack and how best to use it in the forthcoming confrontation.

Tank was doing his best to lead. It wasn't easy, and to say he had his doubts was nothing short of understating everything that currently swam around his head. It hadn't been his idea to come down here, but once suggested, it did seem like the obvious solution to the problem of how to get within range without being spotted. And so while he plodded through the dragon excrement and goodness knows what else, his mind drifted off towards his friends, near and far, wondering exactly how they were doing, and if he'd ever see them again.

Whispered words echoed in the darkness over the

bubbling, steaming river of slurry. Steadily the line of beings drew to a halt, the dragon in front of Tank turning around to face him.

"It appears we've reached the nearest dragonhole cover. What do you want to do?"

Signalling for those behind him, Janice and Hook included, to remain where they were, Tank waded out further into the ever-moving conveyor of waste, skirting past those dragons further down the line until he reached those at the front, crouching down below a huge circular dragonhole cover the size of a car. Ancient words adorned the circumference, most unreadable and caked in filth.

"As far as I can tell, this is the nearest cover to the council building from this particular sewer. There are others, but I would think there's a much greater chance of being discovered if we were to try and get much closer. This one comes out about a block away from the square that sits directly outside the council building, and is located in a secluded alley that runs along the back of a line of shops. I can think of no better place for us to exit."

Tank nodded his approval. Dymo had done an excellent job in getting them here, he knew. Of all the dragons to have on his side, an ex-sewer worker had seemed like something of a mismatch, but he'd proved his usefulness ten times over in what he'd done. Tank was grateful for his counsel, but now it was time to listen to the fighters on the team, the ex-King's Guards, all of whom were now standing with him below the gigantic dragonhole.

"What do you think?" asked Tank of the group.

"From what we know, it does seem like a good place to get topside. And if things take a turn for the worse, we should be able to retreat back down here and lose ourselves in the sewer system."

'What a delightful prospect,' thought Tank.

"Should we all go up above?" he asked.

"I don't see why not," piped up another of the former

guards. "If the plan is to gain access to the council building, then there doesn't seem much point in either splitting up or only taking a small contingent with us. I'd guess it's all or nothing."

Tank's thoughts exactly.

So with seemingly little choice, the young rugby playing dragon ordered them to take a look and do their best to make sure they weren't walking straight into an ambush. Tentatively, two of them lifted up the dragonhole cover, while two more assessed the situation. It seemed to take forever, with Tank's nerves becoming more and more frayed. Eventually they gave the all clear and without a sound, two of them darted out into the scorched ruins of the capital to see if there was any way forward.

With a brief lull in proceedings, nearly all the beings there broke out either food or water, or both. Janice and Hook shared some freshly baked bread that they'd been given back at the nursery ring, along with a strawberry flavoured bottle of water. Given their surroundings, they did well to keep everything down. All the time Janice kept hold of Fu-ts'ang, aware of the mysterious weapon not only in her hand, but in her head as well. Odd didn't begin to cover it.

Tank waited in silence, not having moved from his position below the heavy, circular, metal cover, his thoughts for his friends churning over and over as he gazed up at the two guards resting at the top of both ladders, just below the surface. It didn't take long, less than ten minutes in fact. Four delicate taps in a row on the surface of the dragonhole was the signal. Cautiously the two guards lifted up the cover... a little at first, wary of being caught out. It turned out to be fine, with the two ex-King's Guards dropping through the small gap provided, splashing down right next to Tank, splattering dragon poo up both his legs. Currently, that was the least of his worries.

"It's clear," said one.

"As far as we can tell," added the other. "And we've been as far as the square. There are half a dozen guards milling around the entrance to the council building, but they look disinterested and disorganised. Clearly they're not expecting an attack. I don't think we're going to have any trouble in disposing of them."

Tank nodded, pleased that things seemed to be going their way. He did find it a little strange though, given all the evidence of death and destruction they'd seen so far across the capital. Somewhere there must have been a massive force, and he'd assumed it would have been here. Of course, most of it could well be inside... the council building was, after all, huge. But to leave it virtually unguarded, vulnerable to a counterattack from behind, sounded like a childish mistake. And given the kind of planning and organisation that had so clearly gone into this devastating surprise attack in the first place, the more he thought about it, the more he didn't like the smell of things. And he wasn't just talking about down here, in the sewer.

"We should attack now... while we have the chance," announced one of the guards, forcing him out of his reverie.

"I... I... I don't know," stuttered Tank, trying desperately to weigh up everything in his mind. Defending the king was their number one priority, but the lives of everyone here mattered... to him at least.

"It does seem like now is our chance," added the other one. "Maybe they're waiting for reinforcements to arrive. If that happens, then we're pretty much done for. It certainly didn't smell like a trap to me. More like overconfidence on their part, something I say we crush with all our might."

Backed into a corner, that's how he felt. Of course he trusted the two that he'd sent up there. Why wouldn't he? He was as sure as he could be that they didn't want to throw away their lives. But nothing about this felt right.

From Richie leaving, to avoiding all the marauding patrols of psychopaths, skulking down here in the sewers, and now this. It didn't feel right at all. But he could come up with no other options. And so with the clock ticking down, he very reluctantly agreed that they should all move forward with a view to gaining access to the council building.

With the dragonhole cover slipped fully out of place, dragons and humans alike skirted through the gap, concealing themselves in the shadows of the alleyway and the deserted doorways at the back of the row of shops. Two minutes... that's all it took for all of them to make their way out of the sewer and up above ground. With the dragonhole cover replaced, it was agreed that one of their kind, a librarian named Kymoto, would stay behind and keep an eye on their exit, in case they needed to use it in a hurry. As the shy librarian disappeared up onto a first floor balcony, the guards at the front of the group silently sloped off in the direction of the square, each and every member of the small band alert now, with no telling where the danger might come from; the same could be said of Janice and Hook, both far too aware of the risks involved, their mouths on occasion hanging open wide, not just at what they were part of, but at the scale and sheer size of the buildings around them. It was almost as if they were in the financial district of London up above, with huge skyscrapers towering over them. They'd thought they'd gotten used to the underground landscape, having taken in first Salisbridge and then of course the area surrounding the Nursery Ring at Hampton Court. But this was something else altogether.

Slowly... that's how it progressed, and of course silently. Minutes... that's how far away the square and the council building were. Moving like this took them at least four times as long. But soon enough, they were there, peering out from beneath the shadows of an all encompassing alleyway opposite, skulking, observing and single minded in their attempt to avoid any and all deceptions.

Along with the contingent of ex-King's Guards, Tank was at the front now, determined to be the one to give the order, if that's what it came down to. Part of him thought they just wanted to circumvent him and ignore the authority that had been so unjustly thrust upon him. And although he didn't like it, or hadn't wanted it, now that he found himself in this position, he thought it only fair that it was his call, and his alone, as to whether or not they went ahead with things. And so he bided his time and listened to those around him laying out their ideas on exactly how they should deal with the rearguard and gain access to where they needed to go.

So it was that ten minutes later they were all ready to go. Five of the ex-King's Guards had skirted around the council building until they'd reached the nearest side to the entrance. They were within only a few seconds of the unruly, disorganised rabble that guarded the way in. Once the signal was given, Tank's group, comprising of a mixture of dragons and humans, would charge across the square, effectively creating a distraction, while at the same time the ex-King's Guards would ambush them from behind, stopping them from calling for help from inside the building. Focused on his breathing, Tank waited for the telepathic nudge that he knew was due any time now. Sure enough, what felt like a little tickle on the left hand side of his brain came only a few seconds later, and so pumping his fist in the air, a rather crafty lightning mantra at the forefront of his mind, he yelled, "CHARGE!" at the top of his voice and sprinted out of the darkness and into the square, heading for the council building's entrance at top speed. Sure enough, that got their enemies' attention, with all those visible rushing across the square to meet Tank, and his comrades who were right on his coattails. As Janice hefted Fu-ts'ang while at full sprint, Hook tried to keep up, the base of his heavy water pack slapping furiously against his lower back as he ran. Brilliant bolts of bright blue electricity arced violently from Tank's fingertips as the ex-King's Guards cut off their opponents' escape route back into the council building. Catching the first sloppy dragon directly in the throat, the sizzling electricity pierced his dark yellow scales in several places, causing him to scream in agony as he lost his footing and slipped to the cobbled floor. And then... it was chaos. Not the kind of chaos that had taken place in the market place in Salisbridge. No! This was just the swift killing of half a dozen guards, all over in mere moments really. They never stood a chance. And that was how it was supposed to go.

With their enemies down, the ragtag group of dragons and humans paused to catch their breath after the furious few moments of intense fighting.

One of the guards approached Tank, talons dripping with dark green dragon blood.

"We should head inside. The longer we stay out here, the more vulnerable we are."

Tank was just about to agree, when the dragon's words became more accurate than one of Richie's shots at goal.

Drifting across the square, carried by what little breeze existed, it started very much as a singular being's chuckle. As one, the group of heroes turned this way and that, trying to find the origin. But as they did so, the chuckle increased in pitch, with more beings joining in, and not just a few. A couple almost instantly became dozens, and then dozens became a multitude, with the laughter having taken on a chilling, sadistic air.

Standing amongst the bodies of the enemies they'd just slaughtered, Tank's heroic band instinctively formed a circle and watched as a fighting force six or seven times their strength, numbering well over a hundred, mainly slithered into view. Nagas poured out of nearby buildings while dark dragons hefting huge black swords dropped from the sky all around them. If Tank's group had been terrified during the events that had played out in Salisbridge the previous day, this had taken fear and dread to a whole new level.

Knowing they were massively outnumbered, and exactly what these sick, heartless, brutal murderers did to anyone left alive, Tank vowed there and then to fight until his dying breath. Little did he know that everyone else in the rest of his team currently had the same thought. As the chortling continued, striking fear deep into his heart, he swore to take as many of them with him as he possibly could. With the words already spoken deep within his mind, and the full force of his rage and willpower behind them, he cast an arc of superheated air straight out in front of him, toppling the deadly dragons and nagas like dominoes, and then leapt into the fray, concentrating only on staying alive.

Earth's surface. Salisbridge, England.
Pulling in through the tall, blue, metallic gates of the secure police yard at the back of the station, he still couldn't get his head around all the strange things that seemed to be going on of late. All the explosions that had ripped through the planet and devastated lives and property, in particular the one here at the sports club, which had turned out to be much smaller than all of the others, was where it had started for him. Strange things had gone on. First and foremost, he hadn't been allowed to see the immediate damage after the bomb had gone off and destroyed the clubhouse itself. Odd, suited men from some government department he'd never heard of had turned him away from the site. Of course he'd checked them out, and it was all above board... supposedly. But he couldn't shake the feeling that something else was playing out. What? He had no idea. But he was sure some sort of coverup was underway. And then the two young fellows who'd been arrested immediately after the clubhouse had been destroyed... they'd remained in custody for some time, before unexpectedly being released by the sergeant,

with no explanation given, only that they hadn't been guilty of any of the charges and had in fact tried to prevent the act of terrorism that had taken place.

And now this! Salisbridge was more like a tight knit community than a city, and for somewhere like this to experience all these odd goings on was unusual and disturbing both at the same time, and he was sure... no coincidence. Side lights flashing to indicate that his car was now locked, he punched the four digit code into the keypad. A barely audible 'click' informed him of his success after which he pulled open the heavy door and squeezed through, just as two uniformed officers made their way out. Nodding to both, he continued down the corridor and up two flights of stairs that led directly to his office. Slipping off his jacket, he slumped down in the heavy office chair, its form by now moulded to his particular shape. Still he was plagued by it all, sure that he was missing some stand out link that connected everything together. Logging into his computer, he sat back and played Saturday night's CCTV footage of the Poultry Cross.

'There they are,' he thought, 'exiting the Indian restaurant, slipping on their coats. And then all of a sudden they stop. Probably being told to by the young woman... what was her name? Ah, that's right. Richie Rump. With the onlookers having stopped, the young Rump woman staggers her way alongside the ancient monument, towards the base of the support holding the camera. Moments later, a hand appears in view for a split second, before something... gum as we now know it to be, is placed over the lens. After that... NOTHING! No sign of any of them.'

Parents, sisters and work colleagues had all called in to report each of the individuals as missing. Interviewing the staff and owners of the restaurant had got them nowhere. Interviewing the other diners, who'd been tracked down via their credit cards, had only led to a confused overall picture. Reports of a scuffle, someone collapsing, no medical attention sought, followed by an argument and then supposedly the whole group walking out of the place armed to the teeth with half the kitchen, something the staff and owners categorically denied. By their own admission many of the other patrons were well on their way to being drunk, but enough of them had come up with pretty much the same story without being prompted. It was hard to know what to make of it all.

Closing down the video footage, he tapped his fingers on his desk in front of the keyboard. They'd thoroughly searched in and around the Poultry Cross... checked all the other CCTV cameras in the area for that time period, and come up with zilch. Nothing! Nada! Squat! Where on earth could they have gone? Abducted? Hard to believe, especially given everything they were carrying. And that left what? No answers. Not for the parents, siblings, or colleagues. This was one of the most bizarre cases he'd ever worked on in his twenty one years on the job. And that combined with all the other weird goings on had him on edge, and kept making him second guess himself, something he knew was never good. To do his job he had to maintain his focus and impartiality, and consider all possibilities. But so far that had led him nowhere. Having told those he was in charge of that were investigating the case to consider every option no matter how unlikely, daft or trivial, his only hope now was that some opportunity presented itself from all of that... because one thing was for sure, he had absolutely no idea where to go next or what to look into. As far as he was concerned, all of them had vanished completely off the face of the earth. If only he knew.

23 SUB-ZERO SUCCESS

With a roundhouse kick so powerful that it shattered the naga's spine, the bloody battle beneath Antarctica drew to a close. It had been a resounding triumph despite a number of life-threatening injuries sustained by Yoyo's young dragons. But the danger had been neutralised, the jailer vanquished to hell, and his mysterious fighting force dispatched from this plane of existence. As Yoyo and the rest of the young dragons tended to their injured, Flash and Fredric came together in the middle of the cavern, the latter having wrapped himself in the laminium chains that were no longer his captor, but now in fact his saviour. He looked magnificent, his taut, bulging muscles glistening for all to see, in the same tattered rags that had covered him for decades. Words seemed hard to find for them both, at first anyway.

"You came back. I knew you would."

"No being deserves to be held in this place, least of all a mighty dragon like you. I'm sorry it's taken so long."

"Given how long I've been here, the time that's passed since your last visit seems almost insignificant."

"I'm sorry for everything you've been through. And I'm not the only one."

This piqued Fredric's interest.

"The king has done everything in his power to try and free you, since I reported back to him after my brief visit and he learned of your captivity."

Fredric's eyes glazed over, and very briefly he became lost in his own thoughts, caught up with his best friend back in a time long, long ago.

"As well," announced Flash, "there's someone else."

Startled back to the present, Fredric found it hard to think who else it could be.

"Your grandson... PETER, he's been involved in

everything. He's one of my best friends."

Raw, unadulterated emotion flooded the founder of the Crimson Guards from head to toe, forcing the hairs on his arms to stand to attention and his legs to go momentarily weak. It was all he could do to hold back the tears.

"My boy!" cried Fredric. "How is he?"

'Here we go,' thought Flash, having no idea how the next few moments were going to pan out.

"When I left... yesterday, we found out he'd been captured by the being that seems to be in charge of this whole New World Order thing and goes by the name of Manson. As far as we can tell, he and the 'White Dragon' are to be used as bargaining chips against the king, who as far as we know is holed up in his private residence, surrounding by a huge fighting force that has pretty much taken London, made up of dark dragons and nagas, who are being held ransom by the captivity of their king, and they more than likely have a grip on the rest of the planet."

"RRRRRAAAAAAARRRRRRRRHHHHHHHHHH," bellowed Fredric, so loudly in fact that icicles dropped from the ceiling in far flung parts of the cavern. Astounded, those still able to turned to look in his direction.

"I'm sorry," added Flash. "I know it's not what you wanted to hear, but I figured you'd rather know the truth."

"You're right, of course... always the truth. But what can we do from here to affect events on the other side of the earth? I assume we're somewhere beneath the Antarctic?"

"We are. In a place called Law Dome, and quite far from the nearest form of civilisation."

Out of nowhere, a soft voice echoed across the confines of the icy cavern.

"FLASH!"

It was Yoyo. Both Fredric and Flash looked over to where the healer knelt, tending to two of his injured youngsters.

"What is it?" asked Flash from where both he and Fredric stood.

"They're dying... and there's nothing I can do to stop it."

Instantly Flash took off, Fredric hot on his heels. Sliding to a halt only moments later, the ex-Crimson Guard took in the scene that lay before him. Two of the young dragons, one who he remembered as Hillier, lay prone, blood seeping onto the ice, mortal wounds obvious for all gathered around to see. Closing his eyes, Flash racked his brain for anything that would be of some use, any unusual or unconventional magic. But before he got any further than that, a powerful arm tugged him out of the way.

"Let me have a look," commanded Fredric, the golden chains encompassing his torso rattling slightly as he moved. As one, the young dragons circling their injured friends moved back, in awe of the mighty being that had been trapped in this icy hellhole for all this time.

"There's nothing that can be done. I've tried all that I know. Nothing can save them now," mouthed Yoyo, glancing up at Fredric, glistening transparent tears rolling down his cheeks.

Putting a comforting arm on Yoyo's shoulder, a sudden burst of familiarity blossomed inside Peter's grandfather.

"I know you... don't I?"

"You do seem familiar," replied Yoyo. "I do believe I may have patched you up once or twice."

"I think you might be right. But now's not the time for all that. Let me take a look. With the laminium from these chains, nothing seems out of reach for me."

Yoyo got to his feet and stepped back, joining the rest of his shivering youngsters, the damage to their suits irreparable. Nodding at Flash, Fredric closed his eyes and let his mind wander out over the injured dragons. Much as he had with Flash during the battle with the jailer, Fredric's mind encompassed everything, right down to the finest detail or molecule. Nothing now seemed beyond him. With the speed of a supercomputer and the dexterity of a magician, the Crimson Guards founder used his mind to great effect, multitasking on a phenomenal level. Curing two badly injured dragons simultaneously, as well as healing the wounds of everyone else in the cavern... 'epic' would be the only way to describe what was happening. Never before in history had one dragon had so much magical power. It really was mind blowing, and took the breath away from every dragon there.

Witnessing one of the most miraculous events he'd ever seen, it was only then that Flash realised something inside him was... WRONG! For the briefest moment, his mind harked back to his last visit to this frosty hell, and wondered if once again he'd been poisoned by one of the nagas during the battle, because he was sure the feeling deep inside him was somehow related to that. But a more detailed assessment found something absolutely mind-boggling, and only then did he realise what had happened. Not only had Fredric saved his life when the evil jailer had all but killed him, but somehow, using the power stored in the laminium chains, he'd transformed his DNA back to its original state, back to before he'd encountered Antarctica and any of those damn nagas. In effect, Flash was now the dragon he once had been. Everything he'd missed had been returned to him. No longer was he damned in this falsehood of a human form. Happiness ebbed and flowed inside him. Any thought of taking his natural form though was cut short at the thought of what the blistering cold would do to his prehistoric body without any sort of protection. That dream would have to wait just a little while longer.

Releasing a long, slow breath that all but froze in the chilly air, Fredric opened his eyes and watched the injured dragons do exactly the same. Gasps of amazement from those all around rang throughout the surroundings, accompanied by mutterings of thanks. Yoyo offered out his hand, which Fredric duly shook. All the fighting force had survived, and were now fully healed and fit to carry on. But carry on to what? That was the question.

Clasping Flash on the shoulder, Fredric ventured,

"With me."

And so it was that Peter's grandfather strode across the icy cavern, weaving in and out of the butchered cadavers, heading straight for the naga king himself.

Having watched in total silence, barely able to believe what he'd seen, the king of the nagas now looked on with a semblance of a smile crossing his reptilian face for the first time in many years.

"Majesty," declared Fredric, bowing his head ever so slightly.

"Youuu offffff allll beingsss need nottt callll meee thatttt."

"If you would allow me..." offered the founder of the Crimson Guards.

With a nod of his head, the naga king granted his permission to his fellow captive.

Grasping the chains constraining the king, Fredric tapped into his vast supply of willpower, and with the words that Flash had passed onto him, the ones that had changed his life and granted his freedom, let rip with the mantra. A small glow along the length of the chain and a slight change in colour were the only clues that anything had happened, until a guttural roar from Fredric echoed around the cavern as his muscles bulged, seemingly about to rip through his skin. With his chest expanding and a terrifying snarl on his face, SNAP, the chains broke in two, freeing the naga king once and for all.

Panting heavily, Fredric tossed the remnants of the now laminium chain across the icy cavern, straight at Flash, who caught them easily with one hand.

Slithering and sliding, the naga king extended himself to his full height, something he'd struggled to do with the chains fully encompassing him.

"Thhhhaaaannnk yoooouuuuu."

"No problem," replied Fredric, aware that time was not on their side.

"I aaaaaammmmm theeeeee kkkiiiiiing offfffff theeeeee ennnnnnntiiiiiiirrrrre clllllllannnnn offfffff naaaaaagasssss... buuuuuut yooooou maaaaaay callllllllll meeee byyyyy mmmmmmy giiiiivennnn naaaaaammmmmme... Vasuki."

"I am Fredric, and it's a pleasure to be standing here beside you... free. After everything we've been through. But now is not the time to dwell on that. We need your help, Vasuki. It appears that for whatever reason most of your kin are currently allied with a cruel and wicked being named Manson, intent on taking over the earth and transforming it forever. Is there any way that you can get a message out and let them know that you are free and that their obligation to this psychopath is null and void?"

Ever more creased lines stretched across the naga king's forehead as he scoured his mind for anything that would help. It was almost impossible to see how he could contact even one of his kind without knowing exactly where they were, let alone all of them.

A misty, hazy silence encompassed them all. With the naga king racking his brain, abruptly Yoyo chipped in.

"We have to leave this place. It's too cold. We won't be able to survive for much longer."

Flash turned expectantly to Fredric, who was only now weighing up the whole situation. Even with the immense amount of power from the laminium chains, it would be difficult to sustain everyone here for any length of time. But what played on his mind the most were the events taking place on the other side of the planet. If only they were there, then they wouldn't have to worry about being destroyed by the biting cold and could help defend the dragon king, his friend, from whatever fate was now trying to throw at him.

24 STEEL YOURSELF

Stepping over debris and climbing over mountains of rubble as a group was odd in itself. But not as peculiar or strange as climbing over it all without making any noise, almost as if someone had hit the mute button or the sound had been abruptly cut off on the television news. Still they ploughed on, wary of being ambushed amidst the devastation of what was once a proud and esteemed city. It felt that way no more. Fires blazed, choking smog and smoke made up the air wherever they were, and the scent of death was almost a constant. Weaving their way through the desolate remains of an underground monorail station (they weren't even sure which one, that's how bad the damage was) the old shopkeeper and the humans remained firmly in the middle of the small renegade band, constantly on the lookout for danger. Abruptly the dragons at the front stopped, the leader holding up a closed fist, not for the first time in the last few minutes. With the tension palpable, the eclectic mix of prehistoric beasts and their human charges readied themselves for what at some point would be inevitable... a fight! It hadn't happened so far, thanks mainly to the noise cancelling mantra and the highly skilled nature of those dragons at the front in charge of cutting their way through the ravaged infrastructure. But luck had most definitely been on their side, an ally that was almost certain to desert them at some point in the very near future.

Snaking his long neck out to one side in an effort to see what was happening down at the start of their line, the master mantra maker let out a stifled gasp on witnessing the lead dragon suddenly pulled around the corner of a blazing shop, before being physically thrown up into the air, twisting and writhing uncontrollably, most undragonlike. Like an atomic dust cloud, albeit on a much smaller scale, debris and dust scattered up into the air, before anyone else even had a chance to react.

'THIS IS IT THEN!' was pretty much the single thought that all of those accompanying Gee Tee had simultaneously. Magic humming, crackling and flaring, weapons readied, the group charged as one, determined to use the element of surprise to their full advantage.

"STOP!" came the flustered and rather out of breath shout from their front dragon, belly down on the floor, looking rather more the worse for wear than he deserved to. As one, the old shopkeeper's force hesitated, still ready to act, all wondering what on earth was going on.

From out of the shadows, surrounded by scorching fire just the way he liked it, a young dragon, shiny and supple, cut through the choking black smoke, wings spread out behind his back, muscles rippling, magic arcing across his fingertips. Most stood rooted to the spot, some in awe, most in fear. The look currently emblazoned across the newcomer's face was enough to inspire terror inducing nightmares.

With not a thought for his safety, the master mantra maker wriggled free of his rather constricted position in the middle of the group and with one flap of his aging old wings, propelled himself straight to the front of the line, landing with the delicacy of a feather.

"Tame your temper child. We're not looking for a fight," quipped Gee Tee, tucking back his wings and showing off both his hands in an effort to look as non-threatening as possible. It was only then, close up... that he noticed it. For all intents and purposes, this loner looked young... almost impossibly so. But close up, in the light cast out from the blazing building, there was something else, something the old shopkeeper's know-how recognised immediately: an intelligence and experience, much like his own. Like could easily recognise like and this was no youngster. This was something much more formidable.

"STATE YOUR BUSINESS!" demanded the mysterious dragon seriously, all the time magic lighting up the end of his fingertips.

Taking a breath to compose himself, with everyone else looking on, the shopkeeper replied,

"We're looking to thwart what's going on in and around us. We could certainly use some help."

Surprised at how the encounter hadn't played out as he'd envisaged when he'd caught sight of the dragon poking his head out from around the corner, briefly he wondered how this day could get any more bizarre. It took him no time at all to reach the conclusion that it really couldn't. A dream, was all that he could think, but he knew that not even the darkest dragon mind could conjure up the nightmarish visions that had plagued him since he'd awoken, seventy-two hours ago. This was as real as it gets... unfortunately for him.

"HOW CAN I BE SURE OF THAT?"

"Easy really... my name is Gee Tee and my Mantra Emporium is the stuff of legend. Surely a dragon of your knowledge and experience has heard of me?"

Bewildered humans mingled with even more perplexed dragons. Surely he couldn't have been referring to the young, silky dragon standing before them? But of course he was, and those watching didn't have the benefit of the hundreds of years of experience the master mantra maker had.

"I've heard of you, if of course you are who you say you are."

"Who else would possibly claim to be me?" Gee Tee snorted. "Grumpy, uptight, a stuck up menace to dragon society in general, as well as a cheap old phoney are just some of the nicer things that have been attributed to me over the course of time."

A smile spread out across the newcomer's face.

"I'd heard that too."

"So there it is. You now know that it's me. But you're

something of a conundrum youn... I nearly said youngster. But that's not you at all, is it? Perhaps an introduction would go some way to avoid any mistrust. I have my suspicions, but I think it might be better if they all hear it from you."

Fingertips their normal selves, all hint of magic dispelled, the famed dragon in front of them reached the only decision possible.

"Most of you will know me, even if you don't fully recognise my reconstructed body. I'm STEEL... and I've been known to partake in a little laminium ball."

Stealthy gasps were let loose from everyone's mouths, apart from the humans of course, who still had little idea about what on earth was going on.

"YOU DIED!" accused one of Gee Tee's team. "Nobody could possibly have survived beneath the lava as long as you did."

Nodding his head in understanding, the brave laminium ball captain thought hard about how to address the dragon's very real concerns.

"I understand your scepticism and in a lot of ways share your apprehension. I don't know the exact details of what happened, but I'll gladly tell you what I do know. Apparently after I bobbed to the surface, but a charred collection of internal organs, some of my scales bubbled up, collected by one of the quick thinking medics. While what little remained of my life was held in place by a series of powerful mantras, a group of geneticists was called in to see if there was anything they could do. Given who I was, money was no object, and so over time these free thinking, experienced individuals were able to clone brand new scales for me from those that had been saved. After a series of life threatening operations, the scales were grafted onto my newly healed skin, and then using a pattern of laminium enhanced laser therapies, it was deemed that the new me was about as good as it was going to get. I was told all this three days ago when I was brought out of the catatonic state that I'd been in ever since the match. Also, it was made clear in no uncertain terms that I would need to rest and recuperate for at least the next six months. Needless to say, that's gone straight out of the window."

"How did you survive?"

"I don't know. They tell me that what little there was left of me refused to give in and die. That's all I know. You think all this is a shock to you. Imagine being in my position, waking up in a new body that feels very much how I'd imagine one of the human's rubber gloves would. And then only a short time later, I'm fighting nagas, slaying dark dragons and then finding the domain that I love and call home is all but under attack. To say I'm still a little confused is something of an understatement. But I'm here, and I'm not running away. I want to know what the hell's going on, and would like nothing more than to get my hands on those responsible for inflicting these dastardly events."

This seemed to have the desired effect on those who had any doubt about the brave laminium ball player's story. Of which Gee Tee was not one. He'd long since made up his mind.

"So will you join us?" asked the shopkeeper.

"With a view to doing what?"

"The world needs to know what's going on. Currently no communication is possible. As far as we know, the crystal node in Fleet Street has been taken down by the enemy's force. We're going to put that right, and put them out of their misery."

"I do like the sound of that," added Steel thoughtfully.

"So what do you say?" reiterated the master mantra maker.

"Do you have room for a few more?"

This raised several eyebrows.

"You can come out now," ventured Steel. "SLOWLY!"

Creeping out of the surrounding buildings, eagerly complying with their elected leader's instruction, a dozen or more dragons made their way into the light of the scorching fire, led purposefully by the two recent additions, Jar Man and DomCon, both ready to fight, both ready to die for the cause.

"These are all who survived from the medical facility. Good doctors, nurses and healers. Handy in a fight and particularly on the kind of mission you've just told me about. I'd be happy to join forces, just as long as you're not going to throw away dragon lives needlessly. I for one value each and every one of them, and while I understand the reality of the situation we all find ourselves in, I'm keen that they, and all of your other dragons, live to see another day."

"I couldn't have put it better myself," declared Gee Tee, offering his hand out towards the famed laminium ball captain.

"Good," added Steel, shaking the proffered hand. "Let's get this show on the road."

And so with the two teams blending seamlessly into one, and Gee Tee casting the noise cancelling mantra onto the new recruits as well as introducing them to not only the other dragons but the humans as well, the ragged force filtered off into the shadows, their destination getting ever nearer.

Earth's surface. Salisbridge, England.
Tall, splendid, magnificent, that's how it looked... to nearly everyone, anyway. And just like most days, there were a lot here to admire it today. Overlooking the city and the renowned water meadows, Salisbridge Cathedral glistened in the sparkling sun against the backdrop of a brilliant, clear blue sky. Visitors from across the world milled outside in groups small and large, filling up not only the adjacent grounds but also much of the famed Close surrounding it, most holding cameras, taking pictures of loved ones on their phones, or just the structure from odd

and jaunty angles, doing their best to avoid the scaffolding involved in the major repairs to the outside. These had been going on since the late 20th century, carrying on something of a tradition really, as a major restoration effort had taken place throughout the 18th and 19th centuries as well. Standing since the 12th century, with the extraordinary spire added sometime later, the spectacular place of worship has been the centrepiece of the area for many hundreds of years, throughout that time captivating all those that set eyes on it. Parents and children mingled, students lounged about on the benches and grass, as runners and cyclists weaved in and out of the tourists.

Breathless would best describe those that had never seen it in the flesh, so to speak, before. As well as the groups dotted about the grounds, a long, snaking queue meandered back from the entrance with those eager to take in the ancient delights hidden inside, some taking the tower tour all the way up to the top of Britain's tallest spire to soak up that glorious view. Others would no doubt marvel at the stunning stained glass windows, the cloisters, the north and south transepts and the world's oldest working clock. The inside truly was a work of genius and was well worth travelling thousands of kilometres to see.

Amongst those paying a visit today were a group who considered themselves mischief makers. A more apt description though, would have been... TERRORISTS! But not the usual sort... the magical kind. Three of them to be precise, all females, all ready to use their gifts to rain down destruction on this quiet and peaceful city. Two had queued patiently to get inside and had now split up in an effort to maximise damage to the revered minster. In dark blue jeans and a white knitted jumper, with a camera dangling from her neck, handbag slung over her shoulder, her guide book open in both hands, gradually she made her way up the nave, passing a gorgeous, modern looking font amid row after row of pews, until she reached the pulpit and seats for the choir that faced side on to the pews that were now sprinkled with people. Glancing up at the ceiling and the majestic stained glass of her surroundings, gradually she crept up the steps between the seats that would house the choir. Abruptly, her handbag slid off her shoulder, landing with something of a noise, spilling out a great deal of its contents. But not the most important object. That had been tucked away in a zipped pocket. Letting out a small gasp, she made a big deal of bending down and scrabbling around on the floor, picking up everything she'd dropped. Of course it was all subterfuge. As she hastily threw everything back in the bag, her body conveniently shielding everything she was doing, she unzipped the pocket, pulled the C4 with the duck tape already attached and swiftly placed it against the underside of one of the seats. The tiniest of red lights blinked on to say that it was armed. Her work finished, she scooped up her bag and its contents, turned around and headed back down the steps just as a tour guide arrived to see if she was okay. Expressing her thanks, she told him she was fine, and just a tad clumsy. They both chuckled before heading their separate ways, him off to rejoin the group he was showing around, whilst she sauntered towards the exit, pleased that she'd completed her part of the assignment.

Meanwhile, outside, one of her partners in crime, dressed in a light brown full length raincoat, dark brown knee length boots and carrying a black backpack, had just finished inspecting the statues above the old wooden door on the west front of the cathedral and was slowly working her way around the walls of the building in a clockwise direction. Following the main wall east, she quickly arrived at the north porch. Ignoring the locked entrance, she had a fleeting look over her shoulder to see if anyone was taking any notice of her, and on confirmation that they weren't, she followed the porch's wall along to its corner with the main building, an area showered in shade, and ducked right down into the corner at ground level. Having slid the backpack off and placed it on the floor next to her, she made as if she was tightening the laces on her expensive brown boots, all the time retrieving another tiny package of C4. Arming the explosive and checking to make sure the red light was showing, she buried it behind some wispy, long grass up against the cathedral wall with the light facing towards the brick. It was most unlikely, she knew, that anyone would spot it. They'd have to be right on top of it, and even then it wasn't a sure thing. Having done her part, she straightened up, hefted the backpack across her shoulders and walked off in the direction of the city, all the time taking in her surroundings, and those she shared them with.

The third member of the grisly trio wore white trousers, a dark black jacket and a light blue beret which did little or nothing to contain the mass of dyed blonde hair that flowed down both sides of her head, and, after ambling through the main body of the cathedral whilst doing all the touristy things, pointing at everything to point at, sighing in wonder at everything to sigh at, arrived in the cloisters. Knowing that any wall would probably do, she prided herself on doing the job right, and that meant planting her 'package' close to, or on, the south wall. Whether this would be possible depended on a gazillion different things. Strolling along the footpath, gazing in and out of the stone pillars, still in infatuated tourist mode, all the time looking out for an opportunity, she reached the south wall, having to weave in and out of a group of Asian tourists who were having a snack, to do so. On reaching the wall she peeked down the length of it. Something caught her eye, a little higher up than most would care to look. Determined to get closer, she sidled her way along the wall, stopping beneath what had attracted her attention. Up above her head, about two and a half metres high, one of the huge stones used in the construction of the wall stuck out, forming a tiny little ledge. It was barely noticeable and, because of its height, it would be impossible to see if anything were secreted there. So with the decision already made, she put one hand into her jacket pocket, armed the explosive and waited for an opportunity she hoped would come. Time ticked by, almost fifteen minutes in fact. And that's when it happened. A mother carrying her baby up against her shoulder whilst at the same time steering her child's pushchair, accidentally ran into one of the Asian tourists. This in itself wasn't enough to cause the kind of distraction that she needed, but what followed, was. As the dutiful mother apologised profusely, her child chose that exact point to throw up. And not just a little... with the kind of propensity only usually found in very grown up, very drunk, very large adults, usually after a kebab, or some other late night snack. Projectile didn't do the child's vomiting justice. It was everywhere, having covered at least two of the tourists, with four more suffering from residual splatter, and those around them leaping away frantically. It was an absolute farce, attracting the attention of everybody in the cloisters and turning out to be exactly what she was looking for. Knowing that nobody could possibly be watching her, in a total blur she pulled out the C4 and with a tiny little jump and at full stretch, placed the explosive on the ledge, making sure the red light was sitting fully against the wall so as to not give its position away. With the bedlam from the baby's explosive puke still going on, she strode off around the huge square, heading for the exit at speed, knowing that her part was done. All she had to do now was rendezvous with the others back in town and they'd be able to send the text and unleash the madness that would follow. Then it would just be a case of leaving the city and heading off to their next assignment... simple really.

25 CONFRONTATION BOUND

Just under three minutes... that's how long the battle lasted. I say battle, what I really mean is THRASHING! In all honesty they never stood a chance, and it was only pure luck that all of them hadn't died. Most of Tank's mismatched force lay dead, their remains scattered over the cobbles of the square, green dragon blood and guts splattered up against the pillars that surrounded the famed building. All that remained were Tank, Janice, Hook, one of the healers and a couple of elderly dragons, both of whom were mightily injured. For his part, Tank had fought valiantly, if only briefly, taking down two of the dreadful nagas before being magically overwhelmed and physically beaten, resulting in his left arm hanging limply by his side, the mother of all black eyes and a huge gash to his right leg that exposed not only ligament, but bone as well.

Janice hadn't fared much better. She'd managed to fatally wound one of the dragons, as well as inflicting serious injury to three more, but eventually, much like Tank, magic had taken Fu-ts'ang from her, and without him, she was defenceless and at her attackers' mercy. Broken ribs and a swollen ankle stood out amongst the array of cuts and bruises that littered her grubby complexion as she painfully tried to force in a breath.

Hook had shown just how full of courage he was, taking on a whole force of ten at once, first slowing them down with the heavy water from his clumsy backpack, before eventually beating them senseless with his rifle once they'd breached his defences. For someone facing beings over twice his size, and nightmarish ones at that, he'd acted fearlessly, his bravery far surpassing anything that had gone on anywhere during that day. With his backpack in tatters, he appeared the biggest mess of all, limping badly on what looked like a broken leg, all the time sporting massive cuts to his head that were constantly leaking blood down both sides of his face. It seemed as though every rugby injury he'd ever suffered had all come back to haunt him at once. The remainder of their force were in much the same state, badly hurt, at the mercy of their attackers. But for some unknown reason, they'd yet to be finished off, making them all wonder what lay in store. Nothing good, that was for sure.

Corralled and bunched together, surrounded by thirty times their number, slowly they were marched up the steps of the council building, past the dimly lit pools of lava on either side, the hissing and spluttering of the molten liquid reminding Tank of the last time he'd visited the king. As they filed through the huge, arched doorway and into what remained of the lobby, darkness fell across the group, because the lights as well as everything else were out, after the pitched running battle with what remained of the King's Guard. Nothing had been repaired yet, as that had been deemed secondary to capturing the king. All of Manson's resources were currently being thrown at that. It wouldn't be long now.

26 STARING INTO THE ABYSS

Reminiscent of a New Year's Eve fireworks display, the magical shield erupted furiously in a riot of colour as wave after wave of supernatural attacks detonated unsuccessfully against it. Fifty metres back, Amelia Battlehard stood stoically next to the king, looking on, both dragons keeping their thoughts very much to themselves. Battle tactics for the unavoidable upcoming skirmish and how best to rally her troops raced feverishly throughout her mind, as she mused about just how they were supposed to overcome the insurmountable odds stacked up against them. Momentarily she wondered if any of the other garrisons across the world were headed her way, any and all able to mount some sort of rescue attempt. Almost instantly though, she pushed the thought from her mind. No doubt the dark dragon Manson had all of that covered, given the planning that had gone into everything else. Silently she hoped her colleagues and friends across the planet were fighting gallantly to preserve their way of life and just survive. Deep within her mind, she wished them luck.

A gazillion different things swam through George's consciousness, one after the other, often skittering away before he had a chance to consider each properly. For the most part this was a good thing, as the vast majority of them were much darker thoughts than even he should be thinking. But time and again one such idea kept on coming back to him, centred around living to rally and regroup the dragon world, and surviving to fight again another day. For him it was a distinct possibility, due to the secret entrance only known to him (of course he'd told Flash about it when he was staying here, but they were the only two that knew of its existence) only a hundred or so metres away from where he now stood. He could flee to safety. No dragon here would begrudge him that. At first he'd toyed with the idea, but not for very long, and not particularly seriously. It wasn't for him. Not on this day. And who's to say just what he would find back in the reality of London? For all he knew, there could be almost nothing left, no one to call on, no one to rally around him. NO! He wouldn't run. The very thought of leaving those who had sworn to protect him to whatever fate was rushing their way, was abhorrent. Some time ago he'd decided to stay and fight by their side, die in their defence if necessary, although he had a feeling that, for him, it wouldn't be quite that straight forward. No doubt Troydenn had other plans, plans that featured torture and endless suffering for him. But if he could buy some time, just maybe a rescue or a retaking of the planet was feasible. There must be some pockets of resistance out there somewhere. What about Flash? Where was he? One of the few individuals on the planet that he trusted, he must by now know what was going on. Was he at this very moment mounting a rescue? And if so, just how far away was he? Momentarily, it all threatened to overwhelm him. He knew deep down that he couldn't count on Flash turning up. Perhaps the ex-Crimson Guard had already been taken out of commission, although he did find that hard to believe. Letting out a deep sigh that startled Amelia Battlehard out of her thoughts, he paced forward just a few steps, gazing intently at the events occurring on the other side of the transparent magical shield. As he did so, the current bombardment subsided. All those behind the shield suddenly became alert, on guard for something as yet unseen. Amelia and the king shared a look... one that almost said it all.

'Is this to be it, the beginning of the end?'

As magical beasts of all shapes and sizes retreated back out of view, far beyond the end of the broken bridge that they'd been forced to destroy, three figures abruptly appeared on the edge of what was left of the structure, only a step or two from the infinitesimal drop.

Squinting, the king tilted his head slightly to get a better view through the protective hemisphere, and when he did... GASPED loudly.

"MY GOD!" he muttered.

"Sire?" enquired Captain Battlehard from just behind him.

Shaking his head, the king closed his eyes and fought back the urge to cry, so great was the pain at just what he was witnessing.

Remaining quiet and still, there for him if he needed her, Captain Battlehard realised at this time, he required just that little bit of space. It's a shame things hadn't played out differently, as she would have made a wonderful diplomat.

In his mind, the king raged.

'It can't be! It just can't be! She can't just turn up here and now. Not like this! Not with them like that! Please no!' he pleaded with no one in particular. A tiny part of him hoped this was a dream, a nightmare even, but he couldn't be that lucky. Of course he'd recognised the being shoving Peter and Tim before her as someone responsible for numerous crimes from far off in the past, the estranged daughter of his missing/captured best friend, Fredric, one that went by the name of... EARTH!

'Of all the vicious, malevolent, self centred beings, why the hell...?' suddenly his thoughts were interrupted as a self serving, smug and deeply hypnotic voice floated across the gap that the destroyed bridge had once spanned.

"Enough is enough, old timer," announced Earth, the devious, sickly smile on her magically scarred face visible even from where the king was standing. "There is only one outcome here. And you know it better than most. I've about had it with your time wasting. So now you get to choose. Lower the shield and order your fancy ring to rebuild the bridge. You have five minutes to comply. Should you fail to do so then your favourite little pet here and your saviour, The White Dragon, will be doing a spot of flying, only they might find it a tad hard to revert back to their natural forms on their way down into the abyss with these magic restricting binders on. And oh... wouldn't that be a shame now. Tick tock. Time's a-wasting."

Stomach turning, heart racing, as anger, desperation and fear battled each other within him, the king's head spun as he knew not what to do. Not unaccustomed to nightmares, this was something that genuinely scared the living hell out of him, and that was without knowing the full weight of history was well and truly balanced precariously on his shoulders, right here and now. Putting aside his feelings for Peter, his best friend's grandson, there was the very real and grave matter of The White Dragon. If the prophecy was to be believed, then that same White Dragon was the answer to all of it, the dragons' and the humans' saviour all at once. How on earth could he let him die like this, here and now? Deep down, he knew that he couldn't, he just couldn't. And then there was the small matter of lowering the shield and rebuilding the bridge, which was easily achieved with the power from the ring, but what would happen afterwards? Would that evil witch of a dragon still kill Peter and The White Dragon anyway? There was no guarantee that she wouldn't do just that after rounding up every being here. So what was he supposed to do? What was the right answer to every one of his worst nightmares?

Abruptly, the most delicate cough in the world startled him out of his worst fears. Amelia Battlehard had sidled up to him, an expectant look etched across her face. Turning slowly to look at her, he was lost at sea, adrift without any sort of answer. It was the captain that spoke first.

"Whatever you choose Sire... is fine with us. We trust in you, and always will do. If you believe the key to everything is The White Dragon, then we're with you all the way."

Barely able to believe his heart could break any more, currently it was as close to buckling as was dragonly possible.

"I appreciate your candidness Amelia... I really do. But I struggle to see any other way out. And I fear for all of your lives. That being over there... going by the name of EARTH, isn't somebody to be trusted, quite the opposite in fact. I fear once she has us all outgunned and outnumbered, that she will kill each and every one of you, including Peter and The White Dragon, saving a very long and slow death for me, no doubt at the hands of the charming Troydenn."

"Majesty... we trust in you and have faith that you will make the correct decision. If surrendering now means buying you a little more time in the hope that the dragon domain is fighting back and rallying to your aid, then perhaps it is the right thing to do. Time might well be the key. As you've already told us all... never give up. Keep on fighting with your last breath. As long as you live... there's always a chance."

Of course, she was right. And there really did seem no other way out. It looked as though the choice had already been made for them.

Gazing into the depths of the abyss, his captor's nails drawing blood from the back of his neck, the heavy metal manacles behind his back restricting his magic, causing wave after wave of pain to creep up from his wrists and into his shoulders, Peter caught a quick glance of Tim next to him, in very much the same position. Looking out in front of him without lifting his head for fear of agonising retribution, he could just make out his friend, the king, chatting to a stunning looking dragon standing next to him. Right at this very moment, all he wished for was to be the other side of that barrier, and reunited with the dragon that meant so much to him. But a burning rage stoked the fire within him. He knew what they wanted... Manson and Earth... They wanted the monarch! Wanted to torture and kill him, no doubt. And the very last thing he wanted was for that to happen. If his and Tim's deaths saved George, he would gladly sacrifice himself here and now. Currently, though, that was not an option, not with the firm grip that evil woman had on his neck and his inability to fight back because of the power sapping binders. And as the time ticked down, he hoped with all his might that the stunning dragon standing next to the king was actually talking him into fighting and staying behind the shield, rather than surrendering any advantage he might have.

'Dreamlike' is how he'd describe it, although right at this moment it had morphed itself into some kind of outlandish nightmare. As the bile kicked around the bottom of his throat, threatening to make a mad dash and escape his magically derived body, mainly, he assumed, because of the death defying drop he was currently being forced to look down at by the mad woman... (no, not woman... DRAGON!) forced to look at by the mad dragon, whose fingernails were currently piercing either side of his neck, forcing blood to run freely. It could still all be a dream... at least that's what part of him hoped. That at any moment he'd wake up and be back in his house on the surface, off to play hockey and hook up with the beautiful... RICHIE! Despite his desperate situation, his thoughts turned to her. Immediately he knew it wasn't a dream, and that he really was stuck here, in something of a life or death situation. But he couldn't help wondering what had happened to her. Was she still on the surface blissfully unaware of her past, moving on with her life, still the lacrosse superstar? Or had her world been turned upside down by whatever was going on down here? If it hadn't been, then he had no doubt that at some point in the near future it most certainly would be. Silently he wished her luck, hoping as well to see her one more time.

The muscles in her arms tensed, showing precisely how much force she was using to dig her fingernails into her two captives' necks. Just the sight of their blood satisfied something deep within her, but not as much as knowing that she had the king in an almost impossibly tight spot, one that, as she saw it, he had no option but to surrender to... a word she hardly knew the meaning of. In some ways it was a shame that she wouldn't be able to inflict the world of pain coming his way, but there was no way in hell that Troydenn would let anyone else have even a part of that particular pleasure. So she'd have to settle for breaking him, forcing him to give up and surrender. There was at least some satisfaction in that... knowing that she'd brought the monarch to his knees, and essentially changed the fate of the planet forever. To be at Manson's side as joint ruler of the new world that would emerge from the week gone past, sent a thrill through her like almost nothing else. And that pivotal moment was only seconds away, of that she was sure.

Turning three hundred and sixty degrees, taking in all the dragons that had sworn to protect him, his false human body trembling ever so slightly, he still wasn't sure if it was the right thing to do. Part of him wished he could evacuate the brave dragons here defending him out through the secret entrance, giving them at least some semblance of a chance in the wider world, but unfortunately the magic that held it in place only allowed one being through it at any one time... useful as an escape route to the outside for just him on occasion, but utterly ineffective in a situation like this. As of now though, he could come up with nothing else. Parched, and distraught beyond belief, he just about managed to croak,

"I'm sorry," before he closed his eyes and commanded the ring to take down the shield and rebuild the bridge that would allow the enemy's forces to storm their position. Silently he offered up a prayer, but to whom, he really didn't know.

Out of nowhere, it happened with only a hiss and a flicker. The transparent, crackling, blue hemisphere of energy disappeared into nothing, as Peter's heart dropped like a stone into the abyss he overlooked. That was it. They were all doomed, and not just the king or Tim and himself. The whole planet, that's what Manson wanted. This was the turning point and would give him ultimate control of everything, not just the underground domain of the dragons, but all the humans on the surface as well. Tears trickled from his eyes, very much mirroring the blood running down his neck.

At the sight of the magical shield shimmering out of existence, Tim let out a tiny gasp. It was impossible, and yet was happening right before his very eyes. Unsure whether to be pleased or not about this new situation, all he knew was that their fates were probably going to be resolved very soon.

Regardless of the sneer currently residing between the purple magical scars that crisscrossed her face, deep inside she leapt with joy. She'd done it... forced him to surrender. That was it. That was all they were waiting for. Now the planet was theirs, to do with as they pleased. And the king was about to discover a very new meaning of the word pain, something she absolutely revelled in as she watched the hearts of the dragons surrounding him sink. Satisfaction at a job well done threatened to overwhelm her. Perhaps it would be her turn to win the invading army's 'evil deeds of the week award'.

27 HOLEY MOLEY

Siphoning off just some of the power from the laminium chains crisscrossing his torso, Fredric, Peter's grandfather and founder of the formidable Crimson Guards, had conjured up a small bubble of warmth over on the far side of the chamber, something that Yoyo and his dragons were right at this very moment taking advantage of, given just how badly all of their protective suits had been damaged during the Antarctic battle.

Flash, Fredric and the naga king stood off to one side of the bloody mess in the chamber, the two dragons drawing power from the laminium chains to keep them warm, their companion very much at home in the cold temperatures.

For Fredric, it was nearly all too much. Despite everything that had transpired over the last hour, he found it almost impossible to believe that he'd actually just gained his freedom. After so many decades chained to that blasted wall, it almost didn't seem real, but he'd pinched himself a couple of times just to make sure he wasn't dreaming. And it was REAL! All he had to do now was get all of them back to civilisation and stop that dastardly being and his cohorts from taking over the planet. No problem there then.

Like Peter's grandfather standing next to him, Flash felt seriously overwhelmed, despite it not being the first pitched battle that he'd fought in. If anything, he was struggling to come to terms with having won, notwithstanding the massive odds against it. Yoyo's motley crew had performed admirably, despite their relative naivety. Luck must surely have been on their side for each and every one of them to have survived. More surprisingly though, was the fact that Fredric had restored him to the being he'd been years ago, washing away in an instant any stain of a side effect from Gee Tee's efforts at having saved his life from the deadly naga strike that had caught him off guard on his last appearance, here in Antarctica. Fully restored, he could feel the dragon within him bursting to get out, desperate to take its rightful place out here... in the open. But now was not the time, not surrounded by the life threateningly low temperatures that they all found themselves in. Even with the absurd amount of laminium he was wrapped up in, transforming here was nothing short of a bad idea. Deep inside, he whispered for his prehistoric form to be patient. It wouldn't be long now. Not long at all.

The naga king's strange, echoing voice broke the silence in the icy cavern first, startling both dragons nearest to him.

"Whhhaaaat willllll haaapppen nooow?" he asked, more than a hint of concern about his race drawn out across his reptilian features.

Turning to face Flash, Fredric, the founder of the Crimson Guards, thought it best to try and get as much of a handle as he could on the current situation.

"What is it we need to do? Where do we need to be?"

"When I left," declared Flash, "the meagre force we had was splitting up, with one group heading off to try and restore planet wide communications, while the other headed towards the council building and the king's private residence with a view to a rescue. If I had to take a guess, I'd say we were most needed there, as no doubt that's where things will play out. But how we get back there is beyond me at the moment, with all the dynamic insulating suits broken in some way, shape or form. Maybe one or two can be cobbled together to allow a few of us the possibility of leaving, but even then it will take an absolute age to get back to the opposite side of the world. I very much doubt we'd get there in time to make any sort of difference, not given how long it would take to get us back to Australia, especially with the monorail out of commission. And then we'd have to organise a rescue for those left behind here. Time consuming doesn't begin to cover it," huffed Flash, disappointed that he couldn't come up with a better plan to get them all out of here.

Fredric racked his brain for anything, no matter how obscure, that just might speed their journey up, or give them any sort of edge in getting back to the dragon domain in an effort to save their ruler, and his best friend. Once again though, he was interrupted by the naga king.

"Thhheeereee maaaayybeeee aanottthhhher waaaayy," announced the majestic reptile, instantly commanding the respect of those all around him. "Naggggaaasss havvvveee muuccch covetteeeeed maaaagic. Maaaagic tooo oppeeen annnnd clossssse portallllls acccrrrosss thheee globbbbeeee throughhhh whicchhh beinnngs cannn beeee transsssporttted."

This caught the dragons' attention.

"Go on," urged Fredric, keen to hear what his comrade in arms had to say.

"I caaan opppeen a poortaal at willll, and if muuuch isss knooown byy yooouu abooout thhhe destinatiooon, theen I ssshhould bee able to accccessss ittt telepathicaaalllly. Whaaaat I laaaccck thoughhhh isss a pooowerr souurce."

Despite the cold and everything he'd been through, his mind was now as razor sharp as it had ever been. In an instant, Fredric knew exactly what they would do, how they'd find the precise point they needed to transport to, and indeed just how it would be powered. With his frustrated frown very much turned upside down, he proffered his hand out towards the naga king.

"Fredric Bluewillow at your service," he announced. "How would you like to help take down those that have done this to us, those that would have you as a bargaining chip for your entire race?"

'Snaking' was about as appropriate a word as you could find for the grin that suddenly appeared across the mighty reptile's scaly face.

Grasping the offered hand, an unlikely alliance not seen since the dawn of time was suddenly forged, not only out of necessity, but out of a bond formed in the cold horror of sickening captivity they'd both shared.

"It's a pleasure... Vasuki. Now, let me introduce you to the rest of the dragons here, and then we can get down to the business of escape and of course... RETRIBUTION!"

Earth's surface. The Black Forest, Germany.
It had been an awfully long haul, but finally they'd arrived at their destination. Headlights dimmed, they skirted a half fallen tree and, avoiding the frozen puddles of ice, pulled into the specifically created clearing that awaited them. In the distance, some hundred or so metres away, they could just make out the moon's reflection trailing across the still water of lake Titisee, through the densely packed treeline.

During their last stop in an outlying part of Romania, the low loader that the temperature controlled, lead lined box surrounded by a carbon fibre and titanium monofilament wall, had previously been carried on, had been replaced by something far more sophisticated... a state of the art, brand new electric Mercedes truck, which had allowed them to enter this part of Germany relatively unnoticed. Tucked away deep in the Black Forest, with nobody around for a very long way, the two crews left the comfort of their vehicles and stepped out into the icy wilderness, not hesitating in setting up camp. Huge, camouflaged tents were broken out, erected in almost an instant, with each of them knowing there was little time to waste. They'd been tasked with breaking into the mobile vault in an effort to retrieve its hidden valuables, and knew from the off that it wouldn't be easy, even with a limited amount of magic and supernatural power available to them. The Russians had seen to that. It was deemed easier to transport if they could break it out of its high tech vault, and given that they still had some way to go, each and every one of them hoped their efforts wouldn't be in vain, understanding in no small part just how much their lives were intertwined with the fate of the prized metal they were now supposed to expose.

28 PIPE DREAM

Two brilliant, bright eyes poked out of the darkness, like stunning black diamonds atop a matt, black cloth. Intent only on studying the route before them, the eyes gave no clue as to who they belonged to, not now that she was shrouded in the cloak, the one the king kept hidden for his little excursions out of his private residence, something that should have been impossible, and always had far reaching implications.

Fed up with tracking the devilish twisting and turning pipes, Richie imagined that once things were over, and should she survive, her dreams would only ever consist of pipes. Pipes, pipes and more pipes! That's all she'd seen for over two hours now. Brown ones, yellow ones, white, red, green, and her personal favourite... ORANGE! It was all mind-numbingly boring. Her focus had started to waver on numerous occasions and she'd found it hard to bring it back, despite all her dragon training. The tiniest part inside her screamed out that she'd made a mistake, that she should have stayed and led the group, the one she'd left Tank in charge of. Normally so self assured, that massive hit of confidence had deserted her now and was nowhere to be seen. Even pushing her doubts aside had proved difficult and taken everything she had mentally, something else oddly new to her.

Dropping to her knees, she crawled commando style for about twenty metres before getting to her feet and vaulting a criss-crossing line of different coloured pipes that cut across her path at waist height, once again changing sides of the walls they ran along.

Momentarily she thought about stopping to catch her breath for ten minutes, but she was only too aware of just what might be playing out elsewhere in the domain. Her friends... not only Tank, Peter, Flash and Gee Tee, but the humans as well, they were in danger... mostly placed there by her, with the exception of Peter and Tim.

'DAMN!' she thought. 'How on earth do I keep forgetting about TIM?'

She should have been only too aware of him, in the same way that Janice was focused on the love of her life... PETER! But her lover and now supposedly 'Saviour of the Dragon Domain'... The White Dragon kept slipping in and out of her consciousness. One minute there, the focal point of her thoughts. The next... GONE! No recollection at all. Was it some side effect of having her memories stored in the ring? Would it cure itself over time? Or would it only get worse? These questions and more plagued her thoughts, if nothing else, distracting her from her all too ready dislike of pipes.

Abruptly turning a sharp, left hand corner, she stopped, dropping to one knee, all thoughts of lovers and pipes long since forgotten. There, not thirty metres away, was what she'd been told to look for. A grille, two metres square, slivers of sharp, bright, white light highlighting the dust, cutting through its horizontal slits.

Drawing the dagger from behind her back, heart beating faster, concealed in the cloak, carefully she edged forward, frightened and excited in equal measure at exactly what she might find. Reaching the grille, carefully she pried two of the metal slits apart with the tip of the dagger, creating a gap through which she could see. Relief washed over her, well... in part anyway. One thing was for sure, she was most certainly in the right place at the right time.

Earth's surface. London, England.
It started out as a day like any other in the bustling metropolis that was London. Commuters commuted, children and their busy parents hustled their way through the school run, traffic ebbed and flowed, mainly at the pace of a tortoise, whilst the trains and tubes transported

everyone from the suburbs and the home counties to their offices and places of employment in the city. It was madness, turmoil, an unruly mess, but it kind of worked and made sense in a nonsensical kind of way.

So everything was going... not quite swimmingly, but you know... just about okay, that is until a random tube train, full to the brim with passengers, had the unfortunate luck to be travelling from Waterloo to Bank station on the Waterloo and City line. With the tube hugging the rails at almost its top speed, the driver, a veteran of this particular route, looked out wistfully through the dirt smeared glass, pleased with himself for being on time, virtually to the second. This, as it turned out, would be the very last thought he'd ever have.

With no warning whatsoever, the tube reached the melted part of the tracks the two nagas in disguise had used their magic on only minutes earlier. With nothing there to guide and support the wheels of the carriages, and buffeted by the speed, things started to go awry straight away. During the first one thousandth of a second, the driver felt the front of the transport veer to the left ever so slightly.

'That should be impossible,' was the thought that he didn't quite have time to rattle off, before the right side of the tube somewhere just behind him collided at speed with the wall of the tunnel, instantly throwing him head first through the glass he'd been gazing so longingly through only moments before.

Super hot sparks ricocheted off all the edges of the carriages making contact with the tunnel wall, lighting up individual sections, hurling bricks in every direction, and generating the most horrendous scraping noise (think a teacher scratching her nails down a chalk board times a thousand). Inside the body of the train, screaming passengers were flung into seats, doors and of course each other. The result was a constantly transforming, continually moving bloodbath.

With momentum changing and the lead carriage off its axis like a wriggling caterpillar, the whole train turned over onto its side, smashing windows and doors, ripping up what remained of the rails, still moving dreadfully fast in the direction it had originally been travelling in.

As the first carriage crumpled up somewhat, the second buckled in on itself, tearing seats from their housings, throwing passengers into twisted, broken metal, shaking away the very structural integrity that held the thing together. Blood ran thick amongst all the terrible injuries, shattered bones, morbid cadavers and scattered remains. It was a hellish sight, straight out of most people's worst nightmares.

Emergency lights barely flickered through the thick, choking dust. Screams from those still alive were muted at best, mumbled and incoherent at worst. Those that could move had nowhere to go because they were all trapped inside a metal skeleton cage, unable to get out because the wreckage was so badly damaged. Survivors turned to their phones for illumination, and a chance to get help, and despite the damage they sat amongst, thankfully there was still Wi-Fi, which some used to get a message out. With the emergency services on their way, all they could do was close their eyes in an effort to try and forget the misery and death that they sat amidst.

Being so far from both stations, exactly as planned, the police, fire brigade and paramedics had THE most difficult time in getting to the derailed tube train, wasting valuable resources through no fault of their own, allowing injuries to get worse, more people to go into shock, and with some of those that could have been saved, instead dying through lack of a quick, coordinated emergency response.

As it turned out, it would be one of the most deadly train crashes in the whole of the United Kingdom, with answers for what had happened few and far between. Most importantly though, it started to spread fear and panic throughout the general population, something that from the very off, it had been designed to do, so in that sense, it became regarded as something of a success.

29 A BRIDGE TOO FAR

Tougher than tough, a warrior with few equals on the battlefield, all of this counted for nothing as her fighting spirit crumbled into despair, as the magical shield that had surrounded them hissed into oblivion. Amelia Battlehard watched stoically as the king surrendered, taking in what she knew to be her last moments on this planet. She had no problem laying her life down for her monarch, because that was indeed part of her job. But like this... it seemed madness. Fighting, clawing, scratching the eyes out of her enemy until she bled out and her last breath left the dying husk of her body, that was how she'd thought it would end. But to concede to these savages was nothing short of insanity. Looking on, she hoped that the sovereign had a plan, ninety-nine point nine, nine percent sure that he didn't. Deep within, she prayed for the dragons under her command. They didn't deserve this. They deserved to die with dignity and at least have the opportunity to take a few of their enemies with them.

With the shield lowered, there was nothing to stop another magical attack; he knew, however, that it just wouldn't come. Not that they wouldn't want to of course. No! They wanted him alive. They wanted him to suffer. And no doubt he would, over and over again. Almost broken to his very core and with little hope left inside him, he concentrated on the ring, and commanded it to rebuild the bridge that they'd blown to smithereens only a short time ago. With only the intake of breath from those dragons around him for company, strangely there was nothing from the exotic piece of jewellery. Not a peep. Once again he gave the order. Once again, it was, oddly, ignored.

Energy and magic sapped by the binders that held him in place, blood dribbling around the base of his neck and onto his chest, for the first time in an age he felt totally hapless and lost. Allowing himself to be captured and now used, without putting up even a hint of a fight had cost the king and more importantly, the kingdom, any chance it had to rally against the deceitful acts that had been perpetrated against it. Alright, he'd been taken by surprise, and once confined by the power draining binders he'd had no chance to do anything, but he was pretty sure that others would have found an approach. There was no way in hell that Tank would have stood for all of this. Without a doubt, he would have found a way to escape and fight back. Gee Tee was another. Some fancy spell or other would have set him free, with more of his unusual, ancient magic no doubt inflicting serious casualties on the psychopaths that were behind all this.

Watching George from a distance, head spinning, the breath of Manson's evil queen washing over his left ear, Peter's thoughts turned to his friends: Tank, Richie, Flash, Gee Tee, Yoyo... were they even all still alive? He didn't doubt for a minute that Richie was blissfully ignorant of her surroundings on the planet's surface, just like his love... Janice. Part of him felt sorry for Richie, not able to remember her true heritage. The rest of him envied her for not knowing the double-dealing hell that was now playing out, here, far underground. The others though, they had to at least be in a world of trouble. If Manson had gotten this far, then clearly he had plans for the rest of the world. Nagas would almost certainly have been the order of the day. Fighting back the tears, he tried desperately not to think of them as dead. But given the situation he found himself in, that was the only logical conclusion he could reach. Figuring the rest of his life could now be measured in minutes, rather than hours or days, he vowed there and then that he would look for that one opportunity to make somebody on the other side pay... with their life.

With enough to worry about already, the king had no idea why on earth the ring was failing to comply with his intent. Pushing everything else aside, he used the full force of his will to once again echo his command. The silence in his mind was brutally shattered as the ring screamed throughout his very being, shocking him to his core. Never in all his years had such a thing happened, and it took everything he had left not to drop to his knees. Lost in a melee of psychic screams, the monarch did everything he could to try and understand what the enigmatic band was trying to tell him. Almost instantly it became clear that it was some kind of complaint, rebellion against his chosen course of action, laid out in the most vigorous of fashions. Using what little energy he had left, he tried to lay it all out in front of the contained presence, explain the rationale behind his thinking, in the hope that it could be brought onside. But it wasn't to be, with the fabulously flamboyant loop steadfastly refusing to do his bidding. Without warning, the enigmatic piece of jewellery became silent and inert.

Dropping his head into both hands and letting out an almighty sigh, the king propelled his voice across the void, out towards his enemies.

"The ring has refused to rebuild the bridge. I've done everything I can to try and convince it otherwise, but it's simply out of my hands now. You'll have to do it yourself."

Manson's queen, Earth, cackled uncontrollably.

"Look at you old man, unable to even persuade an outdated magical relic to do your bidding. PATHETIC!" she spat.

Still clinging on to Peter and Tim's necks with her razor sharp nails, Earth looked back over her shoulder towards the array of nagas behind her.

"USE YOUR MAGIC!" she commanded. "REBUILD

THE BRIDGE!"

As one, half a dozen of them slithered forward, the sickening noise of their bodies shifting across the ground inducing terror and fear into Peter and Tim simultaneously.

Painfully pulling her captives back from the death defying drop by the nails dug deeply into their flesh, ignoring their muffled screams, Earth made way for the six nagas, keen to see the extent of their magical abilities.

Slinking around so that each of them faced outwards and the tips of their tails all touched in the middle, the snake-like creatures formed a circle and all closed their eyes. Moments later a loud hum echoed throughout the chamber and the air almost felt like water, thick, heavy, pushing out against everything. Immediately every being there developed a headache, blistering agony blossoming out from behind their eyes and noses, some almost unable to stand because of their acute anguish, as the strange and unusual magic filled the air.

If not for the fingernails piercing their muscles, the two hostages, Peter and Tim, would have dropped to their knees, instead choosing to close their eyes and ride out the wicked waves of pain that assaulted them.

The magic was powerful, he had to give them that, but it was nothing he hadn't experienced before in his many centuries of service to the domain he'd dedicated his life to. Stoic spirit almost crushed, he chose to remain standing, steadfastly ignoring the assault on his false human appearance, a little part of him remaining open to the mysterious ring on his finger, hoping against hope that it would relent and at the very least talk to him. But so far... it wasn't to be.

Wrapped in darkness, the air around her abruptly took on a whole new dimension. Closing in, it felt as though it were trying to crush her, consume her magic, bury her spirit. Pulling the dark cowl down over her face, she smiled as the original pain from behind her eyes, that which had caught her by surprise, faded somewhat. The cloak, however it worked, had provided her with some kind of protection, for which she was eternally grateful. Now if only the others would arrive and join the party, then she could get on and finish this. Impatience was starting to eat away at her.

'Statuesque' would describe the circle of nagas. Not one of them moved a muscle, but clearly they were in contact with one another. Out of nowhere there was a brilliant, bright flash, followed by a booming thunderclap. Dragons on the king's side of the chasm dropped to their knees, afraid for their very existence.

Earth smiled as her eyes refocused, the brilliant, bright white light fading into nothingness as out in front of her, every conceivable shade of brown rock materialised from absolutely nothing, melding seamlessly with that on which they were already standing, a slight crunching ricocheting around all the walls as it did so. It wasn't quick, taking almost four minutes in all, but it was a rare sight and pleasurable to watch the smugness being wiped from the faces of the king's supposed protectors as they realised that now there really was nowhere to run. As the air returned to normal and the headaches disappeared, evil started to slide across the magnificent bridge that had just materialised out of nothing. Clearly, it was over now, and nothing could stop them ruling the planet, once and for all.

Relieved that the torture beneath their faces had subsided, Peter and Tim were cajoled across the bridge, towards the waiting monarch, each of them wrapped up in their own robes of despair and hopelessness, their bindings rattling around behind them.

Resonating across the bridge from far off behind them, a self-righteous, conceited and rather slimy voice caught everyone's attention.

"Ah... my love. It seems that once again you've surpassed my every expectation. What a wonderful ruler and consort you will make. Those fortunate to survive should be honoured to live under your rule."

"Eloquent words, my darling," replied Earth, licking her lips sumptuously, before blowing a kiss off in Manson's direction. "Why don't you join us and get acquainted with the last dragon monarch? I know he's just DYING to meet you."

Manson chuckled at her witty reply as he strode purposefully across the replacement structure, taking little interest in the magic that had created it.

Reaching the king's end of the bridge, Earth thrust each of her tortured captives to the floor directly in front of the monarch, as a large contingent of nagas spread out amongst the pathetic dragon force left. Here and now, the head of state knew that nothing but despair and wickedness was to come. It was hard for him to see it all end like this. Still he fought to contact the ring. Still the enigmatic band was having none of it.

Slowly, and very deliberately licking the blood off her fingernails, Earth caught the king's eye. It was a moment she'd been longing for, anticipating, relishing almost, for many, many decades. Now it was here. And it didn't disappoint. To her satisfaction, he was broken... once a mighty warrior, feared by many, respected by all, she could remember being in his presence as a youngster, being in awe of both him and... hmm, someone else. No longer... now he stood before her. It seemed only fitting that he bow.

"BOW BEFORE YOUR QUEEN!" she bellowed.

Broken, full to bursting with self pity and much more fearful than he would ever let on, he knew only one way to behave, to act. Needless to say, he didn't bow.

Approaching the end of the bridge, the tap, tap, tapping of his walking stick alerting all to his company, he wondered just how the next few seconds would play out, knowing full well that his beloved queen did not generally play well with others.

Eyes locked fiercely on the belligerent king, she could see him revel in what he thought to be the smallest of victories. He would kneel she knew, and it wouldn't take very long. Looking across to a dark hued naga in the middle of a group of dragons, she gave him the most imperceptible of nods. Faster than the eye could see, matt black metal scythed through the air with a ring of alarm to it. As the THUMP that marked the dragon guard's skull dropping to the floor rebounded across the private residence, a look of total and utter surprise remained engraved across the prehistoric beast's face.

Instantly a struggle started, but it was quelled before it had a chance to get out of hand.

Earth locked eyes once again with the king.

"BOW!" she ordered.

Trapped in a well of despair, tumbling out of control... he gave in, slowly dropping to his knees, head cowed for all to see.

"There... that wasn't so hard, was it?" Earth mocked.

For those on the side of light, the last vestiges of hope died there and then, their mortal bodies no doubt soon to follow.

Arm muscles bulging, still trying to break free from the impossible chains, vomit raced up Peter's oesophagus at the sight of the king kneeling before Manson's evil queen. Whatever had been going on, clearly a climax had all but been reached. Death, he knew, was only moments away. Part of him almost welcomed it, not wanting to see the planet and its many citizens burned, destroyed, hunted for sport or George tortured mercilessly. It was easier just to die, to be the first of many and just get it over with. Swallowing loudly, he forced the bile back down his throat, wondering exactly how many minutes he had left.

As the tap, tap, tapping arrived, its source spoke.

"Graciously done, my queen."

Earth smiled at Manson's freely given approval.

Wheeling around, arms wide open, cane pointing high up to different points in the walls, the dastardly Manson pondered a different kind of effort than war, a redecorating effort.

"I must say it's all a bit more drab than I expected. Haven't you heard of colour? I think while you're suffering unbearable atrocities at the talons of someone you know quite well, I might have to remodel. Blood green or blood red might well be my first choice, but I wonder if I'll be bored with it by then... having of course seen so much of it... decisions, decisions."

Every being there who served the king fought to hold their tongues, knowing the words were designed to provoke, cause a reaction. Having seen just how easily one of their brethren had been slaughtered by a single evil naga, each of them knew that now was not the time, should a time even exist. Forcing his teeth together, cowed down on the floor in front of what he knew to be a wicked being, the ruler fought against his overwhelming urge to speak up. It was hard not to, but the thought of getting another being that he was responsible for, killed, kept him in line. For him, it was hard to see just what would happen next. All he knew was that it was the end of the line for dragon monarchs in general. There would be no more. He'd failed, totally and utterly, not just the world here and now, abundant with humans and dragons, but history itself. He couldn't help but ask himself if the great kings of the past would have done anything different, or fared any better.

Pumping furiously through her prehistoric veins, Amelia Battlehard's viscous green blood all but boiled, having witnessed the king's humiliation and the death of one of her own, igniting a rage and anger almost directly emanating from her DNA, coursing through her, unlike anything she'd ever felt before. Only her iron will prevented her from taking action, but even then she knew it was only a matter of time.

'Better struck down in battle, than killed like a defenceless youngling,' she thought.

Wandering casually over to his queen, before leaning in and planting a sticky wet kiss on her cheek, much to her amusement, the psychopathic Manson slowly stepped behind the king's prone frame.

"I think it's time you gave me what I want... old man!"

Out of sight, the monarch's weathered old face contorted in rage, having quite a good idea of exactly what he was talking about.

"GET TO YOUR FEET!" ranted Manson, suddenly seeming to have something of a psychotic episode.

Gingerly, looking frail and showing every year of his time on the planet, George stumbled to his feet and turned to face the purple faced Manson. Across only a few metres, their eyes met, madness and insanity jockeying for position.

"The ring... it's mine now. Give it to me!" he ordered.

An echoing scream of, "NO!" reverberated throughout every molecule of the king's ancient body as the sentient artefact realised exactly what was going on. The pain was excruciating and lesser beings would have dropped to the floor, but not this one. It was almost exactly what he needed, all but waking him from a despairing, self pitying slumber.

30 SHAFTED

In an almost trance-like state, the young lacrosse playing dragon, barely breathing, sat cross legged at the end of the shaft overlooking events playing out below her across the king's private residence. Emotions deeply under wraps, she'd chosen meditation, something taught to her what seemed like a lifetime ago during the fourth year of her fifty year tuition at the Purbeck Peninsula nursery ring. Used primarily to enhance the restoration of dragon magic or mana as it was widely known, the near catatonic state did at least offer the benefit of replenishing energy and banishing fatigue, something she found herself in desperate need of.

Focusing solely on the miniscule specks of dust hanging in the air, occasionally glinting from what little light forced its way through the metal grille in front of her, she found great solace in being tightly wrapped in the cloak that Flash had guided her to. Not a hundred metres or so from the nearest dragon, she knew that without the mantle she might well be discovered, because these were the King's Guard, supposedly the best of the best, although she was sure Flash would have something to say on that particular subject.

Lost in time with just the faintest dribble of magic from the laminium dagger, sheathed at her back, enhancing her hearing, she was confident that when she was required she'd be refreshed, focused on what needed to be done, and aware of the entire situation. Having already compartmentalised her feelings, listening to Peter and Tim's voices had little or no effect on her, at least that's what she kept telling herself.

Against the backdrop of the occasional beat of her very human heart, a familiar voice caught her attention from nearly two hundred metres away. It was the king, and in some respect his words cut right through her, attempting to crush the resolve she held so firmly on to. While devastated that he'd decided to surrender, the tiniest beacon of hope flared up inside her, because if nothing else, it had bought her best friend Peter just a little more time, something she would use to save not only him, but Tim and the king as well.

All she needed now was for Tank's force to fight their way up through the council building and appear on the other side of that blasted magical bridge. After that, it would be no great shakes to dispatch a few dark dragons and nagas, especially given the contingent of King's Guard that were already present, something she hadn't counted on. As the tiniest smile fought its way onto her pale, freckled face, she couldn't help thinking that as much as could be the case in an ever changing situation just like this, things were very much going to plan. She knew wholeheartedly that Tank wouldn't let her down and was one hundred percent sure that right at this very moment, he and his team were heading directly for her.

If only she knew.

What had now become a silent standoff was abruptly broken by footsteps, the shuffling of feet and the slithering of nagas, from back at the start of the bridge.

Manson turned to face the direction of the interlopers, incensed at the interruption.

"WHAT THE HELL DO YOU THINK YOU'RE DOING?" he yelled, his voice magnified by the acoustics of the surroundings.

"SIRE!" the naga leading a long pack of monsters, nervously fired back, as Peter struggled to get his head around the irony.

"We thought you'd want to know about this immediately," stressed the naga in charge, the whole group drawing to a halt right in front of everybody.

"WELL? WHAT IS IT?" raged Manson, about ready to tear someone in two. Almost without a sound, the two lines of age old serpents that had been following their leader slithered off to the side, revealing three badly beaten human shaped captives and three dragon forms, two of them quite elderly.

Goosebumps raced up his arms, as a loud sigh forced its way through his parched lips. Gobsmacked beyond belief as almost every emotion possible gorged on his insides, Peter struggled to stay upright, unable to believe the sight before him.

TANK... his best friend, bleeding from almost every part of his body, looking downtrodden and broken. HOOK... most certainly and inexplicably here deep within the dragon domain, despite him being... HUMAN! And then the last of the three, his love, his soul mate, the being he wanted to spend the rest of his life with. Now he might just get that wish, but not at all in the way he'd hoped for. JANICE... here, now, battle scarred, damaged, bloodied, a right mess. Momentarily their eyes locked. In that instant, her love for him was revealed, despite the fact that he realised she must now know that he was a dragon. His heart leapt as the love he'd suppressed reignited inside him. But it was short lived as the sense of danger all around them closed in.

As Peter's heart leapt, Richie's fell into the deepest, darkest cavern within her mind.

'Tank, Hook and Janice... captured!' was all that she could think, from her vantage point high above the proceedings, as she slid down the wall beside the vent, her bottom slapping loudly on the floor. Momentarily unable to believe it, she wondered what on earth had gone on. Had they been lured into a trap? Overwhelmed? Made some sort of mistake? Knowing Tank inside and out, none of these seemed very likely. Smart and tactically aware, he would never have led the others into anything that even remotely looked like an ambush. Closing her eyes before running her fingers through her long, curly brown hair, she wondered how it had come to this, and just what they were supposed to do now. She'd counted on having the three of them fit... to fight, and armed, something they obviously weren't at the moment, as well as having the rest of their force with them. Given their absence, she had to assume they were dead, apart from the two elderly dragons and the healer from Salisbridge, who all looked like they were knocking on death's door. Alright, there were some King's Guards there, which might make up some of the difference, but could she just appear amongst them? Would it be enough? If she could free Peter and Tim, just maybe with the help of the king's force it might go their way. But uncertainty clouded her judgement. The opposing force looked to be mighty powerful in their own right and that was without taking the psychotic Manson and his deranged queen into account. Centring her balance, pulling in a deep breath, whilst still listening to everything going on down below her, she vowed to wait... at least a while, in the hope that one very obvious opportunity might present itself. If it did... she would be ready, of that there was no doubt.

"Well, well, well... just what do we have here?" scoffed Manson, ignoring the dragon king, limping over towards the new arrivals.

"As you predicted, my lord," ventured the leader of the small group, "we were attacked in the square outside the building by a small but potent force. These six represent all that remains of that force... four dragons and two humans. I thought you would be interested to know that there are humans here fighting alongside the dragons."

Eyeing the group with a sinister, malevolent contempt, a bubbling sense of familiarity rose slowly to the surface of the dark dragon's consciousness. Recognising Tank as one of Peter's best friends, and the young woman from the bar of that blasted sports club that should have gone up in smoke from the laminium bomb that had somehow failed, a sickeningly evil smile snaked its way across his clean-shaven face. He was going to enjoy this. Make them pay. Observe his lucky and bumbling nemesis suffering as he watched them all die.

For his part, he felt terrible. Not just physically, although if you'd taken all the injuries he'd ever suffered throughout his time playing rugby and put them all together, they still wouldn't have even come close to what had happened to him today. A wreck, even by dragon standards, and that was saying something, but it wasn't just his physical state. They were all dead, all because of him. It was his fault; he'd been in charge... their leader. And they were caught off guard. Clearly Manson's force had been lying in wait, specifically for them. How? He didn't know. But they had been. And now they were here, at what looked like the end of it all. Taking in everything around them, his brain told him there was nowhere to go, nothing he could do. And part of him believed it. But a much smaller part, deeper down, recognised that he just might be able to do something, however insignificant it might be, having heard a brief snippet of what was going on when they were brought in. What he needed was a little bit of luck. Pushing the pain to one side, and with his blood still dripping on the floor, Tank wondered just how he could give fate a subtle nudge in the right direction.

Remaining stoic, completely motionless and mightily afraid, surrounded by not only nagas, but dark dragons, their evil looking bastard swords only a hair's breadth away from being drawn, Amelia Battlehard slowed her breathing and reached out telepathically as far as she dared. It was a risk, she knew, especially given the way one of her dragons had been dispatched, but she felt there was no other alternative. Her life up until now had been all about duty, and even with the threat of death hanging over her, it still was. And so she was determined to go out on a high, fighting alongside those she was responsible for. If nothing else, they would do some damage to the enemy, and just maybe do some good for their monarch. As one, a tiny glowing triangle sprang to life in the minds of her fighting force. Outside this tight knit group, it would mean very little to anyone, only ever applicable to a young dragonling in his or her first year in the nursery ring, but to the well trained males and females under her command it meant only one thing. GET READY!

Despite feeling as broken as he could ever remember, that little spark of rebellion and defiance remained. And on seeing Peter's friend Tank and of all things... two humans dragged before him, it ignited something within him, causing him to throw caution to the winds, to once again stand up and be counted, all thoughts of the ring long since forgotten.

"ENOUGH!" declared the king, much to the shock of pretty much everyone there. "I've surrendered myself to you. No one else here needs to die. Let the others go, or I promise you I'll make things difficult."

Manson swivelled around on the spot, both his eyebrows wriggling to a different beat, unable to subdue an almost manic twitch that had developed just beneath his left eye.

Thinking this was it for their king, Amelia Battlehard readied the signal to attack, almost glad the time had come. But it was never going to be quite that easy.

"HAAAAHAAAAHAAAAAAAA," laughed Manson, doubling over in mirth, his change in attitude catching everyone off guard.

George stood puzzled, unable to believe what he was seeing.

For Peter, Tim, Tank, Janice and Hook, this only really confirmed what they'd all been suspecting, that Manson really was a deranged psychopath, probably with more than one personality fighting over the controls to his brain. It was a sight to behold, horrific beyond belief. What was more worrying though was the look of utter adoration sweeping across his queen's face. Madness like this could surely only exist in the depths of hell.

Standing up straight, tears of laughter streaming down both cheeks, Manson shook his head, getting rid of the last few chuckles.

"What on earth makes you think you're in any position to dictate anything?" he chided the king. "Do you really think your pitiful force could put up any sort of resistance against us? Or perhaps you're under the illusion that someone somewhere is coming to rescue you. I assure you they're not. The dragon realm is mine, alright maybe not quite all of it, but it won't be long before those small pockets of resistance are wiped off the face of the planet. In another twenty-four hours it will all be done. And then, we can do as we please. And let me assure you... WE WILL!"

Standing there in two minds, the king pondered which course of action he should take. One screamed to FIGHT! Use the magic of the ring if that were still at all possible, and go absolutely berserk, no matter what the consequences. The other cautioned reason, to wait and see what would happen, to try and negotiate. Both choices seemed downright catastrophic, with the sovereign finding it impossible to choose between them.

As Manson turned away from the monarch, back towards Tank, Janice and Hook, one of the nagas behind them slithered forward, brandishing Fu-ts'ang, a cold blue mist lighting up the air around it.

"The female... she was using this in the attack."

"Interesting," sneered Manson, limping closer to the increasingly afraid Janice, who was, by now, shivering in terror.

"Where did you get this, GIRL?" he fumed, his mood once again having turned itself on its head.

Janice said nothing, her eyes remaining focused firmly on the floor.

Mere metres away, Peter rallied against the chains containing his magic, binding him in place, much to Earth's amusement.

Manson stepped in close, grabbed Janice by the hair, forcing her to cry out in pain, and pulled her head up to his.

Peter gave everything he had. EVERYTHING! Still it wasn't enough.

"WHERE DID YOU GET IT?!" he bellowed right into her face.

Much as he hated to see Janice suffering, Tank recognised this as his one opportunity, and with unflinching resolve, he took it. Abruptly he shook off the two nagas holding him by the shoulders and, almost faster than the eye could see, grasped Manson's arm, squeezing his biceps with all his might, forcing the dark monster to relinquish his grip on Janice's hair, whilst at the same time screaming,

"Leave her alone!"

As Janice dropped to the floor, there was only ever going to be one outcome. Manson whirled furiously, catching Tank full on in the chest with a punch imbued with almost as much magical power as he had. A sickening CRUNCH saw the young rugby playing dragon scythe back through the air in the direction of the watching king. Mid-flight, two things happened, both using magic, but not the dragon kind.

When the three friends had first taken their places above ground in Salisbridge, having mastered maintaining their human forms, Tank, like the other two, had fully immersed himself in as much topside culture as he could. Briefly, the best description of him would have been 'nerd'. Quite by chance he'd stumbled into a tiny little comic book store called the 'The Floppy Tongue' on one of the main routes out of the city, and had fallen completely in love with tales of superheroes and their arch enemies. Comics and books were purchased, alongside action figures and other trinkets, all over a few weeks. Before he knew it, he was attending much bigger events, much further away. At one such event about fifty kilometres away in Bournemouth, his fascination for the human way of life took an about turn. Whilst in the foyer of the building, queuing to get in, he was approached by a well dressed man in a top hat, brandishing a deck of cards. Asked to pick one from the fan-like assortment in front of him, he did just that, watched eagerly by everyone in front and behind in the snaking line. To his utter astonishment, moments later, the magician, for that's what he was, revealed to him exactly what card he held, even though Tank was sure he hadn't seen it. Gasps of amazement and sharp intakes of breath, before a loud round of applause, were the order of the day. In that exact instant, all thoughts of comics, novels and action figures were forgotten for the youngster. Even with his dragon powers, Tank still couldn't figure out how the trick had been done. And that sent his mind racing, well... that and the applause and recognition the artist had received from those around him.

Many books and YouTube videos later, Tank found himself performing in front of Peter and Richie at almost every opportunity, much to the friends' amusement. Whilst he had eventually grown out of card tricks and sleight of hand, the skills that he'd gained remained with him at the back of his mind at all times. What, you're probably thinking, does this have to do with his current dilemma? Everything!

Flying backwards through the air, having taken the fiercest of punches before leaving the ground, Tank had altered his body shape to change his trajectory to get him to where he needed to be. Halfway to his intended destination, he twisted one hundred and eighty degrees, making the movement look natural in an effort to conceal what he was really up to. With the king looming large, and the young rugby playing dragon all but a blur, in one swift move, using all the sleight of hand he'd gained during his time impressing his friends, he reached down and grabbed the forgery of the king's ring that Gee Tee had given him, from the tiny little pocket on the side of one of his walking boots. Bracing himself for impact, he hoped the king would forgive him for what he was about to do.

'BOOM!' Tank hit the king full on in the chest, knocking the monarch to the hard stone floor, taking the wind right out of him, much to the amusement of Manson's hangers on. Having landed fully on top of George, Tank slowly untangled himself and rose gingerly to his feet, having already exchanged the fake ring for the real one on the king's finger, in the melee, hoping desperately that the monarch wouldn't give the game away. Deliberately losing his balance and falling painfully back to the floor on his arse, Tank secreted the real ring back in the small pocket of his shoe, in a sleight of hand even the best magicians in the world would be proud of, before being dragged upright by the two nagas that had previously been restraining him, who'd slithered over to his position next to the king.

With a grunt and a groan, George crawled back to his feet, eyes locked on Peter's friend, the master mantra maker's partner. Despite the unbelievable speed and precision with which it had been done, he knew what had happened and, in his mind, commended the young dragon for his bravery and cunning.

Still some way away from the action, even using her dragon abilities she couldn't see quite what had happened. But something had... something important if she was any judge. It was almost as if her friend had deliberately got himself thrown into the king. That just sounded stupid, she was sure. But that's what it had looked like. Why? That's what she asked herself, but no obvious reason presented itself. Logic would dictate it was to pass on some information, but she was certain nothing had been said. Perhaps they'd communicated telepathically, but she was sure their captors would have been on the lookout for that. It was odd, of that she was sure. Going back to flexing her muscles, and keeping alert, Richie felt sure that the moment of truth was fast approaching.

Giving the naga clutching Fu-ts'ang a nod, Manson ordered him to keep hold of it, knowing that now was not the time for a detailed inspection of the outlandish blade. Slipping back behind some of his colleagues, said naga marvelled at the sheer power contained within the weapon he was holding. Bathing in the cold radiance that it gave off, deep within his mind he coveted the awesome beast slayer for his own personal use.

Earth's surface. New Delhi, India.
It was virtually the same for nearly all twenty or so hospitals situated in and around New Delhi. A steady trickle of patients over the previous eleven days had stretched the infrastructure almost to breaking point. Cases of eye irritation, inflammation of the lungs, chest pains, breathing difficulties and asthma attacks had risen to an all time high, with patients lying two to a bed and, in some cases, stretched out on the floor in the corridors. It was bedlam on an unprecedented scale. Accident and emergency departments were working twenty four hours a

day, with extra doctors and nurses utterly exhausted, though committed to doing their very best for their patients, but still they couldn't get to grips with all the symptoms caused by the noxious smog cloud that hovered over the city, simply refusing to go away.

Today, however, things had ramped up to a totally different level. People from across the region had been presenting themselves all morning, coughing, wheezing, rubbing their bloodshot eyes, clutching at their chests, all deeply distressed. About mid-morning, individuals started showing up with extra indications of illness, as well as those already mentioned. On top of the familiar smog symptoms, people now complained of nausea, vomiting, diarrhoea, a high fever, dehydration and a couple of cases were actually foaming at the mouth. As you can imagine, this changed things a great deal. Government emergency contingencies were rushed into place as parts of the different hospitals were quarantined off, with infectious disease specialists attending as many sites as their limited manpower allowed them to in such a short space of time. As if all of this wasn't bad enough, anonymous leaks to national newspapers spread panic like wildfire, with families and individuals alike running for the hills, or in most cases driving. Every single road leading out of the city was at a standstill, as cars full of people rushed to get out into the countryside. In some cases whole families made up of several generations walked in the pitch black, alongside the mass of congestion, sucking in the poisonous petrol and diesel fumes, which understandably put them at more risk of becoming ill and spreading the airborne toxin to the outlying areas, something that supplemented the diabolical plan.

31 HOODWINKED

Lumbering breathlessly across the renowned bridge constructed purely out of magic by the naga contingent a short while earlier, an aged, primordial, dark shape, seemingly unable to take flight, straight out of history, hushed every other being in the king's private residence. Those few that didn't recognise him were cowed by the menace and power radiating off him in waves.

Very little frightened the king, after all he'd been there, done it... seen everything. But the sight of the being in his prehistoric form, that had tried to overthrow the kingdom all that time ago, terrified him right to his very core.

Battered, bruised, bleeding and yet to recover from Manson's brief interrogation of her, Janice was in a sorry state, suffering from as much pain as she'd ever known in her entire life. On catching a glimpse of the monster that laboured their way though, all her worries were trumped by something far more nightmarish.

Like the young bar worker right beside him, Hook had taken a beating and then some, but his injuries were far more severe. Left arm hanging limply by his side, clearly broken in more than one place, the pain feeding into his brain from that part of his body was agonising. Legs torn open and bleeding profusely made him look as though he'd been mauled by a pack of dogs. That was nothing compared with his head. Thick, dark red blood oozed from gaping wounds at the back and above both eyes, each of which could barely be seen, so horrendous was the purple and blue swelling. All of this was set off by a nose that was more mashed than broken, and what few teeth remained hung on loosely at unusual angles. A mess, he looked as though he could barely stand, wobbling uncontrollably every now and then. But just like his human comrade, everything was put firmly in perspective with the arrival of the ferocious looking beast that was now nearly upon them.

Earth's breath still tickling his ear, Peter's gaze flickered all over the place, barely able to believe what he was seeing. Just the sight of her broken and battered body caused his heart to swell, a vast array of emotions threatening to consume him. JANICE! OH JANICE! What the hell was she doing here? He'd thought he'd lost her, thought that she'd disappeared out of his life forever. But here she was, battle hardened by the look of things, standing alongside Tank and... HOOK, another human of all things, here in one of the dragon domain's most sacred places. Holding on to the love he felt for the young woman before him, he glanced over at the king, hoping for some kind of reassurance, anything that might make him think they'd be all right. Simply put though, absolute terror was the last thing he'd expected to see etched across the warrior monarch's face. Up until that point, a tiny part of him thought this was all a feint, a double bluff, and that the king was trying to hoodwink Manson and his cohorts. There and then, the hope inside him fizzled out, leaving him feeling helpless, powerless and full of regret. It had all gone so wrong, and now not only were the ones he loved about to pay the price, but the rest of the planet as well. In an emotionally charged delirium, momentarily his mind found itself back on the Astroturf on that cold November night, terrified and frightened, a stone's throw from death's door. Through the pain and the anguish he'd had a chance to finish off his bloodthirsty tormentor. And after short lived joy at thinking he'd done just that, the stark realisation of failure hit him only moments before the ice cold snowflakes pummelled his compromised falsehood of a body. If only he'd done it then. It would have drawn to a conclusion. It would have been over.

As the end of the bridge shuddered with every one of Troydenn's laboured steps, most of those held captive averted their gaze, desperate not to catch the attention of evil personified. Only the king watched, forcing himself to out of a mistaken sense of duty, well aware of what was to come.

One of those too afraid to look directly at the monster reaching the end of the bridge, Peter glanced across at his nemesis... Manson, and was surprised to see just the vaguest hint of fear embedded in his face.

'Odd!' he thought. 'Why would he be so afraid?' But there was no time to dwell on that, as the aged matt black beast spoke.

"Ahhhh... how delicious. Do you see how the roles have reversed, old dragon? Now I'm in charge of your fate, and by God you'll pay for encasing us all in that icy fortress. And I don't mean a little. I'll make sure you're tortured to within an inch of your life, and then brought back from the brink. Over and over it'll go. Years will pass as steadily you lose your mind, loathing and regret at handing over the dragon domain to me, and thoughts of what's happening to the entirety of the planet will slowly consume you. And once your mind is shattered, I'll parade your broken husk of a body across the earth so those that are left can see who and what was responsible for this sad turn of events. Don't worry though, those here won't be around to study your shame. They will have long since died."

While the nagas' faces remained deadpan, sickening, twisted grins writhed across most of the dark dragons' prehistoric jaw lines, at the thought of what was to come.

Momentarily, George considered taking his own life, denying Troydenn everything he wished for. But that was gone in an instant. Not only was it a coward's way out, something he most certainly wasn't, but it would have been difficult to achieve without the power of the real ring, something Tank now carried in the miniscule pocket of his right shoe.

Thrusting out his right arm, palm facing upwards, Manson stepped up to the king.

"Hand it over, old timer. NOW!"

A look of utter resignation ingrained on his face, George forced tears from both his eyes, determined to give no hint that anything was out of the ordinary. Slipping the ring from his finger with one hand, and wiping the tears from his eyes with the other, he searched for the words that he needed.

"I don't know what's wrong with it, but it hasn't obeyed me for some time. At first its conscious will rebelled against me. After that, it just fell silent. I have no idea what's going on. Good luck with getting it to work."

Snatching the ring greedily from the king, Manson smiled smugly.

"It'll work for me. I assure you."

Tank and George knew otherwise.

During all this, Janice kept her eyes firmly shut. The reasons for this were threefold. First, she didn't want to see any of it. Having caught one glimpse of the monster crossing the bridge was more than enough to see its evil intent and to know that things had gotten impossibly worse. Secondly, inside her mind, she was fighting against the pain of her injuries, trying desperately to put it to one side. That, however, wasn't really working. And last, but by no means least, she was trying to take a leaf out of Flash's book. And by that, I mean trying to contact what she now considered an extension of her... Fu-ts'ang. Having watched in awe back at the marketplace in Salisbridge as Flash had used just his mind to alter the trajectory of the deadly weapon as it had cut through the air, the young bar worker had wondered if it was at all possible for her to do the same. After all, it had spoken to her, and she did feel the resonance of some sort of connection, almost black and white if you will. Total opposites bonding because of that, the dark soul of Fu-ts'ang, designed expressly to kill, complemented perfectly with the purity of her beliefs.

They say opposites attract. In this case, they couldn't have called it better. Through the haze of the pain, she was almost sure Fu-ts'ang was there, hidden somewhere just in the background. Wishing and pleading hadn't worked so far, unless of course he was just ignoring her. Doubling her determination, she delved further into the depths of her mind, searching for that elusive connection.

Shivering involuntarily, Tim found himself riddled with fear, wishing to be anywhere else. Nightmares and horror movies had nothing on what was going on here and now. It wasn't possible. He'd told himself this dozens of times, but however hard he tried to believe, his surroundings remained, and the dreadfulness playing out in front of him continued. Throughout his suffering, one thought occupied his mind:

'I'm The White Dragon. I'm supposed to save them all. Just what am I expected to do?'

Full of himself as usual, and making a big play of it in front of his very 'captive' audience, Manson ruefully slipped the ring deftly onto his finger, ready and waiting to make its consciousness do his bidding. With everyone but Janice watching, the evil, dark dragon prepared to wrap whatever magic was within the ring, up into his overinflated will, forcing it to surrender to his every wish. But as every being there looked on with wonder and curiosity, the seconds ticked by, and as you might well have guessed, nothing happened.

Despite the seriousness of the situation, it was all the king could do not to smirk or laugh. Just watching him probe the inert ring with his mind, was utterly hilarious. Now he just waited for the impatience to show, his temper to rise, and he knew who would bear the brunt of it. It didn't take long.

"YOU! You've done something to it haven't you?" raged Manson at the king, from only a metre or so away.

"I've told you already. It's answerable to no one. I would have restored the bridge with the magic from it if I could have. But it would not obey my will. It refused steadfastly, before going totally silent. I have no control over it. Only the ring itself will choose whether or not to cooperate. It's happened in the past, but never quite on this scale. I don't know what else to say."

Sensing at least a hint of sincerity in the king's words, Manson turned to face his father Troydenn, hoping he would provide a different insight into the workings of the famed magical artefact.

"I sense no deception from him," grunted the matt black prehistoric monster, weaving his jaw around like a tree being blown in the wind. "I do know, however, that when the ring is passed down from king to king, it can often take days or even weeks before it responds to its new owner."

"Why the hell didn't you mention that before?" bellowed Manson, continuing to screw the ring up and down his finger.

From out of nowhere, one of Troydenn's gargantuan wings swept through the air, knocking Manson's feet from under him, causing him to crash to the ground unceremoniously. A sharp intake of breath from nearly every being there echoed off the walls.

"I don't know why you want that stupid bloody thing anyway. I've told you before it's the trident that you want, not that stupid band."

Much as the sight of both of them scared the living daylights out of Peter, in his mind he egged them both on, recognising the same madness in each, hoping that they would battle each other here and now, making each weaker, with the distinct possibility of death for one of them.

Tank couldn't take his eyes off what was happening,

like one of those awkward videos people post on the internet, thinking they're funny when they're most certainly not. It was a car crash moment. His thoughts, just like his friend's, centred on whether or not a fight would ensue. He hoped so, if only for the distraction it might create. If it allowed him to retrieve the ring, then who knew what was possible? Not having liked hearing that previous monarchs had taken days or even weeks to bond with the magical artefact, he needed it to be instantaneous, here and now. If it was, just maybe some kind of resistance was possible. If not, then they were all well and truly up that creek, with only their hands to use as paddles. That was something that didn't bear thinking about.

'Crikey,' she thought. 'You go for ages without any psychopathic dragons coming along, and then like buses, three arrive almost at once. What are the chances?' Not knowing what to make of what was going on down below her, she let a little more of the power from the laminium dagger fill her now human body, sensing that the time to strike might almost be upon her. If the two bat-shit crazy dragons down below could effectively neutralise each other, a rescue attempt might just be a real possibility, however unlikely. In her mind, it all came down to the King's Guards, dotted around the residence. If they could put up some real resistance against the nagas and dark dragons tasked with holding them captive, and if she could free one or two of the others, then just maybe they could finish off the leadership of the rebellion and... BOOM! Everything would be back to normal. But for that to happen, Manson and the matt black dark dragon had to start fighting each other. Otherwise it was all a waste of time.

Earth's surface. Washington DC, United States of America.

A tiny, high pitched alert echoed out from the speakers sitting either side of the two giant LCD monitors, indicating that the anonymous account he'd set up had received yet another email. Dropping his oddly shaped lower half to the floor, having had both legs draped across the front left edge of his polished wood desk, he reached for the wireless mouse and clicked the icon on the screen.

'Wow!' was all he could think, as yet more money ratcheted up the total he'd so far brought in for his own personal use from the ransomware attacks. It had only been running for a little over four hours, but now stood at somewhere in the region of eight million dollars. Deliberately avoiding law enforcement agencies, he'd let loose the virus across the world, at first targeting institutions that relied heavily on technology such as hospitals, power grids, pharmacies and refineries, creating as much chaos as he could, before moving on to the average home user. The more mayhem the merrier he'd been told, and that had been what he'd aimed for. The money itself hadn't been important to those higher up, it was all about distraction, and that was something he could get behind.

'I'm a genius,' he thought, reflecting on all the coding and other hard work he'd had to put in to reach this very point. He was, however, more than a little paranoid and with that in mind, strolled over to the panoramic window that wrapped itself around the tenth floor of his Georgetown condo. Instead of glancing out at the sunrise that had just started to edge above the glistening, flat water of the Potomac, silhouetting the tiny craft moored out in the middle of the slow moving body of water, he pushed his face right up to the reflective surface and glanced down at street level to the entrance to this particular block, hoping for all to be quiet. It was. There was NOTHING! And that included not a single black SUV skidding up to the lobby, with a dozen agents all converging on his position. That was good, he told himself. And besides, he and the others that had done all the work to put him here were way too smart to get caught out by the FBI or some other federal law enforcement agency. No doubt money had changed hands, palms greased as suspicious photos of important people in compromising positions had been brought to the fore. All of this told him he should be safe, at least for now. How much longer would it go on? This was all part of the effort to have his king released from captivity, but it had been going on way too long for his liking. Those at the top had got it wrong, as far as he was concerned, and were now being used, or worse, played with like an injured bird being dragged into the house through a cat flap, with absolutely no chance of escape. The first to laud and recognise everything their monarch had done for their race, pain tore away at his magical body hidden away behind this false form, at his belief that it was time to let their leader go, and break free from this spell these evil dark dragons constantly held over them. Of course, it wasn't his choice. He was just a tiny link in the chain, able to offer up very little in the way of input. For just a moment, he imagined being free along with the rest of his kind, surfing the achingly cold, white water of the Antarctic, gobbling down whole penguins, rolling in the soft snow. A wave of pleasure at the picture rolled through him, before another high pitched alert jolted him from his thoughts.

32 A ROOM WITH A VIEW

Lying prone, ignoring the blazing fires in the reflection of the window, the view was almost entirely as he remembered. Well... apart from the wicked looking beasts patrolling the perimeter, some strolling purposefully in pairs, others slithering in and out of the wreckage on their own, all armed to the teeth with magic and, by the look of things, all prepared to use it. It had been many decades since he'd been here, for an interview with one of the papers if his memory served him right. They'd wanted to know all about the Emporium's fall from grace and just who might have been behind it all. So he'd headed across London early one morning to meet a very attractive and very intelligent reporter in her office, in one of the buildings he was currently looking out on, right at this very moment. Fleet Street itself, here in the dragon domain, was a series of high rise offices, the tallest over twenty storeys high (second only to the council building in Buckingham), all laid out in concentric circles around the country's main node exchange, a single storey building lying smack bang in the middle of those circles, housing the mystical crystals that amplified the telepathic transfer of information across the world. That was their objective. As the memory of that day splintered into fragments, his thoughts centred on that reporter, hoping she'd not been present when things had gone straight to hell. Back in the here and now, Gee Tee locked his vision on a point out past the nearest fires, trying desperately hard to see the front of the building that contained the telepathic node, the whole reason they were here.

"Well?" asked an impatient voice from the darkness back towards the stairwell, on this... the eighth floor.

"It's well guarded," answered Steel, resting next to the master mantra maker.

"But can you see the node exchange? Is getting there unseen a real possibility?"

Scales covering the old shopkeeper's chin wobbled like a jelly on a unicycle traversing a cobbled street, as he turned to face the newly reborn laminium ball player.

"What do you think?" enquired Steel.

"I think there's still too much we can't see. While it doesn't look too bad from here, there could be an army in there waiting to ambush us."

Steel concurred.

"What do we do?"

"A little reconnoitre, in my opinion, should work wonders. But I don't know who to send."

"I'll go."

"Is that wise, young one?"

Steel chuckled softly at the master mantra maker's reference.

"While my body is yet to harden fully, my mind has a vast wealth of knowledge and experience to draw on. Best of all, I'm topped right up with magic. My mana reserves have never felt so vast. And don't worry. I'll be careful. I've too much to live for now. Who on earth ever gets a second chance at life, especially in a brand spanking new body? It'll be okay."

And so it was decided. Steel would infiltrate the main centre of Fleet Street, with a view to finding out just how heavily guarded the node exchange was.

Slipping down the stairs, the noise cancelling mantra aiding their descent, not giving away their position to the enemy, Steel announced to the others that he was off to look around. Jar Man and DomCon immediately volunteered to go with him, and much as he appreciated the sentiment, he knew it was better if he went on his own. Over the course of only a matter of hours, he'd really taken to the two of them. They were an odd couple to say the least, but their friendship was something to be admired, and their fighting spirit seemed to easily match that of anyone else here along for the ride. Bidding one last farewell, his shiny, new, yet-to-set body disappeared silently into the darkness. The entire group wished him well.

Huddled together on the ground floor, tired, weary, caked in sweat and soot, afraid, all wondering if they'd made the right decision in coming here, the four humans Sam, Taibul, Emma and Angela tried to fathom what on earth was going on. For each of them, their situation resembled a dream. It was hard to distinguish fantasy from reality. As they'd moved through the burnt out wasteland of what remained of the underground dragon domain, it had kept on getting harder. The encounter with Steel had been surreal and none of them had known where it was going. For the most part, it looked as though they'd have to fight, but the master mantra maker, who they had nothing but the greatest respect for, given what he'd done for them back in Salisbridge, had talked around the wise dragon in a newly formed body, allowing them to join in their ragtag band of misfits. Gee Tee had worked his magic... well, not literally, but more in a car salesman kind of way, selling the idea of teaming up to who they had gathered, was some kind of famous sports star. They'd all discussed it and none of them had known what the hell laminium ball was, but that didn't stop them wanting to see a match. Any sport that involved dragons taking on dragons had to be awesome. Didn't it?

Sitting in the dark silence, Sam started to massage Emma's back, not for the first time on this trip. It was just one sign of how much they'd done so far, and just how much more was ahead of them. As he stroked and pummelled her muscles, one thought weaved in and out of his mind, a thought that had remained a constant background presence throughout their journey here. What would happen if he were to die here? Nobody above ground would know, not his family or his friends. Of course there was a lot at stake, he realised that. And if they didn't complete the mission they were on, then just maybe the entire planet might be destroyed, but still... nobody knowing. It hurt just to think about it. As well, he wondered what was going on back up in Salisbridge right at this very moment. Their tiny little troupe of humans, as well as Hook and Janice, had been missing for some time. Surely people would have noticed by now, especially given the almost comical way they'd left the restaurant. Thoughts turning to his young friend's back, he dug his thumbs into her sore, tight muscles, kneading them for all they were worth, hoping to give her some sort of respite from the pain.

'It was all so different,' thought Angela, watching Sam weave his magic on Emma's back. From the acrid smell of smoke and sulphur, to the landscape with its high, cavernous roofs, sometimes impossible to see, to the buildings, or currently, what was left of them. It all seemed so alien. And then there were the dragons themselves. In this case, their teammates! How was that even possible? Taking a sneak peek at one of the nearest prehistoric monsters, she marvelled at the magnificent scales that looked utterly impregnable, the impossible wings that looked both flimsy and graceful, at the ferociousness of the mighty jaws and the soft light of intelligence ever present in the beings' bulbous green eyes. It terrified her, whilst at the same time made her heart sing. Dragons here, underground, and intelligent ones at that, helping to shape the planet and now trying to save it, was a mind blowing concept. And the whole of the human race up there, blissfully unaware of what was going on. How was this even possible? And then there was Richie... a dragon... unbelievable really, but not the most shocking thing about the last few days. Looking back though, at just some of the incredible things the young lacrosse captain had got up to, it kind of all made sense. If, of course, anything could in this bizarre world of supernatural power and ancient enemies. Curling up into a ball, hoping that Sam might turn his magic fingers onto her next, she closed her eyes, hoping to gain just a little rest.

It was all he could do to keep terrified in check. It constantly threatened to overwhelm him, and it was only the thought of letting down the others, his friends, there, that had prevented him falling apart. Young and idealistic, he'd had no idea what was going on when he'd joined Richie's disjointed party and left the restaurant, still wearing his waiter's outfit. The experience so far had been beyond his wildest imagination. And boy, did he have one of those. But all of this... wow! This was something else, barely believable, even though he'd been living amongst it for some time now. And THAT experience back in the giant market place, here underground in the world of the dragons was... EPIC! Okay, it had scared the living daylights out of him, with the blood, violence and gore forcing him to empty his stomach on more than one occasion. But what had gone on, and just how the day had been saved, was nothing short of legendary. Now here they were doing this. Gazing at the other humans, it was then that he realised just how grateful he was for their company. He couldn't imagine trying to do this without them. In fact, it would have been impossible for him to do so. Then and there though, the things that he missed flashed up in the forefront of his mind. Hook, Janice, Richie, his family, the restaurant, playing hockey and the rest of his team. Peter! Goodness, he'd almost forgotten about Peter, the person he owed so much to. Thoughts turning to the other mission, he hoped that they'd saved his teammate from the clutches of evil and that everything was going well for them. Rest... he knew it was important, and so watching Angela curl up into a ball in front of him, he laid his head on his shoulder, ignored the cold biting at his back from the wall he was leant against, and closed his eyes. For Taibul, sleep was hard to come by, with all the fantastical images playing out through his head.

Earth's surface. The Blue Mountains, just west of Sydney, Australia.

Mirroring events unfolding deep underground across the dragon domain, thick, choking black smoke blazed up into the air, visible from almost seventy kilometres away, as what had now turned into four major forest fires razed everything in their paths, leaving blackened vegetation, crispy fried animals and a wake of destruction behind them. Planes and helicopters peppered the area with massive bombs of water to little or no effect, the pilots risking their lives in the deadly and volatile high winds.

Plumes of yellow, red and orange flame snaked into the sky, some reaching heights of nearly ninety metres, often attempting to tickle the underside of the aircraft regularly attempting to curtail their out of control nature. Others transformed into huge red, superheated tornados, spinning precariously in a multitude of different directions, their course as random as a lottery winner, the magnitude of danger increasing tenfold.

Out of control, running north to south for about sixty kilometres, a swathe of fire and astonishing heat, one of the four cut directly across both of the main arteries leading west out of Sydney, the A32 and the B59, melting the tarmac and destroying the road's substructure, rendering a mass exodus in that direction all but impossible. Having already destroyed a huge strip of the Blue Mountain range itself, the fire, with the wind having changed direction, was now encroaching on the densely packed suburbs of Richmond and Penrith. Although used to the odd forest fire or two, residents across the whole of that area, from Sydney to Newcastle, had never witnessed such intense and dramatic weather conditions, with most being stunned into relative inactivity until it was much too late. Alerts went out across the news, ordering those that could to evacuate in either a northerly or southerly direction if at all possible. Main roads, particularly the M1 northbound heading up towards Newcastle and on towards Port Macquarie soon became clogged up with vehicles because of this, becoming every traveller's worst nightmare. And still the blazes burned on. Ferries, and boats conscripted at a moment's notice, jam packed full with passengers, headed out of Sydney harbour, as well as Botany Bay, their destinations unknown, their only objective to keep people safe and away from the end of days blaze that seemed to be swallowing up everything. It was Sydney's darkest hour.

Four hours later, and despite the best efforts of many hundreds of courageous fire fighters, the first of the suburbs capitulated to the unstoppable force of nature, with the demonic fire reducing the outlying areas of Richmond, Windsor and Londonderry to ash in under an hour. Nobody had ever witnessed anything like it, with the death toll already in its twenties.

Kanangra, in Boyd National Park to the south and west felt the full force of one of the other breakaway fires, stripping away bush, reducing walking trails to ash, forcing campers to flee in terror on foot in an effort to get to safety. Australia was suffering a humanitarian disaster of proportions never before seen in the country.

As ninety metre sheets of fire, flame, heat and rage converged on the city of Sydney, unsurprisingly, the culprits of the outrageous attack were nowhere to be seen.

33 SNOW POINT IN HANGING AROUND

It wasn't much of a choice, even he had to admit that. Stay here in the freezing cold wilderness in the hope that a rescue could be arranged at some point in the future. Or jump deliberately through an unknown magical portal that might possibly take you to the heart of the enemy's force. Almost as one, Yoyo and his youngsters snapped up the opportunity to accompany Flash, Fredric and Vasuki and leave this dire hellhole for good. He couldn't blame them, but he worried about what would greet them on the other side. That was, of course, if they made it that far. There was no guarantee. Even Vasuki had expressed as much. Conjuring up one of the magical portals was risky enough, but to use the power from the laminium chains currently winding their way around Fredric and transferring that power telepathically was madness of the highest order. Still... there was absolutely no other choice.

Running through a last minute battle checklist deep within his mind, the ex-Crimson Guard's thoughts turned to those of his friends. Were they safe? Had they managed to achieve their objectives? Were Peter and Tim still alive? A fragment of him hoped that it was all over and that the king and whatever troops he still commanded had thwarted the dastardly plot, captured or killed Manson, and that those he loved (yes... the friends he loved, a whole new concept for him, something he now realised) were safe and sound, waiting patiently for their return. But his experience and cynicism mocked him for such soft thoughts. Nothing was that easy, and this more so than anything else. Just from what little he'd seen, the planning behind this whole scheme had been militarily precise, and if that were the case, then contingencies for almost any eventuality would have been put into place. If that were so, then even with the element of surprise, they were facing an uphill battle. Finishing off his list, he pushed all thoughts of his friends to one side, the professional in him asserting its authority. Now was the time to focus, be ready and prepared, but for what? He didn't know. But with Fredric and himself enhanced by the laminium in the chains, Vasuki hoping to free the rest of his race, and Yoyo and his band of glory hunters all up for the fight, it would take a very special kind of adversary to stand any chance at all against them.

Apprehension at what lay ahead, more for those in his care than for himself, threatened to consume Yoyo, until he fought it off with all his mental resilience. They were here because of him. He'd got them in this mess. But staying in this long lost cavern was no option at all, of that he was sure. It was what awaited them that tore away at his soul. Just the king? Boy, would he be surprised if that were the case. An entire army of soul sucking dark dragons and nagas? That was never going to go well. Being the pragmatist that he was, he assumed it would be something in between. Even that didn't fill him with confidence. But he supposed better here and doing this, than waiting for the planet to be overrun with evil, and the chance to stop them long gone. And so after tending to each, and expressing his love for them one by one, he told them how valiantly they'd fought and how much the courage they'd shown would be needed for what was to come. Now if only it could be just the king in his dressing gown waiting for them below ground in London. That would answer all his prayers.

For Fredric, it was almost as if the clock had been turned back decades. Gone were his doubts, the pain from his captivity and his almost addictive urge for revenge which had now been satisfied. These were replaced by a shining confidence that mirrored the glimmering laminium chains that criss-crossed his well honed bare chest, along with a twinkle in his eye at the thought of not only getting his best friend back, but the grandson he barely knew.

Conflicted and barely able to believe he was free, Vasuki delved deep within himself, searching for the particular type of magic needed to open a portal. It was there, lying dormant, but sprang to life instantly at his command despite the decades that had passed since he'd last used it. Opening the powerful nexus would now be possible. The issue was having the energy to keep it that way long enough for everyone to pass through. Fredric and Flash had assured him they now possessed almost unlimited magical clout from the newly transformed metal of the chains that had kept them bound in this unforgivable hellhole. If so, then it should be possible. Much as his mind was on the task at hand, getting them out of here and back to the underground capital of Britain, somewhere he'd only heard tales about, he couldn't help but question his race's involvement in all this and wonder if he had the ability to turn it all around. Would his freedom free those nagas following this dreaded being Manson, or would they still remain somehow under his spell? He supposed that, shortly, they'd all find out.

34 SUCKER PUNCH

Staggering clumsily to his feet, Manson's scowl would surely have turned most beings to stone. But not his father, the gigantic, matt black dragon currently towering over him.

"YOU DON'T SPEAK TO ME LIKE THAT!" growled the elder of the two.

Manson's rage rolled off him like fog off the sea. It was there for all to see.

"SHALL I TAKE YOUR MIND AGAIN?" mocked the old dragon, pointing a sharpened talon in his son's direction. "I KNOW EXACTLY HOW YOU FEEL ABOUT THAT!"

Fury, wrath and anger caused him to seethe as his temper threatened to consume him. That stupid old man had to go and do it, he thought. Had to come out and belittle him in front of everyone here, but most importantly, in front of his queen, anyone but her. But he'd done it, and now wouldn't back down, still in denial about his power and position in all of this. Still thinking this was decades ago when just maybe he was the most influential being on the planet. Not now though. Things had changed... And although he'd planned on letting his father settle the score with his old adversary, the king, they'd planned for every eventuality... even this. So redistributing all his resentment and irritation, letting it dissipate into the atmosphere all around him, a serene look, one of total acceptance, appeared gracefully on his face.

"That's better. And don't you forget it," threatened Troydenn, more than a little lunacy coming across in his words. Turning to face his nemesis, the being responsible for their icy incarceration, he menacingly asked,

"The trident... where is it?"

With little interest in the weapon, Manson remained silent, not wanting to provoke his father further than he already had.

"OUT WITH IT!" spat Troydenn furiously. "I can't tell you how long I've looked forward to getting my hands on that thing. It will serve as a reminder of everything I've been through, and just how the tables have been turned. I won't ask again, where is it?"

Caught more than a little off guard, George's mind started to race at the first mention of the trident. A weapon steeped in history, forged by another race and keyed to the individual DNA of the dragon monarch of the day, it was as formidable a weapon as there could possibly be, easily matching Fu-ts'ang and Aviva's laminium dagger in both grace and magical power. For most of his reign, he hadn't let it out of his sight, with it always on hand in one form or other, there to boost his confidence, give him reassurance and provide that extra element of protection against any unwarranted threats. One of the supernatural properties it had been instilled with was the ability to transform into another object with just a mere thought from the one whose DNA it had been bound to. And so for many, many decades, George had carried it surreptitiously around with him in the form of his magnificent walking stick, up until quite recently that is. Something inside him had become bored of it, feeling it more of a burden than anything, particularly given that he'd never had cause to use it in anger. So it had been secreted away, deep within the recesses of his private rooms, ironically, not that far away from where he currently stood. Right at this very moment, he wished it were here more than anything, because just maybe it could turn the tide of everything that was playing out around him. For now though, he just had to lie. That weapon in the hands of Troydenn was a nightmarish scenario, even without it being keyed to the psychopathic dark dragon's DNA. And so he did.

"My... my... my predecessor lost it while battling a horde of mentally unstable, rogue vampires across Eastern Europe and Russia. Throughout the decades I've sent many out to search for it, but none have come even close to finding it," he stammered, hands shaking, unable to look directly at the dark dragon.

"REALLY! How convenient!"

"I never inherited it, only the ring, I swear."

"In all of my research about the ring, father," put in Manson, "not once did I ever come across an account of him with the trident. I think he's telling the truth."

Considering this for a few moments, much to the king's relief, which he most certainly didn't show, the matt black monster seemed to concede defeat, turning his attention to other matters.

"NOW show me this supposed White Dragon that I've heard all about for all these years," bellowed Troydenn, "I'd very much like to take a look at the dragon domain's so called saviour."

Standing beside Tim, Peter's focus now was solely on controlling his own body, stopping it from shaking, vomiting or peeing, in the hope that he himself wouldn't get noticed.

For his part, Tim tried to do the same, but with the ominous looking prehistoric beast stalking its way towards him, as Manson pointed him out, his legs shook violently, barely able to support his weight, and tears started to fill his eyes. His heart felt one beat away from stopping altogether.

"So you're it!" spat Troydenn contemptuously, his booming voice ruffling the hair of both Peter and Tim.

"Dragon got your tongue?" he goaded.

Tim, to his credit, at least had the good sense to keep his mouth shut, something both Peter and the king knew to be best.

"Does it speak?" Troydenn turned to ask Manson.

"It does," answered Earth from off to one side. "I do

believe that because it was still only human just a short time ago, it is absolutely terrified of everything in the dragon domain. Also, it's not quite sure that this is entirely real."

"Entirely real!" scoffed Troydenn.

"Indeed," answered Earth.

Giant primordial jaws swivelled slowly round to face George, the dragon king, Troydenn's glistening yellow eyes holding much menace.

"So this is what will save you, your precious White Dragon, the being from the prophecy that was predicted thousands of years ago. It's almost too amusing to take in. And just how is that supposed to happen, pray tell? Will he suddenly transform and take us all out?"

"Rumour has it that he can barely fly," chipped in Earth, adding to the king's consternation.

During all this, Janice still had her eyes closed, hugging her knees to her chest, having not gotten up from being knocked down during the melee in which Tank had been tossed viciously at the king. With her mind set firmly on one goal, she was certain she was getting blessedly closer to full on communication with Fu-ts'ang, or at least, that's how it felt. Although not able to see the dragon killing weapon, she could feel exactly where he was, gripped in two hands by a slimy naga three rows back from the front. She was so close. Giving up now was not an option.

Hook couldn't believe what he was seeing or hearing. He'd recognised the prisoner standing next to Peter as Tim, the treasurer of the Sports club. But all this talk of prophecy and a 'White Dragon', what the hell was that all about? There'd been no mention that Tim was a dragon, or that he was anything to do with a prophecy. Hard as it seemed, for Hook things had just gotten a whole lot stranger.

Keeping a straight face, George wondered where on earth all this was going. Playful, could best describe Troydenn's mood at the moment, having changed from chillingly terrifying at the flick of a switch. He knew it could turn back the other way at any moment, something he couldn't allow to happen. The prophecy (which had to be believed... it just did) described how The White Dragon would save them all. Without The White Dragon they were doomed, it was a well known fact about the prophecy taught throughout the dragon race. He and just about every other of their kind on the planet believed it with all their hearts. If something happened to Tim, there was no saving dragonkind or the earth itself.

"TROYDENN, YOU ARE SUCH A SELF ABSORBED..." that was as far as the king got in providing a distraction.

Out of the blue, Troydenn whirled, almost unseen so fast was he, catching Tim full on in the stomach with the punch to end all punches. Heavyweight champions across the world winced. Tim cried out as he cut through the air, a blur to Hook, who still couldn't believe what he was seeing. Landing with a dull 'THUD' and the sound of breaking bones, some way away, the supposed White Dragon found himself in a heap, almost directly below the vent that Richie had hunkered down in.

Instantly, the king took a step forward. Manson brought his cane around and swept the monarch off his feet. Peter rallied against his chains. Earth gave him a slap that caused his head to ring like the inside of a church bell. Throughout the residence, the King's Guards set themselves ready, only to find vicious looking bastard swords drawn, ready to carve them in two. Amelia Battlehard had been ready to give the order, go all out in one last stand to save not only her king, but The White Dragon as well. But in the blink of an eye, her troops had been neutralised; any attempt now would end up with nearly all of them dead, she knew. From across the shining marble floor, with the ancient text smattered across it, she caught the king's eye. And that said it all. She knew what was coming next.

Giant, purposeful strides reverberated around the hallowed sanctuary as the matt black personification of evil headed Tim's way.

Concealed from view behind the vent, her essence shrouded by the cloak, Richie stood up, banging her head for her trouble, trying to see how Tim had landed. 'Awkwardly' best described it.

Across the way, Manson savoured the moment, Earth likewise.

Fighting her urge to drop down and kick the mighty dragon's arse, Richie kept telling herself,

'He won't kill him, he's far too valuable,' hoping that if she said it enough, it would make it true. Unfortunately for her... it didn't!

Picking up the shattered body of the famed White Dragon, in one swift and deadly motion, Troydenn tore Tim in two.

Time stopped, as blood and guts hung motionless in the air. Voices ceased to sound. Surprise had found its niche and was doing a little jig at how accomplished it had become. Hope died. Love lost. But in that tiny sliver of a moment one thing above all happened... righteous fury ignited!

Turning to face every other being there, the two parts of Tim's destroyed body held high above his head for effect, Troydenn's smile couldn't have been any bigger or bolder... he was in his element and took delight in seeing almost every different emotion possible play out right in front of him. The king's dejected face and crushed spirit were the icing on top of the cake.

Apart from Tim's blood dripping onto the marble from a great height, silence reigned. That is until a huge twisted wreck of a metal plate clanged firmly onto the floor against the wall behind Troydenn's singular victory parade. Everyone, especially Manson, his queen and the dark troops, all glanced up to see what had happened, but only a sullen dark hole remained, nothing at all visible inside.

Having checked for danger and found none, every being's attention turned back to the mammoth monster, the dark destroyer, the primordial pariah. Strangely, he remained totally and utterly motionless, even his twisted grin of sick satisfaction unmoving.

'Odd,' thought almost everyone. That is until the reason why presented itself. Or should I say, herself?!

It was so close. That's all he knew, feeling even now the magic-laden blade within a heartbeat of taking his life. Now that he knew what to look for, he could sense another being beneath him, cloaked in the shadows his massive body created. But something, other than the obvious threat to his life, was wrong. On no account could he tell who or what this other being was. He had to assume it was a dragon, but it made no sense. If that were the case, surely he'd have recognised them, and would have acknowledged the threat long before it had got within his personal space. But if not dragon, then what? Naga? Certainly not human, that was for sure. Those puny, uneducated, self absorbed weaklings were way too cowardly to attempt such an audacious act. Currently though, it mattered not. What mattered was getting his son to act, to preserve his life, even if it put a dent in their plans. There would be another time, another place. The only thing of importance was that he lived.

In but an instant, more swords were drawn. Magic crackled and sparked as it was brought forth, yet to be released. Everyone became on guard.

Having aggressively ripped off the metal vent, Richie had tumbled to the ground behind it, letting it shield her from everyone's view. Moving faster than she ever had before, she'd slipped beneath Troydenn's massive, matt black belly, into the shadow created by his huge left leg, and slid her laminium dagger quite a long way into the evil dragon's weak spot, almost replicating what George had done with his well worn two-handed sword all those years ago. The tip of the dagger was now only millimetres from doing to Troydenn, what he'd just done to Tim. Ironic really, but that was lost on Richie, because she was way too far gone.

He couldn't help it, he really couldn't, despite the fact that he knew it was wrong. A smirk so smug that it could have belonged to a newly elected politician wriggled across the king's face, half of which was currently pressed against the cold marble of the floor. His view of what had occurred was wrong by about ninety degrees, but he couldn't have cared less, amazed at the sudden turnaround of events. Knowing the strength of feeling the young woman holding Troydenn to task had for the former White Dragon, it didn't take a genius to work out that things in the immediate future were going to go very badly for Tim's killer. Where that left all of them though, was anybody's guess.

"What the hell?" screamed Peter's brain as he blinked furiously, effectively doing a double take. "How is it possible she's here? The world's gone totally and utterly mad." It was then that he spotted it, sitting innocuously on her finger, the ring of dark metal, tiny blue triangles just visible through the gloom. It didn't explain how or why she was here, but he did at least understand what had gone on. She'd put on the ring and rediscovered her dragon memories. His friend was back. Back to her true self.

Revulsion at Tim's disgusting death instantaneously turned to hope as his friend stepped out of the shadows, fulfilling her vow to him about being there when needed. How she must have felt, he couldn't possibly even begin to guess. Witnessing the love of her life torn apart in front of her must have been enough to almost drive her insane. Silently he whispered a prayer for her, trusting that she would do the right thing, not just for Tim or herself, but for all of those here and indeed across the planet.

Eyes remaining closed, it was almost as if she could see

what had happened through the link that she'd forged with Fu-ts'ang. Outraged at the death of Tim, a warm trickle of relief filled her body at seeing the young lacrosse player gripping the hilt of her dagger, the blade of which was clearly stuck well into the monstrous dark dragon. A sense of relief swept across her mind, something Fu-ts'ang picked up through their bond, reinforcing that it was good Richie had joined the fight, but that now was not the time to be complacent or unfocused. The time was near at hand, he murmured, and they both had to be ready.

Almost succumbing to the pain gnawing at his broken bones and the despair squeezing at his weakened mind after having watched Tim's body stretched and finally broken in two, Hook's resolve returned ever so slightly at the sight of the being he considered his leader. After all, she was the one he'd followed down here, and the one that had got them all into this mess. For her to be here now was nothing short of magnificent, and something of a fairy tale ending. He just hoped that ending played out in their favour.

Stepping out of the shadows, still maintaining the grip on her dagger, which very firmly remained well inside Troydenn's weak spot, mere millimetres away from ending his life, Richie's face betrayed no sense of the emotional turmoil her body now felt. Anger, rage, confusion, loss... it was all there, buried deep beneath the overwhelming red mist that threatened to lead her down a very unwise path.

"AHHHH... If it isn't the pathetic little lacrosse playing dragon from Salisbridge. I heard you'd had your memory wiped, been cast out and turned into a human... how disappointing."

Part of her baulked at Manson's words, that were no doubt meant to sting her. But she shrugged it off, knowing full well that she was now in control of the situation.

Watching as Manson tried to get a rise out of her, Peter hoped to hell that Richie remembered the much bigger picture that was going on around her. She wanted to kill the monstrosity of a matt black dragon that she found herself nestled beneath, of that he was certain. But if she did, then they had no leverage over Manson and his bloodthirsty cohorts. Instead, she needed to remain calm, bargain to get them all released and then perhaps once back in the wider world it might be possible to regroup, assess the threat, and begin the process of winning back the domain and returning the rightful ruler to his throne. One diabolical act of revenge right now, was no good to anyone.

From the king's prone position one unusual thing rather stood out. Fear! Genuine fear sparkling there in Troydenn's bright yellow eyes. He'd recognise it anywhere and had never seen it or any sign of contrition ever in the being he thought of as his mortal enemy, only a short way away. Something else was going on, he thought. Some sort of subplot if he wasn't mistaken. Perhaps all was not quite what it seemed.

"So... what is it you want, lacrosse player?" challenged Manson, using the same inflection for lacrosse player that he usually reserved for the word 'Bentwhistle'.

It was a struggle, one of epic proportions. She was so close she could almost feel his life touching the tip of the legendary laminium dagger. 'Want' didn't do it justice... 'need', that was it. She needed to kill him. Make him pay. Nothing else mattered, not now that Tim was dead. But that tiny bit inside her, the rational bit, the one tucked away in the back of her mind, surrounded by darkness, with currently no friends at all, grappled for her attention... it screamed at her to take in her surroundings, look at what was going on, who was here and recognise the stakes of the game being played out around her.

For some of the others, for example the king, Amelia Battlehard, and the troops under her command, witnessing the death of The White Dragon from the prophecy they'd all grown up believing in, having had it instilled in them through their formative years in the nursery ring, was a heart wrenching, hope destroying act of utter malevolence, something that was no doubt Troydenn's very intention. Peter though, standing there with Earth still hovering behind him, had just put the pieces together.

'That's it! She is, and always was, The White Dragon. I knew it. Perhaps things aren't so messed up after all.' Just how wrong could one person be?

Taking note of all the beings in range, particularly Peter, Tank, Janice and Hook, it was the rational component of Richie's mind that gained the upper hand and stepped forth.

"Let them all go... NOW! Or he dies," she commanded.

"Listen to her, son. I think she means business," implored Troydenn, sounding more than a little stressed.

Scratching his stubbly chin, tapping his cane on the marble, all the time circling the prone form of the king, Manson appeared to consider Richie's demand. Abruptly though, he turned to face the human shaped dragon interloper.

"KILL HIM. SEE IF WE CARE!"

The look on Richie's face was a picture, but nothing compared with the look on Troydenn's. It wasn't what Richie or the elderly dragon above her had been expecting. How things progressed now was anyone's guess.

Earth's surface. Amazon River Basin, Brazil.
You'd think the rain forest would be used to being bombarded by a little precipitation, given its name, but here and now the circumstances were like nothing that had

ever gone before. Driving rain continued to pelt down, just like it had been doing for over six days without any let up, in warm, moist streams that stung when they hit the skin. Water levels had long since exceeded all records, and with this being midway through what was considered the dry season, people up and down the Amazon were rightly fearful for their lives. Villages had flooded before the end of the first day's rain, with a national emergency being declared along nearly the entire length of the waterway. From Macapa at the estuary, where the river meets the Atlantic ocean, back upstream far beyond Manaus, covering some 1600 kilometres, the mighty Amazon had long since burst its banks, causing whole communities to flee, ruining wildlife and habitats, destroying valuable areas of land and putting human life at imminent risk. Sloths were isolated, even though they can swim, with the few who made it to relative safety having to move far faster than their agonisingly slow average speed, for the first time in their lives. Jaguars bounded away from their natural hunting grounds at speed. Capybaras and anteaters, with their food sources destroyed, had little choice but to slope off inland in search of alternatives. Intensely dazzling poison dart frogs, covered in slippery potent venom, leapt from leaf to leaf, much higher up in the forest's canopy then they normally would be, whilst piranhas and black caiman stalked through the raised water, discovering uncharted territory. It was a catastrophe unmatched in modern times, affecting every single creature located within five kilometres either side of the mighty Amazon. Worse still, there seemed no let up in the magically induced deluge, with forecasters unable to predict when it would stop.

The culprits responsible for the relentless, supernatural downpour, all five nagas in disguise, had fled the area almost immediately, paying passage on a boat that headed up stream, eventually peeling off into a tributary called the Ucayali, which would lead them south, ultimately ending up in Pucallpa, where they were now, after over five days of travel. On the long, tedious journey, all five of them dreamed of slipping over the side into the murky, fast flowing water, but each knew better than to risk their cover identities, now with the end of days, and the supposed return of their king, so close. Instead, they sat quietly, keeping themselves to themselves, avoiding the other passengers, making absolutely no trouble and very little fuss, trying to blend in and be totally forgotten. For the most part, it had worked perfectly. Through their hidden telepathy, they'd discussed what kind of mischief they could get up to on reaching their destination. Fires, imbuing some of the local wildlife with temporary magical powers and murdering sprees were just some of the suggestions considered. In the end though, they decided to wait until they reached Pucallpa to see if anything obvious jumped out at them.

Within minutes of disembarking, the small group were sitting down at a table in the nearest bar, nursing drinks, letting their unfamiliar bodies get used to the feeling of being back on land again. Blending in once again, all five of them used their magical abilities to listen in on conversations, whilst simultaneously watching the news reports blasting out from the television on the wall. Unsurprisingly, all the talk was of the unremitting downpour across the Amazon basin, the flooding and of course devastation. Fear in the voices of the other customers was evident, with each and every one of them concerned about the same thing happening here. Realisation of that very fact brought a smile to all five faces at once. The mischief needed was identified in an instant. They would of course be doing exactly what they'd done before, and not only would it terrify and ruin lives here, but much further down the line it would once again bring fright, horror and panic to those already suffering, further downstream, killing two birds with one stone if you like. Supping contently, all five imagined the chaos it would cause, and the recognition they would gain.

35 A SURPRISE RETURN

Huddled in and around the outreach building on the outskirts of Fleet Street itself, Gee Tee's rather large group lay low in and amongst the shadows, guards patrolling the perimeter; only their breathing could be heard. Amongst them, the small human contingent slept, curled up next to each other, exhausted not only from the journey, but from the stress of constant unseen threats. Their dragon comrades watched over each of them as if they were one of their own.

With Jar Man and DomCon sharing rude and amusing stories in one corner, quietly Gee Tee delved the depths of his knowledge searching for anything that might be useful in their forthcoming attempt to retake the crystal node. Suddenly, from out of nowhere, a hooded, cloaked intruder appeared amongst them. Too startled to even react, let alone put up any sort of defence, the dragon force scrambled to get to their feet. But by the time they had, the need to do so had evaporated.

"Nice to know you're all paying attention," smirked Steel, having folded down the dark green hood that had concealed his face.

"You surprised the living daylights out of us. How on earth did you get in here without the guards spotting you?" queried the master mantra maker, the others all looking on, eager to know the answer.

"I think it's something in these cloaks and hoods. There are a few human shapes wearing these in and around where we want to be. I'm not sure if they're dragon or naga... it's difficult to tell. But inside one of the storage buildings, they had a supply of them. So naturally I appropriated as many as I could."

"What about the node exchange? Is there an army there waiting to ambush us?"

"Not an army, no. But enough of them to make it quite an even fight, if you take into account the hooded and cloaked shapes patrolling the outskirts."

"I see," remarked the old shopkeeper, thinking. "Do you have anything in mind that might help us gain the advantage over all of them?"

Nodding in the direction of Jar Man and DomCon, whilst continuing to smirk, Steel replied,

"I believe I do."

36 TOOLED UP

With Yoyo's youngsters having looted weapons from the corpses of those who'd tried to slay them, whilst a group of the gifted individuals had cobbled together two of the heat insulating camouflage suits from the tatters that remained after the fight, they were almost ready to act and be gone from this place. Hillier and a young dragon by the name of Zebediah had the honour and responsibility of donning the two working suits that would render each of them all but invisible. It had been stressed just how important they would be, should their force find themselves in the middle of a pitched battle. They weren't to focus on one target, but were to move as fast as they could, saving dragon lives where possible in order to keep as many of them and their allies alive, sustaining the size and momentum on their side of the battle. Not all believed that they would blunder into the enemy; most of the youngsters thought the worst they would find would be a bad tempered king who very much disliked having his privacy disrupted. But not Flash, Yoyo, or Fredric. Realists each and every one of them, they'd seen fate in action before, albeit not on this kind of scale, and had a vague idea of how she worked. Each of them figured they'd be walking into a full-scale war.

Surrounded by a wall so white and bright that thirty full sized polar bears could currently be hiding against its backdrop, the icy vault they found themselves in had started to feel claustrophobic for most of them. But in only a few moments, that wouldn't matter. Gathered together as a group, the naga king at the front, Fredric and Flash behind him, followed closely by Yoyo and his band, the atmosphere was quite literally electric, zigzagging lines of radiant magic zipping amongst the stalactites and stalagmites, burning through the ice and snow, crackling into the rock, steam rising into the chilly air.

The upper part of his body weaving from side to side, the naga king resembled a snake that had been charmed, guttural moans and noises that could have been words, at least for another race, slipped from his lips, barely audible over the hissing of electricity.

Chests bare and puffed out, the laminium chains crisscrossed the two former Crimson Guards creating a large X over each of their torsos, not weighing them down at all, quite the opposite in fact. Both dragons were determined to be the first through the wormhole when it opened. Flash because it was his mind the naga king was taking the coordinates from to determine the exit point, which was thought best as he had stayed at the king's private residence. And Fredric because he was desperate to see his friend... the king, and put a stop to whatever heinous crimes were in the middle of being committed. Once a leader, always a leader as far as he was concerned, and so with the wide-eyed young dragons lined up behind a very worried looking Yoyo, magic and mayhem erupted in the cavern, as a blinding bright green circle of light, constantly rotating, appeared, about the size of a tennis ball to start with, getting ever bigger with every second that passed.

His face bathed in the eerie green light from the portal, Fredric turned to face Flash, and with the tiniest of grins at the thought of finally leaving what had been his prison for so long, said,

"Let's do this, shall we?"

37 BLUFFING, HUFFING AND PUFFING

'It's just a bluff. It has to be,' thought Peter, taking in everything that was playing out before him. 'An outlandish one, it has to be said, but nevertheless a bluff.'

Tank felt the same way, momentarily anyway. But the young rugby playing dragon was a good judge of character and an excellent reader of beings of any sort, something that here and now gave him cause for concern.

'I think Manson might actually mean it,' crossed his mind, on studying the evil dark dragon's face from a distance.

You'd have thought George would have had some insight, given how long he'd been on the planet and some of the roles he'd played during that time, but he was as confused as everyone else, including the gobsmacked Richie, whose mind was racing with everything going on.

Just like her best friend, the only real conclusion it was possible for her to reach was that it was a bluff, designed to throw her off guard and buy Manson's opposing force more time to get into position. Well, they could be bloody sure she wasn't about to let that happen.

"I'LL DO IT!" she exclaimed, sliding the laminium dagger's blade another millimetre or two deeper into Troydenn's underbelly, much to the elderly dragon's horror, the battle for her sanity playing out across her delicate freckled face.

"GO ON THEN," urged Manson, his mouth coiling up into a very sick smirk.

"SON!" boomed Troydenn's voice, almost knocking down those closest to the ground with the full force of it. "THIS IS NOT THE TIME FOR GAMES!"

Still smiling, the hateful beast, egged on by his queen, locked eyes with his father. It was then that Troydenn knew. This had been the plan all along. Well, maybe not this... but his death at some point. Having served his purpose he'd been betrayed by his ungrateful, spiteful son. In finally coming to realise he'd been well and truly stitched up, a small part of him couldn't help but admire what his offspring had achieved. Something he probably would have done had their positions been reversed... a deed so very Troydennesque. Never in a million years had he thought the young half-breed had it in him to be so ruthless. Clearly he'd taught him well, and he would die appreciating that he'd learned from the very best there was. Knowing now that there was no way out, at least not with the help of his so-called allies, Troydenn, master of the dark, leader of coups and survivor of that sickly ice palace he'd been imprisoned in for so long, decided to take matters into his own hands. And so summoning every molecule of magic that existed inside his own body, he fed it directly into himself in an effort to increase his speed for what he was about to do, convinced he could fly up and off the blade before whoever it was that held him captive had a chance to react.

More than anything... it was a feeling. Prickly, if she had to put words to it. That's how it felt. But it was a magical prickly, rather than a normal prickly or an imaginary prickly. The supernatural was most certainly involved, and that could only mean one thing... he was about to try and escape. Not on her watch. Without hesitation, and while keeping the blade at the exact same depth within the mighty dragon's weak spot, Richie pushed her hand gripping the hilt of the dagger deeper into the matt black belly of the beast, reminding her of Flash's torture back in Salisbridge marketplace. As her hand pushed through the gloop, and up against an organ or two, she fought valiantly to contain the nausea inside her. There... the tip of the blade remained in exactly the same spot, but now, having pushed her hand deep inside, the whole of the dagger was almost horizontal, making flying up and off the cutting edge all but impossible, even with magical assistance.

But a moment away from reacting suddenly he felt movement... inside him. Anger roared through him at the timing of his enemy's counter. Had they known what he was about to do? He wouldn't have thought it possible. Even so, it seemed unlikely it was a coincidence. Whoever was down there had real power with a mind to match and, as far as he was concerned, presented a very real threat, not only to him, but to his son and that bitch of a queen he fawned over. Why couldn't they see that? Together they were stronger and could defeat whoever it was, but on their own, little breaches opened up in their defences, breaches that if they weren't careful, could become full blown liabilities.

'Oh son... what on earth have you done?'

Manson was able to sense it, he always could when his father was about to unleash something magical... an attack, an escape, a diversion, just something. And then abruptly, he stopped. On closer inspection, he noticed that the young lacrosse player, dragon, human, whatever she now was, had adjusted her point of attack, no doubt preventing him from either fleeing or striking out. Ha! How ironic was that? He'd spent an age mulling over just how he would do it. Poison... that seemed like a good one, but there were unaccountable risks involved. Killing him in his sleep had been next on his list. But he wouldn't put it past the old dragon to lay magical traps just in case of treachery. While his father had taught him a great deal of what he knew, of one thing he was totally sure, that he hadn't taught him everything. And knowing the crafty old scum bag, he'd saved the best for last, for his personal protection, should the time come. A surprise combined all out attack from everyone... himself, Earth, each and every one of the guards... he'd determined that course of action to be the riskiest of all. Troydenn was powerful, even as aged as he was, and he knew better than to underestimate the elderly vulture. Just like books, you should never, ever judge a dragon by their cover.

Glancing away momentarily from what was transpiring, Peter caught the barest hint of fear in the king's eyes, something that immediately made him worry about his friend's predicament. If George had cause to be afraid, then almost certainly Richie had bitten off more than she could chew. In his mind, there was now no way this played in their favour. Whether Manson wanted the old dragon dead, or whether he was just bluffing, either way, Richie was in over her head so to speak. After the debacle with transferring her consciousness into the ring, he just couldn't lose her again. Allowing his mind to fold up into itself he frantically started searching for anything... anything at all that would help him out. He'd done it twice already, on the march to London. But this time he redoubled his efforts, determined not to let his friend down when she needed him the most.

Out of nowhere, the background noise, haze and clutter that had been playing out over the top of their bond ceased. Eyes still closed, a deep serenity consumed not only Janice, but Fu-ts'ang as well. Across the mental connection, they shared everything. Janice's love for Peter, her surprise at the events of the last couple of days, and just what kind of person she was. The experienced killer weapon forged many thousands of years ago briefly got to glimpse through a window into her soul. And was surprised at what it found. Good: pure, honest to God good. If it were at all possible, he/it was slightly taken aback, having never come across this from any of his previous wielders. Mostly they'd had dark, morbid souls. Oh don't get me wrong... some were well intentioned... but overwhelmingly they were killers, takers of lives, perhaps doing the right thing for the wrong reason, or the wrong thing for the right reason. Never before had he encountered such a shining beacon of decency, her goal utterly selfless, attempting to rescue the one she loved. And surrounding that bright, white, noble soul were all the other virtues that she possessed. Courage, bravery, kindness, compassion, a strong will and a high regard for other beings, not just people.

'This one,' thought Fu-ts'ang, 'is like nothing I've ever encountered before. She's special, and not just a little.'

All too well aware of the responsibility he carried in the form of one of the most powerful magical artefacts on the entire planet, tucked away out of sight in the tiniest pocket in the world on the side of one of his walking boots, Tank only had a bad feeling about where this was all going. After having watched Richie let her anger get the better of her and back herself into a corner with nowhere else to go, Manson's bluff, if that's what it was, had now weakened her position considerably, at least in his mind. If she killed the monstrous matt black beast, and there was no doubting in his mind that she wished to, then there would be no hiding. There would be no way out, and undoubtedly Manson's entire force would attack her as one, resulting in one thing only. HER DEATH! If she conceded just a little, then just maybe she could bargain for their lives, that is if Manson's play was a bluff. If it was, then he must have been the best poker player in the world, because right now, as it stood, it did truly look as though the evil dark dragon and ex-hockey player wouldn't mind one bit if Richie exacted her revenge for Tim's very brutal and public execution. Knowing he had to be ready to act, he slowed his racing heart, ran through in his mind how the first few seconds of the encounter would play out, and hoped to hell that once on his finger, the temperamental ring would obey his every command straight away. If it didn't, then they really were in awesome amounts of trouble.

Not daring even to gulp, due to the cold dark metal of the wicked looking bastard sword held firmly against her throat, Amelia Battlehard looked on in admiration at what the young woman, previously a dragon (yes... she knew all about the lacrosse player, and most of the stunts she'd gotten up to on the surface) had achieved. Taking a dragon such as Troydenn by surprise was no easy feat. For a split second, she wondered how she'd done it. Magic... maybe, skill, cunning and guile... quite possibly... or something else. Maybe even a combination of all of those things. However it had happened though, it gave them a worthy distraction, something they hadn't had before. So immersing herself fully into the situation, the dragon captain got ready to give the signal, knowing that more of her troops would die than live during the first few seconds of the fight, given the precarious situation they all found themselves in. Now was not the time to be sorry about that. Now was the time to focus, concentrate, be ready. Later there would be time for mourning. Now was the time to fight, fight for their monarch. And win not only their freedom, but that of the planet as well.

Dagger in almost as far as it would go, and up to her elbow in Troydenn, she fought off the red mist threatening to engulf her, realising that whatever action she took next didn't just affect her, but had massive ramifications for her friends and the king, as well as the entire planet.

'Be calm,' she told herself, inhaling another deep breath, holding it in, and then puffing it out and starting over again.

Patience not really being his strong suit, Manson had become tired and almost bored with the situation. All he wanted was for it to be over. And with that in mind, he decided to take action.

"So," he announced to everyone present, his words clearly aimed at Richie, "you're a spineless coward just like your friends here. It doesn't surprise me. BENTWHISTLE had the chance to finish me off some time ago, but lacked both the courage and intelligence to follow through on such a deed. I can see now that you're made from exactly the same stuff. As well, I suppose being a female must make it so much harder. Having to fight I mean. Generally you're all frightened little children, who are far better off staying at home, cooking, cleaning, minding the offspring, awaiting the return of the warrior of the house."

As goads went, he wasn't sure it would work, not knowing her personality all that well. But what he did know was that she was already steaming mad from watching The White Dragon having been torn in half directly in front of her. A few provocative words might just help rile her up.

Peter and Tank had exactly the same thought simultaneously.

"UH OH!"

Knowing their friend as well as they did, and having a pretty good idea of just how she felt having witnessed the brutal death of the one she loved, there was now no doubt in their minds that things had just taken a huge turn for the worse, if that were at all possible given the current situation. It would be all but impossible for the young lacrosse player to ignore everything Manson had just said. If he'd wanted to provoke her and prod her into killing his father, he'd probably just achieved his aim.

Huffing at the disgust she felt for the words aimed towards her, deep inside Troydenn's belly her hand wobbled almost imperceptibly, as fury and rage roiled off her and a smoke-like fog clouded her normally clear thinking brain. 'WANT!' There it was again, that word, fully encompassing her body, pumping through her blood stream, weaving in and out of every sinew, every fibre of her being. What did she WANT? The answer stared directly back at her, already there, not taking any time at all to form... she wanted to kill him. Here and now. It was an overwhelming urge, irresistible, overpowering, almost an addiction. Normally, she'd have been one of the most equipped beings on the planet to fight off all of these things, loaded to the core with self confidence, belief and faith that she could achieve anything she set her mind to. But not now, not after seeing what had happened to Tim. Her defences were not just broken, they'd been fully swept away by the onslaught of pain. Her suffering was not there for everyone to see, but it was there and had left her vulnerable and in a position to be abused and manipulated. Manson had known that, and was in fact counting on it to achieve just one of his many goals. And no matter how hard she fought (and she tried, by God she tried) there was never going to be any other outcome. Boiling with rage, anger and wrath crushing her soul, eventually she conceded defeat and let the darkness consume her. Mustering every ounce of strength and as much magic as the dagger would let her, in one passion filled act of revenge, as much for her as the one she'd lost, she shoved the dagger as far as she dared into the prehistoric creature that had caused so much trouble for the dragon domain over the centuries, and be damned with the consequences.

Glass splintered, books dropped from shelves up in the library, pages torn, scattering everywhere, as every being there winced in pain at dying Troydenn's last, shrill roar. Eardrums of those closest exploded, apart from Richie who'd gained limited protection because of where she stood. As the grotesque scream subsided, the mammoth dragon's sinister black body wobbled somewhat, before shaking uncontrollably. Still consumed with her act of vengeance, Richie remained rooted to the ground firmly below the dying dinosaur. Her mind screamed, "RUN," but her body ignored it completely.

Exactly the same thought ran through the heads of two beings on totally opposite sides of events playing out.

'SHE'S DONE IT! HE'S DEAD!' For George it was nothing short of sad, despite what had gone on in the past and the fact that his nemesis had promised to torture him for many years to come. A small part of him had hoped to talk him round, maybe even provide some sort of redemption and a turning point in everything that was going on.

For Manson, it was majestic, and he was nothing short of ecstatic. Washed away were his fears. No longer did he have to worry about his father invading his mind, controlling not only his thoughts, but his body as well. For that, he had to thank the young lacrosse player. Perhaps it was time to get right on that.

As the giant prehistoric corpse finally collapsed, almost on auto pilot Richie leapt and rolled from under the mighty beast, jumping to her feet right in the corner below the secretive entrance she'd appeared from a little earlier. Glancing up at the now exposed housing, she knew the only way back up there was to take dragon form and fly, something that in her current condition was a complete impossibility. Having her memories back was one thing; unlocking the bonds of her DNA that maintained her ape like form was something else entirely. As the tiny particles of dust started to settle and the ground stopped shuddering, Manson closed his eyes and directed his commands telepathically towards the guards.

Leaving the King's Guard dragons they were watching over, half a dozen of the vile looking dark prehistoric monsters stalked forward towards Richie, all of them drawing their swords from their black scabbards, a high pitched metal ring splintering the air.

Panic consumed Peter. They were going to kill her here and now and he had to stop it, he just had to. With everything he had, he fought to break free of the magical binders constraining him.

Tank was of the same mind. They weren't going to take her, not as long as he breathed. And so all thoughts of the king's magical ring put to one side, he readied himself for action, knowing that in all likelihood, he'd be dead in only a matter of moments.

Although most of her mind was elsewhere, she knew exactly what was playing out around her. She was in trouble. Big trouble! Janice had a pretty good idea of what was coming. Peter and Tank would not see their friend harmed, and would most certainly lay down their lives to prevent that from happening. Redoubling her efforts, she fought to persuade her friend, the living weapon, to do her bidding.

Broken and feeling as though he'd been hit by a freight train, the rugby player in him bubbled to the fore, watching what was about to unfold in front of him. Although she didn't play his sport, their bond had been forged, as he knew they were pretty much the same inside. And knowing that others around him were almost certainly about to give their all in a futile attempt to save the young lacrosse player's life, Hook pushed aside the pain and prepared for one last hurrah.

Despite things looking as hopeless as ever, Amelia Battlehard recognised her one and only opportunity, and with a polished black blade twitching against her throat, she doubted she would survive long enough to join in. But the others, those under her command, deserved a chance, no matter how remote, to fight for their lives, their king, their domain. Closing her eyes, she prepared to send out the go ahead.

Startled from the shock of seeing his ancient nemesis killed in front of him, all the king could think of was just how wrong things had gone, and how much worse they were about to get. Part of him longed for the ring, but given that it had done nothing but ignore him, he couldn't see how that would help the current situation. Helpless, all he could do was look on and pray for some sort of miracle.

38 GATECRASHERS

A pinprick of light, somewhere in the middle of the private residence, that's how it started. Barely visible, even with the super enhanced senses of the individuals present, it wouldn't be long before the magic feeding it lit up the space, announcing its presence to all and sundry.

Gripping the laminium dagger so tightly that the impression of its hilt almost burned into her palm, Richie faced her attackers with all the gusto she'd lived her life. Unafraid, well for herself anyway, the only reservations and fears she had were for her friends. Unfortunately though, even those thoughts hadn't managed to manifest themselves anywhere near the forefront of her thinking. Still clouded by darkness, anger, fury and thoughts of more retribution, she had little awareness of the trouble she was actually in.

Oddly, it was Janice that noticed it first... with a little prompting from her new found friend.

'Something's happening... something significant. Be ready,' warned the weapon.

And then it increased in size almost exponentially. Everything and everyone stopped and stared in awe as the whirling, twirling vortex of writhing, dark energy manifested itself in the form of a giant, blinding, green wormhole right in the middle of the residence. Magic churned around its circumference as thick, crackling, black tendrils of charged energy tried to snake free. Thunder rolled, shaking the ground. Looking more liquid than either solid or gas, the wormhole's constantly rotating accretion disc bubbled and writhed as tiny concentric ripples echoed out from its centre.

Manson threw Earth a look, wondering if it were somehow her doing. Her puzzled response had him swiftly conclude that it wasn't.

Bruised and battered, his spirit almost torn in two, slumped across the cold marble floor, George, the current dragon king, could only guess at what had appeared before them. There had been legends, documented somewhere on the upper levels of this very library, about extremely powerful beings, able to cast portals from one part of the planet to another. But as far as he knew, those that could do this were all long gone.

'If not that though, then what?' he thought to himself.

Janice could barely keep up with what was going on. Not the appearance of the wormhole though. She'd sneaked a peek through mainly closed eyes. No not that. Fu-ts'ang's excitement. There was lots of babbling, something about the 'lost soul not being broken any more, and about to return,' whatever that meant. All that she knew though, was that she needed to be ready to act. Things were still balanced on a knife edge, and this could well be their one and only chance.

Peter's brain felt scrambled. He'd been using all his mental force to try and access his magic and escape from these blasted binders when 'whooof', out of nowhere, that thing had appeared. It was hypnotic, dreamy almost... the colours, the movement, the slow rotation of the energies inside and out. Feeling as though he could watch it for hours, part of him knew not to get distracted. Not now. Richie was still across to his right, surrounded by dark dragons, their drawn swords reflecting all the colours of the unusual portal that had appeared out of nowhere.

Hook's adrenaline had peaked and was currently being held in check by his tremendous willpower. As he was about to strike, the humongous energy hole had appeared out of nowhere, pausing everything that was going on round about him. Noting that Tank and Peter had reined in whatever it was they had in mind, he'd stalled, waiting to see how events unfolded before he chose to act. Having no idea what he was looking at, by the expressions on the stunned faces of those all around him, it appeared that he was not the only one.

A split second away from sending the signal, just as it had sprung to life out of nothing, given everyone's reaction it had been a good job she'd stopped. Whatever it was, it was just too much of a distraction for her plan to have worked. Even the drooling idiot brandishing the blade to her throat had turned around somewhat to get a view of what was going on. Deep down inside she wished for some help from whatever that thing was. Getting lucky had never felt so good.

A blossoming, yellow sparkle sizzled around the outside of the ring, fizzing and buzzing, jumping and arcing, preceding the main event. And then the liquid parted!

In all his glory, much to the astonishment of the naga contingent of Manson's ragtag army, out slithered Vasuki, a fiery rainbow of magic igniting the air around him. Hushed gasps of surprise filled the chamber. But that was nothing to what happened next.

Following on behind, brilliant bright chains of laminium crisscrossing their bare torsos, out stepped Flash and Fredric, their bulging muscles gleaming against the backdrop of magical energies, ready for practically anything.

Behind them out poured Yoyo's ragtag band of young dragons, all looking much the worse for wear, a mixture of fear and anticipation crisscrossing their prehistoric faces, followed by the renowned healer himself.

The liquid eye of the wormhole parted twice more, but strangely nothing else appeared. Well... not anything visible to the naked eye anyway.

Almost as quickly as it had materialised, the wormhole vanished into nothingness, leaving the air around where it had been charged with magic.

In the annuls of history much would be made of this very moment. Stories would be told, songs would be sung. On the outcome, much depended.

Earth's surface. Nevada, United States of America.
Looking out from the end of Santa Monica pier in Los Angeles, the cool, salty breeze teased his brown, flowing locks as white crested waves washed up onto the beach below him. Scorching sun beating down on his exposed arms, he tried to push aside the warmth that flowed into him, shuddering at how it made him feel, the exact opposite in fact to his longing to be deep beneath the sea he stood so close to. Basking in memories of swimming in cold, blue ocean waters, he pulled his phone out of the pocket of his light blue jeans, brought up the appropriate number and, knowing what a momentous event this was, hit the dial button. All he had to do was wait for an answer and then he could hang up. It happened exactly that way. Job done, he headed down towards the beach, determined to feel the sand, and more importantly the sea, between his toes.

Simultaneously, all five seismic shockers burst into life, the magic captured inside them combining seamlessly with the technology to generate a series of formidable ground quakes that instantly destroyed everything in their vicinity. The solar farm south east of Vegas shattered into a billion tiny pieces. In India Springs, the Joshua tree's roots were decimated immediately, along with half the buildings in the town. East of Vegas, a mountain exploded in a fountain of rubble and debris, killing several hikers and wiping out any existence of the well used trail. Tyres flew hundreds of metres in the air in every direction, shelling unsuspecting residents of Pahrump with huge rubber bombs, something that added more danger to the earthquake they were now experiencing. Though all of this was nothing to what would happen momentarily. You see, all the ground quakes were scheduled to converge at one point and one point only... LAS VEGAS!

Full to capacity with high rolling gamblers and a myriad of tourists, the city itself never knew what hit it.

As unsuspecting visitors snapped away with their cameras, the famous "Welcome to Fabulous Las Vegas" neon sign splintered into a thousand parts, electrical sparks dancing like the devil as it did so.

Not far away, the Hoover Dam in the Black Canyon on the Colorado River suffered a series of devastating fractures to its main structure. Water being water, it soon found its way into the cracks and, with the expanding force of mother nature behind it, applied more vigour than the remaining concrete could handle. In an explosion worthy of any action movie, the entire dam came crashing down in one go, with thousands of tons of concrete crashing into the river below, and the full force of Lake Mead being released instantaneously. Within minutes downstream was flooded beyond belief, along with a tiny part of Boulder City. Bedlam, as well as water, had been let loose.

In a mere moment, the ground quakes united somewhere close to the strip. Not only did the earth move but, for a tiny second, it also appeared to roll. As it did, buildings shook, roads and sidewalks rippled, cars were strewn into the air, fire hydrants burst, gas mains ruptured and electricity cables tore free of their housings. People were thrown in the air and to the ground, and, for the most part, those were the lucky ones, as they'd been outside. Inside the buildings, it was a totally different story. Ceilings tore in two, crashing down one, two, three storeys and more, crushing anything in their way. Windows fractured in a spider web type of fashion, most breaking immediately afterwards, sending dangerous shards of glass ripping through rooms, unpredictable gusts of wind very nearly sucking a number of innocent bystanders out of their penthouse suites.

Across downtown Las Vegas, a hub for business,

containing hotels, high rises, historical buildings, residential and retail, folks poured out of buildings, looking to get out into an open space as quickly as possible, doing their best in the chaos to keep themselves safe. For most it worked, though a few were less fortunate, sustaining major injuries through sheer bad luck.

The famed Las Vegas strip, nearly seven kilometres long, didn't fare nearly as well. Closer to the epicentre, the ground had simply erupted in places, causing massive sinkholes to appear out of nowhere, buckling the spokes on the High Roller Ferris Wheel, reducing the Rialto bridge at the Venetian to dust, and the gondolas that rode the liquid beneath it to nothing more than children's toys. Terrifying high pitched screams accompanied the ear splitting crash to the ground of the humungous Ferris wheel, all its riders dying on impact. Further along, the fabulous Wynn resort came crashing down into its own vivid blue swimming pool, sending up a mushroom cloud of dust, debris and death.

The Bellagio coped little better, its ground floor giving way under the stress, the rest of its massive superstructure rolling into the vast eight acre lake that, up until that point, had hosted the regular choreographed water feature that tourists so loved. Death and destruction accompanied terror and fear on the rollercoaster ride of their lives.

Dizzying red and yellow hanging lanterns in the Palazzo fractured, their remnants hurtling towards the ground, some injuring frightened tourists trying to exit the building, but other than that and some superficial damage, the resort remained unharmed.

What only moments before had been one of the wonders of North America, now very much resembled a scene from a third world war zone. Devastation had rocked the desert like never before, bringing about the kind of death toll only seen in movies. It was horrific, apocalyptic, and not the kind of thing anyone should ever be caught up in. But for the naga agents across the world, some bound by magic, others giving everything for the safe return of their king, it was just another cog in the machine, and something to be immensely proud of.

39 DEESE GUYS AND THEIR DISGUISE

Off in the distance thick, black smoke spiralled into the air from the sporadic raging fires that littered the bleak and desolate landscape that was a far cry from the busy, bustling metropolis that it had been only a matter of days ago. Masked in the darkness provided by the outreach building on the outskirts of Fleet Street, Steel explained his thoughts about what he'd seen, and about the plan that had been slowly developing in his mind as he'd snuck back from his reconnoitre.

"While dragons and nagas loitered with impunity throughout the complex, it would appear that two beings obviously disguised as humans seem to command the respect of all the others. I couldn't tell what they were exactly, but at one point while I was camouflaged they came within mere metres of me, allowing me a detailed look at their faces, and letting me hear their voices, albeit at a whisper."

Gee Tee, Jar Man, DomCon and a few of the other dragons listened as Steel continued.

"Whilst I could only follow them so far, due to the high concentration of guards, it was quite clear that these two commanded not only respect, but a certain amount of fear from every being around them. They also seemed intent on regularly patrolling the outer perimeter of their captured camp."

"So what was it you had in mind?" asked the master mantra maker, intrigued to hear what the laminium ball player had planned.

"Just before we hit them with the full force of everything we have, I thought we could go in, neutralise these two beings, get Jar Man and DomCon here to take their places, and then with me as their prisoner, stroll right into the building, making a big show of me... their prize."

"Hmmm... not bad, not bad at all. Did you get a clear and detailed look at their faces? This will only work if our two friends here can mimic them right down to the very last detail."

"I did," replied Steel confidently. "From almost as close as you are to me now. I can show them everything they need to know for their human disguises. The big question is... will the two of you do it?"

Jar Man glanced over at his much smaller friend, an unseen message sent with just a look. DomCon nodded eagerly in response to his friend's enquiry.

"We're in," announced the strawberry blonde dragon. "It's about time those scum sucking cockwombles were taught a lesson. Share their details with us."

Gee Tee and the other dragons shuffled back out of the way, leaving Steel, Jar Man and DomCon sitting together. Leaning forward, the courageous laminium ball captain craned his neck out into the space between them. The other two did the same, and with their foreheads almost touching, closing his eyes, Steel racked his eidetic memory for the images of his enemies. On finding them, he opened his mind and shared them with his two allies. Jar Man and DomCon absorbed every detail, right down to the creases in the forehead of one and the slight, almost imperceptible, stutter of the other. Knowledge shared and a plan in the making, the three sat back, letting the others rejoin them.

It was then that the mischievous shopkeeper added an extra special ingredient to the ever developing plan.

"There's a little something that might help you out in a pinch, laminium ball boy," quipped the master mantra maker.

"And what's that?" replied Steel, deciding to play along.

"This one's for you and you only. And it's powerful... beyond belief. If used in conjunction with all your will, it most certainly will have the desired effect." Locking away his magic so that he was able to pass on the words of the mantra without unleashing it to devastating effect, Gee Tee passed on his wise words of wisdom.

"VENTOSUS FUROR!" he ventured, only to Steel.

"Never heard of it," stated the laminium ball captain.

"I wouldn't have expected you to," scoffed the shopkeeper. "It's old, positively ancient in fact, and has only come to light quite recently. I've kept it to myself... but no longer. I realise now that the magic and knowledge I possess should be out in the open, shared for all of us to use. It's something I've not done in the past. I've squirrelled things away, kept them secret, to myself. I now know that to be wrong. But this piece of magic is especially powerful and should be not be used in anger or as a last resort. It needs to be thought out before it's let loose."

"What does it do?" enquired Steel, as the others listened eagerly.

"It will cast a powerful explosive wave that will run riot."

"Something we've all done at some point," ventured Jar Man sarcastically.

"Of course," declared Gee Tee. "But not quite on this scale. The concussive wave will shred anything in its path. What makes this one special though, is that you can set the arc of the wave before it's unleashed. If, when you set it off, you picture a full 360° arc, then that's the course the magic will follow, destroying everything in its path. For us today, that would be catastrophic because it would destroy the crystal node, something we can't afford to do. But if you know where the node is, you can purposefully leave a gap in the circle of the wave, making sure none of the magic is released in that direction. It just needs to be pictured in your head before you set off the mantra."

"Nice!" exclaimed Steel.

"It should be enough to take out a whole host of them once you're in there. You just need to make sure that these two," indicating Jar Man and DomCon with a nod of his head, "are standing between you and the crystal node. That way they won't be affected by the blast wave and you'll take out more of our enemies. Sound helpful?"

"Certainly does."

And with that, they all spent the next hour refining exactly what everyone's role was and just what time their attack would take place. Things were coming together.

40 YOU CAN CHOOSE YOUR FRIENDS BUT NOT YOUR FAMILY

RELATIONSHIPS! That's what EVERYTHING boils down to. LIFE is about relationships. It might be between you and your favourite knife that you use to chop up the vegetables for dinner. It might be a special pen to write with, or your bond with a pet. Me? It's the relationship I have with my hockey stick. I might go months without picking it up or even seeing it. But it's with me all the time, an extension of my arms, occasionally invisibly strapped across my back, informing my decisions, influencing all of my actions, guiding me in everything that I do. Relationships, good or bad, are the key to EVERYTHING everywhere. Right at this very moment, that couldn't have been more apparent.

Fredric's heart soared up into his mouth, goosebumps racing down the bulging muscles of his arms as he set eyes on the king, his long time best friend. Anger flared at seeing him like that, but before it had a chance to consume him, another figure caught his eye. Having not seen him for decades, it seemed inconceivable that he could possibly recognise him now, here, in this state and in his human form. But recognise him he did. PETER, his grandson, bound and restrained by those that were about to pay! How was he even involved? Taking in the measure of the boy he'd give his life for, one of the two beings that just the very thought of had kept him sane over all this time, hoping against hope that somewhere in the future he'd get the chance to meet them again, these weren't the circumstances he'd hoped to do it in. Joy coursing through him despite the dire situation he found himself in, the very essence of his being roared in delight at finding both of them. And that's when it all changed and his heart turned BLACK! Not just any black, but the darkest, coldest black that had ever existed. Shivers replaced the goosebumps. His stomach rolled, and despite not having eaten for weeks, nausea threatened to drop him to his knees. What he was seeing just wasn't possible. Everything had to be an illusion. It had to be a nightmare, and he must still be back chained to that icy wall in Antarctica, he just had to be. Because there was no way fate would conspire to put him in a reality this bad. It just wasn't possible.

Still coming to terms with the surprise of the wormhole appearing in the middle of everything, it was then that she locked eyes with one of the new arrivals. A man mountain of a being, whose worn face was framed with dirty, matted long hair, the muscles of his bare torso wrapped in chains, glistening in the low light of the private residence they all found themselves in. Recognition wasn't instant. It took her a few seconds before she realised their connection. But that was all it took before the anger and hatred deep down inside her blossomed into life, fuelling her rage, stoking her revulsion and disgust, contorting her face into the very picture of abhorrence. It all flooded back. How he'd followed her from their home to the bar full of Nazis in the small piazza in Barcelona. The German psychopaths had nearly done her a big favour that day, but as per usual he'd escaped by the skin of his teeth. Luck nearly always seemed to be on his side. It was then that the unexpected memory returned, one that had been blanked out, no doubt through magical trauma. She remembered him slipping through the fire escape at the back of the hotel in Germany, his back exposed, concentrating as he should on the threat in front of him. It felt as if it were only yesterday, so vivid were the images deep within her. Savouring the satisfaction before unleashing the magical hell she had planned for him. But before she could finish the job, he began to realise something was wrong. In that instant she set free her magic, determined to take him down once and for all. And that's where the memories ended. It was a total blank. Up until now, she hadn't even thought about the man staring across at her. It was almost as if every last detail of him had been locked away deep within her mind and his appearance here and now had acted as the key, allowing her access to everything, in particular the raw emotions of just how much she hated him for holding her back. Knowing that somehow she'd failed on that dark, wet night in Germany acted only as a catalyst for her determination. She wouldn't fail again. Today, here and now, he would once and for all... DIE!

Joy at finding his best friend and grandson was tempered with all the pain and sorrow it was possible for one being to experience. Standing over them, shrouded in crazed madness, his daughter, Earth, eyed him from across the room. Throughout his incarceration, he'd never experienced such pain, such heartbreak. Despite his heroic, tough looking exterior, inside he was close to imploding. To see his daughter, the love of his life, a woman who'd not only broken his heart, but had tried to kill him on more than one occasion (yes, that's right, his memories of that fateful evening in Germany had flooded back, and now he could clearly see her reflection, about to let loose her magic, in the brilliant sheen of the car he'd cowered behind) standing over not only the king, but his grandson and her son, was nothing short of the ultimate torture. Anger, pity, shame and the sharp stench of failure threatened to gobble him up. If he'd done a better job with her upbringing, been a better father, then just maybe none of this would have happened. They wouldn't be standing here right now. How many lives would have been saved... hundreds, thousands, more? Tears blurred his sight as his hands started to shake uncontrollably. Try as he might words eluded him as the raw emotions whistled round inside his human shell, effectively neutralising him. His comrades in arms had no idea that one of their own had, at least for now, been taken out of the game.

Deep within her mind, the babbling had almost reached fever pitch. Fu-ts'ang was beside himself, and despite not being able to understand everything he was saying, she got the general gist of it and, like the ancient weapon, she too was beside herself with joy at seeing the mighty form of Flash at the front of the party that had arrived through the magical vortex, which had now disappeared. Although she didn't know any of the others, she did at least have something now that she'd thought she'd lost for good. HOPE!

A cold shiver raced down his spine... never a good thing for any dragon, anywhere, but here and now it seemed appropriate. This wasn't caused by the sheer terror he felt at the situation they all found themselves in. NO! It was his reaction to the arrival of the group that had mysteriously appeared through the magical gateway which had now vanished. Seeing Flash ensconced in what looked like laminium chains, accompanied by a whole party of other dragons, and Yoyo hiding out of the way at the back, buoyed his spirits considerably, despite the fact that a magnificent, regal looking naga slithered forward at the front of them all. And then the hammer came down and hit him, almost shattering his reality. Next to Flash, another human shape stood balanced and ready for action. Taut muscles gleamed as shaggy, matted hair drifted slightly in what little breeze blew around the private residence. An instant familiarity prevented Peter from taking his eyes off the... WARRIOR! That really was the only way to describe him as far as the young dragon was concerned. Rough around the edges, bruised and beaten even, but the strength and power radiating off him looked nothing short of legendary. And that's when he knew. Knew that Flash had been to Antarctica and achieved the impossible in rescuing not only the naga king, but his grandfather, Fredric! That was the being he currently couldn't take his eyes off. Something, somewhere deep inside him urged him on, urged him to rally against what was happening, now that help had arrived. And with that little nudge, something he'd previously forgotten about sprang to the front of his mind. The *alea!* Unbelievably it was still dangling around his neck, his captors having made the mistake of not taking it off him. If he could break it when things kicked off, and he had no doubt now that they would kick off like there was no tomorrow, then just maybe he could play a part in whatever would happen. Closing his eyes, he pushed thoughts of everything else away, and focused on only one thing. How could he possibly break the *alea* and free the magic inside it that had remained dormant for centuries?

Ears ringing, Tank shook his head vigorously, trying to regain some sense of what was going on. In less than a minute, things had all but turned on their head. From out of nowhere help had arrived in the form of Flash and a whole host of others. That they must have succeeded in Antarctica was the only conclusion to be drawn. And if that were the case, the stunning looking naga at the head of the group must be the naga king, and the no nonsense, tough looking human shape just had to be Peter's grandfather and founder of the Crimson Guards.

'My God, how on earth have they achieved such a feat?' he wondered briefly. But now was not the time. Much as he was glad to see his friend and the reinforcements that accompanied him, he had no doubt that a battle to end all battles was only moments away. Part of him hoped that Manson, that evil witch and the rest of the wickedness that pervaded this place would surrender.

Realistically though, he knew it would be a cold day in hell before that happened. Swallowing nervously, mentally he tucked away his fear and tried to prepare himself for everything that was about to unfold.

Anger, adrenaline, passion and rage could no longer be contained, not that they necessarily had been. Watching Tim's murder had flicked a switch somewhere inside her. To be honest, it hadn't taken much. What she'd done to Casey back in Salisbridge had left her feeling tainted. Touched by darkness which had continued to consume her on the solo journey that had led her to this point, in killing Troydenn, she'd felt nothing. Well... strictly that wasn't totally true. There'd been a rush, so brief she'd almost missed it. Momentary exhilaration had been replaced by a deep seated satisfaction, not at the act itself, but at exacting revenge on the dark dragon from another time.

What was odd though, was Manson's reaction. She'd been watching him in her peripheral vision, hoping against hope for some kind of response, assuming all along that he'd been bluffing. On enacting the deed, there'd been no sign of remorse or anything remotely resembling sorrow from him, only a smug satisfaction, and she could be sure because she knew that look, and the feeling, well.

'Strange that Manson would want his father dead,' played over and over in her head, almost taking her mind off the approaching enemies. Flash's timely arrival had given her moments of breathing space, allowing her to expunge at least a small part of the darkness that had taken her, allowing her for the first time since her lover's death to see the situation for what it really was. Before she hadn't cared, wanting nothing more than to take as many of them with her as she could; now though, she could see a way out, a way her friends could survive this, with some semblance of normality a possibility for the rest of the planet. But the one thing it wouldn't be was easy, even with the added assistance of the mighty Flash and the allies he'd brought with him. Momentarily she wondered exactly what he'd been through. To be here, now, and achieve what he had was nothing short of miraculous. Indeed he was a legend and songs should be sung about the ex-Crimson Guard. But they were some way off ballads being composed. First they had to fight, fight for their lives, for their domain, for their planet. And so with the lacrosse player deep within her screaming out that they needed to work together, light pushed away the darkness as she sought eye contact with those she needed to keep her on the straight and narrow.

From behind his ragtag bunch of young dragons, proud and terrified in equal measure, Yoyo sized up the situation that they'd stumbled into the middle of. Instantly he recognised Peter, despite his horrific injuries, standing next to a nightmarish, witch-like figure, purple lines dissecting her face, madness and insanity radiating from her eyes.

'Tank looks in better shape,' he thought, before clapping eyes on the king, a broken and beaten dragon. Aware of just how dire things appeared, he found his composure, readied a number of healing mantras and said a brief prayer, to whom, he wasn't quite sure. It just seemed like the right thing to do.

Ready to send the signal to those under her command, Amelia Battlehard's breathing had decreased to all but nothing in an attempt to focus fully on what was unfolding. It is not a well known fact, but dragons can slow their heart rate and stop breathing for almost ten minutes if they have to. Of course all of King's Guard had trained at this over and over again at the academy, but it's not something that presents as useful in real life. Well, not up until now anyway. Another reason for holding her breath was the dull, black blade that rested against the scales lining her throat. Worried that the slightest movement on her part could result in a separation of her head from her body, it was abundantly clear that the deadly looking swords were sharper than a razor. In the moments since the newcomers had shown up, she'd figured out how to get out of her hopeless situation, or at least how she'd try. Readying the signal, she tapped into the mana that flowed throughout her prehistoric body and prepared to let loose what she hoped would be a rather unpleasant surprise.

'Whole again?' What did that even mean? And why was the weapon (sorry Fu-ts'ang, she should know better than to refer to him as an object) why was Fu-ts'ang jabbering on and on about it, all the time referring to Flash? It didn't make any sense. Just as she thought all this, her mind became still. At first she thought she'd offended the futuristic blade, but she could feel its reaction when that thought occurred to her. That wasn't it. Without any sound or any one specific thought, using only its feelings, Janice got the sense that it was time to prepare, to be ready for what was about to happen. The frightened bar worker had long since been replaced by a being that could get the job done. Powered not by a sense of right or wrong, or fear of failure, her entire being was consumed by love. First and foremost her love for Peter, the being she wanted to share the rest of her life with (be careful what you wish for. This might well be your last sixty seconds) and love for those around her whose friendships she'd made, valued and trusted. For her, giving herself over to the weapon, to do what she had to in an attempt to save each and every one of them, was a clear no brainer. As long as they lived, she believed. Believed that the life she so desperately wanted was possible. And so she would fight, and although only human, she would fight with all the purpose, desire, strength and violence of a... DRAGON!

For him, it was unusual to feel puzzled. For as long as he could remember, he'd always been in control of his destiny, even more so now with the death of his father only minutes ago. Of course he recognised the naga king. Who wouldn't remember one so striking, particularly if you'd kept them prisoner for that many years and enslaved most of their race to do your bidding? Now though, he remembered the human shaped dragon, the unusual one, the one they'd tortured for decades trying to get the truth out of him. The one that he'd at least got to speak on his last visit to Antarctica. What he couldn't understand though, was how they'd been freed, and just what kind of magic had transported them here? Glaring across at the naga king, he assumed it was related somehow to him. While he'd mastered quite a lot of everything magical, he supposed that while the captive nagas had been acquainting him with their magical ways, it should come as no surprise that they'd left things out. Rather deliberately he now assumed. Oh well, it didn't matter. They were here now, and would have little or no influence in what played out. After all, there were only a handful of them. What good did they think they could do? That many wouldn't even scratch the surface of his force.

'Might as well have a little fun with them before they go,' he thought.

"A nice parlour trick, but your arrival will make no difference. The planet is already mine!"

Stony silence encompassed everything as the tang of readied magic hung in the air.

With Fredric too consumed to step forward, Flash thought about responding. But before he could do so, the naga king stopped weaving his head from side to side and did it for him.

"Thesssse beeeeings are of noooo ussse toooo yooou. Yooooou WIIIIILL freeee theeeem aaat onnnnnce!" he demanded, referring to the nagas surrounding them on all sides, mixed in with all the dark dragons.

Rolling back his head and rubbing his belly for impact, the wickedly dark Manson roared with laughter, the sound bouncing around the arena sized room they found themselves in.

"Do you really think you have any say in what goes on here? You might have bought yourselves a few more minutes of life by escaping captivity in Antarctica, but I assure you this is the last place you'll ever set eyes on. You will most certainly die here, and it will be an unpleasant death. What's more, you'll die knowing that your race played a crucial role in securing all this for me. How funny is that? The nagas, helping a new breed of dragon overthrow the old guard and instate a new world order. As their king you must be so proud."

Patience was a naga trait, with his having been tested like never before over the course of his captivity in Antarctica. For the most part he'd embraced it, like you would a lover, learning not to fight it, but letting it help you. But here and now his patience had finally run out on seeing the vast scale of deception the being in front of him had committed. Knowing that almost certainly he'd be dead by now if not for the group of brave dragons behind him, he wondered how many of his kind had been affected, how many were left and if this would be his legacy. Grasping all the magic within him and opening up with his telepathic powers, he let out the biggest, most almighty telekinetic scream that he could, hoping to shock those within range out of the dazed stupor they appeared to be in.

Moments passed. NOTHING! Tilting his head just slightly, he glanced back over at the despicable dragon Manson.

"Oh I'm sorry," scoffed the dark and dastardly dragon. "Are you trying to bring them back to your side? I'm afraid that just won't be possible, either currently, or ever at all... marks out of ten for trying though."

Consolidating his magic whilst trying to tame his rage, the naga king's gills pumped furiously on either side of his neck. It was impossible to disguise his feelings.

"You see, the magic they're gripped by is like nothing you've ever seen. Like nothing ever seen on this planet, if I'm quite honest. And your puny little attempt to shock them out of it, so that they can once again bow down and answer to you, is nothing short of pathetic and was doomed to fail right from the very start. I'm afraid they're under my command now, and there's nothing you, or anyone else, can do about it."

Reaching out to the three nagas nearest to him, Vasuki used every ounce of power he possessed in an effort to get through to them. No matter how hard he tried, he got no response. Nothing! Not an eye flicker, a wink, even some semblance of recognition. All three seemed dazed, confused and almost zombie like. For the naga king, it felt as though he'd just had his ass kicked in a fight. Disappointment had almost overwhelmed him during his incarceration, knowing that because of his mistakes his race were without their leader and were being blackmailed with the threat of his death into doing Manson's bidding. Once again failure blossomed within him, causing his normally well held in check emotions to effectively run wild. With no way to get through to his brethren, how on earth was he supposed to get them to stop, and help his new found allies? Perhaps there was another way, but here and now, he had no idea what it was.

If not for the magical attack decades ago, her face would have been utterly beautiful. Instead of near perfection, it resembled a bodged experiment gone badly wrong, or a child's doll that had been damaged over time by its sadistic owner. Brilliant, purple lines crisscrossed this way and that over the pocked skin, something even the most powerful of magic couldn't undo. Of course she'd tried... long ago, after she'd come to terms with the death of her husband. She hadn't got over it, or forgotten him, quite the opposite in fact. Strange as it may seem, almost everything she did, including, she hoped, becoming Manson's queen, was all for him. Not exactly for him, but to exact revenge for what was done to him by those treacherous, self righteous, stuck up dragons, who all seemed to know what was best for the world and just how to rule it, not from their ivory tower, but from the equivalent deep down within the dragon domain.

Listening to her would-be ruler burst the naga king's bubble, pride shone out across her face, not that it was possible to see given all the damage it had suffered. The only thing that shone out as far as everyone else was concerned was... MADNESS! Clear and evident as ever in both eyes, their pupils resembled black holes; instead of sucking in matter they devoured hope, radiated fear and tore apart anyone they focused on. But like all that suffer from it, she found herself immune from the crazy, mainly due to prolonged exposure. For her, reality was more than a little twisted, even with her schemes, plots and plans of revenge.

And so stuck in her little bubble of insanity, instantly she imagined what she could do to the insignificant little whelp cowering right in front of her, and with little forethought let the magic course up into her hands, holding it their ready to dispatch into the dragon king's little pet. Brilliant sparks of bright red energy leapt across her palm, hissing and smouldering as they did so.

'When it all kicks off,' she thought, 'he'll be the first one to be put down.'

Words had been exhausted on every side. To a creature, they were all balanced on a knife edge, ready to act, ready to die for their leader, and in the nagas' case, compelled by magic to do exactly that.

The king's private residence had seen more than its fair share of history, but this was something else entirely. It would be hard to imagine a standoff that exuded more tension. And so with nearly every being picking their first target and imagining their initial moves, typically it was Manson who got things underway.

Eyes closed, the would-be king of this newly shaped world had already conjured half a dozen black-as-night balls of energy into the palm of his right hand, which he held hidden behind his back. Determined to make the most of the element of surprise, in a blur he brought around his arm and launched the wicked looking balls in the direction of Flash, Fredric and the other new arrivals, powdery black tails trailing in their wake. Pleased with their trajectory and the chaos they would unleash, swiftly he turned his attention back to the dragon king, determined not to make the same mistake as his father, vowing to finish him off there and then. But first he needed access to the damn ring. So far, he'd felt nothing. No connection, no magic, not even a hint of the supernatural power it was supposed to contain. Momentarily he wondered if he was doing something wrong, but he wasn't one for doubts and quickly pushed this aside. Perhaps there was a problem with the ring; after all, the dragon king had seemed genuine when he'd told him about the issues he'd been having. Gathering up his resolve, he tried to submerge the exquisite band on his finger with all his will, madly hoping to take over its consciousness and benefit from all its power.

Cursing deep within his mind, having hoped like hell that this whole thing could have been resolved peacefully, Tank shook off the ringing still resounding inside his head, and using all his rugby player strength, stamina and grace, barrel rolled off to one side, whilst doing so, reaching down to the tiny pocket lining his right boot, in one silky smooth motion slipping the king's real ring onto his index finger. After the third tumble, he leapt up into the air, focused on his surroundings, wary of any possible threat. But on making contact with his skin, he'd forced whatever possessed the ring to awaken, and it did, using all its power to flood his mental defences. Instead of bolting immediately upright from his roll, his legs wobbled with weakness, causing him to overshoot and slide straight into a marble pillar off to one side. It was then that a voice projected into his psyche, numbing his limbs, inundating his mind, swamping his very being. As magic flared into existence all around him, darkness took hold.

From the moment that Manson started to address the naga king, Peter knew that this was it and there was no turning back now. And that crucially, there were only mere moments left until it all kicked off. Knowing that time was of the essence, keeping his body as still as possible so as not to alert Manson's crazy queen to exactly what he was doing, he very slowly tilted his head as far forward as it would go and, stretching out with his tongue, began trying to hook it underneath the necklace to which the *alea* was attached. Now more than ever, he needed as much luck as fate would offer up. With the seconds ticking away, and Manson's dulcet tones drifting around the room, he used all his concentration to complete the bizarre task that he'd set himself. At the back of his mind, tiny doubts nagged at him... mainly about surviving the battle, a few focusing on the unpredictable nature of the magic bound within the ancient *alea*.

Eyes gently closed, knees pulled in tight against her chest, the young bar worker had finally achieved a state of peace and cooperation with the weapon she now regarded as her friend. Their relationship (imagine having a relationship with a weapon) based upon mutual trust and understanding, developed over the course of a matter of hours, honed into what it was in just a matter of minutes. Now that it was done, a sense of utter tranquillity encapsulated the young woman, fine tuning her senses, allowing her to reach out with her mind and get a much better understanding of the bigger picture that they all found themselves in. Flitting across her lips briefly, a smile tempered her nearly perfect face. Peter! He had his head down as far forward as it would go, making it look like an act of submission to the psychopathic queen hovering over him from behind. It was clearly an act, because he was actually using his tongue to fiddle with the necklace that was always clasped around his neck. Janice's thoughts turned to how she could keep him safe when the time came. Through their all encompassing bond, Fu-ts'ang assured her that he would do everything in his power to protect the human shaped hockey player from harm, but reaffirmed that it wouldn't happen straight away. Prioritising was the key, and there were other targets that had to be taken care of first. With a better understanding than most of the true scale of what they were facing, Janice knew the deliverance of death and destruction was right. But would he last long enough for them to provide assistance?

Turning back to assigning targets in her mind, coordinating fully with Fu-ts'ang, she shuddered slightly at the thought of her love, defenceless and alone, against the magically charged witch that stood behind him. Something deep down inside her screamed that he'd be that woman's first objective. If that was the case, she couldn't see how on earth he'd survive. As this concept flowed through their link, Fu-ts'ang deliberately hid his thoughts on the subject, knowing that the young woman was almost certainly right. With all his experience and acumen though, he couldn't foresee another way to get the job done.

Breath held, magic poised, Richie soaked up as much power as she dared from the laminium dagger, stoking anger and rage, ready as she'd ever been to do battle. From two hundred or so metres away, she could make out friends and hear every conceited word Manson spat at what she assumed was the naga king. It made her blood boil, almost literally, with the ancient dragon DNA within shrieking at her to react. Feeling as though her skin was about to explode, that's how hard it was to keep a lid on her emotions, she knew, from taking in everything that had happened, that it was almost time to react. And react she would, to the best of her ability.

Although she couldn't see what he had planned, she could feel him shifting the magic within, preparing for whatever surprise he'd concocted. Pride at what he could, and no doubt would, accomplish made her chest swell. She would be his queen, and a more worthy king it was hard for her to imagine. Although their fates now seemed intertwined, unable to ever be separated, there was a part of her that would always belong to her deceased husband, no matter where she was or what she was doing. The very thought of him massaged the madness within her, like a fire being fuelled by oxygen. For her, that's how the descent into lunacy had started. Okay, she'd been a little unhinged before that, almost certainly stemming from the issues she'd had with her father. But that death, and the way that it had come about, had shattered her soul, driven any last shred of decency from her, forging her future, all paths leading to REVENGE and the here and now. When this planet and its inhabitants knew her pain, when they'd watched everything they so loved being forcibly taken away from them, and when they bowed to their king, her other half (she had difficulty in thinking of HIM as her husband), only then would her lust for revenge be sated. Only then could she rest. Knowing that these moments were only days away at most, the extraordinary power within her bubbled to the surface, easily accessible, ready to strike down the king's little pet in front of her. After that she'd seek the thrill and arousal that came with the lure of a full on killing spree. Joy only ever found her now at times like this.

Instinctively holding back his gag reflex, Peter sucked the *alea* into his mouth as the chain it was on nicked the back of his neck. Between the pain from that and the binders that he couldn't ever remember being without, tears leapt from both eyes, totally missing his cheeks, falling straight to the beautiful marble floor, splashing uncontrollably onto intricately carved letters of the ancient text. Breathing through his nose, head still as far down as it would go, he gripped the *alea* in between his teeth and prepared to bite down, all the time fighting off the fear that threatened to take him. At the front of his mind, the words that he needed stood out like a shining beacon in the middle of the night: "Amplificare Magicus Nunc." Knowing exactly what they meant, he hoped to hell they would... amplify magic now. Remembering Gee Tee's descriptions of how the *alea's* magic could go wrong, he wondered whether he would be saved or whether he would die horribly, possibly even taking his friends with him. In only a few moments he would find out, one way or the other.

Dragons behind him dived for cover as half a dozen sinister magic missiles scythed through the air towards him. Preparing to cartwheel out of the way, it was at that point that the ex-Crimson Guard noticed Fredric paralysed with grief, directly in the path of at least two of the projectiles. In the blink of an eye, the brilliant dragon switched tactics, commanding a wide ranging, pink tinged energy shield to spring into life, powered by the laminium chains crisscrossing his body, easily able to absorb the unusual supernatural attack that had been meant for them. Glancing over at Fredric, puzzled by what could have brought the great warrior to his knees, his thoughts turned to the threats that faced them here and now. In his mind at least, there was no bigger threat than the source of the attack he'd just thwarted. So enhancing his bounds and leaps with the magic from the chains, in a blur he headed straight for Manson, looking to exact more than a little payback for everything the evil, dark dragon had done.

Raising her hands in front of her, a dazzling array of electrically charged magic crackled, fizzed, sizzled and spluttered in a myriad of different colours. Volcanic red, sumptuous plum, red velvet and cool cherry represented but a few. It was, however, all quite red, which suited her just fine because that was her favourite colour and she expected to see a lot of it here and now. Anticipating the taste of human blood, she unleashed the magic she'd been holding in.

A split second before a red death took him, Peter bit down on the *alea* and in his mind screamed the words that Gee Tee had assured him would trigger the last chance or gamble that it represented. Amongst the chaos of his surroundings, he'd almost expected nothing to happen. After all, he was totally reliant on the master mantra maker in all this.

Sucking in a small breath, she shivered despite the humidity and heat. Eyes open now and focused fully on one person only, she watched helplessly as Manson's evil queen summoned her blood red magic and prepared to destroy the love of her life with it. Inside her head, a voice echoed gently throughout her thoughts, providing focus and a measure of calm despite the circumstances.

"Concentrate! You need to concentrate if we're all to get out of this. He'll be alright until we can get to him. He's actually quite resourceful, you know."

Heeding the wise weapon's words, Janice closed her eyes again and immersed herself in magic. Being surrounded by ancient beings had never felt so good.

Watching the dark objects head for Flash and his party of dragons at quite a rate, Hook made the only decision he could: to fight! Having very little left to give, he whirled around and punched the dark dragon standing over him with everything he had left. In all honesty, it was a gamble, like the one Peter had just taken with the *alea*. But in Hook's case it was a calculated risk. After all, they had to procreate? Didn't they? As the pain in his hand from making contact dropped him to his knees, a moment later he had his answer in the form of the most barbaric of howls. Rolling over and over, all too aware of the giant shadow getting ever closer, Hook barely made it out from underneath the body of the flailing dragon as it collapsed to the marble surface with the loudest CRUNCH in the world. Beside himself with laughter at what had just happened, all the time pushing away the pain from his hand, broken arm and assorted other injuries, he crawled into a crouch and began looking for some cover. As he did so, magic blossomed into existence all around.

Drawn to the brilliant, bright reddish magic ignited by Manson's queen directly behind Peter, a feeling of utter helplessness threatened to overtake her. What broke that spell, bringing her back to her current predicament and almost brought a smile to her face despite the dire situation, was Hook off to one side, turning in one swift move and punching the dragon hovering over him right in the 'hoard of treasure'. As the magic from the laminium dagger consumed her totally, all she could think was that the rugby playing human was something special, to say the least.

The time had come, and so without any regrets at all, telepathically, she sent the signal, before turning her attention to the rather sticky situation she found herself in. Bringing one of her hands up so fast it was a blur, even to all those with magical powers, she just managed to get it between the dark, shiny blade and the scales around her neck. Even that would only buy her a matter of moments, so with her other hand straight down by her side, she conjured up a fragmented bolt of dark blue lightning and proceeded to ram it into her guard. The resulting yelp had been reassuring, but not quite the reaction she'd hoped for, having been certain that the beast would have dropped to the ground or been thrown back by her attack. Unfortunately he'd remained professional throughout and still had his lethal looking, sharp as hell bastard sword up and around her throat. Undeterred, and with the blade now cutting into the flesh of her hand, instinctively she kicked out, aiming for the exact same area as Hook, but not quite making the same kind of contact. With magic exploding all around her, it was hard to concentrate and bring forth any of hers now, with her opponent's strength threatening to overwhelm her. Thoughts of the king and how she'd let him down punctuated the tears zigzagging across her scales. As her hand gave out, almost cut in two, she said goodbye to the only world she'd known and waited for her head to be cleaved from her body. Knowing that some dragons prayed to long forgotten gods, it had never really been her thing. Imagining a higher power and believing in miracles was an absolute impossibility for her. But what happened next would make her re-examine every belief she had.

From completely out of nowhere, a rusty, old, bent dagger slashed through the right elbow of the arm holding the dark and dangerous blade, powered by magic with enough force to sever it completely. With a CLANG and a THUNK, the sword dropped to the floor, swiftly followed by half a dragon arm, the dark dragon still having barely realised what had happened, it had all been so fast. More than a little surprised at the unexpected turn of events, Amelia Battlehard swept up the dark sword without a moment's hesitation, and with the blade held firmly, pirouetted, decapitating her enemy in the blink of an eye. Looking around for the king, out of thin air only a couple of metres away, a dragon's head appeared, all on its own. To say it nearly frightened the life out of her was an understatement. With a million questions running through her mind, and a raging battle kicking off all around her, the head in question winked once, roared, "You're welcome," and then suddenly disappeared as quickly as it had arrived. Unable to ponder the total impossibility that had saved her and with the giant black beast of a sword firmly gripped with both hands, she took off at a sprint, weaving in and out of the explosive magic that ravaged the air all around her, all the time heading for the king's last location.

Throughout the complex, King's Guards fought against their assailants valiantly, despite being severely outnumbered, even though most, like Amelia Battlehard, had a sharpened blade to their throats. Some used magic to fight their way free, others used cunning and guile. Most failed, some survived and won their personal duels, procuring a weapon and a very small amount of thinking time.

Ignoring the explosions, animalistic cries and the debris all around her, she opened her mind and let it wander, gaining a bird's eye view of everything raging across the field of battle. Not only was she the eyes now, but in charge of the decision making too. And so it was that as the battle commenced, the sole point of her focus was the group of nagas which Fu-ts'ang found himself in the middle of. Held out in front by one of them, not at all fazed by the cool frost constantly circling the blade, he was suddenly startled when the extraordinary weapon, of its own accord, turned up, its tip pointing directly towards his throat. Halfway through his thought of, 'what the hell is going on?' suddenly the weapon surged forward with all the supersonic speed of a bullet, the blade plunging up through his jaw and into his skull, killing him instantly. His comrade beside him was the only one to have seen clearly what had happened and so started to slither away. Those around began to berate their colleague in the middle of the battle for breaking formation. Before he had the chance to explain about the weapon, Fu-ts'ang and Janice turned their attention towards the whole group of them, slicing two in half before they'd even registered a threat. Finally the nagas in that small cluster got into the game, bringing out their best magic, aiming wonderfully coloured bolts of electricity, fire and even ice at the majestic looking weapon as it manically flew through the air, on the hunt for each and every one of them. It was, however, all to no avail. Fu-ts'ang was far too nimble and agile for any of the attacks. Janice had found peace and a perfect partnership. While she detested the killing, she had no doubt it was necessary, not just for the here and now, but for the much bigger picture. It went beyond all of this and affected everyone, everywhere. This wasn't so much about surviving for the next few minutes, as about the whole planet and saving the entire population of the earth and their way of life. In less than twenty seconds, a pile of dead nagas had appeared in the middle of the chamber, leaving the previously pristine floor and the blade of the deadly weapon slick with naga blood.

As the blood red magic in all its rage left her fingers, the thrill of yet another kill ran through her, chilling her spine, igniting her senses, fulfilling her blood lust. Imagine her surprise when instead of shredding its target, it failed to make contact entirely, bouncing harmlessly off a pale yellow defensive shield that had sprung up out of nowhere. Before she had any chance to react or make any sense of what had just happened, a white-hot superheated nova exploded outwards at waist height, with Peter at its centre, shredding one or two of the goons nearby, forcing the dragon king to remain on the floor, and most joyously of all, tossing Earth halfway across the vast open space of the residence. Peter savoured the moment Earth crashed clumsily to the floor, some way away. Landing in a twisted heap, she looked as though her head had taken the brunt of things. For all he was worth, he hoped that she was dead, and that looked to be the case from where he was standing. But what had happened? Looking down at his feet and off to either side, it became apparent that he was surrounded by some kind of energy shield. Not only that, but the magical binders that had been the bane of his life for as long as he could remember had shattered, their metal remnants scattered across the floor behind him. The *alea* had worked perfectly. Unsure of just how long it would hold, or just how much magic it could absorb, he quickly scouted around, unsure of whether to join the fight or beat some sort of retreat. But where could he retreat to, he wondered. Out of the corner of his right eye he could just make out Yoyo, hidden in the shadows, showering what he assumed were helpful healing spells on the cast of young dragons that had appeared through the wormhole. Should he cover Yoyo, or were there more pressing matters?

Simultaneously, in a huge room packed full of chaos, the two women smiled. Scything down their enemies from a position on the floor through her telepathic contact with the deadly weapon, Janice had managed to catch Peter's miraculous feat and escape from certain death. Hope swelled inside her as her flying comrade Fu-ts'ang urged her to concentrate. They were still massively outnumbered with nowhere to escape to. Now more than ever they needed to even up the numbers, if that were at all possible.

Standing against the backdrop of Troydenn's huge corpse, Richie smiled at what her friend had just achieved. If she had to guess, she'd say he'd almost certainly found some way to break the *alea* and release the ancient magic within. That thought provided her with a measure of comfort. Her best friend had survived an encounter he clearly wasn't meant to and was at least safe for the time being. Eyeing up all the dark dragons determined to end her, she settled on one and, harnessing all her magic, set off at the kind of speed Flash would be proud of.

Whipping around at quite a rate, the naga king put all his might into his tail, using it to fell a vicious looking dragon that had made to slice him in half with a two-handed cut of his giant sword. As the prehistoric beast smashed into the plinth that had been designated the heart of the king's command centre, cracking the spotless marble floor in over a dozen places, a violence born of being held in captivity for all that time bubbled to the surface, consuming the serpent-like monarch in a fit of fury. Before the dragon had time to contemplate any kind of defence, needle sharp jaws clamped tightly around its neck, severing arteries and bone alike. Throat a bloody mess, the ancient beast died where he'd fallen. Anger sated somewhat, the naga king cowered behind the corpse and what remained of the plinth as magical attacks detonated all around him. Dragons fought dragons, nagas fought dragons, as humans fought dragons and nagas. It was total and utter chaos. Aware that he had a duty not only to his kind, but to the dragons that had aided his rescue, ducking down to avoid being a potential target, he opened his mind up as much as he could and let go with the most powerful telepathic cry possible. In peacetime, on another continent, this would have attracted the attention of others like him from nearly one hundred kilometres away. Here and now, he was certain those around him in this building would stop and take heed. But they didn't. There was no lull, no let up in the intensity of the cruelty and carnage. It made no difference at all. Pulling his mind fully back to the present, he wondered just what else he could do, apart from fight alongside the light sided dragons that had rescued him. Ignoring the failure that threatened to tear him apart from the inside, he chose a target... another dragon, for the simple reason that he just couldn't fight against one of his own and, readying his magic, entered the fray.

Still a little surprised at the situation they found themselves in, despite having had it drummed into them in Antarctica before they'd stepped through the magical wormhole, Yoyo's band of young dragons were performing admirably. Terror had gripped them at first, but only for an instant. After that, their 'nothing is beyond us' attitude kicked in and they'd all entered the fight, adhering to Yoyo's strict telepathic instructions not to engage either Manson or Earth. If they found themselves in a direct confrontation with either, they were to flee as though their lives depended upon it. Almost certainly they would.

From out of nowhere a dark green dragon the size of a four storey house, with a black blazing sun, brilliant dark rays exploding out of it at all angles adorning his hip, landed softly in the middle of them, bellowing brilliant orange and yellow flame in a huge semi circle, hoping to slip past the group's defences. Ignoring the small arms fighting going on all around him, Maggotts (don't ask how he got his name) instantly conjured up a magical shield directly in front of the dragon, not only halting the spread of his lethal flame, but reflecting a fair amount back at the assailant. Surprised, and temporarily blinded because of the heat and flare that had bounced back his way, the nefarious looking beast started to choke on the flame that he'd already pulled up from his stomach. Momentarily distracted, he had no idea that the youngsters around him were coordinating telepathically and that they had already decided what form their attack should take. Dropping the shield, Maggotts now peppered the prehistoric creature's wings with tiny little fluorescent, yellow darts, perforating skin and sinew alike, dropping the dragon to his knees as he howled in pain. Taking full advantage of the distraction provided by their friend, Dymist and Wiz, two of the more experienced dragons, both used their power simultaneously to cast a mantra that connected them both by a fizzing, hissing and spluttering, pumpkin coloured streak of energy, the ends of which sat snugly above the palms of their hands, looking in some ways like the most dangerous skipping rope in existence. Having practised in unison during the times Yoyo hadn't been around, the two synchronised their attack perfectly, both bounding off in opposite directions before winding back in, wrapping the sadistic cord of energy perfectly around the attacking dragon's thick, scaly neck. Aware now of the trouble he was in, he ducked, wriggled and kicked out, all the time flapping what remained of his wings in an attempt to get away. But there was now no escape. The youngsters' plan had worked flawlessly and with one giant pull on each end of the magical rope from both Dymist and Wiz, the dragon's head smashed to the ground, followed immediately by its body. Through their telepathic link, both young dragons expressed their joy at having succeeded, but the time for congratulations was not now, and so with Yoyo looking on in astonishment at what he'd just witnessed from the shadows, the two youngsters melted back into the mayhem, hoping somehow to make a difference.

Limping badly, but still smiling beneath all his injuries, Hook weaved his way between corpses, dodging brilliant coloured magical attacks, all the time trying not to choke on the smoke that was starting to encompass the chamber. Briefly he'd caught a glimpse of a dragon tucked up in the shadows, one that he was sure had come through the wormhole, or whatever it had been, with Flash and the others. If that were so, and he was sure it was, then he'd be an ally, something he dearly needed right at this very moment. About halfway to his objective, the mightiest roar in the world from behind him nearly swept him off his feet. Glancing around, terror froze his heart, the smile gone from his face forever. There, stomping towards him, drool dribbling from his razor sharp teeth, an expression of pure hatred etched across his prehistoric features, was the dragon he'd punched firmly in the baby maker, clearly on a mission of revenge. Hook fought against his fear, bravely, fiercely, but whether because of the situation, everything going on around him, or because of his grave injuries, he remained firmly rooted to the spot.

Sensing something, he allowed the little tug at his

consciousness to turn his head away from his young charges. Fifty metres or so, directly in his line of sight, a frightened young human stood rooted to the floor as a very disappointed off (see what I did there) dark dragon plodded furiously towards him.

'That must be one of the brave humans that Flash told us about,' he thought. With the dragon bearing down on the defenceless human, Yoyo pondered what to do. His array of offensive mantras was limited to say the least, and he couldn't think of anything that would take down that dragon at this range. Feeling more than a little helpless, and not able to see where any assistance would come from, closing his eyes, he did the only thing he could and hoped it would be enough.

Heart threatening to jump right out of his chest it was pumping so hard, the pain from his broken arm, his bleeding leg and the blows to his head finally threatened to overtake him. Never having previously faced death or anything remotely like it, he closed his eyes and let his thoughts turn to rugby, his sport and those that he'd called his teammates, Tank among them. Not sorry in the least to have come on this rollercoaster of a journey, he wouldn't have changed a thing, and so with one calm breath he relaxed and accepted the fate he was about to be dealt. Towering over him menacingly, a sickly grin appeared as the dastardly dark dragon opened his mouth in an effort to summon the flame with which he intended to barbecue the insignificant creature in front of him, and drew back his head. It was exactly then that a warm, light embrace smothered Hook, hugging him tight, replenishing him fully and curing every ailment that plagued his body. Thinking that he was being cooked, it was only when he opened his eyes that he realised he'd been restored to full health. In fact full health didn't really do it justice. He felt great, better than great. He felt the best he'd ever felt... strong, full of energy, ready for anything.

And so with that in mind, and his body having shaken

off all the fear that had previously incapacitated him, Hook cartwheeled off to one side as the superheated column of flame that was meant for him vaporised the marble in the exact spot he'd been standing only a split second before. Satisfied with revenge, the dragon was wide-eyed to spot his ape shaped nemesis off to one side, not only un-barbecued, but fully healed by the look of things. It didn't matter though. This persistent pain was nothing more than an insignificant insect and would be dealt in much the same manner. Surging forward, the dragon stamped the ground with all its might, causing a minor quake in the immediate vicinity. Hook toppled like a domino next in line, falling flat on his chest, the wind temporarily knocked out of him. Pushing himself to get to his feet, it was pretty much all he could do to dive up and over, out of the way of the blur of a tail flashing out of nowhere as the dragon turned full circle. Slamming down once again on the painfully hard floor, the tough rugby player turned to face his opponent. Not sure exactly what he could do against him even in his fully fit state, suddenly he wished for the master mantra maker's backpack. But it was in vain, as he'd been relieved of it before they'd been taken into the big council building. Thoughts of running away were contrary to everything he'd been taught and believed in. And so as the ancient beast trampled towards him, the valiant young man bravely stood his ground.

Wishing the young human good luck, having done all he could, Yoyo turned back towards his band of misfits and began shoring up their defences where he could, on the lookout for any unexpected danger, ready to warn them at a moment's notice.

With the naga guards that had been tasked with Fu-ts'ang after his capture neutralised, the last thirty seconds or so had seen the weapon, under Janice's watchful guidance, take out three more nagas and completely slice the tail from one of the dark dragons, leaving him screaming in pain and effectively out of the fight. Now the weapon's seductive voice rang throughout the young bar worker's head.

"Now is the time to... think. Look around, take everything in. Pick out the most immediate threats. We've bought ourselves some time. Let's use it to assist our allies and consolidate our position."

'Wise words indeed,' she thought.

His instructions still echoing in her head, she drifted off into the ether as she had before, this time with little help or resistance, slowly able to view what was happening all around almost from above. It was odd to see her physical body sitting far below, eyes closed, combat raging all around. Pleased that she appeared safe from any immediate threat, she tried to take in the greater details of the skirmish. Richie had just set off at a blistering pace towards all the attackers surrounding her at the far end of the chamber they found themselves in. Immediately Janice knew that was where they should be. But once again Fu-ts'ang's words invaded her privacy.

"Not yet... take it all in."

So she did. Closer to the bridge, the much smaller group of dragons that had arrived with Flash were holding their own against some of the dark dragons and dastardly nagas. It was a sight to behold. Just then an explosion of magic caught her attention... Flash was fighting head to head with the despicable Manson.

'Go Flash, go,' she thought.

Just this side of Richie, a circle of more official looking dragons were fighting off all comers, dragons, nagas, you name it... from the air, and from the ground, all being led by a truly majestic looking female dragon who seemed to be their leader.

'Impressive,' thought the young bar worker. 'Whoever she is, I'd very much like to meet her.' It was then that he caught her attention. No, not Peter, like she'd thought it would be. But Hook, looking very much healed, but how? She had no idea. But he was, and about to be stomped on by a very angry and very determined opposing dragon. Without even the slightest hesitation, for that's where she knew they needed to be, she guided her friend, her cohort, her... she didn't know what, to exactly where the danger was.

Fists out, for all the good it would do him, he very much doubted he'd get a second shot at the goodies, which was a shame really, because he was sure he could do a lot more damage this time, in his heightened physical state. Not really knowing what to expect, he'd picked up a few things from his brief time in this fairytale world, and his albeit brief experiences told him that this attack from the nightmarish looking dragon was going to be magical. The giveaway? Rippling, dark energy rapidly converging into a ball between both hands seemed the likely clue. Unable to even begin to comprehend how to thwart such an assault, once again he peacefully accepted his fate. But once again, the universe had other ideas.

Ready to cast the exquisitely conjured mantra at his ape tormentor, the very pleased with himself dragon only heard the whistle of air being scythed out of the way from behind at the very last moment, leaving him no time to react. His first thought as the frosty blade burst through his chest was that there must be some mistake, and that he'd done something to displease the ever important Manson. After all, he'd witnessed him dispatching others that had earned his ire in very similar fashions. But on glancing over to his right, he could just make out the recently self proclaimed king furiously battling a half naked human form wrapped in what looked very much like laminium chains. As the now unfocused energy from his mantra dissipated harmlessly into the air all around him, his last thought as the life drifted out of him was,

'If not him... then who?'

"JANICE!" he screamed. Well... in his mind anyway, because there was simply no way that he'd be heard over the sound of the impacting magic, the clash of steel and the ferocity of the ensuing battle. Breathing a huge sigh of relief, and with his newly restored body ready to be tested fully, he set off at a sprint towards the dragon in the shadows, hoping to gain at least a modicum of protection.

Caked in the glow of his magical shield conjured up out of nowhere by his breaking of the *alea*, Peter spotted Hook sprinting, for all he was worth, away from a fierce looking dragon that had just been harpooned by a futuristic blade that almost appeared to be made of ice. Unable to make out who had thrown it, the young hockey player turned his attention back to the matter at hand. What exactly should he do? Hook looked as though he was making his way towards Yoyo, something he quite fancied, but the more he thought about it, the more it seemed like a bit of a cop out. After all, he was protected, at least to some degree, so it would probably be prudent to try and offer his friends some help, for at least as long as he found himself in this state. Gazing across to the giant dead end, the furthest part of the lower level from him, he watched his best friend weave and bob, thrust and parry with what he now recognised to be, his, yes his... laminium dagger. It was only then that he corrected himself, remembering that his grandfather was here. Not his dagger, but his grandfather's dagger. Whirling around in an attempt to locate his long lost relative, it was then that he set eyes on her. The love of his life... JANICE! What the hell was she doing still sitting there on the floor in the middle of the magical bedlam that had now been playing out for some time? At first he thought she'd been injured, but as that occurred to him her eyes popped wide open, almost as if she could hear his thoughts. That was it! He'd made his decision, and removing her from the line of fire had suddenly become his number one priority.

Fire coursing through him, that's how it felt. Every atom, every molecule, everything felt on fire... only in a good way. He'd been ablaze many times before, and although not the very worst thing in the world, when it's a dragon intent on doing you harm it still wasn't very pleasant. On one particular occasion, the dragon in question had been so strong and so powerful, it had actually set his whole head alight, making him look like a dragon version of Marvel's Ghost Rider. He knew this because Peter and Tank had made him watch every series of Agents of Shield, pretty much their favourite television show.

So as the supercharged energy from the crisscrossing chains draped around his torso filled every muscle with life, he approached the evil villain Manson, the being he'd been tracking for months, who'd always been at least one step ahead of him. Boosted by the magic in the laminium, even his overstretched confidence knew to be wary when it came to this being. He was crafty, full of guile and Flash had a sneaking suspicion that he was overly familiar with very unusual, much coveted magic, which made him something of an oddity as an enemy. And therein, could lie the problem. Conventional enemies were, for him, much easier to dispatch. For something out of the ordinary, he knew he had to rely on all his skill, cunning and training. This, he thought, was going to be the fight of his life.

Thoughts of the dragon king's ring and just why it wouldn't work were cast aside immediately. A small, magical part of him continuously tested the enigmatic band, hoping it would wake up and serve him, but in reality he didn't hold out much hope. Watching in delight as the battle broke out on all fronts, having released his dark, deadly magic in the direction of those that had arrived out of nowhere, a sliver of concern wriggled around inside him on seeing one of the newcomers deflect it away harmlessly. Realising that it might be a bit tougher than he'd first thought to deal with this unexpected opposition, he whirled around with only one thing on his mind... TO KILL THE DRAGON MONARCH! With his father finally out of the way for good, there was absolutely no need for his nemesis to continue breathing. That would be one less powerful enemy to be concerned about. Pulling back his arm, about to release a sizzling salvo of nightmarish energy at the still prone dragon king, abruptly he was tackled rugby style around the waist (something Flash was immensely proud of, given the news he'd yet to tell Tank about his decision to join him in his sport) and crashed heavily to the floor, a barrage of punches raining down on his face before he'd even come to rest. It had, as far as he was concerned, all been going so well, and then out of nowhere... THIS! As the magically enhanced punches pummelled his face, splintering bones and drawing blood from his nose, a darkness within him fought to escape. Memories of his childhood trapped in THAT cavern in Antarctica came flooding back. The sick brutality, the way his father, Troydenn, had used and abused his mother, being bullied and ridiculed by the other dragons because of how different he was. Shame and fear outweighed the pain from the hits he was currently taking. And then finally... his MOTHER! After becoming useless to them, she was discarded by his father and all the others that had used her like a cheap whore, and died a short time later in his arms, never able to see the exotic powers he'd developed, or how he'd go on to become so powerful. On that unforgettable day, any feelings he had for others were crushed, his soul stained black and his heart disconnected from his body. As the beating continued, his attacker clearly pleased with the job he was doing, the sinister Manson opened himself to all the memories, allowed the grief, heartbreak, shame and fear to consume him. Previously it had given him strength and power beyond belief. Today was no different.

Every one of her dragon senses was being utilised to the full. It was a good job they were all supplemented by magic, because without that it would be impossible to focus on everything that was going on around her. Amelia Battlehard had fallen back on her training, just like the other King's Guards that had survived the brutal slaughter which had started when Manson had attacked out of the blue. Trying desperately hard not to focus on it, she already knew just how many good dragons she'd lost right at that very first point. Twenty-one killed in an instant. Luck had been with the rest of them, and of course in her case an unexpected helping hand. Presently, she was in the middle of the force that remained, having been unable to reach the king. Her guards and two remaining councillors had formed a circle with her at the centre, and as well as dispatching enemies as they flung themselves their way, they were currently moving ever so slowly towards the king's last known position. Unfortunately for her, it was also where the dastardly leader Manson appeared to be, which was presenting something of a problem as the fighting towards that point was heavier than anywhere else in the chamber. Dishing out orders, taking out enemies from above, and correcting any form of mistakes by the others in their line, her brain had never been so active. While knowing that the odds were heavily stacked against them, she was, however, delighted to at least be given a chance. To have died with a sword at her throat would have been a dishonour, a disgrace and something she could never have accepted, and while she mourned the others who had gone that way through no fault of their own, the knowledge of their deaths only made her more determined to rescue the king and ultimately save the domain and the rest of the planet. Much like the young lacrosse player on the other side of the chamber, winning was everything, and today she would give all she could, including her life, to make sure that her side did just that.

With everything not wanting to swim into focus, her first thought was to wonder just why she couldn't see properly. After that, it was about managing the dreadful pain. Slowly, what had happened came slinking back. Sure she'd unleashed her magic into the king's whelp of a pet, what had happened next seemed utterly improbable. From what little she could recall, she'd been impossibly thrown through the air for some distance. After that it was, like her vision, just a blur. Flooding her limbs with warm, pleasant, healing magic, bones cracked back and bonded into place as skin knitted itself together, all the time the pain kept under control. Standing, visibly traumatised, she shook her head half a dozen times in the hope that her vision would recover. It did, but not quite fully.

A thick, all encompassing blackness that didn't seem real greeted him when he opened his eyes. His first reaction was to get to his feet, but all his limbs were weighed down, almost feeling as though they were made of lead. Next he tried to sit, but could barely lift his head away from the floor. Instinctively he reached for his magic, desperately hoping to find something of assistance there, but quickly it became apparent that it had somehow become either lost or had been forcibly taken away. Horror at the thought of being without even the tiniest spark of natural power hastened his breathing, clouding his mind, threatening to render him useless. Most magical beings would have been in trouble, but he'd been ruthlessly trained by one of the best, brightest and most stubborn of beings... one that wouldn't take no for an answer, and one that had ultimately foreseen a day like this. It had been a cruel and calculated move on the master mantra maker's part in taking away his young dragon charge's magical ability, on a quiet day long ago, but he regarded it as 'tough love' and knew that it might at some point in the future save the young dragon's life. Knowing that he'd get no thanks, and certainly not expecting any, it had torn apart his insides to activate a rare and obtuse mantra that had been part of a hoard he'd recovered from the Silla dynasty. A long standing empire that had ruled the Korean Peninsula between 57 B.C. and A.D. 935, founded by the monarch Bak Hyeokgeose, whom legend held had hatched from a mysterious egg in a strange and haunted forest and married a queen, born from the ribs of a dragon. Not quite true of course, but nearly. Instead of being born from the ribs of a dragon, the queen herself was a dragon, and a very powerful and cunning one at that. In spite of the fact that most of the history surrounding this time period had been either lost or deliberately destroyed, Gee Tee had recovered what little was left, all of which made invaluable reading. After that, he'd made it his purpose over a period of decades to go searching for anything of magical relevance from that time period and culture. Token trinkets here and there had come into his possession, along with the odd spell book or two. But his luck had really changed one long weekend nearly eighty years ago, when he'd been exploring a system of underground ruins buried in the centre of an estuary, situated in the middle of a widespread lava formation deep beneath the human city of Daegu in the south east of the region. After a long hike and an even longer flight, he'd donned the mystical necklace/ring combination that had been handed down to him and set off looking for the merest hint of magic. And this time, unlike his previous four escapades, he'd stumbled across something almost straight away. While he'd found the hint of power almost immediately, it had taken him nearly eighteen hours, and that was using no small amount of magic, to unearth the treasure trove itself. The thrill of discovering something covered up or cast away was totally eclipsed by the haul of treasure: trinkets, weapons, spell books, carvings and a huge cache of one-off mantras, one of which was the mantra he'd used on his young apprentice. Of course the work hadn't all ended there. Translation, documentation, testing, research and development as well as finding the most appropriate place to store all the goodies came next, and were almost as time consuming as discovering the stockpile. While the contents were hugely valuable, on the day that he used the one-off mantra on young Tank, he considered none more so than that particular spell. Having your abilities inhibited, your powers removed, was so utterly shocking and devastating, something he could testify to firsthand, that he wished someone had surprised him with it, well... almost. And so it was that although the young rugby playing dragon had been stripped of his magic, finding himself helpless beyond belief, feeling lonelier than the occasion after rugby when all his teammates had stolen his towel and clothes and put them in the middle of the clubhouse and he'd had to walk in wearing only his kitbag to cover up his modesty, it wasn't his first time. So remembering the feeling, and his boss's wise words of wisdom, he gained control of his breathing and started trying to figure out exactly what was going on.

Decades in the making, the plan had not only been timed to perfection, but had been implemented as precisely as it had been laid out, throughout the rest of the dragon domain of course. Dark dragon infiltrators and disguised nagas had spent years scheming, and then eventually sowing the seeds of misery and destruction.

Almost nowhere had been spared. Larger swathes of dragon society beneath the earth were currently suffering horrendous casualties, as well as the indignity of being cut off telepathically from any form of outside help or knowledge about what was happening across the rest of the planet. Subterranean cities such as New York, London, Moscow, Sydney, Paris, Berlin and Madrid amongst others, had been devastated by mighty ground quakes, whilst the destruction of pivotally placed lava dams had wreaked havoc in or around Delhi, Athens, Rome, Wellington, Perth and New Orleans. Death and destruction had visited in the form of chemical, biological and conventional terrorist attacks. Darkness had descended on dragon civilisation in more ways than one. Across the planet the power was out, cities and outlying regions only lit up by the rampaging fires from the torched buildings and the scorched bodies. With the power out, the scrubbers and filters that recycled the stale air of the domain for fresh air from the surface were no longer working, meaning the thick, corrosive black smoke from the fires and evil that had been perpetrated had nowhere else to go. Across the realm smog ruled and magical beings struggled to breathe. Oddly, no nursery ring had been so much as touched. Manson had issued strict orders about this, on pain of death and the beings under his command had made sure to obey them to the letter.

Throughout the history of its race, the dragon contingent had never suffered so much. And this was just the beginning. It wouldn't be long before the humans on the surface followed in their footsteps.

'Lightweights,' she thought, as the laminium dagger held tightly in her right hand swiped across the throat of her first dragon attacker, spewing brilliant green blood in nearly every direction. Evidently they'd fully expected her to retreat and had been taken totally by surprise when instead she'd sped towards them. Deep inside her head, she just tutted at their naivety, wondering how many more of them she could take before their sheer numbers overwhelmed her. Turning on a sixpence, she reversed the dagger's blade in her hand, before using a smidgen of its power to plunge it into the eye socket of the next dragon to set upon her, skipping nimbly out of the way of the sweeping sword blade that had been hell bent on cleaving her in two. With two taken out in quick succession, her inherent cockiness threatened to raise its ugly head, but this was neither the time nor the place, something that quickly became apparent as another five dark dragons stalked towards her.

Approaching the human female that they'd just seen murder two of their own, a cautious apprehension abounded across their telepathic link. Their leader, the biggest brute of the lot, immediately ordered them to spread out in an effort to outflank and overwhelm the tricky human form in front of them.

Sucking up the power bound in the laminium of the dagger, the thought of letting the weapon fall into the hands of these dragons tore at every part of her being. They'd be unstoppable, able to destroy whole dragon communities in an instant. She just couldn't let it happen, and despite having always ignored the odds before, particularly on the lacrosse field, five against one, here and now, looked almost impossible to overcome. Seeing no way out and, slightly more significantly, no way to either hide or destroy the precious weapon she was carrying, the fear causing her hands to shake ever so slightly turned to anger as she chose which of the five would die with her.

In his wildest dreams, he'd never imagined being dropped into a situation like this. The last twenty four hours had been a rollercoaster ride filled with impossible ups and downs. From Australia to Antarctica, the huge battle in the underground cavern, a magical wormhole transporting them half way across the planet in the blink of an eye, and now this. It was all simply mind blowing. Even after Yoyo and the dragon stuck as a human... what was his name? Ah, that's right... FLASH! Even after their warnings that it was a distinct possibility they would all find themselves in the middle of a raging battle, he'd never really believed it. And in all honesty, he still didn't. It seemed like an adrenaline filled dream, being here, cloaked in invisibility, hidden amongst mighty magical beasts, fighting for not just their lives, but the future of the planet. Sprinting for all he was worth, he ducked out of the way of a bright pink salvo of magical missiles, before forwards rolling back to his feet, no mean feat for any dragon at any time, let alone in the middle of a hard fought, pitched conflict. Upright once again, all the time heading in the direction of the young human shaped woman surrounded and massively outnumbered, backed up in the furthest part of the chamber, Hillier scanned the scene in front of him, nervously looking for just the tiniest thing out of place. THERE! The outline of a massive marble pillar, had, for just an instant... rippled! Impossible to spot unless you were looking for it, the off-the-cuff young dragon recognised the imprint of the suit twinned to the one he was currently wearing. Identifying where his friend and colleague Zebediah was headed gave him the exact knowledge he needed. Not sorry at all that he'd stopped to help save the huge battle dragon from the twisted blade that had threatened to decapitate her, he did at least feel a little guilty about slipping up the suit's mask and showing her his face. Throughout the years, he'd always been a little bit of a show off, but that had mainly been a front to hide the insecurities he'd always felt. Speeding around the opposite side of the semi circle of dreaded monsters that were almost upon the human shaped dragon, to where he assumed Zebediah was located, he picked a mantra from the top of a huge list at the front of his brain and prepared to set loose the magic he hoped would turn the tide of a very one sided encounter.

Without hesitation, she'd chosen. The three in the middle had been her pick, knowing that if she harnessed all the power she could absorb from the dagger, there would be a pretty good chance that she could take all three of them from this world. It would, of course, leave her exposed to an attack from the outer two, but this was no longer her concern. Her willpower was now fully focused on doing the maximum damage to the maximum number of opponents, no matter what the cost to her. Take as many out as possible, lessen the odds for her friends after she'd gone, this was all she could do. And so in a blurring whirl of blade and magic, she danced directly into the centre of her surrounding attackers and, reciting one of her favourite mantras, opened herself fully to the mystical energy within. A surgical strike of emerald tendrils spat from her hand, tearing the middle dragon's throat apart in an instant, smouldering smoke filling the gaping hole where a split second earlier his Adam's apple had been. One down, two to go.

Sneaking up on the left hand outer dragon in the line of five that were all about to attack the human shaped dragon, briefly he wondered why she hadn't reverted to her prehistoric natural form. In his mind it made little sense to stay like that; in fact he'd go as far to say it was total and utter suicide, for most beings anyway. Through the madness on his way over here, he'd glimpsed the tiniest bit of what she could do, and if that's what she had in her locker, than there was at least half a chance her life could be saved, but only if Hillier were close by. Not daring to think of the consequences should his friend be elsewhere, he ignored the hastened drum beat of his heart and prepared to strike.

Rewarded with just the tiniest hint of pleasure as her first victim crashed to the ground in front of her, she knew not to dither as her fight was about to get close up and personal, and by then she had to have taken out at least one more. This time, choosing the kind of assault that was abhorrent to almost all dragons, her magic mentally probed the beast to the left of his fallen comrade, as she looked at it. Enhanced and enriched by the power from within the laminium, time slowed as her brain's reaction sped up. Part of her inherent supernatural poked and prodded her next target and surprisingly, to her anyway, it found the tiniest of unprotected gaps in the dragon's personal shield. Instantly taking advantage, her power trickled through the breach and fought its way immediately into the prehistoric monster's brain. With the hardest part done, and Richie all the time travelling towards her next target, it was just a question of what mantra to use next. Usually one for finesse, she knew that now it was a question of practicality, and how much magic to use was totally and utterly irrelevant, given that she was inundated in that department thanks to the vicious weapon she wielded in front of her. Choosing a minor explosive mantra and adding just a little of her willpower to the mix, she rattled off the words inside her head. BOOM! The dragon in question had no idea what hit it, dying instantly, its brain quite literally exploding as it ran.

Two down, with the other three almost within touching distance of her famed laminium dagger, she gave herself over to the magic within as time resumed its normal course, and hoped to take out at least one more of the dreadful, dark warriors.

Fighting wasn't really his thing, and so terrified out of his skin at what was going on around him, Hillier racked his brain for something suitable to assault the dragon he assumed was his to take out. Momentarily flustered, the best he could come up with was a devilish blinding bomb created from pure fire magic, which he threw right into the face of his very surprised target. BAM! It wasn't a huge explosion, as it hadn't been designed that way. Nevertheless it was effective, as a cloud of splintered fiery fragments peppered the beast's face and eyes, effectively rendering him blind and out of the fight for the time being. Pleased with his work, the young dragon weighed up whether to attack another dragon, or finish off the blinded flailing one that he'd just put out of commission.

Most of his young friends had their quirks, or favourite things. That included the type of magic they preferred to use when casting mantras or spells. For Zebediah it would have to have been tricky hexes that would confound or confuse. Hillier he knew preferred to dabble in anything fire based. For him, he'd always been attracted to anything either cold, or magnetic, and during his sparring sessions with Yoyo's other young dragons, had developed a vast array of spells based on these two core elements. While he knew he could do some limited damage to the dragon in front of him with many of the magnetic mantras that were his stock in trade, almost certainly the situation called for use of his cold spells. Dragons' general susceptibility to cold gave him a much better chance of taking out this one swiftly, something he was keen to do, given the fact that he had no idea if his teammate was out there stalking about in an effort to help the cause of the young human female shaped dragon. Without any further ado, he embraced all his magic, targeted his willpower and voiced the words in his mind, watching, satisfied, as a thin sheet of ice started to form at the sides of the scaly monster's head.

Having taken down the other two with magic, it was now time to use the perfect weapon she found herself armed with. In a fleeting slip of concentration, her thoughts turned back to the point at which she'd led the humans deep into the dragon domain and had stumbled, quite by accident, across the master mantra maker in his huge, prehistoric form. It wasn't quite by accident though, as he'd revealed moments later. A vision had taken him there and then, hoping to meet up with their merry little band. Her delicate little mouth threatened to break out into a smile at the thought of Gee Tee handing out terrific weapons to each and every one of her friends... the paralysing water backpack for Hook, an array of grenades for the others, and most unbelievably of all, the mystical and futuristic Fu-ts'ang for Janice. On seeing all this, the wily old shopkeeper had kidded her on that he'd forgotten anything for her, when reality couldn't have been further from the truth, having placed her with what could only be described as one of the finest weapons in the course of dragon history. Exquisitely balanced, finely honed and charged with more power than most developed countries, fighting with it had been an honour, and had boosted her abilities beyond belief. But it could only do so much, and so, almost out of options, she surged forward and with a cunning roll off to one side right at the very last moment, ducking under the fizzing, sparkling blade that had looked to hack her in two, she bounced up back onto her feet. Knowing perfectly well where her target would be, she thrust the elegant dagger straight into the beast's weak spot, with no choice but to leave her back exposed, waiting for the inevitable deadly assault. No fuss, no goodbyes, there was just acceptance. As the hulking brute crumpled to the ground, its mouth barely able to form any sort of response to what had just happened in the lightning quick attack, the young lacrosse player struggled to work out why she was still standing. Slowly turning around, her surprise was palpable... and this from a being not easily perplexed. Looking up at the monster in front of her, memories of what she'd done to Casey threatened to overrun her. Only seconds before, the dragon who'd been powering towards her at a charge, intent on ending her life, was now covered from head to toe in a layer of thick, white frost.

'What the hell?' she thought. Odder still was that the dragon on the other side that she hadn't dealt with, was writhing around on the floor, clutching at his face, flames streaming from his mouth in every direction. Part of her thought she was dreaming, that perhaps she'd been struck down and this was somehow the first step towards the afterlife, not that she believed in such a thing. Quickly, it became apparent that this was not the case.

Watching the bewildered human female wondering just how she'd survived, Hillier and Zebediah both had exactly the same idea at exactly the same time. In an instant, they both lifted up the masks on their camouflaged suits, revealing big smirks zigzagging across both their scaly faces. For her part, Richie jumped back startled, brandishing the dagger about in front of her.

"Whoa, whoa..." shouted Zebediah over the ringing of weapons clashing, masonry exploding, and magic tearing through the air.

"It's alright," piped up Hillier. "We're with Yoyo. He sends his regards. Good hunting."

And with that, the two of them slipped down their masks, their features rippling into invisibility, leaving only a very stunned Richie. Mind blown, she turned around and assessed where she could best be of use. A whisper in her mind gave her cause for concern. The two dark dragons left here had still not been properly dealt with and could potentially rejoin the fight at some point much further in the future. Disgusted with herself on some base level, she knew, as with Casey, she had little choice but to do what could best be described as practical. Seconds later they were no longer a threat, and with yet another stomach churning deed completed, only one of many so far, she gripped the hilt of the dagger tight, and set off at a sprint to see where she could best make a difference.

Deflecting an array of poison spores back in the direction of her assailant from just above the circle of what was left of her force, Amelia Battlehard caught a glint of blurred movement, below and off to her left. Drifting down to the ground, surrounded by her overrun force, she watched as one of the individuals she felt so responsible for smashed the hilt of his stolen sword up against the jaw of his attacker, stunning him momentarily, before ramming the dark, deadly blade as far into his chest as it would go, directly piercing his perceived weak spot. Normally this would have been enough. But not here, not now... not against THEM!

"DAMN!" she cursed, having warned each and every one of them about the deceptive weak spots some of these dastardly foes were able to create. To be honest, it shouldn't really be an issue. Things had changed so much over the last fifty years or so, with the fantastical weapons their human charges had invented with a view to killing everything in their way. A hundred years ago, nothing their charges had would have even scratched them, but now that was so not the case. Barely a day went by that another different and more effective machine gun didn't roll off the production line, capable of firing armour piercing bullets. All of her kind knew not to mess with those. One or two had over the years, ending up brutally slain. And that's what made this whole 'weak spot' business so totally and utterly absurd. Modern, much younger dragons knew little, and cared even less about it. Dragons of a certain age, who'd all been through the same training, were far too focused on where the weak spot was when fighting another of their ilk, and even though instructed otherwise in this case, prehistoric ingrained urges were inclined to run riot. She was only too aware how easy it was, in the heat of pitched battle, to throw all rational thinking totally out of the window. Directing her thoughts straight at her comrade, she screamed telepathically for him to watch out! But before he'd had a chance to realise exactly what was going on, the despicable dark dragon, having feigned death briefly, brought his brute of a tail around, smashing it viciously into the side of the King's Guard's face, toppling him to the ground. Instantly Amelia spat out a vicious streak of blue tinged flame in his direction in the hope of at least creating a momentary distraction and buying her brother in arms a few more valuable seconds. But that's not how it panned out. With the sword still buried in his chest, clearly not suffering from a fatal blow, the prehistoric monster stamped on his enemy and, in one very swift and calculated move, dragged his long, razor sharp, curved talons down the length of the body below him, exposing all the organs within, letting loose a fountain of dull green blood.

RAGE stoked her primal instincts at the sight of yet another one of her force lost, and it should have been preventable... that's what hurt her the most. Exploiting the killer's momentary lack of concentration as he tried to remove the blade he'd been impaled with, the dazzling captain launched herself in his direction, on him in but a moment. Realising just how costly his mistake was, he flapped his wings, trying fervently to take to the air. But to no avail. Amelia Battlehard had gotten right up close and personal, too close in fact to launch any kind of magical attack. Panic stricken, the monster's head flailed about in an attempt to head butt his surprise attacker, but the thoroughly riled Captain had other ideas entirely. With one swift kick that totally blew apart his kneecap, Amelia Battlehard gave in to the unthinkable, knowing that she had to finish things fast. Ignoring the howls of agony she'd just induced, just a little afraid of the repercussions of what she was about to do, her jaws opened as wide as dragonly possible and, moving them either side of her enemy's neck, she clamped down with all her might, rallying against the stomach-churning urge to be sick. As needle sharp, pointed teeth carved through scale, bone, cartilage and muscle, her will dissolved. Pulling back, having not quite severed the dragon's head from its body, a foaming brown nausea spewed everywhere. Shaking her giant jaws from side to side, ridding herself of the last of it, watching the monster of a corpse crash to the ground, the shaken but not stirred captain launched herself back into the air, once again taking up her place up above the circle, urging her comrades to close ranks and tighten up, all the time looking to protect them from above.

Earth's surface. Salisbridge, United Kingdom.

It wasn't what you knew, or who you knew, it was what you knew about who you knew, and that had never been more obvious than when applied to what was happening here today.

Under the watchful eye of the cathedral's magnificent, ancient spire some way off in the distance, vast, heavy machinery had been brought in to clear the huge amount of rubble that covered the enormous sports club site. Over the last few days, against all odds, working around the clock, they'd done all of it. It had been a heroic effort by everyone involved, but then it should have been, given the extraordinary amount of money they were all being paid, courtesy of the man financing the whole rebuilding effort... Al Garrett. In reality, it should have been impossible to get all this done in such a short time frame, but in Salisbridge, Garrett was THE man, and if he wanted something done, generally he got his wish In this case his connections on the city and county council paid dividends, most of them owing him huge favours, with one particular councillor having to be reminded of a certain dubious incident that involved a notorious madam, adult nappies, an oversized cot and a dummy laced with gin. It wasn't pretty, and it wasn't Garrett himself that got his hands dirty, but it was mightily effective in granting all the licences he needed, as well as helping him avoid a whole tickertape parade of red tape. And so it came to be that in the brilliant, bright sunlight of a cloudless, blue sky, the first of the new foundations for the enhanced, feature packed new sports clubhouse, was about to be laid. A small gathering including the mayor, local and county councillors, the new chairman of the sports club and various committee members of each sporting section, as well as Garrett himself, had all come down to witness the groundbreaking moment. In reality it wasn't really much, just some concrete poured into a hole, but it was the sentiment that mattered. Washing away memories of the old clubhouse and the viciousness with which it had been destroyed, replacing all of those and the building itself with something contemporary that would hopefully become a family friendly, community environment for all to use, was Garrett's hope and greatest wish, not really because of the time and money he'd invested in the project, but because of the promise he'd made to Peter. That thought right there sent his mind spiralling off in a dozen different directions, primarily just how worried he was about the two youngsters who had disappeared... Peter Bentwhistle and Richie Rump. It was so unlike both of them, and most worrying. Of course he'd used some of his unofficial resources in an effort to track them down, with very little success. It was almost as if they'd dropped off the face of the planet. How was that even possible in this time of social media and big brother, nanny state policing, he wondered. Racking his brain for what to do next, his train of thought was suddenly interrupted as the mayor began his speech.

"Honoured friends, we are gathered here today..."

One text journeying through the ether, directed to three separate locations all within spitting distance of each other, started the chaos, mayhem, destruction and unprecedented loss of life in the heart of the medieval city that, for the most part, kept itself to itself. Three rip-roaring explosions, one from beneath the innocuous looking seat, one located amongst the long grass against the cathedral's wall and one centred on a high ledge, discharged with the full force of the military grade explosive that had been used, disintegrating everything contained within the minster, including the huge crowds of tourists that had come from across the globe to visit, all the superb stained glass windows, the famous clock which was amongst some of the oldest working in the world, all the sacred texts and of course, each and every wall. In no time at all, the full force of the detonation tore across the outside of the grounds, indiscriminately murdering men, women and children of all ages, races and religions. As if that explosive force and the wave of debris weren't bad enough, the main attraction started to come crashing down in all its glory. One hundred and twenty three metres high, the iconic spire, octagonal in shape, the tallest in Britain, now without any support or foundation, hurtled towards the ground, the full force of its towering weight behind it. Those few that had momentarily survived the initial blast, praised their luck and their God, ecstatic at being able to pull in another breath. Deities, luck and, more importantly, fate had other ideas, as over forty thousand tons of stone belonging to the rest of the building and its spire collapsed on top of the devastation that had already been caused, with an almighty BOOM, shaking the entire city to its core, throwing up a cloud of smoke and particulates into the air, triggering an unmatched, concentric wave of concussive force that shredded through everything in its way, taking out many of the surrounding buildings in the famous Close in which it was situated. Spontaneous fires burst into being as gas lines split. Surrounding buildings, not only in the Close but the city itself, wobbled precariously, some toppling to the ground, others staying upright just long enough for their inhabitants to escape out into the open. A surge of flotsam and jetsam carried along on the air by the force from the detonation extended out across the water meadows as rivers burst their banks, sheep ran amok and trees were flattened like pancakes. Anarchy and disorder the likes of which the city had never seen sparked into being. Residents, shoppers and tourists alike all ran towards the outskirts, one key thing cemented in their mind... SURVIVAL! Bedlam and mayhem ensued, as planned, turning the city into a scene from a war ravaged battle zone.

BOOM!...

Every head immediately turned away from the mayor in the direction of the city centre, as the mud shook beneath their feet and the freshly poured concrete rippled in disgust. A collective gasp reverberated through the air as they all watched the medieval spire in the distance collapse. A second BANG rumbled across the air, not quite as loud as the first, though still causing the ground to tremble. Exclamations of horror and shock at what they'd just witnessed were quick to ring around the ground.

"Oh my God!"

"What in the name of..."

"Aaaaahhhhhh..."

"I can't believe it!"

"Sweet mother of Jesus..."

Watching in absolute disgust as a cloud of grey engulfed what had only moments before been the pride of the city, Garrett kept his counsel and offered a silent prayer to those he knew would have been inside the cathedral itself, and in and around the immediate vicinity. Wondering who the hell would commit such a heinous act of aggression, the industry leader decided it would be best to leave as quickly as possible and get back to Cropptech with a view to finding out more and supporting the staff he knew would be crushed by what had just happened. Excusing himself from the startled congregation, he marched swiftly towards his car, noting that Fred, the man at the wheel, had already started the engine for him. Sliding out into the main road in the direction of the Cropptech main site, Garrett couldn't fault his driver for wanting to get a move on. One thing he knew for sure was that he'd feel much safer once he got to his office.

41 STEELING FLEET STREET BACK FROM THE ENEMY

A ring of towering, gigantic, lighthouse-like structures stretching up into the darkness, the tops of which were higher than any dragon could see, the buildings themselves constructed from conglomerate, with white, egg-like stone protruding from a yellow, sandy layer: subterranean Fleet Street was a marvel to behold. Or at least it would have been if not for the surrounding devastation, burning pyres of decapitated dragons and the throat scorching, nose blocking, eye wateringly thick, acrid black smoke that permeated everything. Nausea inducing might be the best way to describe the smoke, but it had at least one benefit. As a means of cover, it was almost second to none, something that should pay dividends in allowing the three dragons to get as close as possible to their intended target without being spotted.

Moving his head from side to side before stretching out his wings once or twice, Steel couldn't shake the uneasiness he'd been feeling since the details of the mission had been agreed upon. It wasn't so much the plan, but the thought of flying into what had now been turned into a compound. Before the laminium ball bomb and his dice with death, flying was his thing and he doubted there was anyone better at it than him. It felt as though it was the only reason he'd been put on the planet... to fly. But now he wasn't so sure. His experience and the logical part of his mind told him that he'd be fine and it would be exactly as it had been before. But this new body felt supple where it should not give, thin and less protective where it should be thick and strong. Not really wanting to take to the air, he'd argued that sneaking in from the ground, just like his reconnoitre, was the best way to push forward. Of course the master mantra maker had gone on to describe in perfect detail just how they could use the sickly black smog to cover their descent into the compound, making a compelling case with which the others totally agreed. In reality, he did too, it was just the whole flying thing that he was reluctant to do. Continuing to stretch his calf muscles, realising that the eyes of their whole force were upon him, he knew he wouldn't be able to put off the moment for much longer. This was it, it was now or never. So facing his newly found fear head on, he stopped stretching, marched forcefully over to Jar Man and DomCon, who were both chatting to Gee Tee, and firmly announced,

"It's time. Let's do it!"

Nodding their agreement, the little and large of the dragon world waited to follow the famed laminium ball captain's lead.

"Good luck!" remarked the master mantra maker.

"To us all," replied Steel, bending his knees before fully revealing his wings.

In a single bound, the recently healed dragon took to the air, disappearing in no time at all into the thick blackness of the air above them. Not wanting to lose their de facto leader, Jar Man bolted after him, quickly followed by DomCon who was by now fully focused on the deadly mission ahead.

Inside that brilliant, complicated and sometimes selfish brain of his, Gee Tee hoped for nothing more than to see the three of them once again. But he knew the risks of what they had planned and very much doubted fate would be so kind.

Both long time pals had immediately caught up with their newly found friend and leader and were now circling at quite a rate, hot on his tail, quite literally, with Jar Man only a mere metre or so in his wake, and DomCon just behind his buddy. From where they were, it was practically impossible to know precisely how high up they were flying and exactly where the ground was. But both now trusted Steel with their lives. That was just the kind of dragon he was, able to inspire in seconds, pull other dragons along by the scruffs of their necks and make them all feel wanted and part of the team. He was... extraordinary.

Exhilarating didn't begin to do it justice. Oh how he'd missed this. Being at one with the air... even this air, with all the toxins, pollutants and smoke, it made his heart leap up into his mouth, sent a chill of excitement along his tail, and made his scales tingle. For the first time since he'd woken up in that medical facility, he actually felt... alive!

Mind back to the matter at hand, and using his laminium ball experience, he reached out with all his magical senses trying to get a picture of the ground and his surroundings, despite only being able to see ten or so metres in front of him. He knew he was roughly in the right place, because they'd circled up and over one of the lighthouse-like buildings, carefully concealing themselves behind the acrid black smog at the time, before dropping slowly into what he believed was the middle of the compound. This was where he'd seen and evaded the patrolling guards and the two higher ups, when he'd gone in alone on the ground. And this was where he'd hoped to drop in through the cover and gain the advantage of surprise, but his enhanced senses were currently providing him with very little in the way of help. So cutting back on the speed, he brought his tail down and his head up, cutting their level of descent, and continued in the huge arc, hoping to hell that he would spot the enemy long before they spotted him.

Exactly to plan, that's how their assault on this part of the city had gone. Charged with taking Fleet Street and the priceless crystal node that controls the flow of information across the world, the two of them had followed their orders to the letter, knowing that any deviation, no matter how small, would probably see Manson cut their life expectancy considerably. But it was done, and now it was just a matter of keeping it safe, not that they expected any kind of coherent resistance. Strolling through the darkness with his partner, occasionally flicking through to his night vision, just to make sure there were no unwanted guests, he puffed out his chest, proud of the job he was doing, awaiting his role in the new world order that wouldn't be long in coming. If only he'd bothered to look up.

Blowing out a huge mouthful of the toxic air, he fought off the urge to cough that presented a very real hazard. At that exact moment, his head and belly broke through the pungent clouds that had been caused by the dark horde ravaging the land, dropping into a night time like darkness, one where at least he was able to see some distance. But of course, so could his adversaries.

With the tip of his friend's tail almost flapping in his face, and concentrating fully on the mission, the rage within him threatened to spill over. It was all he could do to keep it under wraps. What on earth had they been thinking, joining up with this merry band of suicidal delinquents? DomCon was a dragon who found it hard to express his feelings, instead relying mainly on his friend to speak for them both. But what he lacked in coming forward, he more than made up for in fight. Although he found it hard to make new friends, he was fiercely protective of those that he regarded as such and would, without question, lay down his life in an instant to keep them safe. Now was not just one of those times, but the mother of all those times if these beings were to be believed, and he could see no reason why they shouldn't. But going into the compound almost blind didn't sit well with him. What he did know though, was that his friend and comrade, Jar Man, was going to go with or without him, and that was the crux of the matter. Honour, pride, friendship and a sense of duty wouldn't allow him to let his buddy go on his own. So here he was, about to descend into goodness knows what, in the hope of taking on a ridiculous human shape, in an effort to fool a collective enemy into thinking he was one of them. Brave or stupid, he had no idea which, he just longed for things to be over and return to normal. Part of him even missed the flamingo jokes, but there was no way he'd ever let anyone know that.

Trying their best to walk softly across the debris from the destruction that had taken place during their capture of Fleet Street itself, both ape shaped infiltrators tiptoed around some of the bigger stuff, eager to show those beneath them in the chain of command just how guard duty should be done. In all honesty, they preferred it out here, to being back in the temporary headquarters they'd set up, right next to the main crystal node. It was quiet, peaceful even, and they didn't have to deal with any of the complaints from the other dragons (let me tell you, there were quite a few) as well as those otherworldly serpents, the nagas who were... well, strange to say the least, and that very frightening woman. The further away from them, the better, as far as they were both concerned. Slinking around what remained of a humungous bronze statue, of who they couldn't have cared less, the strangest feeling of imminent doom encompassed both of them. Only then did it occur to them to look up. And so they did.

Poking through the thick, dark layers of cloud caused by the many fires blazing all around them, they could just make out a calculating prehistoric head, followed rapidly by a matching belly and a razor-sharp set of talons. About to reach out with his mind and raise the alarm, abruptly they were both hit by a barrage of psychic energy that Steel had unleashed the instant he'd spotted them. And a good job too.

Crushed firmly to the ground momentarily, disorientated, the two stumbled to their feet, much quicker than the laminium ball captain had anticipated. Worried about the sound from the scuffle travelling and the arrival of reinforcements, Steel landed softly between the pair of them, readying mantras at the forefront of his mind, knowing exactly how to silence them both. Before he had the chance they were upon him, using some kind of shared magic to pin him in place, battering him mentally with an array of unrecognisable spells. Unable to combat such despicable teamwork, Steel dropped clumsily to his knees, all the while trying to block out the telepathic onslaught that was currently aimed in his direction. Although not ideal, the situation had turned into something of a blessing, because both of the human shapes, having more than a degree of success against their one lone attacker, had forgotten all about summoning any help, clearly of the belief that they were more than a match for the kamikaze dragon that had dropped in upon them from above. And their overconfidence allowed Jar Man, and DomCon to sweep down from behind and take each of them out in one swift move, both catching the human shaped corpses before they even thought of touching the ground. Changing from dragon to human on the run, all the time still holding on to their prisoners, Jar Man and DomCon retreated as far into the darkness as possible, ably followed by Steel who was still struggling a little from the attack that he'd just suffered. Close to one corner of the compound, the trio had little choice but to take the lives of their two adversaries. It wasn't pleasant, and there was a long, awkward pause in the run up to doing it. In the end, it was DomCon that stepped up, garrotting both of the infiltrators' throats with a finely sculpted piece of wire he'd acquired from the master mantra maker before they'd left.

"Where the hell did you get that?" whispered Jar Man, stunned at what his friend had just done.

"Does it matter? Let's just move on," was the frank and rather dour reply.

"It had to be done," chipped in Steel, placing his hand firmly on DomCon's shoulder. "Good work, but there'll be worse to come if we're to get through this."

Both dragons nodded in agreement as they hurriedly changed into their victims' clothes. Sixty seconds later and it was done. The corpses had been hidden behind what was left of a wall, the surrounding rubble used to cover them up completely. It wasn't perfect, but someone would have to get awfully close to notice anything out of place. And so with DomCon wrapping the garrotte around his neck, firmly out of sight below his newly gained jumper, the two put the fake binders Gee Tee had somehow come up with around the wrists of the mighty Steel and, as one, they set off in the dark towards the headquarters, knowing that scores of their enemies lay in waiting.

With his mind reeling, and having had only a few precious hours of sleep, the youngest member of this eclectic group, the young hockey playing waiter from Salisbridge, Taibul, excused himself from the human contingent, deciding that now was the time to take a leak. He'd been warned that they would soon be on the move once again, this time taking on a force they might well not be able to defeat. Gee Tee had, however, stressed just how important taking back Fleet Street was in relation to the much bigger picture. It wasn't all doom and gloom though. The humans, all of them here, had great faith in not only the master mantra maker, who'd worked absolute miracles back in the Salisbridge market place, but in the dragon they called Steel. He'd been a natural leader, and despite his surprise at finding a contingent of humans, here underground, had welcomed them with open arms after hearing about their heroics from the previous day. So winding his way through darkened, rubble filled corridors that your average family saloon would have no trouble traversing, the youngster searched for some suitable shadow in which he could relieve himself.

"Brave lad... that one," whispered Angela, nodding in the direction Taibul had taken off in.

"He's a team sports player. That about says it all," ventured Emma.

Eyes closed, head leaning back against the hard rocky exterior wall, Sam nodded in agreement.

They were all missing not only their homes, but their respective sports and of course their friends, who were somewhere else below ground, involved in goodness knew what kind of shenanigans. It was Emma who voiced what everyone was thinking.

"I hope they're okay!"

Sam lazily opened his eyes.

"You mean the others?" enquired Angela.

"Richie, Tank, Hook, Janice, Peter, and all the others that we've met since being down here... I hope they're all okay."

"It stands to reason that they'll be okay," Sam said.

"How so?" both of the women responded.

"Think about it. They had an experienced fighting force alongside them, and more importantly... the element of surprise. Manson, whoever the hell he is, and the rest of his contingent, fully assume that Tank is dead and that any kind of resistance has been nullified. He and his force will be overconfident and unprepared, certainly not on the lookout for any kind of confrontation. If they can sneak in without being seen, then just maybe it'll all be over before it's started. That's what I'm hoping for, because anything else just doesn't bear thinking about."

"But humans... up against dragons?"

"We weren't too shabby back in Salisbridge, were we?"

"That relied an awful lot on luck," Angela stated. "As well, they don't have Gee Tee with them. We do. And we all know what a pivotal part he played in events."

"Give them some credit," chipped in Emma. "If Tank can lead like he plays rugby, the whole thing will be over before we know it."

That made them all chuckle.

With Taibul returning and with nothing else to do but wait, their thoughts turned to their families, who by now would be worried sick about their whereabouts.

42 ALL CREATURES GREAT AND SMALL

Top of the list of things he wanted to know at the moment, was where the hell was he? As he reached around in the pervading darkness, he couldn't quite fathom what was wrong. Not knowing how he'd got there, didn't help. One moment he was in the middle of the mother of all battles, and next he was here... wherever the hell here was. What he did know though, was that time was of the essence. Somewhere, nearby he assumed, his friends were fighting for not only their lives, but for the dragon way of life and the protection of the humans on the surface. So stumbling forward, not for the first time, he decided to do something that he considered so utterly ridiculous, it bordered on the insane.

"Hello? Is there anybody there?"

Not really expecting any kind of answer, he was more than a little perturbed when haunting laughter drifted out of the darkness.

For the most part out of sight, he called on all his experience, knowing that without it, some of those he cared for and loved would already be dead. Ignoring a ground shaking explosion that hit a wall about fifty metres from where he was tucked away, furiously spewing red hot shards of marble in his direction, Yoyo gave over his full attention to what was happening in and around the group of dragons he thought of as his kin. Of course he didn't have all of them covered, the exceptions being Hillier and Zebediah... wherever they were. He hoped they were cloaked and able to avoid the worst of the battle magic. But he couldn't focus on that now. The group needed him, and so he was here for them, like he'd been ever since the fighting had started.

Noticing the youngest dragon of his young horde, Pixma, had let a hole in her defensive rear shield develop, without even thinking about it, the Australian dragon healer recalled the words he needed inside his head, added the desired amount of willpower and watched as the gap disappeared. Right at that moment, he caught a slight movement in his peripheral vision. Noting a brown coloured naga sneaking its way through an array of cadavers, heading in the general direction of his team, Yoyo's internal sense of danger kicked into overdrive, almost overwhelming him with a sense of urgency. Not knowing what the beast's end game was made things difficult, especially as he was constantly deflecting away the odd magical attack here and there already. With one eye on the rogue naga, Yoyo used a controlled blast of kinetic energy to push his young charge Tarko forward, allowing a missile of deadly poison spores to narrowly miss her legs, whilst at the same time throwing up a huge chunk of rock that had fallen from high above to detonate some kind of magical grenade harmlessly away from them all. Diverting his concentration in these precious few seconds had allowed the devious naga to outflank the whole group, giving him the perfect angle to launch his attack. Worse still, Yoyo could only stand and watch, because his magical abilities were being used up elsewhere in the battle. Telepathically, he urged any of the youngsters to turn around, spot the threat and react to it. Probably because of everything going on, and the fact it was their first time in battle, none of them took heed of his warning. And so, working furiously with his mind, his hands and arms almost a blur the way he was dishing out his magic, he watched in horror as the sly naga started to cast his supernatural power. Focused fully on the deadly monster about to unleash his attack, and with a sinking feeling of epic proportions set to burst his gargantuan scaled belly, he was surprised to catch a glimpse of the naga's eyes almost popping out of his head. Wondering what on earth had happened to disrupt him during his crucial spell, it was only when he looked down at the reptilian beast's chest that he noticed the blade of a rather futuristic, cold enshrouded weapon poking directly out of it. Full of relief and delight at the outcome, for a moment he wondered where the weapon had come from. If he'd had to take a guess, and that's all it really was, he would have said it was somehow related to the young human woman sitting on the floor in the middle of the chaos, looking more than a little bruised, battered and broken. But just how and why she was doing it was a mystery to him, if that really was the case. All he knew was that they'd once again escaped tragedy by the skin of their teeth. Glad that they had, he turned his concentration back to the matter at hand, but not before sending a writhing tendril of healing energy in the mysterious human's direction, restoring her back to full health in but an instant, knitting her broken ribs back together, reducing the inflammation in her ankle and repairing all her cuts and bruises.

Assessing the threats and the young dragons' propensity to deal with them was all he could do, but up until now their teamwork had paid dividends, keeping them all relatively safe. Deep inside he knew it wouldn't last. The odd glance across the far side of the rebuilt bridge told him that. Reinforcements appeared to be mounting, in both dragon and naga form. As soon as they swarmed across, which they inevitably would, sheer numbers alone would see them defeated. It was all a bit of a disaster, but he vowed to keep on fighting, defending and healing until his last breath, hoping against hope that help of any sort would appear. To be honest, it didn't seem that likely.

Chilled to the bone by the icy cold, white marble floor he found himself lying on, and despite the magic screaming through the air all around him, the current dragon monarch only had eyes for one being... his best friend, comrade in arms, the dragon he thought of as a brother: FREDRIC! Seeing him stride through the magical wormhole had brightened his soul, lifted his spirit and energised the magic within him. But almost immediately things changed. For some unknown reason, the dragon giant and founder of the Crimson Guards had dropped down to his knees, looking a shell shocked wreck, startled beyond belief. Was it the humans here, fighting alongside the dragons? Or maybe he recognised his grandson, his emotions becoming all too much for him. Whatever it was, it didn't bode well. The others needed him in the fight... and NOW! Commanding his broken and beaten body to roll over and up into a sitting position whilst ignoring the blazing pain that burned throughout his human shaped limbs, it was then that a kind of emptiness washed over him, forcing him to feel half the dragon he'd been. Gazing down at his hand, it became immediately obvious what had provoked such a strong reaction. THE RING! Currently now in Tank's possession, George wondered what he'd done wrong. Throughout his guardianship of the precious magical artefact, it had always been stubborn, distant, even aloof at times. But for the most part it had agreed with his decisions, supported his actions and provided him with its inherent power on the occasions that he'd needed it. Not only that, but it had been his constant companion. When he'd not been able to share his thoughts and rationale with anybody else, the ring had come to his aid, giving him good, solid advice, clearly built up from a long history of experience. So why, over the last month or so, had it all gone wrong? Nothing had changed as far as he knew. Of course he was under an extraordinary amount of pressure, but that was nearly always the case. At least that's how it felt. Shoving the puzzling dilemma towards the back of his mind, and ignoring the ear splitting explosions all around him, George reached out with his psyche, searching for one consciousness amongst many, one that he'd interacted with more times than he could remember, one he was sure would recognise him in an instant.

Unkempt, bruised, battered, and clad in laminium chains, Fredric, now free from the captivity of the icy hellhole in Antarctica, knelt down on the floor, head bowed, his long, matted, scraggy hair concealing most of his face. Having survived the tortuous ravages of decades in confinement, it was ironic that his first taste of freedom should break him almost immediately.

Floating on the air, dodging and ducking brilliant bolts of blistering magic, George's mind finally reached his friend. Not wanting to startle him, the king rubbed his mind across the back of Fredric's head, something akin to a human handshake. Normally a reaction would be instantaneous, but not now. Stumped momentarily, the floating will changed tack, deciding that perhaps startling was what he needed. Now he tapped... tap, tap, tap... hoping a more concerted effort would have a noticeable effect. Not so. Searching his memory, scanning the vast array of knowledge he'd accumulated across his time walking the planet, he discovered another tactic, one he'd only used once, many, many decades ago. Enclosing Fredric's head, the consciousness poked and prodded this time, but once again to no avail. It was as he thought though: his friend had erected a mental barrier, something only usually done in times of danger or close quarters combat, like now. To the king's mind, it felt very much like a dome made from brick, mortar filling the gaps and all. So with that in mind, and with what felt like his last chance at reaching his friend, his consciousness dropped onto the top of the brick and effectively turned into liquid. More than anything, this required an awful lot of magic, something the king lacked by not having his majestic ring any more, and a mighty amount of concentration. This he could manage. And so having held the liquid in place with quite a lot of effort, slowly he allowed a few tiny drops to trickle down the side, searching and scouring for any gap at all, no matter how infinitesimal. One by one, he let even more go, each and every drop trickling across the course surface of the brick, some following the maze of the mortar, until finally every last inch of the surface of the protective dome had been covered.

'Blast,' he thought, frustrated at not having found a way in. It was then that he realised what he had to do, back across the other side of the chamber, deep within his body. Recalling his consciousness, he used a little of his magic to create a soothing wave of healing energy that he let run riot throughout his being. With not quite so much pain inhibiting his aged limbs, he staggered to his feet, looking for some way to cross the distance between himself and his pal without getting fried. In all his time, he'd never done anything like this.

From one king to another...

Flattening himself close to the brilliant white marble floor, he soaked up the refreshing cold, almost missing the icy confines of Antarctica. ALMOST! With no time to dwell on that, he rolled three times to his left, raised himself up to full height, ducked out of the way of the oncoming razor sharp blade his dragon opponent scythed in his direction, and in his mind, conjured up the words he needed. Foreign to all but his own distinctive race, the language, combined with just enough willpower and magic, produced a spectacular result. From just above the dark grey dragon, a dozen needle sharp, ice encrusted stalactites rocketed down, inundating their target, piercing it in over nine places, the most lethal of which punctured the beast's skull. Instantly dead, the prehistoric corpse toppled forwards. Effortlessly, Vasuki slipped out of the way as the giant shadow did its best to consume him.

Momentarily free from any opponents, again he reached out for his brethren, something so instinctive it was positively built into his DNA. But again there was nothing. Well, not nothing exactly, more of a kind of static, perhaps a magical interference. Resigned to not being able to help his kind, at least for the moment, the powerful, strong and proud king glanced around to see where he could be of most use. Charging towards the nearest dark dragon that had just touched down from the air above and was about to launch an assault on the still kneeling Fredric, Vasuki vowed two things to himself. One... he would help his new found dragon comrades right to the very end if need be. And two... he would not spill naga blood here today, even if it meant sacrificing his own life. While these two things might be contradictory, he was determined to do no more harm than had already been done to any member of his race.

Slithering across the marble, the naga king sank his long, needle sharp fangs into the prehistoric beast's scaled tail, and was rewarded with a very satisfying scream of epic proportions. Relinquishing his hold on the magic he'd prepared, he let it loose and watched as forked lightning tore open the supposedly invulnerable scales of his opponent. Heading in for the kill, he kept his telepathic senses open to everything around him, hoping for some sign or contact from any of his race. He wasn't optimistic though.

From two true kings, to one wannabe pretender...

Powered by pure, unadulterated evil, Manson's rage reached tipping point, and in a magical act so astounding, he used the power of his mind to rip Flash off him and tossed him angrily against the nearest wall. Flash impacted with the force of a sledgehammer being wielded by a power lifter, all but leaving an imprint of himself in the cracked, fractured and smashed construction. Sliding almost comically to the floor, the 'clink' of the chains wrapped around his torso barely audible over the magical racket that played out across the rest of the chamber, the courageous ex-Crimson Guard valiantly surged to his feet, greedily gobbling up as much of the magic as he could from the laminium he wore.

Jumping up, shaking himself off, whilst at the same time using a miniscule amount of magic to repair his false human features, Manson was both surprised and annoyed to see Flash almost immediately get back to his feet. This on its own was enough to set alarm bells ringing throughout not only his head, but the rest of his body as well, and he was unable to remember any being he'd ever met that would have got up so quickly from a hit like that. Whoever this newcomer was, he was good... and powerful, he thought. Cursing his luck, unable to believe these new found obstacles that had been placed in his way, he delved as deep inside himself as he dared, searching for the most wicked of his magic. Finding it almost instantaneously, he found himself faced with a choice. Five deadly spells sat lined up against a wall in his head, each giving off matt black wisps of evil looking dark vapour. Selecting not quite the worst, he conjured it up in his mind and, with barely a glance, spat it out in the direction of Flash, who by now was running steadfastly towards him.

Head pounding like a pneumatic drill and blood gushing down his cheeks, Flash surged forward with all the speed he had. A blur didn't do him justice. On closing the gap to about half way, a succession of black tendrils rippled from the would-be king of this world's right hand, expanding out much as a spider's web would over time, only this happened in a split second. Caught off guard by not only the speed in which his opponent had reacted, but by the look of whatever strange mantra had been used, the ex-Crimson Guard had to re-evaluate all his options in far less than the blink of an eye. As the remarkable magic closed in around him, powered by the metal he wore, Flash leapt up and over, just off to his right, forgoing an immediate opportunity to get to his chief target. Sailing through the air, he felt ever so slightly smug at having skirted the dark dragon leader's attack, and was already preparing his next move. Thoughts of that disappeared in an instant as a liquid fire tore up his left leg, from ankle to shin, so bad in fact that he wished he were dead. Instead of forward rolling and bouncing back up to his feet, Flash crashed to the ground face first, breaking his human shaped jaw instantaneously, not that he noticed at all. The pain from the tendril of magic that had sliced open his left leg was all consuming. Nothing else existed or mattered. Thoughts of everything else were long forgotten as the ex-Crimson Guard writhed around, almost bound inside the laminium chains that circled his chest.

In all his years, he'd never felt this afraid. Genuine terror clawed at his insides, desperate to escape. But still he kept his calm, outwardly anyway. Surrounded by pitch black, barely able to see the hand he knew was attached to the end of his outstretched arm, he'd tried everything he could to shed some light, in more ways than one. A simple mantra that should have produced a burning ball of light in the palm of his hand was snuffed out before it got started. Three other mantras he'd tried after that suffered the same fate. Next, he'd scrolled through his various forms of vision, hoping against hope that might at least give him a fighting chance to see where he was. No joy again. Desperate, worried and with fear nibbling away at his insides, he could only come up with one more thing to try, and in his human guise, it wasn't ideal. Delving into the core of his very being, he rummaged around for that tiny little spark that all dragons have, no matter what their shape or form. It took longer than he would have liked, all the time the fear inside him willing him to fail. Eventually though, he found it, and not wasting any time at all, brought it up through his stomach and into his throat. It felt so different doing it as a human. Well... it would, wouldn't it? Dragon bodies are designed for this very purpose. The human structure is not. Feeling his tongue and the skin at the top of his mouth begin to char, with all his might he pushed out the flame, his eyes wide open, determined to take in anything of his surroundings. But as the bright yellow and orange licks of fire passed over his teeth, sending shivers of hurt surging down into his gums, in turn triggering a rapid succession of tears from his eyes, the absolute blackness won, easily slaughtering his last attempt to see his surroundings. Out of breath, mouth fried, and more in need of a drink than he could ever remember, Tank slumped to the floor, landing with a huge bump on his ass, despairing at the situation he found himself in. He was supposed to be helping his friends, and here he was transported somewhere else, of no use to them at all. Just when he thought things couldn't get any worse, the haunting laughter started up again. Fear and terror chased each other around his insides, inciting panic and alarm throughout his falsehood of a body. Unable to fight it off anymore, he curled up into the foetal position, sobbing for all he was worth.

Panting like an over enthusiastic dog that had been chasing its own tail for an hour, and sweating more profusely than a marathon runner in a desert, Hook skidded to a halt beside Yoyo, delighted to be out of the main firing line and pleased to see a friendly face. At least, that's what he thought he was looking at, as the two had never actually met.

Offering out his hand, Hook introduced himself.

"Hook," he remarked, ever so orotund.

Taking his eyes away from the battle, although still using his arms to cast, deflect and temper magic in and around his group of dragons, Yoyo smiled at the young human.

"Yoyo," he ventured.

"Pleased to meet you," put in Hook. "Was it you that healed me?"

"It was, and you're very welcome."

"What can I do? I don't have any magic to offer up, but I'll help in any way that I can."

"You can cover me and make sure no one sneaks up behind us. I get so lost in the moment at times, with everything that's going on, it's sometimes hard for me to focus on the here and now. If an enemy approaches, give me a shout and I'll take care of it. Do not engage them yourself."

Hook nodded, turned and started to take in the fight, noting where all his friends were, determined to make sure nothing devious or underhand found itself in a position to harm Yoyo. Turning back towards the action, the dragon healer marvelled at humans sharing the dragon domain, and not only that, but fighting alongside dragons, and their monarch. Things were getting crazy!

Gingerly wobbling to her feet, Earth rose just in time to see her king and current soul mate, far across the chamber, launch a magical strike straight out of the naga's supernatural handbook, looking on happily as wisps of waspish shadow energy encompassed his onrushing attacker. Amazingly, and with more agility than she would have thought possible, the human shaped male leapt up and over at the very last moment, avoiding the attack. 'Ah... but he hasn't,' she thought, noticing the tiniest tendril on the outer edge of the magic slice through the lower part of his leg. Confident that her other half's opponent had been brutally dealt with, she turned away for a brief moment, brushing herself down, before checking that the healing energy she'd infused herself with had done its trick. It had. Pleased to go into battle looking her best, stoked by the rage and power bubbling just below the surface of her fair skin, thoughts of her appearance faded, only to be replaced with where she should strike first. It was then that a recognisable voice whispered inside her head, urging her on, begging to be set free. As the disembodied words flitted around her mind, she wondered how long it had been. Years since they'd last seen each other... oh how she'd yearned for him. Cartwheeling out of the way of several stray missile blasts and the explosive debris they tossed her way, she told him how much he'd been missed. Expressing the exact same sentiment back in her direction, both practically purred in satisfaction. With just a thought, using an image instead of words this time to give life to her magic, down beside her on the cracked, charred and discoloured broken white marble, appeared her familiar, the two-headed serpent looking eager to please. Dismissing him with the tiniest movement of her index finger, he knew not to stray too far, after all his primary purpose was to keep her safe, but how he did that was very much down to his own discretion. And having been away for so long, every instinct in his body screamed at him to fulfil his role by killing all her enemies, an instinct he was only too happy to comply with.

Watching her companion's thick, muscular tail disappear into a choking cloud of magical smog, Earth turned her attention to the raging enchanted encounter in front of her. Spotting two of the King's Guards together, seemingly having a great deal of success fighting back to back against a series of probing naga attacks, she readied her magic, let the darkness within consume her, and bounded over the rubble in front of her, intent on satisfying her blood lust.

Parrying another strike, she feinted one way and then the other, before ramming the hilt of the dark edged sword up into the monstrous beast's jaw. It was momentarily stunned, so without hesitation she thrust her weapon as hard as she could through its pale green stomach, watching in satisfaction as blood spurted from the wound and gurgled from its mouth. With no time even to celebrate her small victory, and keeping her back firmly planted to that of her comrades, she brought her stolen sword up and prepared for the next attack. It was only then that she noticed the dragons and nagas in front of her part like trains at a set of points. Directly down the middle was the one being here that she feared the most. NO! Not Manson. Maybe it should have been him, after all, he was clearly a psychopath. But in some respects that made him predictable and certainly fightable. This foe though, she considered much, much worse. Having watched his evil queen throughout the entire time they'd been captured, she'd hoped to hell not to catch her attention, and thankfully hadn't. But that had all changed now. With Earth marching steadily towards her, the young guard powered up her defensive shield, sent a brief warning to her partner, and with all the determination that she could muster, let loose a dizzying array of magic, all of it meant to destroy the crazy monster heading her way.

Instinctively Manson's queen lit up her personal shield, allowing it to harmlessly absorb the pathetic display of sorcery spat at her by the disappointingly average guard who now looked on in absolute horror.

'Good,' she thought. 'What's the point of having power if not to terrorise others?' Almost within a sword's reach, Earth stopped and smiled, the kind of sickening smile only pure, malevolent evil could muster. It had the desired effect, goading the guard to step out and leave her partner's back exposed. Without hesitation, the vile queen willed her magic into existence, producing a brilliant swarm of bright blue mosquitoes that, after acknowledging their own mortality, dive-bombed head first straight towards the quaking guard. Putting all her willpower and mana into her barrier, she died with a look of total and utter surprise ingrained into her scaled face as the supernatural insects not only penetrated her personal shield, but violated her scales with almost no resistance. Before the first guard's body had even hit the ground, Manson's queen was already using her exquisite gift for evil to drill beams of super powered light into the exposed back of her partner. With a roar louder than most planes taking off, the wounded dragon dropped to his knees before a horde of dragons and nagas swamped him. In an instant he too was dead.

Alongside Troydenn's massive, motionless skull, Yelevel, one of the dragon councillors that had retreated back into the king's private residence when the council building had come under attack, danced a dance she knew well. A former knight in her younger years, for but a brief while she'd served alongside George, although some time after his encounter with the famed dragon at what was now known as the city of Salisbridge. Presently she found herself dicing with a particularly punchy naga who had a whole array of magical mischief up his sleeve. So far, she'd managed to avoid being caught by any of it, but was not only running out of ideas, but of mana as well. Knowing that she needed a brief respite to recover just a little spurred her on to finish off the serpent-like beast as quickly as she could. Detonating a brilliant, bright flash bang at almost point blank range, knowing what was to come allowed her to close her eyes and escape the worst of the dazzling explosion. Acting on instinct alone her human form closed the few metres' gap as her slippery opponent tried to wriggle out of the way, unable to see where his enemy was. Leaping for all she was worth, she almost slipped as she landed on the top part of his scaled tail. Grabbing onto his right ear with her right hand to steady herself, she knew speed was of the essence. By now the naga could feel her atop of him and started dancing about like a cat that's just realised it's about to be taken to the vet. Yelevel held on firmly, rising up and down and rolling with every movement, focusing her centre of gravity and maintaining her balance. During a momentary respite, she struck. Using the stolen knife she'd acquired from the guard that had held her hostage originally, with her left hand she rammed the blade fully into the beast's left ear with all the strength she had. Rewarded for her efforts by the start of a high pitched scream and the naga's now inert body slumping to the floor, the councillor leapt up and over the bleeding corpse, landing beside the massive matt black cadaver of Troydenn. Catching her breath fleetingly, having bought herself a little bit of space, she scrutinised the magical madness going on all around her. All things being equal, she should really have picked a target and ploughed on into the battle. It's a shame that she didn't. It might well have saved her life. With her back to the giant corpse for cover, and the energy within her recharging at quite a rate, she glanced around in front of her, selecting her next target carefully. Unbeknown to her, Earth's two headed wicked serpent slithered out from under Troydenn's neck where it had been hiding. Spotting its prey, the nightmarish beast wasted no time. In one lightning strike, both heads each clamped their razor-sharp teeth around a leg, injecting venom and holding on for all they were worth. Yelevel didn't have a chance. By the time she realised what was happening, the pain prevented her from finding the appropriate magical response, while the poison dulled her senses. In a matter of seconds it was over. The councillor for New Zealand was dead, Earth's familiar was vaguely satisfied and the battle raged on.

Waves of pure, supernatural power roared through the air, hexes and enchantments ricocheted off the walls and floor, as a rainbow of different coloured smoke drifted across the king's private residence. Throughout it all, a young human woman began to feel the cold chill of the marble she'd been sitting on for some time. It hadn't of course been all plain sailing. Fu-ts'ang had deflected away a number of wild magical assaults that hadn't been intended for her, but had put her in danger anyway. And while things had gotten way past crazy, the dark dragons and nagas didn't see her as a threat and so focused their rage and their magic on other more dangerous looking targets. Little did they know that she'd played a significant part in the damage they'd suffered. Her tally of kills was significantly higher than anyone else's here. Of course, it wasn't just her. They were a team... one pure mind working with an experienced, calculating one that had a singular grasp of what needed to be done. And what a team they were. If Manson had known just what was going on, and the way in which Janice was guiding Fu-ts'ang, she'd be their number one target for sure. But he didn't, and with so much chaos and mayhem around the chamber, it was unlikely that he'd find out any time soon.

Turning her attention to half a dozen nagas closing in on Yoyo's young band of renegade dragons, the youthful bar worker guided her partner in their direction. Slicing through the air, barely noticeable to most of those around apart from the slight frosty trail he left in his wake, Fu-ts'ang arrowed in on his first target... or should that be targets? Skipping around a wayward volley of scattered magical shots, the deadly weapon swept in low, disguising his trajectory by passing through two giant clouds of smoke given off by one of the huge ear splitting explosions that regularly lit up their surroundings. Lining himself up, much to Janice's approval, and with the deadly, icy white frost circling the blade, the weapon rushed forward, cleaving not one, but two naga tails in half, in a single strike. Both beasts smashed against the marble floor, emitting the most nauseous of ear-splitting sounds. Pleased with his work, Fu-ts'ang whipped back around in a tight arc, sights set on the next target.

With their concentration focused on saving the lives of the band of young dragons, Janice and her partner failed to heed the approach of a brutal looking dark dragon. Brilliant burgundy merged gently with yellow across the whole of his body in a stunning combination, apart from his face which just looked as though he'd flown into the side of a house. Scales were missing, while some just flapped around as he walked, barely holding on with anything at all. The most disturbing things though were his eyes. One was almost totally bloodshot, while the other was... MISSING! A dark yellow eyelid was fused in place, with two thick black lines running diagonally across the scales and gunk that sat there instead of the normal tennis ball sized eyeball. As if that wasn't enough, some of the scales on his tail had been removed, and metallic spikes of various sizes and degrees of deadliness had been inserted. Stalking towards the unwitting Janice, one or two of the spikes dragged across the marble, the loud scraping noise of them doing so masked by the violence going on all around them.

Jumping out of the way of a dazzling purple net that sizzled to the ground next to him, briefly the young hockey playing dragon considered reverting back to his natural form. Almost immediately though, he dismissed the idea. For the likes of Tank, it kind of made sense. His dragon body was huge, almost that of a laminium ball player. For Peter it was somewhat different... almost embarrassingly so. In his dragon form, he could fit quite neatly underneath one of Tank's mighty wings. So while he was reasonably agile and nimble in the air, that wasn't really a part of the battle he wanted to get involved with at the moment. Things were hard enough here on the ground... having glanced across the newly rebuilt bridge, he could see a massive force of dragons and nagas gathering there. He had little doubt that in no time at all, when Manson gave the command, the air above them would be filled with enemies. And while he was comfortable in the air, to him it seemed like the natural alternative was to stay in his human guise and help as best he could on the ground. Besides... it wasn't like he was the only one. Currently, George the king, Fredric his grandfather, Richie his best friend, Tank when he'd last seen him, and Flash were all in their falsehood human bodies, and so he figured he was in good company.

Evading monstrous heaps of rubble being dropped from the air by some of the dark dragons, Peter instinctively rolled off to one side as a spluttering, brilliant white, errant spark cut through where his head had been only moments ago. Thanking his lucky stars, and still reasonably sure he was protected by the shield from breaking the *alea*, even though he couldn't see or feel it, a sense of urgency started to niggle away at him. Glancing over his shoulders to make sure there was no immediate threat, it was then that he realised what the warning meant. Spotting the hulking, great, one-eyed prehistoric monster through the explosions and the magical melee, creeping ever closer to the love of his life, he knew he had to act. Without a thought for his own safety, he leapt over the lifeless remains of a silver shaded naga and sprinted straight into a cacophony of the supernatural, heading directly towards her.

Stomping towards his completely off guard prey, the humungous beast stopped when he knew he was in range. Ignoring some of the errant magical attacks that harmlessly bounced off his remaining scales, the sensation brought forth childhood memories of being tickled, causing him to pause momentarily. For a being so full of anger and violence, it was an odd turn of events, but one which fortunately allowed the young hockey playing dragon to close in on the threat he recognised to his beloved Janice.

Familiarity blossomed, causing her to open her eyes as her heart skipped a beat. There, directly in front of her, through the haze of the many different types of magic, her one true love appeared, poking through the multicoloured mist, rushing towards her at speed. Ignoring Fu-ts'ang's protests, her mind wandered. About to get up and throw herself into his onrushing arms, abruptly a cold chill ran down Janice's spine, filling her with dread. Slowly she swivelled her head and looked up to see the back of the gargantuan dark dragon, his head looking around at her, just like she was watching him. Roaring loudly with delight at the look of utter terror on the female bar worker's face, the prehistoric monstrosity raised his ferocious club-like tail in the air, and prepared to bring it down right on top of her.

Confused at his partner's temporary lack of concentration, Fu-ts'ang skewered the last of the six nagas that had been attempting to flank Yoyo's contingent of misfits, straight through the heart, all the time willing his comrade to come back to him. Unexpectedly he found their telepathic link cut. Stunned by the sensation of terror which had been the very last thing he'd got from Janice, the ancient artefact willed himself on, desperate to intervene. But it wasn't as simple as that. For his spirit to have physical control over the outer cage it resided in, he had to have a partner. Those were just the rules and had been that way for thousands of years. And so glancing at the young woman he now thought of as his friend, across the field of battle, he looked on helplessly as a mighty red and yellow spiked tail came crashing down towards her. The absolute dread on her face would have broken his heart, if he still had one. Clinking to the floor, the frost enshrouded weapon shivered ever so slightly as the prisoner consciousness bound inside it roared in fury and frustration at the futility of his situation.

Mouth dry, head pounding, heart threatening to burst through his chest, much like the alien in the film with the same name, he put everything he had into running as fast as he could. Not as fast as either Flash or Richie, he was still a blurred streak to almost everyone around him. Dropping his shoulder, he weaved around a bright blue bolt of magic that went on to strike a naga another twenty metres off his position. Unable to worry about how that turned out, he kept moving, aware only of what he was trying to do.

Frozen in place by fear, Janice cowered beneath the jaw dropping shadow of the wicked tail that was about to crush her. From out of nowhere, suddenly she was thrust to the ground. Barely able to breathe, she turned over to find the one being she'd climbed down into this fantasy world and fought dragons for. Peter! Shocked and elated both at the same time, without hesitation she leaned in and kissed him passionately on the lips. His surprise was palpable, but that didn't stop him getting caught up in the moment, losing himself entirely in his one true love. That is until the monstrous dark dragon decided to have a second crack at them, bringing his gargantuan spiked tail crashing down atop of them. Clinched in a warm embrace, the earth quite literally moved for them both, as what remained of the *alea's* shield saved them from a very unsavoury end.

As the two lovers scrambled to their feet, and with what magic was left of the shield protecting Peter hissing, spluttering and sparking all around them, holding each other's hand, they backpeddalled furiously as the crazed looking dragon, having turned around to face them, stomped forward. Gripped by blind panic, and just as they thought it was over, a distorted movement off to one side had their mouths hanging open. Before their attacker had a chance to react, a cartwheeling Richie landed on his tail, weaved around the deadly spikes and sprinted straight up the top of it. The floundering dark dragon waved his arms, flapped his wings and shook his head in an attempt to rid himself of this recently arrived menace. But it did him no good. Richie's balance was perfect, and just like a rodeo rider atop a bucking bronco, there was no shaking her. With the ancient beast about to take flight, figuring that just might get rid of her, the young human shaped lacrosse player reached around behind her back, pulled free the exquisite laminium dagger and in one single, very deadly move, buried the weapon deep into the top of the dragon's head. As his giant jaw slumped forward, the beast exhaled for the last time. Withdrawing her dagger, Richie back-flipped to the ground, barely missing the fountain of green blood spouting from the fatal wound. Landing with a THUD beside her two friends, she used the bottom of her t-shirt to wipe the blood from the blade as the dragon's dead body crumpled to the ground with a CRASH.

Temporarily stunned because of what had just happened, it didn't take long for the two lovers to recover. Janice was first to react, throwing herself at Richie, enveloping the petite lacrosse player in the mother of all hugs. All smiles and laughter, the sporting superstar returned the gesture, telling the bar worker just how good it was to see her. Looking on, Peter could hardly believe what he was seeing.

'Since when did the two of them become so chummy? What on earth have I missed?'

Breaking off their emphatic greeting, the two women separated, allowing Peter to step forward. Grinning from ear to ear, he proffered his hand in the direction of his best friend. Without hesitation, she leapt straight at him, wrapping her arms around him in a giant bear hug. In the midst of all the magic and mayhem going on all around them, it was as surreal as moments get.

"Thanks for the save," Peter shouted.

"Thanks for hanging in there so long."

"I'm sorry about Tim... he was a good... man. I mean dragon. I mean... person."

Letting her best friend go, Richie stepped back so that both friends could get a better look at her. Taking in her face, Peter was staggered at the pain, anger and torment he could see. Since he'd last seen her, she appeared to have aged considerably.

'Surely the death of Tim on its own hasn't done that to her?' he thought.

Free from facing impending death, Janice immediately turned her thoughts to Fu-ts'ang. Reaching out with her consciousness, he couldn't hide the elation he felt when their minds merged into one.

"I'm sorry," she whispered.

"SORRY!" he replied. "I'm just glad you're okay and disappointed that it wasn't I that came to your rescue. Your friends, however, were adequate substitutes."

They both chuckled at this, before the frost enshrouded ancient weapon reminded the young human that they had work to do. Closing her eyes, Janice's vision of the battlefield swam into view, as Fu-ts'ang sped off in search of his next target, delighted to be of use once again.

Wrapping his arm around his love's waist, occasionally startled by the odd explosion nearby, Peter shouted in the direction of his best friend.

"What do we do now? Can we escape?"

Leaving all thoughts of Tim for another time, the tiniest of smiles wriggled across the lacrosse player's face.

"Escape... no! I don't think it's possible."

"Then what?"

"I think it might be time to rally my troops. Don't you?"

"Your troops?"

"That's right! I'm the leader of this rabble... how about that?"

Peter could barely believe what he was hearing.

"And just how did this come about?"

"I think we'll have to save that for another time. As you can imagine, it's quite a long story. But suffice to say, it was a unanimous vote. And no... it wasn't something I wanted. But since I am their leader, I say it's time to get the party started."

Laughing manically, much to Peter's horror, Richie started to turn in a circle, taking in everything around her, keen to grasp the entire nature of their situation. After all, a leader should totally understand the much bigger picture.

Over the sounds of his sobbing, a gentle voice whispered sympathetically.

"Please excuse my actions. It was never my intention to be quite so mean."

Wiping away tears from both eyes with one of his giant hands, Tank uncurled himself, sat up and glanced around for the voice's master. But all he could see was darkness, much like before.

"Who are you and where am I?" the young rugby playing dragon managed to sniffle.

"You're where you've always been... lying on the cold marble of the king's private residence, smack bang in the middle of one hell of a confrontation."

"I don't understand."

"I'm sorry. I thought you wanted to know where your body was."

More than a little confused, Tank tried once again to get his head around exactly where he was.

"So if my body is there, then where on earth is this?"

There was a bit of a pause, with the voice clearly thinking about its answer.

"Let's just say that your personality is my guest for the time being, shall we?"

"Your guest... sounds more like your prisoner," replied Tank, swallowing hard, his mouth drier than a Martini in the Sahara. "You haven't answered my other question. Just who are you, and why are you stopping me from helping my friends?"

"I'm not stopping you," replied the voice haughtily. "It was, after all, you who made contact with me."

Confused and fed up with being surrounded by darkness, Tank struggled to make sense of what the voice was saying.

'I made contact with him? How on earth does that work? The last thing I can remember doing is...'

And then it came to him. Not where he was, but whom he was addressing... the king's RING!

"You're... you're... you're the king's ring."

"Up to a point... you're correct. I have been passed down from one dragon monarch to another over the course of time. I do not though, belong to anyone, not even the current incumbent of that office."

'Well... that told me,' thought Tank, taken aback at the brusqueness of the ring's reply.

"I merely augment the dragon king's own power with that of my own, and offer advice based on the experiences of my long life, but only as long as I agree with the decisions being made. Should, for example, a monarch go insane and start murdering his own subjects, I would not and could not be made to go along with that. Although bonded with an extraordinary piece of jewellery, I am for all intents and purposes a sentient being."

Tank was taken back at this revelation, although he shouldn't have been, because unbeknown to both of them, they'd met before. A sentient being... wow that was something... but why wasn't the jewellery in question helping the king and the others in the fight for their lives? Slightly nervously, Tank asked the question.

"Recently I've had cause to question the king's judgement."

"Because of the voting at the Council meetings?"

"Ahhh... of course... I'd forgotten he'd told you and your friends all about that. I'd had misgivings for a while, not just about the voting, but about a few other things as well. It all came to a head in a conversation we had, that is to say I and the current king. Like him, I can be quite stubborn when I want to, a trait that has in the past gotten both of us into a great deal of trouble."

"You do know the voting in the council chamber was being rigged?"

"I understand that might have been the case."

"But what about now?" asked the rugby playing dragon.

"What about now?"

"Shouldn't you put your differences to one side and help them fight against the pervasive evil that's trying to infiltrate and ultimately take over the domain? Your vast reserve of power might be the difference between life and death for everybody."

"Why?"

"Surely, if you're sentient like you say you are, then shouldn't it be obvious?"

"How so?"

"You just used the example of not going along with a murderously insane king in killing his own subjects as an example of your own free will. But by not doing anything here, unquestionably that's the same as helping commit murder. Isn't it?"

"Perhaps this fellow Manson and his ilk are not as bad as you think they are. Perhaps the domain needs a new way of thinking and in particular a new leader."

"You must have seen what they've done, what they're responsible for?"

Silence and darkness walked hand in hand.

Tank waited, irked at the ring's attitude and the fact that he'd been taken away from helping his friends. On most levels it didn't make sense. Surely it should do what's right, whether or not it had had a tiny little spat with the incumbent bearing it. Why wasn't it helping? Puzzled at the ring's response, part of him was impatient to get back to the reality playing out all around him. But if nothing else, the young rugby playing dragon was full of common sense and with the maturity that had now started to blossom within him over the last year or so, held a deep rooted belief in himself and the decisions he made. And right now it occurred to him that if he could get the ring back on side, then just maybe the tide of the battle could be turned, and that with the king and the enigmatic band reunited in one common cause, Manson and his minions could once and for all be vanquished.

All consuming darkness closed in around him. Not an unfamiliar situation, he'd found himself here before, on many an occasion. But not quite like this. Here and now he felt powerless... powerless to resist. A nagging pain from the lower part of his body somewhere relentlessly assaulted him, stopping him from focusing, preventing him from finding his magic and the almost limitless supply of power he could feel wrapped around his physical body. Locked inside his mind, he fought to break out and regain control. Time served no purpose here, he knew. Seconds, minutes or hours could be passing outside in the real world, and none of it would apply here. He was pretty sure it wasn't hours, but a part of him was still afraid it would all be over by the time he got back there, if such a thing were even possible. Bounding out of the way of the pure black that mirrored his every move, he'd taken to running away now, instead of his usual fighting back. In the past he'd fought off what he always supposed had been the pain tormenting his physical being. It had been hard, and he'd needed all his tricks and wits to do such a thing, but it had been possible, as he'd proved on a number of occasions. But this was somehow different, almost magnified in strength if he had to guess. And so continuing to evade by running up walls, jumping off ledges and barrel rolling beneath outstretched shadowy fingers, Flash pushed on, feeling his heart rate increase, ignoring the pounding in his ears that distracted his thinking. He knew he had to live up to his name, even though his very being only existed deep within his own mind, right at this very moment.

'Oh crap!' he thought, deflecting yet another multiple set of attacks on his young band of dragons. That wasn't what had caused his outburst. No! He'd just witnessed his young friend, the dragon whose life he'd saved far beneath Perth, Australia on that fateful day, get his leg sliced in two by some very curious magic, and land hard in a heap, barely moving at all. Feeling more than a little depleted of mana, Yoyo knew that he now faced a very difficult and very immediate choice: keep on supplementing the defence of his young dragon contingent to the detriment of Flash, or take the risk of saving the former Crimson Guard at the cost of his young charges. It was the toughest decision he'd ever faced, and over the course of his life he'd had to choose which dragons had lived and which had died on the operating tables of the battlefield. Pushing any doubts aside, he made his choice based solely on the bigger picture, and what would best give them the likely outcome of winning and surviving. Stepping out from his relatively sheltered position so that he could get a better view of his unconscious subject, he cleared his mind, letting it converge on one being and one being only. FLASH! As his consciousness reached the ex-Crimson Guard, it cast its keen, specialist eye across the whole of his body. When it reached the deep gash on his leg, it almost gasped, as if such a thing were possible. A matt black, tar-like substance had infiltrated the wound and was currently eating away at the surrounding flesh, muscle and bone. That wasn't the most worrying thing. Unlikely as it may have seemed, even to Yoyo's brilliantly unorthodox mind, the substance in question was replicating, and doing so at a particularly fast rate. The healer knew that if he didn't do something, and fast, then Flash's time on this plane of existence would surely be over. Looking at the prone form of his comrade lying below him, Yoyo locked on and prepared to use his remaining magic to expunge the evil that had permeated his friend's physical form.

A fraction of a second was all it took for the experienced healer to realise just how much of a mistake he'd made. There was no doubt that he'd chosen the right mantra, but the enormity of the task dwarfed what he was capable of doing with the amount of mana he had left. There just wasn't enough to give, and that now left him trapped. Try as he might, with all the knowledge available to him, he just couldn't wriggle free. Flash's death sentence had now just become his. But as his hope turned sour, his mind reflected on the last thing he'd seen before bringing forth his magic. Flash had been wearing the chains... laminium chains. That was it! The chains were the answer. But just how could he get his hands on the powerful metal... that was the question.

Crouched in the shadows of a hidden little alcove, Hook was still exceedingly thankful for the return to full health that Yoyo had provided, and was determined to do everything he could to keep his new found friend safe. Watching along the wall that provided them with some semblance of cover from part of the raging battle in that general direction, he was suddenly startled when a huge scaled hand grabbed him by the shoulder. Pulling away by spinning around abruptly, Tank's rugby playing teammate was surprised to find Yoyo standing there, eyes glazed over, sweat pouring off him, barely able to move.

"What's wrong?" yelled Hook, over the noise of the skirmish.

"I need Flash brought over here."

"I can't hear you. You'll have to speak up."

Hardly able to move his scaly lips, Yoyo put all he could into his words.

"You have to get Flash over here so that I can touch those chains. If you don't, we're both dead."

Yoyo's eyes closed as the sweat continued to pour, and despite Hook's best efforts, he could get no reaction out of the dragon healer. Swallowing hard, the young rugby playing human hero, who'd already proved himself a dozen times over in his brief stint underground, glanced across to where Flash's body lay some twenty or so metres away. The distance wasn't much on a rugby or hockey pitch, but right here, right now, with magic raining down hell, psychopathic prehistoric monsters running riot, and the sound of swords clashing ringing through the air, it was enough to turn most beings' legs to jelly... but not his. Using the passion, strength of purpose and courage he usually only exerted playing his sport, Hook set off at a dead run towards the unconscious looking ex-Crimson Guard. Peppered by explosive fragments from the marble flooring all around him taking a direct magical hit half way across, it didn't deter the rugby strongman. Reaching his target, he grabbed Flash's arms and started to pull him along the floor. Blessed with huge upper body strength, this task should have been nothing more than a tame training ground test. But he hadn't figured in the weight of the chains. Not knowing what they were made of, the one thing he could attest to was that they were unbelievably heavy. He had no idea how Flash could even stand with them on... no doubt due to some sort of magic that he couldn't begin to understand. Pulling him as far as he could, he stopped for a breather, sweat dripping off every part of his body. Looking up, he realised he'd only managed to pull the young dragon about a tenth of the way. Horror and panic threatened to take over. It would take an age at this rate, all the time exposed, leaving them vulnerable to attack. What he needed was some help, but where to find it amongst everything going on was well beyond him. So without further ado, he got on with it, dragging the dead-weight body another two metres, and then another. But with each metre, the chaos and the fighting around them intensified. It was far from plain sailing.

Siphoning off some of the magic from the laminium dagger that was surely only on loan to her, Richie used the additional power to boost her telepathic range and, opening her mind in a calm and controlled manner (something quite new to the rebellious young lacrosse player) shouted as loud as she could.

"Light sided individuals... fall back to the wall nearest the staircase. There we will regroup and coordinate our attacks with a view to taking the fight to them. As quickly as you can... your commander, Richie Rump."

'Boy has she got some chops,' thought Peter, his friend's every word reverberating around inside his head. Wondering how they would all know to obey the command, he assumed most of the guards here would probably never have heard of her, let alone trust her enough with their lives mid-battle. But a quick momentary look made him think again. Yoyo's group of young dragons who were fighting furiously with magic and conventional means, occasionally helped by their two invisible friends, had heard the call and were slowly shuffling in the direction of the rendezvous. The circle of ably equipped King's Guards continued fighting valiantly on, outnumbered and overwhelmed but currently holding their own, mainly due to Amelia Battlehard's command of the situation. Hovering above them, putting out fires, both figuratively and literally, the captain of the guard glanced over in their direction. Richie pointed with her thumbs, indicating the direction that they all should be travelling in. It was something of a standoff, with the captain of the guard reluctant to trust anyone she didn't know. But given the situation, and the fact that quite probably they'd all be dead if not for her unexpected intervention, she knew better than to look a gift horse in the mouth. So, one excruciating footstep at a time, their fighting force moved back in the right direction, all the time trying not to trip over the blood soaked cadavers that littered the battlefield.

Grabbing Janice by the hand, Peter poked his head out

from behind the huge dragon corpse all three of them were crouching behind, and tried to figure out the best route back to Yoyo's position. It was then that he spotted him, smack bang right in the middle of everything. HOOK! Before he could even think, 'what the hell are you doing?', he realised not what, but just who the rugby playing human was dragging. FLASH! Instantly he grasped Richie by the upper arm, trying to make himself heard over the racket of rampaging magic and very real explosions. Try as he might, he just couldn't. So instead, he pointed, hoping his new found leader would get the message. She did.

Screaming at the top of her voice for her two friends to follow, the lacrosse playing wizard broke into a sprint, tumbling here and there occasionally to avoid the odd long range attack. Following in her wake, the two reunited lovers had a hard time skipping up and over some of the debris, consequently arriving at Hook a few moments after their leader who was, by then, crouched over Flash's unconscious form.

Looking up into Hook's newly repaired face, whilst at the same time deflecting away numerous bright yellow magical spears that would really have ruined their day, and their lives, Richie asked what they were all thinking.

"Where's Yoyo? Why hasn't he healed Flash yet?"

Before Peter had a chance to respond, Hook cut in.

"Yoyo's in a bad shape. I think he tried to heal Flash, but somehow it's all gone wrong. He told me to get Flash's body to him so that he could touch the chains straddling his torso."

Placing her dagger beside one of Flash's chains, it immediately became obvious what the metal they were made of was. Laminium!

'Impressive,' thought Richie. Where or even how the ex-Crimson Guard had gotten such power she couldn't even begin to fathom. Her abilities had been greatly enhanced by the laminium in the dagger, and that must have been only a fraction of what made up the chains. The magical potential alone was staggering. And so if that was the case, why on earth couldn't Flash heal himself? Then she spotted it... the dire infested wound on his leg, leaching a dark, stinking matter, its covering increasing with every second that passed.

'No doubt naga magic,' she thought.

"Peter... you and Hook take an arm each. I'll take his good leg. Let's get him over to Yoyo in double quick time."

Both nodding, and with Janice accompanying them, using Fu-ts'ang to guard their path, Peter, Hook and Richie carried their injured friend back to Yoyo. Of everything that had happened in the middle of the raging fight, and that includes Janice sitting on the floor, eyes closed, all alone for quite a while, this was almost the most bizarre. But in no small part due to a considerable amount of luck, they made it back, placing their friend at the feet of the statue-like healer. Puffing and panting, having exerted considerable strain, Hook told them again that Yoyo needed to touch the chains. No sooner had the words left his mouth when Richie, enhanced by the dagger, picked up the injured Flash, careful not to touch his toxic wound, and slowly walked him across to the healer. With Flash in place, Peter gently lowered Yoyo's right hand, and despite him being in a trance-like state, he found very little in the way of resistance. The instant his dragon hand made contact with the magical metal, Yoyo let out a long sigh, accompanied by the words,

"Oh my."

Taking a step back, Peter asked Richie if she needed a hand with Flash. Smiling, she declined. With Janice still using Fu-ts'ang to great effect and Hook watching out for any kind of sneak attack, Peter found himself encouraging Yoyo's contingent of misfits to head his way faster. Marvelling at their mastery of so much dragon magic, particularly given their apparent age, he couldn't help but notice just how lucky they were getting. Opponents' feet would give way at just the right time, while swords either slipped away or were mysteriously blocked for no apparent reason. Absolutely convinced something else was going on, he really couldn't fathom what.

Yoyo felt fulfilled... spiritually, magically, in every possible way. That's how this abundance of magic impacted him. Clearing his mind from the fog that had clouded it, and glad he didn't now have to face the consequences of embarking on a mantra and not having enough magical energy to complete it, he turned his attention, not for the first time, to the dragon in front of him. Prior to even delving into the depths of Flash's injury, something tickled his senses, brushed his brain. But before he could latch onto it, it was gone, scooting off into the ether. A feeling of change somehow played over him. Was he supposed to change? Had the battle somehow changed? He didn't know and right at this very moment, didn't actually care. Dismissing the strange sensation as just one of those things, the dragon healer once again cast a mantra, this time not even vaguely concerned about the amount of mana needed to see it through. Pure, raw, unadulterated magic seeped out of Yoyo and flooded Flash's damaged body. But a connection remained... one tiny strand of the supernatural held the link together. Through that bond, information filtered back and forth. As the power invaded Flash at a cellular level, an unrivalled level of detail found its way back to the dragon healer. Over the course of twenty seconds or so, Yoyo built up an unparalleled picture of Flash's physiology. In this case, magic trumps science every time. Studying the information for but a few seconds at most, it became clear just how invasive the enchantment he'd been struck with was. It was multiplying and spreading at quite a rate. Normally Yoyo would have been encumbered by the amount of mana available to him, but for the very first time in his life, this wasn't the case. And so with that in mind, he let his imagination run rife, dreaming up the most outrageous and majestic solutions to the almost unimaginable problem. In two blinks of an eye, he had it. Desperate didn't begin to cover it, and under normal circumstances he wouldn't have even dared dream of it. But normal had caught the bus out of here long ago. Only drastic measures remained.

Breaking his concentration, he returned to reality, Richie, Peter, Janice and Hook all pleased to see him.

"Thank goodness you're okay," exclaimed Peter, clutching Yoyo's free hand.

"Yes, yes, yes. I'm sorry, but we don't have time for all this at the moment."

With Peter wondering what he'd done wrong, the healer's eyes fell on Richie and more importantly the dagger she held.

"Ah... you must be Miss Rump. It's a pleasure to finally meet you. I've heard all about you."

'That could mean anything,' Richie thought, but went along with it anyway.

"I'm afraid I'm going to need you to do something that you really don't want to," insisted Yoyo.

"And what's that?"

"You must cut Flash's leg off somewhere above his injury. Make sure you're not too close to the magical infection itself and use your weapon's magic to cauterise the wound or all this will be for nothing."

"ARE YOU KIDDING ME? CUT HIS LEG OFF?"

"I don't have time to explain everything, but it will be all right if you follow my instructions to the letter. There's no time to waste."

Richie shook her head, cursing under her breath.

"It'll be alright Rich. I trust him implicitly. You can too," urged Peter.

"Okay... I'll do it. But this had better work."

"It will, little one, it will," assured the healer, about to get back to work. "Just remember to cut off the correct one, and things will be fine." And with a wink and a smile,

Yoyo's face turned blank once again, all his concentration focused on the wellbeing of his patient.

Richie turned to Peter.

"Well... that's reassuring. Make sure you cut the right one off."

All Peter could do was grin.

"Sounds like good advice to me," he chipped in.

Turning away, she handed Flash's body over to Peter, and blocking out the sounds of fighting all around her, the superstar lacrosse player wiped the dagger once again across the front of her t-shirt, why she didn't know... it wasn't as if it was sterilised. Kneeling down level with the wound, she sucked up yet more of the dagger's seemingly unlimited power. Gripping the hilt tight, before taking a calming breath, there was no way on earth she'd normally do this to one of her friends. But circumstances required her once again to do something totally and utterly against what she believed in, and so telling herself it was down to her and nobody else, she dragged the dagger across Flash's leg, just below the knee, scything through bone, muscle and cartilage all in one fell swoop. Landing with a mighty CLUNK, the bottom half of Flash's left leg dropped to the cold, marble floor without any sort of fuss. No blood, no mess, just a nice clean incision with the magic from the dagger sealing both sides.

"Ughhhhhh..." groaned the ex-Crimson Guard, still for the most part not with them at all.

Surprised that Flash hadn't made more noise... Peter knew he would, had somebody just cut off one of his limbs. There and then his job of holding Flash up straight was now made more difficult with him effectively only having one leg to stand on. Using all the strength he had, the young hockey player wondered just how long it would take Yoyo to weave his extraordinary magic.

Eyeing the infested stump that only moments ago had been attached to one of her closest friends, Richie could still see the darkness within the gaping wound multiply.

Eerily creepy, she wasn't quite sure what to make of it. Part of her wanted to kick it away, while another part wanted to destroy it entirely. Not sure if either option was a good idea... (what if she obliterated it and Yoyo needed it back?) she settled for keeping a close watch on it.

Things all around them were getting louder and closer, with Janice still using her precious partner, the weapon that resembled a frosty buzz saw, Fu-ts'ang, to carve a path for the group of young dragons. Only about twenty metres away now, it was plain to see they had all suffered numerous injuries, with two of their kind being dragged along the floor, bleeding profusely, to what they hoped would be relative safety.

Through the connection the two shared, Yoyo could sense the molecules within his friend's body start to return to normal now that the esoteric, dark magic had been removed from the equation. Keen to get the ex-Crimson Guard back into fighting shape, he knew with access to this much power and mana that virtually nothing was beyond his will. And so, without a moment's hesitation, he immersed himself in the supernatural and, using the blueprint from the magic he'd showered Flash with earlier, began to create another limb that he hoped would be an exact replica of the one they'd had to cut off. Igniting the magic one molecule at a time, it was a dizzying prospect and one that under normal circumstances, he wouldn't even have attempted to take on. But as well as enhancing everything magical within him, the powerful metal of the chains had also boosted his self confidence and belief. There was nothing he couldn't do or achieve, and Flash's little scratch was nothing more than a temporary inconvenience.

Hurried by a trio of wicked looking nagas, what was left of Yoyo's band of young dragons backed their way up against the wall, all the time making sure their injured were covered and protected.

"We need Yoyo right now!" screamed Wiz in Richie

and Peter's direction.

"He's a little busy, but it shouldn't take long," replied the lacrosse playing dragon, trying to sound as calm and as reasonable as possible.

"They're hurt... really badly. He needs to heal them NOW!"

That was it. Richie had finally reached the end of her tether and despite the severity of the circumstances, was about to go off the reservation. Knowing what to look out for with his friend, Peter managed to step in just in time to defuse the situation.

"Why don't I take a look at your friends?" he suggested, while uh... Rich, perhaps you could help out with... THAT!"

As a group, they all looked around. Beyond the trio of nagas fighting furiously with the group of prehistoric youngsters from Perth, five of the meanest looking dragons they'd ever seen had taken to the air and were currently approaching the group at speed. Trapped against the marble wall of the lower floor, as a unit they were sitting ducks, something their leader, Richie, now realised. While it did offer them a modicum of cover, and it was the only part of the chamber to do just that, it hadn't occurred to her that a situation quite like this might arise. Silently cursing her stupidity, she leapt up and over Yoyo's charges, planting herself fully in front of them to face the oncoming aerial foes. Leaning back, almost as far as she could go without toppling over, she narrowly avoided having her throat cut by one of the nagas and his trusty shadowy sword. Disappointed to say the least, and now harbouring a thirst for vengeance, the petite lacrosse player stabbed the naga straight through the middle of its face, watching it die full of surprise. Before the beast's slack body hit the floor, it was back to the job at hand, the five dragons streaking in at top speed, almost a blur, even to her magical senses. Knowing that they would make run after run at them with a view to incinerating the group with bursts of their deadly flame, she could only think of one thing that would prevent all-out slaughter. Drawing on all the power her weapon possessed, Richie brought up her personal shield, letting it flicker into being all around her. Absorbing the magic into her entire being, she commanded the shield to expand. Much to her surprise... it did, covering the entire group in the process, as well as decapitating the remaining two nagas who'd been mid-attack as it sprang into life, Richie hadn't been sure of success at all. It had, if nothing else, bought them all a little more time. Smiling at the outrageousness of it all, the one problem it threw up concerned her greatly. The others... the group of King's Guards, were all outside the shield, and although slowly heading in this general direction, were still some way off. Tank was nowhere to be seen, while George, the dragon king, was right at this very moment dodging and ducking, rolling and weaving his way across the combat zone, heading directly for his best friend... FREDRIC! And then there was the dazzlingly bespoke naga that had come through the magical wormhole with Flash and the others. Assuming it was the naga king that had been previously mentioned, whoever he was, he was more than holding his own against dark dragon opponents, laying waste to nearly a dozen so far, and those were just the ones she'd witnessed. He'd need a safe haven, along with all the others. What she'd done was trap all of them here behind a shield, without any way to get out and help their allies. Oops.

Sprinting as fast as he could, the aching in his magically designed bones increased tenfold, almost forcing him to stop. Determinedly he ploughed on, knowing that only death itself would prevent him reaching the best friend he hadn't seen in decades. And while his spirit had been crushed by that wicked Manson dragon fellow, it was able to recover somewhat as he ran. Skipping around a small blast off to his left, he dipped out of the way as a string of electrically charged bolts came zipping past him. Sucking in another deep breath to fuel his falsehood of a body, George wondered where on earth the burning he could smell was coming from. Gracefully sliding to a halt directly in front of his friend, it was then he realised the source of the acrid smell. HIM! He was on fire, well... technically his clothes were on fire, but you know what I mean. Throwing himself to the cold, white floor, the current dragon king rolled over and over, all the time patting his arms and legs. After only a few seconds, the flames were out and so instead of standing, he knelt in front of Fredric, having to shout to be heard.

"My friend... it's so good to see you. I never gave up hope you know. I always thought we'd meet once again."

Nothing! The king's words had no effect at all on the motionless form of Fredric, whose head faced the ground, as a river's worth of tears trickled to the floor. Brushing aside the long and dirty matted hair, George reached in and put his hand gently beneath his friend's chin, slowly lifting his head up so that it was level with his.

"I know you're in there, and I know you're hurt. And I think I can guess why. But you need to snap out of it right now. We're in need of your extra special skill sets. I don't think we'll last much longer without you. Do you think you can help us?"

Peter's grandfather's inert form barely moved. If not for the soft, gentle breathing and the steady stream of tears, he might well have been mistaken for a larger than life statue.

Deflecting away a few powerful supernatural bursts heading his way with just the wave of his hand, George was still a force to be reckoned with, even without the ring, his magical companion for so long. Single-mindedly he fought off the blistering attacks that were converging on them both, his resolve determined to keep them safe. But as one part of his mind dedicated itself to doing this, another much smaller part wondered what he could do to shake his friend out of his shocked, trance-like state. If he didn't do something quick, then the rescue efforts of those that came to save him would all have been in vain.

"Well? Wyvern got your tongue?" ventured Tank into the thick, all encompassing darkness, somewhat fed up at not having had a reply yet.

"Well... what?" a much softer, sombre voice came back.

"You claim to be sentient, to be able to make informed decisions based on all the experience you've accumulated over the centuries..."

"I am sentient," beseeched the ring firmly, "and my experience makes me a better judge than almost anyone else on the planet."

"If that's so," replied Tank, "then tell me about Manson's group. Is it right that they've killed and maimed so many innocents... not just dragons, but humans as well? And what about their vision of the future, surely you must know about that. There won't be any room for the ordinary dragons that currently inhabit what's left of the domain. They'll be slaughtered by the thousands, which compared with what awaits the humans on the surface, is probably quite a good option. They'll be hunted for sport... doesn't that seem like a pleasant way to go?" Tank added sarcastically, his patience finally starting to run out with his magically enhanced captor.

"You don't know that's what'll happen."

"I DON'T KNOW?!" Tank screamed. "I DON'T KNOW?! I've been there, seen the pyres of dead dragon bodies set on fire, witnessed the sheer cruelty of his minions, and been a victim of what he has planned for every being on this planet. DON'T YOU DARE TELL ME I DON'T KNOW!"

Letting his words ring off into the distance, Tank's hands and legs shook with the rage he felt, his temper spilling over. Lacking clarity of thought, he only knew one thing: it was time to get out of here and back to his friends. This had been nothing more than a huge waste of his time. While the being controlling the ring might have power to wield, it certainly didn't have the right attitude, as far as he was concerned. Gathering his thoughts and any remaining spark of magic, the rugby playing dragon's mind turned to just how he might leave, hoping to hell he didn't have to fight.

With the young dragon Wiz watching over him, Peter placed his hands on both of her injured friends' bodies. To say he wasn't sure of what he was doing was something of an understatement. Of course he'd had rudimentary medical training, back at the Purbeck Peninsula nursery ring, but that was a long time ago and it had only covered the very basics, such as what to do in an emergency, something that in peacetime rarely presents itself to any dragon at all. And so here he was, two young dragons on the edge of life itself, ready to drop into the chasm of death, because he needed Yoyo to heal Flash to give them any sort of chance at turning the tide of the raging battle going on all about them.

Remembering what he'd been taught all those decades ago, the young hockey player did the most obvious thing he could... he flooded both of them with magic. Normally he'd struggle on this front, but his reserves were almost fully topped up because he hadn't been able to use any supernatural power over the last few days due to being constrained by those damn binders. And since the *alea* had broken him free, he'd used very little. In theory it should at least give them half a chance, as flooding them with magic should boost their immune systems and allow their own bodies to start repairing the devastating injuries they'd suffered. Both dragons moaned simultaneously, startling both Wiz and Peter.

"What have you done to them? She demanded.

"Nothing. I mean not nothing... no. I've flooded them with energy. It should help them heal."

"Is it? Is it helping them heal?"

And this was where it got tricky. He didn't know. How could he? After all he wasn't a dedicated healer like Yoyo. To reach even the most inexperienced level of healer took many, many decades. All he was doing was guessing. It was all a sham to buy Flash some time with Yoyo. To say he felt bad did no justice at all to the meaning of the word. About to 'fess up and take whatever he had coming to him from the concerned and spirited Wiz, it was then that Yoyo spoke through gritted teeth.

"It's okay Peter. You've done a good job showering them in your magic. But I can take over now."

Not wanting to... really not wanting to, because he was afraid of the answer, he just had to ask.

"What about Flash?"

Yoyo's face kind of grimaced.

"Don't worry, I've got him covered too. Boosted by the laminium in the chains around Flash's chest, I'm more than confident I can heal all three of them. Why don't you see if your friend Richie needs some help?"

Never having been more relieved, he left Wiz and Yoyo, heading over towards his friend who had created the most magnificent shield around them all. Glancing down at the dagger in her hand, he just hoped it held enough magical energy for her to power their defence indefinitely.

Juggling five balls in the air at once was the only thing Yoyo could compare with what he was doing. Just as he'd gotten the hang of regenerating a new lower leg for Flash, two of his happy gang had turned up with life threatening injuries, and there was just no way he couldn't attend to them immediately. But that was the beauty of the laminium chains... he didn't have to pick and choose. With so much magic and mana available to him, he could continue to heal all three of them at once. It wasn't easy mind you... far from it in fact. He'd had to compartmentalise his mind into three sections... one for each of his patients. In the first one, he continued with the leg; that was coming along nicely, even if he did say so himself. Next, he began to heal Trayrin, the more badly injured of the two. This was beyond difficult. Her internal organs had been severely damaged, so much so that there wasn't even an option to patch them up. They had to be fully repaired, here and now. And so that's what the second part of him was doing. Montague or Monty as he was known was next. Not as badly injured as Trayrin, he still had significant damage. A broken jaw, shattered kneecap, broken left arm and a perforated spleen. He probably wouldn't die from the damage, but his condition wouldn't allow him to be mobile or move in any way, shape or form, which wasn't ideal given their current situation.

And so, overwhelmed by the sheer amount of supernatural power deluging his prehistoric body, Yoyo went about his work, thinking that without the ravaging battle they were caught in the middle of, and the crisis that might involve the end of the earth as they knew it, he could hardly remember being happier.

That though, could all change at a moment's notice.

Most of his dark force settled for attacking the remaining group of King's Guards that were trying with every step to edge closer to the main group that had somehow managed to hide themselves behind a huge, formidable defensive shield. Just as they should, he thought, not exactly pleased with how things had gone, but slightly happier now that events seemed to be getting back under control, with the balance tilted much more in his favour. His mood, however, could change in the blink of an eye, something those who fought under his banner could attest to. That was how the madness worked... never predictable, which was, of course, its very nature. Lucid right at this very moment, he brushed himself down and turned just in time to be greeted by his queen. Resembling a giddy schoolgirl, she threw herself into his arms. For his part, he caught her, holding on to the embrace for quite some time. When their bodies parted, they lowered their foreheads towards each other, making telepathic communication that much easier.

"I'm sorry for my part in all of this. I should have reacted quicker. He caught me off guard," whispered Earth deep inside her love's head.

"The arrival of the newcomers through that blasted portal certainly threw a spanner into the works. Never mind. Things seem to be much more under control. Don't concern yourself about getting caught out. Let's just end all this, so that we can start ruling over our new subjects once and for all."

Smiling wickedly, she whispered a long, snake-like, "YEEEEEESSSSSSSS!!!" and bounded off into the distance.

Through the relentless onslaught of magical attacks and from her position above her circling troops, she could just make out the one being she'd been tasked with protecting, off in the distance, kneeling beside a ragged looking human shape, draped in glistening chains, having appeared through the magical wormhole with all the others. Briefly she wondered what he was doing there, but almost instantly cast that thought aside. Whatever the king's reasons, she knew better than to question them. If it was important to him, then it was important to her. And with them both attracting additional attention from the enemy's force, telepathically she sent out a shout for the meagre force she commanded to engage more and more of their vile opponents, in the disillusioned hope that it might keep the dragon monarch safe for just a tiny bit longer. Spitting roaring flame at a dive bombing dragon off to her left,

Amelia Battlehard couldn't help but wonder how much longer they could hold out. Unless reinforcements showed up straight out of nowhere, just as they had done previously, then they were all fighting a losing battle. And with nowhere to retreat to, it could only end one way.

Barely able to contain his temper, Tank took a long, deep breath and composed the words he wanted to say. For him, time had run out, having already given the ring's sentience enough time to respond, he'd heard absolutely nothing back. So it was time to leave, and not knowing how, all he could do was ask.

"I wish to leave this place," he declared. "Please can you show me how?"

As his words floated off into the distance, silence returned. Controlling his breathing whilst suppressing what little magic he had, that was just itching to escape, inside a worry that he'd offended his captor or host, depending on how you looked at it, nagged away at him. About to repeat the exact same words, he was slightly startled to hear a reply.

"You're a very interesting character."

Not sure of what to make of it, all he could think of saying was,

"Thank you."

"You talk with such passion and belief, which I find quite remarkable and intoxicating in someone so young. You remind me of... hmmm..."

This time Tank remained quiet.

"Are we taking it in turns to stay silent?"

"I'm not at all sure what you want me to say. I'd like to be able to get back to my friends and help them in their fight."

"What if I told you it would make no difference? What if I told you you're doomed to fail?"

"I'd still want to return to them and try."

"But why chase a lost cause? You could stay here indefinitely, safe and sound."

"I won't desert my friends, and would gladly lay down my life for theirs."

"Even if they're going to die anyway?"

"In a heartbeat."

"I believe what you're saying to be one hundred percent true... extraordinary!"

"Please can you help me return now?"

The ring went on...

"The king was once like you, you know."

A puzzled expression that shouldn't have showed up at all given just how dark it was, wormed its way across the young rugby player's face.

"You're surprised at that?"

"Which king? Do you mean George?"

"Ah... yes, I'd forgotten that you are one of the few to know his true history. George... he was once like you... possessed of a fierce and undying loyalty to those around him. Never afraid to stand up for what was right. Constantly putting himself in harm's way to save those that couldn't save themselves. All mightily admirable qualities in any being, don't you think?"

"Sure."

"But slowly, over time... things changed. Maybe because of the position he found himself in, or just because of the political circumstances surrounding him... who knows? Those qualities were buried, hidden away deep within his very being. It made it hard for me to like him, to share my thoughts and experiences with him. I purposely became withdrawn, occasionally withholding my power, purely out of spite, just when he needed it most. I knew it was wrong, but I just couldn't help myself."

If anyone had been able to see through the all encompassing blackness, they'd have seen Tank, mouth hanging open, listening intently to every word that was being spoken. Of course, they couldn't.

"Over time we drifted apart... stupid really, given our bond and joint pledges to protect not only the dragon domain, but the human world as well. He threw up robust mental barriers that effectively closed me off from any of his thoughts. I returned the favour to the same extent. Tit for tat, some might say."

"Surely the two of you could have worked things out?" blurted Tank unexpectedly.

"We could have... should have, even. But we didn't. Our differences became irreconcilable, and for my part in that I'm hugely sorry. And if that wasn't bad enough, suddenly humanity and dragonkind find themselves facing an extinction level event. How could I have possibly known all this would happen? I just assumed George would at some point discard me, and lock me away for the next dragon monarch. I never thought it would come to this."

"It's not too late to do the right thing."

"Says you."

"It isn't. Join the fight, right now. You could be the difference between winning and losing."

"I think all you're describing is losing. And if that's the case, then almost certainly I'll end up in the hands of that psychopath Manson, forced to do his bidding, being partly to blame for an inconceivable number of deaths. What kind of fate is that?"

"But at least you'll have tried, given your all. If we go on to lose and you end up in Manson's hands anyway, not only will you be burdened by everything you've mentioned, but for all eternity you'll wonder: what if? Join us now and help make the difference. Together we can all send this creep and his goons packing."

One giant swing of his tail felled yet another dragon stupid enough to attack him from the ground. It was a good job for him that they hadn't peppered him with assaults from the air, as they were doing to so many others throughout the chamber. Riding the shockwave of the huge, prehistoric beast crashing to the floor, Vasuki sank his needle sharp teeth through the dragon's tough, scaly neck, clamping them as far shut as he could. Like a drill striking oil for the first time, brilliant, bright green blood gushed up into the air, showering him immediately. With the beast dead and the air tasting of spent magic, the naga king slithered off at speed, concerned about just how exposed he was, here in the middle of the makeshift battlefield. However, he had nearly reached his intended target.

Batting away yet another charging dragon, George, the current dragon king, whirled around ready to discharge yet more magic and mayhem, only to find an onrushing naga heading his way. As pure, ethereal energy flickered from his fingertips, something about this particular being gave him cause for concern. Sky blue around his head and gills, gradually the blue on the snake-like beast got darker the closer it got to the tip of its tail. It wasn't just that. It looked somehow... regal. And then it hit him. It was the naga king... who'd come through the gateway with Fredric and the others. His attention had waned somewhat, focused only on the fact that he'd been reunited with his best friend after all this time, even if it was in the most dire of circumstances. Commanding the power within him to stand down, he lowered his arms to his side, trying to make himself as least threatening as possible. It seemed to work.

Sliding to a halt, using his tail as a brake, Vasuki bowed his head in George's direction. The dragon monarch responded in kind.

"I ammmm Vasuki," announced the king of everything naga.

"George, Your Majesty."

"Whaaaat issss wrong wittthh Fredriiiiic? Why doessss heee juussst kneelll theeere?"

It took him a moment to adjust to the naga king's speech, but that's all.

"Truth be told, I'm not quite sure. I could take an educated guess, but that's all it would be. He won't respond to me no matter what I do. I've tried contacting him telepathically, but it makes no difference. In all honesty, I'm at a loss."

"Mayyyyy I?"

"Of course," answered George, a little wary.

Slithering forward, Vasuki leaned in towards the seemingly paralysed Fredric. Closing his eyes, whilst swaying ever so slightly, the reptilian started to mumble what George assumed were words... assumed because they came across to him as just sounds, and strange ones at that. Guttural and instinctive, they did at least cause the hairs on his arms to stand on end. Willing his friend to return to the present, the dragon monarch wondered just how it was that Vasuki knew Fredric's real name. Assuming they'd formed some sort of captive's bond whilst imprisoned, at the very thought of this, his heart nearly imploded as a crushing cloud of sorrow threatened to overwhelm him. Bravely, and while staving off two more magical attacks from the air, he pushed his feelings away, firmly shutting them out, knowing that dealing with them here and now was not the answer. On the lookout for more danger, he willed his friend to snap out of it.

Breathing the biggest sigh of relief he could ever remember, Yoyo wiped a whole lake of sweat from his forehead, and whilst continuing to heal the two young dragons he thought of as his own in the compartmentalised portions of his mind, he opened his eyes and looked down at the patient he'd given his all and more to. Flash looked serene... sleeping like an angel. Of course it was the healer's doing. After all, if he was going to build the ex-Crimson Guard a brand new leg out of nothing, he couldn't have his courageous friend wriggling around. But it was done, and from the outside it looked as good as new. But the proof, as they say, was very much in the pudding. More than a little concerned, he would have liked to have Flash rest some more, but the current situation they all found themselves in would not permit it... and so without further ado, Yoyo woke his friend up, hoping against hope that all would be well.

"Uhhhhh... where am I?"

As if to remind him, half a dozen bright violet energy missiles streaked against the shield Richie was still holding in place.

"What in the name of...?"

"It's okay Flash... you're safe for the time being."

"YOYO!"

The prehistoric healer smiled at the mention of his name, despite everything going on all around them.

"Uhhhh... I remember being tagged by some sort of magic I've never seen before. It hurt like hell. Did you manage to rid me of it?"

"In a manner of speaking... I had to fabricate you a new leg."

Looking utterly aghast, all Flash could manage was,

"WHAT?"

"It's a long story, youngster, but needless to say you should be as good as new. And while we're on that subject, is there anything you wish to tell me?"

Fretting about his leg, Flash couldn't work out what his friend was going on about.

"No... I don't think so."

"You should know that I've used up every last ounce of magic that the laminium chains were imbued with, healing you and the others. I didn't think it would come to that, but it did and I'm truly sorry, my friend."

"You shouldn't have to say sorry for once again saving

my life. The debt I owe you seems to mount up every time we meet."

That made Yoyo chuckle.

"It certainly seems that way, doesn't it?"

"That it does, that it does."

"Good enough. Now there's no time to spare. I think your particular talents are needed if we're to stand any chance at all of getting out of here in one piece."

Gingerly, he stood, tentatively putting pressure on what had been the damaged leg. Surprisingly, and it shouldn't have been like that after the way Yoyo had previously saved his life, it felt perfect, as if nothing bad had ever happened. Turning towards his friend, he mouthed a great big, "thank you," before disappearing off in the direction of Richie, Peter and Janice.

Standing in front of them all, holding off the approaching horde of evil, Richie gripped the priceless laminium dagger with all her might, despite the fact that its hilt glowed red hot, currently burning the skin on her hands. That's how much magic she was drawing from it, and that's how much it meant to her to protect everyone she loved.

"Let me help you?" whispered a soft, familiar voice in her left ear.

Glancing back, she was pleased to see one of her two best friends standing there beside her.

"I don't think there's much you can do right now Pete. If I stop for even a moment, I don't think I'll be able to get the shield back up."

"But it's burning your hands!"

"It's a small price to pay."

Knowing that to a certain degree she was right, after all without the shield they would all probably have been captured by now, he knew he still couldn't stand there and just watch. Thinking about what he'd done only moments ago with the young injured dragons, the hockey player within him closed his eyes and sought out his friend, which given she was standing right next to him wasn't that difficult. Slowly at first, he began to dribble a small amount of healing energy into her hands.

Having been fighting the pain for some time, it came as a pleasant surprise when it started to desist. It took her a few moments to work out what was going on, but she couldn't help smiling when she did. Peter!

"Where did you learn that?"

"Back in the nursery ring... did you skip class that day?"

"I think I'd probably already graduated by then. Didn't they keep you behind for an extra decade?"

"Oh... ha!"

Pouring as much healing magic as he dared into his friend, for her part, she just stood and lapped it up. Half a minute later, her hands were fully repaired, with the dagger having cooled down considerably.

Abruptly, something slapped Peter really hard on the back.

"What have I missed?" bellowed a smirking Flash.

"FLASH!" cried Peter.

"FLASH!" exclaimed Richie.

"FLASH!" declared Janice.

With Richie unable to, both Janice and Peter hugged their friend tight, pleased to see him in one piece and back in the fight.

"How's the shield holding up Rich?" asked the ex-Crimson Guard.

"Okay for now, but it's consuming an awful lot of magic. Reserves in the dagger feel like they are well below fifty percent."

Flash nodded his understanding. It was a worry and quite a prolific problem, but difficult to know how to solve given their current circumstances.

"Any other imminent threats I need to know about?"

Richie swallowed uncomfortably, knowing that she

would have to tell them about her misjudgement.

"When I raised the shield, I totally forgot about those three," she said, nodding out beyond the transparent protective barrier.

All three of them turned to face the direction in which she'd nodded.

To their horror, they could make out George and Fredric, just being joined by the naga king.

Flash's heart jumped up into his mouth, particularly when he spied the new aerial force heading their way at speed. If he didn't do something immediately, two very different realms would each lose their king.

Cauterising wounds, knitting bones and internal organs back together, Yoyo seemed to have a production line of casualties. It was hard going, and not just because of the dangerous situation they all found themselves in. It wasn't as if he was the youngest of them here either, quite the opposite in fact, and that at this very moment contributed greatly to his concern. He felt tired... truly tired, more tired than he could ever remember being, with his limited supply of magic feeling as though it were nearly depleted by everything he'd done so far today, and he still had charges that needed his care. As well, he'd been paying attention to what had been going on around him, just as his experience had taught him to do. The young girl that had been ostracised, Richie Rump as she was known, had been doing a fine job of protecting them all and keeping them safe, but he'd done the math and knew that the laminium in that dagger would only keep powering the shield they all hid behind for a limited period of time. By his best estimate, they didn't have much time left at all. What they'd do then was anybody's guess. And so with what little magic and mana was left within the group being consumed at quite a rate, a concerned Yoyo redoubled his painstaking efforts to get his charges back on their feet, pushing away the nagging worry at the back of his mind, that he'd gotten them involved in something that would ultimately lead to their untimely demise.

43 I LOVE YOU! I KNOW!

The security presence was much bigger than any of them had anticipated. So far they'd passed through three outer rings, each made up of about twenty dark dragons or nagas, most in their natural forms, with the occasional human shape thrown in for good measure. Passing near enough to smell the rotting body odour on most of these false figures, the three infiltrators found it impossible to discern from which race they originated. Luckily for them, they didn't need to know. All they had to do was maintain their stern faces and throw in the occasional nod. So far, it had seemed to do the trick. Reaching an unguarded section of darkened corridor on their journey towards the main control room, DomCon tried to lighten the mood.

"I feel like Boba Fett having just captured Han Solo in Cloud City."

"Does that make me Darth Vader?" asked Jar Man sarcastically.

"If I had to choose... I'd say you were more like Chewbacca," replied his friend.

"Really?" whispered Jar Man, tilting his newly formed head to one side inquisitively.

"Because of the smell," chuckled DomCon.

"Who cares about that?" declared Steel softly. "I'm Han Solo!"

"How do you even know about Han Solo?" asked Jar Man. "After all, you laminium ball players haven't been taught how to assume human form and aren't allowed anywhere near the surface."

"Not that this is really the time, but it might surprise you both to know that a great deal of laminium ball players are fascinated by the humans and the earth's surface. There are some very unscrupulous black market dragon traders that, for a price, will deliver pretty much anything you want. And don't forget... currency for us is no object."

"And so where do you fit into all of this?"

"I do love their films and books. To say I have a modest collection of each might be something of an understatement."

"NICE!" exclaimed DomCon a little too loudly.

"Since we all seem to be on the same page with this, I think that each of us should adopt these names as a pseudonym from now on," suggested Steel.

"Just call me Boba," stuttered DomCon, totally in character.

"That'll make me Chewie then I suppose," grumbled Jar Man light-heartedly, the creases in the forehead of his false form squidging together.

"Again... who cares? I'm Han," added Steel.

And as quickly as it had arrived, the merriment was over, with all three dragons getting their serious game faces back on.

Not so far away, the master mantra maker and the rest of the light sided infiltrators packed up their things and prepared to move out. In the depths of the shadows, the wily old shopkeeper delved deep into the secret pouch that circled his all encompassing belly, checking to make sure the single most important item they were carrying as a group was still there. It was! Glancing down at his masterpiece of magic, much as a parent would at their precious child, he marvelled at the sparkling, golden sheet of parchment, watching with awe as the rainbow array of colours swirled gently across it. Splicing with Tank had been as good as it could get, as far as he was concerned, and that day would be etched in his memory for as long as he remained alive, which in his case might not be that long at all. Taking one last look before shutting the pouch tight, he swore to himself there and then that he'd get the job done and unleash the mantra across the entire crystal node network in an effort to halt the nagas' nastiness.

As the group of humans finished the snacks they'd been provided with and took one last sip from their water bottles, the lumbering form of Gee Tee wandered silently up the debris strewn corridor towards them, occasionally stumbling over rocky wreckage and scraping his tail against what remained of the walls. Each and every one of them knew there should be noise accompanying his actions and found it more than a little odd that there wasn't, despite the fact that they'd had some time to get used to it.

"Ahhh... my human friends. How are you all doing?"

"Uhhh... okay thanks," volunteered Angela.

The others all nodded.

"Good to hear, good to hear. Now... I just want you to know that nobody expects a repeat of the heroics from Salisbridge. Songs will be sung about what you did there, should we turn the tide of evil away and regain control of the planet. Your bravery and courage are the reason we've got to this point. Without all of you, everything would already be lost. So... find somewhere to stay safe. If you see an opportunity to help out and use your remaining grenades... do so! If not, help in any other way you can. Nobody expects you to go into battle against a horde of malevolent dragons with just your bare fists. Use your heads."

Having felt lost and alone for the most part, with Tank, Richie and Hook all missing, the four surface dwellers all broke into huge smiles simultaneously at the dragon shopkeeper's kind words.

"I must go now... they expect me to be on the front line when things kick off. An old dragon like me... whatever next?! So I shall bid you goodbye and good luck. You've all been a credit to your race and I hope that after this is all over, we can share a drink or two. You have my thanks for what you've done so far."

And with that, the gentle prehistoric giant, turned and lumbered noiselessly away.

Checking the straps on the bandoliers that held their grenades in place, Emma and Angela valiantly held back tears, while Sam and Taibul stoically chose to just let the master mantra maker's words sink in. It was hard for each of them to believe they were actually here and not in some kind of abstract dream that they would wake up from any second now. The true danger of what they'd wound up amongst was only really starting to become apparent now, which in itself was odd given everything that had happened below ground back in Salisbridge. Outnumbered, outgunned, outdragoned but not to be outdone, they'd all contributed to something that had not just saved the lives of their friends and the other dragons, but may just have tipped the scales in the battle for the planet. But it had all been achieved on instinct, adrenaline, surprise and a blind loyalty to the human Richie Rump, someone who, at the time, they'd all have laid down their lives for. To find out she was a dragon was gobsmacking to say the least. Unfortunately though, she wasn't here now, despite all four of them yearning for her. With her around, failure was impossible to comprehend. Each of them had wished her luck when they'd parted. Angela and Emma missed their friend and captain awfully and often wondered where she was, what she was doing, and whether or not all of it was a lie, the whole 'lacrosse' thing, the 'let's be friends' thing, and the 'I can behave in any way I want' thing.

With signs of movement up ahead in the cool darkness, she pushed aside thoughts of her friend, instead choosing to fully focus on her family. If things went wrong, would they know what had happened to her? Would her body ever be found? Would her part in the story of saving the planet ever be told?

Seconds later a low, guttural grunt from one of the dragons somewhere down towards the front signalled it was time to move out. Taking up their positions some way down the line of battle ready creatures, the four of them followed the gigantic beasts out into the darkness, unsure of what was to come, knowing that all they could do was their best. But would it be enough?

Following the dark, rocky corridor around a right hand bend that almost had them doubling back on themselves, Boba and Chewie stared straight ahead, while Han's head focused firmly on his razor sharp talons, as they approached a towering stone door, guarded by about a dozen deadly dark dragons.

"Password?" demanded the monster in charge.

'Uh, oh,' all three of them thought at once, as the guards eyed them suspiciously.

"D... d... d... do y... y... you reaaallly think weeee've gooot time for th... th... th... this?" stuttered DomCon doing a great job of keeping in character.

"Password!" demanded the guard once again.

This was going to hell, and they hadn't even made it into the inner sanctum yet. If they had to fight here, they'd alert every single guard in the compound to their presence and the party would be over before it had even started. Worse still, those inside could potentially destroy the crystal node, foregoing any chance at all of letting the world know exactly what was going on.

'Calm,' thought Steel. 'Remain calm.'

As sweat dripped from places he wasn't even aware he had, Jar Man had a decision to make. Knowing only too well the importance of getting them inside, and exactly how much depended upon it, he took the biggest gamble of his life and, strolling up to the dragon in charge, mustered all the strength he had and hit him as hard as he could.

CRASH!

With almighty speed the guard hit the wall, sending chunks of masonry flying every which way. Instantly the others adopted fighting stances, drawing their weapons, readying their magic, prepared to attack at a moment's notice. Before they could, Jar Man let rip.

"You insolent little whelp! I should pull your head off and poo down your neck."

Dazed, barely able to think straight, it took everything for the dragon in charge to sit up straight.

"Don't you realise just who we have here? Look at him! Don't you know?"

Swallowing nervously, the dragon on the ground had at least for the time being lost control of events playing out around him.

"This is Steel... one of their most famous laminium ball players!"

"Ohhhhhhhh!!" came out of the mouths of two other guards, clearly a sign of recognition.

"And you know what that means?" continued Jar Man.

The dragon captain continued to look stumped.

"Laminium ball players are renowned for their aerial skill and dexterity. Almost certainly he's been sent to scout ahead, find out the full extent of our force and capability, before reporting back. With that being the case, time is of the essence, which I would have thought would have been plain to see. And you think I have time for passwords? I need to inform the hierarchy NOW! Not in an hour, not in thirty minutes, not in thirty seconds. NOW! Let me in immediately or you'll know the real meaning of the word suffering."

Steel was more than impressed with the strawberry blonde dragon he now thought of as Chewie. And so with Jar Man maintaining his facade of righteous anger, and DomCon continuing to snarl at the lot of them, they waited to see what the outcome of their outrageous bluff would be.

In less than five seconds they had their answer.

"WELL?" screamed the guard captain in the direction of those under his command. "WHAT ARE YOU WAITING FOR? LET THEM IN!"

Lowering their lethal looking weapons, two dragons opened up a hidden control panel and began punching in two different sequences of numbers. On completion, a huge ROAR of stone on stone assaulted their ears as the giant door in front of them started to swing open. Maintaining their defiance, the two dragon friends marched their prisoner into the darkness beyond at their earliest opportunity.

Once the massive, forty metre tall door had slammed closed behind them, making sure there was nobody within earshot, Steel turned around to face Jar Man.

"I love you!" he whispered, adding a conspiratorial wink for good measure.

"I know!" replied the strawberry blonde dragon hiding in human form.

DomCon chuckled.

44 PAIN RELINQUISHING THE CHAIN

Deep in the midst of the magical mayhem, three beings huddled together, concern for one of their number the prevailing feeling amongst them.

"Yooooouuuu muussssst coooome baaaack toooooo usssss," the snake-like voice hissed throughout his mind. "Everyyythiiinnnngg depeeeendsss upooon iiittttt!"

Still he ignored it. Not on purpose, but because he was lost... lost in his own misery, lost in his own family, lost in his own mind. Vasuki's words were little more than insignificant background noise playing out far away. As far as Fredric was concerned it meant less than nothing. The words themselves were barely recognisable against the backdrop of the grief that had stalked him during his time imprisoned in Antarctica, which had got a firm grip on him now and was determined not to let go.

Rattling off a series of super powerful mantras in quick succession, George blasted a hole through the wing of one dark dragon sending it spiralling out of control, melted the sword and the hand grasping it off another, before electrocuting a bold naga who'd slithered out from behind the nearest stack of rubble, leaving a smoking and sparking corpse in its place. While not being truly tested, things were starting to heat up, in more ways than one. And he didn't dare glance over to his left and back across the magically recreated bridge. The last time he'd done that, he'd become hugely concerned at the numbers gathering on the far side of it. In his mind though, things were becoming a little, how should we put it... reckless. Covering for Vasuki's conversation with his best friend, he was having to cast mantra after mantra, and while he didn't feel particularly drained, having the ring back on his finger would at least have provided some reassurance in that department. But he'd only gone and blown it. Relationships had never been his thing... not with dragons, people, and most amusingly, not with inanimate objects. Complacency, it would seem, had bred failure. If he could have his time over again, he'd have done so many things differently. But what being wouldn't? Pushing the regret he felt to one side, a brief lull in the action enabled him to take in what was happening elsewhere within what was HIS private residence. Marvelling at the all encompassing shield that had sprung up around his rescuers, it was no surprise to find the beautiful, young former dragon, Richie Rump, powering it with what looked like Peter's, nay, Fredric's, laminium dagger. Wonders would never cease, he thought, turning his attention away from the shield. Across the way he could just, behind all the bloody battle chaos, make out Amelia Battlehard, a couple of the councillors and what remained of his guard, all putting up a staunch fight against what appeared to be overwhelming odds. Momentarily he wondered if he could help them. Realistically though, he knew he wasn't going to leave his friend, not having just found him after so long. As well, he knew what the guard captain was doing... drawing the enemies towards them and away from him, effectively buying him some more time. Deep down inside, he hoped it would be enough.

You don't just get to be king of the nagas for no apparent reason. You have to be special, and Vasuki was certainly that. Possessed of no small amount of unusual magic, he had a knack for not only leading and negotiating, but communicating with other beings, something that currently fuelled his frustration. Fully aware of the dire situation they all found themselves in, he'd tried everything to get through to the former prisoner, a dragon he now thought of as his ally. But his efforts had all been in vain.

Fredric remained on the ground, tears still streaming from his eyes, mind locked solid, thoughts inhabiting a faraway place. Reluctantly, Vasuki rose up to his full height and turned towards George.

"It'ssssssss noooo goooood. I caaannooot geeet through toooo hiiiim."

Fighting off the hopelessness of their situation, a hell bent naga, and two dragons peppering him with projectiles from the air, it was tough for the dragon king to hear that his naga counterpart had failed. Options, he knew, were in short supply.

Grasping Richie by the arm, almost able to feel the thrumming power from the laminium dagger she held out in front of her coursing through her muscles, Flash was keen to acquire the young woman's attention. Having caught her eye, he conveyed his thoughts.

"I need to get out there Rich! I need to help the king!"

Fully focused on maintaining the shield, safeguarding them all, she glanced over at him.

"I can't take it down... not even for a second. We'll be overrun, of that there's no question."

"What about creating a gap for me to charge out of?"

With beads of sweat gradually building up on her forehead, the dagger wielding lacrosse player thought fleetingly about his request.

"I don't think so. I don't have the kind of fine control I would have had as a dragon. For me to conjure up a gap big enough for you to pass through, I'd have to go even bigger again, and that would give our enemies a chance to attack. It's just too risky."

Knowing that she was right did little to quell the urgency with which he felt he should get to the king. Trapped and with no place to go was a situation he'd been in many times before, but not when the king's life was quite literally in his hands. Drifting down through all his experience and knowledge, the ex-Crimson Guard searched furiously within himself for anything that might help. Rumours of vibrating mantras that could move a being through solid objects from decades ago sprang up. Almost instantly he ignored those. Next, some illicit experiments with phasing mantras, again with the aim of passing through solid objects, from back in his time with the Crimson Guards. None had proven even vaguely successful. Last but not least, a long out of date report of a reclusive wizard dragon that had boasted about succeeding with a teleportation spell. Unfortunately for him, it was mere speculation with absolutely no details. That left him with... NOTHING! Well... maybe.

Each one is different, coded to that particular individual's DNA. The words might be similar, the intent and willpower behind the magic almost identical, but what happens when that mantra is set in motion depends purely on the dragon in question. The mantra that holds one of the prehistoric beasts in perfect human form was designed millennia ago. Sure, it's been updated across the centuries, with little additions here, a little editing there, all of course designed to make it more sturdy and robust. Refinements have been made available, something every nursery ring student knows off by heart. They should anyway, especially as they spend over fifteen years of their long lives studying that aspect of dragon magic. With the right words and intent, faces can be sculpted to practically any design. Hair of almost any type and colour can be added, be it flowing long locks running down past the shoulders, to a short buzz cut that never needs cutting. Beards and goatees are now a breeze, whereas once they weren't available at all. Like all things, there are fads. For a while a full facial covering of stubble was perhaps the most popular add-on mantra of all for young male dragons. But it didn't last long. Most soon return to either clean shaven or a full-on hairy beard, at about the time they need to consider two of the most amusing hair traits... at least to them, anyway. Ear and nasal hair always causes much hilarity at whatever nursery ring it's being taught. Dragons have virtually no understanding of such things. While it might afflict a few (with Gee Tee being one of those, due mainly because of his super extended age) most won't have to face that threat for many, many centuries, if ever. To see a dragon suffering from either of these would be rare, especially nose hair. Why? Shouldn't it be obvious? Not only does the scorching flame of hell itself come out of their mouths, it also escapes in small amounts through their noses, whether they like it or not. In a hair versus fire fight, I think we can safely say there'll always only be one winner. So from that point of view it's of little concern. Next in the amusement stakes when it comes to add-ons for a dragon's human shape would be bellies, followed closely by reproductive organs. If you thought a gaggle of giggling schoolgirls at a girls only school being taught sexual reproduction was a teacher's worst nightmare, I can assure you it's ten times worse for any of the *tors* tutoring this particular subject to dragonlings. Dealing with the topic can last for months, with all the usual crude jokes, (elephant trunks, you've got your tail on the wrong way, all that sort of thing) and of course they've all been heard before. The nursery ring staffroom can be quite a depressing place throughout this period of time.

Surprisingly, particularly given the crisis he found himself in, all this shot through Flash's mind in less than the blink of an eye. Crucially though, it gave him an idea.

His training had been different. It needed to be because of what was expected of him. Exceptional... that's what he was supposed to be, and so everything was covered in minute detail. From mantras to offensive magic, evasion to spycraft, channelling energy and healing to killing in the sky. It was all there and about as comprehensive as it could be. Right now, he was grateful that it had been.

Brushing Richie's shoulder gently, so as not to distract her too much, he leaned in close so that he didn't have to shout over the cacophony of magic that was exploding in and around them.

"What about a small gap? Could you open up one of those?" he ventured, an appealing look smothered across his face.

"How big would it have to be?"

"I don't know. What do you think you can safely do?"

Dividing her focus between maintaining the shield and Flash's question, her mind raced with figures and equations, working out where best she could form a hole and just how big she could make it without letting too much of the magic currently bombarding them from the outside, in.

"Maybe the size of a football at best, but it'll be sketchy. As well, I won't be able to hold it long, especially if our friends out there spot it."

"I understand," replied Flash. "Can we get on and do it?"

Turning to face her friend, whilst holding the laminium dagger firmly out in front of her, the tiniest of smiles weaved its way through the freckles of her pale skinned face.

"I have to ask... how in the hell do you think...?"

Holding up his hand, Flash cut her off there.

"Trust me... you really don't want to know!"

Brushing himself off, whilst at the same time harmlessly deflecting away a couple of stray bolts of magic heading directly for him, the monster that was Manson blew out a long breath as he assessed his force's situation, all the time twisting the dragon king's ring around his finger. For the life of him he couldn't work out why he didn't have access to the power it held. If he'd had control over it by now, something that he'd planned for, all this would be well and truly over. But he didn't, and it wasn't, and that in itself was odd. From everything he knew, all the research he'd done, he should have at least felt its presence. But there was nothing, no trace of magic, no inkling that any intelligence either existed now or at some point in the past. Pushing all thoughts of this aside, he returned to the moment and a few of the other conundrums.

It had all been going so well only a short time ago. And now this! Fate, he knew, could be a fickle mistress, but sometimes she just downright sucked. Now was one of those times, and the more he thought about everything he could see all around him, the more puzzled he became. The reinforcements arriving through that strange magical portal that almost certainly had the stench of naga power written all over it. Clearly those slithering serpents hadn't offered up all their magic. They'd pay dearly for that at some later date.

The brilliant bright intensity of shocking blue electricity bouncing up off the huge defensive shield hiding the vast majority of his enemies caught his eye from across the way. Glancing over, his mind veered off in another direction. Her! How in the hell was she here, and doing all of this? As far as he knew, she'd been stripped of all her dragon powers and her memories. And yet here she was, a spanner in the works of everything he was trying to achieve. Alright, she'd killed his father, the one being on this planet he'd hated the most, and he supposed he should have been grateful in some sick sort of way. But he wasn't. It should have been him, and it should have happened a long time ago. But when it came to his father, he'd always found it all but impossible to stand up to him. Something inside him, gut wrenching and twisted, had always prevented him from being strong, being counted... saying his piece. For decades he'd had dreams about killing the infamous Troydenn. He'd take his time, string it out and let him suffer for months. NO! Years! Torture him until he begged for mercy, only then putting him out of his misery. But now any hope of that had gone. A quick glimpse over to his left at the humungous, matt black corpse that lay splayed out on the pristine, white marble soothed his aching gut. Pleasure and pain tugged on opposite ends of his heart strings, if such things even existed inside him. Pleasure because he was finally free, pain because the foul psychopath of a beast that had called himself his father hadn't died by his hand.

Turning back to events across the way, the tiniest part of him, hidden deep inside, marvelled at the young female powering the magnificent shield. In very different circumstances they could have been friends... she could have been his queen. As soon as the idea nestled into his head, he dismissed it immediately. That would never have happened because he'd seen her defiance up close and personal, and there was simply no way at all that they'd have had anything to do with each other. Pondering the best way to deal with the 'Rump' girl and all those cowering behind her protection, he sought to get an overview of everything that was going on. Off to his far left, dark dragons and nagas under his command bombarded a circling group of what remained of the forces he'd found here. No doubt it was a stray contingent of King's Guard from the council building putting up a valiant last stand. Instantly he dismissed them as no threat. They wouldn't last much longer against his unstoppable legion.

Over to his right, something much more interesting caught his eye: three beings he was more than a little familiar with... all of whom he had some history with... the king of this godforsaken realm, the one he'd already broken, the one he'd intended to make suffer for many, many months to come. George, as he'd once been known, a brave and courageous knight centuries ago, according to his father. What he was doing away from the shield, deflecting and defending the other two, was anybody's guess. And that brought him of course to them. Prisoners from Antarctica, both of whom he'd overseen personally, and hoped would die in the prison he'd been confined to when growing up. How they'd escaped was an utter mystery. Worse still... he hadn't heard anything at all from Joshim, the jailer that he held accountable, the one he'd left in charge of the trap he'd set, just in case anyone was stupid enough to try and mount a rescue attempt. What it all meant, he had no idea. Vasuki, the naga king, was supposed to have been taken care of by now. His appearance could upset the plans he'd set in motion with the rest of his race. It was a good job they'd been magically enthralled. If not, their king might have taken half of his force away from him. As it stood, that really wasn't going to happen. And the other one, why on earth was he just kneeling there, in the middle of all the chaos, the other two protecting him? It didn't make any sense. Had he been injured? It didn't look like it. Then what? Something didn't add up. He didn't know what, but there was something missing from the information he had at his disposal. And that made him nervous. Without all the facts, acts and events became harder to predict. Wildcard elements came into play, as they'd already done over the course of the last hour. It was time to put a stop to all of that. No random fluke was going to prevent him from ruling this world, putting his stamp on the planet that had, for the best part of his life, turned its back on him. Now was the time to act. And act he did. Holding his arms aloft, he closed his eyes and let out the loudest telepathic shout out of his life, encouraging, no... ordering his dark, demonic troops on the council building side and the bridge itself, to swarm on over and finish off the puny pocket of resistance remaining. Satisfied that he'd ignited the fuse that would lead to the conclusion of events, the tiniest smile snaked across his chiselled jaw.

Shrouded in long forgotten, ancient magic, the deranged being known as Earth, Fredric's daughter and Peter's mother, skulked in and out of rubble, using both debris and magical explosions for cover, getting closer all the time to her main objective. Stifling the laughter building up inside her so as not to give her position away, it amused her greatly to see the dragon that had once been her father reduced to this. Assuming he still thought of her as his daughter, even after her memories had come flooding back, she still couldn't come to regard him as ever having sired her. To see him on his knees now, a supposed mighty warrior reduced to this, bought her tremendous joy. It was all she could have wished for in the middle of this almighty battle. But it still wasn't enough, and that, she was about to put right.

Through the blossoming explosions that constantly rained down on the shield Richie held in place through force of will, powered by the exotic laminium dagger, Flash, preparing yet another of his party pieces, caught the briefest slither of movement, outside and vaguely in the direction he'd planned to travel. Off in the distance, unnoticed by the trio he intended to get out there to protect, a dangerous woman, protected by magic by the looks of things, cloaked head to toe in brown, appeared to be traversing the battlefield with singular intent. Right there, right then, it was all the motivation he needed. As a pinprick of a hole started to appear at his feet, the ex-Crimson Guard closed his eyes and commanded the bonds of his now fully dragon DNA to unshackle. On doing so, he gave them a totally unfamiliar command, one from far off in the past, one that he hoped would still work, one that he prayed would get him out in front of things and into a position to serve the being he'd pledged his life to.

With the bulk of Manson's force having headed through the council building and out onto the courtyard before the bridge on the other side, a small contingent remained in case any sort of resistance force should show up. It was unlikely, but this plan had been long in the making and no detail, however small, had been overlooked. Well... almost.

On the third floor, two dragon guards stood stoically at their posts, ready to fight tooth and claw, ready to unleash the magic that rallied within them. On guard, they fully expected trouble. What they didn't expect was the sound of soft buzzing, lazily drifting up from one of the stairwells next to their posts. Both giving the other puzzled looks, the bigger of the two indicated to his colleague with a nod of his head that he should check it out. Confused about what could be making the sound, the smaller dragon plodded over to the edge of the stairwell, leaned over the railing and looked down. From out of nowhere, up popped two nifoloa, and in one swift, coordinated action, both picked a different eye and stabbed their single large tooth into it, releasing a huge amount of toxic venom. Before the prehistoric, dark dragon had been dragged over the side by the bright, blood red hands of the gaki, it was already dead.

Stunned at what he'd just witnessed, the larger of the two guards readied his magic and, thanks to his training, was prepared for anything. At least he thought he was. As a dozen more nifoloa joined their two nest mates in a swarm that would chill any being's blood, two four armed, scaled apes swung up from the staircase, landing with a thud beside the single toothed, vicious magical insects. As if that wasn't bad enough, a pack of eight blue-maned asena trotted casually around the corner, green blood dripping down their jaws, matting the thick fur surrounding their necks, a wicked understanding of the poor dragon's plight reflected in their blazing blue eyes.

As the realisation dawned on just what he was up

against, regret welled up inside one of Manson's nameless sycophants. Nothing was worth this, none of the promises of power, wealth and position. At that very moment, all he wanted to do was survive and with that in mind, he opted for the most undragonlike thing possible... to run away, or in this case... FLY AWAY! Turning on his heels, bending his legs, he pushed off with all his strength in an effort to take to the air inside the building. It was then that a cloud of tiny gnats tumbled into his line of sight, flitting this way and that, surrounding his face. Ignoring them as little or no threat, just as he'd been trained to do, surprise, fear and terror consumed him as the first of the little buggers breathed a steady stream of fire right into his left eye. Rocked by the attack from something so innocuous, his take off faltered momentarily, ending any real hope he had of escape. A split second later they were on him... ALL OF THEM! Scorpion men stung him, double-headed eagles dive bombed and pecked him, pixiu raked their claws across his wings as he tumbled to the floor, conaima took giant bites from the muscles on his thighs and belly. All of that, and the camaheutos and skrikers hadn't even gotten involved. Of all the ways to die, this was by far the last way any being should go. After a few minutes, the feeding frenzy was over and the coordinated attackers continued to move upwards, following the trail of magic.

Cold, calculated cunning battled against the rage that constantly flooded her veins as she negotiated the obstacles in her way. It had been slow going, but she was about to reap the rewards for her patience, having almost reached a position to strike from. She knew exactly who was going down first... her father! And this time, unlike events in Germany that her mind had blocked out for so long, there'd be no escape, no intervention by the fickle mistress of fate. This time, he'd be going straight to hell.

Not quite the fiery red mass it had threatened to become, the laminium dagger that Richie held out in front of her to power the shield that for the moment kept them all safe, had cooled down considerably, affording Peter the luxury of just dribbling a little healing magic across his friend's hands every now and then to keep them fresh and undamaged. Concentrating solely on this, the young hockey playing dragon was well aware that something was going on, something that involved Flash, but he hadn't a clue about the details. None of them did. So as Hook followed Yoyo's instructions in an effort to assist the injured, Janice's consciousness swirled in and around that of her new found friend and decidedly deadly weapon, Fu-ts'ang, they, like Peter and Richie, almost missed the single most amazing, most astounding bit of magic on display so far today. And that was saying something.

As the pinprick sized hole in the shield expanded to that of a table tennis ball, Flash's strong, stocky form instantly folded in on itself. Remarkable, it was made even more so by the fact that as far as the friends knew, a human sized shape was almost the smallest a dragon could become. Peter might have known differently if he'd thought about it; after all, his first experience of Gee Tee's Mantra Emporium had involved one of THE most embarrassing experiences of his life, in which he'd stood almost naked in front of Tank, who'd been sitting high up on a wall, transformed, using an ancient magical mantra, into a gigantic grinning spider. If not for the shock of the experience, the young dragon might have thought to wonder about the size difference. It had been a giant spider, but it was still about half the size of a normal human being, something that should have been almost impossible. Anyway, he hadn't thought to enquire of either his friend, or the famed master mantra maker, about this and so his surprise now was palpable. Usually unflappable, even in a situation like this, the young lacrosse playing dragon was also so flabbergasted she almost dropped the dagger, something that would have ended them all. Luckily, she didn't. And what bombshell had them so up in arms, so totally and utterly dumbfounded?

Flash's physical form had continued to crumple in on itself, looking as though it might disappear altogether, but before this could happen, the colours of what remained of him began to change. Greys, whites and subtle yellows transformed into majestic blues, stunning shades of green, brilliant bright oranges and reds that looked like a phoenix rising from the flames, with finally just a hint of purple, all taking place in less than a blink of an eye. So captivated were the friends with the rainbow brilliance of colours forming before their very eyes, they'd failed to notice the newfound shape their magical pal had become. But they noticed now, and as their jaws dropped open simultaneously, they marvelled at the beauty, elegance, complexity and simplicity of it all. With that, and the hole in the shield staying steady at about the size of a tennis ball, Flash, decked out beautifully as the single most striking hummingbird in the whole of history, hovered in mid-air, wings flapping almost faster than their enhanced dragon senses could see. He nodded once in their direction before diving headlong through the gap Richie had provided him with, lost instantly in the dizzying array of ethereal explosions still inundating their last line of defence.

A stray dart of poisoned magic spun counter clockwise through the air as it headed in her direction, deep behind two piles of upturned marble. Normally she'd just bat it away with a touch of the supernatural, much like you or I would swat a fly. But using even the slightest touch now might alert her enemies to her presence and so she calculated the lost projectile's path to the nearest millimetre and let it zip past her left thigh, tearing a hole in her fluttering brown cloak as it disappeared into the recesses of yet more debris. Ducking down, wary of each footstep, she made sure not to touch any of the rubble strewn around her. As her painstaking journey reached its conclusion, she peeped out from her hiding place, sheer delight on her face at what she saw. There, only twenty metres away, was her so-called father kneeling on the cool, white marble, tears spilling down his face, with the current dragon king of this world and a very fancy coloured naga, trying hard in her opinion to look important. This was it! Her chance had come. None of the trio had any idea she was here, so wrapped up in their own world had they become. A fatal mistake this would prove to be, as far as they were concerned. Raiding her mind to bring forth the perfect spell, a smile of epic proportions drifted into place across her purple scarred features, as the deliciousness of it all sank into place.

For Flash, time had slowed to almost nothingness. As well as taking on the hummingbird's form, some of its unique qualities had also merged with his dragon consciousness. The appreciation of time was one of those. Flapping his wings at around fifty beats a second instantly gave him a much greater understanding of his surroundings. Magic oozed, blasted, shot, fragmented and exploded all around him, but he was in absolutely no danger because of the form he'd chosen. As agile as anything and able to fly at around eighty kilometres per hour, there was a reason the hummingbird was renowned, the very same reason he'd selected it all those years ago.

A grumpy old dragon, even in terms of all the other instructors, this one had been there from the beginning, and it showed. Flash, unlike most of the other candidates, had little time for tomfoolery or jokes. He was there to learn, something he was well aware of, due in part to the number of times it had been drummed into him. But most of the others, his classmates and future colleagues, all liked to muck about. Considered a loner because of this, he spent most of his evenings studying by himself, and most of his tutor time sitting as far away as possible from anyone else. Today was no different, apart from the fact that the ill-tempered tutor had dragged him into a challenge, something the other students were absolutely delighted about, much to his horror.

"And so now, we will see just how much you've learned on this subject," announced the dragon tutor known as Fleetingsmeet, all plummy and upper class. "Transcend here and Flash will see just how small they can go. The winner will have tomorrow off. After you gentledragons," offered up the tutor with a wave of his hand.

Transcend, cheered on by the rest of the class, minus Flash of course, released her DNA and allowed her bonds to relax. In an absolute muddle, causing eye strain for even the most fervent of her supporters, the physical form that she'd clung on to throughout the lesson so far, ran amuck briefly, before buzzing into place, a much smaller place than her previous incarnation.

"Bravo, bravo," shouted Fleetingsmeet in delight over the howling and the clapping, at the sight of the small ape.

Flash stood stock still, a totally blank expression covering his entire face.

"Not joining in?" enquired the tutor sarcastically, as the crowd basked in Flash's failure.

"Hardly worth bothering yet, is it?" he replied.

Transcend, her hackles up and buoyed by the crowd's support, once again released the restraints of her DNA, recognising a challenge when she heard one, sure she could go one better than the ape. As the same magical mixing and writhing started to occur, this time there was a pause, almost as if her physical form was against what she was trying to achieve. A battle of wits might well have been taking place; if that was the case, she eventually won, but at what cost? Much slower than before, her physical form shimmered into place, the last pieces taking an age to reform. Moments later a large house cat purred softly in the crowd's direction, producing screams of excitement, much to Fleetingsmeet's displeasure. As more clapping ensued, a sudden squawk from the cat stopped them in their tracks. One of its paws had totally lost cohesion. It didn't seem to be able to regulate its form. And then letting out one long sigh, the change they'd seen twice already reoccurred once again, the end result this time being Transcend back in her recognised human form, looking more than a little worse for wear and flustered.

"Well done my dear, well done. A super example of what we were trying to achieve. It's only a shame that your opponent ducked out of the challenge."

Something inside Flash stirred.

"Funny," he uttered, "I never think of any of us as opponents. Only brothers and sisters in arms that I've yet to work with, and as for the challenge... ACCEPTED!"

Accessing the magic inside him as simply as you or I would blink, he started the process of change, at the same time whispering the words in his mind, giving himself over totally, applying all his will. He had no doubt that it would work, because truth be told he'd tried it before, on his own, in his room. That night it had been about testing his limits, the strength of his magical endurance and imagination. Inspired by something he'd read a while ago, an article about the Aztec God of War Huitzilopochtli often being depicted as a humming bird, something piqued his curiosity, and he made it his mission to find out what he could about Huitzilopochtli. When he did, it made him chuckle, and I bet you can guess why. Of course, the Aztec God of War was... a dragon! Not just any dragon as it turned out, but a mighty powerful one. And what's more, rumours abounded throughout the ages about him being able to change his form into a... hummingbird! Brilliant, he thought on discovering this, knowing that it was the perfect form to aim for. Not only did he achieve his goal, but the creature itself was spectacular, its dazzling colours as close to perfection as he could have hoped.

And so it was on that fateful day in the classroom that the change occurred, much to the surprise of not only his classmates, but Fleetingsmeet as well. For the next twenty minutes or so, the soon to be Crimson Guard flew around the room, dive bombed the tutor's fish tank and precariously hovered in place right in front of all their faces, one by one, much to the whole class's delight. For everyone involved, it was a day to remember. And remember he did.

Arcing energy from a series of crackling, electrical, blue bolts startled his tiny form out of the memory he'd been enjoying and back to the raging battle he now hovered in the middle of. Whilst in no danger from the form he'd chosen, he was only too aware of how costly lack of concentration could be, having seen others lose their lives time and time again. Jinking left, out of the line of fire of some vicious looking ice shards, he turned his head to follow their trajectory, watching them splatter harmlessly against the powerful shield his friend so confidently held in place. Thoughts about what would happen when her magic ran out tried to infiltrate his mind, immediately swatted away by his strong will and self control. He couldn't divert his attention to that, not now. The king needed him which was his one and only priority, and maybe the answer to the shield problem. If he could get George, Fredric and Vasuki behind Richie's magical barrier, then the king's ring might well be able to power it indefinitely. Unaware of the deep flaw in his plan... that the ring hadn't been behaving for its rightful owner for some time now, and that his friend, Tank, was in possession of the real band, Flash swept back round on himself to avoid yet another mystical barrage, dropped down like a stone towards the deck and, building up all the velocity he could, corkscrewed off in the direction of the trio that desperately needed his help.

Side slipping dark dragons and brutal looking nagas, each of whom paid him little or no attention at all, Flash's beautifully designed form climbed up and over a particularly large and angry prehistoric monster, before plummeting down its back at quite a dizzying rate, running almost straight into a vile, blood stained naga that seemed for all the world to be carelessly throwing his magic around on an almost industrial level. Paying little heed to the foul creature, with the king his utmost priority, the ex-Crimson Guard wondered how any magical being could be so stupid.

'He'll have wasted all his power in no time at all. What an idiot!' he thought, as he drew to a halt, wings beating ten to the dozen. The dumb assed naga conjured up a huge bubbling ball of ethereal energy, and in one powerful, slick motion, tossed it in the direction of the magical shield. As the brightly coloured ball left the naga's grip, the merest glint of light caught the little hummingbird's attention.

'Oh my God!' thought Flash, taken aback at what he'd just spotted. 'It can't be? Can it?' Vectoring in for a closer look, Flash's surprise was there for all to be seen if anyone had been looking. 'It is!' he thought.

On his first trip to Antarctica, something that now seemed like a lifetime ago, he'd gone totally and utterly prepared, as any decent dragon agent would, despite the fact that it was supposed to be a very straightforward assignment. Things had, of course, gone south in almost the blink of an eye. Out in the harsh, snowy wilderness, he'd been captured by two ingenious and resourceful nagas, totally unaware of their true nature. Looking back, it had been one of the most worrying times of his life. Right there and then, escape seemed almost impossible, and a lifetime of imprisonment in that hellhole looked like a fate far worse than death. Fortunately he'd had a little help in the form of the two beings he'd recently returned the favour for: Fredric and Vasuki. Not only that, but he'd had his trusty Polar Surveyor Redesign watch. Luckily for him his captors had forgotten to remove it from his being, and that had helped him break free. At the time though, they'd had the forethought to remove two other items of his, a prized laminium necklace and a matching ring. As he fluttered to a halt, hovering in mid-air as gracefully as any being that could take flight, both missing items swam into view, adorning the depraved serpent sitting there before him. Relief at seeing his prized possessions again swept through him, followed quickly by anger.

'How dare that loathsome being wear those things?' he mused. Quickly though, his mind moved on to the much bigger picture, and whether or not he could regain his lost jewellery. If he could, then it would temporarily solve the problem of powering the shield. Whilst the necklace didn't contain nearly as much laminium as Richie's dagger, it did contain quite a lot and would be able to power that size of barrier for some while, providing of course that it hadn't already been depleted. Mind set on a course of action, all the while aware of the king's plight, Flash lost himself to the action and wondered just how best he could use this tiny little form to inflict the maximum amount of damage on the raging, repellent serpent-like monster, curled up there before him.

'Limited' adequately described his options, with only one really standing out. So with no time to lose, he got on with it.

Trading stealth for altitude, knowing time was of the essence, he pulled up into a climb, racing upwards for all he was worth. Reaching the fifth floor, he figured this was high enough for what he had in mind. Ignoring the multitude of rainbow coloured, magic infused blasts exploding all around him, he took one last look at the scene below him and lurched into a dive. Feeling the full force of the air exerting pressure on his multi-hued feathers, he concentrated his vision on his rapidly approaching target, knowing that he'd probably only get one chance to do this right. Carving a path through the atmosphere, the exhilaration of flight threatened momentarily to take over. Sadness at not having flown in some time, due to the catastrophic injuries he'd suffered by one of the kind he now found himself approaching, was washed instantly away when he remembered what Fredric had done for him back in the Antarctic icy prison. Then the moment arrived. Unable to blink for fear of missing his target, it was then that he knew he'd gotten it right. All the naga had to do was not move his head in the next few moments, and it didn't. With little regard for the tiny little body he currently inhabited, the ex-Crimson Guard flew with all the speed he could muster, using his beak to crash headlong into the naga's right eye. The results were... eye watering in more ways than one. The beast's yell of excruciating pain could be heard above the sound of the explosive magic going off throughout the private residence, and given the number of creatures and the firefight involved, that was quite something. It wasn't the only pain in evidence though. The entire length of Flash's deliciously dark beak felt as though it had been pounded on an anvil with a blacksmith's hammer. This had been negated though by the most satisfying 'POP' in the world, on contact with the creature's vertically slit pupil. With no time to waste, Flash placed his sharp but delicate claws on the naga's cheek, and used them for leverage before pulling out his beak. Free to fly, he had to muster all his wits to avoid flailing, flimsy arms and the muscled length of tail that was smashing its way through the air, mirroring its owner's descent into madness.

Changing from a hummingbird into a magpie in all but physical form, the ex-Crimson Guard went straight for the ring, relieving its current owner of it with his tiny little talons on the very first strike. Darting swiftly up, he knew he might get only a single pass at the necklace. Pumping his wings furiously, he tossed his head up, arched his neck and headed straight for the clasp with his still ringing beak.

'SNAP!' First time it came free and proceeded to tumble down the naga's brightly scaled chest. Punching through the air, Flash hooked onto it with his open beak and pulling a slow loop, pitched away, back in the direction of his friends and the ever present shield, leaving the dastardly naga tormented with pain, wondering what the hell had just happened. Immediately a new problem presented itself, one he hadn't foreseen. How on earth was he going to get the valuables back through the barrier? Seemingly with little choice, he reached out telepathically for anything familiar. Risky at best, particularly given the amount of power he was using to hold this form together, he could think of little alternative, especially knowing that he had to get to the king. Whilst the shield did dull the feel of the presences he would normally have recognised instantly, one amongst them stood out. YOYO! Skimming down a dark dragon's wing, raking its skin with his claws once or twice on the way, all the time holding tightly to the ring and the necklace, he reached out with his mind, giving everything he had to contact his friend.

"YOYO! YOYO!" he screamed, deep within himself.

Binding together a ruptured deltoid with what was left of his mana, the experienced healer slumped back against the wall, depleted and spent. Whatever happened now, he knew he'd play very little part. Mainly because of his age, it would be some time before the living magic within him replenished, and by then events would surely have played out. All he could do was lend a helping hand, guide others with his vast experience, and of course... pray. Not something he'd normally do, but of one thing he was certain, if ever a situation called for a prayer or two, then this was most certainly it. Closing his eyes, drawing a deep breath, it was then that he heard it over the cacophony of everything else going on. Subtle at first, barely even there, quickly it got louder. And that's when he recognised it.

FLASH!

Sitting bolt upright, his eyes as wide open as they'd go, the experienced healer returned the call deep inside his head.

"FLASH?"

"I'm outside the shield Yoyo."

"I know youngster... I saw, a hummingbird, deeply impressive."

"There's no time for that now. I have items that will help you and Richie with your magic. You have to get her to open a gap in the shield... NOW!"

No sooner said than done, Yoyo bolted to his feet and bounded over to the young lacrosse playing dragon.

"You have to open up the same gap you did before for Flash!"

"WHAT?" bellowed Richie.

"He wants to give us something. It's important."

Deeply sceptical, and about to tell Yoyo what he could do with his request, it was then that she spotted him in all his hummingbird glory, twisting and turning, diving and gliding, swooping and darting in between all the magic that would have been instant death to a larger form. Immediately she siphoned more power from the dagger, focusing her concentration on maintaining the uniformity of the barrier but with one exception. In almost exactly the same place as she'd let him through, the tiniest of holes once again opened up. This time though, it was a lot more raggedy around the edges, shaped nothing like the uniform circle it had been before.

Not needing to be told twice, and with Yoyo shouting in his ear, he dive bombed the hole on exactly the approach he needed. At the very last instant, he thrust the ring from around his feet, and with a flick of his delicate little neck, flipped the necklace to follow. Allowing himself just enough time to see both items land safely on the other side of the barrier, he watched as the gap closed, before wheeling tightly around and setting off in the direction of his monarch.

With Richie sweating nervously while continuing to power the shield, fully aware of just how much energy was, or in this case wasn't, left within the dagger, Yoyo scurried over to see what Flash had just delivered them. Picking the items up from the white, blast-stained marble floor, he could hardly believe his eyes when he realised exactly what they were. Hurrying back to the young lacrosse player, he approached her from behind, much to her surprise.

"Don't worry my dear, Flash has provided us with a temporary respite. That boy is always full of surprises."

And with that, he placed the necklace gently around Richie's neck and then locked the clasp in place.

The realisation of power struck her by surprise. It was as if she'd been cleansed, reborn almost, with her tiredness and fatigue banished, replaced by a clear head and refreshed muscles. Turning to smile at Yoyo, all the time continuing to power the shield, she watched hungrily as he slipped the laminium ring on one of his big fat fingers, the same power she'd just experienced washing over him. A nod from both was all it took for Yoyo to sprint back over to his injured charges, buoyed now by almost youthful exuberance.

She had it... a scorching hot beam of pure plasma that would melt the flesh from his bones instantly. Perfect! Relinquishing the rage she'd been holding in check, she took one last look at the being she hated most in this world and, pushing the disgust from her mind, conjured up the words in her head, preparing to put every last ounce of her will behind them. As her hatred boiled up through every atom in her body, a change occurred within her physical form, something she'd only experienced twice before. It started as a sensational tingle that massaged her entire scalp. After a few moments the massage turned into a coordinated kind of tugging, which in itself transformed into an all encompassing ecstasy. It had happened once again, and this time she didn't need a mirror to see the results. Tiny sharp-toothed serpents had replaced her long, flowing, brown locks, snapping and hissing, writhing uncontrollably. To her, it was rapture, bliss, pleasure personified. This was her crowning moment as queen, one that both she and the world would never forget.

Dodging flame, electricity, pure unadulterated energy, ice, poison and in one poorly judged case, an ambush by a two headed serpent lying in wait, the hummingbird that embodied all that was Flash poured on as much speed as it dared in an effort to reach the sneaking assassin. Unfortunately the circuitous route he'd had to take in order to avoid all the obstacles and the highly volatile offensive magic had left him approaching from behind the trio of magic wielders. George, the king and Fredric spotted him all at the same time, even though the latter was torn apart by grief, kneeling on the floor, his face flooded with tears. Flash, however, could see exactly what they couldn't: their revenge fuelled assassin about to unleash whatever fresh hell she'd concocted on their very sorry arses, and from the looks of things, he wasn't going to get there in time. Having planned to put himself in between the very real threat and his king, throw up the most powerful shield he could and then attack with all his might, things, he knew, had just gone out of the window. Delicate little wings burning like the most potent form of lava, Flash gave it his all in one last attempt to gain as much speed as possible, before tucking in his feathery appendages and like an aerodynamic dart, he screamed through the air in a reckless attempt to achieve his goal. As his graceful little form parted the air like a bullet from a gun directly above the king's head, the words in his mind began unlocking the interchangeable bonds of his DNA, and as the change started to occur, all the time on the move, his consciousness tried very hard to line up the words to the mantra for his shield, knowing that he'd have almost no time at all to do exactly that.

Batting away a thick tendril of ice that a huge naga had attempted to swat him with, all the while crushing another's windpipe with an oddly worded spell that had suddenly come to him from far off in the past, out of nowhere a tiny blur of colour caught his eye. Readying yet another mantra, one that would throw a wicked electrical net over the threat, neutralising it forever, the presence of a strong arm gripping his calf forced him to re-evaluate. Glancing down, he was surprised to find himself looking straight into the watery eyes of his best friend. Before he could utter even one word, Fredric spoke first.

"Don't! It's Flash."

George nodded, having only just realised himself. Simultaneously, the two of them turned, watching the ex-Crimson Guard fly overhead, wondering what the hell he was doing in a form like that, amongst all this chaos and mayhem. As they followed his flight, the tiniest movement of a brown cloaked figure in the background caught their eye, the nature and scale of the threat becoming utterly obvious instantly, but by then, it was far too late.

All he needed was the last little bit of DNA to lock into place... that's all. But for some reason or other, it seemed to be taking an age. In his original plan, he'd considered changing back into his dragon form, something he now knew was possible, and something that most certainly would have given him an edge. But it was all about time.

Changing back into the larger form would have taken a few more moments, moments he no longer had. Willing the process to go faster, he fought off the impatience inside him, concentrating instead on readying the mantra for the shield that he needed to deflect away whatever vile magic the attacker had planned for Fredric, Vasuki and the king.

'Come on,' he thought, 'come on.'

Sickly yellow in colour, the pure energy being brought forth out of nowhere in front of her hands carried a vivid undertone of danger, and as the disgusting, corrupted magic within her obeyed her will without question, the spell that would lead to the death of her father was ready to be released. Revelling in the glory that was about to be hers, goosebumps racing up and down both arms, on the verge of near ecstasy, a small but noticeable smile setting off those purple lips, she let go, watching intently as the broad beam of death hunted down its target.

Both friends, freshly reunited, watched in horror as a dense shaft of energy lanced in their direction, one too broken to be of any use, the other, the king, caught off guard, unable to conjure up any suitable defence in time, both dragons knowing that this was it, their final hurrah, the very end for both of them. Deep down they wouldn't have had it any other way, but both regretted the lost time and not having the chance to catch up and get to know each other once again. Regret, sorrow, anguish and pain all ripped at their souls in one infinitesimal speck of time. That and the thought of having handed the world over to these despicable beings was a torture far worse than his time in Antarctica, Fredric thought, awaiting the end. They say that in the moment before death, your life flashes before your eyes, and that's what the two of them had anticipated. Reliving all their misdeeds, lies and in Fredric's case, the beings he'd had to kill, all supposedly in the name of peace and rightfulness, along with his supposed failure with his daughter. Not sure where it had all gone wrong or how it had come to this, even during his decades in the icy, Antarctic hell hole, he'd never been able to figure that out. For George, it would have been more the political untruths, a necessity in what he'd found himself caught up in. But he'd also sent dragons to their deaths... good dragons, honest dragons... beings that hadn't deserved to die and were just following the orders of their monarch. But here and now, they were wrong about all of that. Something did indeed flash before their eyes and it wasn't their past. Of course the flash was... FLASH!

Crackling into existence seemingly out of nowhere, directly in between the two best friends and Earth, the well built human form of the ex-Crimson Guard tumbled comically in the air as time slowed for everyone involved.

Finally it happened, that one last strand locking into place. But all was not well, and he didn't know why. Perhaps he'd been stuck as a hummingbird for too long or maybe he'd just used up too much magic. Either way he didn't know. What he did know was that his psyche was suffering from some kind of lag, and although he'd cast his defensive spell the very instant he could, his magic had yet to even start creating it. With his mind in disarray and the fatal magic heading his way, all he knew was that he was going to take a hit. Having sworn his life to his king there was no way in hell he'd let him down.

Eyes fully open, fists clenched, rapture rushing through her, no being on the planet had ever been as surprised as Earth when completely out of nowhere, Flash's physical human form popped into existence directly between her and the target of her malevolent revenge. Choking at what she'd just seen, and with the first wave of magic having already left her, biting bile rose from her stomach, scratching at the lining of her throat, as the storm of her anger unleashed the thunder and lightning throughout every atom of her body. They would pay. They would all PAY!

With nothing else to do but look on, both had accepted their fate with the decency and dignity that all great beings possess. Almost as surprised as their nemesis, Fredric's daughter, only twenty metres or so away, the pair's eyes not only widened, but lit up on seeing Flash touch down on the scorched, white marble between them and a terrifying death. As one, the two of them willed him to power his shield into being and give them one last chance at life.

Poised defiantly, legs one in front of the other, facing the formidable shaft of energy locked on to his position, Flash fought off the instinct to dive out of the way, knowing that if it was just him, that's what he'd do in a heartbeat, but here and now that wasn't the case. Willing his magic to save him and bring the shield up all around him, he knew it would be close. But as every moment passed, the realisation that it wasn't going to happen became ever more real, and with that, terror's grip started to close in on him.

On the edge of madness, fuelled by fury, Earth lined up her next deadly attack, ready to relentlessly bombard the beings in front of her in an all out effort to kill the father she hated so much. It would be done, today, here and now. And if it wasn't, she'd die trying.

Moments, like a rising tide, cannot be held off, and this one had arrived with a vengeance. Striking him fully in the chest, the ex-Crimson Guard had no idea what hit him. Unbelievably though, and with his magical shield yet to make an appearance, he stood there, strong and defiant, his broken and bleeding body sopping up every last drop of the lethal magic intended for someone else, despite the damage it was causing him.

All everyone could do was look on. George and Fredric, Vasuki, who'd only just turned to face the threat, more than a little late to the party, Earth raging at the injustice of it all, and from behind the faraway shield on what seemed like another planet, Richie, Peter, Janice, Hook, Yoyo and his young assortment of outcasts, all dumbfounded, all incredibly proud of their friend's valiant sacrifice and bravery. There were no words to describe what they felt.

Everything that happened next, all took place at once. What remained of Flash's crumpled, charred and blood soaked body crashed to the marble, surrounded by tiny wisps of burnt smelling smoke. Instantly George commanded his magic to shield them from another attack, a green tinged energy barrier springing into existence that encompassed all three of them. Earth, lost in the deepest, darkest despair she'd ever known, went ballistic, hurling wave after wave of the most deadly magic in the direction of her father and the others. Richie's concentration faltered just for a moment, the flickering shield that protected them all almost disappearing into nothing. But a kind telepathic word from Yoyo stopped that from happening. Briefly he reminded her that Flash would have wanted them to survive, that he wouldn't have wanted his sacrifice to have been for nothing. This was enough for her to regain her composure. Peter, Janice, Hook and the other young dragons all stifled a cry on seeing his body drop to the floor, the pain of seeing the ex-Crimson Guard in that condition almost too much.

Knee joints on fire from having been prostrate for so long, face swamped by salty tears, the agony of it all tore right through him. Freed from the icy prison that had held him captive for decades, escaping oncoming madness by only a gnat's genital, this day was something he'd dreamed of, hoped for, fought for, clung on to for all that time. But the joy of being rescued had now turned to complete and utter horror, and he could see now that he was partly to blame. It didn't matter where he'd gone wrong... but what he did know was that she was his mess, and he should have sorted it out all that time ago. And so casting off the shroud of grief that had pinned him to the floor for so long, he delved into the laminium that criss-crossed his torso, filling every fibre of his being with power, charging every one of his finely tuned muscles, and delighted at being anywhere but that damned prison.

Desperate to go on the offensive, George ploughed all his magic into holding the shield protecting them all, as the unimaginable waves of wicked supernatural energy either deflected away or were harmlessly absorbed. Mind racing with thousands of calculations every second, he wondered where this young child had learnt the vicious incarnations she was now spouting in their direction, how long she could keep it up, and just how he'd get round to any sort of attack with this kind of intense bombardment. On that last point, he needn't have worried.

With an ear piercing battle cry, one that caught the attention of the entire battlefield and scared the living daylights out of Vasuki and George, in one swift move, Fredric leapt to his feet, somersaulted up, out and over the shield he'd been cowering behind, and with an ice cold determination, set his sights on the source of the attack. His... DAUGHTER!

Lost to insanity, at least for the moment, Earth hadn't even seen her father leave the protection of the shield she was trying to batter into submission, that's how far gone she was. It was only on noticing an ever approaching blur out of the corner of her left eye that she realised the trouble she was in. He was coming for her, and he was MAD! Perhaps that's where she got it from.

Steaming, thick, red blood pooled across the scorched white marble next to Flash's torn apart chest, his body deathly still, a satisfied smile chiselled into his adorable features as death inducing magic thundered all around him. Fate had found her scapegoat and just perhaps, given everything that was going on, it was better this way. Better to go out like this than with a whimper. Better not to be around when the planet's ownership changed.

More than a little shaken at his friend's change in circumstance and never, ever wanting to hear that roar again, his mind raced uncontrollably, thoughts of what to do next consuming him fully. Off in the distance, he could see the courageous Amelia Battlehard and her contingent fighting valiantly, totally outmatched, part of him wondering if he should assist them first of all. And then there were those behind the shield who had risked everything, those currently protected by a dragon whose memory he'd had wiped and had banished to the surface. Having known all along she was special, seeing not only what she was doing now, but what she'd done since she'd shown up nearly blew his mind. What a dragon! That was when he caught sight of it through his rippling shield, beneath all the magic that was being currently cast in his direction. FLASH! Was he dead? Just injured? Or indeed, saveable? His head told him there was nothing that could be done, and that even not dead, he would be too close to it to bring back. But his heart and the fierce loyalty that made him such an exceptional king told him otherwise. In that moment, he was truly torn. That is until a voice right beside him spoke up.

"Leeeett meeee seeee toooo himmm. It'ssss theee leasssst I caaan do."

"Are you sure?" answered the king, his voice a little wobbly.

"Iffff I caaaan saaavee himmm I willlll. Afterallllll heee rescueeeed ussss frooooom thaaaat prisooooon."

The king had wondered what had happened, and now he knew. Even more reason to rescue the brave former Crimson Guard.

"If you can save him, I'll be forever in your debt."

"Ittttt issss I aaaand my raaaace that aare innnnn yooour debt. GO! I wiiiillll dooo my beeeeest."

Nodding his approval, in what was almost a blur, even to those magical beings all around him, he turned, converting all the energy from his shield into speed, and disappeared off in the direction of Captain Battlehard and her overwhelmed comrades.

Enhanced by magic and with a whiff of freedom soaking through his gills, Vasuki slithered off to one side just as the king's shield dissipated, hoping not to get caught by the barrage of magic. Right at that very moment however, it stopped, much to his surprise. Too intent on helping his dragon rescuer to pay any attention to why it had ceased, he slithered off across the battlefield, once more opening himself up telepathically, again broadcasting a plea for any of his race to hear, hoping against hope that they would kowtow to his wishes and stop all this madness. For the moment though, his plea fell on deaf ears.

It was all she could do to drop the assault and bring up any kind of defensive shield in time. And that was the only thing that saved her life. Immediately he was on her, pounding on her shield with his powerful fists, his fingers spitting half a dozen types of fire, the words shouting from his mouth totally incomprehensible. Paralysed but for a moment, mainly due to the shock of seeing her father in this state, something that had never happened before, it wasn't long before her sense of self preservation kicked in, followed quickly by the injustice and then the anger, fury and rage. The magical scrap of a lifetime was about to begin.

45 DEFINITELY NOT WINGING IT

Knowing that the enemy's forces would be more alert and on the lookout for an attack from the sky after Steel's supposed capture, Gee Tee's ragtag troupe of dragons had decided to attack from the ground, on foot, gaining the element of surprise the rationale behind it.

Stalking through the dark, a thick layer of smog and toxic, black smoke engulfing everything, a contingent spread out five across led the way, with the master mantra maker at their centre. An unusual formation to say the least, the old shopkeeper had come up with the plan, because the visibility had been so limited. Bumping into an adversary out of absolutely nowhere was a real possibility, and with one dragon out in front, it could quite possibly lead to the alarm being raised, something they just couldn't afford to happen. With five spread across, and with Gee Tee in the middle, if they stumbled across one, or even two guards accidentally, they could handle it, quickly, quietly and without any fuss, ably assisted by the master mantra maker, that is unless the opposing force were using exactly the same formation, something they all thought extremely unlikely. It was unconventional to say the least, but thinking outside the box was the only way they were going to succeed against such overwhelming odds, if indeed that was at all possible.

Noiselessly skulking between buildings they'd already cleared, the dragon/human hybrid force deliberately moved at slightly less than walking pace, determined to use stealth, not be caught off guard, and be able to take down anything in front of them very, very quietly and at a moment's notice.

Midway along the line of dragons behind them, very nervous humans, each with makeshift masks made up from torn fragments of material they'd found along the way, fingered the bandoliers that held their remaining grenades in place, each wondering what the hell they were doing here, each re-examining their life choices up to this point, apart from Taibul who hadn't really had much of a life to re-examine. For him, it was all about hoping for more... more of everything. More years to experience and relish, more hockey, more banter with his friends, and if he was honest with himself... more of this! Emma, Angela and Sam, the friends he'd bonded with on this outstanding adventure, were all very much afraid, surrounded by terror, and still astounded at being here. He, however, was secretly lapping things up. Dragons... how cool was that?! Being here, in a secret underground world that had existed forever... brilliant! Tied up in a plot to thwart an evil force taking control of the world... absolutely amazing! It gave him goosebumps just thinking about it, but in a good way. Here and now, all he wanted to do was play his part, a small cog in a mindbogglingly humungous machine, but ready to do anything he could to help all the beings around him, dragon and human alike. And so, grinning like a Cheshire cat, something none of those around him could see in the cloying, choking darkness, he trailed in Emma's wake, alert and poised, ready to act when called upon, his mere eighteen years of age filling him with confidence and excitement, instead of the trepidation, fear and horror the others felt.

As one, the five at the head of the line stopped; the others behind immediately followed suit. Directly in front of the master mantra maker a fire raged furiously, the heart of which flickered from blue to orange, to red and yellow and back again, only seen through a shimmering heat similar to that of a glassmaker's forge. Mesmerising in itself, this was something that under normal circumstances most dragons would have stopped to fully take in, bathe in the heat and lose themselves in the warm radiance and hypnotic colours. But not here, and not today, especially given the fire's purpose. One of many, the flames encompassed a horde of dragon cadavers, burning its way through what remained of their disfigured and brutally maimed bodies, searing muscle and sinew alike, roasting flesh, stripping away skin and scales from the skeleton, reducing everything but the bones to ashes, systematically destroying all evidence of the atrocities that had been carried out. Bile rose up the throats of all the dragons at the front. As one, the shopkeeper included, they all forced it back down, fighting against the nausea, just as they would if it were a physical opponent. It was tough on them all. Unlike the pyres back in Salisbridge, the biggest of which probably embodied no more than eight or nine dragons, the one in front of them had more than that just at its base, and rose up for as far as they could see, disappearing into the thick, throat scratching, acrid black smoke at six or seven dragon bodies high. From the looks of things, it had been an absolute massacre. Setting the feelings of grief, pain, loss, anger and disgust to one side, Gee Tee used a light touch to send a telepathic message back to the others, not wanting them to experience the same kind of horrific surprise that he'd felt when they'd stumbled upon the smoking desecration.

Soundlessly, a huge, scaled jaw cut through the darkness that surrounded them, appearing as if by magic in between the four friends. With tensions running high, Sam reached for the first of his grenades, with both Emma and Angela following his lead. Taibul, recognising the dragon from the ranks further behind them, stood down.

"Easy... little ones, we're friends, not foes. Remember?"

Clipping their grenades quickly back into place, all three shook their heads, each letting out a long breath, the relief palpable, tension eased momentarily.

"Sorry," whispered Angela, her voice taut and full of nervous energy.

"Apology accepted," mouthed the prehistoric beast quietly.

"You should all know that we've stumbled across a

mass of burning dragon bodies. It's not only shocking but quite horrific. We just thought you should know so that you can prepare yourself. We have to go right past it. There's no other way around."

"We all witnessed the ones back at Salisbridge. Is it worse than that?" piped up Emma.

"I'm afraid so," replied the dragon, "and by quite some margin apparently. I'm sorry that you have to witness all this."

"And we're all sorry for your loss," put in Angela, her voice filled with regret.

"Good to know, little ones. Steel yourselves."

And with that, the huge, scaled skull disappeared back into the thick smoke behind them, leaving them all to wonder about what the others had encountered and just how bad it could be.

Pretty damn bad as it turned out. Despite their dampened, makeshift masks, the sickly, vomit inducing smell still seemed to race up their nostrils and launch a full assault on their delicate (more so than the dragons around them) senses. Digging deep, it took everything they had not to be sick, and from the few dragons in their own force that they were able to see, it didn't appear any different for them. So with sweat from the furious fire that nobody appeared to want to put out dripping down their faces, before running down their collar bones, disappearing off into goodness knows where, they did their best not to look at the towering pile of cadavers, fully aware that their own fate might well be the same. With the same courage they'd shown back in Salisbridge during the fight of their lives, and much to their dragon comrades' satisfaction, they soldiered on through the nose blocking, eye watering smoke and devastation, determined to play their part.

An accident, a total and utter coincidence was how it

could be described. But that was why they'd set up this way, and that was why they were ready and unfazed... their adversaries, not so much.

Two serpent shaped nagas slithered through the overpowering, choking smoke, around a corner and ran straight into the ferocious dragon that had been stalking just to Gee Tee's left. Surprise and astonishment were the first reactions to the encounter, from both beings. Unlike their enemies, they'd fully expected to bump into trouble, and so faster than the eye could see, they reacted as only dragons could.

Instantly the telepathic warning of engagement ran through every dragon's head in the small, compact, fighting force. Those at the back tucked in, forming a shield around those in the middle, including the four humans. As one, the front four engaged, their movements shrouded in silence thanks to the mantra that had been bound to them all much earlier on. For Gee Tee, it was all about keeping his head and delving deep into the well of experience that only he could call upon. And so he did. Reacting slowly to their newfound discovery, the darker coloured of the two drew open his mouth in an effort to strike back with some kind of ear splitting scream. With a flourish of his fingers and an effortless use of his will, the old shopkeeper stood back out of range of the physical fighting and directed a three word mantra straight at the serpent's mouth. Immediately it closed tight, engendering a stifled snort and much more surprise than that of the original encounter. With super speed and the brutality to match, the four versus two encounter was now in full swing, the lighter coloured of the two nagas propelling her tail around in a one hundred and eighty degree arc, sweeping the feet of one dragon away, watching in satisfaction as he hurtled to the ground, dumbfounded at the lack of noise on impact. And that tiny distraction was just enough to end her life, because in that fraction of a second, dragon number two had glided up out of nowhere and rallying against every ounce of decency in his prehistoric body, clamped his wickedly sharp teeth around the slippery beast's neck. Muscles tensing and using all his might, he bit clean through, tearing the monster's head from the rest of its elongated body. Witnessing the fate of his partner, the other naga, the much darker scaled one, reacted as only he knew how... he screamed. Or at least he tried to, but the wily shopkeeper's mantra was still in fine working order, fastening his jaws shut, preventing him from uttering a single sound. Sensing what was almost inevitable, and in a fit of utter rage at what had just happened to his longstanding friend, the remaining serpent went berserk, flailing and scrabbling, using his scaled tail as a club, casting what little magic he knew would work from deep inside his mind. Knowing better than to underestimate an enemy that had long since graced these lands, two of the dragons jumped back out of range, allowing their comrades more space and freedom to fight in, determined to offer support in the way of magical healing if required. Ravaged by bloodlust and the unfettered belief that he was going to die, the naga, despising the heat and longing for the cool, dark waters of the Antarctic, let the madness consume him. In one foul, blurred strike, he head butted the first dragon to approach him, the thick, sickly 'THUNK!' of contact echoing out over the crackle of the fire slowly consuming the mutilated dragon corpses. Instantly disappearing off into the darkness, with brilliant, thick, green blood spurting from his nose and a wound beneath his right eye, the red tinged dragon thudded to the floor, once and for all out of the fight. Having seen his chum caught well and truly off guard, one of the outer two dragons stepped in, straight away having to lean back like a limbo dancer to avoid the chest height haze of a tail that came whizzing in his direction. Mad at not having finished this floundering clown, after the tail passed him by he dived in, talons first, latching onto the scales at the base of the monster's back.

As the penetrating scream of pain escaped the naga's lips, the remaining dragon that had stepped back, had the forethought to wrap the sound up with magic, preventing it from leaving the immediate area, keeping their presence a secret, shrouding everything that was going on, in silence. Razor sharp talons firmly attached, the dragon flapped his wings for momentum, and then with everything he had, pushed all his weight forward, forcing the writhing and wriggling beast onto its chest, all the time watching out for that darting and probing tail.

In Gee Tee's mind, it had to end NOW! They'd already exhausted too much of their energy on this fight, and if they were to stumble upon a much larger force of these fiends, then this encounter did not bode well. Willing up much more magic, mana and willpower than he'd hoped to expend, he tapped into an ancient Algerian spell that had once caught his eye. Never having used it before, he was unsure of the specific results, but felt that right now it would serve his purpose. Focusing in on the squirming serpent, the words appeared at the forefront of his mind. Reading them aloud in his head, allowing some of his passion and power to seep through, he looked on in fascination as the prone naga's skull started to crumple in on itself. Two of the dragons fighting hopped back out of range, surprised at the stomach churning turn of events, while the other, talons still firmly implanted, looked on dispassionately. Moments later, it was done, the beast's skull firmly caved in, looking like some misshapen pottery attempt. As the dragon unhooked his talons, one of the others spoke up.

"What shall we do with the bodies?"

The master mantra maker thought for a moment. They didn't really have time to do too much, but if they were discovered it would raise the alarm and then they'd lose their element of surprise. What to do? What to do?

"Quickly throw them onto the pyre. If you can cover them up a bit, then do so, but time is of the essence and we can't spend too much of it doing this."

"They shouldn't go in with our kind. It's not right," piped up one of the dragons off to the side.

"I fully share your sentiments," stated Gee Tee thoughtfully, pushing his odd shaped glasses as far up his nose as they'd go. "But we don't have time to worry about right and wrong, good and bad. We have to get the job done. Not only do our lives depend on it, but the lives of millions of others, dragons and humans alike. Maybe even the fate of the planet. When and only when we've done that, can we return and clear up this mess, give our kin the proper, respectful send off they deserve. Until then, we must push on."

It wasn't the answer the dragon, or indeed the rest of them had hoped for, but it was just about enough. And so reluctantly, as one, they got to work, using magic to clear up the mess, depositing their enemies' corpses within the lower tier of the mountainous pyre that still burned fiercely, making sure they left no clue behind as to what had happened for others to find. With that all done, and with the dragon who'd been knocked out and badly injured by the naga's head butt revived and restored, the force returned to their previous positions and very slowly continued on towards their target, the building that housed the Fleet Street crystal node, all the time hoping to hell that Steel, DomCon and Jar Man were holding up their end of the bargain.

Usually well lit, before all this, anyway, the wide, high ceilinged corridors were masked in shadow, a foreboding presence staining their entirety, and as the three friends traversed them, nerves started to fray.

"I have a really bad feeling about this," murmured DomCon, his dour demeanour blending in with his surroundings.

"Everything's fine. They let us through didn't they?"

replied Jar Man, his face neutral, staring straight ahead.

"Something's not right. I think they might be on to us."

About to answer his friend, the slightest telepathic tug on his mind was enough to still his mouth.

"Both of you calm down and please... don't speak like this. We have no idea if anyone's watching. If I were them, I'd have rigged up some kind of underhand security. If they see anything out of the ordinary, it's over before it gets started. We must maintain our discipline; play our roles right up until the very end. Only then can we reveal ourselves, which hopefully will prove too late for them to do anything about. I would suggest from now on that there isn't any telepathic contact. Who knows what abilities these damn nagas have? If they have a knack for anything mind related, using telepathy might well give us away. I'll say it now and be done. It's an honour fighting alongside both of you, and know that I'll do all that I can to make sure our mission here is a success. Also, if push comes to shove, I have your backs, just as I know you both have mine. End all contact now. Good luck."

And with that, silence returned to their minds, pierced only by the plod, plod, plod of Steel's huge feet on the brown, rocky surface as they made their way further into the enemy's stronghold.

46 MACABRE MAGICAL MADNESS

To most humans multitasking simply means doing two things at once, but to most dragons it means much more than two, something Amelia Battlehard was ably demonstrating right at this very moment. Hovering in place above what was left of her meagre force, she tried not to notice the dark dragons leaping into the air on the council building side of the bridge, or the flurry of nagas swarming across it. Instead she chose to bat away yet another sizzling cone of flame meant to incapacitate her, with the edge of the dark bladed sword she'd wrestled from the hands of a dying adversary. It had been some time since she'd hefted the weight of a bladed weapon in battle but the feel and possibilities came back to her almost instantly. So now she was defending not only herself, but the dragons below, swatting away attacks like a child would an errant bubble, as well as getting in a little punishment of her own when the chance arose. Swinging round to face the onrushing threat of a spiky looking dragon zipping quickly in her direction, murder written into his face, Captain Battlehard left it until the very last second to roll beneath the blunt and obvious attack, all the time maintaining the shield above her comrades below, not allowing them to become vulnerable to an aerial strike. With the 'disappointed off' attacking dark dragon already contemplating coming round for another pass, a valuable lesson in keeping up your concentration at all times was about to be handed out. Mid-way through her avoiding tumble, Amelia Battlehard's spatial awareness kicked into overdrive, alerting her to the fact that for a few brief moments there was nothing else in the air around her small group apart from the murderous dragon now flying right over her. It was a small gap to be sure, the reinforcements she'd spotted only moments ago would be here in no time at all, but the opportunity to rid the battlefield of one more enemy was just too good for her to pass up. Momentarily dropping the shield covering her allies, she soaked up the extra power that flooded her, and with two quick beats of her wings, threw herself after 'Spiky', who'd just started to bank into a very lazy turn. Pouring on as much speed as she could muster, she caught up with him as he came out of the looping curve, facing back from where he'd just attacked.

'Where on earth did she go?' was his first thought, seeing the small band of enemies undefended from above. 'Perhaps I did some damage to her after all. Or maybe in avoiding my brilliant assault, she damaged herself,' were both subsequent thoughts on the matter at hand, as he looked this way and that, over both shoulders, at the air all around him. Either way, he decided, now was the time to go back and put these second-rate beings out of their misery once and for all. If only he'd noticed the underside of his wings being buffeted just that little bit more than usual. But like most of Manson's force of part-timers, he was more brawn than brain, something that would prove a little costly.

Realising that whatever she was going to do, she'd have to do it fast, without hesitation she let the battle take her, and fuelled by thoughts of those already killed, and the danger to her monarch, she did something most dragons would find utterly impossible. Her burst of speed had put her directly beneath her spiky, would-be attacker. That was why he couldn't see her anywhere, and that was what was about to cost him his life. Instinctively Captain Battlehard, all the time mirroring her opponent's moves from below, inverted, difficult at the best of times, all but impossible when flying in the shadow of another dragon. But she pulled it off with consummate ease, being the forward thinking, risk taking daredevil that she was. With the delicate current of air now tickling her back, and looking straight up at her attacker's slightly larger body, any number of means to take him down whistled through her mind. In the end, she chose the most obvious, still wary of her unprotected charges. Clenching the talons on both her feet together, in one fell swoop she thrust them simultaneously into the wings of her enemy and raked them across, then down, as far as she dared. The result was immediate. In that instant, 'Spiky' had no idea what hit him, until his crazed and confused face passed within inches of a very pleased with herself Captain Battlehard, who watched the tumbling, out of control death dive with a great deal of satisfaction. Only then, and with one less enemy from a hundred to deal with, did her attention return to what she was supposed to be dealing with: covering those who she'd pledged to defend, in an effort to draw fire away from her king, hoping to at the very least give him a fighting chance. But to her absolute horror and astonishment, George, now looking magnificent in his natural dragon form, the rightful monarch of this failing dragon domain, had appeared in her position, directly above the small cluster she'd been defending, rallying his troops, preparing himself to take on all comers. Swiftly she plummeted in his direction, pulling up at the very last moment.

"Sire... what are you doing here?" she enquired.

"I'm doing what every great monarch would do in this position. I'm fighting with my kin. I wouldn't ask you to do anything I'm not willing to do. Look around you Amelia, what do you see?"

Tentatively, the young captain glanced about. Before she had a chance to say anything, the king spoke up.

"Evil everywhere," he announced, "all wanting to kill us, except for me of course. I'm sure they have very specific plans for me. Well, as far I'm concerned, it ends here... and NOW! No quarter given, no laying down arms, no surrender... WE FIGHT WITH EVERY LAST BREATH... for ourselves, for each other and for those defenceless creatures who can't do it themselves. Across the globe, the human population has virtually no idea what's going on here and exactly what impact it will have on them if we fail. And it will have an impact. They'll be hunted down, killed in packs and on their own, used by these atrocious beings as sport, slaves or for other perverse pleasures. I'll tell you now, that only happens over my dead body. With my dying breath I will defend and protect every last noble being on this wonderful, beautiful, bountiful planet. I'm in charge, and so help me God, I'm going to make these scum sucking cockwombles (he'd heard Peter and his friends use this world, and had instantly taken a liking to it) pay for every single dragon and human they've slain."

A little taken aback at first, the start of a small smile slid across Captain Battlehard's scale encrusted face at the thought of the king having his mojo back. The passion and commitment with which he spoke roused her hopes, and although it didn't quite fill her with confidence, mainly because of just how badly outnumbered they were, she did at least know that dying for this dragon and the cause he supported was not only the right thing to do, but the only thing to do. Glancing down, she realised those below her had heard every single word and were on exactly the same page. As Manson's reinforcements started to arrive, George and Captain Battlehard hovered back to back, covering their buddies beneath them, readying themselves for the onslaught.

"RICH!... we need to get out there!" he screamed. "Flash is hurt!"

Swallowing awkwardly, she continued to let the magic from the necklace that Yoyo had thrust around her neck flow continually through her, using it to power the shield under which they all sheltered. Steadying herself and ignoring the build up of heat not only in her hands from the dagger, but now around her throat, she moved her head barely a centimetre to look one of her two best friends in the eyes.

"We can't do it Pete. You know that. I'm sorry."

"But..."

"PETER! Dropping the shield means instant death for all of us. What would you have me do?"

She hadn't meant to be so harsh, but that's exactly what she had to be, having seen the sacrifice Flash had made for his king, watched in slow motion as his burnt and smoking body toppled to the floor, fought off the need to cry out in pain and ignored the urge to drop the shield and go to his rescue. Now she felt trapped in the most precarious position she'd ever known. Every fibre of her being called out for her to fight, use all her magic to harm those vile, wretched monsters for all that they'd done, and all that they continued to do. The merest glimpse over her shoulder, however, told her to stay put and continue to keep Yoyo and his young dragons, Hook, Janice and of course Peter, safe, by maintaining the shield that was still being constantly bombarded by onrushing dragons in the air, and nagas on the ground. It was an impossible situation.

"I'm sorry Pete," she called out, turning once again to look out at the battlefield, "but I just can't do it. You know that, maybe not in your heart, but your head fully understands."

And truthfully, he did, he just didn't want it to be so.

"What can I do to help, Rich?"

"Continue to funnel your magic and keep my hands and throat cool. If you can do that, it'll be easier for me to concentrate. And if you spot anything that you think might help get us out of this situation, don't hesitate to let me know."

Nodding his agreement and understanding, he trickled the tiniest amount of healing magic across his friend's hands and coated her neck, absorbing the residual build up of heat, all the time holding the hand of the woman he loved, hoping to hell that she was having better luck attacking than they currently were.

'So many targets,' he thought, momentarily confused. Immediately she agreed with him, but her firm and concise thinking was exactly what he needed to regain perspective, maintain focus and remind him of his purpose.

Their bond was extraordinary and had reached dizzying new heights, getting stronger with each second that passed. Both could read the other's mind, hear the other's thoughts as if they were right there, and now they were starting to sense emotions across the connection. It was truly awe inspiring, at least that's how Janice viewed it. For Fu-ts'ang it was all of that and more, with the more being set free, after centuries of being locked away in Gee Tee's magical vault deep beneath the Mantra Emporium. Like a bird finally being released from its long term cage, the ecstasy Fu-ts'ang felt at coursing through the air, the wind whipping across the razor sharp edge of his cold, cutting blade, was like nothing he'd ever felt. And of course Janice was now starting to feel it, something so rapturous it was hard to ignore. But ignore it she did, all, of course, for the sake of the mission.

"You have to continue," she urged the dragon slaying weapon from the relative safety of her warm and slightly strange mind.

"There are just too many of them. Perhaps we should flee?"

"FLEE?!" bellowed Janice's harsh response. "Even if I wanted to, how would I go about that? I'm trapped behind this shield and without me, your essence would go back to being entombed in an inanimate object. PLEASE! We need to fight, not just for ourselves, but for every other being here. We're making a difference, you and I. We can continue to do so."

Not a selfish being, just one that had been lonely and

lost for so long, and one who'd do practically anything not to go back to his previous state, her words struck a chord. It wasn't just the way she said them, more the passion and the feeling behind them. Intoxicating was the only way for him to describe it, so with all thoughts of escape put to one side, he shot straight through the back of the nearest naga that had been pounding the shield with cream coloured bolts of magic, not satisfied until his eerie blue tip exited the scales at the front of its chest cavity. Achieving this under the petite bar worker's guidance, he pulled out at speed and as the naga's dead body slumped to the ground, both of them selected the next target, before his dynamic and deadly streamlined shape disappeared swiftly in that direction.

Explosive magic ringing in his ears, wayward projectiles zipping all around him, he rocked up right next to his target, sliding to a halt on the shiny white flooring. Immediately he wrapped his tail around as much of the body as he could and without wasting any time at all, he lowered his head on to the being's forehead, only to feel... NOTHING! Whatever should have been there was gone, almost as if nothing there had ever existed. This, he knew, was definitely not the case. After all, this one selfless being had risked his own life to rescue him from the confines of the icy prison in Antarctica, giving him hope for not only his future, but for his entire race.

At one with the ancient magic that flowed through every molecule of his being, he commanded it to flood the smouldering body and seek out what he was looking for. Very slowly, a crystallising blue haze started to create a shell on the motionless human shape, working its way down from the head, until every last millimetre had been covered. Still nothing!

Acutely aware of the danger surrounding him, a sense of ethereal power closing in on his position startled him away from the task at hand. With his head still planted firmly on Flash's brow, he glanced across to face the threat. Sure enough, a barrage of flaming orange spears headed his way at speed, their intense heat causing them to shimmer as they cut through the air. Bringing up his right hand, momentarily he held it fully open, stretching his fingers as wide as he could, seeming to get a lock on the target heading swiftly towards him. Simultaneously closing his fingers, locking them into a tiny fist, the fiery projectiles seemed to get sucked in towards each other before causing one hell of an explosion, about thirty metres from where he crouched. Shielding his eyes from the blast, he felt an array of fast moving magical shards pepper his body and tail. Only then was he grateful that he'd had the forethought to offer up the extremity to his would-be rescuer for protection.

Interspersed with the recurring ground quakes, tons of debris started to fall from the surrounding walls and the hidden ceiling, making the already lethal battlefield of the king's private residence deadlier than ever. In the last thirty seconds or so, a tidal wave of rubble had slipped down the wall adjacent to where the light sided force were shying away behind their extremely well defended shield, and with the kind of force usually only associated with Mother Nature, had washed away half a dozen unsuspecting dark dragons who were caught so off guard they hadn't even had the chance to take to the air, providing a temporary respite for the beleaguered force.

But what the huge fight gave with one hand, it easily took with the other. From out of nowhere, crashing through the air at quite a rate, tons of speeding debris shaken loose from the ceiling nearly set the air on fire as it plummeted down towards the circular group of dragons atop which the king and Amelia Battlehard fought back to back. In the end, it was only George's outstanding awareness and battle hardened experience that had saved them. That and the fact that as a unit, they'd all instantly obeyed his command to move, suffering no more than a few scratches and bruises. Luck, at least for the time being, was well and truly on their side.

A fast moving blur, that's all anyone would have seen, and that's including all the beings with magically enhanced senses, so fast were they moving. Wrapped around each other, on opposing sides of the fight, each looking for leverage over their opponent, just the tiniest of edges, hoping to gain the merest advantage, in this very moment the ultimate dysfunctional family was baring its teeth, quite literally in this case. With both of their personal shields having melded into one, flickering and sparking as they crashed together, constantly creating weak points in some prime spots, failing altogether in others, the two combatants, father and daughter, went at it hammer and tongs. Grinding to a halt momentarily against a huge mountain of rubble that had fallen from the ceiling, Fredric had the upper hand as he lay on top of his daughter, left hand pinning her right hand, the thumb on his right hand only a centimetre or so away from his daughter's left eye as he tried to gouge her with all his might, all the time avoiding the venomous, vicious viper strikes from the serpents her hair had changed into. Just the thought of his daughter being able to generate these horrors was enough to make him feel nauseous. It was disgusting, disgraceful, despicable and on most levels truly terrifying. How the best part of him had ever turned into that, he had absolutely no idea.

Quelling the panic rising within her, she summoned all her strength to escape... but it wasn't enough. Desperate times called for desperate measures and so, unable to break free from his grip, she thrust her head upwards and bit down on his thumb as hard as she could.

Instantaneously he yelled in agony and wriggled what remained of the bloody stump out of her mouth, his body reacting as it should, shooting his hand up out of the way, but not before the passing fingernails raked at the criss-crossing purple lines that tormented her lunacy ravaged face. This time it was her turn to let out a cry, much to her father's satisfaction. But that spark of pain provided the impetus for her to fight back, because of course she was used to the pain; it had been a constant companion for as long as she could remember, and now felt as though it were her friend. Instead of making her weaker and fearful, it actually made her stronger and more determined than ever to put her father down, once and for all.

Ignoring his half torn off thumb, consumed by the total need to destroy this runt of the litter, Fredric flexed his muscles, putting all the power he could behind a well timed punch aimed directly at her face. Before it had a chance to connect, a huge jolt of kinetic energy exploded between them, tossing him back some thirty metres or so in the air. Landing with a 'THUNK', the former Antarctic prisoner shook his head in an effort to stop his ears ringing, blood trickling from both nostrils, rather a large chunk of rock sticking out at an odd angle from the top of his left thigh. Delighted at the result of her lesser known naga magic, Earth stood up from the pile of debris and, with a sickly smile, brushed herself down, the snakes in her hair writhing, wriggling and hissing wickedly.

Face and body feeling as though they were on fire, and not in the way a dragon might like, Fredric angrily ripped the chunk of rock from his bloodied thigh, tossed it off to one side and promptly used the laminium in the chains that still adorned his chest to heal all his wounds. Dust and tiny particles of debris spewed out of the thigh wound before the falsehood skin knitted itself back together. Simultaneously, the thumb that Earth had bitten down on fully regenerated, the bone growing back right in front of his eyes, before a layer of skin spread out of nowhere to cover it up. Impressive, but not as much as his nose clicking back into place all by itself, the blood from the nostrils running back up inside.

Despite her utter revulsion for him, she did at least admire his talent for wielding the magic at his disposal. The problem he had though, was just that... the magic at his disposal. She had pretty much all that, and everything the nagas had deigned to teach her on top. As they stood there, facing each other across thirty metres or so, she knew one hundred percent that she had him. Never mind the laminium chains he was drawing power from wrapped around his bare torso, they'd never get the chance to make a difference. In the end, all it would come down to was... MAGIC! Who had the most powerful spells, and just who could weave them the best. His time, she knew, was most certainly running out.

Amongst the carnage and pandemonium, Vasuki remained bent over Flash's prone form, having exhausted nearly all options. The regal looking naga king had done all that he could to try and heal the gaping wounds caused by the pure beam of plasma Flash had absorbed to save George, his rightful king. In doing so, he'd all but literally broken the human shaped form he currently resided in, if that were even still the case. Vasuki could not magically either heal the wounds outright, or even encourage them to heal of their own volition. And with such extensive injuries, there was no way this human shape could survive much longer. If Flash's consciousness were indeed still locked away in there, it looked very much as though that was where he was going to die.

Racking his knowledge filled, experienced and ultimately cunning brain, the newly returned leader of the nagas searched frantically for any sort of alternative, desperate for the being in front of him not to die. Rummaging through huge amounts of irrelevant and useless information, finally, just as he thought all avenues had been exhausted, he found something... interesting. Sure he couldn't heal Flash's human figure in its current condition, this something might just be able to skip a step in the animation process, so to speak, and return the ex-Crimson Guard to all his prehistoric greatness. There was however, one proviso. His consciousness had to be intact... in there somewhere. If that had flickered out, then it was well and truly over, and no magic on this planet or any other would be able to return him.

Ushering those immediately under his command out of harm's way when that giant part of the roof collapsed nearly on top of them, they'd only just managed to regroup in any meaningful sort of form. In some aspects they'd been lucky, although it didn't sound like that. Two nagas and two dark dragons hadn't fared so well, having either been killed or injured so badly as to no longer be a threat. Scattering so quickly on the king's command, had left them briefly vulnerable individually. Amazingly, all of them had come through unscathed. There'd been a fleeting moment when he and Captain Battlehard had to fly down and help fight off three demented dark dragons determined to take down one of the more seriously injured of the group, but they'd gotten there just in time and had been able to whisk him back to the main force before they'd been compromised any further. Now they found themselves in pretty much the same position as before, only about fifty metres off to one side of the pile of rocky remains, slightly nearer the shield housing their comrades. As the king allowed his magic to bubble up to the surface, casually swatting away a naga who'd tried to sneak up close from behind the bodies of several of his comrades, his thoughts turned to prolonging the life of those fighting all around him. Was it worth trying to make for the shield? How would that benefit them and would it just prolong the inevitable outcome of this very one-sided affair? As supernatural missiles and unrecognisable magic once again bombarded their position, his mind pondered those very questions.

Facing off in what was proving to be a properly epic battle, father and daughter stood amongst all the wreckage, each waiting for the other to make the first move, both full of anger and rage, each for different reasons.

Bloodlust slowly simmering, Fredric's calm and common sense was, in a very small amount, starting to return. Without taking his eyes off the kin that was trying to kill him, knowing that even for a fraction of a second that could be fatal, the cool, calculated tactician in him tried to observe everything else going on around him. Vasuki leaning over Flash's decimated body almost crushed his spirit... almost, but not quite. Then there was the king hovering in mid air above a group of his guards and at least one councillor, filling him with pride and reminding him of times gone by. Some of the adventures they'd had were out of this world, and even more precarious than the situation they currently found themselves in, unbelievably. That was when his heart nearly broke. His grandson! Peter! Channelling his magic behind the shield, fighting alongside his friends, giving his all to make a difference at a time and place like this. Fredric's chest swelled with pride; his insides though, were a completely different matter, with the boy's mother right across from him, trying to tear him limb from limb with her spiteful, dark magic. Oh yes... he recognised what she'd been using for what it truly was. Dark, dastardly and evil best summed it all up. No dragon should be caught using it, for various reasons, but mainly because of how corrupting it was. Any being using it for any length of time would be driven completely insane. Perhaps that's what had happened, he thought, eyeing his adversary, all that time ago. No matter. It was done, and as far as he was concerned, there was no going back. Not now, not ever... not even for the boy's sake.

Speaking of the boy... man... dragon, you know what I mean... presently still applying the cool, healing magic to his friend when the need arose, Peter looked out from the protection of the shield at everything going on in the rest of the king's private residence. It was utter pandemonium. Nothing in his upbringing or dragon training had ever prepared him for something like this... how on earth could it? Glancing over at Flash's motionless body, currently guarded by what he assumed was the naga king fresh from Antarctica, he knew for certain the ex-Crimson Guard wouldn't have been fazed by any of this at all, no doubt being able to take it all in his stride. At least he would have, had he been in any state to do so. And there was the king, fighting tooth and nail above the group of dragons that had, for so long, valiantly held off Manson's force, bringing the bridge down in the process, trapping themselves right in this very place, only deigning to give up at the threat presented to his life and that of The White Dragon... TIM! There, unnoticed, amongst all the debris and rubble, magic and mayhem, lay the crumpled body of Richie's one true love, lost and forgotten, a victim of circumstances well beyond his control. Out of nowhere, a tiny tear dropped from the corner of the young hockey playing dragon's eye, traversing the smooth skin of his cheeks, before encountering the resistance of the usual stubble, slightly longer than normal because of his continued and unexpected incarceration. There it zigzagged down his chin, occasionally weaving this way and that, searching for the path of least resistance, which it found just before reaching the drop off. Once there, it had little choice, its momentum carrying it off the precipice, the single, tiny drop riding through the air, the loneliest entity in the entire vicinity, (at least the magic had magic for company) its molecules clinging to each other for dear life, as the ever approaching floor rose up to greet it. And then with the teeniest splash in the world, it was over, gone, barely noticeable, long since forgotten, much like Tim's stint in the dragon world. At the very best, he would no doubt be a footnote in the tomes of dragon history, and that was if they somehow made it out of here alive, something right at this very moment he doubted a great deal. For a split second he wondered what sort of effect Tim's death as The White Dragon might have had on the beings here all around him. Were they resigned to dying and Manson winning? Had their belief been decimated? Or had they not believed the prophecy, that every dragon knew so well, in the first place? For him, it didn't matter. Glancing up at one of his two best friends, the one currently keeping every dragon here safe, powering the shield with a little assistance from the borrowed laminium she both wore and held in her hands, the pride he felt at not only being her friend, but knowing her since a dragonling, and having been lucky enough to have her in his life, swelled his chest a great deal. It would have, had she just been his friend, just been Richie Rump through all of this. But ever since that very first, unexpected moment when he'd witnessed the full force of the damage inflicted upon her back, on that fateful Saturday morning in her flat in Salisbridge, damage that the most potent dragon magic couldn't cure or heal, he knew there and then, however impossible it seemed, that she was the true White Dragon and not her lover, Tim. Convinced beyond belief, Gee Tee's agreement of his assessment was all that he needed to be one hundred percent positive about his friend's pivotal role in the historic events going on all around them. And now, in the midst of this utterly hopeless situation, it was what kept him calm, stopped his confidence from shattering and gave him hope. Hope that they would prevail and that the dragon domain would stand firm. Hope that the majority of the humans and dragons of this world would survive these dark days, going on to thrive in the future. Again adding a little of his fairly tame magic, at least that's what it seemed like, to the thunderous power rushing through his friend, he marvelled at the supernatural power she controlled. If it had been him, there was no way the shield would still be in place. In fact, he didn't think he could have conjured something so stable and so big in the first place. What he did think though, was this. He'd do everything in his power to keep his friend alive, because he was convinced she was the key to everything, to the survival of not only every being here, but almost certainly every creature across the face of the planet. And if it ended up costing his life... so be it. Leaving the love of his life... Janice, he stood up and walked across to his friend, vowing to himself to protect her at all costs. No pressure then!

Instinctively, he knew that he'd found exactly what he was looking for from within the long, complicated strands of DNA he was immersed in. All Vasuki had to do now was touch the magic within the human shape and let it show him how to flick the switch that would start the transformation back to his rightful prehistoric self. Hoping that what was left of Flash would recognise him as a friend and not react to his serpent-like form as an enemy, the naga king picked through the twisted and broken fibres all around him, searching for that ever elusive spark of mystical power, reasonably sure he could achieve his aim of saving the broken being before him.

Magical mayhem exploding all around them, the two, father and daughter, faced off, each disgusted with the other, each driven by righteous fury at what had happened, neither willing to acknowledge the trigger point in their interconnected lives that had led to this very moment, neither willing to back down or budge even an inch. Today, there would only be one winner. One survivor! Each of them was sure the reasons that they firmly adhered to justified their actions, not just now but far off in the past; both knew deep down that if that one event had gone the other way and if destiny had intervened, things might have been so different. It hadn't, and now here we are, the fate of the planet hanging over the edge of a precipice, two close family members on opposite sides, willing to give their all to destroy the other, one ready to save it, the other hoping to destroy it. If you think your family's peculiar, then you should say a prayer for this one, because nothing good is going to happen here today. One way or another, evil will prevail.

With a snarl on her face and all the ferocity of a starving predator, the twisted Earth drew forth as much magic as she could hold on to in one go and, breaking into a sprint, launched it all at her father. Flaming cranberry coloured projectiles closed in on his position, his deranged daughter not far behind. Momentarily he paused, waiting for his young blood to show her hand. So that was it, he thought, watching the malevolent magic head his way, all the time in the background keeping an eye on his approaching adversary. Hastily, his body tossed up between staying put, deflecting the incoming energy away and departing the immediate area. Instinctively, he chose the second option. With the kind of speed Flash would have been proud of, Fredric let out a snort of contempt at his daughter's pitiful effort, before diving off to his left, his unruly, long, matted locks swaying this way and that, almost having a will of their own, much like his approaching offspring. Through all the magic zinging around the battlefield, Earth checked out her dad, confident she knew exactly what he was thinking. Sure enough, instead of holding his ground, he chose to tumble off to one side.

'So predictable,' she thought, knowing full well that would at some point be his total and utter undoing. Landing tentatively on his feet, careful not to slip on any of the debris he'd stumbled into, the former Antarctic prisoner siphoned off the power he needed from the chains adorning his torso, and as cool and calculating as you like, released a line of explosive magic, tearing across the marble floor. Curving around in an arc to follow the path of her loser father, surprise screamed loudly in her ears as the floor between the two of them started to explode, the detonations shredding the exquisite, white, shiny marble, on their way to make her pay. Intuitively and aided in no small part by the supernatural power deep within her, she leapt off to one side, somersaulting over a trio of dead nagas, skidding to a halt behind their grisly cadavers. Not totally surprised to see her sidestep his latest attempt, Fredric focused his mind, intricately moved his fingers and, putting not quite all his will behind it, cast the next spell.

'Hopefully that might have more luck,' he thought, as the magic in question did his bidding, bringing forth a gigantic, sizzling, electrical net, about thirty metres square, precisely above her serpent wriggling head. 'Let's see how much she likes that!'

Surprised at his magical ingenuity, hundreds of options of how to defeat it raced through her mind in barely a second. One stood out. With a cast iron mental grip, her wayward and excitable magic took hold of the nearest pile of rubble that had fallen from the ceiling a short time ago. Directing all her power, she willed the huge stack to come to her. It wasn't quite as instantaneous as she'd hoped, but as her father's net started to drop, the mountain of rock slid across towards her.

Grinding his teeth in frustration, the founder of the Crimson Guards looked on as the massive mound of debris slid across to his daughter, the top of which pierced his net as it fell towards the ground, arcing and spitting electricity all over the place. As soon as it slid to a halt, avoiding all the sparking and flickering voltage, Earth quickly dived into a recess in the mass of rock, hidden away from the lattice trap that had by now totally fallen to the ground, spitting and hissing violently, bright blue energy crackling everywhere, magic that, had it caught her, would have incapacitated her for a very long time. Pleased to have countered all that he had, her nerves were starting to fray, whether through anger or fear or even a mixture of both, one thought alone inhabiting all of her. It was time! Time to finish it, and of course... HIM! With the click of her fingers, a deluge of water rained down out of nowhere, flooding the surrounding area, shorting out what was left of the powerful grid designed to take her down. Striding out of her hidey hole, looking both magnificent and mad, with cool, foamy water sloshing around her ankles, the resolve in her eyes was clear for Fredric to see, even at forty metres. Gnawing fear spread across his belly for the first time in decades. Imprisonment had been what it had been, and throughout all the torture he'd always known that he could have been killed. Quite early on he'd come to accept that, something that had fashioned his resolve and steeled the chilly confidence that the near solitude had provided him with. This, however, was something different all together. So far she'd matched him, magic for magic, and he had the ominous feeling that she was only getting warmed up. This did not bode well. Glancing around to see if support of any kind was even vaguely in the offing, it instantly became clear that it wasn't, and obvious to him that he was well and truly on his own. Wishing to just live a quiet, happy and productive life with his best friend George, and the grandson he loved so much, with a force of will stronger than most beings would ever know, he pushed the dangerous thoughts aside, and harnessing the laminium wrapped around him, brought forth some of the vilest magic he knew, hoping to very quickly end things once and for all.

Standing so close that the static electricity from all the power she was channelling made his slightly shorter hair stand firmly on end, over the noise of all that was happening on the other side of the shield, he asked,

"What can we do to turn the tide of everything that's happening, Rich?"

Aware of his presence next to her for some time, she'd been lost in powering the shield and keeping them safe up until now. It was only when he spoke she realised quite how drained she felt, despite the laminium from the necklace and the dagger augmenting her own reserves. Head twisting to face her friend, she shook it from side to side to loosen up her neck muscles that had started to tighten. Wishing for a soothing massage, once again she turned to face her friend.

"What do you mean?"

"We can't stay like this forever? Can we?" he asked.

"There's enough power in the laminium for the time being," she replied.

"And then what? The shield runs out and that's it. We're just ripped apart by that horrific force continually bombarding us at the moment. Shouldn't we at least try and fight back? What about the king, Flash, the naga king and... my grandfather?"

Ignoring the strain powering the shield had on her body, Richie's face broke into a sympathetic smile.

"I've tried to come up with something, I really have. But powering this monster of a barrier takes a lot out of me, not just physically, but mentally as well. It's as if my head's full of a fog that I just can't clear, no matter what I do. As you may well have surmised, I haven't been able to come up with anything that either allows us to go on the offensive, or gives us the ability to help those outside the barrier we care about, without risking life and limb for everyone already trapped with us. I'm open to any suggestions."

"What about extending part of the shield outwards to encapsulate either the king and his group, or the naga king and Flash?"

Pete, I'm already at about the limit of what I can do. Even a tiny little bit more, like creating that hole for Flash, pushes me right to the very edge and risks the shield collapsing totally. I'm sorry."

"It's alright. It was a bit of a stupid suggestion anyway."

"Not at all," Richie replied. "We need to think on our feet, pool our resources, think outside the box if we're to do anything but die here today. Perhaps you should ask Yoyo and the others if they have anything we could use. I'd do it quick though, if I were you. There's a whole new wave of reinforcements massing outside the council building on the other side of the bridge. If they get over here, I don't see the outcome being anything but us dying in the most horrific of ways."

Nodding at his friend, he turned, brushed past the blonde haired human he loved more than life itself and rushed off in Yoyo's direction, hoping that the experienced dragon healer had something useful to offer.

For a moment, the king's back had become vulnerable. Amelia Battlehard, hanging in the air behind him, had taken a sword strike to her cervical ribs at the base of her neck. A painful scream from directly behind was what alerted the monarch to his fighting partner's dangerous dilemma. Ignoring the pressure from several mental attacks that were nibbling at his consciousness, George unleashed a wave of pure energy from his bruised and bloodied fingertips, in the direction of two dragons intent on having his head. The magic honed in on its intended target, bursting the creatures' subcutaneous air sacs that are located deep beneath the skin, acting as bellows not only for the lungs, but to pneumatisize (fill with air) the bones. Two simultaneous ear ringing 'SPLATS!' accompanied the gore infested, bloody explosions, as internal organs drenched the surrounding area.

Immediate threat seemingly dealt with, the king turned to his collaborator in a world of significant hurt. Wrestling Amelia's sword from her limp hand, with all the strength he could muster George thrust it up into the jaw of the prehistoric beast that had dropped down out of the air and was about to take a bite out of the fearless captain. The look of horror as the beast tried to recoil was accompanied by a satisfying gurgle as it spiralled out of control towards the deck. Knitting together the captain's wound as best he could without stopping to take a look, the king thickened the air around another would-be attacker's windpipe, causing him to suffocate mid-flight, and watched as the speeding body of his foe dropped straight onto a particularly vicious naga fighting one of the guards below. The wicked looking serpent never knew what hit it.

Really, George should have known better, being the seasoned fighter that he was, but his genuine concern for Captain Battlehard's welfare momentarily blinded him to the danger of the situation, leaving him vulnerable to a surprise strike from one of the dragons that had tumbled to the ground some time ago.

Clambering out from underneath numerous corpses and extraneous body parts, still clutching the dark bladed sword that he'd been handed some weeks ago, he wiped away the green blood oozing from a vertical cut that ran from just above his right eye to beneath his chin. Caught off guard, the assault that had started and finished with said cut, knocked him unconscious, sending him into a dizzying spiral before crashing firmly to the ground, all of which he remembered very little of. What he did remember though, was the mission, and to whom he'd pledged his loyalty. So with that in mind, and infuriated beyond belief, he scouted about the immediate area to see exactly how he could repay those that had inflicted the hurt he currently felt. Not fifty metres away, he saw the circular group of dragons made up of a lone councillor, what remained of the King's Guard, and of course Amelia Battlehard and the king. Fighting for all they were worth, sizzling shields protecting the main group around their circumference, Captain Battlehard and the current dragon monarch defended them aerially as supernatural magic detonated all around them. Wading through the broken carcasses, his head still ringing, the sound of the raging battle alone increasing the pain he felt from his headache, the dark dragon set his sights on destroying his enemy's defensive line, determined to do as much damage as possible. And then he spotted his chance. The female of the two fighters situated at the top of what looked like a dome, had unexpectedly taken a sword to the base of her neck. Watching intently, he waited to see what would happen next. He doubted her partner would intervene, because it would mean leaving a weakness, an opportunity, one to be exploited for those looking to do so, and he seemed way too savvy for that. Or was he? As those thoughts finished playing through his head, unbelievably the dragon (he had no idea it was the monarch, as he'd been one of the first to fly over from the council building once things had already kicked off) did exactly what he thought impossible, dropping his opponents in an instant before rushing to the female's aid. This was it, he thought, this was his chance. Without hesitation, he dropped into a crouch and, using the attacking dark force of nagas on the ground as cover, sprinted for all he was worth towards the dome, covering the distance in all but a split second. Coming up behind the ring of nagas spitting poison, battling with swords and magic, all the time trying to take out the beings that formed the ever moving dome's magical shell, in one fell swoop he leapt into the air and, hugging the surface of the shield that curved upwards, he snuck up at speed towards both hovering dragons, approaching the male from behind.

Closing Captain Battlehard's wound properly, eager for them both to retake their defensive positions, George felt a surge of pride at how well the dragon he now tended to had fought. Surely they could prevail if each and every one of them battled like that. And then he sensed it. Astonished, dismayed and terrified all at the same time, he knew without a doubt that it was far too late for him to do anything about the sneak attack one of the dark dragons had just launched. Barely able to turn half way towards his adversary, he wondered if this was just the beginning of the end, as the tip of the matt black blade thrust down towards his neck, a smile of deep satisfaction etched across the unhinged dragon's face at just the very thought of the killing stroke. Stuck in a moment, George steeled himself to meet his maker, if such a thing should ever happen. But something in that instant changed. The look of utter delight on the dark dragon's face transformed at first into puzzlement, followed immediately by anguish, as the apex of a frost shrouded cutting edge burst through his chest, hissing and spluttering, throwing tiny particles of cold into the air all around it. Mesmerised completely by not only the beauty of the weapon, but by the cool, elegant blanket of brilliant, white frost that continuously circled the blade, it was only the echoing clang of the dastardly, black sword bouncing off the top of the shield, that startled the king back to reality. Shaking himself alert, he wondered who had just saved his life, hoping to see Flash's smiling face appear from behind the deceased form of the prehistoric monster that had come so near to ending his life. But he was about to be disappointed. With the tiniest of wriggles, the blade pulled itself free of the monster that it had just impaled, allowing the despicable creature to slump on to the shield, spewing brilliant, thick, green blood this way and that. With the dragon out of the way, the futuristic foil floated closer to the king, all the time pointing upwards, as if to say it offered no threat to the incumbent monarch of this world.

'Fascinating,' thought the king, eyes glued to the most amazing weapon he'd ever seen. 'Does it have a will of its own? Is someone controlling it? How was it made, and by whom?' All these questions scurried through his mind at almost the speed of light. At the moment though, the answers would have to wait, because right at that second his tingling, magic enhanced sense of danger kicked in, shocking him out of his reverie, forcing him back to reality, which in this case represented half a dozen murderous looking dragons, all speeding towards the top of the dome, all looking to tear the duo apart. Readying his ethereal birthright, George watched with a certain amount of amusement as the weapon seemingly bowed in front of him before turning to face his attackers, and then zipped off at speed towards them. Mere moments later, when it was time for the king to use the power he'd already prepared, half a dozen had been whittled down to two, something he was not only grateful for, but more than confident he could cope with. And so ripping off one of his attacker's wings, whilst continually blasting the other with freezing cold darts of ice, he wished his ultramodern ally good luck, as a part of him wondered if the famed master mantra maker had anything to do with it. He wouldn't have been surprised to find that he had.

Eyes closed, bathed in an inner tranquillity she'd never, ever known before, the love of Peter's life was bowled over at having saved the dragon king's soul through her newly found bond with the ancient blade. Fu-ts'ang... not quite so much. In his case, it was more a mutual respect kind of thing; having taken the tiniest of glimpses into the soul of the dragon monarch, he knew beyond any doubt that he was a righteous, kind and good being. Whether that was enough to turn the tide of what was happening here, he had no idea. The cold, logical part of him screamed out that it wasn't, and that if he didn't leave now he'd be captured, put in the hands of these foul and wicked criminals and used for dreadful and despicable deeds. He might have been right, but he just couldn't leave. Besides, he wasn't able to go on his own, he'd have to take the girl with him, and having shared her memories and feelings across their link, he knew there was no way in hell she was leaving, not without her love and the rest of their friends. Accepting that it was now a full on fight to the death, Fu-ts'ang continued on his destructive rampage, fulfilling his purpose, destroying evil in all its forms without hesitation, all the time having one eye on friends and allies strewn across the battlefield with a view to protecting them at all costs, thanks in no small part to the human whose mind he shared.

Sliding to a halt on the shiny marble next to Yoyo, he waited patiently for the experienced Australian healer to finish his ministrations, gawping at the stunning looking ring that now adorned his right hand. It didn't take long.

"PETER!" exclaimed Yoyo, "what on earth can I do for you?"

Grinning inanely, the young hockey playing dragon relayed Richie's appeal, asking his friend if he had any idea of exactly how they could get themselves out of this seemingly impossible spot and take the fight to those that were trying their best to crush them. Scratching his chin whilst at the same time wriggling his jaw, Yoyo pondered Peter and Richie's request.

"No, no... that wouldn't work at all," he mused. "Hmmm... maybe, maybe... NO! What about... no, that probably wouldn't cut it. Hang on a second... that might just work. Yes... out of all the options, that's the one that gives us the best chance... I'm sure of it."

"Sure of what?" urged Peter

"I've nearly healed every dragon here. We're almost all ready to re-enter the fight. What about if we kept the shield up around us and, as one, moved out into the battlefield, all the time attacking, making our way towards those we care about, able to offer protection and a temporary safe harbour?"

It wasn't quite the idea Peter had been hoping for.

"It would never work. Richie says she can't maintain the shield whilst moving, even powered by what's left of the laminium in the necklace and the dagger."

"I wasn't thinking of letting our superstar leader do it all by herself. We can share the load around. Now that they're healed there's enough of us to take on some of your friend's burden, and knowing my lot as I do, I suspect they'll all have a few ideas about how to build on the shield that she's developed. It won't be easy, but I do believe it's most certainly doable. What do you think?"

"If you're sure, then it sounds good to me. I'll let Richie know."

"Just give me a couple of minutes to finish up here and inform the others of the plan. When I'm ready, I'll contact Richie telepathically."

"Sure thing," replied Peter. "Good luck!"

"Right back atcha!" remarked Yoyo, smiling.

With that, Peter turned and headed back towards his friend, buoyed ever so slightly by Yoyo's plan, knowing from all his life experiences and in particular the hockey, that if you work together you can far exceed what you can do alone. Deep down inside, he just hoped it would be enough to overcome these insurmountable odds.

Arms stretched wide open, standing atop the largest pile of rubble within the private residence, Manson, eyes closed, willed his force on, urging them over the bridge and out of the council building, all in an effort to finish things off. Bored and unable to see how this would end in anything but a victory for him, thoughts of how he would dominate this world, ruling not only the humans, but what remained of the dragons as well, played through his mind. They'd be his slaves until the end of days, subjugated and robbed of any life they would ever have had. Part of him especially liked the thought of using humans as sport. Dragons chasing humans through cities both on the surface and here underground, with a specified destination in mind... If the human reaches it before the dragon catches up with them, then he or she may prevail that little bit longer, perhaps to try again another day. Should the dragon catch up with the human... that would then be another matter, with a tasty morsel of a snack always being appreciated, no matter what time of day. In his experience, human flesh tended to taste a little like chicken, rather nice if chargrilled. Once he was king, he'd make sure it was available everywhere, twenty four / seven, for every one of the beings that had helped him achieve his goal. There'd be queues at slaughterhouses kilometres long as they looked to keep up with the demand for delicious human kebabs. Children, he found, were especially tasty. Stomach rumbling at the mere thought of food, gently, and very slowly, he allowed the magic to flow out of him, to wander through the air, connecting with as many of the beings that had pledged him their allegiance as he could, implanting one thought, and one thought alone. ATTACK, ATTACK, ATTACK!

Rolling like giant marbles through everything in their paths, Earth and her father tumbled at speed, fighting hand to hand, each once again doing their best to physically hurt the other... gouging, scratching, punching and kicking, with the deranged daughter even at one point head butting her father, much to his astonishment. Spinning across the battlefield in blind panic, their rounded shields colliding with corpses and cadavers, debris and rubble, and even the odd living being or two, who were either too consumed by their actions or just too slow to get out of the way, the dysfunctional relatives fought tooth and nail, both firmly believing in their righteous cause, Earth long since lost to the madness that consumed her.

Pitching forward, the crazed witch lunged at her father, driving him back, whilst at the same time connecting her hand with his face. It was more of a backhanded slap than anything else, but it carried the weight of just some of her magic, rattling his eyes and everything else within his skull. Dazed for but a heartbeat, suddenly all the breath was forced out of him by a violent knee in the crotch. Nearly causing him to go cross-eyed, but not quite, it did at least stir a very real anger inside him, provoking him to fight back with everything he had. Wrestling in close proximity wasn't ideal as far as he was concerned, but long ago he'd been trained for all eventualities, so he allowed the memories of that time to come flooding back, hoping to allow his body to fight instinctively. To some degree it worked.

Pleased to have caught him just a little off guard, particularly at having inflicted pain 'there'... her short lived victory came crashing down around her as the sharp incisors in his gaping mouth closed in around her purple-lined, delicate nose, and bit down as hard as they could. A sickening 'CRUNCH' that would have caused most beings to spontaneously vomit resounded between them, followed quickly by an almighty, high pitched shriek. Encouraged by the sound, Fredric shook his head viciously, a great white shark tearing apart its prey, shaking loose blood, bone and sinew, all the time keeping his human mouth firmly clamped around what was left of her nose. In her heightened, frightened, terrified state, her magic took over, exploding out between them in a kinetic rage that mirrored everything the insane woman felt. Crackling into nothingness, their shields disintegrated as both father and daughter flew violently apart, both crashing thunderously down on opposite sides of the residence.

Slightly concussed and feeling sick from the contact of his daughter's knee, it was the founder of the Crimson Guards that rose to his feet first, battle weary and tired, despite the power the chains surrounding his chest offered up. Up until then, his body hadn't really realised it was in a fight. Now it certainly did.

From her prone position, Earth rushed a spoonful of her magic into what she assumed were broken ribs given the vicious 'CRACK' they'd made on contact with the floor, understanding that it was more important here and now for them to heal than her nose. Mended ribs would allow her to move more freely, something she really couldn't do without right at this very moment. If an appropriate opportunity showed itself to heal her nose, then she'd take advantage of it, but not before.

Wary of her aching arms, she pushed herself up and got to her feet, shaking dust and rubble from her tattered brown cloak as once again she faced her father. This time it was his turn to grin, and as the blood ran from what was left of her nose across her mouth, some of which dribbled down her chin, a vicious snarl burned itself into her already nightmarish face. Fully consumed by the bubbling lunacy, almost as if a switch had been flicked within her, thoughts of everything but killing her dad faded into nothingness as she channelled her hot-to-the-touch magic, once again devising an attack strategy, determined this time to make him pay for everything.

Arriving back just in time, Peter could see the heat radiating off the laminium dagger and the necklace. Washing both items with a handful of cooling magic, the young hockey playing dragon outlined Yoyo's plan for his friend. Considering it carefully, still the group's de facto leader despite everything that had happened, Richie was bereft of any alternatives. Not the ideal situation she knew, but they had to do something, or risk just sitting here, watching their friends die, and being killed once the magic powering the shield ran out. It was that simple. Do nothing and die, or do something and just maybe... you never know.

"Okay Pete... let's do it! Tell Janice to be ready, and make sure you keep her safe."

"I will."

"I've just telepathically confirmed everything with Yoyo. With all that's going on, I can't promise to keep an eye on you both. Sorry."

"Don't worry about that. Keep doing what you're doing. I'm one hundred percent certain that will be enough to give us a fighting chance."

"You sound very confident, against all odds, how come?"

Decision time he knew. Should he tell her what he'd seen and shared with Gee Tee? Would it alter her mindset and fate itself if he did? It didn't seem likely it would, and perhaps knowing would spur her on to greater deeds. As well, this might be his very last chance to do just that... decisions, decisions. Ignoring her studious stare, he searched inside himself for the right thing to do. It didn't take long for the answer to reveal itself.

"I have something to tell you Rich, something you may not like, or even agree with. But it's important and I believe it to be one hundred percent the truth."

"Go on," she urged intrigued.

Not knowing the best way to wrap up what he needed to say, and wary of time ticking down, he did what he was best at and just blurted it out.

"It wasn't Tim that was The White Dragon, it's you."

In all the time he'd known her, he'd never seen her so surprised.

"That's impossible," she stuttered, shocked to her core.

"I'm sorry... but it's not. You're the one who's going to save us all. It's you, and I'm not the only one that thinks so."

"Why is it me? You saw Tim turn into a totally and utterly white dragon, like no other in the history of our race. You helped teach him to fly... why would you think it wasn't him?" she croaked, her hands holding the dagger shaking ever so slightly.

Regretting spilling his guts like this, concerned because in places, the shield was fluctuating and sparking more now than at any other point in the proceedings that had led them here, he knew he was going to have to explain everything to her. Determined to keep things brief, aware of just how upset she'd become, he pushed on.

"The scars and wounds carved into your back from the explosion at the clubhouse are shaped like a dragon. And because of the pigment of your skin, the dragon itself is... WHITE! You are THE WHITE DRAGON!"

Struggling to focus, maintain her composure and ultimately hold the shield in place with her mind, the lacrosse playing dragon's intellect refused to believe what she'd just been told.

"IMPOSSIBLE! You're making it all up!"

"I swear to you Rich that I'm not. It's all one hundred percent true."

"Then you're just mistaken Pete. I'm not The White Dragon, Tim was, he's gone, and it's all my fault."

Terrified that the shield was going to come down, leaving them all at the mercy of the surrounding dread force of nagas and dark dragons, the only way forward Peter could see was to convince his friend that everything he believed was true, so with that in mind, he continued, ignoring the looks Yoyo, Janice, Hook and the other dragons were giving him.

"The day I picked you up from your flat to take you to lacrosse was the day I saw your back. In that moment I knew it was you, Rich. The revelation rocked me to the core, stopped me from sleeping and when I did eventually sleep, it haunted my dreams. In the end I could think of only one thing to do, one thing that might just give me peace of mind, and the confirmation that I needed."

"And what was that?"

"I shared my thoughts on the subject with another being."

"But not me?"

"No."

"Why?"

"Because I needed somebody objective, somebody whose experience far outweighed my own. If I'd have told you, the conversation would have been exactly like the one we're having now. You'd have told me it wasn't so, and I'd have told you that I believed it to be with every atom in my body, and we'd have gotten nowhere."

"So who did you tell?"

Pausing, running his hands through his hair, more than a little dismayed at the turn of events, he wished to God that he'd never even opened his mouth. Not wanting to, he told her anyway.

"Gee Tee!"

"And what did the all seeing, omnipotent shopkeeper have to say?"

"Honestly? He laughed in my face."

"Really?"

"Really."

"You obviously convinced him though."

"I did, and you wouldn't believe how."

"Try me."

"I shared the memory of seeing your back with him."

"What?"

"The actual memory... I shared it with him."

"Is that even possible?"

"That's a stupid thing to ask when it comes to the Emporium and its owner."

"Agreed, but I'd still like to know how."

"Using a mantra designed by Leonardo da Vinci allowed him to relive everything from that moment, the sounds, smells, my emotions as well as my deepest, darkest secrets."

"REALLY?" exclaimed Richie, hopefully. "Mild mannered Peter Bentwhistle, love machine to the stars, and all round super spy. That's it... you're James Bond aren't you? That's your real identity." She mocked, mercilessly.

"Funny! But it did backfire a little. He found out about Janice."

"Owwww... that couldn't have been good."

"No... it wasn't. Moving on though. As you've already gathered, we shared the memory and once we'd finished, and it took some time, the shopkeeper was a changed dragon."

About to interject, Peter held up his hand in an effort to let him carry on.

"Sceptical before, he immediately revised his decision, agreeing that almost certainly you were The White Dragon the prophecy refers to. After that, it was difficult to know what to do. He convinced me that going to either the king or Council was a bad idea. At the time, I seemed to have totally run out of options."

Richie's face fell at hearing him recall this part of the story, so sad was his voice.

"What did you do?" she asked over the sound of the continued magical bombardment.

"It was then that he showed me the Nissix ring."

"The one on the chain that you begged me to look after?"

"That's right."

"The one containing my dragon memories, the one I'm currently wearing?"

"Yes," he nodded sadly.

"He just gave it to you?"

"NO! I stole it."

"You're kidding?"

"No. I really did steal it."

"Why?"

"Because he showed it to me, wowed me with what it could do, knowing full well that I would relate it to your predicament, and then refused to give it to me when I asked. I think at the time, it might have all been too much for him."

"So you just took it?"

"I did, and I'm reasonably sure he knew I did."

"I think you're right. When we met up below ground on the outskirts of Salisbridge, he wasn't surprised to see me wearing the ring."

"You've seen him?"

"Yes... we travelled up to London as a group together."

"Then they're on their way here to back us up, right?"

"I'm sorry to say they're not. Right at this very moment, they should be mounting an assault on the crystal node at Fleet Street, in an effort to retake it and restore communications across the planet. Any hope of them coming to our rescue should be forgotten because it just isn't going to happen," she stated, totally dashing his hopes.

"Well, that's about the long and the short of it. With everything going on, I haven't had a chance to discuss the prophecy with the master mantra maker, and so we've done nothing about it. But he, like me, is totally convinced that you're The White Dragon. What is it?" he asked noticing the strange, faraway look that had descended over her face.

"I'm just remembering the last conversations I had with him. What you've just told me brings a whole new light to some of the things he said. I hope they're all okay."

"I'm sure they'll all be fine."

"I do hope so."

It was then that a tiny little nudge, like a gentle rap on the door deep within their minds, made them aware that Yoyo and his street band of dragons were almost ready to start. It was time to recover their friends and bring a little bit more pain and misery to the enemy. Bring it on!

Slipping away, that's how it felt, almost as though he were being pulled into a never ending, bottomless abyss. Of course he fought, after all, that's what he did best, but despite his heroic efforts, nothing he did made any sort of difference. Hope seeped out of him at an alarming rate, leaving his rational mind to come to terms with the fact he was about to die. Not for the first time. Clawing at the myriad of thoughts scrabbling around his head, as his life force ebbed away, he searched for answers to questions he hadn't even thought of yet. Confused, dumbfounded, frustrated and more than a little frightened, the courageous dragon rallied against the inevitable, his intellect fighting on every front. Talons pierced hardened rock in an effort not to be dragged further towards the end, but it still wasn't enough. A force more powerful than anything in the universe had its grip on him, and one way or another, death would get its man, or in this case... DRAGON!

Hope having all but disappeared, fear surrounded him, commanding him to surrender, mocking him for trying to escape the inescapable. Unable to organise his thoughts in any meaningful manner, exhausted by the assault of constant pain, slowly his will started to relinquish its refusal to give in, accepting the fate ahead of it, long in the calling. It was then that what little remained of him shuddered ferociously, almost crying out in fear and terror as it recognised something slippery, scary and serpent-like. In a desperate attempt to get away his mind scratched and fumbled, dug and groped at everything around it, panic overwhelming the fear and genuine alarm he felt.

Gaining a little more purchase in his escape from an untimely demise, images of a huge, golden-coloured snake-like creature, thick, bright yellow fluid dripping down the scales at the side of its head, somewhere in a cold, snowy environment, flooded his synapses, causing what remained of his physical body to jerk and writhe in absolute terror, like a possessed demon. Any ground that he'd made up in his attempt to outrun death was instantly lost as he slid back towards the metaphorical cliff edge, beyond which lay the abyss, and of course... HIS CERTAIN DOOM!

To say it was not going well was something of an understatement, thought Vasuki as he trawled through Flash's unruly mind, searching for the trigger he needed to save the brave dragon. Amongst the magical background of the king's private residence, the naga king arced over the wrecked body of the ex-Crimson Guard, his scaled forehead directly atop Flash's, the contact of their skins breaching any inbuilt supernatural defences, providing the best opportunity to save the dragon defender. It was then that their exploits caught some very unwanted attention.

Pride swelled his chest. It wasn't something he often experienced, least of all because of another, but as he watched the woman he loved battle for all she was worth against the unkempt prisoner from Antarctica, who, it had to be said, was considerably more powerful and able than he could ever had imagined, it somehow vilified his decision to crown her queen and give over all of himself to her. She was magnificent, he thought, a rightful mate and the perfect mother to all the offspring she would provide him with.

Watching with glee as she launched yet another foul and depraved magical attack, something behind their personal duel caught Manson's twisted attention. Through the rubble, dust, smoke and haze of supernatural power that saturated the huge chamber they all found themselves in, he looked on with incredulity at what the naga king was doing to Flash.

'That's odd,' he thought, his mind speculating about what on earth was going on. Strangely though, he couldn't come up with anything that would explain what the hell they were doing. He couldn't abide anomalies or anything out of the ordinary, because as a general rule they interfered with the best laid plans, and given that his plans and machinations had been long in the making, the only decision available to him was to go and investigate. And so without further ado, he did.

Reliving his Antarctic experience was enough to destroy what remained of his defences, letting him slide ever closer to the chasm of no return. Curled up in the foetal position, his petrified mind no longer cared whether he lived or died. Luckily for him, someone else did.

Committing to the process, Vasuki gave himself over to saving the dragon that had rescued them from that icy hellhole in Antarctica. Delving deep into what was left of the ex-Crimson Guard, the naga king dropped his defences, ignoring everything going on around them in the physical world, and pushed on in the hunt for the trigger he needed. Urgency threatened to overwhelm him, but he had no idea why. Shrugging it off, he set free the magic that had been his since birth, and allowed it to soak into every last fibre of the being he was trying to rescue.

Batting away a stray wave of electrical energy, the malevolent being that had caused all this in the first place, casually strolled through the carnage, weaving in and out of huge piles of debris, nonchalantly deflecting massive chunks of ceiling, that continued to fall down in his path, harmlessly out of the way. Senses taking in everything around him, he momentarily spied the love of his life in the tiniest bit of trouble. Watching from a short distance away as the former dragon prisoner grabbed her by the throat, ready to throttle the life out of her, Manson decided, against his better judgement, to intervene. Thrusting out his hand in the battling pair's direction, a tiny dark dart, full of potent magic, sped away from him, heading directly towards his love's adversary. Through the dust and the smoke, he looked on, eager to see the results of his handiwork. He wasn't disappointed. As the deadly barb neared its target, the prisoner clearly sensed the danger and with no other choice available to him, relinquished his grip on Earth, before bounding off to one side in a dramatic display of gymnastic ability. With his love free for the moment, the despicable dark dragon decided she'd had enough of his help and turned his attention back towards his intended target, determined to put a stop to whatever abnormal supernatural behaviour was going on.

Still curled up in a ball, what was left of the valiant ex-Crimson Guard now rolled towards the precipice, gaining speed with every rotation, Death looking on, rubbing his hands in anticipation.

Lost in the pull of the magic, Vasuki allowed himself to be consumed by it all, once again experiencing the euphoria that it entailed, even deep inside something as alien as this. The rush was fantastic: think rollercoaster, waterslide, fairground ride and helicopter trip all rolled into one. Briefly he was not only lost for words, but lost in the moment. If his will hadn't been stronger, he could very well have been lost forever. But he was king for several reasons, one of which was his strength of purpose, something those who had met him and served under his command, never doubted for a second. Singlemindedly bursting the bubble of ecstasy he'd found himself in, as the rush of adrenaline washed away he reached out along the tendrils of magic that embedded themselves deep within the young dragon, searching for what he needed. Almost instantly, he found it.

It hadn't been subtle. He hadn't had to sneak or cloak himself using any of his inherent power. All he'd done was stride resolutely across that part of the battlefield, mindful of all the wayward magic, falling debris and slippery rubble. Approaching the naga king, who was leaning almost over on himself, his whole reptilian body forming what looked like a giant S, his pale blue, scaled forehead pressed firmly against the smoking remains of the human he'd briefly battled earlier, Manson once again wondered what the hell was going on, and what on earth could be important enough to totally disregard your own personal safety in the middle of a pitched battle like this. Contemplating the answer for a split second before discounting the question totally, he drew to a halt five metres away, his smug smile once again making an appearance at the thought of finishing off both of these beings once and for all. Running through a list of the most formidable spells he had at his disposal deep within his mind, he carefully chose something that was appropriate to the situation.

Joy at discovering just what he was looking for was immediately tempered by his inbuilt sense of danger screaming furiously at him. Knowing to trust that particular sense wholeheartedly, he grasped the magic he needed, commanded it to follow a very specific set of instructions, before gathering himself up in an effort to return to his own body and the chaos of the battle, hoping that he wasn't too late to face whatever danger lay out there. In the blink of an eye, it was done.

A row of dominos would be a fitting description... DNA dominoes. And all the naga king's magic had to do was knock down the first one. It did, and with impunity, they all began to topple.

That first split second back was the worst. It always felt as though your mind had been forcibly pulled through a hole half its size. It was nauseating at the best of times. Today was not one of those. Heaving his heavy head up and away from Flash's, Vasuki rose to his full height before turning to face the threat that his body had been screaming out for him not to ignore. By the looks of things though, that was far too late.

Rolling brilliant, bright emerald green balls of magic around in both his hands, Manson arrogantly stood only a short way off, amused to see the king of the nagas suddenly realise the trouble he was in.

'This will be fun,' he thought to nobody but himself.

Like any good domino construction, the lines turned this way and that, splitting into two, and then two again, before twisting off in totally the opposite direction. As each came crashing down, nothing known to either man or dragon could prevent this unstoppable force from reaching its inevitable conclusion.

Something in him changed instantly, forcing the pain to disappear, flooding his essence with hope. Immediately he dived out of the ball he'd been in, smashing to the ground, metaphorically speaking. With the relentless force still exerting itself on him and pushing him ever closer to the fateful drop off the edge, his will reasserted itself. Powered by the new found hope, he staggered to his feet and began walking in the opposite direction. It was like striding into a hurricane, but slowly, inch by inch, he made progress in the opposite direction.

Never before in the history of the universe had Death been so caught off guard or surprised. When he finally came to terms with what had just happened, and the fact that he wouldn't be needed right here today, like the fickle entity that he was, he just shrugged it off and moved on to the next one. There were plenty of others close by that required his services.

"Mourning your friend there?" mocked Manson, the magic in his hands ready to be used at the first sign of trouble.

Vasuki chose not to answer. What would be the point? Caught off guard, knowing full well he was unable to bring forth any kind of defence in time, the serpent-like king rose up regally to meet his fate head on, hoping against hope that his magic had made the difference.

"Your brief glimpse of freedom was short lived. What's it like to suddenly have hope after all that time, and then find it pulled out from under you? Must be disappointing to say the least? Naga got your tongue? Ha ha."

'Coooommmme onnnnn, coooooommmme onnnn, coooommmme onnnnn,' thought Vasuki. 'Ssssurrrrellllllyyy iiit mmmusssst hhhhavvvve wwwwooorkkkkeddd byyyy nnnnowwww.'

Only a few branches of the DNA domino tree left to fall now, and if anyone had been looking at the smoking, corpse-like body of Flash, they'd have spotted wisps of crackling purple energy sparking over his skin. Vasuki had his back to the ex-Crimson Guard's remains, obscuring Manson's view totally, whilst everybody else in the chamber had more pressing matters on their minds.

Wondering what was going on behind him, not daring to look round despite every atom in his body desperate to do so, the naga king's experience told him one thing and one thing only. Buy some more time! And so against his better judgement, he tried to do just that.

"Whhhyyy dooooo yoouuu dooo aaalll oofff thisssss?" he hissed. "Suuurely theeere isssss noooo neeeeeed."

"HO HO," replied Manson, anything but Father Christmas. "There's every need. It's my destiny to rule the planet, just like it was my father's. He might have failed, but fate wills me on to succeed. Benevolent beings like you are weak and have had your time. A new era is about to be ushered in, one that you were never going to be part of. Thankfully, due in no small part to your race, the world will belong to my Queen and I. And once it does, your kind will be wiped from the face of the earth. How's that for ironic?"

Fighting off a rising tide of fury, Vasuki wrapped himself in the diplomatic persona he hadn't used for decades.

"You're aaa smmaaart, creedible drraaaagoon. Yoou caan't poossssibly waant toooo hurrrt aaallll oooof theesssse beingssss. There muusssst beeee sooome kiiind ooof cooomprooomisssse weeee caaaan reach?"

"COMPROMISE?!" shouted Manson, infuriated. "Do you know how many dragons I've killed? Thousands, if not tens of thousands, and that doesn't include their precious pets on the surface. You can probably add hundreds of thousands of those to the tally. Do you really think those in the dragon domain will be happy to do a deal with me? I DON'T THINK SO!"

"Hoow caaann yooou knooow without trrrrying?"

"Hmmmm..." murmured Manson. "What are you really up to? I don't believe for a second you think an agreement is possible. Buying some time in the hope of a rescue, are we?"

Hopes dashed, with his feeble ploy all but revealed, the naga king was out of time and at the mercy of a being who had no concept of the word.

With the tiniest 'tap' in the world, the last one fell into place, ending the cascade and launching the mother of all chain reactions. Locked and loaded, the torrent of magic within writhed and wriggled before finding the right path and once that happened the change was electrifying and much, much quicker than it should have been. Instantaneously, the being that had been on the verge of death was all but reborn, back to his prehistoric best thanks to the repairs made by Fredric to his damaged DNA, back in Antarctica, but with one crucial difference. Before the naga attack at the bottom of the world, the one that had almost proved deadly, the one that Gee Tee had saved his life from at the cost of his dragon form, his natural shape had been nothing too special. Not huge, not small, somewhere in between. Of course his training had made up for any shortcomings in his stature, as had his quick and lithe mind. But here and now, something was different. The feeling of the change was the same, his mind recognised that instantly. But something about the volume of it all felt odd. The reason would soon become apparent.

About to decimate the being in front of him, that he thought of as substandard, with the powerful magic he juggled in both hands, shock and fright forced him to take two steps back as a mighty primeval dragon sprang into being out of nowhere behind the naga king, its prodigious gaze focused solely on him. The tables had been well and truly turned on Manson and, for a change, not only did he feel out of control, but terror and fear ran riot throughout his monstrous, human shaped body.

Magnificent did not do him justice. Much, much bigger than his previous prehistoric incarnation, his new outer shell felt as though he'd just slipped into a tight fitting pair of gloves. Shiny, bright silver scales inundated his upper body, trailing off into gun metal grey around his head, the underside of his wings and down across his sternum. Nordic sky blue accentuated a whole host of features, running along the inside and outside of the wing phalanges, down his tail along the whole neural spine, culminating in the entire caudal spade at the end of his appendage. The same colour outlined his entire cranium. Quite literally, he was a dragon to die for.

Euphoric at being back in the form that he'd entered this world in and being saved from death by the skin of his teeth, Flash, all dragoned up, let out an almighty "ROAR" in the direction of the evil Manson, causing the twisted mastermind to drop the powerful magic he'd been playing with and roll out of the way. In that instant Vasuki recognised his chance and so, slithering out from in front of the newly formed beast of a dragon, he brought his unusual naga magic to bear, creating a defensive shield of frost around his entire snake-like body, as well as readying a wicked looking, shimmering, spear of ice to go on the attack with.

Stomping forward, causing the ground to shake and the marble to break, Flash stretched out his new born wings, scything them through the air, twisting them this way and that, delighted to feel the wind tickling either side of them. It felt so good to experience this again, he thought, especially since it looked for some time like he'd never do so. Pushing his feelings to one side, the logical, literal, agent part of him took control, knowing the trouble they were all in, determined to end things once and for all. And he knew exactly how. If he could kill Manson here and now, things would end, of that he was sure. The dragon world would go back to what it had been before. Simple really, at least that's what he told himself. Without hesitation, knowing exactly what had to be done, he... ATTACKED!

Fizzling out into a puddle of green, Manson watched the supernatural, abnormal dragon magic he'd just dropped, disappear. Of course there was more to come. Unfortunately, he'd expended a great deal of mana in conjuring up that particular spell, hoping to provide a spectacular death for the king of the nagas, something every member of his race that was here could witness. But it wasn't to be, well... not just yet. As far as he was concerned, they'd only delayed the inevitable. With that in mind, he turned to face the more immediate danger, the immense silver dragon that had sprung up from the body that blessed naga had been hunched over. So that was their plan, that's what he'd been up to all along. Cursing any kind of anomaly, he let the magic within him rise to the surface and, in his mind, conjured up a whole host of evil. Get ready!

Against insurmountable odds, George the dragon king, Amelia Battlehard and the small group of defenders they found themselves aligned with were valiantly holding off all comers, to some degree, quite pleased with themselves at not having lost a single member of their tight knit band since the monarch had joined. Unfortunately, chaos continued to reign, getting continually worse with every second that passed, so much so that it was all but impossible for any of them to see out beyond their assailants. As yet more dark dragons dropped from the air, wielding their huge, shadowy, bastard swords, and nightmarish nagas slithered in to back them up, a sea of scaly bodies ten deep surrounded the circle of light sided dragons on the ground, as a dozen dark prehistoric monsters pounded away at the king and his courageous charges from the air. Things were as grim and hopeless as George had ever known in the many centuries he'd been alive. As despair suffocated faith and hope, sensing victory closing in all around them, the dark force mounted one last sustained push.

"Let them in," she'd been told. She didn't like it; it wasn't natural. It went against everything she believed in, especially in the situation she currently found herself in. Sharing your mind with other beings was just... WRONG! Despite vehemently opposing this part of the plan, and against her better judgement, slowly Richie Rump lowered her mental defences, readying them to spring back up at a moment's notice. Any doubts she'd had though, were assuaged after a few seconds. It was an odd feeling, like being in a room with all the others, hearing their beating hearts, feeling their breath, sensing their agitation and suspicion.

'It's going to fail, it's going to fail,' was all she could think, ready to reinforce her barriers and cut off the connection. And then a calm, soothing, confident persona materialised, immediately setting all the others at ease, washing away any concerns and worries that they had. YOYO had that effect on most beings he came into contact with, none more so than this ragtag, eclectic bunch of misfits. They trusted him entirely and up until now he'd never led them astray, only ever having put his faith in each and every one of them. For him, there were two battles going on... the physical one out there, with magic ravaging and raging, the two forces using everything in their arsenals in an effort to defeat each other, and the internal battle threatening to consume the mild mannered healer. He'd promised to protect them, promised them they'd have a life, a future... everything a normal dragon had. But here and now that promise looked hollow, emptier than a politician's pledge. If he could go back, would he have gotten them involved? He wasn't sure, which in itself was a terrible thing for him to think. Without them, Flash would have attempted his rescue alone, and that would have led to disaster and almost certainly a bloody death for the ex-Crimson Guard, the naga king and, of course, for Peter's grandfather, Fredric. Effortlessly pushing his doubts to one side so as not to disturb the fragile meeting of minds deep inside Richie's consciousness, Yoyo vowed to do everything in his power to keep his young charges safe, even if it meant giving his own life.

"Let them feel the power from the dagger and the necklace flowing through you," asserted Yoyo, "give them just a tiny taste, just to get used to it."

Finding things almost too bizarre even for her, and given everything she'd been through in the last few days that was saying quite something, rather unwillingly, she drew them in and let them feel the magic flowing through her, that currently held the shield keeping them all safe, firmly in place.

The first youngster exhaled sharply, so enraptured was she at the touch of so much ethereal energy. The next one, startled, gave a yelp, and then the next and the next. Before long, they'd all experienced it, all got an idea of what they were dealing with, each of them wondering what should happen next.

"You know what we need to do," announced Yoyo, the sound of his voice booming around deep within the lacrosse playing dragon's head. "It's up to you to implement the plan, but bear one thing in mind... time is of the essence."

Silence ensued, filling Richie with a disturbing sense of dread. Before she could act on it, the voice of one of the young female dragons very meekly resounded across whatever space it was they were all sharing.

"A division of labour is what we need if we're to

expand the shield so that it's protecting us on all four sides, and rolling along at the same time. We should designate very specific roles to pairs of dragons, taking some of the burden off Richie, who we still need to power it through the necklace and the dagger."

'Oh, I like her,' thought Richie, stopping abruptly in case all the others could hear her. Luckily they couldn't.

The youngster continued.

"One pair can be responsible for maintaining the shape and integrity of the shield, making sure it's in contact with the surface at all times. Another can help with the movement, no small feat in itself. Some of the quantum mantras we've studied should help with that. Combine your brainpower and that should be a relatively straightforward task. One pair can be responsible for keeping our leader here cool, siphoning off the heat build up from the magic and applying any healing needed."

She sounded so authoritative that Richie didn't have the heart to tell her that Peter had been doing just that.

"One pair can be responsible for any debris, rubble and bodies we travel over, making sure that nothing untoward gets underneath and inside with us. If it does, I don't need to tell you the consequences. If it still has its head, make sure that it's dead!"

Slight chuckling reverberated everywhere at this.

"As for the rest, make sure everyone in here is safe, that their physical bodies are all keeping up with the shield's movement and if any of the pairs have a problem, assist them straight away. Keep your eyes open for anything unforeseen. I'd like to tell you what, but clearly I'm unable to. I'd like to leave Yoyo in reserve, and use his wealth of experience to provide an overview and tell us what we're doing wrong, or even right. How does that all sound?"

Richie was the first to pipe up.

"Brilliant!" she announced, causing the young female dragon's consciousness to blush, if such a thing were even possible.

With an ethereal nod of his head, Yoyo confirmed that he thought it was a sound plan, and so without further ado the youngsters paired themselves off and divided up the tasks, quickly and efficiently.

Richie realised that any doubts she'd previously suffered from had been well and truly sunk. These guys and gals were good, she thought... really, really good.

47 INTO THE HORNETS' NEST

Ominously, they reached what would have been a gigantic entrance had a huge stone disc some twenty metres across not sat in the way. On the plus side, at least there were no guards this time; on the down side, they had no idea how to negotiate the hastily erected barrier.

Wondering about any secretive recording devices as mentioned by Steel a little earlier, Jar Man tried to appear as though he knew exactly what he was doing. Leaving the prisoner in DomCon's capable hands, the strawberry blonde dragon wandered straight up to the humungous granite disc and, without hesitation, placed his hand directly on it. Nothing! Taking two steps back, he proceeded to look it over, top to bottom. Miniature symbols that he didn't recognise had been carved around its circumference. Silently, he hoped to hell magic wasn't involved otherwise they'd never get past it, and would end up trapped in this gaping corridor. Eventually somebody would notice they'd never reached their destination and would trigger the alarm, and the element of surprise would be over. Stepping forward again, he ran one of his unfamiliar fingers across a couple of the symbols, making sure to feel the indentations as he did.

"PANTS!" he shouted at the top of his voice, pulling his hand back faster than a leopard powered by energy drinks.

"Y... y... you okay?" stuttered DomCon, rushing round in front of Steel.

"Guard the prisoner!" ordered Jar Man, cuffing his slightly diminutive friend around the back of the head 'Gibbs fashion' in an effort to keep up appearances.

"It just gave me a little shock, that's all."

An unexpected voice rang out inside their heads.

"Stay away from their magic. Goodness only knows

what it can do.”

Giving a little nod in the direction of their falsely restrained friend, the two so-called guards pondered their next move. Suddenly they were interrupted as a tiny hole opened up, and a dark metal globe on the end of a dark metal arm thrust itself in their direction, stopping just short of 'Ginger's' face. Standing stock still, all they could do was look on. Out of the blue, a pale green, circular light, very much resembling an eye, appeared on the surface of the globe. Fighting back nerves, he held his breath.

A deeply monotonous voice spoke.

“Present your request!”

'Yikes!' thought DomCon.

Fortunately his mate was much quicker, not only on his feet, but behind his eyes.

“We were told to bring the prisoner here for interrogation.”

“Hmmmmmmmm...” answered the voice. “One moment.”

Facing straight ahead, not daring to look away, Jar Man maintained the stoic look on his face, very much hoping it resembled that of the guards they'd already passed. Moments later the utterly boring voice rang out once again.

“Access will be granted imminently.”

And with that, a loud, grating rumble filled the air, as the gigantic, magic infused disc slowly rolled back to reveal a well lit assembly hall. Swallowing hard, Jar Man strode forward, doing his best to ignore the somersaults his stomach had been performing for some time now. Giving the prisoner a shove to encourage him to move, DomCon played his part to perfection. Out of the corner of one eye he could just make out the energy infused crystal node in the far corner of the antechamber. Using all his concentration, he did his very best not to stare at it.

'Finally!' thought Steel, shrouding his mind in magic,

just as any prisoner brought forward here would do. They were now exactly where they needed to be. The end game could begin.

Passing the grenade over to his left hand as carefully as possible, he wiped his free hand against the back of the black jumper that he wore, hoping to get rid of most of the sweat, before returning the weapon to his dominant hand. It was hot here... baking hot, with absolutely no relief. The dragons around him seemed to be lapping it up, all extremely comfortable with the intense heat; if anything it seemed to give them more get up and go, make them more eager for confrontation. Following behind the three other humans, he'd lost sight of the master mantra maker and the other dragons spread out at the front when they disappeared into the darkness. Spooky, eerie, ghostly, spine-chilling were all words he felt summed up his existing situation. Moving through a place like this was bad enough, but doing so in complete and utter silence gave him the 'willies', so to speak. On top of which he kept on catching stray glimpses of some of the dragons he was travelling with, which made it all the more alarming. Part of him thought that he should have been used to them by now, and to a certain degree he was, but given that fantasy creatures he only knew from computer games, movies and books were right at this very moment alongside and behind him, his perception was all over the place. Knowing that he needed to concentrate, because almost certainly there was going to be another crazy battle similar to the one at Salisbridge, he pushed the part of him that was terrified to the core away to the back of his psyche and embraced the equal amount of him that loved every second. Wiping the sweat from his chin on his shoulder, Taibul carried on bringing up the rear of the human contingent, determined to do everything in his power to keep them, and his new found dragon allies, safe.

48 SWAMPED

Sensing the danger a split second before it hit them, George thrust out a wing and shoved Amelia Battlehard out of the way, before diving off in the opposite direction. The mammoth chunk of rubble missed the end of his tail by millimetres, crashing perilously onto the top of the magical dome protecting the fighting force beneath it. Fearing more debris falling from the roof cloaked in shadows, far out of sight, George thought he'd best tell those below him to move themselves out of the way quickly, even if it meant breaking up the safety of their shared barrier. Opening his mind to do just that, tearing a wing from a dive-bombing dark dragon with a compartmentalised part of it as he did so, it was then that he spotted what had actually happened, and the slight change in tactics his adversaries were now adopting. Clusters of dragons were picking up parts of the roof that had all ready fallen to the floor, before flying high up above the king and his group of light sided fighters and dropping said debris from a great height towards their protective shield. As the king watched dispassionately, two more dragons circled around, ready to make their bombing runs. Knowing that the shield couldn't possibly take this kind of bombardment for long, the rather angry monarch decided to take matters into his own hands.

With multiple spells constantly on the go, stretching the mana inside him this way and that without thinking about it, he applied a shocking touch to a dragon opponent that had dropped in from the sky just behind him, hoping no doubt to take him by surprise, before performing a one-hundred and eighty degree roundhouse kick to send the prehistoric monster's body flying off the top of the dome, tumbling onto some of his comrades below. Intently watching the next dragon from a group circling some way off head towards him, all the while deflecting dazzling bolts of magic from both himself and Amelia, he conjured up two potent and very different mantras and, without hesitation, despatched them towards their targets. The first, what he liked to refer to as an Arctic blast, was plain for all to see. Five frosty bolts materialised from the palm of his right hand, rocketing off into the mayhem of magic, dedicated fully to searching out their target, the next dragon on the bombing run. Simultaneously, his second attack appeared without warning above and around the rest of the dark dragons circling, all clinging onto humungous chunks of debris, waiting for their bombing runs to start. Still multitasking on an epic scale, George couldn't help but turn his attention to his adversaries far off in the air, pretty sure he'd like the result of his spectacular effort. As acid rain cascaded down on top of all of them, burning straight through their scales, annihilating their soft organs, screams, screeches and shrills of terror carried throughout the private residence, momentarily catching the attention of every being fighting there. Pleased with himself for a very small moment, he turned his attention back to the more immediate threat, having fleetingly lost track of his Arctic surprise, whilst at the same time crushing the skull of a naga who'd almost gotten the edge on the only surviving councillor down beneath him. Receiving a mental nod of thanks from his ally, he went back to tracking his frosty projectiles.

Gripping the twisted chuck of debris, steel girders, marble and all, the cruel creature thought nothing of dropping his load on top of his target, in fact it gave him great pleasure just thinking about the results. Flapping his mighty wings twice as hard as he normally would because of the load he was carrying, causing tiny vortices in the air behind their tips, his bulky cargo proved to be his undoing, because the king's mantra had one little addition that most magic being cast in and around the battlefield lacked. It had a slight semblance of sentience built into it, taking into account how magical creatures might act, defend and dodge its ultimate purpose. A hint of sadness trickled through the dragon monarch briefly as he remembered this. His ring, the magical one he had once thought of as his friend, handed down from dragon monarch to dragon monarch, had taught him this. Apparently, no other beings on the planet knew how to do it, and it was a secret each and every king was sworn to take to their grave, something he fully intended to see through. Ever since gaining this knowledge at the very beginning of his reign, part of him delighted in knowing something his friend the master mantra maker never would. A much smaller part wanted to share the secret with his estranged friend, understanding just how wondrous he'd find it, but of course he never had. Sad at missing the ring he'd reluctantly given to Tank a little earlier, he wondered where the young rugby player was, realising only now that he hadn't seen hide nor hair of him. Wherever he was, at least Manson didn't have the enigmatic and powerful band. If he got hold of it and could bend its will to his own, this battle and their lives would all be over in a split second.

Looking on with great satisfaction, George watched the result of his handiwork as yet another dark beast dropped on top of the shield in front of him, taking an almighty swipe with a lethal looking sword. Arching back so as to avoid the vicious blow, all the time with one eye on the approaching bomber, the king, letting the rage he felt bubble to the surface for just a moment, moved in with lightning quick speed, and in one fell swoop, head butted the monster so hard that every bone in his skull cracked. Flopping clumsily to the ground, the incompetent dragon's lifeless body slid down the side of the shield, once again hampering his attacking colleagues below.

Zooming in a blur far beneath their target, dodging in and out of all of the explosive magic going off around them, one of the chilly bolts got caught in the wake of a huge flaming fireball which destroyed it immediately, leaving only four of his brothers left. Of those four there wasn't a leader, only one singular purpose driving all of them on together... to destroy their target. Banking hard left in a turn so tight no being there would have been able to follow them, they approached the target on exactly the same line but from below, knowing full well they'd never be seen due to the payload he carried. Hammering every last ounce of speed from the magic that drove them on, their sentience felt fulfilled as it achieved its ultimate purpose and made contact with not only the underside of the mighty beast's wing, but along the back of its tail as well. Instantly frozen, not knowing what the hell had just happened, the hapless monster plummeted to the ground at breakneck speed, slamming itself and the debris it had been carrying into one side of the group attacking the shielded dome, providing a temporary respite for some of those inside. Thrilled at the outcome, the king turned his focus back to the air around him, lighting the next attacker on fire with a brilliant burst of flame, enhanced in no small way by the magic that was his birthright.

Colliding together again at speed, not a single magical defence in sight this time, Earth knew nothing about her surroundings or anything of the world outside her personal battle. Raking the sharp, purple coloured nails of her left hand across her father's exposed torso, she hit him hard with an uppercut to the chin as he frantically tried to grapple with her. Dazed for but a moment, it was long enough for the brown-cloaked, deranged dragon to press her advantage. Words from an alien script tumbled out of her mouth, conjuring up one of the nagas' most popular forms of magic... electricity! With ten centimetre bolts of crackling energy lancing out of eight of her fingers and both thumbs, she pressed her left hand against his bare chest, delighted at feeling the sticky, red blood that oozed from the wounds she'd just opened up with her nails. As the blood caught fire and rippled with an electric current, her right hand lunged for his throat, squeezing as tight as she could, forcing the electricity into his skin, watching in rapture the surprise on his face, the pain behind his eyes and the voltage jumping and writhing across both his upper and lower teeth. As the smell of burnt flesh and blood washed up his nostrils, Fredric let out one almighty yell, sounding like something otherworldly. Startled for a second, but not taking her eyes off the prize, a ruthless snarl developed across the bloodcurdling features of her face, forcing the purple criss-crossing lines to pump furiously, making her look more intimidating and evil, if that were at all possible.

With loss of consciousness and the inevitable death it would bring only a few seconds away at most, Fredric struggled to bring any of his magic to the fore through all the pain he felt, despite the laminium chains wrapped firmly around his chest. That was it... the laminium chains. Shying away from mounting any kind of defence now... it was far too late for that... instead he searched deep inside the metal that had turned the tide in Antarctica, hoping he could set it alight and use it to part the two of them. All he knew was that he couldn't take much more, and that he had to put some distance between them. It just might work, but it just might kill both of them, something he was willing to risk, not because he had no choice, but because he'd easily give his life to stop her reign of evil, something he should have done a long time ago. Finding what he needed at a quantum level, he shut his eyes, let down his guard and left himself to fate's mercy.

Throwing back her head full of ecstatic serpents, laughing manically as the electricity continued to burn its way into the blackened skin across her father's chest and around his scraggy throat, it would have been clear to anyone watching that she'd lost her way and would almost certainly never return. Insanity had consumed her totally and utterly.

The explosion was unparalleled. Everything that had previously taken place on the battlefield paled in comparison.

A concussive force wrapped up in a brilliant, bright, white ball of magical energy materialised briefly, before exploding out in every direction. Fredric and Earth were both tossed back into the air at an incredible speed, each of them travelling over one hundred metres, both taking the initial impact of the detonated laminium. Originating from the centre of the blast, a powerful ring of supernatural force and energy discharged across the private residence, tearing beings apart, destroying debris and what little infrastructure remained. Those paying close attention managed to fly out of the way, though most of the nagas were not so lucky, having their lives ended prematurely by something that had been designed as a last resort. Vasuki was one of the few lucky ones; having seen it coming, he'd managed to use his very unusual magic to erect a force field that had dissipated most of it. Still he'd been knocked to the ground, alongside both Flash and Manson.

For the two remaining teams of light sided dragons, it had been something of a blessing in disguise. As the horizontal ring of power cut its way across the combat zone, it killed almost everything in its path, and given how crowded the area had become with enemy forces, it was Manson's dark allies that had suffered the greatest losses. Most had died instantly; some had limbs or extremities ripped out from under them.

Those behind the shields survived by the skin of their teeth, the magical protection that they sheltered behind faltering momentarily, shimmering and sparking as the massive amount of energy threatened to overload and overwhelm. In the end, both barriers stayed strong, mainly down to the fact that the burden of each had been shared amongst those behind them. Had it just been one individual carrying the weight of the load on their own, they wouldn't have been so fortunate, something Richie was only too aware of, counting her lucky stars that she'd teamed up with Yoyo's youngsters when she had.

At the point where the magically rebuilt bridge connected with the king's residence, dozens of nagas and dark dragons that had been streaming across at Manson's summons, to join in the truly one-sided fight, lay dead, decapitated and just plain shredded. Faster than a speeding bullet, Earth thundered into their remains, landing hard enough to shatter the marble surface beneath them, the cracks and fissures themselves spreading out onto the bridge.

Over two hundred metres away, Peter's grandfather Fredric, the founder of the Crimson Guards, smashed equally hard into something solid, this time part of the wall about twenty metres along from where Peter, Richie, Janice, Hook, Yoyo and the others were sheltered.

"Nooooooooooooooooo..." screamed Peter in utter horror, watching the being he'd hoped to get to know much better land harder than a problematic Soyuz space mission.

Arms and legs at impossible angles, the mother of all burns in the shape of a hand imprinted deep within his chest, a burning, blackened band circling his neck and with no hint of the laminium that had only moments ago covered him, dust and smoke rose into the air as brilliant red blood spilled down the perfect white wall, producing what was likely the most gruesome scene from the whole sorry play.

Without hesitation, Peter sprinted across to the part of the shield that was nearest to where his grandfather lay.

"Let me out!" he cried, banging fruitlessly against the magic. "Let me out!"

Even with so many of the enemy defeated, there were still dark dragons circling in the air above them, and not just a few. Leaving the safety of the shield would be futile, something all the voices inside Richie's head agreed upon almost immediately.

Turning to face his friend with a mixture of sorrow, anger and regret etched into his almost schoolboy like features, the hockey playing dragon begged to be let out.

"I have to go out there, Rich. Please. I have to get to him."

Swallowing hard, and with the voices in her head dead set against anyone leaving, Richie Rump struggled to maintain the focus on the shield as she composed her reply.

"You can't go Pete. You'll be killed. None of us can go with you, and we'll never be able to walk the shield over there in time. Without any kind of protection, it's just not going to happen. I'm sorry."

Boiling red with rage, fury radiating from every part of him, he cried out with all his might.

"LET ME OUT!"

Hands shaking, threatening to come apart on the inside, the lacrosse playing dragon knew the voices of the others made total sense and that it was nothing short of suicide to go out there on his own. She just had to make him understand. It was then that a gentle hand laid down on her shoulder, surprising her more than a little.

Janice!

"I'll go out there with him. It'll be okay, Fu'ts-ang will protect us. We can bring his body back in here. It won't take long. Let us through. There's no other way."

Processing the information in a fraction of a second, the de facto leader of the dragons made her decision instantly, ignoring the protests of those that had taken up residence inside her mind.

"GO!" she ordered the young human bar worker. "Good luck!"

Pleading for protection from within her mind's eye, Janice hoped the space age weapon would stop killing long enough to offer up its help, but without even checking that was the case, she sprinted forwards towards Peter and the barrier, which fizzled into nothingness just as they reached it, allowing the two of them to leave the relative safety of the others. As fast as they could, they dashed towards what remained of Fredric.

Reforming the defences behind them, Richie shouted out within her mind, determined to be heard over the squabbling that had broken out.

"BE QUIET!"

Instantly they were, and most of them weren't very happy about it.

"Make sure we're ready to go. When they come back with his body, we'll move off towards the king's position."

One of the impudent young dragons spoke up.

"We should just go now and leave them here. They knew what they were doing. I thought the whole point of this was to rescue the king. Metaphorically speaking, Yoyo buried his face in his hands.

"We're going nowhere until they come back, is that clear?" growled Richie furiously. "They get left behind over my dead body. Understand?"

More than a little shaken, a tiny female voice could just be heard to squeak,

"Okay."

With the tension raised higher than a wayward balloon filled with helium, Richie focused on controlling her breathing, regulating her temperature and letting the magic from the dagger and the necklace flow through her, all the time keeping one eye on what Peter and Janice were both doing.

Gliding to a halt next to what was left of the wall, Peter reached down to lift up a slab of marble that had slipped across his grandfather's face. Tossing it carelessly off to one side, he looked back down at the being he longed to get to know better, hoping against hope that his time on earth hadn't yet drawn to an end. Right on cue, Fredric's broken, battered and bruised body started to cough and splutter, all of its own accord.

"Thank God," uttered Janice, with no small degree of relief.

"We have to get him back behind the shield," Peter declared. "If we don't, then we're all as good as dead."

Only then did he turn his attention skyward, feeling something untoward watching him from a great height. He wasn't wrong. They'd caught the attention of two ferociously scary dragons, both far bigger than Tank's huge bulk, both now starting their descent, eyes firmly fixed on their newfound prey. Instantly Peter's legs froze to the spot, while his arms shook uncontrollably. Some hero he was turning out to be. Janice was also rooted to the spot, her attention fixed intently on both prehistoric winged beasts zipping through the air towards them.

'Do something,' she willed in Peter's direction, hoping against hope that was enough to kick start him into action. It wasn't, and he remained steadily glued to the floor, mouth agog, eyes wide open.

There appeared no way out, and that death had finally found two of the many heroes here today, as both homicidal dark dragons' downward flight reached the point at which both could use their mighty flames to incinerate the childlike human forms before them. They chose not to. It was a mistake. Flying side by side, they each acquired a target, satisfied that not only would their thirst for violence and murder be quelled, but their hunger as well. Grasping each other's hands, too afraid to attempt anything else, Peter and Janice closed their eyes, already petrified beyond belief. It was a shame, that's for sure, because they missed a move so superbly executed that it should go down in dragon lore, providing that the light side lived long enough to record that history. Out of nowhere, a shimmering, speeding bolt of brilliant, white frost cut through the molecules of the air, parting the very atoms themselves. Fast didn't begin to describe it, with it making most bullets look like snails. Not even aware of the danger they were in, both dark dragons opened their mouths to the fullest extent and savoured the expectation of their next meal. If kebab was what they dreamed of, then kebab it would be. Taking both dragons sideways on at ninety degrees, Fu-ts'ang hammered into them with no thought of his own safety. Like a knife through water, that's how easy it was for the centuries old weapon to pierce the dragon scales of both beings, impaling them both on the blade and compressing their bodies with the force of his approach, nailing both beings to the marble wall, slightly further along from where Fredric lay half-buried in debris. Surprised and more than a little grateful, the two young lovers opened their eyes, astonished to find a dragon kebab, with their friend, the magnificent Fu-ts'ang, the skewer.

"Oh my God," announced Janice, her voice wobbly, her hands shaking beyond belief.

"Wow!" was all that Peter could get out, looking at the devastation the ice shrouded weapon had caused. "How in the..." he didn't get to finish, because the realisation of why he was there, and what he had to do, hit him head on.

Fredric! Ignoring the impaled dragons bleeding profusely and wailing more than a little, the hockey player turned around and started pulling the biggest chunks of rubble off his grandfather, determined to help get him back to his feet. As Fredric's moans and groans became more incomprehensible, Peter paused momentarily and, forgetting all the rubble for just two seconds, placed both his hands on his grandfather's forehead, pumping as much healing magic as he dared into the stricken dragon. It had no effect... nothing! Leaving one hand on his forehead, continuing to heal, with the other he grabbed more of the debris and tossed it away to one side, all too aware of his surroundings and the continued danger they were all in.

High above, wicked, dark dragons schemed and plotted

telepathically as they continuously circled the battlefield, looking for the best way to answer the rallying cry their leader had already let out. Some had their eyes on the dome of magic users on the ground, guarded by a force shield and two dragons from above, while a few others had witnessed the brutal skewering of their colleagues only a short while ago and had vowed revenge on those that had sought to take away their brothers in arms.

From only a short distance away, Richie Rump, impromptu leader and infamous lacrosse hotshot, continued to power the shield that kept them all safe and host the array of different dragon personalities deep inside her head. At the moment, most of them seemed to be bickering, mainly about Peter and Janice's reckless actions in leaving the confined safety of the barrier. She hadn't said it yet, but there just wasn't time for all this. How could she make them see that? With her focus spread thin... powering the shield, listening to all the voices inside her and keeping an eye on her best friend and his partner in crime, her composure started to crumble, threatening to yield to her fiery temper that was an intrinsic part of her very nature. Worried for her friends, the obvious answer to it all popped right into her head totally out of nowhere.

"If we're going to move the shield to save the king and his cohorts anyway, can we not just walk it on over to where Peter, Janice and Fredric are now, on the way? Surely that would make sense, buy us a little time, keep them safe and rally a few more beings to our cause?"

The silence was deafening. Moments passed, with what seemed like brains whirring.

Finally, the young female dragon who'd instigated the plan in the first place, spoke up.

"We should be okay to go, and there's no reason not to do that. In fact, it makes perfect sense... everybody ready?"

Lots of virtual nods and yeps later, Richie could feel a

little more weight from the shield being taken from her, the burden spreading out amongst them a little more evenly.

"Remember," shouted the young female dragon throughout their minds, "head over towards Bentwhistle and the two others first, and then we cut across the battlefield in a direct line towards the king. Be aware of your responsibilities, and if you have a problem, share it immediately. Good luck!"

And with that, and at walking pace, the whole of the shield started to move what was effectively sideways, very slowly getting closer to the stricken Fredric, Peter, Janice, and Fu'-ts'ang who was still skewering the two near dead dragons to the white, marble wall.

Janice, oblivious to pretty much everything else, opened herself up to her newly found friend, the weapon that had just saved them from a very gruesome end.

"Are you okay?" she whispered, wondering exactly what kind of response she'd get.

It took more than a while for the answer to come.

"What you did was exceedingly reckless. You could very easily have both been killed. What on earth were you thinking?"

"I'm pretty sure neither of us were thinking, only acting on instinct. The dragon buried beneath the rubble is Peter's grandfather. He's been imprisoned in Antarctica for decades, and was one of the ones that showed up out of the blue to rescue us."

"And might I say, what a fine job he's done," fumed the frost shrouded weapon sarcastically.

"There's no need to be like that. We all need to stick together. Getting uppity at each other will help no one."

Suitably berated, and more importantly knowing the young woman was right, Fu-ts'ang apologised immediately, informing the bar worker that the dragons he'd impaled on the wall were still alive, and that he was reluctant to pull out and let them free at the moment.

"What about you?" she replied. "You can't stay like that indefinitely. And besides, we need you in the fight."

"When the relative safety that's approaching you arrives, I'll let them drop to the floor and rejoin the fight. You didn't think you were getting rid of me that easily did you?"

"Never!" she answered, only then noticing Richie and the shield creeping ever closer.

"Go and help your love," ordered the weapon. "If you need me, call out. Once I'm free of these two, I'll try and help cut you and your friends a path towards the dragon king, at least I assume that's where you're headed."

"I suppose it is. I haven't really been informed."

"For now little one, all I'll say is that it's been a privilege, an honour and a pleasure. Like I said, if you need me... YELL!"

And with that, their link went dead.

Rushing over to her love, immediately she started helping with the rubble that was half burying Fredric. As she knelt down beside Peter, for just a split second their eyes met and through the dirt and dust in the air, despite the danger they were all in, with only a look, their hearts intertwined. There and then they knew that there'd be nobody else for either of them, and that they were meant to be together forever, however long that would be given the seriousness of everything going on around them. Content, at least for now, both turned back and with everything they had, tried to free Peter's last known relative. If only he knew the truth!

Some of those high up above had witnessed everything, including the weapon that seemed to have a mind of its own, being stuck firmly in both dragons it had skewered, and, by the looks of things, the wall. Instantly a decision was made, and four psychotic dragons peeled away from their holding pattern, heading swiftly for the ground.

Eyes closed, firmly grasping the dagger, ignoring the heat radiating out from both of the mind bogglingly valuable laminium items, ever so slowly she stepped in the direction of her friends, feeling the shield following all around her, To say it was odd was something of an understatement. It felt as though they were all trapped inside a jelly that was being dragged along with them. It wasn't, it was the shield, and it wasn't moving nearly as fast as she would have hoped. In the middle of all this, her danger sense screamed out at her. Immediately becoming ultra alert, she scanned the area, quickly determining the threat: more of the enemy coming in from above, and she knew that their current pace wouldn't get them to Peter, Janice and Fredric in time.

"Stop!" she shouted within her head for all to hear. They did.

"What's going on?" asked the female in charge.

"We need to all squeeze up as much as possible and extend the shield out in the direction of our friends... NOW! They've got company coming in from up above and won't stand a chance if we don't act."

"Knowing just how futile arguing with Richie would be, and encouraged to do so by a little nudge from Yoyo, the youngsters within the shield, Yoyo and Hook, all bunched up towards Richie, leaving a huge area of barrier behind them deserted.

Within her mind, the lacrosse playing superstar opened herself up, not only to the massive amounts of magic flowing through her, but to Yoyo's young band of rebels, hoping to hell that once again they knew what they were doing. Peter's life quite literally depended on it.

At the same time as the shield around the area with nobody in it began to constrict, the shimmering, transparent barrier in front of Richie began to stretch out in the direction of her friends. Looking up as far as she dared, Richie couldn't tell what was going to reach her friends first... their defensive barrier, or brutal death by murderous dragon. It was going to be close.

Ridding Fredric's body of as much rubble as they dared, and only too aware of what was going on, instinctively both Janice and Peter grabbed one of his arms, and without any kind of formality or warning started dragging his broken body towards the safety of the approaching shield, all the time keeping their eyes on the ground, not wanting to see what was hurtling towards them from the air.

Able to see what the despicable shapes on the ground were retreating towards, all four dark dragons poured on as much speed as they could muster, determined not to let their prey, and lunch, escape the grisly fate they had in store for it.

Hauling for all they were worth, ignoring the thick trail of brilliant red blood Fredric's legs left on the stone covered ground, and his babbling wails and cries of pain, Peter and Janice gave everything they had to reach the safety of the magical barrier the others sheltered behind.

Shuffling forwards, feeling the hot breath of those behind her tickling the back of her neck, Richie Rump assessed the dynamic of the situation with all her limited experience and immediately came to only one conclusion. They weren't going to make it. Not by far, but they simply weren't moving quick enough. Continuing forwards as fast as she dared, her focus shifted. Contracting the shield behind them, so that it closed in around Yoyo's group of dragons, instantly lessened the power she needed to draw from the laminium, momentarily anyway. Knowing it was but a fleeting pause in proceedings, the lacrosse playing dragon exhaled deeply in a sigh of relief, before once again closing her eyes.

Four wide-eyed predators moving at a mind numbing blur were but a split second away from annihilating their prey, the vicious snarls of delight and victory matched only by their stomachs rumbling in anticipation of something tasty to eat for the first time in a while. Savouring their triumph, each of them opened their jaws as wide as they could, brought their legs forward and opened up their wings wide, to provide some resistance and slow their rapid descent. As their shadows cloaked the ground in and around their quarry, a stuttered crackle pierced their ears.

As every atom of her body drew in magic from the necklace and the dagger, her mind projected what she needed out onto the battlefield, using every ounce of her impressive force of will. With a slight shimmer and a rustle, the magical barrier extended out in front of her, enveloping her friends, providing much needed solace. A 'BANG' akin to the sound of two vehicles colliding at speed jolted reality all around them. Straight away it was followed by three more, as the proceeding dark dragons followed their friend, smashing straight into the shield, all four knocked totally unconscious.

Wondering whether or not it was safe to leave the quartet of prehistoric beasts alive knowing that they could come back to haunt them at practically any time, Richie was secretly glad when the decision was taken out of her hands. With just the tiniest of wiggles, Fu-ts'ang backed up out of the two skewered dragons, their corpses dropping forcefully to the floor and, in a stunning display of aerial manoeuvrability, proceeded to stab each of the unconscious dragons on top of the barrier, precisely through their hearts, leaving them well and truly dead, and exactly nothing to chance.

Able to take her mind ever so slightly off powering the shield, Richie felt a flood of relief as her anguish faded to nothing and she was able to ask her friends how they were.

"He's hurt pretty bad," announced Peter, referring to his grandfather.

Squeezing through the others, Yoyo knelt down next to Fredric, shrouding both of them with his wings, giving the young hockey playing dragon a wink and a nod.

"He'll be okay. Just give me a few minutes."

"Do we have that long?"

"I don't know," replied Yoyo. "Do we?"

Before Richie had a chance to respond, the young female dragon who'd come up with the plan and had sorted everyone out, cut in.

"I'm not sure we do have that long. They're being overrun. Every second we waste puts them in increasing danger."

Yoyo and Peter shared a look, neither of them wanting to endanger the king.

"What about if you carry him, while I heal him?" urged Yoyo. "That way we can help with his recovery and head out towards the king without delay... the best of both worlds if you like." Keen to assist, he did briefly wonder how he was going to lift Fredric's rather impressive human shaped body aloft. Even enhanced with magic, it seemed a tall order. But he didn't want to let anybody down, and so in one fell swoop, ignoring the thick, red blood that oozed from the gashes on his well defined chest, he lifted up the man he loved dearly, despite barely knowing him at all, cradled him in his arms and began to follow the others as Yoyo healed. Protected by the magical barrier, they shuffled off in the direction of the king and his small legion of followers.

49 COMMITTED TO THE END

Hunkered down behind yet more of their dead brethren, to a dragon, man and woman, they all fought down the nausea that threatened to ride up their throats and give away their position, so overwhelming was the smell from all the guts and gore. With little fuss and more than a few stealthy killings, against all odds they'd made it this far, and from their hiding place in the shadows could now see the Fleet Street entrance to the building that housed the giant crystal node, the one that they hoped would help them re-establish communication across the planet, the one their friends were currently inside. All they could do was wait, and pray that things somewhere deep within the building were going exactly to plan. If Steel set off the mantra they'd know, because the results of the magic would be visible even from here, which would be their signal to attack with everything they had.

It was dark... oddly dark. Immediately all three of them switched to their magical infrared vision, hoping to cut through the clutter and get a better idea of just where they were and just what they were dealing with. Strangely, it didn't help very much. Steel knew why. MAGIC! He didn't know what kind of magic, and couldn't explain just how he knew, but he'd never been more certain of anything in his life. It was almost as if he could taste it on the air itself. Something here was wrong, very, very wrong. Things, he thought, were not going to be as easy as he'd hoped.

Swallowing nervously, mainly for effect but partly because that's how he felt, he assumed whoever was already in here could see him perfectly well and, knowing exactly what kind of an advantage that gave them, he hoped to hell the other two were ready for what was about to play out. They'd all need their wits about them if they were to come out of this alive.

Shambling forward, bound by his restraints, appearing resigned to his fate, Steel, head bowed low, used his brilliant dragon eyes to give him a two hundred and seventy degree view around him. And he didn't like what he saw. Sitting at control stations, barely visible in the supernatural gloom that hung heavy in the air like a cool, morning mist stuck to the surface of a river, dragon cadavers, broken, battered and ravaged, littered the room. They must have been taken by surprise somehow, which in itself surprised him because they were nearly all at their work stations, most of them journalists, most of them seemingly in the process of typing up a story for whatever telepathic paper they worked for, no doubt to go out later on that day via the crystal node they'd come here to gain access to. One or two had even tried to write messages in their own blood on the screens they sat in front of, after the vicious acts that had eventually so disgustingly taken their lives. Fury and revulsion at the despicable acts raged throughout his body, trying to tempt him into breaking free of the false restrains with a view to gaining revenge for these poor beings who'd just happened to be in the wrong place at the wrong time. Logically he knew better, knew to bide his time and get a clearer understanding of the situation before he tried to act. Allowing his hands and arms to shake a little, knowing that's what his enemy would have expected of him in a situation like this, he took as much of it in as he possibly could, in his mind readying Gee Tee's mantra, really, really looking forward to using it to destroy these sick sons of bitches. As the glowing crystal node appeared out of obscurity the further he strode into the room, looking very much like a giant, green, glowing, crystalline egg, hope at regaining the kingdom buoyed him just a little.

Straight faces were permanently engraved on their false human forms, with both friends realising that their lives, at this point in the operation, probably depended on it. Ready to act in a split second, but outwardly appearing docile, the two of them couldn't help but wonder what barbaric acts had taken place. Like their shackled friend, they too wanted revenge. When it came, and they knew it would, there would be no stopping them.

Through the murkiness stepped a tall, human, female figure, clad fully in a black, figure hugging jump suit, short, spiky, flaming copper hair adorning her head, both eyes resembling the event horizon of a black hole. If danger had an emoji, she would most certainly be it.

It was all that Jar Man and DomCon could do to hold on to their composure, against the fear and just downright evil that radiated off her. Bowing their heads in respect, they waited for her to speak.

"What is this?" she demanded, her honeyed words reverberating in and around the murk that surrounded them.

Taking the tiniest step forward so as to address her properly, Jar Man summoned up all the courage he could muster, and without faltering, replied,

"A spy we captured in the grounds, no doubt scouting out the location."

"No doubt," she spat, "No doubt! Who the hell are you to make that distinction?"

"I... I... I... I meant no offense," stammered Jar Man, genuinely terrified.

"You'd better not or I'll have your liver torn from your flesh where you stand. Understood?"

Nodding profusely, all the big dragon could manage was a squeaky, "Yes" in reply.

Shielded from the outside by the most powerful spells he knew, DomCon had already lined up some offensive mantras within his head, figuring they might just be needed in a hurry.

"Has he been interrogated?"

"No... no... no... not yet he hasn't."

"Why have you brought him to me then? He's of no use here. We have professionals for just such a job."

"I... I... I... I was told to do so."

"Really..." she left it hanging in the air, expectancy of boundless possibilities floating throughout the room.

Steel wasn't fooled, not for one second. It wasn't only her killer looks that had him worried. Undoubtedly she was dangerous beyond belief, he could feel it from the off, and was pretty sure both of the others did as well. Standing exactly where he needed to be, the laminium ball captain prepared Gee Tee's mantra in his head and gathered up all his force of will. All he needed now was for Jar Man and DomCon to get between him and the crystal node so that he could unleash the explosive spell whilst at the same time keeping them safe. Not willing to give them a nudge telepathically, or even the merest glance for fear of getting caught and exposing their plan, he hoped the two would take a hint now they were here, and manoeuvre themselves into position between him and the crystal node, post haste. Time, he knew, was running out, not only for them, but the rest of the world as well.

Huddled together as one, all hugging each other against the backdrop of decapitated dragon corpses, bloody entrails, bowels and innards spread out around them, there was no concern about inappropriateness, or the fact that their friendships, up until a few days ago, had been solely based on their sports and the ground in which they played. A bond had formed between all four of them ever since the moment they'd followed Richie down those steps beneath the Poultry Cross and entered the dragon domain proper. A life changing moment for each and every one, they now had no secrets from each other, constantly supporting one another where able, their only desire to see this through in one piece and help their prehistoric comrades defeat the scourge of evil that threatened civilisation both above and below ground. As terror and fear swirled around the four humans hidden in the middle of the dragon force, and with courage in short supply, their dependence on each other was something akin to the sports they participated in on the surface. Impossible to win a team sport individually, they knew the value of working together as one in a combined effort to achieve the right outcome.

Strolling casually around Steel's recently formed body, gazing intently at his wings, belly and chest, 'Red', as Jar Man had started to refer to her in his head, suspiciously eyed the newly formed scales across the prisoner's chest, unsure of what to make of them or how they contributed to this unusual situation.

Knowing that he was being watched from all sides, and with Jar Man having turned somewhat to allow 'Red' her inspection, Steel caught his eye and ever so slowly cocked his head to one side, hoping that his disguised friend might take the hint. A cursory returning wink told him he had. All they had to do now was find a way to pull it off without their adversaries realising what was going on.

BAM! The swiftest punch in the world caught Steel directly above the kidneys, sending waves of nerve shredding pain rippling throughout his body, dropping him instantly to his knees. So brutal was the unexpected violence, both DomCon and Jar Man immediately took two steps back, despite wanting to help their friend and get into a position for him to unleash the magic.

Gulping in huge breaths of air, writhing in mind bending agony, the laminium ball captain struggled to wave away what had just happened. His whole body felt like it had been hit with the full force of a giant's hammer. Nothing now made sense, the letters from the words readied in his mind scattered throughout his consciousness. There was no spell, no mantra, and no magic. For now, it had been blasted away, replaced by distress and misery. Curling up into a ball, his mind retreated into the darkest depths it could find, as more punches of similar ferocity rained down. Darkness replaced light, as hope vanished completely.

50 RACIST

Bolstered by his limited supply of magic, Peter carried his grandfather's broken body in his arms, marching behind Richie who was leading them off in the direction of the king. Walking next to him, Yoyo continued to heal the significant injuries whilst on the move, a type of precision healing he'd not really had to do before, but improvisation was his forte and something he wasn't unaccustomed to. Perilous didn't do it justice. Whilst not moving particularly fast, the persistent bombardment constantly drew their attention away from the rubble, debris and dismembered dragon corpses that they all had to negotiate on the floor. Twice having almost tripped, with one of his charges catching him at the very last moment, Yoyo was saved from a full-on face planting. That wasn't the only danger. As predicted, their opponents had tried to infiltrate the shield by lying on the floor, playing dead. Fortunately the quick thinking dragon youngsters were as good as he'd described, and had seen the ploy long before the creatures in question had the chance to do any damage. They'd been routinely dispatched, dead and torn apart long before the moving shield passed over them. So far the plan to move towards the king was a success, with Richie's mind hosting all of the consciousnesses working like a dream. It wouldn't be long now.

As the healing magic flowed into Fredric, he not only became more lucid, but his injuries started to repair themselves. The gash on his chest closed back together, after copious amounts of red blood retreated back inside his human form. Black charring that criss-crossed his chest in the shape of the laminium chains he'd had to sacrifice in order to get away, and the burnt skin around his neck, slowly disappeared, whilst the bones in his broken arm and ribs knitted themselves back together, all under Yoyo's expert guidance.

Aware enough now of what was going on around him, he stared into Peter's eyes, something he'd been desperate to do for so long, part of the motivation that had helped keep him sane in the icy hellhole of Antarctica. As he motioned to be put down, Peter obliged as gently as he could. Unsteady on his feet, it didn't stop the founder of the Crimson Guards from clasping his grandson by the elbow and pulling him in tight. Words wouldn't do that instant justice, a moment both dragons would cherish for the rest of their natural lives, however long that might be.

"My boy..." was all that Fredric could manage, as brilliant, glistening teardrops streamed down his face.

"Grandfather!" the youngster uttered with a certain sense of fulfilment. "I'm so sorry. You shouldn't have been there for so long. When Flash said he'd found you, I tried to get them to launch a rescue mission, but the Council wouldn't have any of it."

"Slow down, son. It's alright. I understand, and it certainly isn't your fault. Besides, we have more pressing matters on our hands. Let's just concentrate on what's in front of us."

Nodding, the young hockey playing dragon acceded to his grandfather's wisdom.

At exactly that moment, a delicate, little pale hand appeared between them, offering a transparent bottle to the barely recovered Fredric. It was Janice, offering out some water she figured might be much needed, something she'd purloined from one of Yoyo's charges.

"Thanks," declared Peter's grandfather, before downing the whole bottle in one, still constantly on the move with all the others.

"And just who would you be?" he asked, tossing away the empty water bottle on the floor.

"This is Janice and she's..."

"A HUMAN!" Fredric snarled.

Scared at the look that had just come over the human

shaped dragon's face, the young bar worker retreated back as far as she dared.

"What the hell is a human doing here, in our domain?"

Sensing the tension in the situation, Hook sidled up beside Janice in an effort to give her some moral support.

"TWO OF THEM!" Fredric bellowed, incredulous.

"Grandfather... calm down. PLEASE!" urged Peter.

"What the hell is going on?" the Crimson Guards founder persisted. "Has the world changed this much since I've been away? They should not, under any circumstances, be here!"

"But..." started Peter.

"No buts! Humans shouldn't be anywhere near our world. It just isn't right!"

Head downcast, looking almost tearful, young Peter felt torn apart inside as the battle raged on around them all. Confusion, trepidation, fear, anger and every mixture of love possible surged throughout his body, rolling the insides of his stomach, forcing his legs to weaken. Hearing his grandfather speak like this about the woman he loved, shattered his heart in two, decimating him entirely.

Stepping forward, Hook had heard enough. But Yoyo's outstretched wing prevented him from getting any further.

"Fredric," ventured Yoyo softly. "You know not of what you speak, and given the trouble we find ourselves in, there isn't time to bring you up to speed in detail. Needless to say, those here without fangs and flames are valued as much as those with. While I wasn't there personally, I do know that Janice and Hook here helped provide a rescue, without which, none of us would be here. Without them, Flash would be dead, and you'd still be rotting away in that prison cell in Antarctica. There's more to it than all of that, but take my word, both these beings are as worthy as any dragon I've ever met. They're courageous, fearless, cunning and ruthless. Oh, as well, that weapon out there that saved your life... she's the one controlling and guiding it. Without her, you'd be well and truly dead at least twice over. Please... take my word on all of this."

All the time on the move, gaining ground on the besieged monarch, Fredric ran both freshly repaired hands through his long, straggly hair, taking in everything that was so new, eyeing his grandson, noticing the distress he'd caused him.

Looking up from his self pity and emotional conundrum, courage from somewhere inside he didn't realise he had, raised its head.

"They're my friends, grandfather, and I love each of them to bits." (One a little more than the other... obviously.) "As Yoyo's already explained, we wouldn't have this fighting opportunity without them."

Considering his kin's words, the hulking founder of the Crimson Guards brushed himself off, before turning to address both Janice and Hook, towering over them as he did.

"You both have my sincerest apologies. You must excuse my lack of manners; I'm afraid that the events of today are proving to be a little too much for me. That said... it's no excuse for the way I've acted towards you both. If what I've been told is true, and I've no reason to doubt it, then it will be an honour to fight beside you. The very last thing I am is a racist, and in the past I've fought tooth and nail to protect humankind. I'd give my life in a heartbeat in an effort to keep humanity safe. It was, for me, just a shock realising what you were, and that you were down here fighting beside those of my kind. In my day, that wouldn't have been possible under any circumstances. You have my thanks, and once again my sincerest apologies."

Leaning forward, Fredric grasped Janice's delicate little hand, raised it up and planted a faint kiss on the back of it. After that, it was Hook's turn. Hoping that he wouldn't get the same treatment, he was duly reassured when Fredric clasped his hand in the mother of all handshakes. Donald Trump would have met his match with this one, was all that he could think.

Pleased with the outcome, and proud of the class his grandfather had shown in admitting being wrong, a major doubt sought to engulf the young hockey playing dragon. If he'd acted like this on finding humans battling alongside them, how on earth would he respond when he found out about his love for the petite blonde bar worker? Scared almost out of his skin, he shared a split-second look with the love of his life before turning away to face Richie, and beyond the shield, the king and his comrades. As they edged closer, there was just so much for him to worry about.

Dazed, confused and momentarily crippled, Earth lifted her spinning head up as far as it would go... not very far as it turned out. Coughing violently, mainly due to the dust she'd swallowed, she tried to stand up from beneath the debris that pinned her into position. Nothing moved, not even a jot. Summoning her magic, she let rip with a kinetic burst that should have, in theory, thrown all the rubble off her. Nothing happened. Remaining motionless and paralysed, inside a tiny seed of fear started to spread its shoots throughout her, weaving this way and that, vying for control.

Licking one of the warm offshoots of blood that tricked across her lips, desperately she tried to calm herself. Losing her temper here and now would not benefit her in the slightest, she knew. Sifting past her thumping head, she attempted to call on just the slightest spark of magic, but her focus was shot. Here and now, it just wasn't going to happen. She was totally and utterly trapped.

Suddenly, from above and behind, a minute scraping noise caught her attention. This was it she thought... the end of the road. One of her enemies no doubt, looking to capitalise on her precarious predicament. Anxiously trying to turn her head this way and that, frantically attempting to catch a glimpse of whoever it was, a wave of relief washed through her when a thick, toothy jaw slithered into sight, followed instantly by its double. Her familiar!

"Good girl, good girl!" she exclaimed. "Come to help your mistress have you? Your timing couldn't be better. See if you can move some of the bigger chunks of rubble will you, and I'll try and work myself free from this end."

Slithering across her chest in an 'S' shaped motion, the familiar chose the biggest piece of marble it could find, and widening both its jaws as far as they would go, grasped hold of it, pulling it off to one side. This it started to repeat, over and over again.

Under siege, raging mad and constantly on the move, Manson was a mass of conflicting emotions. This should have been over by now. Not only should the coronation have already taken place, with him crowned king, and Earth, his new wife, queen, but all of their enemies should have been vanquished forever, except that blessed dragon imposter George, remaining alive for him to torture for as long as it amused him. Instead though, here he was bounding, leaping and somersaulting out of the way of this blasted silver dragon that had sprung up out of nowhere, from the human shaped body that bloody naga king had been tending to. It just wasn't fair, or right.

Pinned down momentarily by a wayward piece of rocky debris, he fought back against his fear as a huge, raging fireball, spat at him from said dragon, headed his way at speed. Falling back on his experience and knowing that there was no time to avoid the very obvious attack, with closed eyes he opened his mind, found the guttural words of the unfamiliar language, and put all his willpower behind the effort. Through the sheer force of his psyche, he compelled his eyes back open, determined to face the consequences head on. Within only a few metres now, the heat scorched his face, that's how close it was. And then, suddenly, the roaring comet of superheated magic skipped in an instant, off to one side, missing him by the width of a fly's tongue. Forcing himself to swallow and shaking his foot free of the rubble he'd got caught up in, a short-lived flashback rendered a bright green Astroturf pitch right before his very eyes. Of course, he thought, harking back to the day when he'd taken Bentwhistle down a peg or two in the hockey match they'd played against each other, when both Salisbridge teams had met during a supposed friendly. Despite having already used his magic during the course of the game, his team were on the verge of losing as he approached the goal. Wanting to make sure of securing at least a draw, he could remember in stunning detail casting the spell that he'd just used as he wound up to hit the hockey ball. Following its trajectory all the way, pure delight and ecstasy had rocked him back and forth at the ear splitting sound of the ball hitting the backboard of the goal. Not only that, but the confusion Bentwhistle had suffered as a result of not being able to stop his magically driven shot, was by far the icing on the cake. Right there and then, he'd lost his temper and given the hopelessly naive dragon a hint of what was to come, something by all rights he really shouldn't have. It hadn't, however, affected what happened next, only the freak weather had done that.

Surviving once again by the skin of his teeth, the heat from the attack searing his chin smarting like hell, his temper, with yet more cause to erupt, threatened to spill out. Unfortunately there wasn't time for that, because that damned naga king was working in conjunction with the dragon, and both of them together had him almost pinned down. Thoughts of the past fortunately presented him with another option. Grunting out parts of the nagas' decidedly basic language, in conjunction with intricate finger movements, his mind harked back to his time in charge at Cropptech, the company he hated so much. It had amused him no end to observe the lengths the suspicious Bentwhistle had gone to in an effort to figure out just how he'd been avoiding the security cameras in and around the huge corporate facility. In a million years, he'd have never worked it out. Unlike the almost backward dragons living beneath the surface in their precious domain, the nagas had harnessed their God-given abilities in much more advanced ways, one of which included an incredible piece of supernatural wizardry. On finding out what they were going to teach him all that time ago, at first he'd thought it a joke, a prank, something he had little time for. But no, it was real, and had been demonstrated to him there and then. You see, this one spell, the one he'd used to avoid Peter and all the cameras at Cropptech, was a teleportation spell. Limited to a range of about seventy metres or so, it could easily bypass physical objects and transport its user that sort of distance in any direction, up, down, left right, pretty much anywhere. All the caster had to do was imagine exactly where it was he or she intended to end up and then BOOM, it would happen in an instant, the only drawback being that it was hugely magically intensive, consuming more for every metre it moved the user. Magic that allowed him to move about covertly then, is exactly what he used now to avoid the imminent attack, transporting himself only a short distance this time, looking on as half a dozen icy missiles zinged past his left shoulder, slamming into the ground, forming their own slippery little lake in the middle of all the action.

Cursing himself for coming over to investigate the peculiar turn of events, he wished to hell that he'd stayed surrounded by the subordinates in his army. Briefly going on the offensive, bright blue and purple arcs of electricity rocketed from his fingertips in the direction of the naga king, forcing the serpent-like beast to use all the coils in its body to roll unnaturally out of the way. Tumbling head over heels to avoid more magical attacks from the well armed and informed silver dragon, reluctantly he brushed away his pride and telepathically sent out a call for help to all and sundry. Knowing that he only needed to last a matter of seconds before dozens of reinforcements arrived, spurred him on to go on the attack once again. So blasting the winter lake that had formed on the ground from the ice bolts with a huge fireball of his own, he somersaulted up and over the gigantic plume of steam that erupted from it, and hiding behind it, readied ever more offensive magic, determined to bring these insolent whelps to bear when his backup arrived.

Nagas and dark dragons of every shape and size flooded out of the council building and onto the courtyard adjacent to it, the serpent-like creatures queuing up to cross the bridge and join the action, while the dragons waited patiently for enough air space to take flight, that's how crowded it was. Manson's magical call to arms had ignited the supernatural power within all these beings, forcing them to do their master's bidding, whether they liked it or not. Very few, if any, of Manson's attacking force remained in the council building, which would have been unwise on a tactical level, especially given the current infestation of magical and mythical creatures slowly scouring what was left of it, attracted to the scent of magic, following it wherever it would lead them, keen to sate their hunger, all now working together as one. Somebody, at some point, was in for a big surprise.

"If you let me out now, I can go and help them," suggested Fredric to everybody within the supernatural barrier that edged ever closer to the king's position with every second that passed.

"I can't lower the barrier, not even for a split second," replied Richie, slightly more relaxed with channelling all the magic with help from Yoyo's band of young dragons. "Our best bet is to roll on over and absorb them into our shield. If we do that, they'll instantly be protected, and then we can start on the offensive. Letting you out now would place all of us in unnecessary danger."

Despite appearing agitated outwardly, Fredric knew she was right.

"How else can I help?" he asked, genuinely wanting to play his part.

"Keep an eye on the so called corpses we're travelling over. Make sure there are no surprises left in or on them, or that any of them are still living. I'm sure by now their forces can guess our plan, and would like nothing else but to try and stop us reaching our goal at all costs."

Nodding in agreement, Peter's grandfather sidled up to Richie at the front of the shield and, after recognising his own dagger and fuelled by magic, checked every single corpse, naga or dragon, to make sure nothing was missed. Inch by inch, they edged closer to their leader, and the dragon Fredric thought of as his best friend.

Things were getting mightily hairy for the remaining councillor and the King's Guard soldiers fighting in the circle beneath the monarch and Amelia Battlehard. Besieged by dragons and nagas as far as the eye could see, as soon as they cut down one of the dreaded beasts, another would instantly appear in its place. There was no let up, no break, no respite... something had to give, it was inevitable.

A timely kinetic mantra helped her use the air surrounding the dragon's head to warp and crush the skull beyond belief; another enemy collapsed to the floor dead. Unable to even take a breath before yet another took its place, this time of the serpent-like variety, in the blink of an eye Dixie Sadheart reinforced her part of the collective shield, deflected away a barrage of pink and white magic she didn't recognise, and dug deep into what remained of her reserves of mana. So busy was she lining up spell after spell, mantra after mantra, that she didn't even have time to be worried that her reserves were almost depleted. Using a skill she liked to think of as 'ignite', the words inside her wrapped themselves in a good deal of her willpower, and instantly the naga in front of her burst into superhot yellow, blue and red flames. Batting them away madly with its tiny little hands, the beast in question rolled off to one side as the scales around its monstrous face started to melt. Readying her next attack deep within her mind, a particularly vicious mental probe that should in theory strike one of the monsters dead without anyone knowing why, a sharp, piercing pain ripped through her knee and lower leg. Stunned, shocked and panicked all at once, the fearless and courageous dragon looked down past her belly, to find one of the supposed dark dragon corpses chewing on the lower part of her extremity. Trying desperately to shake it off, her momentary lapse in judgement and the pain caused her to forget about her part of the shield. As it sizzled into nothingness, naga arms, teeth and whole bodies tore through the gap, overwhelming poor Dixie, who died almost immediately, whilst infiltrating those light sided dragons' last bastion of safety.

Blowing out an intensely powerful jet of fire that scorched an approaching attacker's wing, forcing her to spiral out of control, smashing firmly into the marble some way away, Amelia Battlehard immediately realised what had happened beneath her. Assessing the situation, not wanting to leave the dragon she was there to protect without a wingdragon, it was only when a telepathic 'GO!' from the monarch entered her mind that she chose to act. Instinctively, she slid down the side of the shield, coming to a halt next to the gap Dixie had left. Brutally smashing the hilt of her stolen sword into the side of a naga's head, rewarded by an almighty 'CRACK', she kicked his body back into the crowd, moved across to plug the opening, and with one effective command, ignited a shield of her own design. In only a few moments after the breach,

Captain Battlehard had taken the deceased dragon's place, once again shoring things up. But there was a problem. In the time it had taken for her to get there, some of the enemy had gotten inside their impenetrable fortress, and were now attacking the other dragons from the interior of the dome. This did not bode well.

Much too slow for her liking, it was at least working, and because of that, she fed nothing but positive feelings into her link with the familiar that she loved more than any other being on the planet. With a particularly nasty and heavy rock having been removed, she could at least appreciate being able to take a full breath once again, even though it hurt like hell.

'Broken ribs,' she thought to no one but herself. So, with a few full breaths, her head began to clear and her thinking straightened out. Moments later, her magic was there, where it had always been. Wasting no time, she flooded her body, in particular the legs she knew were there but couldn't feel, with all the power she dared, ordering her familiar to slither off to one side. After it had complied, she used a forceful kinetic blast to shake the remaining debris off. It worked a treat. Now to find her bloody father and finish what had already been started.

A female's life was always one of compromises, constraints and in general a juggling act, Amelia Battlehard thought as she rammed her stolen sword up through the jawbone of one of the usurpers that had infiltrated their safe haven, whilst at the same time fighting off a stream of nagas hurling strange magic that even she didn't recognise at her side of the dome. Bad enough those two events on their own, she also had the task of keeping an eye on George, the king, fighting solo above her: multi, multi, multi tasking as she liked to think of it. Inside herself she knew they were running out of time. There were just too many of the enemy to continue to stave off. They needed either a rescue or an escape plan; neither looked very likely though. And with that last thought, whilst assaulting yet another naga, looking straight out in front of her, in the distance, through the horde of attacking serpents, she caught sight of something incredibly unusual and heart warming. A moving shield filled with the dragons she'd last seen cowering over the other side of the battlefield, was only a matter of moments from reaching their position. Briefly her heart leapt, but given everything she was trying to deal with, it really didn't have the time to do it properly.

'Just maybe,' she thought, 'we might get the tiniest bit of respite.'

Throughout all the centuries he'd inhabited the planet, and all the battles and dirty deeds he'd been involved in, never had he ever seen anything like this. It was an impossible battle, the air filled with deadly flying beasts the like of which the earth had never seen before, well... not in such numbers. It was no better on the ground, with barely a square metre free from murdering monsters either in their disturbed dragon form, or nagas slithering in long lines, controlled using dark magic, forced to ignore the pleas of their king and do the dreadful bidding of the newcomer Manson.

Constantly at risk of being flanked without his fighting partner encouraged his magic to freely flow through him now, his molecules soaking it up before spitting it almost straight back out in some form of offensive magic. Not knowing how long he could keep up this level of supernatural trickery and damage, he could only really concentrate on the moment, and then the next one and the one after that, barely able to think about staying alive in order to protect the ones that had pledged their lives in an effort to keep him safe.

With four dragons all on opposite sides about to close in on him, the raging magic within found the most appropriate mantra almost without his help. Whispered words backed up by his indomitable will instantly turned the air surrounding him into thick grey clouds, heavy with ionised particles. Their vision obscured, all four murderous dark dragons closed in on their opponent's last known position, but unknown to them he'd hovered much higher up in the air, using the newly formed clouds as cover. Converging on the apex of the shield, it only then became apparent what was going on.

Waiting for the inevitable, knowing that the mantra he thought of as a lightning conductor was about to kick in, a flicker of a brief smile crossed his face. In some ways he loved everything about being in battle: adrenaline surging through his veins, the taste and smell of everything going on around, the confusion, misdirection and of course the vicious and cruel bloodlust he knew to be part of his dragon DNA. It wasn't right, that much he was sure, and the king inside him would have gone to great lengths to avoid any sort of conflict, but here and now, without any choice, he found himself fully immersed in all of it, his supernatural power going ballistic, fulfilling its natural intent. It was rapture, pleasure personified, and most definitely satisfying a dragon's most basic purpose.

FLASH, CRACKLE, BANG... no, not the latest incarnation of the cereal characters, but George's sleight of hand coming to fruition. In an onslaught of power filled lightning blasts designed to culminate at the top of the shield, all four dark dragons found themselves being electrocuted over and over again. An added by-product of this trickery was that George had enabled the power from the strikes which missed the monstrous beasts, and there were many hundred in such a short space of time, to be absorbed by the barrier covering his allies, in the hope of reenergising it, allowing those inside one less thing to worry about. As the last of the thunderous bolts of lightning fizzled into nothingness, and the smell of roasted dragon flesh wafted through the air, the current monarch dropped back down on top of the domed energy barrier, resuming his previous position, fully focused, ready to protect those whose side he stood by.

Relieved to see not only her king return, but the extra power added to their shared defensive barrier, without thinking about her actions she blasted one of the wicked creatures that had stolen away behind them inside the shield, with a thick stream of superheated flame she'd conjured up at a moment's notice, watching with satisfaction as its twisted, charred form wriggled, smoked and writhed in tortuous agony for the last few moments of its life. It proved to be a good tactical choice within the confines of their small fighting force, as the other dragons soaked up the excessive heat from her attack. Turning to face back out, she conjured up an explosion of acid directly behind the naga now attacking her part of the shield with some sort of sonic screech. Snake-like body parts and thick, green, gooey acid flew in every direction as the detonation decimated not only her immediate attacker, but the two behind him and both either side. Momentarily pleased with her handiwork, she willed the walking shield she hoped was trying to rescue them to hurry up. The sooner the king was back by her side, the better she would feel about the whole situation they found themselves in.

'Damn!' thought Flash, frustrated and ultimately disappointed at the turn of events, having not managed to finish off Manson, something he'd not only been close to doing, but actually looking forward to. In a matter of just a few short seconds, he and Vasuki had been swarmed over by what under normal circumstances he would have considered a small naga and dragon army. Here and now, it was of course only a tiny contingent of Manson's massive force, but it felt like much, much more. Having just agreed with the naga king to take the forces attacking them in the air, leaving the ground for him to deal with, Flash in his breathtaking new dragon persona leapt up, and with one flap of his giant aerodynamic wings, glided into position above his serpent-like friend, belting out fireballs and torrents of superhot flame in almost every direction, falling back on his Crimson Guard training, determined not to go down without a fight, all the time keeping an eye on the smirking form of Manson in the distance, who now watched with studious satisfaction. All that did was rile Flash, something most beings who knew him would be super wary of, and for Manson, it just might prove to be his undoing.

Lines of nagas six deep had no idea what approached them from behind, well... at least not until it was too late. Led by Richie holding out the laminium dagger in front of her, the sizzling, thick shield of magic walked straight into them, crushing some, electrifying others, Yoyo's band of young dragons mentally and magically attacking even more, whilst Fredric and the great healer himself picked off the odd stray one that might have caused a problem. In essence, a huge swathe of the nagas were massacred in but a few moments, creating a straight path to the domed shield of their allies, something the light sided rescue force took full advantage of.

Marching straight ahead, Richie stood face to face with Amelia Battlehard, the two female dragons each giving the other a deep nod of respect. Wondering what the plan was, Captain Battlehard was shocked when the young lacrosse playing dragon, shield and all, just walked through her defences as if they didn't even exist. Once there, and in conjunction with Yoyo and all his charges, they immediately extended out the invisible shield, forming a barrier around the one all the King's Guards had put in place previously. In a split second, Fredric killed the remaining two infiltrating nagas who were wrestling with a couple of the king's protectors. Knowing that they were now guarded by something far more serious than the meagre barriers they'd all conjured up between them, the disheartened, dismayed and exhausted fighting force slumped to the ground, exhausted, wary, tired, and nearly all out of magic. Acting on instinct, Yoyo instructed the spare young dragons not tied to powering the shield to start healing the wounds of those they'd just rescued, while he did the same, attending to the most serious himself.

About to open her mouth to ask about the king, staving off multiple attacks from outside the shield, directly above them, she watched gobsmacked as a gap at the top of the barrier opened and, without warning, George was drawn in, much against his will and to his great surprise. As the king crashed clumsily to the marble floor, the magical barrier again became whole, closing up and thwarting those dark dragons that were hoping to get inside. Explosions, fireballs and colourful magic rocked the huge, supernatural defensive structure, but not at any point did its integrity waver or even look like doing so. For the moment, they were safe. How long it would last was anyone's guess.

Straining the muscles in his powerful legs to get to his feet, the king, a furious expression chiselled into his prehistoric face, whirled around to see exactly what was going on. Before he had a chance to vent his anger at being so unceremoniously dumped to the ground within the shield, a huge human shaped body threw himself at the king's mighty belly. Surprised, purely because of royal protocol, it was only when he looked down to see the thick, matted, long, ragged hair of his friend that his demeanour transformed.

"It was me who pulled you through. Sorry!" announced

Fredric, looking up into the mighty jaw of his friend the monarch."

"REALLY?" stated George sarcastically. "I'm shocked!"

Not knowing what the hell was going on and deeply disappointed that somebody had gotten past her to get so close to the king, Captain Battlehard fingered the hilt of her appropriated sword, ready to leap into action at a moment's notice, should she be required.

Tense for but a split second, the silence was squashed when the two long lost friends both burst into laughter, each giving the other the biggest hug in recorded history, with ribs surprisingly remaining intact.

"I'm so sorry," began the king.

"It doesn't matter, and besides there's really no time for that. Let's just do what needs to be done and get the kingdom back to where the hell it should be."

"Right, as always," declared George, releasing his friend and for the first time taking in everything going on within their little conclave.

Glancing across to the dragons he'd just been fighting alongside, he spotted Yoyo and gave him a little nod. The experienced healer returned the sentiment. Turning back round, he took in all the others for the very first time.

"And just who are these fine folks?" solicited the king, referring to Yoyo's young dragons, who for the most part had their eyes closed, helping Richie with the magical barrier.

"They're with me, Majesty. I can vouch for every single one of them. They're good dragons to have in a fight."

"I'm sure you're right, Yoyo. I look forward to fighting alongside them to see exactly what they're capable of. A full on dragon education doesn't always cover everything. Sometimes life skills are much more important."

'How the hell does he know?' wondered the master healer, all the time tending to one of the badly hurt dragons that had been fighting alongside the king.

Despite most of their consciousnesses sharing Richie's mind, nearly all Yoyo's charges started at the fact that the king knew who they were, and that they hadn't been to a nursery ring. Each of them wondered if there would be consequences of some sort, should they make it through all this.

"Peter... my boy. It's so good to see you. I'm just sorry it can't be under better circumstances."

"So am I, sire, so am I."

Disappointment replaced the joy George had briefly felt.

"Not 'sire', not today," he announced for everyone there to hear. "Today I'm George to all of you. Not king, not monarch, not sire. Today we fight as one, for each other, for our way of life, to keep the planet safe and out of the hands of evil. If we are to survive this, we can't put one being above all the rest. We have to work together, everyone as equals, including, dare I say it, our... visitors from up above. Perhaps somebody would like to fill me in?"

Having already grasped that this was the dragon king, Janice's cheeks started to glow red in embarrassment as the monarch stared at both her and Hook. She had no idea what to say, how to address him, or if there was any other royal protocol she should abide by. Being the centre of attention and stared at by everyone there was her idea of absolute hell.

Wanting to jump in, his over keen sense of self preservation kicked in once again, making him shy away from speaking out for the one he loved. Mentally, Peter berated himself for lacking the courage to stand up and tell everyone here how he felt. He knew it was wrong, but he just couldn't help it. The heart wanted what it wanted, and he wanted her more than anything in the world. Besides, he told himself, if he opened his mouth now, it would just cause a huge distraction, something they could all do without, maybe even causing some kind of rift. Concluding that the best thing for everyone was for him to keep quiet, he waited in awkward silence, hoping that somebody else would brief the king.

"I'm assured these two both have the heart of a dragon, and have played pivotal roles leading up to our rescue," ventured Fredric, clapping his best friend on the shoulder for good measure. "They're brave, fearless and inventive and without them, neither of us would be here. That should be enough for now."

"Hmmmmmm..." uttered George, not entirely convinced.

"He's right, George!" announced Richie, from what was considered the front of the shield, without turning around. "They accompanied me from the surface, helped with the rescue in Salisbridge and escorted us here. Without them, things would have gone very differently, I can assure you. Please don't be mad that they're here. They're good people... good beings."

Scratching his huge, prehistoric, dragon chin, George considered what he'd been told for a few seconds.

"It would appear you're held in high regard by Miss Rump. Part of me wonders whether that's good or bad," he pondered, eyeing the lacrosse playing dragon whilst remembering all the reports about her that had crossed his desk. Deep down though, he knew she could be trusted not only with his life, but the fate of the planet as well. Despite sanctioning it, though it hadn't really been his decision, he still felt guilty for allowing the dragon priesthood to wipe her memory and banish her to the human world above. For whatever reason it clearly hadn't worked, and she'd been the one to come back and rescue them all. In a strange way, he thought, it kind of made sense, it having to be her.

Over the 'CRACKLE', 'BOOM' and 'THUD' of the multicoloured, for the most part unrecognisable, magical barrage constantly deflected by the energy barrier they all sheltered beneath, Fredric brought up the dragon (there were many here of course, but this was a metaphorical one, much like an elephant, only bigger, stronger, much more powerful and full to the brim with flame) in the room.

"What on earth are we supposed to do now?"

Standing right beside each other, George in his hulking great prehistoric figure, Fredric shrouded in tatty fabric around his waist that looked as though every moth in the world had taken a nibble at some point, but apart from that pretty much bare in his well muscled, shabby and unkempt human visage, both friends shared a concerned look.

"Surely we've been in tighter situations than this?" asked the king.

"If we have, I'm struggling to remember them, but I have been a bit out of it lately, with my memory not being quite what it should. You could well be right."

In the middle of the huddle of beings, an arm shot up. Everybody turned to look. This time it was Peter's turn to brighten up in the cheek department.

"You don't have to put your hand up, Peter," chastised the king, in the nicest possible way. "We're not in the nursery ring now, you know."

This amused Fredric no end.

"Speak my boy, speak," urged George.

"Why don't you ask Richie what to do? She was chosen by everyone to be the leader."

It wasn't often that the young lacrosse playing dragon's mind had cause for alarm. It most certainly did right at this very moment. What the hell was he doing?

"By everyone?" enquired Fredric, before the king could slip in.

"Apparently so," replied Peter enthusiastically.

Maintaining her focus on the shield, Richie shook her head in disbelief.

"Do tell," said George.

"After the battle at Salisbridge, all the dragons and

everyone there all came together and decided she should be in charge. So far she's done a sterling job."

"Hmmm..."

"It's true. She extracted all the information out of that traitor Casey, before leading everyone up to London, splitting up into groups once here, deciding the makeup of each group."

"Whoa..."

"What?" asked Peter.

"There's more than one group?"

"Oh yes... Gee Tee took a group over to Fleet Street in an attempt to capture the crystal node and restore worldwide communications in an effort to discover the scale of things and just maybe form some kind of resistance."

"Have you heard from them?

"No one here has. I think we'd probably know if they took Fleet Street, as there would be nothing stopping them getting a message out... quite the opposite in fact."

Still siphoning off power, guiding it into their defensive barrier, Richie couldn't believe what he was telling the king. She'd heard Janice recounting most of the story to Peter after they'd first found safety behind the shield and hadn't really thought much of it. Was now really the moment to retell it once again? Surely they didn't have time for all this, and to boil down what had happened to just a few short sentences didn't do the events justice at all. In fact, if anything, it muddied the waters. As far as she was concerned, George should just go back to being in charge, because his experience alone made him the most qualified to do so, without the fact of him actually being the monarch. Unless... Oh no! Please don't tell me he's going to mention that... not to the king. PLEASE!

As it turned out, her fears, pretty trivial at a time like this, were well founded.

"There's another reason why I think you should ask Richie what we should do," blurted out Peter, almost unable to stop.

"And what's that?" enquired the king, starting to get a little frustrated at not being kept in the loop.

"She's THE WHITE DRAGON!" he announced to all and sundry.

"WHAT?!"exclaimed Fredric, totally caught off guard.

"I think you must have suffered a blow to the head, my boy," concluded the king.

"It's true. I'm not delusional. I shared my thinking with Gee Tee and he believed me."

This stopped them all in their tracks.

"The famed master mantra maker thought she was the real deal?"

"YES!"

"Oh... and we all know just how well grounded he is," offered up Fredric, his face swimming with insincerity.

"Enough," barked the king, intrigued. "Tell me why you believe her to be The White Dragon and not the actual 'White Dragon', Tim."

In some ways, it was a good job Richie had been in charge of the shield because if she hadn't been, almost certainly she'd have got up and left, no matter the horde of vile beings outside wanting to taste her blood. So, blocking out all the sound from the voices around her, she lost herself in the job at hand, concentrating on nothing but the invisible barrier that continued to keep them all safe.

"To retell the story would take far too long," quipped Peter matter-of-factly. "What I will tell you is that by accident, I looked at the scars on her back. It was plain to see, once I did. I would advise you to do the same."

With those that were paying attention from Yoyo's band of young charges all holding their breaths, Janice and Hook failing miserably to come to terms with exactly what was going on, it was left to Fredric and the king to sum up just what they thought.

"You must be mistaken Peter," ventured Fredric softly. "What you say is just not possible."

"I'm afraid he's right my boy. It just can't be true."

"You've both just quoted Gee Tee's exact words."

"Then how is it he changed his mind?"

"He saw what I saw."

"Really?"

"Really!"

Tired, weary, wounded, with his supply of magic running low which in itself made him cranky, George had never seen his friend's grandson with as much conviction as he had now. While he didn't think it at all possible, he was totally convinced that Peter believed it to be true with every atom in his body. And that left him with no other choice. It was a good job there was nobody from HR about.

Plodding across the busted marble flooring, which only that morning had resembled an ancient Italian masterpiece, the king rocked up directly behind Richie as she continued to hold Aviva's laminium dagger outstretched in her hands, the intensely powerful magic flowing throughout her entire body. Opening his right hand, he studied the tip of his index finger, watching intently as a razor sharp nail about four centimetres long popped out from beneath the surrounding scales, looking like an elegant assassin's dagger.

Asking forgiveness from whatever deity might be listening at the time, not really believing that any such beings exist, with one swift vertical stroke of his right arm he tore her shirt in two and watched as both halves drifted off to their respective sides. As light from a dozen fireballs exploding against the barrier and a brief spattering of fizzling fiery rain drizzled all around them, it brought into being the stark contrast of the scars on the young dragon's pale, human shaped back. Instantly the king stepped back, shocked, exhaling sharply as he did so.

"Amazing!" was all that Fredric could be heard to say.

A collective intake of breath from all Yoyo's charges echoed inside the confined space they shared.

Yoyo turned to take a look.

"Well I'll be..." he uttered.

Janice and Hook stood there, mouths wide open, wondering about the significance of a dragon carved into the lacrosse captain's back.

Peter looked on, having seen it all before, convinced beyond any doubt that he was right. His friend was The White Dragon, and had been so all along. It was never Tim, always her.

Stock still, facing the nightmarish beasts that continued to blast all sorts of magic at them, Richie could do nothing but face the reality of the situation. She knew that one of them would take a look, but hadn't suspected they'd all get a peek. Not one to be easily embarrassed, after all, being the life and leader of a lacrosse team meant lots of banter and practical jokes, and given that she was more than able to hand it out, she'd been taught a long time ago by her human lacrosse mentor, if that were the case, then she'd always better be able to take what came her way in return. Here and now though, she just felt ashamed and afraid. After what had happened during the course of the last few days, it was the last thing she needed. Hands starting to shake just a little, her composure began to fracture, with all the terrible deeds that had happened coming back to haunt her. Torturing and killing Casey, killing the evil dragon Troydenn and worst of all Tim's death at the hands of Manson's devilish dad, washed through her. Tiny cracks and fissures began appearing in the energy shield that kept them safe. Everyone froze, knowing they'd be dead in about two seconds flat if the barrier came down around them now. However, they needn't have worried. A most unconventional rescue was underway right at that very moment.

"Wow!" stated one.

"How cool is that?" ventured another.

"That is the most brilliant thing I've ever seen," cited one of the young females. "I wish that was on my back."

And so it continued, with all the young charges in Richie's head chipping in on the conversation, each utterly clueless about the effect they were having on the superstar lacrosse playing dragon.

Listening to the awe with which they described the injuries she'd sustained to her back, broke the spiral of despair she threatened to get sucked into. Hearing the youngsters express genuine wonder, surprise and admiration transported Richie out of the dark and back into the light, ridding her of any embarrassment she might temporarily have felt, at the same time shoring the shield right back up, much to everyone's relief. In true Richie fashion, and while still having her back to everyone else, she quipped,

"If somebody could do me up, that would be just great. It's starting to get a little chilly."

It was enough to break the awkward silence, and without further ado, George released a little of his magic from the top of the razor sharp finger, which immediately knitted the young female's garment back together. Everything was back as it should be, except now, each and every one of them considered her to be The White Dragon from the famed prophecy. Would that fact be enough to spare their lives, and could she save them from the surrounding doom?

Pumped full of adrenaline, Flash let out the mother of all rallying cries, whirled through the air above Vasuki and sliced yet another attacker in two, his long, razor sharp talons all but taking off a dark dragon's head, only a few exposed strands of sinew holding it in place as it hurtled towards the ground. Instinctively he doubled back on himself in a confined aerial somersault, something that took absolute precision and guidance, so much so that most highly trained dragons couldn't perform it. But because of his specialised training... he could. Confusing the next two opponents to close in on his position, without breaking sweat he zapped one with brilliant zigzagging bolts of luminescent pink energy, the pure, ethereal power instantly rendering the monster incapacitated, another hulking beast sent spiralling to the deck, as he turned to face the other head on. With an almighty 'CRUNCH' their jaws met and their prodigious prehistoric bodies tangled up with each other as they rolled through the air. Despite the dark dragon's smaller body, she was feisty and agile enough to cause Flash more than a few problems. As their jaws locked together, each tried frenziedly to bite the other, their huge curved teeth clashing, rattling their massive mouths, stretching the almighty muscles in their necks almost to breaking point. Withdrawing his head sharply, the ex-Crimson Guard swiped her across the eyes with the tip of his wing, hoping to distract her briefly in an effort to gain the upper hand. It didn't work. Closing her dark, prehistoric eyelids, she let out a piping hot burst of flame which immediately had the effect of blinding and temporarily distracting Flash. Following the supernatural sixth sense that had almost always kept him safe in battle, Flash smashed his mighty head against his spirited foe, catching her with a glancing jab to the jaw. It was enough for her to release her grip and tumble just out of reach. Ignoring the pounding in his head, he used the power in his gigantic wings to bring his thick, spiked tail around, hoping to catch her with another blow. Pulling an extremely tight turn, the murderous female just about managed to avoid what would have been an absolutely devastating stroke by the ex-Crimson Guard. With his exposed back to her, for a split second he proved to be vulnerable. Using a dark spell from an array that she'd only been taught quite recently, the aggressive female conjured a curled up, barbed line of spiky, shadowy energy, and released it towards Flash's exposed rear, mimicking the way a human whip would work. Slapping against the scales across his back above the point at which his tail joined, the deadly, sparkling energy flayed scale and skin in a long line, causing our hero to cry out in agony. Sadistically satisfied, Flash's opponent took her eye off the ball, at least momentarily, and with his training telling him now was the time to strike back, he did so in spectacular fashion. Rolling around to face her head on, the words in his head, backed up by unshakeable willpower, imbued his dragon form with not only strength, but a transitory burst of speed, in effect turning his whole body into a battering ram. One moment he was there, the next he was gone, his prehistoric form moving so fast that none of the magically enhanced beings on the battlefield could see it. Most importantly, neither could his enemy. Colliding into her midriff, it was Flash's turn to feel momentarily satisfied at the sensation of bones and organs shattering into a million pieces. With a howl like that of a dog with its favourite lickable body part trapped in the garden gate, the female dark dragon drifted off towards the marble surface, her face a contorted visage of torture.

Robes soaked in disgusting, human coloured blood barely visible through their dark brown colour, covered from head to toe in dust, reeking of smoke, toasted flesh and supernatural power, Earth strolled casually up the side of the pile of debris Manson perched atop, taking in all the action, getting ready to enjoy the impending death of his enemies. Sharing a glance, neither said a word. They didn't have to; their thoughts, like the expressions on their faces, told their own stories, their destinies intertwined almost as if fate had fashioned them that way.

Directly below Flash, much the same battle was taking place on the ground as Vasuki, king of the nagas, fought furiously with members of his own beloved race, very much against his will and better judgement.

Using an expanding, circular, sonic wave, Vasuki threw back a ring of three of his kind all trying to attack him at once. Knowing that they weren't down for good, he proceeded to press his advantage. At the first sign of naga reinforcements he'd tried to be a good king, do the right thing for his kin, trying to only stun them, take them out of the fight temporarily. Of course it hadn't worked. They'd got up and joined back in with some of their allies, almost costing him his life, but teaching him a very valuable lesson. On the field of battle, there could be no holding back. You had to give it your all, at all times. It was do or die, there was simply no other way. And so it proved to be. Without hesitation, driven on by a sense of self preservation and a determination to stop the abomination of a world that the murderous Manson was trying to create, the naga king ruthlessly used his superior magic to cut down swathes of his own race, in an effort to stop the violence. Unfortunately it wasn't working. The more he destroyed, the more appeared in their place, driven on by some kind of forced magical will. Inside, it broke his heart.

Aware of Flash, his rescuer from that Antarctic nightmare, fighting furiously above him, he too threatening to be overwhelmed, the thought of fleeting respite filled his thoughts. Through the throng of vicious antagonists, he'd briefly caught sight of the giant shield that had moved over to the other side of the arena, now no doubt protecting the king and those that had been fighting alongside him. Realising just how hopeless their position had become, inside his serpent-like head he hatched a plan, one that might cost him his life, but could well save his rescuer above, who he knew had given everything to come back to that Antarctic prison. Opening his mind out into the arena as he continued to stave off attacks, he searched frantically until he found what he was looking for. In a mental kind of knock on the door, he screamed out inside his head, hoping to be noticed.

"FLAAAASSSSHHH! FLAAAASSSSHHH! It'ssss meeeeee... Vaaasssuuukiii. Opeeennnn upppp!"

Suspicious beyond belief, fully knowing that it might be a tactic used by the enemy in an effort to dominate his mind, particularly with a horde of other nagas on the rampage, he wondered how they would know him by name as he glanced down in the direction of the ground at Vasuki himself. One look was enough to confirm Flash's suspicion that it was no ruse. Filtering the contact through a tiny hole in his fortress-like mental barricades, the ex-Crimson Guard asked Vasuki what was so important that it couldn't wait.

"We'lllllll beeee oveeerruuuun sooooon. I caaann clearrrrr ussss a path onnn the grouuuund. Buuuuut weee haave toooo goooo nooowww."

Using a gravitic attack to crush all the bones in an oncoming dragon's wing, Flash swirled round to face the next mid-air attacker, there and then realising the king of the nagas was right. Enemy reinforcements were swarming in from every direction... dragons in the air, nagas on the ground. There was simply no way they could outlive those kind of odds, something the still smirking Manson far below him was no doubt counting on.

"DO IT!" Flash sent out through the link. "I'll be ready."

"I wiiiilllllll neeeeed toooo use uuuppp every laaast biiiiiit ooooof my maaaagic. I miiiightt noooottt maaake it."

"I understand," replied Flash, wondering what the hell that might mean.

Summoning up a brief icy storm that froze two potential attackers mid-flight, the ex-Crimson Guard circled around only to find himself face to face with the most gruesome and frightening being he'd ever encountered, and that included his little dalliance in Antarctica that still haunted his dreams to this day. There, only a few metres away, closing in at a dizzying speed, was a battle scarred, dark brown and green, three-headed dragon, spitting fire from each of his disfigured jaws, madness rolling around each of his six eyeballs. Any other being approached by this would have frozen up completely. Not Flash. Using a tiny sliver of magic to hugely increase his mass momentarily, he tucked in his wings and let his prehistoric body drop like a stone. It did, narrowly avoiding the creature's violent attack. Out of its reach, Flash returned his mass to its normal density, used his tail as a rudder, flapped both of his powerful wings, and whilst barrel-rolling, at the same time circled as tight as he dared, pulling around and back in behind the macabre beast, hot on its tail so to speak. You'd think with three heads, it would have awesome all round vision, but that didn't seem to be the case with this monster. The way in which its necks were fused together provided all three heads with limited mobility, something that Flash was now about to use against it. Powering his mighty wings as hard as he could, turning on a short burst of speed, Flash glided right up to the back of three heads without the monster even noticing. Pleased at having negotiated his wake without any problems at all, the affable ex-Crimson Guard gathered up all his strength, courage and in this case... rage. Without hesitation he plunged down towards the fiend's exposed back, jaws wide open, fangs bared, ready to take a huge bite. Hitting with the kind of precision you'd expect from a dragon with his experience, his jaw crunching through scale, sinew, soft tissue and bone about half way down his adversary's spine, it was a spectacular attack, almost certainly the most audacious and brilliant aerial assault that had played out that day. With no warning and the ferocity of prehistoric apex predators that had roamed the planet long before his race had been conceived, it was over in a moment, 'Three Heads' plummeting clumsily to the hard surface, far, far below.

It was then that his mind filled with a familiar voice, from the ground.

"Threeeeee... twoooooo..."

'Oh crap,' thought Flash.

"Onnnneeeeee..."

An explosion, the likes of which dwarfed anything that had gone on previously, thundered out concentrically from a single point on the ground below him. That point was Vasuki. Everything on the floor that hadn't been protected by magic in a two hundred metre radius was decimated. Life ended instantly on an epic scale. Manson and his monstrous bride would have died, if not for Earth's split second intervention, wrapping her personal shield around them both, providing immunity from the superheated wave of fire, fury and magic. The timing of her arrival had been nothing short of miraculous. Nagas were indiscriminately cut in half, their bodies burned and torn asunder. In the air confusion reigned, the concussive blast bursting the eardrums of many dragons, affecting their balance and of course their flying aptitude, Flash included. Knowing exactly what had happened, he was only too aware of what he needed to do. Unlike every other being left alive, he turned tail and headed at speed directly towards the epicentre of the blast, ground zero... Vasuki.

'Damn, he wasn't kidding,' thought Flash as he approached his target. There, lying on the ground, totally silent and still, the naga king's body resembled a statue that had tumbled to the floor, never to be picked up. Considering his options in double quick time, and noticing that a path leading directly to the shield and his friends had been fully cleared of all and any enemies, he had but one thought. SAFETY! However temporary it might be. And so with outstretched talons, and with the tenderness and care associated with mother crocodiles when they carry their newborn babies to the water in their jaws, Flash swooped down, picked up Vasuki's motionless body and, zipping along no higher than a metre off the ground at quite a blistering speed, headed directly towards the shield which his friends, and the monarch he would unquestioningly die for, hid behind. As his elegant, powerful and quite stunning body cut through the air on something of a collision course, a stray thought tickled his brain.

'I wonder if they'll recognise me?'

Rocked from their thoughts about The White Dragon prophecy, each and every being behind the protective shield flinched as a wave of utter devastation rippled out from a point directly behind their enemies.

'That's where Flash and the naga king were,' thought Peter, concerns for his friend overriding every self preservation instinct he had.

'What the...?' thought Richie, not knowing what to make of all the nagas being sliced in two directly in front of her.

George and Fredric turned to face the commotion, ready to fight at a moment's notice.

Yoyo continued to heal, unperturbed. His band of misfits were somewhat startled, but maintained their composure enough to carry out their duties.

As the smoke, debris, blood and body parts cleared, a dramatic, eye-catching and remarkable sight had them all shaking in their boots.

Faster than a speeding bullet, a striking, unrecognisable, silver dragon, its talons hooked into a naga body directly beneath it, headed their way at breakneck speed, seemingly with no intention of stopping.

"That naga corpse must be some sort of bomb," screamed one of Yoyo's young charges from somewhere near the back.

"I think we may be in trouble," suggested Fredric from George's side.

"Don't panic," Peter told Janice. "I'm going to change into my dragon form to protect you... stay sheltered behind me."

And with that, the young hockey playing dragon

released the bonds of his DNA and started his transformation. It was anybody's guess whether he'd be ready in time.

Reinforcing the front of the shield with every ounce of magic she could muster, something scratched her soul, stabbed her dragoness, prodded her psyche... something familiar.

'It can't be, can it?' she thought, as the mother of all collisions rumbled towards them like a runaway freight train. It was all on her. Nobody else had the power or time to do anything about it; all their lives quite literally depended on her next actions. And so with timing down to one thousandth of a second, she dropped the shield in front of her as the glorious winged beast passed through the barrier, narrowly avoiding all the beings gathered there, and glided to a halt in less time than anyone there thought it possibly could, just in front of Yoyo and the wounded he was working on. Gently it dropped its cargo to the ground. To everyone's surprise it was Vasuki, the naga king. Almost failing to remember, Richie reignited the wall of the shield she'd brought down to let their flying visitor in. Once again they were all surrounded by magic and, at least for the time being, relatively safe.

"What have you done, child?" yelled the king at Richie. "Why did you let it pass?"

"It's Flash... Your Majesty," she replied, sarcastically.

"I'd know that Crimson Guard in a heartbeat. Not only can he not assume his original form, but that looks nothing like what he once was. Everyone on me," announced the king. "Ready your magic!"

Despite her severe injuries, Amelia Battlehard was the first to do as the king asked, a blistering ball of brilliant, crimson energy clasped firmly between both her hands, ready and waiting to be used.

"Whoa..." came a soft, startled voice from behind the newest prehistoric addition to join the group.

"Peter?" announced the perfectly formed silver dragon,

noticing the bent whistle shape on the scales of the prehistoric being crouched over Janice.

"FLASH!" stated the young hockey player, hardly able to believe his eyes.

"Of course it's me. Who else do you think could pull off something as stunningly wicked as that? Yoyo, I know you're tending to injuries, but could you take a look at Vasuki please? He used up all his magic in buying us a chance to get over here. I couldn't feel his presence anywhere inside his body. I'm not sure he made it."

Apologising profusely to the dragon he was attending to, Yoyo leapt up, heading straight for the naga king, slapping Flash's stomach as he sprinted past.

"Nice body, my boy. I bet you're pleased to have that back. Congratulations!"

"It wasn't the one I was born with, hence the little standoff we find ourselves in."

"Indeed," acknowledged George, "indeed."

"It's me sire... honestly!"

"If it wasn't you, that's what I'd expect you to say."

"It's Flash, Your Majesty. I wouldn't have let him through otherwise," declared Richie.

"How come he can once again take dragon form? And why is it I don't recognise him? I know what his lost form looks like, I have after all sent it on missions many times over."

"I think I may be able to answer your first question," interjected Fredric.

George turned to face his best friend.

"Really?"

"During the battle to break free in Antarctica, Flash was fatally stabbed by that son of a bitch of a jailer. Luckily at the time he'd just transformed the chains into pure, unadulterated laminium, and so using our connection I repaired the damage he'd just suffered, and in the same instant I noticed an underlying flaw in his DNA, and so repaired that as well. Up until now, I didn't think anything of it. I'm guessing that what I did allowed him to retake his natural form. It might even explain his change of appearance."

It could explain things, thought the king. But he had to be sure, totally and utterly sure. If this was some kind of infiltrator, then the lives of everyone here were on the line, and he wasn't about to risk that again.

"Tell me something only I'd know," he ordered the giant silver dragon.

Without thinking, Flash just said it.

"You talk in your sleep, sire. Over and over again you go on about a failed mission, and how it was your fault you'd sent your best friend to his death. I take it that friend is Fredric there, and I'm pretty sure it wasn't your fault. Also you like to listen to 80's music when there's no one around, or at least you think there's no one around."

Chuckles from Yoyo's charges broke the ice, because they too had taken to listening to 80's music in their private space, deep beneath the computer repair shop in Australia.

"Oh... one last thing. You're utterly hopeless with technology, and can't use it worth a damn."

"Ahhhh... that one I recognise. You've always been like that," laughed Fredric, slapping his friend hard on the middle of his scaled belly, which everybody there thought was most certainly not royal protocol.

"You certainly make a compelling case, Mendrik," ventured the king, in one last gamble.

"It's Dendrik, as well you know, sire. Dendrik Ridge!"

"Owww... he's James Bond," whispered Janice, or at least that's what she thought, not knowing about the heightened sense of hearing nearly all the beings surrounding her had.

"Who's James Bond?" asked the king.

Janice blushed. Peter answered.

"A fictional super suave spy from a series of movies that the humans above absolutely adore."

"Oh?"

"That does sound a little bit like me," joked Flash, hoping that everyone, including the monarch, had come to realise it was actually him.

"One last thing please Flash... change back," ordered the king.

Of course, it made sense, but the ex-Crimson Guard really didn't want to give up his new found, mighty, magnificent dragon persona, not after all this time being unable to change back to his base DNA. Reluctantly, in front of everybody, he did so.

In but a moment, the human shape they were all familiar with, down to the very last freckle on his arms, emerged before them, much to George's satisfaction.

"It's good to see you well, Flash. I'm sorry I doubted you. But I just had to be certain. I'm sure you understand."

"I do, Your Majesty. I understand just how much you value everyone's safety."

The king nodded appreciatively, knowing that he'd been let off the hook just a little.

"Before we go any further, I don't suppose there's any spare clothing that I could borrow, is there?"

"I think now that we know it's you, perhaps you'd better change back. In either form you'll intimidate everyone with your size," declared George.

Janice chuckled. Peter blushed. Everyone else just looked on.

Moments later, the gigantic silver dragon was back.

"Can I ask what's going on?" queried Flash.

"We were just wondering if Miss Rump here could guide us in a new direction," responded the king.

"She's certainly a capable leader and not afraid of making the big calls. Next to you of course, sire, I'd follow her into a fight, anytime, anywhere."

Surprised at such a ringing endorsement from the battle hardened ex-Crimson Guard, the king's estimation of the highly unconventional, spirited young dragon went up a notch or two.

"How do you suggest we proceed Miss Rump?" asked the king, as every being there looked on.

Taking her time, composing her thoughts, finally she came up with something they could all get behind.

"I'm sick and tired of hiding from these bastards. I think it's high time we taught them a lesson in not only manners, but in the evolutionary pecking order of things around here."

If they hadn't been sure about her qualities as a leader before, then that little line absolutely did the trick, buoying each and every one of them, including the king and Fredric. It was just what they needed to hear. Now all they had to do was implement it. Surely that couldn't be too hard, could it?

51 CAPTAIN COURAGEOUS

"Your concern is unwarranted," whispered Gee Tee. "There's still plenty of time for them to get it done. Above all, we have to be patient. If we try rushing in and Steel hasn't set off the mantra, the chances are we'll be overwhelmed, which will be the end of our little resistance, and of course us. Keep your head down and wait for my signal."

Deferring to the master mantra maker's wealth of experience, the dragon second in command, by the name of Rhombus, stalked silently back to his position amongst all the dismembered dragons they still hid amongst.

Pulling in a long, deep breath, ignoring the nausea inducing qualities of the smell as he did so, Gee Tee gave everything he had in an effort to maintain his outwardly calm facade. In truth, he felt anything but. The deed should already have been done he knew; they'd had plenty of time to reach the inner depths of the building, the control centre if you like, where the crystal node itself was secured. Something must have gone wrong, he thought... but what? And if that were the case, what the hell were they going to do about it now? Going storming in there when they're fully alert with a full contingent of defenders would only get everyone here killed, and so in his mind was not really an option. All he could think to do was stall his cohorts, wait, and hope that whatever was going on in the bowels of that building could be turned around to their advantage, and put the original plan back on track. Without Steel using that mantra and taking out those in the inner sanctum, they were without a doubt, an inclined plane wrapped helically around an axis... or in other words, SCREWED!

Both friends had thought it a terrifying experience infiltrating this base of operations and reaching so far inside the labyrinth, but anything they'd done previously paled in comparison with what was happening now. Previously ready to fight, both had been unable to manoeuvre themselves between Steel and the crystal node at the right time, and had now lost any advantage they may have had. That first unsuspecting vicious assault on the laminium ball captain had caught them all by surprise. After that... things were pretty much all over. Given how many nagas had slithered out of their hiding places in the darkened inner sanctum, both of them together stood absolutely no chance. Not without Steel and the mantra from Gee Tee only he possessed, that should, if used correctly, take down every being there. But they both knew the moment had passed, almost certainly never to present itself again. Too scared to acknowledge each other with even the slightest look, all they could do was watch as their friend continued to suffer the most brutal torture imaginable. Half an hour of cruel punches and kicks was how things had started, the two of them finding it hard to conceive how any being could have survived that, or whether there would be any point in continuing the violence. But their mindset was nothing like that of those around them. Having used their friend as a defenceless punch bag, the vicious dark dragons pulled him up off the ground and shackled him to the wall, where he was still currently restrained, the evil woman, 'Red', right at this very moment pulling off scales, one at a time, from the most sensitive areas of his newly reborn body. It was chilling for the two of them to watch, but they could do nothing else, not without giving the game away and in turn their true identities. The anguish and suffering they felt at being so helpless mirrored their friend's physical pain. Both thought the courage he showed in adversity was a testament to the true hero he really was, on and off the laminium field of play.

With Steel well and truly out of commission, being tortured beyond belief by the wicked red headed woman who clearly had no scruples, morals or decency, the mantra couldn't be cast, and the rescue effort by the others was doomed to fail. In short, their plan to take back the crystal node had failed spectacularly. There would be no help from the rest of the planet, no rescue, no rebellion. It was for all intents and purposes... OVER!

An overly ornate room inside the dragon council building opened out onto the courtyard that fed the bridge that had been magically rebuilt. Stuffed full of dark dragons and nagas eager to do Manson's bidding, both the courtyard and the room could hold no more creatures. They were full to capacity, with not even the slightest amount of room left, full of testosterone and beings vying to taste both victory and violence.

Only a short way away, the corpses of two nagas were being fought over by half a dozen magical species as their de facto leaders, the ra-hoon, looked on in delight at those they'd co-opted by either force or submission. Having sent out hunting parties into every part of the strange, futuristic building, they now knew that these two were the last pair of stragglers. All the remaining beings were grouped together... they could taste the staggering build up of magic, the apprehension threatening to send them wild. But they were clever, cunning and above all... patient, something they knew served them well, time and time again. And so with a sea of dark yellow gnats flitting around the corridors, and the slavering asena taking huge chunks out of the nagas' giant tails, dripping blood across their brilliant bright blue manes, the ra-hoon started to plan the attack they knew would satisfy their lust for the magic they liked nothing more than to feed upon.

Against the backdrop of loud, methodical stomping, echoing up from far in the distance (emanating from the crazed rock demon haunting the lower floors), orders had been given and it was time for the assortment of mythical beings to move out. Malevolent, dark brown lizards scuttled along the walls on all fours, tasting the air with crackling, green bolts of vicious, forked lightning as they did so. Nifoloa buzzed as trios of pixiu whipped through the air around them, pulling tight turns in the confined spaces, blasting out superheated cones of fire in front of them. Bounding along the floor and walls, frightening looking scaled apes beat their chests in pleasure at the thrill of what was to come, one of them only able to use two arms instead of the usual four as the other two had been ripped off during a previous encounter. Rowdy two-headed eagles dive bombed the gnats, as slithering snakes in a writhing mass hissed hysterically. Over all this, the sound of the scorpion men crunching their pincers together moved them all along towards their ultimate targets, with the ra-hoon, who resembled unicorns, in the background, waiting for the perfect opportunity to harvest the magic they so desired.

52 AN ABRUPT END

Menacing, evil grins of sickening, ancient beasts out to do them harm, letting rip with a constant barrage of colourful, deadly magic surrounded the glistening, supernatural shield they all found themselves sheltering beneath. Twisted nagas stood side by side with demonic, dark dragons, their provisional brothers in a perverted magical alliance, their only goal now to feast on the innards of the beings cowering behind the energy barrier, that at some point would run out of power. It was only a matter of when, not if.

Ignoring the murderous scowls of the cruel and vicious monsters baying for their blood, Fredric had at least managed to find a mantra in his extensive database which had silenced all the noise being made from the outside. No longer were they bombarded by the constant sound of explosions, unrecognisable magic, dragons stomping on top of the shield above them and the intimidating, blood curdling screams of individuals intent on doing them all harm. Unfortunately, neither he nor anyone else there had managed to turn the transparent barrier opaque so as to obscure everything happening on the other side. It would have helped stave off the fear a great deal if they had.

So far quite a few suggestions as to how they would go on the attack had been rejected, mainly because it meant individuals risking their lives instead of working together as a team, something they all seemed to think was the key to their survival. As they continued to rack their brains, Peter asked a question.

"Is there anything in the king's library that could be used to help? Any magical artefacts, antediluvian spells or antiquated mantras?" he added, knowing full well the library was stacked full of all these things, thanks to his unofficial visit, very much against procedure.

Both the king and Fredric shared a look that set them both thinking the same thing. Probably, they both thought, but there was simply no way to fly up to it in their current situation.

"Good thinking, my boy," quipped George, "but unless we can get up there unhindered it's probably not viable at this time. It could be worth considering later, particularly if we manage to strike a large enough blow to their force. Any sort of distraction may give one of us an opportunity to sneak up there and gather anything of use. I'll have a think about the most powerful things that should be rounded up and pass it out to everyone, then if the opportunity arises, anyone who's best placed can go forage."

Everyone nodded their agreement that it was the best idea they'd had so far.

"If only I had my ring or the trident," mused the king softly, from totally out of nowhere. And that thought led him to a forgotten question that would have consequences for nearly all of them. "Peter... where's Tank?"

Those three words caused reality to come crushing down on all of them like a ton of bricks, ripping away the young hockey playing dragon's fleeting smidgeon of happiness which he felt at being accompanied by the woman he loved, despite the desperate nature of the situation they both found themselves in. Immediately he turned towards Richie, who craned her neck right round to look at him. TANK!

'Oh my God,' she thought, realising that she hadn't seen him at all, having been so caught up in the rage and grief that had flooded her body in the aftermath of Tim's death. Scouring his memory, Peter couldn't recall at what point his friend had stopped being there. The last thing he could remember was seeing Tank tumbling end over end beside one of the soaring marble pillars that lined part of the private residence. After that... NOTHING!

Standing together atop a mountain of churned up, shiny, white marble, the would-be rulers of this wicked new world marvelled at the staggering amount of sheer luck their opposite numbers seemed to be availing themselves of, as the hulking silver dragon and the king of the nagas disappeared behind the temporary safety of the magical barrier the cowards all hid behind.

"Fluky bastards!" observed the queen in waiting.

"Quite so, quite so," agreed her psychotic other half, fingering the ring he'd appropriated from George.

"What's that you have there?"

"A magical trophy from the spoils of battle... the dragon king's ring, my love," announced Manson, not taking his eyes off his enemies for one second.

"Really..."

"For all the good it's worth. I was assured it provided the user with a near limitless supply of magic and some rather unique mantras from across the ages."

"And..."

"So far... absolutely nothing. It seems totally dormant. I've tried flooding it with my magic in an attempt to force my will upon it, I've tried to bond with it, pretend that I'm their new official king, which of course is pretty much the truth, and to prove to you just how desperate I've been to access all that knowledge and power, unbelievably, I've even... asked nicely. Two possibilities come to mind. I've been lied to, or it's tied directly to the king in ways that I can't begin to imagine. Either way, it's of little use now. Fancy rendering it useless for me?"

"It would be my absolute pleasure."

Faster than the eye could blink, Manson slipped off the ring and tossed it high up into the air. Unfurling her right index finger nonchalantly, Earth set the air on fire, dispensing a high voltage bolt of crackling, blue electrical energy, releasing so much power that what little hair Manson had left on his head, stood fully to attention, while the serpents entwined around Earth's head bathed in the spooky glow of the current. A fireworks display of supernatural sparks exploded high in the air above them both as the supposed magical band disappeared off into the ether.

"Nice shot!" remarked Manson, grinning inanely.

"I just imagined it was the dragon king himself. That was more than enough motivation."

"I know exactly what you mean, my dear. How about we take care of our problems once and for all... together?"

"That sounds positively... delightful!"

Reeling from the realisation that Tank hadn't been seen in any way, shape or form since almost the start of the battle, the sudden cessation of hostilities beyond their imposed new home caught them all off guard, as dark dragons and nagas alike all stood down, most turning their backs and retreating some distance.

"Something's going on," announced Hook.

"Perhaps they're going to surrender," piped up Janice hopefully.

Normally a glass half full kind of woman, their current situation offered the lacrosse playing superstar very little in the way of optimism, something that came through when she voiced her opinion.

"I very much doubt that. There's absolutely no reason for them to do so. They're up to something... I'd stake my life on it."

Not very wise words given the circumstances.

"Perhaps this is our chance to get to the library," offered up Peter.

George and Fredric shared one of their telling glances, and although nothing was said verbally, a whole conversation played out with just their eyes, as it did telepathically in their heads.

"I don't like this one bit. It reminds me of that siege in

Burton," sighed Fredric.

"You just had to bring that up, didn't you?"

"It wasn't me who thought it was a brilliant idea to go up against thirty well armed thieves and bandits. Oh, it'll be alright, I remember you saying."

"It turned out okay in the end, didn't it?" defended George.

"Only because of lady luck. All things being equal, you should have died that day. I'm glad you didn't, but the outcome was never in your hands. You should have realised that before you went in."

"It was a lesson learned, that's how I look back on that day."

"And what does your experience tell us is happening out there now?"

"Nothing good, I'm afraid," replied the king.

"I concur."

"And..."

"We need to be ready to fight with everything we have," added Fredric seriously.

"I thought you were always ready to fight with everything you have."

"I am," his friend replied. "I'm talking about everyone else."

"I see. Do you want me to tell them?"

"It's probably better coming from you."

"So be it."

And with that, their private conversation was done.

Clearing his throat with a fiery roar to gain everyone's attention, George stood up to his full dragon height, the eyes of everyone except Richie, Yoyo and a couple of injured personnel all upon him, waiting for whatever pronouncement he had to make.

"I think we can all agree that some kind of pivotal point has been reached somewhere outside. I don't know what it is or what they're going to do, but we need to be ready to respond with the full force of our fury and magic.

Only that will do, only that will give us a chance and even that might not be enough. From behind this shield, while it's still intact and with enough power to keep us relatively safe, we need to go on the offensive. It might well be our only chance. So we'll have a look at what's playing out but you all, as a being, need to be ready to move on my command. Ready your magic, prepare to use it all in the most heinous of ways if need be. Now is not the point to be shy about using it, or have any regrets about mantras you may have or have not cast. If we survive, there will be no recriminations, no judgement... NOTHING! Today we do what we must to survive, all of us. I will say no more, other than: good luck. I'm proud to fight alongside each and every one of you, and yes... even those non-dragons amongst us. Don't forget, every living being on this planet is counting on us. If we don't succeed, the entire earth will become a breeding ground for evil, and its face will change forever. BE READY!"

Disappointed that he might never spend another day amongst the domain that he loved and had dreamed of returning to over the decades he'd been incarcerated, the goosebumps running up and down his arm were a sign to him of just how proud he was of his friend, and that he was exactly in the right place, at exactly the right time. One last stand in the fight to uphold good with his best friend right beside him was more than he could have hoped for in Antarctica, and so looking to make the beings outside the shield pay dearly for every drop of blood they'd shed, the founder of the Crimson Guards delved deep into his memory and found the deadliest, most dreadful and atrocious magic he could remember. In an instant it was primed and on the verge of being released.

Beyond the magical barrier, telepathic orders had gone out, very different to the call to arms Manson had issued only minutes ago. A huge swathe of space opened up like the parting of the Red Sea as dragons flew back into whatever gaps in the air they could find, and nagas slithered away into any small hole available. As the path revealed itself further, as that's very much what it now was, two beings holding hands strolled indifferently along it, slowly making their way closer to the light sided heroes sheltering behind their shield.

Beyond the barrier, the king had a suggestion for his friend.

"I guess we're going to need to hear what they're saying. Perhaps now's a good time to reverse the effects of that mantra."

In the blink of an eye it was done, with the sound of wings flapping and tails swishing echoing throughout the confined space once more.

Watching the sickening couple approach, Richie fought off the urge to forget about the magic she was channelling and just run out there and kill them. In her usual confident way, she was pretty sure she could do just that, but knew it would be at the expense of every being there. Even she wasn't that cold.

Pulling in a deep breath, she wondered how her best friend was holding up. His history with the deeply despicable Manson far outweighed her own, and she knew for a fact, even in the brightest of times, something this most certainly wasn't, Peter still had nightmares about his evening on the Astroturf. It must hurt him to see the villainous scumbag strolling casually towards them all without a care in the world. Using the tiniest part of her mind, she channelled some love and understanding in his direction.

Deja vu rattled his brain and tweaked his nipple nuts as his nemesis, hand in hand with his vile and murderous queen, strode slowly in their direction. Inside, Peter desperately tried to hold things together, not only his emotional stability, but his bladder's urge to release itself there and then. Fear caused his arms and fingers to shake badly, as his jelly-like legs wobbled ever so slightly, something he hoped the love of his life wouldn't notice.

Brave as he was, with little equal on the rugby pitch, except maybe for Tank, Hook was scared here and now, and not just a little. Watching the couple, who he'd been told were both dragons, amble aimlessly towards them, was like watching a video of a fatal car crash, over and over again. You knew something bad was going to happen, but you just couldn't look away. And despite the brave, fearless and powerful beings he found himself surrounded by, the young rugby playing human was utterly convinced that this was the end, and that they were all about to die. Every atom in his body simultaneously longed to be on the surface.

Pretending not to notice the effects the couple were having on her prehistoric other half, Janice instead preferred, as she always did, to look on the bright side. Right now, that involved closing her eyes and reaching out for a certain futuristic looking weapon that was still carving its way through clusters of dark dragons and nagas on the outer edge of the now packed battlefield. During the eye wateringly slow passage across to rescue the king and his defenders, the young bar worker had tried reaching out to Fu-ts'ang on a number of occasions, only to be summarily ignored. The telepathic connection was there, it was just as if the consciousness of the weapon itself had chosen not to answer... which to her felt odd, because in the short time that they'd been together, they'd most definitely formed a bond, sharing key moments of their past, as well as her hopes and dreams for the future. Why he'd ignore her now was anybody's guess.

"I'm busy killing your enemies child," came across the link, in a slow methodical kind of way.

"I just wanted to know that you're okay."

"Why wouldn't I be?"

"Something's going on here. The leader and his queen are making their way towards our position. It doesn't feel right, almost as though they have a secret we don't know about tucked away. I was hoping you might keep an eye on them for me."

A short blast of silence had Janice wondering if she'd gone too far and asked for too much. That, however, didn't appear to be the case.

"I'll take a look in a moment. Although I've exterminated many more of their kind, for every one of them I kill, two more always seem to take their place, and although the crowded arena provides me with more than a little anonymity, I'm doing little to reduce the actual number of adversaries you're facing. I'm sorry, my friend, I'd hoped to have almost ended it all by now."

"It's not your fault, you've done an amazing job and it's been a pleasure being joined with you. Why don't you conserve some of your magic and take a look at the murderous couple to see if you can fathom out what they're up to? Stay safe and as much out of trouble as you can."

"Touché," replied Fu-ts'ang, vaguely amused, diving off into the nearest shadow, which extended all the way up one wall. Screaming at speed under the cover of darkness, the fabulous ancient weapon continued to head up in an effort to discover exactly what duplicitous plan the happy couple were hoping to enact.

Multitasking as only he could, healing broken bones in two dragons whilst at the same time knitting together torn ligaments and scales for a third, Yoyo's mind wandered off topic just a little. Through what had now become rather a crowded and confined space, he could just make out the vile dragon Manson and his devil bride. Momentarily a shudder juddered down his back, sending a tingling through his scales, something his vast experience considered a warning of sorts. Evil was here and out to get them, and somehow he couldn't shake the feeling that their time had all but come to an end. In an uncharacteristic show of emotion, whilst still attending to his patients, the knowledgeable healer opened up a telepathic connection to all his young charges, something they'd prearranged to use only in the most dire of circumstances, and started to speak.

"Listen up all of you, we don't have much time. I wouldn't have thought it possible to get any more dangerous, but every sense within me tells me that it's about to. Your actions over the course of this unfortunate adventure have proved you all to be a credit to your race. More courageous, daring and cunning dragons would be almost impossible to find than those hidden behind this shield. I could have all day and still not have enough time to explain exactly how proud I am of each and every one of you. Whilst I know that your DNA and mine don't match, and that all of you have had the most horrendous upbringing, for many years now I've regarded you as the sons and daughters I could never have had. Know this! I love everyone of you with all my heart, and while I regret, to my very core, getting you all involved in this, it was at least the right thing to do. What you've done today has made a difference beyond belief. Without all of you, none of us would have got this far. Continue to fight with everything you have, right up until your very last breath, and hopefully we will be reunited again on the other side. As the king has already said, ready your magic and use all your initiative. Good luck!"

Wonder, worry, sadness and joy flooded the invisible link, at least for about a thousandth of a second, before it was terminated and Yoyo's full focus returned to the wounded in his care.

"I'm not liking this one bit," whispered the king to his newly recovered best friend.

"Neither am I. But our hands are tied at the moment. We need to let it play out and just hope we're adaptable enough to deal with whatever's thrown our way. As long as the shield maintains its integrity, we should be able to stay safe, take a pounding and at least be able to give them a bloody nose, something I'm really looking forward to."

"I'd forgotten how much sense you can make," added George.

"I'd never forgotten our friendship, even in the darkest of times. You and Peter were all that kept me going... kept me sane. I wouldn't be here without you."

"I know, my friend. I've missed you terribly. Not a day's gone by without me thinking of you, wondering about your fate. I only hope we can avoid the future our friends out there think they have in store for us, long enough to return the domain and the planet to what it once was, and celebrate long into the night."

"On that we're agreed," replied Fredric, smiling at his friend as they both clasped hands.

Knowing that the eyes of every being in the king's private residence were on the pair of them only increased the magnitude of madness trickling through Manson's veins. Earth, on the other hand, worried little about anyone else, whether they were watching or what they were thinking. One thing and one thing only dominated her thoughts... her father, and all the different ways in which he could die.

Stopping some twenty or so metres short of the front of the magical barrier, Manson looked inquisitively at the cowering heroes, wondering how they would react to what was about to happen. Not that it mattered in the grand scheme of things, he just liked to play things out in his mind, hoping to look back later on and realise he'd predicted the turn of events. With a long, deep breath and a wave of satisfaction rolling through him, his default, smug smile wrapped itself across his lips as he began to speak.

"Here we are, at something of an impasse," he

announced for everyone to hear.

'Imp ass!' thought one of Yoyo's young charges behind the shield, conjuring up images of a wicked demon's bottom, something that briefly brought a smile to his face in this darkest of times.

"In some ways I have to admire your fruitless heroics," continued Manson, Earth standing beside him, all the time grinning inanely. "But as you can now see, it's all been for nothing. You're heavily outnumbered, with only finite reserves of magic, and with nowhere to go. Communications across the planet have been cut off, and by the time the worldwide dragon community realises exactly what has happened, it will all be too late. The dragon domain and the planet at large will all be mine... I mean, ours," he said, turning to face his queen, much to her pleasure.

"Get on and say what you have to say numbnuts," demanded Richie, still channelling the magic from the dagger and the necklace, attempting to be as disrespectful as possible, "before we all fall asleep from boredom."

Being a dragon, you'd have thought that Manson would have had a thicker skin and be relatively immune to a barb like that. Not so.

A rising rush of red flushed from his neck up into his head, warming him up like a superheated volcano at just the thought of being spoken to in that tone, particularly in front of his entire army.

"YOU... YOU... YOU... half dragon, half human, weak willed, lily livered, dumb ass, stupid lacrosse playing halfwit," Manson managed to stutter furiously, determined to regain some sort of respect from those looking on.

From behind the magical barrier, Richie let rip with the biggest cheesy grin she could, knowing full well from his reaction that she'd succeeded in her effort to wind him up and hopefully keep him off guard. Muted admiration from Yoyo's young charges rang throughout her head, as those that accompanied her admired her brilliance.

Wrapping a comforting arm around her king's waist in an effort to keep him from actually exploding, Earth glared daggers in Richie's direction, fully understanding what the young woman was trying to do.

"It's alright, my dear, they're trying to get a rise out of you. Calm down, otherwise you'll be letting them win. And we don't want that, do we?"

Responding well to his queen's sage wisdom, Manson calmed himself down, dispersed all the heat he'd built up and eyed his father's killer with what can only be described as murderous intent.

"Now where was I? Oh... that's right, you're all... DOOMED! No rescue coming, no hope of escape, no life beyond that which I grant you here today. So I will offer you this only once. Surrender now, and stop this travesty."

This time it was Fredric's turn to mock the wicked, dark dragon leader, which he did by bursting into a raucous round of mock laughter, whilst at the same time rubbing his taut muscled belly in a circular motion, much as Santa Claus would at Christmas.

"If you had the ability to take us down, you'd have already done it by now," boomed Fredric's deep, gleeful voice through the magical barrier. "We have enough magic to survive indefinitely, something that clearly throws a spanner into the works of whatever you've got planned. As far as we're concerned, you can kiss our giant, scaly asses."

"DRAGON FILTH!" Manson screamed.

"ENOUGH!" screeched Earth, pulling back her king, who was intent on charging the barrier.

Turning to Manson, very gently she caressed his cheeks.

"You can see what they're trying to do. Hold yourself in check. Don't let them get to you. It's what they want. They're trying to keep you off guard and divide us. You know that."

"I'm sorry, my love, my temper got the better of me. It won't happen again, I assure you."

"It's okay, it's nearly all over. Things will be better then. What say we get on with what we came here to do?"

"I'd like that, I really would."

"Then let's do it," answered Earth, grabbing Manson's hand, turning to face the group of beings standing between them and planet wide domination.

Fleetingly, silence encompassed everything within the king's private residence. No beating of wings, wriggling of tails, hissing of tongues, barely even a breath as events rested on a knife edge. Now was the moment, the one they'd all been waiting for. Whatever had been planned was about to come into play. It was now or never.

Clasping her king's hand, Earth opened herself up fully to him, the madness inside them both colliding, rebounding, their separate forms of magic intermingling, unifying, together becoming more than the sum of their parts. Around their physical bodies the air became infused with magic, looking as though it had been ignited. Yellow, orange and red streaks of light danced and twirled, wriggled and twisted, weaving in and out of the couple's bodies, through their arms, fingers, hands and legs, almost engulfing them, but not quite.

Quiet panic at unrecognisable supernatural power out beyond the shield and their control, threatened to swallow up the light sided heroes, but in solidarity, they stood firm, readying their magic, prepared to fight for their lives.

Losing herself in channelling the power from the dagger and necklace, Richie formed the mother of all cohesive bonds with Yoyo's band of young dragons, melding with each of them, sharing memories, feelings and fears, their magic together giving the barrier an extra element of protection. Whatever happened, they knew the shield would shelter them, at least for now.

Hundreds of dark dragons and nagas watched in anticipation, wondering what was about to happen and whether or not they'd get their chance to attack the interlopers.

Behind the barrier the air crackled, hissed and sizzled as magic thrummed into life, ready to be dispensed at a moment's notice. With the exception of Janice and Hook, everyone else had an offensive spell ready, including Yoyo, who was still multitasking, this time healing deep tissue muscular injuries that three of the King's Guards had picked up fighting alongside their monarch.

"Aaaahhhhhh..." sighed Earth in rapture, the snakes from her head nipping and snapping, this way and that.

"Ohhhhh..." moaned Manson, fully consumed by what was going on.

And without warning, it happened.

For Richie and Yoyo's band of talented young dragons, it felt like having their magic snatched away instantly. Like opening the floodgates of a dam, all of the mana contained within Aviva's dagger and the laminium necklace surged out at breakneck speed, threatening to drain both items dry. Momentarily stunned, Richie's mind leapt into action, fighting to hold onto what was left with all her will and might. Shocked beyond belief, the cadre of youngsters sharing the lacrosse playing dragon's mind reinforced her will, adding all their own power to hers, redoubling their efforts, hoping it would be enough to save at least some of the mana they were relying on to power the shield behind which they all sought safety. It wasn't sufficient. And as if that weren't bad enough, what little power they all still retained individually got siphoned off as well, leaving them completely defenceless in the shells of their prehistoric bodies. In a final, futile glow, the last of the supernatural power was ripped from the confines of the laminium dagger, sending a surge of superheated energy into its hilt, burning and blistering Richie's hands, forcing her to cry out in excruciating pain, as she dropped clumsily to her knees, instantly disconnecting the link in her mind with the other dragons. Looking to stave off the pain from the burns, the young lacrosse playing dragon reached into her well of magic to do a touch of healing, only to find the source of her power had run dry. Unconsciousness took her as she crumpled to the floor. Sharp intakes of breath were all that could be heard as the steadfast energy barrier that had kept their enemies at bay, saving all their lives up until now, flickered into nothing.

George and Fredric, their most powerful offensive magical spells already lined up, opened up their hands and thrust out their arms in the direction of the gruesome twosome. Instead of the brilliant, bright display of colourful, powered magic they'd been expecting, a few dying, supernatural embers sparked across the lifelines of their palms. They too, had had all the magic sucked right out of them.

Witnessing the earth shattering events that seemed to be playing out in slow motion, and against everything the healer in him believed in, Yoyo, still tending to the unconscious Vasuki, leapt to his feet, turned to face Manson and with all the willpower, experience and anger that flowed through him, rattled off the most vicious, most despicable and evil mantra he knew, looking to kill the rogue dark dragon leader there and then. Nothing happened, except a sense of total and utter bewilderment consuming the experienced dragon physician.

One bound from his powerful legs had his magnificent new form surging through the air, heading out through the shield on course to tackle Manson and his psychotic queen. That is until every atom within him had its supernatural power torn asunder, leaving him bereft and alone. Too much for any normal being to take, even for Flash it was a shock. So much so, that instead of maintaining flight, which in theory should have been possible even without all his magic, he just crashed nose first into the marble, tumbling to a halt against a massive pile of debris.

Aghast at what had transpired all around her, Captain Battlehard sought the magic of her birthright and prepared an all out attack with everything she had, in an effort to keep the king and his friends safe. Suicidal at best, she could see no other way out with beings around her losing their magic left, right and centre. Grasping the ethereal energy within herself as she'd done thousands of times before, she attached her iron force of will and prepared to strike with everything she had. Just as the words started to form deep within her consciousness, the magic itself started to slip away. Desperately she tried to cling on, but it was like water slipping through her hands. Nothing she did stopped the undeniable leak through which her power was being drained. In an instant it was done, with every last particle being stripped from her body. Despite her training, panic threatened to take her. It was all she could do to remain frozen to the spot. All around the fearless captain, others suffered the same effect. Those that she'd fought alongside, and Yoyo's brave band of young dragons, underwent exactly the same ordeal, none of them coping nearly as well as Amelia Battlehard. Dragons behind the shield dropped to their knees like chestnuts falling from a tree during a storm. It wasn't just their magic that had been siphoned off either. Any vestige of hope had all but disappeared, replaced instead by a deep sense of terror, dread and overwhelming apprehension.

From his position high up in the shadows, a sense of panic surged through the master weapon smith's soul that was Fu-ts'ang. Utilising more than a lifetime's worth of courage and passion, and without any thought for his own safety, he surged towards Manson and Earth's position, knowing that if he wanted to save his friends, Janice and Flash, as well as the others, there was only one thing to do: he had to kill the murderous couple, and he had to do it now. Faster than a speeding bullet, imbued with ancient Chinese magic and empowered by righteous fury, the speeding blur of the cold, frosty blade extended out like a tail, making him look like some kind of blazing comet in the night sky. Unseen by every other being, as they all had their eyes glued to the now defenceless group of heroes, the tiniest hint of satisfaction ran along the weapon's shaft, knowing that he was about to not only save his friends, but kill two of the most vile beings he'd ever had the displeasure to encounter. As the blistering speed closed the gap between them in units of time so small they were almost impossible to measure, the mighty, feared and dreaded Fu-ts'ang arrived unnoticed within two arms' lengths of impaling the lovers.

Entwined in the bliss that was the combination of their magic, Manson's frenzied state allowed his magical abilities and senses to extend far beyond their normal reach and in doing so, he'd constantly had his eye on the futuristic looking blade that had done so much damage on the field of battle up until this very moment. He'd assumed that it might have sought them out after the barrier had been destroyed, and of course he'd been right. Letting it get as close as he dared, without even turning he whipped his right arm around towards its trajectory and let rip with the surprise he'd been saving up especially for it.

Dark, gruesome magic forked out of Manson's extended fingers, rippling its way through the space between them and Fu-ts'ang, covering the distance instantaneously. The master weapon smith had no time to react, no time to deviate, change course or mount any sort of defence. Black, soulless magic bored into the shaft and the hilt, piercing the weapon's very essence, tearing away its psyche, sending its spirit spiralling into the afterlife, its physical form exploding out into a thousand tiny pieces.

From amongst the group of light sided heroes, Janice's scream rang out, before she too dropped to the floor, her mind in tatters from the surge of feedback through what remained of the link to her friend. Peter draped his monstrous dragon form over the top of her, immediately offering a modicum of protection, cradling her broken mind and body.

As the shards of what remained of Fu-ts'ang tinkled to the ground, Manson and Earth let go of each other's hands. Straight away, the supernatural power that had encompassed both of them disappeared.

Taking two steps menacingly forward, the leader of this dark new world, the one that had schemed and manipulated events for so very long to reach this exact point, bared his teeth in a wicked grin, and declared for every being there to hear,

"Isn't this nice?!"

Close by, the taint of the primordial, abhorrent magic used by Manson and his queen woke up the dormant, roaring lion inside the slumbering kitten. An agreement was quickly established and reality returned. If magic was a rock concert, then all that had happened so far was the warm up. The headline act was about to begin.

The adventure continues in book 5, A Fiery Farewell. Read on for an extract...

Lashing out, Tank caught one naga in the throat with his elbow, whilst planting the sole of his right foot straight through the gills of another, in a death defying display of agility that even the legendary Bruce Lee would have been proud of. But there was no rest for the wicked, or those fighting them, and so pitching forward, he poked yet another firmly in the eye with the tip of his index finger, feeling the soft squelch as his nail pierced the dense, fibrous nerve tissue, semi blinding the beast. Dodging the tip of a tail the size of a human thigh meant to catch him full on in the throat, the young rugby playing dragon lunged forward and karate chopped that one right in the windpipe, knowing full well that it wasn't recovering from that any time soon.

'They're nearby,' whispered a voice deep inside his head.

'Okay... tell me when,' he replied, ducking out of the way of a slashing blade meant to cleave him in two, his errant reply streaks of furious fire lancing out from his fingertips, piercing the monster right through in at least half a dozen places, all performed instinctively under the guidance of his partner For'son. As a torrent of rubble dropped from the air onto the battlefield strewn with bodies, clearly hoping to add his to the tally, he gracefully backflipped twice, before assuming a crouch and letting out a scintillating wave of energy in every direction. Nagas exploded like fish being hunted with dynamite, dragons tumbled from above, huge black lines of fire scorched the, by now, well worn marble flooring. For a split second he had a chance to breathe and take in everything that was going on around him. And then with a little nudge from his partner, he spotted the first of them.

'That's impossible,' he thought only to himself. Of course it wasn't. On the contrary, it was totally possible.

"Underestimate them at your peril," was the reply from the enigmatic band. Unable not to watch in some sickly, horrified kind of way, the two of them looked on as a swarm of more than a dozen flying insects dived straight through the skin of dark dragons and nagas alike, easily puncturing scales and sinew with their one massive out of proportion sharp tooth the size of a man's finger.

"Those, my friend, are called nifoloa and are quite deadly. One drop of their poison and you'll be taking a one way trip from which there's no return."

Swallowing hard, Tank gathered up all his magic.

"Avoid using poison of any sort on them. They're immune to most forms of it."

"Thanks," he replied, readying a haze of frost for them.

Dropping the last of the nagas between them and their intended target, the buzzing grew infinitely louder as the swarm set their sights on Tank, and more importantly, the ancient band that smelt of magic.

Pulling in a deep breath through his nose and exhaling out of his mouth in an attempt to calm himself down, without a sound he whispered the words that had appeared at the front of his mind and applied a little of his ethereal energy to them.

Swooping through the air as a squadron, the tiny mythical creatures vectored around before darting forward with a great deal of speed, screaming through the space towards Tank and For'son. Taking their velocity into account, the magic that the young rugby playing dragon had cast materialised in the form of a huge, icy glass plate, directly in front of him. Unable to alter their trajectory, the demon insects flew straight into a whole world of wicked cold, instantly regretting their decision to attack, falling to the floor as one, their flimsy wings frozen in place, their deadly weapon proving to be a weighty burden. Lying there helplessly, twitching uncontrollably, For'son urged Tank to finish them off with a ball of flame. Unsure at first, the sense of overwhelming urgency and danger through their bond quickly changed his mind. Opening out the palms of both hands, the young dragon discharged two blistering balls of intense fire that instantly incinerated everything lying on the floor. Turning to face the direction from which the nifoloa had come from, Tank's heart sank at what he spotted in the distance. Huge scorpion men with bodies the size of cars and the torso, head and arms of a human, were indiscriminately ripping open nagas, the stinger on their tails puncturing the scales of low flying dragons, causing utter carnage in their wake. And that wasn't even the most scary part. A pack of blue maned wolves fought over the remains of two nagas, gorging on intestines, fighting over the limbs and tails, shaking innards and organs everywhere. Scaled apes used their differing number of arms to beat a downed dragon to death, ripping off parts of its wings, stamping on its head, pulling out its teeth to keep as trophies. Heart stopping as these events should have been on their own, unbelievably there were more. Two-headed eagles dive bombed the slippery serpents on the surface, taking out eyes and gills with little fuss or bother, while in the end the feared pixiu, winged lions of sorts, tore apart unsuspecting dark dragons, having little knowledge or experience of how to fight off this new and exotic enemy. Filling the space up above, huge clouds of fire breathing gnats whipped through the air, squirting flame at anything that moved, including those on their own side. It had been absolute bedlam up there before, now though, a new word was needed to describe the total turmoil and anarchy.

'Things', Tank thought, 'can't possibly get any worse.' That's when the giant asag reared up to its full height, some way off in the distance, the huge, hideous rock demon scouring the battlefield with its purple vision, pummelling targets into the ground with its gigantic fists, sending beings of every sort skittering into the air. From out of nowhere a flash of colour caught the young dragon's eye. Barely able to avert his gaze from the asag,

Tank focused in on the bright blood red and brilliantly neon green that had attracted his attention.

'What in the...' he thought, having never seen anything like it. There in front of him were human bodies with bulbous, bulging bellies and the heads of cattle. Each had three eyes, with sharp talons, horns and bony protrusions littering their monstrous forms, something they put to good use by spinning viciously, cutting open everything around them with the efficiency of one hundred razor blades. It was bone chillingly scary.

"Ah... the gaki. Monstrous legends of the Far East," added For'son. *"Rumour has it that they feed off the souls of evil men and women."*

"Great!" replied Tank sarcastically. *"Are there any other surprises out there that I should know about?"*

"You've spotted most of the really dangerous ones. There are a few others, but they're of little consequence. Only the ra-hoon present a greater threat than those you've seen and they, from what I can tell, seem to be lurking in the crowd somewhere towards the back near the very disappointed rock demon. Resembling a unicorn, only with two horns instead of the usual one, if you stumble across a ra-hoon, you need to run for your life. Under no circumstances should you try and engage it. IF YOU DO YOU WILL DIE!"

"Understood," replied Tank, shaking his head.

"Heads up," declared For'son. *"INCOMING!"*

ABOUT THE AUTHOR

Paul Cude is a husband, father, field hockey player and aspiring photographer. Lost without his hockey stick, he can often be found in between writing and chauffeuring children, reading anything from comics to sci-fi, fantasy to thrillers. Too often found chained to his computer, it would be little surprise to find him, in his free time, somewhere on the Dorset coastline, chasing over rocks and sand in an effort to capture his wonderful wife and lovely kids with his camera. Paul Cude is also the author of the White Dragon Saga.

Thank you for reading...

If you could take a couple of moments to write a review on either Amazon or Goodreads, it would be much appreciated.

CONNECT WITH PAUL ONLINE
www.paulcude.com
Twitter: @paul_cude
Facebook: Paul Cude
Instagram: paulcude

BOOKS IN THE SERIES:
A Threat from the Past
A Chilling Revelation
A Twisted Prophecy
Earth's Custodians
A Fiery Farewell
Evil Endeavours
Frozen to the Core
A Selfless Sacrifice
Christmas in Crisis

www.ingramcontent.com/pod-product-compliance
Lightning Source LLC
Chambersburg PA
CBHW030834190726
48285CB00004B/1220